RUPERT DREADNOUGHT;

OR,

THE SECRETS OF THE IRON CHEST.

BY
THE AUTHOR OF THE "YOUNG APPRENTICE," &c.

ILLUSTRATED WITH NUMEROUS ENGRAVINGS.

LONDON:
EDWIN J. BRETT, 173, FLEET STREET, E.C.
MDCCCLXX.

PRESENTED GRATIS WITH No. 120 OF THE "BOYS OF ENGLAND."

RUPERT DREADNOUGHT

OR THE SECRETS OF THE IRON CHEST!

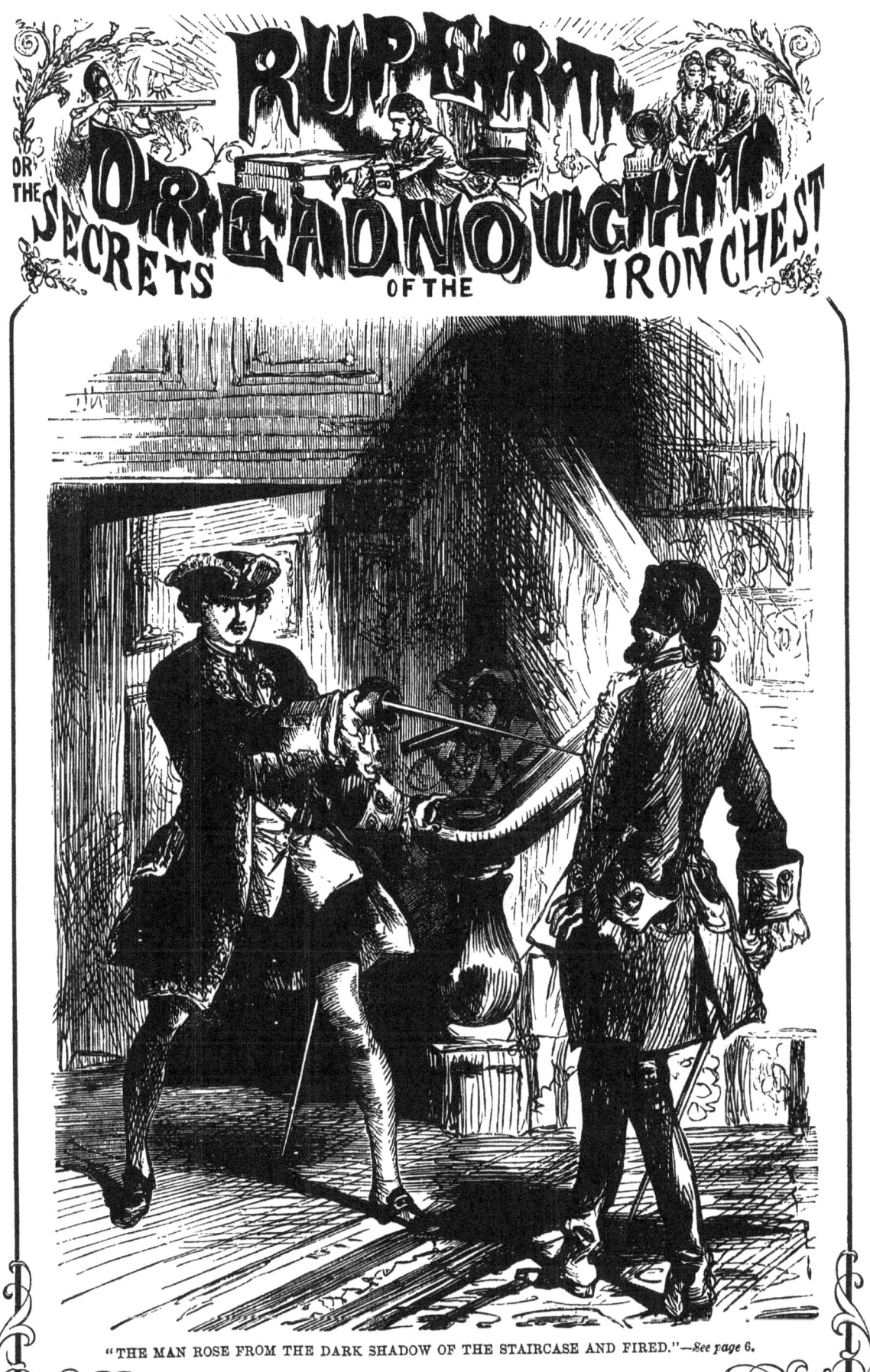

"THE MAN ROSE FROM THE DARK SHADOW OF THE STAIRCASE AND FIRED."—*See page* 6.

No. 1.—"BOYS OF ENGLAND" EDITION.

BOOK I.

LAYING THE TRAIN:

CHAPTER I.

SILENT DEATH—THE OLD HOUSE NEAR THE TOWER—THE REVEL OF THE POISONERS—THE MIDNIGHT HOUR—THE EXPECTED GUEST.

DEATH flapped its raven wings over the City of London, yet revelry was at its height everywhere.

It was New Year's Eve, in the year 17——.

London, in spite of the intense cold, was then under the influence of an epidemic—slow, sure, inevitable.

What it was no one knew.

Some called it the Plague, and imagined that the great decimation of fifty years before was about to be repeated.

But it had not the peculiarities which were characteristic of that hideous affliction.

The patients did not turn black, neither did they die swiftly.

They lost their natural colour truly, but it was a deadly pallor which succeeded to it.

The patient, moreover, died away by slow degrees, lingering generally a month and suffering no pain whatever.

There was another strange phenomenon, moreover, connected with it.

Though an epidemic to all outward appearance it seemed not to be catching.

Nurses never died of it.

Patients had been nursed through all stages of the disorder by persons of every variety of temperament.

But these persons never suffered.

The rich, moreover, appeared to be the most liable to the torments of the fell disorder.

Some few poor persons had been attacked and died, it is true.

But these, when their cases were investigated, always turned out to be heirs in the second or third degree to some large and disputed property.

As the whole of London suffered under the same calamity, a numerous band of doctors were engaged in endeavouring to stem the fatal tide.

But not one had been successful.

Not a single patient attacked by the pestilence had been known to recover!

Then the dread suspicion came suddenly into men's minds.

Was it poison?

Could there be a conspiracy of wretches, so large, so carefully organised, as to spit forth their venom upon a whole capital?

And if so, what was the poison used, that it defied all efforts at cure and discovery?

Again and again were the bodies of patients opened and carefully dissected.

But in vain.

The symptoms in all cases were the same, but no trace whatever of any poison could be discovered.

It was on this New Year's Eve, when thousands were dying everywhere, that the song and the dance resounded merrily in every quarter of the city.

People seemed to have taken up the motto of the desperate reprobate—

"Eat, drink, and be merry, for to-morrow you die!"

No one knew when they would be seized—in the dance—at the supper-table—in the silent night.

So, as I have said, there was everywhere singing and dancing, and merry music; and nowhere seemed it merrier and more enthusiastic than at a large house, whose high, frowning walls sheltered it on one side from the curious gaze of walkers near the old Tower of London, and whose large windows on the other side shed forth a blaze of light over the river Thames.

It was built, in fact, so close to the river, that the waters lapped its walls, and at high water its vaults were considerably beneath the level of the river.

In the huge drawing-room of this house was collected a motley assemblage of men and women.

Both were dressed in the extreme of fashion, and seemed on excellent terms.

But all were masked.

The gentlemen wore masks, which completely concealed their features; but the ladies allowed some glimpses of their pretty mouths to be seen, and their bright eyes flashed through the eye-holes of the black velvet.

Every kind of dress was to be seen in that gay gathering, from Turks to nuns, from ancient priests to gay cavaliers.

All seemed full of jollity.

Yet, in the midst of all this merriment, many an anxious look was cast at the clock, which now pointed towards the hour of twelve.

As the hands of the time-keeper approached nearer and nearer, the music stopped, the dancers gathered into groups, and while earnest conversation was carried on in low tones, all seemed to be listening for some one.

There were two persons in particular who seemed most anxious for whatever event it was they expected to happen.

The one was a woman apparently of about twenty years of age, dressed in an Italian dress with short petticoats and low boddice, displaying a pair of exquisitely formed limbs, and a pair of gleaming shoulders, rich with youth and health.

Her companion was also young, but about five years older, and dressed in a huntsman's dress, which showed off a figure replete with manly beauty.

His mask nearly concealed his features, but you could see that he had a heavy moustache, and a pair of eyes which vied in brightness with those of his fair companion.

"This delay makes me nervous, Alford," whispered the girl. "Can it be that anything has gone wrong, and that, for the first time, a victim has escaped?"

"No, no; fear not," replied Alford. "You are a nervous creature, Lesbia. Who that heard you talk in such a manner would believe that you were one of the band which has spread such terror throughout London?"

A slight shudder passed through the frame of the young girl.

"I tremble to think of that sometimes, Alford," replied Lesbia. "I have strange dreams of a night, and phantom forms hover threateningly over me. They are but phantasms of a disordered brain I know, but what then? The deeds we commit are no phantoms, and——"

"Stay!" cried Alford, quickly; "say no more. The clock strikes twelve."

The first stroke of the clock sounded.

Then, in an instant, every voice was hushed.

Men and women both stood motionless; voiceless as statues.

These men and women, young, handsome, gay, knew that another year had come for them—ANOTHER YEAR OF NAMELESS HORROR!

The past year could open up hundreds of graves.

Graves of old and young, rich and poor, hurried to their doom by remorseless villany.

And all this glitter and tinsel of joy, derived its being from the treasures of the murdered.

As soon as the last chime of the clock had sounded, the statues sprang once more into life.

Strong arms encircled slender waists; lips met lips in loving kisses; the music burst forth again, and away the revellers rushed once more in the mazes of the giddy dance.

It was a scene of mad jollity—a revel of demons.

They cast off all thoughts now but those of eager enjoyment, and in the excitement of the moment thought only of pleasure, the evil pleasure of being possessed of other's wealth, of being with the ones loved, yet unknown.

Even this did not last long.

Another hour passed.

Again the clock sounded.

The first hour of the new year had gone!

Then there came a hush over all.

For a solemn voice had spoken above the din and confusion of the music—

"HE COMES AT LENGTH!"

Who was it who came thus?

That he was expected by all was evident.

The dancers stayed their movements, as they had done at the striking of the twelfth hour, and eagerly glanced at the door.

Presently it opened, and a young man entered.

A tall, fine-looking young man, with a handsome countenance withal.

He had no sooner entered than a man detached himself from the crowd of merry-makers—a man dressed in the costume of a Turk—and hurried forward to meet him.

He was habited so as to appear old, but in spite of this it was easy to see that it was but pretence.

"Well," he said, "is it all over?"

"Yes," replied the new-comer, "he is dead. Give me wine, for I faint and shiver with dread."

The old man led him away at once into an inner room, the dancers making a line for them to pass.

But before we follow them and explain this mystery, we must ask our readers to accompany us to the bedside of two dying men.

CHAPTER II.

THE DYING EARL—THE LETTER—THE JOURNEY—THE SURPRISE—THE ATTACK IN THE STREET—THE MYSTERIOUS FRIEND—STEALTHY STEPS—THE MASKED INTRUDER—THE QUARREL—THE HIDDEN ASSASSIN—THE ESCAPE—THE VOW OF REVENGE.

IN a large bedchamber, in a house near the Tower of London, lay an old man at the point of death.

The surroundings of the room showed plainly that Poverty was an unknown visitant.

The curtains that shaded the high windows were thick and embroidered with gold; the carpet soft and noiseless to the tread; the bed draped with all elegance; the furniture and the pictures massive and grand; the escutcheons of the Dreadnoughts over the high hearth, speaking of the grand old deeds of the family.

But yet all had an air of chilly discomfort. The glare of the white drapery, and the silence and the steady flame of the low-turned lamp, seemed to tell of the snowy shroud, the voiceless tomb, the Life passing away!

Near the bedside sat a young man about eighteen years of age.

He was a well-made youth, with regular features, which all would have denominated handsome; but there was on them a strange look—a wild look of sorrow, which augured ill for his peace of mind.

Ever and anon his eyes were cast sorrowfully upon the pale, ghastly face of the sleeper, as if with the passage of that life would pass also the whole hope and purpose of his existence.

In the midst of his watching the door gently opened, and a servant entered, glidingly, bearing in his hand a letter, which the youth took eagerly.

It was addressed to Master Rupert Dreadnought.

"It is from Helen," he murmured, as by a wave of the hand he motioned the domestic to remain, "well I know her dear handwriting; what can it mean? Ah! what is this? in danger?"

The letter ran thus:—

"DEAREST RUPERT,—Come to me at once. I am at the house of Lady Beaumaurice. I have fled from the home which your dear father gave me, and even though he is dying I dare not come to him. I will not delay you; but it is urgent—it is absolutely necessary both for you and for him that I should see you for a moment.

"HELEN."

Rupert re-read the letter, and then leaning over his father, glanced earnestly into his face.

"He sleeps," he said. "Edward, you see to him. An hour only shall I be away. Should he wake, tell him that Mistress Helen Penraven has sent for me on urgent business."

Without further delay, Rupert passed out of the room, and having placed on his hat and sword issued forth into the night.

He had not far to go, not more than half a mile,

and the distance seemed even less to him as he walked along thinking of the strange summons which had called him from his father's death-bed when he had imagined the fair one who had written to him to be safe away from her enemies in the country house of the Dreadnoughts.

He arrived almost ere he had imagined himself to have arrived half way at the stately mansion of the Beaumaurices, and rang a loud peal on the clanging bell.

A servant lazily answered the summons.

"Is Lady Beaumaurice at home?" demanded Rupert Dreadnought, impatiently.

The man stared at him.

"You have not, then, heard the news, Master Dreadnought?" he said.

"What news?"

"Her ladyship died this morning of the mysterious plague."

"Gracious heavens! And Mistress Penraven, is she not here?"

"No, Master Rupert; we have not seen her bright face for more than a month."

"Heavens! what can this mean?" he cried. "I have but just received a letter from Mistress Penraven saying she was here and awaiting me. Ah! I see it all now; it is a ruse—a vile piece of treachery to take me from the bed of my dying father! I must hasten back at once!"

Then, without further parley, he quitted the house and prepared to return.

He knew well that that night was a crisis in his fate; he knew that his father had strange secrets to reveal, and he knew well also that there were those who eagerly desired to prevent the transmission of these secrets.

He felt, therefore, the necessity for prudence.

The way he had to go was not long, but it was very dark and full of intricate courts and alleys, where assassins might lurk in the shadows to pounce upon the unsuspecting wayfarer.

By keeping to the open streets he might have avoided these dangerous ways, but there was no time to lose; his father was on his death-bed; this forged letter was intended to separate them; who, then, could tell what hideous crime might not be perpetrated in his absence?

Loosening his sword in its scabbard, so as to be ready for action, he took one glance round him and plunged away into the darkness.

He had not proceeded many paces before he fancied he heard footsteps near him.

He stopped and glanced round.

But again all was still.

With a fervent hope at his heart that he would be able to reach his father's bedside in safety, he once more advanced, but, just as he reached a dark corner of a street, there was a rush of feet, and a loud voice cried—

"Halt, there! Whither so fast, young sir?"

At any other time Rupert would have looked upon the three masked and ruffianly strangers who now sprung out from the gloom, as some of those night prowlers who, at that period, infested the City of London; but he now saw in their appearance part of a preconcerted plan.

Drawing his sword, he at once planted his back against the wall, and prepared to do battle with his enemies.

He knew well there was no probable chance of aid.

The place was dark as pitch; there was an air of murder around—a silence like that of the grave.

The spot was well chosen for an assassination.

"What want ye with me he cried?" as the ruffians approached him, sword in hand.

There was no reply; only a vigorous attack from all three together.

Their deadly animosity, evident in their savage thrusts, showed they were no cut-purses, but personal foes, or men set on by personal foes to destroy him.

But if they had suspected an easy conquest they were mistaken.

Rupert Dreadnought, young as he was, had a wrist of steel, and it was not long before one of his assailants had to hang back, wounded in his arm.

"Come on, Gilbert," shouted he who was bravest of the three; "this young gallant will soon be tired. We know you well, Rupert Dreadnought," he added, "and 'twould be best to yield."

"Yield!" laughed Rupert, "I know not the word!"

"Then you will die ere you leave this spot. We have sworn it. We know well your father to be dying; we know he has secrets to impart. Mark me, Rupert Dreadnought, those secrets shall never be yours, for, if you enter your father's chamber again to-night, it will be as a corpse to be placed by his side in death!"

"Boast not," cried Rupert; "there is no time for words, and but little for action. Clear the way for me. I cannot waste such precious moments with braggarts and assassins!"

As he spoke, he made a desperate lunge, which separated his two enemies, and would have left him free passage, had not the third man, who had been wounded, come up on the instant.

It was now that something strange and mysterious occurred.

Before this nothing was to be seen but the four combatants, whose bright swords wreathed round and round like serpents; nothing was to be heard but the clash of steel, and the hard breathing of the three men, as they strove against the one, and their blood ran in curdling streams over the pavement.

But now one of the shadows seemed to detach itself from the rest, and a mysterious figure (man, or boy, or woman, it could not be seen, so dark was the spot and so sudden the appearance) dashed in among the three men, and, rushing between the legs of one, hurled him in the air so that he fell with a crash, stunned and bleeding, on the rough pavement.

Then it disappeared as quickly as it had come!

Rupert's eyes followed the apparition inquiringly until it was lost to view, but little did he think who that strange friend was, or what an important part he would take in the unravelling of the wild secrets of his life!

The tide had now turned.

Startled by the sudden appearance of an unexpected friend, the two assassins lost confidence, and taking

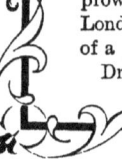

advantage of an unguarded moment Rupert made a brilliant lunge and ran one of his adversaries through the body.

"Now," he cried, as the assassin fell with a thud and a groan upon the jagged stones, "now we will see if Rupert Dreadnought will not return home safe and sound to hear his father's dying curse upon his enemies!"

But the battle was virtually over.

The third man made but a feeble resistance, and, presently, making a feint, he stepped back, and turning suddenly, fled away through the darkness.

Rupert made no attempt at pursuit.

His mind was busy with his father's approaching death, and eager to hear his dying instructions; and, keeping his sword still unsheathed, he hurried once more towards home.

The old earl had not been disturbed since his departure, and when the youth entered he dismissed the servant and resumed his place at the bedside.

Presently the sleeper moved, and the aged eyes opened.

"Are you there, Rupert?" he asked.

"Yes," said the youth, turning eagerly, "yes; I will never leave you."

The old man put forth his thin hand, which the youth pressed eagerly.

"Good Rupert; good son," said he. "I am dying fast, but my sleep has refreshed me; and now, while I have strength, I would speak to you. Draw near, and lean over me that I may pour into your ears a tale of terrible sorrow—the foundation of a life-long vengeance. Is the door fast?"

"Aye, father, well fastened."

"And have the servants their orders?"

"Yes. No one shall be admitted; fear not. At my sword's point I will defend the peace of your last bed!"

"Have any of my hungry relations come here and been refused?"

"None as yet. I have been summoned this evening, on a false errand during your sleep, and have been attacked by assassins in the street, but they have not attempted as yet to come here. They have, perhaps, thought it best after all *not* to do so. However, fear not; if they do come——"

The old man started.

"Hark!" he cried. "Stealthy footsteps approach. See—quick!—who comes!"

The youth, with his hand upon his sword, sprang at once to the door, and opening it, listened.

Up the broad, marble staircase, the steps of some one approaching were distinctly audible.

A moment's thought decided Rupert, and, closing the door behind him, he advanced towards a part of the corridor where a lamp shone above, and illumined with its dull light a square landing.

Here he waited.

Not for long.

In a few moments a man's form emerged from the gloom.

Another form, gliding stealthily, followed him, and, unseen by Rupert, concealed itself in the shadow of the staircase.

The new comer was a man wearing a mask, dressed in the garb of a gentleman, but with a kind of flashy gaudiness about him, which proclaimed the parvenu, the man risen from the dregs of society.

RUPERT DREADNOUGHT.

He advanced with a swagger towards Rupert.

"What want you, sir?" demanded the youth, haughtily.

"I come to see Lord Desmond Dreadnought," replied the stranger.

"'Tis too late," replied Rupert, "you cannot see him."

"Is he, then, dead?" said the other, in an anxious tone.

"He is not; but death is hovering over him with eager wings, and he desires, before he passes away, to commit to me a sacred trust. He will see no one."

"Tell him my name; say that a friend of Everard Dalby is without. Go quickly."

"I refuse; I have sworn to guard his death-bed from intruders, and with my good sword here I will keep my trust."

"Insolent boy!" cried the masked intruder, "who are you who thus bar my passage? Stand aside, ere I chastise you!"

"And is it thus you would force yourself to the chamber of death?" cried the youth, who at once suspected his connection with the midnight assassins. "I will tell you who I am. I am Rupert—soon, alas! by the death of a good father, to be Lord Dreadnought. Therefore, I have command here, and, if you value your life, retire at once and intrude not upon time.

"Stand back! I recognise no right to bar me from his presence!" cried the other. "I must and *will* see him! I come with news that he would long to hear. So, while the spark of life still lingers within him, let me see and speak with him."

"I have told you that yonder chamber of death shall on *no* pretence whatever be entered by a living soul save me," replied Rupert Dreadnought, firmly, as he stood still erect and sword in hand. "If you do not quit this house quietly, within five minutes, my servants shall cast you into the street, for I will *not* measure swords with you."

A sneering smile curled upon the lips of the stranger.

"Coward!" he muttered.

For an instant the young man's sword was raised.

But only for an instant.

"No," he said, as he dropped it, pale and angry withal, "I will not be forced into a quarrel. Ho there, John and Leonard!"

Hardly had he uttered these words when the man who had glided so mysteriously after the masked stranger rose from the dark shadow of the staircase, took aim and fired.

In the hurry of the moment, however, the aim was defective, and the ball whizzed by without effect.

Then, ere Rupert could attack the villain, he plunged down the stairs, and disappeared, but not before one glimpse had revealed to him that it was the villain who had attacked and fled from him in the street.

In an instant after a door was flung open, and two men appeared armed with short daggers.

In spite of the modern times, the old Lord Dreadnought invariably kept armed retainers about him.

Why, this was a mystery.

In fact, his whole life had been one which no one could fathom.

The two men glanced in some surprise at the scene before them, and the foremost said—

"What is the matter, Master Rupert, and who fired the shot?"

"My father is dying, as you know. He has a wish to see no one but myself. This man intrudes, and brings with him a hired assassin. Quick, seize him and bear him away, and at the same time see if you can trace the cowardly villain who attacked me. At another time I may meet this man, and demand of him an explanation of the planned murder which so signally failed this night."

The face of the stranger underwent a fearful change as Rupert uttered these words.

His features assumed a ghastly pallor, as if the denial which Rupert had given him had foiled the purpose of a life.

"Curses on you!" he cried, shaking his clenched fist at the young heir. "Curses on you! We *shall* meet again when there are no menial curs to bar my path to you. Farewell, Rupert Dreadnought, and remember."

He dashed down the stairs as he spoke, while the youth returned gently to the sick chamber.

His father was eagerly awaiting his coming.

"Who was that with whom you were having so loud a converse?" said the old man.

"One who calls himself a friend of Everard Dalby," replied Rupert; "he said he came on most important business; but still I took your word and bade him go."

The dying man smiled.

"You did well, my son," he said. "But why that shot? Did he refuse to go?"

"He did, and some hired assassin made a coward's attempt against my life."

"And you forced him hence?"

"I did; yet not by my own sword," replied Rupert. "Its stainless blade shall never drink the blood of braggarts save at the last moment when no chance is left, and the instinct of self-preservation is uppermost, as it is with all. I sent him hence by calling forth our menials, and threatening to cast him forth into the street as we should cast a dog."

"And he went?"

"Aye, in a moment."

"And the assassin?"

"They are even now upon his track," replied Rupert.

A strange smile flitted over the brow of the dying man.

"Well, well," he said, "I rejoice at this. But this is no time for smiles. I have not long to live, and now I must unfold to you the strange history I have so often spoken of. You love me?"

"Yes, by the Heaven above us, yes!"

"I do believe it; but by thy sainted mother—by all thy hopes of happiness in the future—by your wish for my dying blessing—you must swear one thing ere I reveal to you the secret of my heart. Swear this, and there shall be a glorious task before you—a recompense on earth and in Heaven!"

His father glanced eagerly at him as he spoke.

"Tell me, father," replied the youth, kneeling, "and I will swear. I need but to know *your* wishes to accomplish them."

The old man placed his hand upon his son's head.

"Brave, generous youth," he said. "I knew what your answer would be. I have many enemies—men who have made my life most bitter, who have plucked every rose from my path and in its stead planted a thorn, who have made existence a curse instead of a blessing, and robbed me of every pleasure I might have culled—and against these and theirs I exact from you an oath of vengeance!"

"I swear it!" said Rupert, raising his hand to Heaven. "I swear it!"

"A deadly, an unremitting, unceasing vow of vengeance!" said the old man.

"Yes, never ceasing until death, so help me Heaven!" said Rupert Dreadnought, solemnly.

"Then, good and worthy son," resumed the old earl, "while I have yet strength within me to remember my sorrows, I will tell you my story."

CHAPTER III.

EARL DREADNOUGHT'S STORY.

It was a story of a cruel wrong that the old man had to tell—the old, old story of a stern father—a young love—a false friend.

With its details we have nothing now to do.

They will be sufficiently described in other portions of our history.

Suffice it to say that Rupert Dreadnought listened with a beating heart to his father's tale of love—how he had wooed and won his heart's treasure—how his father had forced him abroad—how his beloved Alice had been left in the care of *Robert Penraven, his bosom friend*, who had promised to watch over her, and guard her for him.

Then came the revelation of treachery.

"Fighting against the enemies of my country in foreign lands," said the old earl, with faltering accents, and with tears rolling down his cheeks, "I received a letter from Penraven telling me of Alice's death, entering into all the sad details, and endeavouring to console me."

"I cannot now attempt to describe to you my feelings on receipt of this letter.

"I need only say that I felt mad.

"The whole world appeared a blank, and I cared not how soon a friendly bullet shortened a career that had no longer in it any object.

"I never heard again from Penraven.

"Indeed, I did not trouble to tell him where I was, and the letter he had promised in a day or two never arrived.

"I became soon distinguished in the army; wherever the fight was thickest there was I.

"I was always ready to join the maddest forlorn hopes—always the first to scale a rampart—always ready to head a desperate expedition.

"But Providence seemed to keep a special watch over me.

"I was never even wounded.

"I have seen dear comrades struck down at my side; I have been in the midst of a carnage where a mist of blood seemed to hover in the air, and the very atmosphere smelt thick and faint.

"But never a bullet or a sword-thrust reached me."

"I became sickened at length of fighting, as it were, against a charmed life, and I determined to return to England.

"The lapse of time had something to do with this.

"I had had plenty of time to think, and I saw how impious it was to fight against fate.

"When I *did* return, I found how foully I had been deceived.

Alice was *not* dead—the story had been invented by Robert Penraven to deceive me, and keep me away from England, that he might have the field open to himself.

"Alice Rainford I blamed at first quite as much as I did him.

"But she was not so much to be censured when the truth came to light.

"Her father had fallen into difficulties—she had received *a printed notice of my death*, and had accepted him to save her father and herself from misery.

"The villain had woven a deadly scheme of treachery, and he had succeeded in persuading her to become his wife.

"The ceremony had not yet taken place when I reached England, and discovered the enormity of my friend's villany.

"I at once proceeded on the wings of injured love, towards my old home, resolved to thwart his plans, but the villain heard of my coming, and took plans to baffle me.

"Aided by some gipsies, and a villanous brother (who is the father of Oscar, your enemy), he seized upon me, carried me away to a lonely house, and there for a long time I languished, helpless and alone.

"I will not dwell upon the hideous misery of that time.

"Heaven forgive me for the thoughts that rushed into my mind.

"I was a murderer then, in thought, if in nothing else.

"I resolved to devote my life to vengeance, but that unfortunately I have been unable to fulfil, and I leave that task to you.

"At length I was released.

"I sought my enemy everywhere in vain, and in the search I met with one who soothed my aching heart at last, and recompensed me in some degree for the treachery which had been the ruin and desolation of my youth.

"That one was your mother; Helen, my ward, is my Alice's youngest child."

"Her child!" exclaimed Rupert, in astonishment.

"Yes, indeed. She was sent to me by Alice herself, after she had discovered Robert's treachery, and begun to experience his cruelty.

"I leave her to you as a sacred trust. See to her happiness. If you can love her, marry her.

"That is my first wish. Now for the GREAT WORK OF YOUR LIFE.

"Set out to-morrow, see Helen Penraven, place her in a place of safety, and, as I have said, visit her often; and if you can make it consonant with your feelings make her your wife.

"But *not* before five years.

"During that time you must work out your oath of vengeance. Go, my son, towards yonder pilaster."

The youth obeyed.

"Touch the rose which is on the left hand side."

"It is done, father," said Rupert.

"Now, then," said the earl, "you will see a chest."

"I do."

"Come here, then, and I will place into your hands the key of the mystery."

With much wonder in his heart, the youth obeyed the words of his father, whose failing voice now betokened the swift approach of death.

"See," said the old earl, as he drew something from beneath his pillow, "see, this is the key; but remember you have sworn to do my bidding."

"I have."

"And I trust you, my son," said his father, fondly, "yes, I trust you. In this iron chest there are five compartments. Each compartment contains a parchment detailing my wishes, and the money wherewith to accomplish them. Each reveals to you a mission of vengeance which you have sworn to carry out. But, remember, until one vow is fulfilled the second must not be investigated. When you have seen that Helen is in safety, then open the iron chest, read carefully the matter contained in the first compartment, but beware of looking at the second. While you are seeing to Helen's safety, bury the key in the back vault of this house under the third stone from the door. It will there be in safety. Come, my son, come nearer; I feel exhausted; but I feel also happy in the thought that you will fulfil my wishes."

"Yes, to the last letter, dear father," said the youth, with tears in his eyes.

The old man held his son's hand in his, and remained silent a moment.

Then he said faintly—

"It is come, Rupert; it is come! Farewell. REMEMBER YOUR VOW!"

And, with these words, the spirit of the old earl passed away, and the NEW EARL, pledged to A LIFE OF MYSTERY, sank at the bedside to weep!

AND THE CLOCK STRUCK TWELVE AS HE KNELT!

CHAPTER IV.

THE SECOND DEATH—ANOTHER VOW OF VENGEANCE—THE INSTRUCTIONS OF THE DYING MAN—THE APPARITION!—THE DEATH OF A TRAITOR.

WE must now turn to the room where the second man lay dying—the man whose nephew had entered so strangely the mad revel of the Poisoners.

At his bedside sat the youth some two hours before he had passed in among the dancers.

There was a wondrous likeness between uncle and nephew; the same dark-looking features, the same savage, piercing eyes, the same thin-lipped mouth.

He, too, had been listening to a commission of vengeance, though given in a different way.

For it was Robert Penraven—Sir Robert Penraven, who was lying on that bed of death, not half a mile distant from the room where his old enemy, the man he had ruined in happiness for ever, lay dying also!

"Oscar," said the old baronet; "Oscar, you see I am fast dying."

"Yes."

"Repeat your oath, then."

"Yes, yes, I repeat it once more; but why this exaction? I *shall* perform it."

"My adopted child, forgive the petulance of deadly sickness," replied Penraven; "but I wish to speak of Helen, your cousin. You must rescue her, tear her from the hands of my old enemy."

"He is dying."

"Yes; but he leaves a son on whom your vengeance must fall swiftly and surely. He has concealed Helen somewhere; those papers will tell you where. When the breath leaves my body, fly at once to the spot indicated there, and convey her to some place far from London, where none of that evil brood shall see her."

"I will."

"And mark me," said the baronet, "if she loves young Dreadnought, *kill her* rather than allow her to mate with one for whom my hate is unextinguishable even in death. Remember this."

"I do, uncle," replied the youth, looking impatiently at the clock.

What could this look signify?

Was he eager for his uncle's death?

Had he assisted in hastening it?

This at present is a mystery we cannot pretend to penetrate.

But it seemed truly as if he was anxious for the moment to arrive which should see the breath pass from the body.

The old baronet observed his anxious looks.

"Why do you so eagerly gaze at yonder clock?" he asked at length.

The youth started.

He had no idea that in his dying state the baronet would observe him.

"I am thinking of Dreadnought," he said.

Penraven's eyes sparkled with demoniacal glee as he answered,

"You are sure he is dying?"

"Yes, sure. I am reckoning the minutes as they fly."

"And the messenger will come?"

"Yes. I have so arranged it."

The baronet smiled.

"Good boy, good boy," he said. "Give me some more wine. I must not die before I know that my greatest foe is gone."

The youth rose immediately, and approached a table whereon were bottles of sparkling wine.

Pouring out a large quantity in a deep glass, he approached the bed, and his uncle drank eagerly.

The draught appeared to revive him, and he, too, looked at the clock.

"It is approaching midnight," he said. "When did you hear last?"

"About an hour since."

"And he was then dying fast?"

"Yes."

"And so must all his brood!" exclaimed the baronet, to whom the wine had given a renewal of false strength. "So must all his hated brood. Not one of the detested stock must be left. Ha! what is that?"

As he spoke there was a loud knocking at the door.

"He comes!" said the baronet, excitedly.

The next moment the door was flung violently open.

A chill wind invaded the apartment, shaking the curtains, and nearly extinguishing the lamp that stood by the bedside.

Then a man entered.

He was a roughly-dressed fellow, wearing a sword, but evidently of no gentle blood.

But it was not at him, rudely as he entered, that the dying man looked.

It was not his appearance that made him start, and, half rising in his bed, clutch his son's arm, and, with starting eye-balls, glare upwards.

It was a far stranger and more terrible vision which he beheld with his glaring eyes!

Entering behind the messenger of death, and floating above him, with one hand extended over the man's head, and pointing threateningly, warningly, was the white, misty form of the dead Earl Dreadnought.

'His eyes were fixed on those of the man who was so soon to join him, but who seemed truly as if he were roused into new life through very horror.

"See—see, Oscar!" he cried; "the ghostly form that follows him! See, 'tis my old enemy approaches. He glares at me! He points with shadowy hand! Oh! mercy—mercy! save me from this horrid thing!"

RUPERT OR THE DREADNOUGHT SECRETS OF THE IRON CHEST

"YOU HAVE DONE WELL!" SAID THE CHIEF OF THE POISONERS.

The man who had entered the room of the dying man stood transfixed with wonder and alarm, as the excited speaker pointed over his head at some unreal thing which no one else could see.

"What means this?" asked he.

"I know not," said Oscar; "but is the Earl Dreadnought dead?"

"He is. He died but a few minutes ago, and I have hastened to inform you."

"And was your presence suspected?"

"It was not; but, see, your uncle beckons, and, by the look upon his face, his days are numbered too."

The old man was now of a green and ghastly pallor, as with deadly fear.

The dews of death upon his brow were big and heavy.

The eyes stared wildly—the hands clenched fiercely together, as if in mortal agony.

"Oh, it is terrible!" he muttered, as Oscar bent over him. "He comes to summon me. See how he glares and smiles in triumph on me! Oh, this is death—death! Oscar—REMEMBER!"

Then he fell back with a groan, and the youth, listen as he might, could hear his voice no more!

Over him, too, the shadow of death had fallen, and the two youths, bound to deadly vengeance by a terrible vow, were alone in the world!

Leaving the messenger to keep lonely vigil by the side of the dead, we will follow Oscar now to the Poisoners' Revel, and see how he fared there, and how he fulfilled the first promise he had made to his adopted father.

CHAPTER IV.

THE POISONERS ONCE MORE—ROSALIE ST. AUBYN—THE SUMMONS TO THE SECRET CHAMBER—THE MYSTERIOUS MASK—THE TRAITOR—THE OATH OF RETRIBUTION.

As the young man entered the brilliantly lighted room where the Poisoners were holding their revel, the company, male and female, as I have said, moved aside to allow him to pass, and murmurs of various and mysterious import might have been heard from all sides.

Sir Oscar Penraven, however, took no notice of any one, but walked onwards with firm step towards a part of the room, where sat a man dressed in the dress of a cavalier of the time of Charles I.

This man was seated apart from the rest, and seemed to possess a kind of authority over those around him.

He greeted Oscar Penraven with a haughtiness that evidently foreboded evil, for the brow of the young man became pale as marble.

"He is dead," said Oscar.

"You speak of your uncle?" said the cavalier, in a stern voice.

"I do. He passed away but half an hour since."

"And the property?"

"Is left as you desired it—to me; and is at the disposal of your dread tribunal."

"It is well. And when will the title deeds be given over to me?"

"The day that sees my uncle buried," returned Oscar, "will see the papers also in your hands."

The cavalier mused a moment.

Then he glanced at the clock.

"It is time," he murmured.

Then he beckoned Oscar to him.

"Leave this room," he said, "and pass into my private study. You know well the way. I have a secret of the utmost importance to reveal to you, and I will follow you, therefore, in a moment."

The young baronet moved away sick, and faint at heart.

He felt that some strange event was about to happen.

The manner of the old man had told him this plainly enough.

He had not much time for the indulgence of these thoughts, however.

A fairy vision sprang before him.

It was a young girl dressed in a light, fantastic garb, which showed the whole of her rounded shoulders, and a leg as far up as the knee, well formed and large, while a pair of eyes of bewitching brightness gleamed through the holes of the mask.

"Oscar, or rather, Sir Oscar," she cried, "whither go you so fast?"

Oscar started, and a smile overspread his pale features.

"Whither? To the study of our chief, Dr. Henzollern," he answered; "he has need of me; but wait for me, Rosalie. Even in this terrible hour a smile from you has power to give me joy."

He raised her plump white hand to his lips as he spoke, and kissed it.

A roseate hue overspread the neck and bosom of the young girl, showing how pleased she was at the compliment.

Strange, that in such a scene of terrible revelry, such a frail and modest thing as a blush should have survived!

"Yes, I will wait for you," replied the young girl, tenderly pressing the hand of Oscar Penraven; "but be not long."

"I will not. Wait yonder, near our President's chair. Farewell, for the nonce, dear Rosalie."

So saying, he passed behind a curtain, and disappeared.

The young girl watched him till he was out of sight, and then turned once more towards the dancers, murmuring—

"He will come again. I know it."

"*If he be alive!*" said a voice by her side.

She started sharply round, and saw standing near her a tall man, masked like the rest, and dressed in a fantastic garb, which resembled the costume of the old buccaneers of the West.

"Did you address me?" she said, in a voice of some dread as well as anger.

"I did."

"And why? You cannot know my heart."

"I do; better than you know it yourself," returned the man. "That youth," he added, in a low voice, as he laid one hand upon her shoulder, and with the other pointed towards the door, "that youth whom you are striving to lure into your toils may never return. 'Tis a dangerous place this for traitors, so beware!"

"I am no traitor," returned the girl, quickly starting from his grasp, with neck and bosom crimsoned with anger and alarm; "leave me, or I will pronounce a word that shall consign you to an instant death!"

A low laugh escaped the lips of the mysterious stranger.

"I, too, Rosalie St. Aubyn," he said, "could pronounce that word, and seal your fate also. But

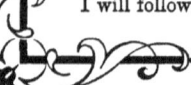

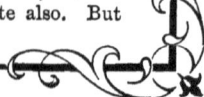

remember my words. This is no place for traitors. If they are discovered, *they die!*"

Then before she could make reply he strode away, and passed behind the curtain, beneath which Oscar Penraven had disappeared a moment before.

"This man has cast a dread upon me," said the girl, shudderingly, as she passed towards the fire which played merrily at one end of the apartment. "He knows my name and yet I know him not; neither could I through his mask catch one glimpse of any feature save his red gleaming eyes. I shall advise Oscar of this. And yet what meant he by *his* terrible words of warning?"

Meanwhile, leaving Rosalie St. Aubyn to doubt and wonder, we must follow the young baronet into the study of the President of the Poisoners.

It was a dismal room, hung with black tapestry, and filled with heavy furniture, and strange old books, while on stands and shelves were an infinity of miniature phials with liquids of every imaginable colour.

When Oscar Penraven entered there was no one present, but no sooner had his foot touched a certain plank in the flooring than a bell rung, and two men entered.

One was the man with the red, gleaming eyes, who had so alarmed Rosalie St. Aubyn, the other was a stranger.

These two ranged themselves on either side of another curtain, which evidently concealed a door, and in a moment after the President entered.

Advancing to the table which stood in the centre of the room, he said, in a solemn tone of voice,

"Oscar Penraven, you have hitherto acted honourably and truly towards our Society."

"I trust I have," replied Oscar, firmly, yet respectfully; "my wish has ever been to aid you, as I have proved in the last few hours."

"We know it, and therefore at the dread meeting which took place this day in this room," continued the President, "your name was not set down in the list of traitors. You remember, however, that about a month since you enrolled the name of one Lawrence Gascoigne, for whom you became guarantee?"

"I did."

"You had good reasons for believing him faithful?"

"We have been friends since youth," replied Penraven.

"Good. We were satisfied at the time that you did not hastily or without judgment enrol his name in our catalogue of true men. We therefore acquit you of blame."

"Blame! for what?" exclaimed Oscar, in a tone of genuine astonishment.

"You will know in a few moments. Were you aware of his means of subsistence?"

"I believed him to be independent."

"He was not; he was a spy in the pay of the Government!"

The words fell like a thunder-clap upon the ears of the young reprobate.

"A spy!" he repeated, under his breath, "impossible!"

"It is true," continued the President, "but fortunately for us his thirst for gold was so great that he defeated his own purpose. Listen, and I will tell you the story of his treachery.

"Three nights since, I and another member of our Society were traversing a dark and dismal street, where even now some ruins can be seen, relics of the Fire of London, when we thought that we heard voices engaged in earnest conversation.

"We stopped suddenly beneath the shadow of a wall, and listened, for it is our business to learn the secrets of all.

"'I thought I heard footsteps,' said a voice, which I at once recognised as that of Lawrence Gascoigne.

"'Oh, no, it is your fancy,' replied the other, who was an utter stranger to me. 'You are so infernally nervous that it's ten to one you spoil the whole affair.'

"'No, no, I am not nervous,' replied Gascoigne, 'though well I might be, knowing the terrible vengeance which will fall upon my head if I am discovered. Listen patiently, and I will tell you all quickly.'

"Then I listened, my blood curdling the while, as he told the whole story of our Society—its foundation—its rules—its terrors.

"'Well,' said the officer, when Gascoigne finished, 'you tell me enough to take my breath away. The reward which is offered for the discovery of these villains is enormous. We must share it between us. But there is one whom I must first consult.'

"'Who is he?'

"'Gerard Offley, the cleverest of all the secret agents of the Government.'

"'Is he a true man?' asked Gascoigne, the traitor, in a trembling voice.

"'Yes, yes, we may depend upon him, especially when such a reward is in view. It would be only madness on his part to tell others, and so lessen his own chance of a large share.'

"'True. And when will you bring him?'

"'I will meet you here at ten to-morrow night at this very spot, and we can then make arrangements for descending upon the gang of Poisoners at their next revel.'

"The traitor then departed, and we saw the other spy passing away in another direction.

"'Your doom is sealed,' thought I.

"But I restrained my anger.

"There was every chance that the other man would reveal at once to Gerard Offley the reason of the secret meeting, which had been arranged for the next night, and it was best, therefore, to permit the assemblage of spies to take place at the appointed time.

"Accordingly, I and my companion quitted our hiding-place, and on the following night we repaired to the ruins again with a dozen companions.

"This force I so disposed that there could be no escape for our enemies.

"They knew exactly what to do, for their orders were most precise.

"At length the hour of ten came, and precisely as it struck, your good friend Gascogine made his appearance.

"A few moments after came the two Government agents.

"'This is my friend, Gerard Offley,' said the one I had seen on the night before.

"'Glad to see you,' said Gascoigne; 'you are to your time.'

"'George Beckford never fails,' returned the Bow Street runner, pompously. 'Now, Master Gascoigne, let us hear your story once more.'

"He did so.

"The officers listened intently—eagerly to every word.

"'When will their next revel be?' asked Offley.

"'To-morrow night.'

"'And this friend who introduced you, this Penraven, is to be captured and suffer with the rest.'

"'Yes,' returned Gascoigne, 'yes, he would never forgive me, and might prove a dangerous foe in the future.'

"Impossible!" murmured Oscar Penraven.

"It is true," replied the President of the dread tribunal. "Well, this villain, who was ready to sacrifice his own friend's life in this heartless manner, proceeded then to detail to his hearers the same that he had detailed on the night preceding in regard to the revel of to-night.

"Gerard Offley listened eagerly, and when Gascoigne finished, he exclaimed—

"'We will break in upon them when they think themselves most secure.'

"'As *I* do upon *you*,' I exclaimed, in a loud voice.

"This was the signal agreed upon.

"When my voice was heard they were to fall upon and kill the officers, except Gascoigne, who was to be reserved for a more terrible fate.

"'You have betrayed us, villain!' cried Gerard Offley, as the shadows seemed to take life, and the men surrounded them.

"They gazed at him with murderous eyes.

"But they had no chance of acting, whatever might have been their feelings.

"My friends rushed forward; bright knives flashed in the air, and Offley and Beckford died upon the instant.

"For an instant Gascoigne stood at bay.

"But it was not for long.

"A heavy blow struck him senseless to the earth, and when he again awoke he was in yonder iron room, from which that curtain and a thick door separates us."

"And why is he there?" asked Oscar, trembling, for he guessed the fearful import of the President's words.

"Listen," said the latter, "and, though your oath should tell you, I will explain."

CHAPTER V.

THE VICTIM—THE IRON ROOM—THREE CHOICES OF DEATH—THE TERRIBLE TASK—THE SILENT COMBAT—THE STRUGGLE IN THE DARK—THE TRAP-DOOR—THE REVEL ONCE MORE.

"YOU remember," continued the President, "the oath that you took when you first entered our Society?"

"I do well."

"If anyone introduces a friend, and this friend becomes a traitor, the person introducing him is bound by oath to kill him. Is it not so?" asked the President, gazing fixedly into the eyes of the young baronet.

A shudder passed through the frame of Oscar Penraven.

Nevertheless he answered firmly—

"Yes, it is so."

The President pointed to the door before which hung the curtain.

"Go, then," he said, "your victim awaits you. See, there on the table are your weapons—a bottle of poison, a knife, and a pistol. It may be that when he sees his doom to be inevitable, he will relieve you of the necessity of shedding his blood by voluntarily taking the fatal draught. But remember, his death must be certain—and by your hand! Go, we await you here."

The youth who had so lately quitted the still chamber of death, shuddered again as he approached the place where his victim was confined.

He knew the task, terrible as it was, was inevitable.

Nothing but his own death could relieve him from it.

So he advanced boldly, in spite of the fact that he fancied he heard the rustling of wings near him, and felt a chill air invade his very veins.

The room where the victim sat communicated, as the President had said, with that in which he had just made his unexpected announcement, and, as soon as the two sentinels had withdrawn the bolts, there was little difficulty in making his way into the iron room.

As soon as he had entered the door was barred again, and he was alone with his victim.

It was a small room, with nothing in it but a small table, a chair, and some heavy hangings in one corner.

All the walls were painted black, and here and there small gratings were placed in the walls to admit the air and also to permit the chiefs of the terrible Society to see and hear all that passed within.

Neither Gascoigne nor Oscar Penraven were aware of this.

The former started from his chair with a smile as Oscar entered.

"Ah, my friend," he said, "they have then permitted you to see me."

"They have," returned Penraven, avoiding the outstretched hand. "You see for the last time the one whom you would have betrayed and destroyed for money."

A fear of something—an indefinite dread crept into the heart of the prisoner as Oscar spoke.

He looked eagerly into his friend's face.

"What do you mean?" he faltered. "I never intended to destroy you——"

"Hold!" cried Oscar Penraven, "hold! I know all; and *you* know the terrible vow which binds us to each other."

"I do."

"You know also that it was I who introduced you to the Society."

"It was."

"I believed you faithful, and I took the oath for you, swearing that you were a good and true man, and bidding myself to take your life with my own hands if you turned out a traitor."

"A mere mockery to alarm the weak-minded," said Gascoigne.

"It is no mockery," returned Oscar Penraven, solemnly. "I come to fulfil my vow. See here my weapons; poison—the dagger—the pistol!"

Gascoigne staggered back to the farther corner of the room, and pressed his hand to his brow, upon which now the large beads of perspiration had burst forth.

"You are mad!" he cried; "you cannot mean it; this is murder—cool, deliberate murder."

"And pray what would your act of treachery have resulted in? What, but cool and deliberate murder? Besides, what oaths have you taken yourself? Are we not members of a band of poisoners—sworn Agents of Death, bound to him by terrible vows of slaughter? What is our trade but murder?"

Gascoigne groaned.

"Choose," said Oscar; "here is a poison which will bring to you an instant death, sure but painless. I offer it you now in the name of old friendship. Drink!"

"Truly a friendly offering," said Gascoigne, eying his adversary with eager glances. "I refuse it."

"You refuse?"

"I do. I will fight for my life."

And, with these words, he sprang towards his foe.

But Oscar Penraven was too quick for him, and a sharp stab in the arm warned the spy to be more careful of his foe.

It was for him a most fearful position.

He had, with the courage which is so often found in those who assume the administration of the country's laws, resolved to risk his life in order to discover the cause of the hideous calamities which were decimating the metropolis.

It would be wrong to say that in all this the spy had not an idea of gain.

But of this desire we must all of us plead in some degree guilty.

All of us desire money, no matter how wealthy, no matter how old we are, and no matter how useless it will be to us when gained.

Every man, no matter how spendthrift he may be, loves gold, if it is only for the pleasure of handling it and spending it before the admiring crowd!

Now he had lost all his aims!

He gazed at his friend, the one (bad though he might be) whom he had purposed to betray, and waited.

What could he do?

Even if he succeeded in betraying this friend—now his enemy—would it avail him?

Yet how useless to think thus.

OSCAR PENRAVEN.

The first danger is always the worst, and it was naturally the first impulse to save himself.

He looked, therefore, with savage determination at his enemy, and was just about to make a dash at him, when Penraven fired.

But the ball took no effect.

There was a flash, a report, and the ball spun back from the iron wall.

The poison had been refused, the pistol had missed its aim.

There remained only now *one* weapon, the dagger.

With this he now prepared to attack his foe.

Gascoigne's eyes glittered with terrible meaning.

But Oscar was not dismayed.

Young as he was, he knew that his own life depended upon his acting promptly, and he at length rushed headlong upon his victim.

Gascoigne was an older and a stronger man; but he was unarmed, and was, moreover, weakened by the knowledge that he was surrounded by foes, in the centre of a band of determined murderers, who (if Oscar failed) would in all likelihood rush upon him like a pack of bloodhounds.

The struggle, therefore, hideous and terrible as it was, was not of long duration.

The dagger, short, easy of use, and sharp, was a fearful weapon, used as it was against an unarmed man, and in the course of a few moments the spy lay gasping in horrible agony in one corner of the iron cell.

"Oh! in mercy spare me!" cried the wretched man, "for the sake of old friendship! For the love of God, spare me!"

There was no answer in words.

Oscar Penraven had his work now to perform, and he knew that there was no use in attempting to shirk it.

It was life or death to him.

Either he or the wretched spy must be the victim of that night.

So he nerved his arm for the deed.

The hot breath of the murderer rushed in horrid gusts upon the cheek of the dying man.

The steel lightened the darkness—the voice of the dying gurgled out a curse. Heaven whispered its promise of revenge and justice through the tremulous tones of the passing spirit, and then—

All was over!

During the struggle, the lamp had been extinguished, and the place was therefore buried in utter darkness.

But, even through the gloom, it seemed to Oscar Penraven as if the ghastly white face of the dead man was glaring at him, and telling him of a vengeance to come!

Oscar, strong and full of nerve as he was, trembled as he imagined to himself this horrible vision.

He was old truly in sin.

But yet he was but a youth.

His frame might be tall and powerful; his mind might have been schooled in crime; but, nevertheless, age is something, and he could not be so coolly villanous as those who had served a long apprenticeship in crime.

Resolved, therefore, to escape as quickly as possible from the scene of horror, he stooped to pick up the weapon which had fallen from his hand in the last struggle.

As he searched, his hand came in contact with the face of the murdered man.

He started back, and uttered a wild, piercing cry.

A cry, driven from his bosom as it were by intense horror!

In an instant, as if by magic, the place was illumined by a bright ray of light, which came with a rush through the open door.

The President and the two sentinels were standing there, gazing with evident interest at the scene.

"You have done well," said the Chief of the Poisoners, addressing Oscar Penraven, who was standing leaning upon the table in the centre of the room. "You have done excellently well; the villain is dead!"

"Quite dead!" returned the youth, shudderingly.

"And our secret is safe. Come," added he, addressing the two men by his side, "come, let us bury him, and let the thought of this night's work be buried for ever in oblivion!"

The men advanced with him into the room, and then, closing the door, proceeded to bury the dead.

It was a strange burial!

The flooring of part of the chamber, being touched by a spring, moved away, and disclosed a chasm, dark and mysterious, and emitting a dank and fetid odour, while the rush of waters could plainly be distinguished beneath.

"Whither does this lead?" asked Oscar Penraven, with a shudder.

"Below is the river—the swiftly-flowing river," replied the Chief Poisoner, "and this body, borne away by the rushing tide, will carry with it our secret for ever. Come, is all ready?"

While this brief conversation had been going on, the two attendants had raised the body of Gascoigne, the Government spy, and approached the yawning gulf.

One moment they steadied their awful burden over the abyss.

Then they loosed their hold, and it fell with a dull sound—down among the plashing waters, which sent back an echo like the yell of a warning avenger!

Little did they dream who the AVENGER would be.

Oscar Penraven gazed at them silently.

For the first time in his life his hands had been stained in blood!

It was a commencement of a career of crime, a good schooling in murder, and when the President clapped him on the shoulder, and bade him follow him, he started as from some fantastic dream.

"Is he dead?" he asked.

"Aye, dead and buried, too! It was well done. But come, let us rejoin the dancers, and presently we will drink to the health of the new Baronet of Penraven."

Oscar shuddered.

He had wished for wealth, freedom, and distinction.

What cared he for it now?

There was a mist of terror before his eyes which took from him all memory of the death that had given him his wish.

"I am bloodstained," he said. "My hands are yet hot from crime; I cannot go into a scene of revelry like this."

"Foolish boy!" exclaimed his Terrible Companion, "foolish boy! They will know nothing of this deed. A few glasses of wine, moreover, will revive your spirits, and you will look upon this death scene as some hideous dream. Come."

He said the last word somewhat sternly, and taking Oscar Penraven's arm, led him through the black-tapestried room, beneath the curtain, and into the ball-room, where the Poisoners were still whirling round and round in the giddy mazes of the dance.

They were old in crime.

The hideous doings of the past year, and the awful prospects of the new year, had no effect upon *their* merriment.

Here soft eyes greeted him, a soft arm passed into his, and a soft voice murmured to him—

"You have been long, very long, Oscar, and you look pale and ill. Drink!"

The maddened youth seized eagerly the proffered bumper, then another and another was tossed down his parched throat, and in a few moments, reckless, intoxicated with terror and strong wine, he whirled away with his fair companion among the gay and hideous throng

CHAPTER VI.

THE IRON CHEST—HELEN PENRAVEN—THE WARNING VOICE AND THE WARNING HAND—IS SHE IN DANGER?—THE PURSUIT—THE BATTLE ON THE DARK HEATH—THE SUDDEN RUSE AND FLIGHT—MURDERERS ON THE TRACK.

WHEN Rupert Dreadnought rose from the spot where he had knelt by the side of his beloved father, now lying in the still majesty of death, he had re-registered the vow which he had taken.

Once, and once only his eyes turned wistfully towards the iron chest which contained the wonderful secrets which were to be his guiding stars in after life.

But his mind was firmly resolved.

His first task was to seek Helen Penraven, the daughter of his father's enemy—the cousin of his own sworn foe—the one upon whom already his youthful heart was set.

He knew well where Helen had been placed by his father.

It was in a house some miles from London; in a lone and sombre spot, yet in itself a garden of beauty.

It was in such a place as this of necessity that she would be most safe, and the young girl herself was quite as eager as they to escape for ever from the hands of her stern and terrible father, and a cousin whom she feared no less.

A few hours' sleep was absolutely necessary to the young lord ere he went upon this journey. His vigils had been long and frequent.

Scarcely for an hour had he allowed his father to be under the care of any but himself.

What terror would have been his had he known that the disease of which his father was dying was an unnatural one—the prevailing epidemic—the Breath of Poison!

Little dreaming, however, of such a horror, he had tended him with eager hope, and now exhausted nature demanded a short repose.

It had been Rupert's resolve, at first, to make his journey at once, but the bright sun of the morning deterred him.

His life was one now of secret vengeance, and if he were to be followed by enemies, the day was the very worst time he could choose.

After mature consideration, therefore, he resolved to put off till the night his journey to Sandmount.

The sun, however, which had promised to be so bright soon changed its mind.

One of the thoroughly English rains began falling about noon.

Plash! plash! plash!

Regular and unceasing, the steady and monotonous shower deluged the streets.

Plash, plash, plash, fell the big drops on the flooded thoroughfare.

Scarcely a single figure, as evening came on, might be seen struggling through the heavy rain, which at times makes the most fashionable avenues in London appear to be deserted, like that city of the dead of which we are told in old legends where nothing of seemliness and shadowy splendour was wanting save the activity and pulsation of actual life.

Plash! plash!

Drearily it plashed against the window-panes of the room where the dead man lay.

But towards night it seemed to clear up suddenly, that is to say, the rain ceased; but as the atmosphere warmed a steam of humid vapour rose from the ground and concealed from the one side of the road the view of the other like a November fog.

"Good," thought Rupert Dreadnought, as he prepared to start upon his journey; "this will effectually baffle all pursuit. No one, however well-sighted, could see me through this mist."

He forgot the consequent danger to himself from the same cause.

A horse was ready saddled at the door, and as eight tolled from the clock of the neighbouring church, he set forth rapidly upon his journey.

From the spot where he started, it was no long journey into the dark, wild roads of Essex, and he soon found himself dashing along on his steaming horse over a lonely and tree-lined road.

The mist was not quite so dense here as it was in the City of London.

But still it was very dark, and on a road where no lamps were it was dangerous travelling to the unwary.

Rupert, therefore, had soon to slacken his pace, and proceed cautiously, for here and there heavy market carts had made deep ruts in the road, and large stones and pieces of timber lay about, which greatly endangered the horse's legs as he stumbled and staggered on.

There was no definite reason for such continuous and rapid exertion.

He had no right to suppose, in fact, that Helen was in danger, except from the fact of the forged letter which had so strangely called him from his father's dying bed.

And this, moreover, hardly gave him sufficient reason.

It might simply have been the idea of the moment, and have no reference to any imminent peril to *her*.

But a warning voice seemed urging him continually forward.

A warning hand seemed to beckon through the heavy mist.

The old earl, grim in the majesty of Death, appeared hovering near, leading him still onward to the point where the first step in his mysterious mission was to be taken.

With such incentives, therefore, it was not wonderful that he urged his steed on to his full speed as long as he was able.

Frequent stumbles, however, as I have said, warned him to be more careful.

He slackened his pace.

As he did so, he fancied that he heard the sound of horse's feet behind him.

It was very faint, and soon died away in the distance, though in what direction it passed it was difficult to say.

He stopped and listened a moment.

But it did not recur again, and he allowed the matter to pass away from his thoughts.

About two miles had now to be travesed, and at a cross-road, where four roads met, he had to leave the highway and ride out over a broad moor.

Just before he reached this cross-road, the fog began to lift, and when he arrived at a point where more than one suicide lay buried beneath the heavy clay, the moon broke through the shimmering haze, and showed to the astonished eyes of Rupert Dreadnought three shadowy horsemen on the other side of the road.

In an instant he reined up, and prepared to defend himself.

But there was no need of fear, at any rate at this moment.

No sooner had the three strangers beheld him than they dispersed in different directions, and the far-off clattering of their hoofs soon told that they had passed away.

Though there was no reason for immediate alarm, however, Rupert felt certain that the mysterious appearance of these men had reference to himself, and he accordingly loosened his sword in its scabbard and ere he advanced another step he examined the priming of his pistols.

Then, with a feeling of renewed confidence, the bold young adventurer went forward on his journey.

He was now out on the lonely moor, but the bright moon had risen and dispelled the mist, and he could, therefore, gallop swiftly and fearlessly forward.

Taking advantage, therefore, of the temporary cessation of the dismal weather, he put spurs to his horse, and dashed away at full speed.

No one interfered with him now, and although distant sounds now and then caused his horse to start and prick up its ears, the animal steadily pursued its way.

At length in the distance he could see looming out of the darkness the outlines of the house where he hoped to see Helen Penraven.

There was a portion of the heath just before he reached the house where a mass of trees clustered and formed a miniature wood.

So dense was it that any terrible crime could have lain hidden in its gloomy depths.

Just as Rupert neared this place, he descried once more the shadowy forms of horsemen, and ere he could see more than that they were now four instead of three, his foemen were upon him.

Who they were it was impossible for him to say, for they were all masked and attacked him savagely yet silently.

He was for the moment bewildered.

There was no apparent method of escape, but yet the idea of surrender never crossed his mind.

This, however, was apparently more the object of his adversaries than immediate murder.

They surrounded him but made no effort to slay him.

"What means this mummery?" he shouted, in an angry voice. "Tell me what want you with me, or let me pass in peace."

It was a strange voice that answered him.

"Surrender!" it exclaimed, "we give no explanation."

"Tell me to whom I surrender, at least," replied Rupert, who resolved to endeavour to temporise with his strange enemies. "This is but sorry courtesy, even in warfare, to meet a foeman in a dark spot and demand surrender without word of explanation. Is it money you require?"

A derisive laugh echoed loudly over the dusky heath.

"Money; no, we demand no money," replied the man, who had made himself spokesman, "neither do we desire your blood."

"What then?"

"The surrender of yourself to us. There are weighty reasons why you *must* go with us. If you refuse to do so, wounded and helpless you will be taken. Yield while you are safe."

A rapid train of thought flashed through Rupert's mind.

He glanced round him.

Already, as I have said, he could see the dark outline of the house he sought.

There, without doubt, his beloved awaited his coming.

What could be done?

To surrender was madness.

Much as they affected to desire to save his life, they doubtless only wished to spare him now for future tortures worse than a brave man's death.

In this moment his mind was made up.

He would either cut his way through them and dash away at full speed towards his destination, or he would perish in the attempt.

Suddenly, before they had any idea of his intention, he pulled the bridle sharply, made his horse rear, and then applying the spur, went plunging away along the hard road.

"After him, my men!" exclaimed a voice, which he fancied he recognised, "let him not escape."

Several shots were fired at him as he dashed away along the road.

But none reached him.

Fortune seemed to favour him.

As he dashed away, the moon became obscured, and he was enabled in spite of their pursuit to make his way towards the wished for goal.

The gate was closed as he reached it.

It was a high iron gate, and there was no chance of leaping it.

There was no time to ring, or, indeed, make any summons, and he glanced wildly round for a means of entrance.

Chance gave it to him.

The wind had been violent on the night before, and a wide gap was visible in the high fence, where the woodwork had been blown down.

Rupert at once turned his horse's head, leaped the broad ditch, plunged across the dark grounds and reached the wide-porched door in safety.

The men whom he had left behind him on the road did not for the moment attempt any pursuit.

They remained on the spot where he had left them as if to reconnoitre.

They knew well, of course, his destination, and they were perfectly aware, therefore, where to come up with him, but this apparently was not their wish.

Eagerly they discussed the subject, and at length their leader turned his horse's head in the direction which Rupert had taken.

In the course of a short time they came in sight of the house, and stood where they could see the bright lights in the windows.

"Now, my men," said the latter, "we must enter and secure him, and Helen Penraven also. If he resists, his blood be on his own head."

Then the four men, like hungry wolves eager for their prey, advanced stealthily towards the old house on their mission of murder.

RUPERT OR THE DREADNOUGHT

SECRETS OF THE IRON CHEST

"NOW," CRIED RUPERT, "LET US CUT OUR WAY THROUGH THEM!"

CHAPTER VII.

THE TREACHEROUS SHOT.

A LOUD ring brought a servant to the door, and our hero leaped almost from his horse into the hall.

The servant glanced in surprise and some alarm as he beheld him.

Rupert shut to the door impatiently behind him before he addressed the wondering domestic.

"See to the door," he cried; "there are enemies about. Tell me at once if they surround the house. Where is Mistress Helen Penraven?"

"I will conduct you to her, Master Dreadnought,' replied the servant, who knew not that he had so lately become an earl. "She is upstairs at this moment, dreading a visit from her cousin."

In a few moment he had passed up the stairs, and was in the presence of her he loved, who, with a start of pleasure, sprang forward, and was locked in his arms.

She was a beautiful creature.

It is almost a temptation to describe her.

Yes I will, for my readers will see her before them I hope for many a long day, and her portrait, therefore, ought to be impressed upon their minds.

Rather below than above the middle height, she was attired in a tight-fitting velvet dress, which displayed to advantage her exquisitely moulded figure.

It was tight round her pretty waist; it fell in voluptuous folds over her finely-moulded limbs, and being cut low according to the fashion of the times, it revealed to the admiring beholder the whole of a soft white bosom, whose outlines might have charmed the eye of any sculptor.

Her arms, bare nearly to her shoulder, were clasped by simple gold bracelets, while over her creamy neck soft, brown ringlets fell in careless profusion.

Her eyes were dark blue, contrasting exquisitely with her hair, while her bright complexion and rosy cheeks rendered her an object of intense admiration.

Rupert's eyes wandered over her exquisite person with the true delight of a lover.

"Dearest Helen," he said, "how glad I am to once more clasp you to my breast, and yet—"

The lovely girl raised her tiny hand and playfully placed it over his lips.

"Nay, say not so," she said; "you have ever that word 'yet' to spoil all."

"Alas! this time, dear Helen," he answered, "it is no jest. My father, the one in whose kindness and goodness we have so long trusted, is dead!"

"Dead!" murmured Helen.

And she shuddered.

It is a terrible word for all.

But more terrible than can be imagined for the young.

Life in its prime and beauty seems so bright, and joyous, and full of hope that death—a sudden cutting off from all human ties and love, is something hideously depressing to a youthful mind.

"Dead!" she murmured.

"Aye, Helen," replied Rupert, "he *is;* gone at length from among us. He has left to me, *the last of our race*, moreover, a strange and terrible mission; a work to be fulfilled which will take years to accomplish. And during these years I am forbidden to claim the guardianship of you, my dearest love, by making you my wife."

It may be deemed by some unmaidenly, but a glance of disappointment beamed from the eyes of the young girl at these words.

A feeling of bitter loneliness invaded her gentle bosom.

She had for a long, long time been taught to believe that ere long she should become the loving worshipped wife of Rupert Dreadnought, and that his strong, encircling arms would shield her from all harm.

Rupert could see by her eyes, and her change of manner, how truly sad she felt at his words.

The look struck to Rupert's heart.

For an instant his resolution faltered.

Here was a young girl, warm with youthful love, ready to marry him; ready to yield herself up to him at once, while he had wealth, position, everything achieved for him by his father.

Why not marry her now, and be in a position to claim the right of guardianship?

The thought was only for a moment.

He remembered his vow.

"Grieve not, dear Helen," he said; "my father dying bound me by a vow, and this vow in the sight of Heaven I must keep."

"Yes, Rupert," replied the young girl, sadly; "yes, a vow made by you to your dying father must be kept; and *my* father—what of him?"

Rupert shook his head.

"Alas!" he answered, "my bad news is good news in this instance. Your father also is dead."

"Dead!"

"Yes; the same hour that launched my father into Eternity, saw him, too, pass away, no doubt in hate and ill-will with all. His legacy to his nephew I know not, but, if I am not incorrect in my surmise, there will be a deadly feud on both sides."

"In which, for *my* sake, Rupert, you will risk no danger."

And, as the words left the coral lips, the bright eyes beamed up tenderly in his face.

He pressed her tenderly to his breast, and kissed her rosy mouth, as he murmured—

"For *your* sake, dear Helen, I will not imperil myself in vain."

Scarcely had the thrilling kiss been given and returned—scarcely had the words been spoken, when there was a sharp report, and Rupert staggered back with a cry of pain.

CHAPTER VIII.

IN UTTER DARKNESS.

THE shot had sped so suddenly, that for the moment Rupert felt so confused as to be totally unable to see whence it came, but it was not long before he was enlightened.

Before Helen could run to his aid, there was a rush of feet and the room was filled with masked and armed men, who dashed in between the lovers and separated them.

This was all he saw, for in another moment all was blank—utter, impenetrable darkness and oblivion.

When he awoke from this condition, the surrounding atmosphere was as gloomy as it had been fancifully made by his dream.

All was utter darkness.

The air around, too, was dank and chill.

Where could he be?

Was he entombed alive?

Were this coldness and this atmosphere those of a charnel house?

Had the vow made to his father come at last to so abrupt an ending?

Was his young life to be crushed thus in its very beginning?

He spread out his hands to their full extent.

They came in contact with nothing—nothing but cold, chill air.

What was to be done?

He could think of no plan of safety.

Then suddenly a hope entered his mind.

The time had passed without his being able to count the hours.

It might, therefore, be night, and the blessed light of day might reveal to him some method of escape.

He was just wondering in his own mind what was the intention of his cowardly captors, when a deep, sonorous voice sounded near him.

"Rupert Dreadnought," it said.

"I am here," said Rupert. "Have you come to triumph over me?"

"I have not," replied the unseen and mysterious speaker. "I am come to let you know your fate."

"Speak on," said Rupert. "I fear you not. But tell me who are you?"

"Your sworn foe," returned the other. "I am Oscar Penraven."

"Helen's cousin!" murmured Rupert. "'Twas so I suspected. Tell me why I am here?"

"On the night when your father died," said Oscar, "you took a solemn oath. Is not that correct?"

"It is."

"I know its nature. I know that I stand first on your list of enemies. You wish the hand of my cousin Helen; you wish to take her away from my protection; you have been commanded to do so, and you have sworn to obey; is it not so?"

"It is," replied Rupert; "but ask me no more. I shall refuse to reply to questions which affect the solemn secrets of others. I refuse this, and shall reply to nothing further on this subject."

"'Tis well. Listen to your fate," returned Oscar, with cruel emphasis. "You love Helen. She shall never be yours!"

"Heaven will shield her."

"Aye, Heaven will help those who help themselves; but I will take care that you see not the light of day before the one great event happens which shall crush your hopes for ever! There is a husband already chosen for Helen; and while you remain thus hidden from the world, you will have the satisfaction of knowing that she is being wedded to one who will take her for ever from even your eyes."

"And who is this husband?"

"Myself. When this marriage is consummated, you will be delivered up to a tribunal of those who were your father's enemies, and whom you have made also your own enemies by accepting the responsibilities which death might have destroyed for ever."

There was silence after this.

With these mysterious words, Oscar Penraven quitted his post of observation, and Rupert was once more alone.

Presently there was the sound of a key turning in the lock, and in another moment a man entered with some provisions.

A vague suspicion of poison crossed Rupert's mind.

But this was speedily dismissed.

There was a more terrible lot in store for him, and to poison him would be to shorten the misery to which it was intended to doom him.

For the sake, therefore, of preserving his strength for future exertions, he partook of a hearty meal, and soon after fell asleep.

CHAPTER IX.

THE WHITE HAND.

When he awoke from his slumber, he was startled by a ray of light which shone full on his face.

It was sunlight, but the atmosphere through which it had passed had taken from it all its warmth and cheeriness.

It was a sign, however, that he was not utterly excluded from the outer world.

He sprang up, therefore, and examined the aperture.

It was a small opening in the side of the wall, but it showed, at least, that there was some communication with the outer world.

In his utter wretchedness—imprisoned in the lonely darkness without a voice to cheer him, he stood by the small chink of light and gazed up at the few inches of sky which constituted, as it were, all his world.

As he did so, the bright sun and the bit of blue seemed to warn him against despondency, to tell him of bright days in store, and to bid him hope and work.

As he looked, the light was suddenly shadowed, and a white hand was thrust through the opening.

He could not, of course, recognise the taper fingers, but a note was thrust into his hand.

He opened this eagerly, while the hand once more disappeared.

It was in a female hand, tremulously and hastily written, and read as follows:—

"Have courage. Though hidden from the world, you have not lost all your friends. Be at the window at ten to-night, and you shall receive instructions how to escape."

A bright glow of pleasure invaded the heart of the prisoner.

He was not forgotten then.

Whoever his fair protectress was, he recognised in the deed the hand of Helen.

It was she, no doubt, who had sent him the friendly warning.

And yet——

Might not treachery be afloat?

He rejected this idea, however, almost as soon as formed, and resolved to await in hope and confidence the coming of the hour of safety.

Yet how could he tell the hour?

The darkness would fall, and time fly by without possibility of reckoning.

As darkness came on, however, he stood by the aperture and waited.

The hours went by on leaden wings, as it always does with those who wait and watch.

At length a faint rustle was heard without.

Eagerly he listened.

Then a voice—a soft female voice—one, however, which he did not know, said,

"Rupert Dreadnought."

"I am here!" he cried, eagerly.

The hand was introduced once more into the aperture; but in the utter darkness, Rupert could not see it.

How gladly would he have pressed it to his lips, but this was rendered impossible by the fact that on *his* side of the wall bars were placed to which the hand could not reach.

"Here is a letter," said the voice, "take it quickly."

"If I do it will be impossible to read it," said Rupert.

"I have not forgotten that," replied the voice; "here is flint and steel and a taper. Quick, take it, for I hear footsteps approaching."

Rupert lost no time in taking the flint and steel through the small opening.

Just in time.

He had hardly succeeded in doing so when there were hurried steps without, and a rushing noise among the bushes, as if his unknown friend was making an attempt to escape and enemies were pursuing her.

Then there was a faint scream, the report of fire-arms, and all was once more still as before.

"Pray Heaven my fair friend has met with no mishap," he murmured. "Strange mystery this. It was *not* Helen."

Though his heart, however, was yearning to discover the mystery, he was still cautious for a time.

As his friend had been watched, and perhaps seen, in her act of kindness, it might be dangerous to strike a light, and he remained, therefore, for some time clutching the letter.

At length, however, some time having passed, and his impatience getting almost the better of him, he struck a light, lit his taper, and opened the letter, which contained a key.

It was from Helen Penraven, and read as follows:—

"My dearest Rupert,—I write these few lines in haste (and in fear too, for I am watched each moment) to give you the means of escape. The messenger who brings this is trustworthy, and if you receive with this a key, a taper, and flint and steel, you will know you have received all I send. God bless you, Rupert; that is all I can now say of our love. I must give you directions how to escape. The key I send you is a master-key. Now you are in possession of a light, you will find a doorway in the corner of your cell. Open this, and it will admit you to a long and dark corridor, which will lead to another door. This door is also to be opened by this key; and you will then find yourself in the fresh air. Be careful then, for if you plunge forward you will fall into a deep moat, and the splash would arouse those who would destroy you. It is Oscar Penraven himself who has sworn to marry me; therefore, when you escape, make haste to my succour. For three days I shall be in safety; a longer delay will be fatal to all our hopes.

"Yours for ever,

"Helen."

Again and again Rupert Dreadnought pressed the missive to his lips.

Then placing it in his bosom, he rose up and began to examine the walls of his prison.

They were black, murky, and dripping with moisture.

For a long time it was impossible to see any indication of a door, but at length in one corner he saw the shining of metal, which turned out to be a lock.

He lost no time in inserting the key, and, then, having first put out the taper, he opened the door which was to lead him to liberty.

His heart beat loudly as he passed out into the dark passage and unhesitatingly plunged forward into the gloom.

He met with no obstacle.

As he went on he heard occasionally the loud laughter of men making merry, but there was no light to indicate whence the sounds proceeded, and he did not trouble himself to make discoveries.

The passage was a long one and full of oozy slime, but he soon arrived at the further extremity, and feeling for the lock, inserted the key, and found himself in the open air.

The difficulty now was the moat, but he hesitated not.

Letting himself gently down into the water, he waded across, rose in the neglected garden, and in a very short space of time emerged upon the high road.

He had no horse now, and he would therefore be compelled to walk to London, unless some friendly hostelry should afford him the means of conveyance.

Nothing dismayed, however, he plunged along the road, and was soon making his way across the dusky heath.

CHAPTER X.

IN WHICH ALLAN OF THE GLEN MAKES HIS FIRST APPEARANCE IN LONDON.

On the edge of the moor where it suddenly ceased, and where three roads branched off from it, there stood an inn which, from its dark and uninviting appearance, seemed scarcely a place for a traveller's entertainment.

Nevertheless, it *did* drive a thriving trade in consequence of being the only house of the kind within a radius of some miles.

Here, accordingly, Rupert Dreadnought stopped, and contrived, after much bargaining, to obtain from the landlord a horse which, although its beauty was a thing of the past, was yet able to carry him at a tolerable speed towards London.

He met no adventures.

His enemies, secure in the idea that he was immured in the underground vault, had no idea of watching for him; and so, until the streets of the metropolis were reached, he scarcely met a soul.

At the first town hostelry he dismounted, and in order to break all clue to his proceedings and his whereabouts, left his horse there in the stable.

Then he advanced on foot, and soon found himself in a long, narrow street, in the oldest part of the city.

He was just turning a corner when a loud outcry was heard; and, as he passed round, a blaze of light revealed a curious scene.

Before a low but brilliantly-lighted house of entertainment were a crowd of men, women, and boys, laughing, shouting, and screaming, and moving about with quick and confused motions.

They were all of the lowest class, and much excited by drink, and their language was of the vilest and most blasphemous description.

It was quite evident from their words and actions that some unfortunate individual was the object of their ridicule and torture.

"Let him have it."

"Kill the Scotch fool!"

"Ha—ha! there he had it."

"Ah! he has drawn his knife—crack his sconce!"

It was evident by their cries that they were all attacking one, and Rupert Dreadnought, ever ready to aid the weak, drew his sword, and forced his way through.

He saw now the object of all this disturbance.

Against the wall, defending himself with his short Scotch sword against the insensate crowd, was a tall, fine-looking youth, with light hair, fair, sun-freckled face, and bright gleaming eyes, whose full highland dress proclaimed him to be a native of Scotland.

His face was red now and convulsed with passion, and one or two of the crowd around him bore evidences of his anger.

HELEN PENRAVEN.

"What," cried Rupert, as he dashed in among the drunken crew, and placed himself at the side of the young Scotchman "what, all you upon one! Cowards and savages, come on *now*, and try the metal of my sword!"

There was a hush among the crowd as these words were pronounced.

Then came an ominous whispering and growl of discontent, and one of the ragamuffins sprang away as if on some errand.

"Good luck to you, master," cried the Scotch youth (in his broad dialect, which, during the course of my story, I shall purposely omit), "good luck to you. Do not risk your life for a poor lad like me. I've a strong arm, and it'll be a strange thing if I cannot make good my way through these cowards."

"Oh! I never desert a friend," cried Rupert; "it is *not* in my nature. Stand back there, we desire no delay. Back there, or blood will be spilled."

The crowd moved slightly back at the sight of Rupert's bright sword.

Then after a moment it recovered itself, for there was a rush of feet and two stout, tall fellows sprung into the midst of the combatants, sword in hand.

The new comers were ruffians of the lowest stamp, dressed in faded clothes of elegant cut and material, with here and there large rents, which, as well as their red and bloated faces, spoke of past and recent debauches.

"Hillo, my young brawlers!" cried the taller of the two, "what do you here disturbing our peaceful neighbourhood?"

"Talk no folly," said Rupert, angrily, "but let us pass. I have no time for drunken combats in the street. This inoffensive lad has need of my protection, and he goes with me."

The man who had constituted himself spokesman of the crowd, turned round at this and appealed to them.

"What say you, good people!" he cried, with a sort of mock solemnity, "of what have these fellows been guilty?"

"That Scotch stripling yonder has plundered James Whitethorn's shop," cried one.

"He is a Scotch thief!" cried another.

"The other is a confederate of his."

"Kill them both."

"They have broken the sanctuary of the Golden Acre. Kill them."

These threatening cries were received by the two bullies with evident satisfaction.

Not so by Rupert.

The Scotch youth knew not what the Golden Acre signified; but Dreadnought was well aware of its character.

It was one of the most fearfully criminal parts of London.

A kind of self-elected sanctuary of vagabonds, it harboured thieves, bankrupts, forgers, coiners, even murderers of the deepest die, and being more confined in space than the world-renowned Alsatia, it was very easy to call assistance at a moment's notice.

There was no doubting that their position was one of great danger; but it was also as evident that the slighest show of hesitation or fear would be their destruction.

Rupert turned hastily to his companion.

"You have courage and you have a sword; can you use it?" he asked.

The eye of the young Scotchman brightened valiantly.

"I can," he said. "Let us begin."

They were brave words, and Rupert understood at once that he could trust in the speaker of them.

"Good," he said. "We will cut our way through our enemies, and then we will make for yonder hostelry where the red light illumines the street."

One glance told the Scotch youth what the speaker meant.

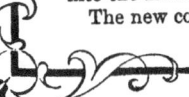

Nearly the whole street was involved in utter darkness for a long distance, but at the further extremity there was a cheerful light, which showed the opening into a wide square.

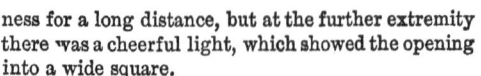

In an instant, now, the Scotch youth darted forward, and both he and Rupert Dreadnought were at once engaged in a desperate conflict.

The bullies who had been brought forward to fight the battles of the people of Golden Acre were no cowards, and they could fight as well.

This both our heroes soon discovered to their cost, for, far from being able as they had anticipated to make one dash and penetrate the mob, they found the crowd closing in on them, and aiding by a variety of troublesome antics and even blows the half drunken brawlers.

Boys rolled upon the rough pavement and crawled between their legs; women flung mud at them as they sought to disable their adversaries, and it soon became evident to both that unless some assistance came or some change came over the scene they would find a terrible and abrupt termination to their adventure.

But not for a moment did Rupert regret what he had done.

He certainly in this hour of peril, as in other hours of need, thought of Helen's sweet face, and prayed that nothing might happen to separate him from her.

But there was no cowardice in his heart, no desire to evade the contest.

Bravely the swords clashed and rang together.

Yet no progress was made.

A babel of voices sounded round them; women shrieked; men shouted; boys yelled; and all laughed at intervals as the two bullies gained some unexpected advantage in consequence of some stealthy stone or brutal knock from a stick.

Seeing that for a time, at least, they must husband their strength, the two strangely connected companions placed their backs against the wall.

"Ah! ah!" shouted one of the brawlers, "ah! ah! they yield. At him, Franklyn."

"Right, right, my man is safe, Brandon," shouted the other, with a swagger. "Now, now, together."

Neither Rupert nor the Scotch stranger spoke, but a contemptuous laugh escaped their lips, and as a reply, the former suddenly sprang forward, and cut the boaster across the arm.

Just as he leaped backward with a yell of pain, Dreadnought made a second pass, and in an instant his blade had plunged through the villain's heart.

A yell, a shriek of execration arose from the crowd, and one man, who, from his dress and his brawny arms, seemed a smith, leaped forward, seized the sword of the dead man, and attacked Rupert savagely.

But aid was coming from an unexpected quarter.

There was a sudden rush of wheels, a sudden blaze of light, and a carriage, driven at full speed, came dashing round the corner of the street.

The crowd which was now spread across the street at once necessitated the pulling up of the horses, and the coachman reined them in with such suddenness that the animals nearly fell upon their haunches.

As the carriage stopped a head was protruded from the window.

Then a loud voice cried—

"What does this mean? Why do you not drive on?"

One glance, however, proved to the speaker that what he desired was an impossibility, and opening the door he sprang out among the brawlers, followed quickly by a friend.

As they dashed in among the wondering crowds, there was a flash of light, and a sudden cry of recognition.

"Ah, Rupert Dreadnought! well met, and just in time!" cried the foremost.

"Ah, Stanley Sherrington!" exclaimed Rupert "you are just in time. Now for a good rush!"

Once again, and now with renewed vigour, the two friends dashed upon their enemies, and this time with good effect.

The cowardly gang—many of them now wounded—began to give way.

The Scotch youth, who had but an indifferent weapon, but who, on the other hand, was no mean swordsman, had now succeeded in severely wounding his adversary, and the bully, finding himself undoubtedly getting the worst of it, began to give way.

This was the critical moment.

"Quick, to my carriage!" cried the one whom Rupert had spoken of as Stanley Sherrington. 'Now, while the cowards are drawing back! Have no compunction—strike right and left!"

Rupert and his new companion at once obeyed the injunction of their unexpected friend, and, dismayed by the fearful fate of the bully, the yelling mob at once began to retreat.

As they did so the swordsmen quickened their steps, and not noticing in their haste that a second ominous whisper was going the round of the savage conclave, they made their way towards the carriage.

Hardly had they reached it and entered, when a loud shout again arose.

The cowards recovered their speech, now that the gleaming blades could no longer be seen.

"The horses! the horses!"

"Drag them from the carriage!"

"Smash the Scotch rebels!"

This was a new turn of the tide.

A dangerous turn too!

They at once recognised the peril, and prepared to act.

"Now, Rupert," said Sherrington, "put your head out of one window while I do the same out of the other. Here is a pistol. I will give orders to my coachman to drive on while you shoot any man who attempts to stop the horses. I will fire away at the crowd at the same time."

This plan was at once adopted, and as Stanley Sherrington shouted to the coachman, the blacksmith and the remaining bully dashed forward.

"Now!" cried Sherrington.

The coachman whipped his horses; then there were two sharp reports, and with a loud cry the two ruffians fell back among the mob.

The carriage now dashed away, the frightened horses needing no whip nor incitement of any kind to exertion, and it was but a few moments before they had passed the bright, red lamp, and left the Golden Acre and its fierce and bloodthirsty inhabitants far behind them.

CHAPTER XI.

THE ADVENTURE IN THE OLD HOUSE.

It was at the corner of a wide and handsome street that Stanley Sherrington ordered his coachman to pull up.

"Why stop you here?" asked Rupert; "we are not near your home."

Sherrington laughed.

"No, no," he cried, "we are not bound for home. I and my friend, Hubert Redfern, are compelled to meet our free companions at yonder tavern. A glass of something strong and hot, Rupert, would not suit you ill now, I imagine, after our recent battle. Let us enter together."

"And who are your companions, Stanley?" asked Rupert Dreadnought.

"We belong to the Mohocks, a good and brave Society," said Sherrington; "we seek amusement everywhere and in everything. We wage war against drunken citizens and meddlesome watchmen, and we sometimes even exact black mail in the way of kisses from the fair sex. We force the rich sometimes to disgorge at the voice of Poverty, and do good deeds between whiles, in fact, to pay for absolution for the bad. There is our character written out in full."

For an instant Rupert Dreadnought hesitated to join him.

It seemed scarcely right while the body of his grand old father was lying in the stately silence and majesty of Death, yet unburied, in his chamber, to enter a scene of wild and reckless gaiety.

But he was in need of aid.

In need of it at once.

Who more likely, then, to assist him in his perilous and daring enterprise than these reckless spirits?

"Good," he said; "I will accompany you."

"But your strange and ill-clad friend here?" whispered Sherrington.

The Scotch boy caught the words.

"I will go my way," said he, meekly; "or if there is danger threatening the one who saved my life, I will remain all night to shield him from it."

There was such a depth of earnestness and sincerity in the words of the Scotch boy that it touched the hearts of the hearers.

"My young friend," cried Rupert, "are you in need of service?"

"Yes, sir, I am," replied the Scotch boy, eagerly. "And if you have the chance of giving me aught to do, there is no one in the world I would more gladly serve under."

"Have you no friends in London?"

"None, sir."

"Well, well, here is my address," said Rupert. "Come to me to-morrow night at eight, and you shall have your wish. I will find something for you to do."

A wild gleam of pleasure shot from the eyes of the wild-looking Scotch boy.

"May Heaven reward you," he said; "you are the first friend I have met in London."

"Stay, however," added Rupert; "mayhap you are hungry. Have you money?"

"I have not," replied the Scotch youth, with a look of the utmost shame. "I was spending my last coin in purchasing food when I was accused of theft."

"Come, come, Rupert," cried Stanley Sherrington; "the Mohocks are waiting."

He also had listened with some interest to the conversation with the boy, but he became impatient as he saw the evident inclination of Rupert to hear more.

"Fear not; I shall not detain you long," returned Rupert, as he hastily wrote a few words on a scrap of paper, and gave it to the boy, together with some money. "Go with this to my house; show it to the servant who admits you, and ask to be taken to the kitchen. Make yourself at home there, and you shall in the morning tell me your story."

With many thanks, incoherent from their very sincerity, the Scotch boy remained standing some few minutes after the young men departed into the house of entertainment.

Then, with a bewildered feeling of pleasure and gratitude in his heart, he walked away

We shall follow his footsteps at present, and narrate a strange adventure that befell him in Rupert's house.

What happened at the meeting of the Mohocks, and who the Mohocks were, we will describe at a future period.

The appearance of our young Scotch adventurer was, as may be imagined, far from prepossessing at this moment.

His clothes, torn and stained before, were more torn and stained now than ever, while here and there marks of blood showed plainly on his face and his habiliments.

When, therefore, he presented himself at the door of Rupert Dreadnought's dwelling, it was with some difficulty that he could make the domestic believe that his master had sent him.

"We want no beggars here," cried he, in a contemptuous voice. "I will not take your letter. Some begging petition, no doubt."

"Have a care," cried the Scotch youth, reddening with anger, "or as sure as my name is Allan of the Glen, I'll force your insolent words down your throat. I am a friend of your master's—have fought side by side with him, and I demand admittance."

The domestic, who was one of the fat and pompous style, cared not for an encounter with the ragged wayfarer, and seeing Allan's hand gliding naturally to his sword, he thought it best to be civil.

So he took the paper.

The words there contained soon altered his manner.

"This way, young sir," he said. "You must forgive my words. You will confess that appearances——"

"Are against me," laughed the youth; "but lead on, I shall forgive you with a truer heart when I taste some of that good fare which I can smell even now in your kitchen. Bread and a little spring water has been all my fare of late."

The entrance of the strange guest into the room where the servants were indulging in a hearty supper was, as may be imagined, the signal for a general stare of astonishment and a general volley of exclamations.

A whisper, however, from his companion settled matters, and with some amount of ill-grace among the well-fed, well-clothed lacqueys, he was admitted to a place at the hospitable board.

Once installed among them, he lost no time in making friends.

His voracious appetite being appeased, he became talkative, told his adventures, and interspersed his words with snatches of his native melodies.

Instead then of despising and ridiculing him, the servants looked upon him as a valuable acquisition to the circle, and were sorry when the hour came which summoned them to bed.

It was in a chamber not far from that in which the dead earl lay in the majesty of death that Allan of the Glen was placed to sleep.

It was a comfortable room though small, and looked out upon a garden in the rear of the house, pleasant with flowers and greenery of all kinds.

He did not spend much time, however, in admiring the things around him, neither did he trouble to undress.

Two or three times he looked almost suspiciously at the snowy white bed as if scarely knowing what to do. But he did not enter it.

Its excessive cleanliness seemed to frighten him, and at length, with a sigh, he rolled himself up in the remnant of his plaid, and lying on the hearth-rug, fell off into that sweet, sound sleep, which only comes to tired youth.

Poor lad! The hard floor was a welcome and soft couch to him.

He had slept beneath haystacks, and by the roadside, in the sunshine and the storm; and the soft bed of luxury provided for him would have afforded him no rest.

He was a light sleeper, however, and had scarcely enjoyed an hour's slumber when he was awakened by a slight noise.

All was in complete darkness, for he had extinguished the light; and so, as he rose up on one hand to listen, he was somewhat confused as to where he was.

Quickly the thought came to him, however, that he was in the house of his benefactor, and then was seen a mysterious vision.

Outside the window was a man who was endeavouring to open it.

Again the noise was heard that had awakened the sleeper.

It was the mysterious stranger gradually wrenching away a portion of the woodwork.

A feeling of joy entered at once the heart of Allan of the Glen.

Here truly was danger, but here also was a chance of serving his new master and benefactor.

He raised himself up quietly, and, crawling to the window, hid himself behind the tapestry, drew his sword, and waited.

The night was very dark, and, although everything around was very still, the man was under no fear of being discovered from without.

A heavy pouring rain was descending in a steady deluge, sending the pedestrians from the streets, and turning what had been a scene of gaiety a few hours before into a scene of cold wretchedness.

So the man worked on.

It seemed an age to Allan as he listened anxiously and watched, but it was not, in fact, long before the steel tool of the mysterious workman had forced its way, and ingress was free to him.

By the dull light Allan could see that he was masked, and that, although he wore a sword, he had not drawn it.

In fact he considered himself quite in safety, and when he had glided in, he noiselessly closed the casement after him.

In an instant Allan's views were changed.

Sheathing his sword, he remained still behind the curtain and watched.

The man drew from his pocket a dark lantern, and opened it.

It shot forth a brilliant light, and every object in the room was plainly visible.

The man glanced first at the bed; and saw it was empty.

"Good!" muttered the masked intruder. "I am in luck. There is no one here."

He glided, as he spoke, towards the little door which communicated with the apartment where lay the dead body, and as soon as he had entered, Allan of the Glen followed him.

There was heavy tapestry in the chamber of death, and the man was fully occupied with his own thoughts, so that the Scotch youth found no difficulty in following him, and concealing himself once more.

The man glanced round, and seeing a lamp upon the table, lit it.

Then he gazed intently at the walls, as if studying their configuration.

At last he uttered a low cry of pleasure, and sprang forward.

"I have it now," he cried, as he glided his hand rapidly along the smooth surface of a pilaster, and then touched a knob.

In an instant a door flew open, and discovered a dark closet, while a cold rush of air swept round the room.

Allan of the Glen at once conceived an idea of action.

He would imprison this man in the closet until the return of his master, and the secret of the mysterious visit would then be discovered.

He lost not a moment.

Springing forward impetuously, just as the man peered into the darkness, he seized him, and ere the stranger could turn or offer any resistance, he had pushed him forward with all his strength into the darkness.

What happened next occurred so quickly that Allan had not even the time to slide back the panel!

There was a wild cry, the sound of a heavy body bumping against projections, then a loud splash, and all was as still as death.

RUPERT; OR THE DREADNOUGHT; OR THE SECRETS OF THE IRON CHEST!

"HE IS DEAD!" SAID RUPERT, AS THEY BORE HIM FROM THE SECRET PANEL.

For a moment Allan stood as if petrified with horror at what he had done.

Then he rushed back to the table, seized the lamp, and, returning, raised it above his head, and gazed into the darkness.

All he could see was that he himself was standing on a small ledge, and that below him was a deep, dark well.

He could not see the bottom, but he could guess what was there.

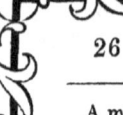

A mangled, ghastly corpse!

What should he do now?

Should he awaken the servants, and tell them what had happened?

Or should he await the return of his benefactor?

The latter, which was, of course, more consonant with his feelings, was, however, only possible if he permitted the man to die (if there were yet a spark of life in him) or left his mangled body there.

He was relieved of his anxiety, however, in a manner he least expected.

There was a quick step along the corridor, and in another moment the door opened, and Rupert Dreadnought entered.

CHAPTER XII.

THE DISCOVERY—RUPERT DREADNOUGHT'S MISGIVINGS—THE DESCENT OF THE WELL—THE DEAD BODY—THE MYSTERIOUS PAPER—THE ROBBERY OF THE RING—THE WARNING.

RUPERT glanced with astonishment at Allan as he entered.

The Scotch youth's face was white with fear and anger with himself, and he was leaning against the table for support.

Rupert's heart sank within him, and his eyes shot fire.

What did the scene mean?

Why was Allan standing there, with the secret panel open, and desecrating by his presence the chamber of death?

Had he already become ungrateful?

Was he giving this return for his benefaction?

"What means this?" he cried. "Why are you here?"

The Scotch youth sank on one knee.

"Oh, forgive me, sir!" he cried; "I am not here for any evil purpose. The story I have to tell you will prove that I have but sought to do you a service, and, I fear, have done you an injury."

"Quick, then, to your tale," said Rupert Dreadnought, who, although half convinced by the manner of the lad, was yet unable to understand the meaning of the scene, "be not afraid, if you have done wrong unknowingly I am not the one to blame you."

Briefly then the youth told his tale.

Rupert listened in utter wonderment.

The panel which was now opened he had imagined to be that which concealed the Iron Chest with all its *wondrous secrets*, and now that he looked in there were nothing but dark, murky walls and a deep, and apparently fathomless, pit.

"You have done no wrong," said Rupert, "I commend you for it. If you had *not* been here Heaven knows what mischief this midnight robber might have done. He came here for no good purpose and his end is his own reaping."

As he spoke he went to the door and called aloud for the domestics.

In a few moments three of the male servants made their appearance, half dressed.

They stared in utter astonishment at the open panel.

"Go, fetch a rope, a long and strong one," said Rupert, quickly, "it is for life or death, so let there be no delay."

A stout rope was soon brought by one of the men, and they proceeded in a body to the panel.

"Below there a man is lying," said Rupert Dreadnought, "he came as a robber and he has doubtless met his fate. Which among you will have courage to descend?"

The Scotch boy almost interrupted him as he spoke these words.

"Stay, sir," he cried, "it is I who did the deed, I alone will descend. Give me yonder dark lantern that the stranger has left upon the table. I will bring him up whether alive or dead."

There was no attempt upon the part of any one of the domestics present to dispute with him the task.

They were awestruck by the scene which, as it had been but half explained, to them seemed strongly and wildly mysterious.

The Scotch youth smiled in spite of everything, as he adjusted the rope around his waist and fixed it round his left arm.

"This puts me in mind of my Highland home," he said, "when my comrades used to let me down from craggy mountain points to rifle the nests of the wild mountain birds."

The retainers watched him with eager interest, as he approached the dark panel and prepared to descend.

"Before you do this," said Rupert Dreadnought, as the Scotch boy passed himself over the edge, "let me give you a caution. I know nothing of this place. I never, till now, was aware of its existence, and it may be fathomless and filled with deadly vapour for aught I know. Therefore, if you find your strength giving way, at once give a signal and let us raise you quickly again to the surface. Your life is too good to throw away upon a midnight robber—an assassin for aught we know."

"Fear not for me!" cried Allan of the Glen, "you risked your life to save mine. I risk mine now that you may know what danger threatens you."

Then he turned to the servants.

"Now lads, be quick," he said, "and lower me rapidly."

The brave youth was soon descending at a rapid pace, and both Rupert and his domestics gazed down with interest at the light of the lantern as it grew less and less in the deep distance.

Presently it became so small that they could scarcely see it, and the strain on the rope become so great that it seemed as though it must break.

"'Tis a fearful depth," said Rupert, as he leaned over the dark opening, "no man can be alive after such a terrible fall."

As he spoke the rope grew slack.

He had evidently reached the bottom.

"Throw down another rope," cried Rupert Dreadnought; "with a man, perhaps dead, in his arms, this one is not sufficient to bear him safely to the surface."

At this moment there was a sharp tug at the rope.

Then another, still more impatient.

"Quick," exclaimed Rupert; "in such a place he might suffocate."

The servants, eager always to obey their young master, at once flung down the rope, with increased eagerness, it may be said, because they were themselves anxious to solve the mystery.

The second rope was soon apparently adjusted, and they began slowly to raise the two men.

It was at once easily seen that the midnight intruder was either dead or insensible.

Had he not been so, he would have aided in the ascent, whereas what they were bringing to the surface was a dead weight.

It was not long, however, before the curiosity of all was gratified.

The Scotch youth, white as a ghost, and shivering as with cold through his battle with the dense miasmatic vapour, staggered upon the brink of the black pit, and dropped by the side of the masked man, whom the servants lifted in and placed upon the ground.

"He is dead," cried Rupert, as he felt the heart of the latter.

Then he removed the mask.

The white marble features (stained here and there with blood from the wounds which he had received against the rough edge of the pit) were those of a perfect stranger.

"What can this mean?" murmured Rupert Dreadnought.

"Perhaps, sir—" said one of the domestics.

Then he stopped hesitatingly.

"Speak out," cried his master; "what is it you suspect?"

"Perhaps the story you have heard is not the correct one."

"In what way?"

"Perhaps, after all, this Scotch youth," returned the man, lowering his voice, "may have some knowledge of this man, and, in endeavouring to secrete him, may have killed his friend."

Not for one moment did this suspicion enter the brain of Rupert Dreadnought.

"No, no," he said, "*he* is no traitor. I am certain of it. Let us search this man; perhaps upon his body we shall find documents which explain the mystery of his presence. For *my* part, I believe him to be no common robber."

The search was at once made, but for some time nothing could be found. At length one of the domestics took from his pocket a torn, ragged piece of paper which he handed to his master.

Rupert Dreadnought at once took it, and read as follows:—

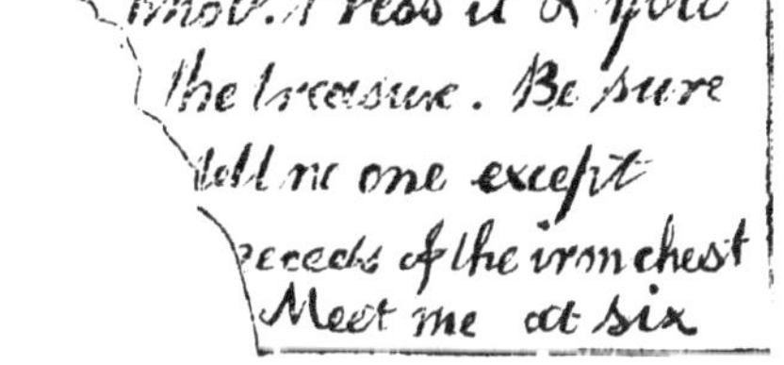
the second pillar you
knob. Press it & you
the treasure. Be sure
tell no one except
ecrets of the iron chest
Meet me at six

"This is a strange thing," said Rupert, "a very strange thing. There is no name here, or anything, in fact, which will afford a clue to the mystery."

The document, torn as it was, proved, however, that the person who had so mysteriously entered the house was no common robber, but an emissary of the enemy.

"Take this carrion out of my father's death-chamber," said Rupert, sternly, as he ceased the examination of the stranger's body. "Place him below; then fetch in the watch, and see if his features are known to them."

The Scotch lad, who had now recovered from the effects of the foul air, approached Rupert as the men bore the body away.

"My benefactor," he said, "how can I thank you for your kindness to me, and how excuse my conduct?"

There was real pain and sorrow visible in the youth's features.

Rupert placed his hand kindly upon his shoulder.

"My lad," he said, "in the first place you have acted quite properly in this matter. You had every right to believe that this man was a thief; the paper contained in his pocket proves you were correct. He came here for plunder; he has met his death. To-morrow night I shall be able to let you prove to me the gratitude I believe you truly feel."

The Scotch youth seized his benefactor's hand.

"Oh! I thank you for this," he cried. Yes, I *do* indeed feel gratitude. I who am fatherless and motherless, and have never yet known a home! how can *I* avoid feeling gratitude to one who has saved my life? I shall wait eagerly for to-morrow night, and then, if needs be, I will lay down my life for you."

"To-morrow, or rather, to-day, for morning approaches, I will hear your story," said Rupert. "This day is fixed for the funeral of my beloved father; and in the evening, when darkness closes in, I am about to proceed upon an errand which may prove a perilous one. Now retire to bed, and be assured of my firm friendship."

The Scotch youth then turned away with a murmured blessing, and Rupert Dreadnought proceeded towards the bed wheron his father lay.

Reverentially he uncovered the face of him whom in life he had so greatly loved.

"Now, perhaps," he said to himself, "I can with respect take from his finger the large emerald ring which he bade me guard with my heart's blood. No doubt among so many secrets this may point to some other mystery."

He drew down the white satin coverlet, on which, embossed in golden threads, glittered the semblances of an earl's coronet, and raised his father's hand.

The ring was gone! while clenched in the stiffened fingers of the dead was a piece of paper, on which were inscribed these words—

"Rupert Dreadnought, mysterious enemies surround you! The ring you coveted so much is gone. It is in the hands of those who will use its mysterious agency to your destruction. You are no match for those who have sworn to be your death, and to ruin while you live every plan you desire for our ruin. When we meet—when you are face to face with him who now wears your father's ring, you will tremble, in spite of all your boasted courage, at what I shall reveal to you."

"Curses be upon these treacherous hounds!" he cried; "nevertheless I will not swerve from my duty. In spite of all," he added, as he placed his hand upon the cold brow of his father, "I swear to proceed with my task; in spite of the world."

He little knew when he said these words the secret which the ring contained, or the power it placed in the hands of his enemies.

CHAPTER XIII.

THE ORPHAN OF THE GLEN ALMOND—THE MYSTERIOUS FLIGHT—THE CHASE OVER THE SCOTCH MOORS—THE BATTLE—TWO TO ONE—THE FALL OF THE LOWLAND TRAITORS—ELSIE OF THE GLEN—THE STRANGE ADOPTION—THE HIDDEN PEOPLE—MARY MACPHERSON—THE DISAPPEARANCE—THE DISPERSION OF THE OUTLAWS—THE FUNERAL OF THE OLD EARL, AND RENEWAL OF THE OATH OF VENGEANCE.

THE story which Allan of the Glen related to Rupert Dreadnought on the following morning, if told in his own words, would enable little of his true history to be known by the reader.

So we will tell the story ourselves.

Early one morning, about fifteen years before our story opens, the inhabitants of the town of Perth were aroused by the furious clattering of horse's feet, and those who succeeded in reaching their windows in time saw a sight which made them wonder.

Mounted on a powerful but somewhat heavy horse was a man whose features they could not distinctly see, but his general appearance betokened one belonging to the lower class of society.

On one arm he carried a child apparently about three years of age, and with his disengaged hand he clutched a long and heavy sword.

Following close at his heels and evidently mounted on swifter horses, were two men, who, with loud curses, called upon him to stop.

The only heed he paid to them was to urge his horse to still fiercer exertions and wave his sword now and then defiantly over his head.

This was all that the townspeople of Perth saw.

They went by like a flash of lightning, and until they had reached the open country there was nothing to be seen beyond a simple pursuit.

Shots, certainly, were exchanged, but they fell harmless, and had the stranger with the child been able to hold his own there was every probability that there would have been no bloodshed.

His object seemed rather to escape than rancorously to seek their destruction.

Riding hard as he was, over somewhat dangerous and uneven ground, he nevertheless kept looking again and again over his shoulder to see how the distance between him and those who followed diminished or increased.

His horse, strong as it was and able to do an immense amount of work, was no match for their lighter and swifter steeds, and at length, though most unwillingly, he was compelled to draw rein.

"Hold!" he cried, wheeling round his horse and confronting them so suddenly that their rushing steeds fell nearly on their haunches, "hold! What want you with me?"

"The child!" cried the foremost of the horsemen.

"I refuse to yield, him," answered the man, defiantly.

"Then you will meet your death," said the other; "there are two of us to one. Our horses have proved more than a match for yours. Yield the child, and we will no further molest you."

The man in the cloak laughed loudly in disdain.

"Whenever did one of *my* name yield to a braggart's menace?" he cried. "No—no, I yield not."

"And yet the child fared better with its wealthy friends."

At these words the eyes of the pursued flashed fire.

"Friends, say you! rather talk of deadly foes," he shouted. "*I* am his best friend—I, his father. Friends, indeed, who would educate him to despise his kindred—to laugh at his father, whose greatest prize lay in the flashing of his bright sword! No—no," he cried, casting an eager glance round the country, and carefully taking in the details of each vale and mountain, "no, no, rather let his home be among the wild crags, and his only mate the eagle, than hear him lisping amid your Lowland traitors."

"Come, come," cried the foremost horseman, "come, come, time presses. Either yield the boy at once, or prepare to meet thy doom."

"Once more I ask you, what want you with him?" asked the mountaineer, hugging it more closely to his breast.

"We cannot waste time," said the horseman; "we wish to take him to those from whom you wrested him by stealth; we desire to restore him to wealth, and save him from beggary and starvation. Now, no more delay; restore him."

"I will not yield him," answered the man. "No, no; surrender is a cry which with my dying lips I'd laugh to scorn. I will fight you both. I will place the child on yonder grassy mound. Then I will fight you one by one, and if I cannot beat you both, you wretched Lowlanders, then may the noble name I bear be for ever buried in the dust of oblivion and disgrace. Will you consent to this?"

"Upon your honour as a Highland gentleman not to attempt to fly," said the Lowlander, "we will confer together on the point."

"I will not move an inch," said the Highlander.

The Lowlanders neared each other and conferred together for a few moments in a low voice.

Then the one who throughout the affair had been spokesman, advanced.

"We accept your terms," he said. "We will dismount, and I will fight you first."

The Highlander, who, with his wild and chivalric notions of honour, could not for a moment conceive it possible that any treachery was intended, at once proceeded to comply with the request.

He dismounted, and carrying the child to the grassy mound he had indicated, he kissed it, and bade it be quiet no matter what it heard or saw.

Then he advanced, sword in hand, to meet his first opponent, taking no notice of the fact that the other man had dismounted also.

The fight began, but he soon found that the game of his adversary was a treacherous one and that neither he nor his friend meant open fight.

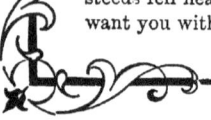

While the man in the road parried and warded the bold strokes of his foe, the other began gradually, but not unseen by the Highlander, to approach the spot where the child lay.

The ruse was apparent in a moment.

One was to steal the child while the other kept the Scot at bay.

In an instant, just as the Lowlander was close to the child, the Highlander drew a pistol and fired.

The traitor staggered, uttered a loud cry, and then, throwing his arms above his head, fell back upon the ground.

"Ah, ye villains!" cried he, "ye think to cheat me of my child, but a father's arm, when raised in such a cause, is not easily beaten down," and he attacked his foeman furiously.

The Lowlander was no match for him, and after many rapid passes he succeeded in stretching his enemy desperately wounded on the ground.

Then, taking the child once more in his arms, he rode away.

After riding as rapidly as he could for about an hour, he reached a point in the mountains where a path led abruptly from the high road down into a deep glen.

The glen — Glenalmond, as it was called—was well known, and avoided by the Lowlanders whose business called them along that lonely highway.

ROSALIE ST. AUBYN.

By some it had the reputation of being haunted, and well it might in those superstitious times, for terrible crimes were said to have been committed there.

Travellers were said to have been inveigled into its shadowy recesses and cruelly murdered.

Certainly peaceful travellers along this route *had* disappeared, but when at length the authorities were roused, and the place was explored, the glen was found not only free of all signs of foul crime, but free of all inhabitants.

Save one, or rather two.

These two were an old hag and a huge wolf-dog.

Both were ugly and forbidding; both were fierce, and disliked by everyone.

But there was no sign in her wretched hovel, perched as it was among the trees on the slope of the glen, of any wrong doing, neither was there a shadow of possibility that she or her dog either could have effected the mischief which had been done.

She spoke civilly to the officers, laughed a hideous laugh of merriment at the idea that the glen was a place of ill-omen and butchery, and finally dismissed them, convinced that she had nothing whatever to do with the matter, and, in fact, knew nothing of it.

They were wrong in two ways.

In the first place there had been no murders committed.

In the second place the old woman *was* cognizant of all that had transpired, and was chief actor in the disappearance of the travellers.

But there was another and a very simple explanation.

All those who had vanished so strangely were well known, not only to be carrying goods of great value, but *to be enemies of the Pretender*, whose firm friends these "Highland bodies" were.

But, as I have said before, they were not murdered.

Pounced upon suddenly, they were carried to old Elsie's dwelling, and there bound.

At the back of her hut was a door communicating with a second room, and into this without delay the captive was led.

Then one of his captors raised one of the rough stones, and descended about ten steps, which led into a corridor cut in the solid rock, and leading upwards by a rapid ascent.

After about a quarter of an hour's scrambling along the rough-hewn path, the captive would be astounded to find himself on a high table-land, surrounded by trees which served to screen a kind of colony.

It was a hidden hamlet, of which old Elsie's hut was really the gateway!

Here the captives were kept until their disappearance had somewhat blown over, and then they were carried away by night and shipped abroad.

A new method of filling a royal treasury, or, rather, the treasury of an expectant king.

It was near Glenalmond that the stranger and the child halted.

He gave then a long, shrill whistle and waited patiently.

In a very few moments a black object made its appearance on the summit of a block of sand-stone, and a grey face peered over.

This face was Elsie's.

It disappeared as quickly as it had come, and in a few moments an answering whistle told the anxious stranger that the road was clear.

He at once urged his horse up the narrow, rocky defile, and in a few moments was in front of Elsie's dwelling.

Here he fastened his horse and entered.

"Here, Elsie," he said, "is my child. I give him into your charge. Let no one have him; rather take his life than cast him again into the clutches of his kindred, who desire only to murder him that they may have his property. Let him dwell among the Hidden People; let him be one of them till I can come to claim him."

As he spoke this hurriedly, giving no further explanation, he drew from his pocket a purse of gold, and placed it in her hand.

"This," he said, "will help to keep the boy till I come again."

"And when will that be?"

The stranger smiled.

"Ah!" he said, "I know not."

Then he thought a moment, looking fondly at the boy the while.

Then he brought his clenched fist fiercely down upon the table.

"Remember, Elsie," he cried, "no cozening with Lowlanders. Let him be brought up in the free Highlands, on the brisk mountain air, as little knowing of their ways as the mountain deer, which will be his companions. I must go now. God bless you, Allan."

He knelt down on the hard ground as he spoke, and embraced the little one fondly.

"Stay," cried Elsie, "stay. What is your name?"

"That must remain a secret," he said, "until *a stain now on its honour* is removed for ever. Call him Allan. If years roll on years, there is something by which I shall know him again."

He then, without further comment, quitted the room, and leaping on his horse, dashed away once more on the high road.

A little sand strewn on the rocky path obliterated all traces of his deviation from the high road, and when search was made for the wild and reckless rider, not a trace to his whereabouts could be found.

Allan remembered well the scene on the Moorlands.

It was indelibly impressed on his memory by the pistol shot, and the desperate sword contest so terribly interesting to a child's mind.

But after this all was monotony, until, at length, as he grew up towards manhood, he fell in love, and the sweet companionship of Mary Macpherson lessened the dreariness of his life.

At length the hiding place of the Hidden People was discovered by an astute officer, and the authorities came down upon them with a large number of troops.

"I won't keep you much longer now," said Allan of the Glen, as he sat in Rupert Dreadnought's chamber, narrating the story of his life. "The rest is a scene of horror.

"The soldiers made their way through the subterranean passage and found the Hidden People ready armed to receive them.

"A desperate and bloody battle ensued.

"Men, rather than be taken prisoners, were seen to fling themselves from the lofty crags and secure certain death in the chasms below.

"When I saw most of the leaders taken prisoners, and all hope lost, I leaped across a wide fissure in the rocks and made my way round to the glen where I hoped to see my Mary.

"In this I was deceived," said the youth, with a trembling voice, "she was gone. I have never seen her again."

"Never seen her!" exclaimed Rupert. "Whither, then, had she gone?"

"I know not—I have never known," replied the youth. "I have sought her everywhere in vain, and at length, disgusted with my own native land, which had robbed me of my father and my bride, I quitted it with scarcely a farthing in my pocket, and came to England.

"*You* met me when I was weary and fatigued, and set upon by bloodthirsty assassins."

"And why were you accused of theft?" asked Rupert Dreadnought.

"I know not. I gave my last piece to the man at the shop near which you found me for a piece of bread, and, thinking I had more, the villanous rabble at once set upon me calling out 'thief,' to turn the sympathies of all against me. Here my story ends. Your kindness saved me."

"Yours is a strange and eventful history," said Rupert Dreadnought, "and contains a myster which even yet you may unravel. You have noy proof that your father is dead?"

"None whatever, save his prolonged and unaccountable absence."

"Then you may yet find him. While there is a shadow of life there is also the shadow of hope. I will aid you in your search for him. But now the time approaches for the mournful obsequies of my father. After that I must set myself to work to accomplish his last wishes."

We will not pause to describe the funeral of the old earl.

Suffice it to say that the obsequies were carried out with great pomp, and that a numerous retinue of weeping friends followed him to the grave.

Among them was Allan of the Glen, transformed by new clothes into a clean-looking, handsome youth, whose features alone betokened his Scotch descent.

The young orphan remained by the grave after the others had departed.

Allan waited near, but did not obtrude his presence on his master's sorrow.

When all had departed from the vaults of the grey old church of St. Andrew's, Rupert Dreadnought knelt, and after invoking his father's blessing on his head, he renewed his vow.

There was no shrinking, no qualification in his oath.

Boldly, and in the sight of heaven, he renewed it as a vow which he had a right to keep when once registered by his father's death-bed.

After this he himself locked the vault, placed the key in his pocket, and quitted the church with Allan of the Glen.

He shook off his tears and his grief as it were as he passed out once more into the bright and open light of day.

"Now," he said, cheerily to Allan, as they rode back towards the old house, "now we must commence the work. To-night Helen Penraven must be saved!"

CHAPTER XIV.

THE BURIAL OF THE KEY—THE DEPARTURE FOR THE HOUSE ON THE MOOR—THE MOHOCKS—THE PURSUIT—THE BATTLE—THE ESCAPE—THE ARRIVAL AT THE HOUSE—A TERRIBLE DISCOVERY.

PURSUANT to his father's earnestly expressed desire, Rupert Dreadnought, when he arrived once more at his home, proceeded at once to bury the key.

The vault he knew well.

It was one in which it had been his father's custom to keep some rare and curious wines, and it was with the excuse of seeking for some of this that he descended, with Allan of the Glen, into the damp cellar.

Allan had never seen such a place, and stared about him like one lost.

But the necessity for work soon roused him, and at this special kind of labour Rupert soon found him an able assistant.

The youth who had so often raised the heavy flagstone in old Elsie's hut, was not long in raising also the loose stone which lay third from the door.

Underneath the stone was a soft, black soil, emitting an aromatic smell.

"What can this be? Let us search further," said Allan, as he raised a little of the earth with his broad-bladed knife.

Rupert caught his wrist.

"Profane it not," he said; "*there may be a mystery here, but it is not yet time to unravel it.* No, this path of vengeance must be trodden slowly, cautiously, methodically, as my father directed me."

Then he placed the key of the IRON CHEST upon the earth, covered it over, and replaced the stone in its proper position.

Taking up a bottle of curious wine to deceive the domestics as to the object of his descent to the vault, he then passed up stairs and led Allan into his own private room.

It was a gem of a place.

Just such a place as suited the character of its clear-headed, brave, young owner.

Guns, swords, pistols, ancient breastplates, and other pieces of mail were scattered about, or hung against the wall.

To qualify these was a goodly array of books upon every conceivable subject, even Love.

"My lord," said Allan, "this is a place where I could be happy for years."

Rupert stopped him.

"Stay," he said "there is one thing I must impress upon you."

"What is that, my lord?"

"What you have just repeated. You must no longer call me my lord. I wish for the present to drop the title entirely. While I have work to do and a vow to carry out, I am plain Master Dreadnought, unless, indeed, circumstances compel me to change my mind. Now, then, Allan, since you know this, select your weapons, and we will proceed to the rendezvous, where I expect to meet some of my brave friends and companions."

Allan had soon made his selection.

A pair of large horse-pistols, and a short, strong sword, something like that he had wielded among the Hidden People, were his weapons, while Rupert Dreadnought chose the finest and thinnest of all the blades, and two short, light pistols.

"You can ride?" he asked, as they descended the stairs, after drinking up the wine to warm their blood in preparation for their long journey in the cold.

"Yes, well."

"That is good," said Rupert. "Our horses are fresh and fast, and my friends are not the right sort of men to let the grass grow under their feet."

Within a few moments they were in the saddle, aud making their way with all haste towards a spot beyond the Tower of London, where Sherrington and some of his Mohock* friends had promised to await their arrival.

There were no great number of passengers or vehicles in the street, and it was not long, therefore, before they reached the rendezvous, where six shadowy figures on horseback were gathered beneath a high wall, which sent its gloomy shade far across the road.

"Ah! here comes our worthy leader," cried Sherrington, who had been foremost of the party, "we have been long expecting you."

"I am not long behind my time," said Rupert Dreadnought, "we will at once advance."

They accordingly waited no longer, but immedi-

---

* "A set of men have lately erected themselves into a nocturnal fraternity under the title of the Mohock Club, a name borrowed, it seems, from a sort of cannibals in India, who subsist by plundering and devouring all the natives about them. The President is styled 'Emperor of the Mohocks,' and his arms are a Turkish crescent, which his Imperial Majesty bears at present in a very extraordinary manner, engraven upon his forehead. Agreeable to their name, the avowed design of their institution is mischief, and upon this foundation all their rules and orders are framed * * * * In order to exact their principle in its full strength and perfection, they take care to drink themselves to a pitch that is beyond the possibility of attending to any notions of reason or humanity, then make a general sally, and attack all that are so unfortunate as to walk the streets that they patrol. Some are knocked down, others stabbed, others cut and carbonadoed. To put the watch to a total rout, and mortify some of those inoffensive militia is reckoned a *coup d' éclat.* The peculiar talents by which these misanthropes are distinguished from one another, consist in the various kinds of barbarities which they execute upon their prisoners. Some are celebrated for a happy dexterity in 'tipping the lion' upon them, which is performed by squeezing the nose flat to the face, and boring out the eyes with their fingers. Others are called 'dancing masters', and teach their scholars to cut capers by running swords through their legs, a new invention, whether originally French I cannot tell. A third sort are the tumblers, whose office it is to set women on their heads."—*See Spectator, No.* 324, *March* 27, 1711.

[This account and what follows may, of course, be received as somewhat exaggerated, but there is no doubt that the Mohocks in those days were pests and scourges of society. There were many, however, who, like Stanley Sherrington and his friends, had joined the society under a misapprehension, and who, while joining in their *fun*, endeavoured always to discourage their more mad and violent freaks.—*Author of* "RUPERT DREADNOUGHT."]

ately starting off at a quick trot, were soon in the open country.

Darkness had fallen, but the moon and the stars were brilliantly gleaming, and only occasional clouds intercepted the gentle rays which they cast upon Mother Earth.

I have before described the route from London to the old house where Helen Penraven was immured, and I need only say, therefore, that no interruption occurred until they reached the inn at the cross-road, where Rupert on the night of his escape had borrowed a horse.

On passing this they saw something moving in the distance.

It was difficult at first to say what this something was.

Dense clumps of trees, as will be remembered, grew on the hedges of the road across the heath, and at first it seemed, truly, as if one of these were moving.

But presently, as the moon burst suddenly from behind a cloud and inundated the scene, the truth was evident.

A party of horsemen held the road.

A spy had informed Oscar of Rupert's intended journey, and the enemy were on the alert.

Rupert hesitated not, but only glanced round him at his companions.

The Mohocks whom Sherrington had brought with him were all tall, young, stalwart men; and there was not much fear as to the result of an encounter with those who might be hired assassins.

"Let us dash onwards," cried he; "if they are friendly they will make room for us, seeing we are in haste. If they are foes we will cut our way through."

"Bravely spoken!" cried Sherrington, "let us put spurs to our horses then, and draw our swords."

Keeping their glittering blades as far as possible out of sight, the little squad of brave, determined hearts rushed eagerly along the high road.

It was as Rupert had at first imagined.

The body of men who held the road were foemen.

Masks concealed their faces and they were all attired in black.

In order to make a pretence of not being the first to commence the quarrel, they jogged their horses leisurely towards Rupert and his friends, and when the latter came up with them there was a perfect shout of feigned astonishment.

"How now, gentlemen," said a strange voice, "what means this conduct on the king's highway?"

There was no answer.

Almost as the words left his lips the horses and men met with a crash and the conflict commenced.

The opposing body, however, were by far the more powerful in the way of numbers, and they had moreover so disposed their horses that it was impossible for any but an overwhelming force to burst through.

Instinctively, as it were, recognising the fact that all parley was now useless, they began the contest at once.

Yet in the contest there was a strange similarity to the former one.

The masked men seemed desirous of barring their foemen's progress.

But nothing more.

They appeared not to fight to kill.

They were soon, however, compelled to change their tactics.

Rupert's friends gave no quarter.

It was a demand and a blow with these wild youug spirits.

"Let us pass," was the demand.

Then came a whirling gleam of steel, and men fell back cut to the chine, with scarcely a cry to mark the moment of their death.

Blood flowed freely on every side, streaming down the flanks of the horses and over the roadway.

Horses, riderlesss, went plunging away through the darkness, over the dark moorland.

Both sides suffered.

But the Mohocks were used to desperate fighting, and, with the exception of a few unimportant wounds, they got off comparatively free.

Suddenly, just as the battle was at its height, there was the report of a gun at a short distance off.

It acted like magic.

In an instant the masked men drew away from their opponents.

There was no more desperate fighting on either side.

As soon as they had retreated far enough, they suddenly broke and dashed away in different directions over the moonlit moor.

"Hurrah! they fly!" shouted the Mohocks.

Rupert restrained their ardour.

"Stay," he cried, "there is treachery afoot! Silence!"

In an instant the little band ceased their outcry.

"The report of the gun, my friends," said Dreadnought, "was a signal. That signal came from the direction of the house where Helen Penraven is immured. You understand me now, no doubt, my friends: while we fight here, treachery is at work with her. So let us lose no time, but hurry on, and let these cowards fly whither they please."

This was scarcely what the Mohocks liked, but they had for the time being submitted themselves to the command of Rupert Dreadnought, and so they cheerfully complied with his request.

On, therefore, they once more pushed, and, within a very short space of time, they drew up before the half-ruined wall and ragged hedge which surrounded the house where Helen Penraven had been placed in supposed safety by the old earl.

Waiting for no summons at the door, Rupert Dreadnought leaped the ditch, and dashing through the brushwood, made towards the house porch.

RUPERT OR THE DREADNOUGHT; OR THE SECRETS OF THE IRON CHEST

"WILL NOT SOME FRIEND TELL RUPERT I AM IN DANGER?" SHE CRIED.

He had no need to knock.

It was wide open.

It was easy to see that enemies had been busy there.

On the floor, gagged and bound, were two men servants, while one lay dead in the entry.

The former were at once released and eagerly questioned.

"Who has been here?" asked Rupert Dreadnought, as he helped one of the men to a chair.

"I know not who they are," cried the man, "for they were masked, and not one of their voices was familiar to me; but Mistress Penraven is gone—a prisoner—with them."

A muttered curse escaped from the lips of young Dreadnought as the man spoke.

"Are you certain of it?" he asked.

"Yes; I saw her struggling in the arms of a brawny ruffian and rushed forward to aid her, when I was knocked down and gagged; while one of my poor companions, as you see, was shot down, and lies yonder. She screamed loudly, but it was all in vain. No help was near."

"And did she say nothing?—did she leave no message for me?" asked Rupert, distractedly.

"No; only as she was lifted up by her captor and placed before him on the horse, she cried out, in an agonized voice,

"'Oh! if Rupert were here! Will not some friend tell Rupert I am in danger?'"

Without asking more, Rupert seized a lamp from the hall table and passed up towards her room, followed by Allan of the Glen and two of the Mohocks.

They searched everywhere.

In vain.

In not one of the chambers was there the slightest clue to be found as to the identity of her captors.

However, on this point there could be little room for doubt.

It was a plan of Oscar Penraven, and it was he who must be discovered and punished.

Yet how fix the guilt on him?

That he *was* guilty there could be no doubt, however; and, after giving instructions to the serving-men what to do, Rupert led away his little band, and once more made his way towards London.

CHAPTER XV.

RUPERT'S DESPAIR—TOM THE WATERMAN—THE MYSTERIOUS CARRIAGE—THE SHRIEKS OF A CAPTIVE—TOM TO THE RESCUE.

THE feelings of Rupert Dreadnought, when he returned home to his quiet, deathstricken house and thought over the utter failure of his plan for rescuing Helen, I will not pause to describe now.

As may be imagined, they were intensely harrowing.

At the very outset he was thwarted.

His father's express injunction was that nothing should be attempted until Helen was in safety, and the failure of the night's expedition, therefore, postponed indefinitely the opening of the first compartment of the IRON CHEST and the commencement of the first MISSION OF VENGEANCE.

However, there was nothing like despair in his heart.

Angry with himself and with circumstances, as he might be, he never for one moment faltered.

All he thought of as he rode home—all he thought of during the night and the next dreary morning, was how he could save Helen—where he could meet Oscar Penraven face to face, and wring from him the secret of her concealment.

It was a terrible thing now even to dream of delay.

Helen Penraven had been named by Oscar as his bride.

What villany might he not put in practice to secure the possession of her?

Force, of course, would be used; and without a single friend to aid her, or even give her advice, how could she be expected to go through the ordeal unscathed?

It was now that Rupert for the first time felt the loss of his father.

He had ever been accustomed to lean upon him, as it were, for advice, and it was indeed a change to miss his familiar voice—to miss his familiar face and form, and have to think and act entirely on his own responsibility.

"This night," thought he, "I will seek out Oscar's dwelling and force the secret from his dastard lips."

He little knew how useless on this occasion would be the endeavour.

In order to explain this we must carry our readers to a little hut on the edge of the river, where lived three persons who will play an active part in the development of our story.

These three persons were Mistress Braxley, her niece Agnes, and her son Tom—known at home and all along the shores of Father Thames as Tom the Waterman.

Not that there was any speciality about Tom's watermanship.

There were plenty of watermen on the river, plenty of strong arms and willing hearts, but Tom had been called the "waterman" when first he dabbled, infant like, in the muddy water and tried to pull his father's huge oars, and so the name had stuck to him ever since.

There were plenty of "Toms" there and thereabouts, but there was only *one* "Tom the waterman."

And this one was a fine, tall, curly-headed fellow, strong-armed and stout-hearted, the support of his widowed mother, the esteemed friend of his companions, the beloved of his cousin Agnes.

On the night of the abduction of Helen Penraven from Sandmount, Tom the waterman had been engaged very late.

A more than usually large number of persons had that night crossed from the Kentish side of the river towards the Tower, and more than usually mysterious had been their manners and their words.

Tom was used to mysteries.

His best customers were men running from the law or pursuit of various kinds, loving couples who were hastening from the anger of parents and cared not for the publicity of London Bridge, and masked and cloaked men who said little, paid well, and left strange doubts as to their occupation.

These latter had been his customers all that evening.

Four times his boat had been chartered, and each time two masked men had crossed the Thames.

His reputation must certainly have preceded him with these men, for although Tom expressed himself unable to accomplish so much work alone, they declined to allow him to seek help, preferring to assist him themselves.

With their aid, therefore, four journeys had been accomplished, and then a fifth journey brought over one man only—a tall, young, elegantly-dressed man, whose features, like those of his companions, were concealed by a mask.

The others, when they were landed, at once proceeded along the Essex Road.

The young one remained behind, and lighting a cigar, strolled away some distance beneath the shadow of the old houses, keeping as far as possible out of reach of all passers-by.

Tom the waterman was nearly worn out by the fatigues of the evening, and when the last passenger slipped a gold piece into his hand, he inwardly resolved that he would row no more that night.

Such, however, was not the intention of those who had employed him.

Just as he had moored his boat, and sat down upon the broad, dry steps, to take a whiff or two before entering his little home, the youngest of the masked men returned and spoke to him.

"Young man," he said, "we shall have need of your services again."

"I trust so, sir, since you pay liberally," returned Tom; "but not to-night."

"Yes, indeed, to-night," replied the stranger. "It is a lady who requires your aid, and you will not, I am sure, be so ungallant as to refuse her."

Tom laughed lightly at the tone in which the speaker addressed these words to him.

"Well," he said, "how long will it be before the lady will be here?"

"In two hours, so you have time for rest," returned the masked man. "Go, join your comrades in yonder tavern, and recruit your strength with rest and drink. I will apprise you when the hour arrives."

"Good!" said Tom, who, for a long time had not made so fortunate an evening's work. "I will be here before the two hours, since you needs must have *my* boat, and row you across. Meanwhile, I will say good-night!"

The stranger nodded haughtily as the free-and-easy waterman walked away, and Tom, whistling to himself a merry tune, passed towards his mother's home.

He soon reached it, and pushing open the door, entered a small but comfortable room, where his mother and his cousin were seated by the fire, while near them was a table with substantial viands yet untouched.

"Ah, dear mother!" he cried, as he kissed her cheek, and then saluted Agnes in a similar way; "waiting supper for me! That's too bad! I vow I won't touch a morsel the next time you act thus. Why, you two ought to be in bed, and not waiting up for a strong, hearty fellow like me, who can wait upon himself."

"Don't talk so, but eat, Tom," said his mother, kindly, as Agnes pushed a well-filled plate towards him. "Why, what's that, Tom? gold?"

"Aye, and plenty of silver with it," returned the young waterman, who had piled his night's earnings on the table; "and I've not done yet, for before I can turn into my bed this night, I've to ferry a lady over the old river."

"A lady at this time of night!" said Agnes, a pretty, bright-eyed girl of eighteen, with a well-turned plump figure, and long, curling, dark hair; "what a curious thing!"

"Yes, it's altogether a curious thing," said Tom, who was eating and talking at the same time without raising his eyes from his plate. "The men that I've ferried over to-night are all masked, and seem full of money. I wonder what the lady's like; if she's handsome I'm safe to fall in love with her."

The blush on the cheek of Agnes Mayland as she murmured "Foolish fellow," told that she did not quite relish his joke; but Tom did not observe it, and rattled on accordingly without intermission in his cheerful, jolly way until the clock struck.

He jumped up at once.

"I've none too much time," he said. "An hour's gone already. I'll run over now to the 'Three Sailors' and have a glass, and mind when I *do* come back I shall expect to see all the lights out, and you two fast asleep."

Then the happy, genial fellow kissed his mother and cousin again, and went out into the night.

The "Three Sailors" was soon reached.

It was a little, low-pitched, oddly-built, but cleanly little tavern, standing not very far from the bridge, and just in such a position that Tom must see the return of the masked strangers with the lady, so he lounged near the door with some of his companions, and smoked, and drank, and listened.

He expected naturally that the mysterious lady whoever she was, would come in a carriage, and his ears were opened therefore for the sound of wheels.

Presently they were heard driving very rapidly, but they stopped suddenly, and all was again still.

Then came another sound.

A shriek; wild, piercing, prolonged.

"That was a woman's cry!" exclaimed Tom, whose gallant heart was at once moved; and, as he spoke, he sprang out, and glanced eagerly around him.

Bnt nothing was anywhere to be seen.

"It's some poor thing cast herself off London Bridge maybe," said one of his companions who stood near him.

"Oh! no," said Tom the waterman, "my hearing tells me better than that. The cry did not come from that direction, but directly the opposite. Let's get some weapons, and wait here."

"Weapons!" exclaimed his friends, in undisguised amazement.

Tom's quick mind had at once realised the situation.

This cry was a woman's.

Might not she be the very one of whom the masked stranger had spoken?

Might she not be borne hither against her will?

"Yes; weapons," he repeated; "don't waste time in asking questions. Run in and get your oars, and sticks, or anything. Depend upon it we're wanted."

Tom, who was like a king among these rough river-men, was at once obeyed.

In a few moments they re-appeared, armed with staves and oars, and hardly had they done so when there was a second loud and piercing cry, then a rush of feet, and the masked men who had crossed the river in Tom the waterman's boat dashed from out the darker portion of the street, one of them bearing in his arms the form of a woman.

This was Helen Penraven.

"See, my friends!" cried Tom, as he rushed forward, "did I not say we were wanted?"

CHAPTER XVI.

THE FIGHT BY THE RIVER—OARS AGAINST SWORDS—THE CAPTURE OF THE BOAT—THE FLIGHT OF THE MASKED MEN—THE MYSTERIOUS WARNING.

"SAVE me! save me!" cried the wretched girl, as she saw in the dim, uncertain light the body of watermen advancing towards her.

"Curses on you, Frankland!" exclaimed the youngest of the party—the one who had remained behind; "did I not tell you to drug her food?"

"I will explain another time," replied the one addressed as Frankland; "here are the watermen; let us get quickly across the river or her cries may arouse the neighbourhood. Quick!"

"Draw your swords!" exclaimed the young stranger; "these come as enemies, What means it? How now, Master Tom Braxley; is your boat ready?"

"No more this night for you!" cried Tom, boldly. "If I had known what evil I was doing, I would have lost my arm sooner than used it to bring you across the river to-night. Release that lady!"

"Insolent ruffian!" cried the masked stranger, drawing his sword. "What mean you by such words as these? Quick, to your boat; and if you do not want your tongue cut out, or your ears shorn off, be silent upon what does not concern you."

A derisive laugh from Tom was the only answer to this braggart speech.

Then, at a signal from him, the sturdy river men rushed upon the masked strangers.

But the latter were well prepared.

"Bear her to the boat!" shouted the clear, ringing voice of the leader. "We will cover your retreat. Keep back these insolent knaves," he added, "but let us have no unnecessary bloodshed. We must not have our names mixed up with street brawls."

The man who bore Helen Penraven across his shoulders had not now so much work to do.

There were no more struggles on her part.

The peril of her situation, and the sight of the drawn swords, had made her swoon, and she lay a dead weight in his arms.

The other masked men formed before him, and as the river men rushed upon them with their oars uplifted, they were met by a stern resistance.

"On, on, my men—on!" cried Tom the waterman, beating down the sword opposed to him. "On, on—or we shall be too late! Drive them into the water!"

"By Heavens! this insolence surpasses belief!" exclaimed the young leader, as he fiercely rushed at Tom. "Are you mad thus to interfere with gentlemen? Quick, there, Frankland!"

As he spoke, the sword he had lunged so savagely at Tom's heart was dashed to the ground by a stroke of the oar.

The oar was then let drop, and Tom closed with his enemy.

The masked stranger was a powerful man, but he was no match for the young waterman, who soon held him on the ground at his mercy.

But the battle was a useless one.

The masked men had decidedly the advantage, and, although they gave way as they retreated towards the river's brink, it was but to cover their friends while they lifted the young girl into the boat.

As soon as they had succeeded in this manœuvre the boat was pushed off, and the young leader cried, in a sneering tone, to Tom, who still held him—

"Now, then, my friend, is it murder you intend?"

"No," said Tom, releasing him, "but you, I fancy, intend worse than murder. Providence, unfortunately, did not aid us in rescuing yonder poor girl from your clutches; but, mark me, she'll escape you yet. If not, a terrible retribution is in store for you, as sure as Heaven is just."

Then, as the young masker sprang to his feet, Tom cried, turning to his men,

"Bill Flaxman, where is your boat? Let us pursue them."

And then, leaving the masked stranger to cross by the bridge, or as he best could, they rushed through the dry arch to the spot where Bill Flaxman's boat lay.

This boat was a long, sharp-pointed one, but it was capable of holding several men; and in a few moments the skilled watermen had taken their seats, and were pulling with a will from the shore.

The others, however, were very far ahead, and were using the most strenuous exertions to reach the opposite shore, evidently being influenced by an intense dread of discovery and capture.

Tom soon saw that all pursuit was useless, and when half way across the river he gave the word to return.

They had hardly turned the head of their boat before they saw their enemy's wherry reach the opposite bank, and the captors of the young girl leap ashore and make hastily away.

When Tom and his companions returned to the spot they had left, the masked men were gone, and no one who was near could give any account of their whereabouts.

Tom was in no humour now to join his comrades in any further carouse, so he refused all inducements to retrace his steps to the inn.

Saying "Good night," therefore, he passed hurriedly towards his home.

His mind was strangely disturbed.

His thoughts were full of the lovely being he had seen.

In fancy he could again behold the sweet, appealing look she had given him when she cried—

"Save me—save me!"

Her voice, sweet and thrilling, seemed to penetrate into the inmost recesses of his heart, and he vowed that he would yet trace the enemies of the lovely unknown, or perish in the attempt.

He was so absorbed in these fancies that he was at his own door before he had any idea that he had travelled so far.

He was just entering, when a deep, sepulchral voice near him said—

"Beware, Tom Braxley, you have stepped upon a dangerous track; abandon it while you are yet safe."

He turned sharply to see who was the author of this mysterious warning.

But in that brief instant he was too late to learn much.

The words had been spoken quickly and sharply, and, as he turned, all he could see was a tall, dark figure in a cloak, gliding swiftly and noiselessly away.

He darted after it as it passed round the corner of the street, but, *when he reached the spot, it was gone!*

Tom was not reckoned to be a very superstitious man.

But, to say the least, this was far from being a pleasant adventure.

The whole evening had had its air of mystery about it.

What meant this last scene of all?

Who could be his mysterious adviser?

Tom had hitherto kept himself most wonderfully aloof from all kinds of intrigue.

Considering the curious character of some of those who had from time to time made use of his boat, it was indeed wonderful that he had been able to preserve himself so entirely from scrapes of all kinds.

And yet here was he—honest, prudent Tom Braxley, being dragged into the mazes of a mystery more intricate than all!

He turned into bed that night with a heavy heart, but his resolution was in no way shaken.

CHAPTER XVII.

A MEETING OF MOHOCKS—A RIVER SCENE—TOM THE WATERMAN FINDS A CLUE AT LAST.

We have said that after the failure of his first attempt at carrying out his dead father's wishes in rescuing Helen Penraven from the power of her cousin, Rupert Dreadnought—though not giving way to despair—was sorely angry and disappointed.

But he had not the slightest idea for a moment of giving up the chase.

Better, it would have been in his eyes, to have died in attempting to save his beloved, than live to see her the wife of another.

Better by death to cancel the vow of revenge which he had sworn, than live for vengeance alone, without the prospect of so sweet a reward.

The only friends, who, upon the moment, he could depend, were Stanley Sherrington and his Mohocks.

These were desperate characters to mix up with, yet they had befriended him, and behaved as trustworthy comrades before.

Why should they not do so again?

So, in the evening, accompanied by Allan of the Glen, he made his way towards the old tavern where the Mohocks held their meetings.

Arriving here, he set Allan to watch at the door, while he, having given the pass-word, as conveyed him by Stanley Sherrington, advanced up a broad staircase, and made his way into a large room.

Stanley was in the chair, and, around him, sitting at little tables, drinking, smoking, and singing, were a number of young men, all belonging to the best classes of society, but debased and lowered to vulgarity now by excesses of every kind.

THE CHIEF OF THE POISONERS.

An insane notion that what they were banded together to perform was courageous as well as funny, led them into the most outrageous acts, but it was then only, of course, under the influence of drink that they were able to bring themselves to the commission of deeds which would have qualified any one of them in these days for Hanwell.

The entrance of Rupert Dreadnought, who was looked upon as a new member, was received with shouts of applause.

They little knew in what contempt he held them, or how eager he was to release Stanley Sherrington from their clutches, or, it is very probable, they would have commenced upon him the same style of attack that they practised upon their unfortunate victims in the street.

"Welcome, brother," cried one half-inebriated fellow.

"Hurrah! for the new Mohock!"

"Three cheers for the new cannibal!"

Such cries, amid shouts of mad laughter, greeted him, as he walked up to an empty chair near Sherrington and sat down.

"Sherrington," he said, "can you come away? I want you."

Sherrington shook his head.

"No," he said, "I dare not."

"Dare not!"

"Yes, indeed. It is the correct word. If any here saw in me any signs of quitting hurriedly there would be a revolt."

"And what the consequences?"

"My death, perhaps."

Rupert smiled.

"You are jesting," he said; "you make your Society more terrible than it is."

"Not I," replied Sherrington, "it is a fact. In

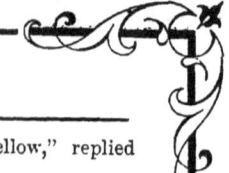

their mad fury they would set upon me, and without, perhaps, intending it, they would accomplish my destruction. What you have to say you must reserve until presently. Is it important?"

"It is a matter of life and death."

"Then as soon as I can escape from them I will listen to you," said Sherrington: "they are bent upon a strange expedition to-night, and until that is over nothing reasonable can be done."

"And what is their purpose, then, to-night?" asked Rupert Dreadnought.

"You know well, of course, the pretty village of Twickenham?"

"I do."

"Well, there is a grand ball to be given to-night at Lord Hawksworth's. The guests are expected to leave the rooms about midnight, and most of them, in order to reach their homes, have to pass along Love Lane."

"And are these to be the objects of attack?"

"One section of them. There are six young ladies who will attend the ball, who belong to the school kept close to Hawksworth House by Miss Primrose. They will, of course, be escorted home by some gay gallants, and upon these it is proposed to make an attack. The young ladies will be seized, carried to the river side, and conveyed across the water in boats."

"But this is nothing better than murder," said Rupert; "in this cold weather, and with only their ball dresses on, they will die of cold and misery."

"Ah, well!" cried Sherrington, "I have done my best to dissuade them, but with no effect. I am bound by the oaths of the Society to aid them, and so I am compelled to take my share in all their foolish pranks. I shall do my best to prevent mischief. *You* will second me, I am sure."

Rupert Dreadnought started in astonishment.

"I!" he cried, "I! What have I to do with it? I shall not think of accompanying them in their mad expedition."

Stanley Sherrington leaned over him and whispered in his ear:

"Don't be mad, Dreadnought. Don't speak so loud. You are talking treason. You don't know what a desperate set of fellows you are mixed up with. They stick at nothing. You are one of us for the time being and cannot recede."

"Cannot! I fear them not," said Rupert Dreadnought. "Against such a set of inebriate fools my sword would be quite enough to clear my way."

"Yes, yes, but do not risk it," replied Sherrington. "I have an idea. We can rescue these girls."

"How? Tell me," eagerly asked Rupert.

"Listen, and then you must quit my side," answered his friend. "Full of drink as they are, they will observe us. We are going to take two boats on the river."

"From what starting point?"

"From London Bridge. Tom Braxley—Tom the waterman, as they call him, supplies them. We shall be rowed up the river to Putney, and shall arrive there about midnight. On our journey——By the way, before I say more, do you know Tom the waterman?"

"I have never seen him, but I have heard my father speak of him as an honest fellow," replied Rupert.

"He is," said Sherrington, "and not the one to aid in any madcap folly that is likely to end in bloodshed or disaster of any kind. Take him into your confidence. Remain behind when we land, and I will slip back to you. We together, masked, will lead the watermen to the rescue and save the girls."

"Good. I understand your scheme well."

"Say no more now, then. Ah! what means that? I fear even now we are suspected."

A tall, ill-looking young fellow of brutal appearance, heavy-browed, heavy-mouthed, and unlike altogether the sort of being one expects to find in circles of refinement, had left his seat a moment before, and in a low whisper imparted some information to those at the little tables.

Then he rose again and quitted the room.

Sherrington was not taken aback.

He was a good and cool hand in cases of sudden danger.

Rising to his feet, he cried—

'Gentlemen and brother Mohocks,—According to our rules our new brother here has to make his appearance three times at our club, and to partake in at least one adventure before being elected. This is his second appearance, and having heard from me what is proposed to be done to-night, he has agreed to accompany us."

Loud cheers followed these words.

They had no idea what signification they had.

All they cared to know was that their new comrade was about to join them in their madcap excursion.

Whatever suspicion the one who had quitted the chamber had sought to rouse in their minds was now at once dispelled, and when he re-entered the clock's voice—telling them it was ten—closed all further conversation.

"It is time to start," cried Sherrington. "Drain your glasses, gentlemen, and prepare."

Inebriated as they were, they at once started to their feet, and within a few moments they had taken from a large cupboard at one end of the vast room a number of masks and weapons of various kinds.

In a few moments all were ready, and they sallied forth into the street.

At the door stood Allan of the Glen, who, at a whisper from Rupert Dreadnought, sprang away and disappeared into the house.

The night was a very fine one, and as they neared the river they could see the moonlight shimmering brightly and gracefully upon the tiny wavelets of Father Thames, and casting a kind of unknown splendour upon the roof-tops of old houses, which, in the merry sunlight, looked dark and dismal enough in very truth.

Underneath the arch of London Bridge, where, not long before—in fact not very many hours before—Tom the waterman had had his conflict with the abductors of Helen Penraven, the young fellow was waiting, with three comrades and two fine boats.

Neither Tom nor his friends had the remotest conception who their employers were, or it is questionable whether they would have cared to carry them, but as it was these young gallants were soon seated and the boats flying over the moonlit river.

Sherrington and Rupert Dreadnought sat close to one another, and near Tom the waterman, who could consequently overhear all their conversation.

"Tell me, Rupert," said his friend, in a low tone, "what want you with me to-night ?"

"I want your aid again to find Helen Penraven."

"Have you any clue to her whereabouts ?"

"None."

"Then how do you expect to find her ?"

"I come to you for advice," said Rupert. "Now, all *I* know is *this*. Helen was seized last night by a number of masked men, one of whom placed her before him on a horse and rode away with her across the moor. At the roadside inn they changed their mode of conveyance, and placed her in a carriage. They then dashed away on the road to London, and from that moment I have lost the clue."

Sherrington smiled.

"And how, think you," he said, "can *I* unravel the mystery ?"

"I do not fancy you can," replied Rupert, "but among the desperate spirits who compose your club may be some friends of Oscar Penraven."

"This I will discover for you," said Sherrington. "I can see your drift; and depend on me to aid you in everything which lies in my power."

It may be imagined with what intense interest Tom the waterman listened to this conversation.

Here, at length, was a faint clue to the mystery.

Here, at any rate, he had found one of the friends of the captive young lady, if he had not discovered her whereabouts, and he determined to communicate with Rupert directly they landed at Twickenham.

It was approaching midnight as they reached the shore and the young men landed.

"Let us go in couples," said Sherrington, "and hide ourselves in the lane. We shall in this way avoid exciting so much suspicion."

The Mohocks, who, on this evening, were under his direction, at once obeyed, and it was not long before Rupert and Sherrington were left alone.

As soon as the coast was really clear, Rupert turned to Tom the waterman.

"Tom Braxley," he said, "I believe you and your fellows are brave; my father has told me as much."

"Your father, sir !" exclaimed Tom, in surprise.

"Yes, Earl Dreadnought, who is now, alas, no more !"

"Is the good earl dead, then ?" said Tom, sadly. "Yes, he knew me well; and you then, sir—that is, my lord—are his son ?"

"Yes, I am his son," said Rupert; "but we have no time now to talk of my poor father. I and my friend are here to prevent the perpetration of a great wrong, and to prevent, maybe, the shedding of blood. Those persons whom you have brought here are the Mohocks. They are about to assail innocent and unoffending people. Will you aid us in preventing such an outrage ?"

"Yes, willingly," said Tom the waterman; "but we have no swords."

Rupert gave a low whistle.

In an instant a dark form rose from the bottom of one of the boats, and in another moment Allan of the Glen sprang ashore with four swords in his hand.

"Here are your weapons," cried Rupert. "Be brave, and follow our directions, and you have nothing to fear."

Rupert was in the act of adjusting his mask when Tom the waterman touched his arm, and whispered, hurriedly,

"My lord, we have no time now, and in the fight we may be separated. Come to my house, near London Bridge, to-morrow night, at any hour you name (ask for Tom Braxley, and any one will tell you where to find me), and I'll give you information about a certain lady."

"Helen Penraven !" exclaimed Rupert, in astonishment and excitement.

"I know nothing of her name," said Tom, "but I saw her carried away last night, and——"

"Now, then," cried Sherrington; "now then. The clock has struck the quarter to midnight. We shall be late."

As he spoke, he advanced a short distance down the dark lane.

"To-morrow night at ten expect me," said Dreadnought, and then, with Allan of the Glen, they passed on rapidly after Sherrington.

The house of Lord Hawksworth was soon reached.

The Mohocks had reached the place before them, and were concealed behind the hedges and in dark corners, but Rupert Dreadnought and his friends remained in one body under the shadow of a large hayrick which stood at the corner of Love Lane.

It was not long before the unsuspecting company began to issue forth from the house where they had been enjoying themselves.

For some time no movement was made among the desperadoes.

Presently, however, there emerged from the house six young ladies, each leaning on the arm of a gentleman, while an elderly, prim-looking person brought up the rear.

Their appearance was the signal for a general rush, and a series of yells more worthy of demons from the infernal regions than of human beings.

"The Mohocks! the Mohocks to the rescue !" was the cry which brought terror into every female heart, while it caused the gentlemen to spring aside and draw their swords.

As Sherrington had calculated, the defenders of the young girls were quite ready to do their utmost, but the swords they wore were but light dress ones, not intended for serious battle, and in a few moments they were driven off, and the ladies at the mercy of their insane tormentors.

Each one was seized in the arms of one of the Mohocks, who had just succeeded in imprinting one kiss on the cheeks of their unwilling captives, when a diversion occurred which they little expected.

A loud outcry was heard, and the shrill shrieks of women resounded along the river's banks.

They were not long, however, left in the hands of their tormentors.

"To the rescue, to the rescue!" and like lightning Rupert Dreadnought and his brave fellows rushed to the scene of outrage.

The Mohocks little expected this.

This was evidently an organised attack upon them.

Such a thing had never before occurred to them.

However, they resolved to stand it out, for though their acts were cowardly towards the defenceless they were able also to stand their ground against armed foes.

They had no chance, however, and this they saw at once.

Compelled, of course, to relinquish their fair prizes, they found themselves attacked not only by Rupert Dreadnought and his stalwart allies, but also by the gentlemen whose swords they had before beaten down.

It was of no use now shouting their rallying cry.

Little availed now the encouragement of leaders, and within a few moments it was quite evident that flight or surrender would be the next necessity.

A peculiar exclamation from one of them decided this question, and in an instant, without any intimation, they turned and ran with three of their members badly wounded, and one of their number carried in the arms of his comrades.

"Now, ladies," said Rupert, raising his hat, "we can safely leave you."

"Oh, no!" cried one (whom he had snatched from the embrace of a tall Mohock), as she clung to his arm, "oh no, do not leave us. See us to our door. They will return if they see you depart."

"We will see the ladies in safety," said Sherrington, and so, much to the chagrin of their gallants, the young damsels were escorted to their homes by our heroes, who had now removed their masks.

As they neared the door of the house, Rupert's companion spoke.

They were walking last, and as he turned to glance at her the moonlight was full upon her face.

It was a lovely face, and as Rupert gazed down upon it, her eyes seemed to gleam through and through him.

"I know you!" she said.

"Know me!" he exclaimed, in unfeigned astonishment.

"Yes. You are Rupert Dreadnought," she said, still looking up into his eyes.

The voice she said this in was wonderfully low and sweet, but there was something in it which thrilled to Rupert's heart.

Not pleasantly—not with love's sweet pain.

No, it was an undefinable sensation—a sensation almost of alarm.

"And what is your name, my little fairy?" he said, leaning slightly over her.

"My name?—oh, that matters not," she said, with a light laugh. "I must not tell. We shall meet again."

"Your Christian name, then. That will not harm you."

"Rosalie."

Oh! if Rupert had but known who it was who eaned upon his arm—whose life he had saved—who was living among a number of innocent girls!

Rosalie St. Aubyn, whom Oscar Penraven had met at the Poisoner's Revel!

Little did he dream who it was whose arm hung so gently on his own!

He would have gladly attempted to discover the mystery.

He had not much time for further converse, however.

They had reached the door of the school; the mistress thanked them, the young damsels pressed the hands of their preservers, and they were gone.

Rupert Dreadnought little knew what strange tracks he had trodden in, but still the gleaming eyes and the strange beautiful face of the young girl haunted him as he went!

As they expected, they found on reaching the river bank that the Mohocks had taken possession of the boats, and they had therefore to proceed to the next boat-house and return to London in hired wherries.

"To-morrow night at ten, remember," said Rupert to Tom the waterman, as they parted for the night. "I shall be with you to the minute."

CHAPTER XVIII.

TOM'S HOME ONCE MORE—A DISAPPOINTMENT—A GOOD HEART—THE DARK RIVER—TOM AND HIS NEW PATRON GO ON A PERILOUS ERRAND—THE OLD RUIN—THE DANGEROUS ASCENT—ON THE BRINK OF A DOUBLE PRECIPICE—THE VISION OF BEAUTY—ALLAN'S MOUNTAIN EDUCATION COMES INTO USEFUL PLAY.

THE clock had scarcely struck the hour of ten the following night, when two figures, muffled in cloaks, knocked at the rude door of Tom the waterman's dwelling.

Business had been very slack that evening, and Tom was indulging in his usual hearty supper, as Agnes opened the door.

Tom at once sprang up as he saw two figures, suspecting to see but one.

He was naturally somewhat alarmed, for the mysterious figure, which he had seen only for a moment upon the night of the abduction of Helen Penraven, had been flitting about the house, and he knew that his enemies were capable of any crime.

As he beheld the strangers, therefore, he advanced towards the door, with his hand on his long knife.

"HER LITTLE WHITE HAND WAS DEVOURED WITH KISSES."

"Ah! my lord," cried Tom the waterman, as, advancing to the door, he recognised the features of Rupert Dreadnought. "I am glad you have come. I have seen——"

He stopped a moment, and glanced questioningly at Allan of the Glen, whom in his cloak he failed to recognise.

Rupert smiled.

"Ah!" he said, "you do not know my companion. It was he who gave you your swords last night.

He is a friend and faithful servitor of mine. Tell me," he added, as Allan entered, and Agnes closed the door behind him, "what is it you have seen since I saw you?"

"I saw one of the masked strangers pass the bridge this night," said Tom the waterman, "but he was on horseback, and I could not follow. However, it proves to me that it is on the other side of the water that their haunt is."

"True; but tell me, since you talk now in enigmas," said Rupert, "how much you know."

Brifly Tom the waterman told the story of the abduction he had witnessed.

There was no longer any doubt remaining in Rupert's mind.

The coincidence of time and everything tended to prove that the girl who had thus forcibly been carried off was Helen Penraven.

"By heavens!" cried Rupert, with blanched lips, "this is a terrible blow; this losing of all clue to her whereabouts."

"But why not go openly to your enemy and accuse him?" said Tom the waterman.

"It would be useless," said Rupert Dreadnought; "he would simply deny all knowledge of the transaction, and I have no proof by which to confute him."

"The lady, I presume, is some relation of yours, my lord," said Tom, almost nervously.

Poor Tom!

His heart was soft as his arm was strong, and the bright face of the girl whom he had attempted to rescue from the masked strangers had haunted him day and night.

Wild dreams of ambition floated before his mind, and he saw himself winning his way to glory for her sake.

So he listened eagerly for his reply.

"No," returned Rupert Dreadnought; "she is no relation of mine. She is dearer, nevertheless, than life. She is my betrothed bride, and, more than that, the care of her is left to me by my father as a sacred trust."

Tom's heart fell as Rupert Dreadnought spoke.

His vision melted away at once.

She the betrothed of the rich, handsome, daring, young lord!

Of what use, then, was his mad fancy?

"We will start at once, my lord," he said, as he turned away. "I know the spot where they landed, and from that point we must track them."

Very few preparations were necessary.

Tom was soon indued in his rough coat, and in a few minutes they had reached the side of the river, and were pulling rapidly across its dark waters.

The clue which they had to follow was certainly a very slight one.

But they did not despair.

The neighbourhood surrounding the place of disembarkation was a thinly populated one, and the appearance of masked men would doubtless have attracted considerable notice.

Pulling straight across the Thames to the point, they drew their boat under the shadow of an old building, and creeping up into the light, appeared as if rising suddenly from the water.

The thoroughfare was a narrow, well-lighted one, and they were just debating as to the best mode of procedure, when a man suddenly emerged from a tavern, and walked hurriedly away.

"My lord," cried Tom the waterman, excitedly, "my lord, let us follow that man. I am certain, though now he wears no mask, that he is one of those who were engaged in the carrying off of the lady."

"Lead on, then," said Rupert; "but please remember that I am plain Master Dreadnought."

"The title of Earl of Dreadnought, of which no man need be ashamed," said Tom, warmly, as they hurried on.

"Truly; but until my father's wishes have been carried out I will not assume it. But come, let us separate here. We may be suspected if he discover us following him so quickly."

The man, however, seemed entirely absorbed in his own meditations.

He walked on straight and rapidly, looking neither to the right nor left, until, reaching a turning partially enveloped in gloom, he darted round the corner.

In an instant Allan of the Glen was after him.

He was not lost to view, and when Rupert and Tom came up, he was seen entering the door of a large, gloomy-looking house.

Allan, who was crouching in the shadow of the street opposite when the portal was opened, saw that the hall was full of armed men.

It was useless, therefore, for the moment to attempt a forcible entry.

Indeed there was no proof that it *was* the prison where Helen Penraven was confined, or that Oscar was in any way connected with its inmates.

At present, all they were acting upon was mere surmise.

Chance, however, gave them a method of discovering the truth, which they would have been long, indeed, in finding for themselves.

The street in which the house was situated did not properly deserve such an appellation.

It was a rough-looking lane, whose roadway was cut up by heavy waggons, and where the houses, few and far between, had a dismal and deserted look about them, as if there was a curse upon the vicinity.

Next to the house where the man they were following entered, was a building half in ruins, which seemed to be leaning against it in its decrepitude.

Years before it had been destroyed by a fire, which had almost entirely gutted it.

Now little was left but the bare walls and a staircase, which wound its tottering way up to the summit.

"See," said Allan of the Glen, "see yonder ruin. We can climb to the top, make our way to the other house, and see whether we cannot effect an entrance. The lights are all at the top of the house, and the summit of the ruined building overlooks one window."

The plan was a good one, albeit less feasible to their minds than to the wild mountain boy who had leaped after the goats from crag to crag of his native hills.

However, there was not much room for hesitation.

Tom the waterman was still certain that he had

seen the form of the man before, and even to discover who and what this man was would be to advance one step further on the track of the mystery.

Allan of the Glen led the way, and with slow and cautious steps they began the ascent.

The staircase, left open for years to the winds and rain, was very rotten and shaky, and every now and then birds and bats, startled by the unusual sounds, swooped out of dark corners, and went soaring away with shrill cries.

But there was no fear of discovery.

Not a soul was moving in the lane or the dark, murky, misty land which stretched between the ruined house and the river, and unseen and in safety the three adventurers reached the topmost landing.

Here a difficulty presented itself.

The staircase ended here abruptly, and a wall of some height rose all around them.

What was now to be done?

"Let me mount on your back," said Allan of the Glen, "I am the lightest and most used to climbing, and the wall will bear me the best."

In a moment he was standing upon the strong shoulders of the Thames waterman.

Hardly had he done so when he uttered a cry of astonishment and glided down to his former position.

He had never seen Helen Penraven, but he had heard from Rupert a full description of her beauties.

"She's there!" he cried.

"What! Helen Penraven!" exclaimed Rupert.

"Ah, that she is, Master Dreadnought," said the Scotch boy, whose heart leaped with joy at the thought of having been the first to make the discovery, "she's there, unless my eyes very much deceive me; mount on my shoulders and see for yourself."

In an instant Rupert had mounted and ascertained that Allan of the Glen was in no way mistaken.

Opposite the wall against which he was leaning was a room brightly lit up by a lamp.

As *he* was, therefore, in complete darkness, he could see all that was passing within, in spite of the bars which crossed the casement.

Helen Penraven was indeed there, sitting near the table on which was the lamp.

She was leaning her head on one hand while with the other she was turning over listlessly the leaves of a book.

Rupert felt his heart leap within him as he dropped down again by the side of his companions.

"She is there," he said, in a voice of subdued excitement, "and we must speak with her, but how?"

"I can creep along the wall," said Allan, eagerly, "that is nothing to me."

"Where *you* go *I* can go," returned Rupert; "something must be done, however, to enable us to ascend without each other's help. A double weight might crumble away this wall. I think I see a method by which we can ascend singly."

Drawing his sword he began knocking away at one of the bricks, from which time and fire had crumbled away the mortar.

In a few moments the brick slipped from its place, and fell, with a loud plash, into some water at the basement of the building.

By this means he soon formed a means of passage to the top.

The enterprise was truly a perilous one, for the width of the wall on which they had to pass was only a few inches, and on either side was a sheer precipice some forty feet in depth.

In an instant Rupert made up his mind.

"Allan," he said, "that wall will not sustain both. I shall go alone."

The Scotch boy, with his adventurous spirit, had looked forward with pleasure to this hazardous enterprise, and was disappointed sorely at this speech.

"It would be less dangerous for me than for you, Master Dreadnought," he said.

"No," said Rupert, "you and Tom must remain here and watch. Helen is there and I must speak with her."

So saying he leaned over, obtained a footing on the wall, which swayed beneath his weight, and began his dangerous journey.

The distance was not great, but it was impossible to walk erect, for the bricks moved under his feet, and he was in danger each moment of being hurled to destruction.

Stooping, therefore, he contrived to crawl quickly over, and, reaching the other side, he raised himself up by carefully feeling the wall; and, grasping the bars, was safely within reach of the casement.

He was now only a couple of yards from where Helen was sitting.

"Helen," he said, gently tapping at the window.

The young girl heard the tapping, but not the voice, and did not move from her position.

Bats and night birds had been tapping at the casement all night long.

"Helen," he cried, in a louder voice, and again he tapped more strongly.

The young girl heard the voice this time, and started up in wonder and alarm.

Could it be a spirit that was addressing her?

She knew the voice well, but how was it possible that Rupert Dreadnought could be near her?

One glance at the window, however, was enough to show that he was there in reality, and she sprang eagerly towards the casement.

It was evident in a moment that it would be impossible to rescue her that night or to speak loudly, and in a moment Rupert took a desperate determination.

"Helen," he said, raising himself so that his face almost touched the window, "Helen, resume your seat and read your book as if nothing had happened. Then I will break a pane of glass with the point of my sword. They will enter, probably, to see what is the matter. I will conceal myself, and when they are gone we can resume the conversation."

Helen at once understood his meaning, and though her heart was beating wildly in her bosom, she resumed her seat.

Drawing his sword, Rupert then dashed it through the window, splintering it so that it appeared as if the wind, which was very high, had sent a stone through it from the summit of the old wall.

In an instant after—almost before he had time to sheath his sword—there was a light in the window beneath, which showed to the watchers above the forms of several men ascending a staircase.

"Have a care, Master Dreadnought," cried Allan, "the ruffians are ascending towards the room, and, as I live, the one who ascends first is one of those who attacked me in the 'Golden Acre.'"

"Hush!" cried Rupert, "and keep behind the wall. They can see you from the window."

Through the open casement Rupert could now hear all that passed.

The door was flung open violently, and a man entered.

"What was that noise, Mistress Penraven?" he said. "Were you trying to break from prison?"

"No, indeed, it would be useless," said Ellen, "surrounded as I am by ruthless ruffians. Some one has flung a stone through my window, or the wind has broken it."

The man grunted some surly reply, and approaching the casement, peered out.

All was as still as death.

"It's a bat or something has done it," he said; "it can't be mended to-night. Will you change your room?"

"No; I'll remain here. Draw the curtain across it. That will do for me. I like this room, for I can see the river, and some little sign of life."

The man said no more, but sullenly quitted the room, and in a few minutes the flash of lamplight on the ruined wall showed that he had once more descended the stairs.

A moment after, and Helen Penraven reappeared at the window.

"Rupert," she said.

His voice could now be heard distinctly through the open window.

"I am here, dearest," he cried; "your hand, my sweet one, that I may kiss it."

The plump little white hand was at once extended, and devoured with kisses.

"Now tell me," said Rupert, tenderly holding the hand within his own, "now tell me in what position are you. That ruffian cousin of yours told me that in two days you would be his bride."

"He lied to you, Rupert."

"Thank heaven it *is* so," returned Rupert Dreadnought. "But tell me what has changed his determination so suddenly?"

"Not his own will, you may rely upon it," said Helen. "It *was* arranged that to-morrow I was to be married to him."

"Forcibly?"

"Of course," said the young girl. "You could not suspect that I should yield, no matter what pressure was put upon me. I was to be kept here; a priest was to be brought to me, and in this room I was to be made his wife."

"Curses on him!" muttered Rupert, as the young girl paused, overcome by emotion.

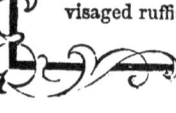

Horror and disgust filled her heart even at the mention of the fate which had threatened her, and was now only put off for a time, unless her lover should be enabled to rescue her.

"Proceed," pursued Rupert; "I am eager to hear more. You have not yet told me why he delayed his hideous design."

"Last evening when he was in this room telling me of his determination a man entered—the dark-visaged ruffian who was here but now.

"He came in without knocking.

"Oscar turned savagely towards him.

"'How dare you enter this lady's room unannounced?' he cried.

"'*When we are sent we need no announcement*,' returned the man.

"In an instant Oscar's manner changed, and, as the man handed him a letter, he opened it eagerly.

"His face altered as he read, and his brow again became as black as thunder.

"'Accursed be this interruption to my cherished hopes!' he said. 'Why could not this letter have been sent before, or not at all? I have traitors somewhere about me, Marksby.'

"The man shrugged his shoulders.

"'If you think *I* am a traitor, prove it,' he said.

"'Oh, no; you value your life too much to run the risk,' said Oscar.

"'And,' replied the ruffian, bowing with every appearance of humility, 'I love my master too well.'

"A grim smile overspread the features of Oscar Penraven.

"Then he turned to me.

"'Helen,' he said, 'I am compelled to leave you. You were to have been my wife in two days. I am summoned away from your side for a week. During that time reflect on what I offer you. Wealth—distinction—the position of a queen in the place of a weary waiting for happiness with one who may die a violent death long before the conclusion of the time which he is compelled by his vow to wait.'

"I made no reply.

"But he could see how full of joy I was at his words.

"The short reprieve which he was giving me, was Heaven, compared with the horrid prospect which had opened up before me; and as he leaned towards me and imprinted a kiss upon my lips, I had no time to prevent him."

"It would have been his last moment had I been near," said Rupert, fiercely.

"He left me then," continued Helen, "and I have not seen him since."

"Oh! that I could release you now," said Rupert, "this may be but some ruse upon his part. How many guard this house?"

"It is full of armed men," replied Helen; "an attack upon it, unless you were in numbers, would be but a mad risk."

As she was speaking, Rupert, forgetful of the fact that he stood on so frail a support, tried the strength of the bars.

They yielded not.

They at least were set in solid masonry and he saw at once that any attempt on his part to wrench them from their holdings would result in instant death to himself.

So he desisted.

"I will return to-morrow night, dear Helen," he said, "with force sufficient to wrest you from your captors. In the meantime, dearest Helen, be firm. Let nothing force upon you a consent. Even if they declare us to be in deadly peril trust them not. Put your confidence in Heaven, my love, and all will be well. Farewell, dearest, I go now to hasten my preparations for to-morrow."

The little hand was again covered with kisses; and then, with another "Good-bye, God bless you," the lovers parted.

The young girl drew as near to the window as she could, and gazed out, as her lover gradually and carefully withdrew, along the trembling and treacherous pathway.

When he joined his companions, who were eagerly awaiting his return, he waved his hand once more to the gentle girl, as she stood in the casement, and then hurriedly descended the stairs.

Next night, at this hour, a red flame ascended to the sky, and the whole of the dismal and misty country around the deserted house was awakened for the moment into life.

But before we describe how this happened, and what hideous treachery caused it, we must follow Rupert, and then Oscar, on their night wanderings.

CHAPTER XIX.

THE INN BY THE RIVER—THE CONSULTATION—THE HAGGARD STRANGER—THE HORROR OF A MOMENT—THE STRANGE COMPACT.

Hurrying away from the old house, Rupert Dreadnought and his companions made their way into the high road, and, weary and agitated, entered a small tavern which stood near the river, and, indeed, close to the stairs which had served them for a landing place.

ALLAN OF THE GLEN.

Here they ascended the stairs, and passed into a room which looked out over the Thames.

This was the public room, but at the moment we speak of it, it appeared to be tenantless.

Wearily they threw themselves down by the fire.

"We are on a strange adventure, Master Dreadnought," said Allan of the Glen, "and I fear that we are only at the beginning of it."

"Not so," cried Rupert, "we *must* bring it to an end. I cannot bear this suspense. I will either release her at once or I will die in the attempt. This week shall see her freed, or I shall never live to carry out my father's instructions."

"And where is this enemy, this Oscar Penraven, now?" asked Tom the waterman.

Before Rupert could answer, the door opened and a man entered.

"What are your orders, gentlemen?" he said, at the same time glancing uneasily round the room.

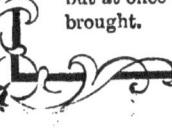

The tired travellers did not observe this movement, but at once ordered some wine, which was promptly brought.

The man hesitated after he had been paid the score, and looked earnestly at a dark corner of the room, which concealed the opening of a recess.

But after a moment's hesitation he appeared to change his mind, and thanking the guests for a gratuity given him, and bidding them ring if they required anything, he quitted the room.

The conversation was at once renewed, though in a lower key than before.

"You were asking where this Oscar Penraven was," said Rupert Dreadnought; "I cannot answer you. All I can say is that he has received a mysterious summons which compels him to quit yonder house for a time, and leave his prisoner in peace. To-morrow night I must arm my servants and attack that place."

"Why not call in the assistance of the constables?" asked Tom.

"Because, legally, I have no right to interfere," said Rupert Dreadnought. "She is the daughter of Sir Robert Penraven, the guardian left for her by him is Oscar Penraven her cousin, and from him, therefore, I have no claim to take her."

"But you *must* take her, or she will be lost, whoever she be," said a voice close at hand.

It was a strange, sepulchral voice, and the three men started round simultaneously.

The speaker was stranger still than the voice itself.

He was tall and thin, his face was pale as death, except where the scars of ghastly wounds presented themselves, and his clothes, which clung to him with the peculiarly tight embrace which seems to denote poverty, were torn and ragged.

It was his eyes which gave tone and life to his being.

Red—gleaming—fierce—ravenous as those of an animal, they seemed as if they penetrated through and through those upon whom he gazed.

Rupert Dreadnought gazed in some wonder at the strange apparition which so suddenly appeared before them.

"Pray, sir, whom am I addressing?" he said, after a moment.

"An enemy of Oscar Penraven," the stranger answered, "one who will hunt him to the death."

"If you can destroy him why do you not do so at once?"

The ghastly apparition smiled.

"No," he answered, "that would not be revenge enough for me. I will follow him like his shadow. I will thwart his plans. Ever when the cup of happiness is close to his lips I will dash it from him."

Rupert gazed at him curiously.

Was he really what he seemed?

Was he in truth the enemy of Oscar Penraven, or was this simply a ruse to get Rupert into his power?

"If you are, indeed, Oscar Penraven's foe," replied Rupert, "then you and I are brothers in arms, if I may so speak. But in these times it behoves one to be careful. How do I know that what you say is true?"

"And how do I know that what *you* say is true?" said the mysterious stranger, with a smile.

"I did not express my feelings at first for your benefit," replied Dreadnought. "I knew not of your presence when I was speaking to my friends, whereas *you* volunteered *your* statement."

"True, true," replied the ghastly stranger. "You are young, but you are full of prudence. But come hither to me a moment and I will reveal to you what will curdle the blood in your veins, and at the same time will cause you to place that implicit faith in me without which it is impossible for me to do you any service."

Rupert rose at once, and was about to follow his strange friend to the other corner of the room when an idea struck him.

"Tom, and you, Allan, also," he said, "leave me alone with this gentleman a moment. Remain close at hand within call."

The stranger watched their departure, and then staggered to the door to see if they were listening.

"It is unnecessary," said Rupert; "they are honest men."

"I have found so few in my time," said the other, "that I doubt every one. However, I'll come to the fire (it's very cold), and we won't detain your friends long. In the first place, am I right in supposing that you are Rupert, or, rather, Lord Rupert Dreadnought, son of the late Lord Desmond Dreadnought?"

"I am."

"And did your father die a natural death?" asked the mysterious man."

"He died of old age."

The other shook his head.

"No, no," he said, "it seemed so, but such was not the case. He died of the mysterious malady that carries off all our rich people—*he died of poison!*"

"Poison!" cried Rupert Dreadnought, excitedly. "How know you this unless *you* were an accessory to the crime?"

A smile of scorn wreathed over the features of the stranger.

"If you are so hot-headed and suspicious," he said, "nothing can be done. In regard to your half accusation I shall say nothing except that it is absurd; and if I am to be met in that way I cease my speech with you."

The manner in which this was spoken convinced Rupert Dreadnought that he had been too hasty.

"Forgive me, sir," he said, "but the thought that my poor father had died of poison nearly turned my brain. Proceed, and I will not interrupt you. Are you certain of what you say?"

"I am morally, though not practically, certain," said the stranger, "but when I have told you my own story you will say that this moral certainty is as good as positive proof. Listen."

The strange and terrible story which he unfolded to Rupert Dreadnought I shall not here narrate.

Let it suffice that as he spoke our hero watched him with eyes full of a stony horror—a face pale as ashes—while ever and anon muttered ejaculations fell from his parted lips.

When the ghastly stranger finished there was silence for a few moments.

"This is horrible!—most horrible!" cried Rupert Dreadnought; "it seems almost incredible that in the heart of a populous city like London such terrible things could be. But so it is—you astound me, and all I can say is that, while believing all you have told me, I am, notwithstanding, confounded."

"I pledge my word that every syllable of what I have told you is correct," said the stranger; "but now I have told you—have trusted you before hand, let me ask you for a pledge of secrecy. It would ruin all my plans were it known that I was in any way cognizant of the fearful facts which I have narrated to you."

"I solemnly pledge to you my word of honour, as a gentleman, not to divulge a single syllable of anything which you have told me," replied Rupert Dreadnought; "but tell me by what name shall I know you, and where are you to be found?"

The stranger hesitated for a moment.

Then he said—

"You can call me Mark Redfern. Here, for the present, is my home. When do you propose to attack the house?"

"At ten o'clock to-morrow night," said Rupert; "this neighbourhood then is quiet. Most of its quiet inhabitants are then asleep, and we shall be for some time at least undisturbed."

Mark Redfern, as he styled himself, paused and reflected for a few moments.

"This is a very hazardous matter," he said; "it is an offence against the law, and you may get the constables against you as well as your enemies. But still there is great danger in delay, and I will not counsel it. Be here, if it is possible, at half-past nine o'clock, and I *may* have a plan to suggest. As you imagine," he added, with a smile, "my plans are generally quiet. I prefer stratagem to open warfare."

"Very good," returned Rupert Dreadnought; "I will collect my forces and bring them to the spot. I and my two friends will meet you here at the hour you name; and now adieu. Consider your secret still your own, with the exception of *one* thing—you will now have one who has vowed before Heaven to destroy Oscar Penraven, and who will risk his life with yours to carry out the Oath of Vengeance!"

Rupert then quitted his ghastly companion, and in a few minutes more he and his friends were crossing the cold river.

CHAPTER XX.

OSCAR PENRAVEN AND THE CHIEF OF THE POISONERS—A NEW OBSTACLE—THE STORMY SCENE—OSCAR'S DEFEAT—HIS TREACHERY OUTWITTED.

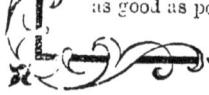

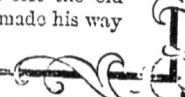

We must quit Rupert Dreadnought for a time, and follow Oscar Penraven's steps as he left the old house where Helen was confined, and made his way towards the spot where the sender of the peremptory missive awaited him.

This was no other than the Chief of the Poisoners—the Head of the Society which was the scourge and terror of London.

It was to the house where the Poisoners had held their revel that Oscar now directed his steps.

He found the Chief waiting for him in the little room where he had heard for the first time of the treachery of Gascoigne.

The Chief was alone as Oscar Penraven entered.

He greeted Oscar cheerfully; but in his manner there was something which spoke either of anger or of doubt.

"You have sent for me," said Oscar, coldly.

He was there on compulsion; he was bound to do the bidding of his superiors, but there was but one thought in his mind.

This was the lovely bride which he had been forced to leave.

He looked upon her as his bride, for although there was no chance of her yielding to his wishes, he never dreamed that anything could step between them when he was willing to use any amount of violence to secure her.

"Yes," said the Chief. "I have in the first place an important communication to make to you, and on the other hand I have an important mission for you to execute for the Society."

Oscar bowed in acquiescence as he seated himself close to the President's chair.

"In the first place, you have deceived our Society."

The President said this in a solemn voice.

Oscar started.

In his own heart he was utterly unconscious—evil-minded as he was—that he *had* been guilty of deception.

"In what way?" he said.

"You have a cousin," returned the Chief, "named Helen Penraven?"

"I have."

"She is possessed of an immense property?"

Oscar smiled.

"I believe her to be penniless," he said.

The Chief of the Poisoners eyed him narrowly.

"You will swear that she *is* so," he said inquiringly.

"I will not swear that she *is* so," replied Oscar, "I will swear that I believe her to be so."

"You are in error, then," said the Chief; "she is heiress to a hundred thousand pounds."

Oscar was visibly moved.

He had never known the fact before; and it made him all the more desirous to hasten on his marriage.

"You surprise me," he said; "I had no conception of this."

"I believe you," said the President; "but I have another thing to add to this—the Society does not demand her death."

Oscar turned pale.

He had not even thought of this hideous alternative in regard to Helen.

"I love her," he said.

"For herself alone?" suggested the President, with a sneer.

"Yes, for herself alone. In a few days I hope to be her husband."

The President frowned.

"You forget one important fact," he said, "our members are none of them permitted to marry until they have done five years' good service to our cause. Your attachment to this Society is only of short duration; it dates, indeed, only two years back."

Oscar bit his lip.

He began now to feel the tyranny to which he had willingly, with his eyes open, subjected himself.

"Why," he said, in a tone of irritation, which he did not attempt to conceal, "why is this act of tyranny?"

"You forget your vows," said the President, ironically; "when you accepted the position you hold you did not speak of this as tyranny. But enough, the marriage is impossible. Her money is ours, it belongs to the Society."

"I say she *has* no money," returned Oscar, doggedly.

"She is your cousin, the daughter of your uncle. How could it be that he, with all his wealth, should leave her penniless?"

"The money you speak of is already in the hands of the Society," replied Oscar; "therefore my adopted father's wealth is all disposed of. Where can this money, then, come from?"

"It is through a private will known only to a few," replied the Chief of the Poisoners. "Listen to me attentively and you will hear a strange story.

"Sir Robert Penraven, *your* uncle, had a son by a former marriage.

"This son, a wild, harum-scarum fellow even in his boyhood, was shipped away to India (when your uncle desired to contract a second marriage) and placed under the care of a gentleman in Calcutta of the name of Radford.

"To this son your uncle has by a private will left one hundred thousand pounds, which sum he kept separate from the rest of his immense fortune.

"In the event of this son's—Richard Penraven's—death, the hundred thousand pounds comes to Helen Penraven.

"Now this Richard *is* dead."

"You have proofs of this?"

"Yes; but it will not do to allow the world to consider him dead. He must live again."

Oscar started.

He did not quite understand the drift of the Chief's words.

"I do not understand you," he said. "Will you kindly explain yourself?"

"I will," replied the President. "It is easy enough to do so."

"In the first place," he said, "this man being dead the money goes to Helen and we cannot touch it."

"Yes."

"If, on the other hand, he is not dead, we can."

"I cannot see it."

"Well, of course the real heir *is* dead," continued the President. "We give *you* the mission of discovering a new one. Nay, do not interrupt me. I can make all the plan perfectly easy, perfectly comprehensible.

"This Richard Penraven would, if he were now alive, be about eight-and-twenty. Now our object is to discover some one about this age, one who knows India, and one who would have no objection to aid you in the fraud. We have done all this for you. Such a man exists already in our Society."

"And who is it?"

"Alford."

This was the one who, it will be remembered, was speaking to Lesbia at the "Poisoners' Revel," described in my first chapter.

"Ah! I know him well," said Oscar, "he is just the man required. But since you are going to rob him of his inheritance as soon as he obtains it, what is his inducement to aid you?"

"Simply this," replied the President; "we shall give him ten thousand pounds out of the hundred, and, his identity once established, he will immediately come in for three other legacies of large amounts, which we will not touch."

"Does he know of this scheme?"

"Not a word. It is for you to make him acquainted with it."

"And the proofs of identity. Since the real heir is dead, how can you prove he is alive again, and how can you establish his identity?"

Oscar catechised his chief as severely as was possible.

He had no liking for the task that was set him—a task, be it said, from which he could not shrink.

"In the first place," replied the President, "I and one other, alone, know of the death of this young fellow.

"It was a disgraceful death, which alone, however, saved him from a shameful punishment.

"I, by accident, I need not say how, have become the possessor of the whole of the papers necessary to establish his claim to the properties.

"These I will place in your hands at once."

As the Chief said this he rose, and, approaching a bureau, took out some papers.

"Here," he said, returning to the table, "here is, in the first place, the certificate of his birth; here is a memorandum in his father's handwriting speaking of a peculiar birth-mark. Here is a copy of the will in the possession of Mr. Gregory Bramble, of 4, Grays' Inn Square, London; and here are correct copies of letters received by Mr. Bramble from your uncle, from young Richard, and from the gentleman in Calcutta in whose care he was placed. He has only now to present himself, with a forged letter of introduction from Mr. Radford."

"I see; and where is Alford now?"

"Here is his address."

"And what is to be *my* reward?"

"In that case," said the President, "I will see that the Society waives the celibate clause in your case, and you will be free to marry Helen Penraven when you choose."

"When, *as you fancy*, you have robbed her of all she is worth," thought Oscar.

"Very good," he said, aloud; "I will start on my mission at once."

He rose as he spoke, gathered up the papers, and saying—

"In three days I will report what progress I have made," quitted the room.

"He is an unwilling worker," said the President to himself, as Oscar departed; "but for his own sake he will work with a will."

CHAPTER XXI.

THE CURSE OF THE GUILTY.

The demoniacal smile which played on the features of Oscar Penraven as he left the old house by the river which had lately been the scene of mad revelry, showed plainly that he had some secret buried deep in his heart—some secret which not even the Chief of the Poisoners was a sharer in.

His plans, for the present, were entirely upset.

He had hoped, before many hours had passed, to clasp to his breast sweet Helen Penraven, either as his willing or his unwilling bride.

Now, however, it depended entirely upon the success of his mission whether she should be his bride or not.

With so sweet a prize in view, it may be imagined that he felt an inclination to deceive even the dread tribunal.

But this was a plan more easy to dream of than to realise.

Had Helen loved him, and been willing to become his wife, it would have been far different.

As it was, however, a bride who had been forced to his arms, would not be likely to do much to assist him, and he at once cast from him as impossible and absurd all attempts at deceiving the Poisoners.

Without hesitation, therefore, he proceeded towards the house where he expected to find Alford.

Alford was a strange man.

He had, as we have seen, a certain position among the Poisoners, and had been present at every revel which these demons in human shape had taken part.

He had brought money into the hands of the diabolical confederation.

Yet he subsisted only on rewards!

It was, nevertheless, in a comfortable room that Oscar Penraven found Alford sitting.

The latter started in some wonderment as Oscar entered.

"*The third hour and the Cross*," said Oscar Penraven, quietly.

Alford smiled.

"The hour of the Cross is far distant let us hope," he said. "I see you come from the Chief—not on any private errand?"

"You are right," said Oscar. "I come on strange and mysterious business."

"Sit you down by the fire, then," rejoined Alford, "take some of yonder wine—it contains none of our ingredients—and begin your story."

Oscar did as was suggested, and, in a few minutes, began his narrative.

The listener started at several points, but otherwise retained his composure, and did not speak a word.

Then he said—

"And what is the name of this person whom I am expected to personate?"

"Richard Penraven."

At these words Alford started visibly, and sprang with a ghastly smile from his chair.

RUPERT OR THE DREADNOUGHT
SECRETS OF THE IRON CHEST

"ON, MY MEN," CRIED RUPERT; "CUT YOUR WAY THROUGH THEM."

Oscar could not avoid noticing the strange and mysterious action of Alford.

"You know him, perhaps," he said.

"I did; in India," said Alford, resuming his calmness. "And you say he is dead?"

"Yes, that is proved."

"Good; then with the proofs you will give me I shall be easily able to personate him, and obtain his wealth. I knew him so well that I am aware of all his peculiarities, his ways of speech, and his manners of life. Oh! doubt me not. I shall be successful."

"I fancy the scheme *is* well laid," replied Oscar, "and there is only one matter now to be settled. You must write me a letter, saying you are expected in London—say to-morrow—date it back a few days—ask me to call on Mr. Gregory Bramble, and so on, and I will take you on the second day to see him. But, in regard to handwriting?"

Alford smiled strangely.

"Oh!" he said, "I am an excellent imitator of handwriting. I fancy I shall have no difficulty in imitating that of Richard Penraven."

"And then the birth-mark; what about that?" asked Oscar.

Again that quiet, strange smile.

"That also can be managed," said Alford. "I don't do things by halves. Give me the papers; let me study them carefully, and by to-morrow you'll find me so transformed that you won't know me. But, by the way, I ain't specially liberally supplied with money at the present moment. You had better give me some."

Oscar shook his head.

"No," he said, "you are not doing this for me but for the Society; you must apply to our Chief. It is for him you work; it is from him you must obtain the money of which I am to be robbed."

Alford mused a moment.

Then he said,

"This is a very pleasant little arrangement, I have no doubt, and as far as I see is likely to be very profitable, and so on, to me; but there is a very *un*pleasant and very *un*profitable affair mixed up with it which none of you, perhaps, have looked at."

"And what is that?"

"*A murder!*"

"A murder!" echoed Oscar.

"Yes. I will explain to you briefly," said Alford. "When Richard Penraven arrived in India, he fell in love with a young girl named Rose Allerton; she was then only sixteen, and extremely beautiful. He married her; and within six months she fled with an officer. In the heat of passion, he gave chase, and meeting the seducer, shot him through the heart. The officer had a friend with him, who swore to be avenged. His vengeance was stopped by the news that Richard Penraven's body had been found in the river; but now, if I assume the character, I may also assume a most unpleasant responsibility. If I *am* Richard Penraven, I am liable to the deadly hate of this officer's friend; if I am not, I am an impostor."

"This I will represent to the Chief," said Oscar; "and since this will compel me to see him, I will also ask for the money. And now adieu till to-morrow night."

On the following evening Oscar presented himself at the appointed time.

Seated in a chair by the fire was a man of whom he had not the slightest recollection.

He was thin, pale, with a white, cadaverous face, short black hair, and no vestige of the luxuriant beard and moustache which were the characteristics of Alford.

Yet this *was* Alford.

Oscar for a moment was puzzled.

"You don't know me, I see," said Alford, "I think the disguise is good."

"It is perfect, and if it is like the original," said Oscar, "there can be no doubt about its success. *Your* identity is entirely sunk. But there is another difficulty which has only just presented itself."

"And what is that?"

"There has just arrived in London an Indian nabob, who was once a bosom friend of Richard Penraven."

Again, this third time, the strange and satanic smile crossed Alford's face.

"Oh, he will be sure to know me. The story of my death can be easily explained to him. Well, and about this officer's friend, this one who has sworn my death."

"If you allude to Colonel Dellmarr, he is in India," said Oscar, "it will take more than six months for the news to travel thither, and six months for him to come back to England. In the meantime you will have secured the property and your reward and resumed your former self."

"You are sure he is in India?"

"By the last mail, he was said to be far in the interior."

"*Very much so*," muttered Alford to himself with a peculiar intonation.

Then he added aloud,

"To-morrow, then, we will visit the lawyer, and this nabob; is he called Ramsetjie Jehador Khan?"

"The same."

"Where is he?"

"He is at a private house near Whitehall. I can give you the address to-morrow. I expect one at twelve; and in the meantime farewell."

Alford watched him out with curious glances, and as the door closed his whole face seemed to be lightened up with a new light.

"Oh! heaven," he cried, "I lived but for vengeance, and until now all chance of it has evaded me! Living near the one who deceived me—seeing her day after day I have not dared to reveal myself—have not dared even to whisper the doom which is coming—coming inevitably for my enemies. Now all is changed. I shall soon handle a fortune which will enable me to punish the guilty, and then, Alford, even happiness may be yours. The curse I years ago called down upon the guilty is now about to fall heavily upon them."

CHAPTER XXII.

THE ATTACK ON THE OLD HOUSE.

Before we proceed to describe what success Alford attained with Mr. Gregory Bramble, we must follow once more the fortunes of Rupert Dreadnought.

whose whole mind and soul was now wrapped up in the one idea—the saving of Helen Penraven.

It will be remembered that when Rupert parted with the strange, ghastly figure at the tavern, it was with an understanding that they should meet at the same place at half-past nine, and that those who accompanied Rupert should make their way towards the old house, and wait there for his coming.

Rupert was punctual to the hour, and found his strange and ghastly friend already waiting for him.

"Well," he said, "what cheer? Are your men with you?"

"Yes. They are waiting in the shadow of the old house," replied Rupert Dreadnought; "but is there any method of arranging matters without force?"

"I fear not; but I have contrived so that you will not be disturbed, I fancy," he answered, with a quiet smile. "Yet you must proceed as if you were unaware of this. Make as little disturbance as possible; and be as quick as you can, also, in your movements. One thing of importance, however, I have discovered."

"And what is that?"

"Oscar Penraven is not returned."

"That is well," said Rupert; "not that I desire not to meet him, but in such a position as this, it is best that he should be absent."

"Let us be going, then," said the strange man.

"Us!" repeated Rupert; "are you, then, coming?"

"I am," said the other, smiling. "I shall be glad to see the discomfiture of your enemies."

In a few minutes they were *en route* for the place of Helen's confinement.

Arrived here they made their way into the old house, where they found Tom the waterman, Allan of the Glen, Stanley Sherrington, and others waiting for them.

The first move to be made was to knock at the door of the house and demand to see Helen.

Rupert Dreadnought and Stanley Sherrington alone were to show themselves at the door, but if a refusal was given by those within, the others (who were to lie in ambush) were to rush forward and make a dash into the hall.

There was very little chance of their being able to make an entrance into the house by fair means.

But it was worth while to make the attempt.

With a beating heart, therefore, Rupert raised the heavy knocker of the door, and gave a loud and ringing summons on the iron plate.

In an instant the door was opened, but a heavy chain still crossed from the lock to the wall.

A shaggy head was protruded.

"What want ye?" asked the owner of the shaggy head, in a gruff and surly voice.

"You have a lady here—Mistress Helen Penraven—we desire speech with her."

The eyes of the shaggy-haired individual glared in fierce curiosity at the speaker.

"It is impossible," he said.

"Why so?"

"Because my master is from home, and we can't admit any one when he's away."

"Then you confess she *is* here?"

"Of course she is. She's here, and likely to remain so. Is that all you require?"

"Yes; and we *must* see her!" cried Rupert Dreadnought, angrily.

The man chuckled.

"*Must?*" he said. "Oh, we don't know that word here. You *can't*, is my answer; so good-night."

Saying this, he was about to close to the door, when, according to a preconcerted arrangement, one of Rupert's men thrust the hilt of his sword into the aperture.

In an instant the man within the house saw that it was a preconceived plan to attack the house and release the prisoner.

A long, sharp cry rang out from the whistle which he raised to his lips, and in a moment more the hall was full of armed men.

Then followed a strange scene.

Not a blow was struck by one man on another, not a shot fired.

It was merely a struggle to reclose the door.

In this the attacking party had the advantage.

Those within had not anticipated any assault, while the besiegers had brought with them some axes with which now they vigorously attacked the gate.

Allan of the Glen, with a short, stout hatchet, hacked and hewed vigorously at that point in the woodwork of the door where the bolt of the chain was fixed, and those within soon saw that it would of a necessity come to a hand-to-hand fight.

A few shots were now fired from the inside of the house, some at random through the door, and others through the open space right into the thick of the besiegers, slightly wounding more than one of them, but making no perceptible difference in the vigour of the assault.

At this moment, a number of dark figures, attracted by the noise of strife, made their appearance, and approached the house.

"We shall be foiled, after all!" cried Rupert Dreadnought, in a tone of disappointment. "Yonder come the constables."

The strange man whom he had met at the inn turned sharply round.

"Have no fear of them," he said. "I will arrange matters easily."

So saying, he darted away in the direction of the approaching figures, and was soon lost among them.

The constables stopped in a body, had, as it seemed, a hurried conference, and then moved rapidly away.

Whoever Rupert's new friend was, he evidently had power with *them*.

The woodwork at last, beneath the vigorous attacks of Allan and the others, gave way, and the door with a sudden rush burst inwards, disclosing a crowd of well-armed and resolute-looking men.

One of these advanced.

"Now then," he cried, "what seek you? Are

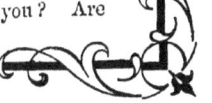

you mad, thus to attack a gentleman's house in the night?—or is your object plunder?"

"You have here a lady, captive, against her will," said Rupert. "I demand the surrender to us of Helen Penraven."

"Sir Oscar Penraven, her cousin, and our master, the guardian in whose care she has been left by his late uncle is not here," answered the spokesman; "but he has left her in our charge, and with our lives we will defend our trust."

The man spoke with a bold eye, far worthy of a better cause.

It was evident the struggle would be a fierce one.

"You refuse even to allow me speech with her?" said Rupert Dreadnought.

"I do."

"Then your doom is sealed by your own hands," cried the young lord. "On, my friends, cut your way through them."

As he spoke, he rushed forward, and vigorously attacked the spokesman of the defending party.

No further words were exchanged.

Nothing was heard now but the clashing of swords, the hard breathing of the several combatants, the groans of the wounded, the cheering cries of leaders.

The attacking party were evidently the strongest, and by degrees the defenders of the house were driven back to the staircase.

The hall now presented a hideously changed appearance.

The balustrades and the furniture were broken, while men lay dying or dead upon a floor slippery with blood.

The longer the battle raged the more fierce became the combatants.

Their faces red with excitement; their eyes wildly gleaming; their fierce exclamations, made them seem more like demons than human beings.

Seeing that the contest was going so entirely against them, the leader of Oscar's men, who had as yet succeeded in escaping without a wound, in spite of the brilliant swordsmanship of Rupert Dreadnought, stooped down and whispered to two of his men.

They both at once darted upstairs.

At the first landing, however, they separated, one hurrying upwards towards the top of the house, while the other, taking a back staircase, descended to the basement, let himself out of a back window, and hurried across the dark, waste land which lay between the house and the river.

This one had gone for reinforcement, while the other had proceeded to the room where Helen Penraven was confined, and trembling with mingled terror and hope, as the sounds of deadly strife were borne to her ears.

Suddenly, in the midst of the combat, when the little band of besiegers were forcing their way up the side stairs to the first landing, a curl of thick smoke ascended from the basement, and rolled blindingly among friends and foes.

It was black smoke, mingled with a white, hot steam.

It told its own story.

The old house was on fire!

A deadly horror invaded the heart of Rupert Dreadnought.

The conflagration would quickly spread among the dry and rotting timbers, and, while they fought below, Helen, at the summit of the old building, would be completely at the mercy of the flames.

"Hold!" he cried in a loud voice. "This is madness. While we fight, the lady for whom we combat will die a terrible death!"

"Fear not," replied the leader of the defending party, savagely. "She will be saved. We see plainly through this ruse. Your men have fired the house. She will be all the more certain to escape your hands."

It was useless to argue with such a man at such a time.

"On—on, my friends!" cried Rupert, desperately. "One grand effort now, and we will drive these hireling hounds before us. On—on, for your lives, and for Helen Penraven!"

Incited by these words, and the example of their young leader, the besiegers concentrated their strength for a grand and final effort, although among the ranks of the combatants could no longer be seen the forms of Allan of the Glen or Tom the waterman.

There was nowhere to be seen any trace of them.

Cruel as were the thoughts which invaded Rupert's mind, however, he had no time to think of them, or to inquire if indeed they *had* met their death, or were fighting elsewhere, or had been carried wounded away.

Eagerly dashing onward, the gallant little band soon made good their footing on the landing, for the retainers of Oscar Penraven were fast losing heart.

Not only the smoke now, but the heat betrayed the spread of the conflagration, and while Rupert and his friends had the street open to them and could fly at any moment, they were being driven to that portion of the building which was being rapidly seized in the eager maws of King Flame.

At every pause there was a quickly whispered conference.

But Rupert did not permit them much time for converse.

As they became less eager for the fray, so the eagerness of the victorious besiegers increased until Oscar's men found themselves pressed up against a huge doorway which was burning to the touch.

"Surrender!" shouted Rupert, "further battle is a mad waste of blood."

He had hardly spoken when the door burst open as if rent by an explosion, and tongues of red and yellow flame lapped over the heads of the combatants.

Some of the unhappy men fell backwards amid the smoke and the steam and were suffocated, others ran to the staircase windows and threw themselves madly out.

Rupert, however, yielded not an inch.

"Now!" he cried to Stanley Sherrington, who had throughout fought by his side, "now to save Helen."

Stanley detained him.

"Stay," he cried, "it is madness to ascend higher. You will be going to certain death."

"Stanley," exclaimed Rupert Dreadnought, "I know not what you say. What if death does await me? If *she* is dead life is no longer of use to me. Follow or remain as you please."

Without waiting for further parley, he broke from his friend and rushed up the stairs, which were almost invisible for the dense smoke, in spite of the red glare of the flames and the light of the frequent lamps in niches of the wall.

He noticed neither the smoke nor the heat.

All he thought of was that his beloved Helen was above in extreme danger, and that if he desired to save her, now was his only chance.

He was not long in reaching the top of the house, and here, of necessity, he found the atmosphere cool and refreshing.

The danger was below.

There all chance of escape seemed likely to be cut off.

Rupert cared not for this.

He knew well that the window of Helen's bedchamber overlooked the ruins.

There being now no danger in discovery, the bars could easily be forced from within, and he could bear her in safety along the wall to the ruins.

But he sought in vain.

Every room was empty.

TOM THE WATERMAN.

The one where he had before seen her was the last he entered.

There was not even a trace of her.

The window was broken and the bars smashed away, but all was dark, gloomy, horribly silent without.

What could it mean?

What but that Oscar Penraven had received intelligence of the attack, and had carried away by the only means that was left to Rupert to secure her safety.

Vainly he sought and resought, vainly he cried aloud from the window.

There was no reply.

Helen was gone; and between her and him again a wide gulf was fixed.

He was in doubt as to whether or not he could make good his escape by the wall or by the staircase, when the question was decided abruptly for him.

There was a terrific crash—then a tremendous rush of smoke and flame.

The staircase had fallen in!

Rupert lost no time in making his way to the window and letting himself out; he crept swiftly, though carefully along the wall.

It was not long before he descended the rickety stairs and reached the front of the house, where his friends, huddled in a crowd, were wondering at his disppearance, and making conjectures as to his probable fate.

To his eager questions none could give a satisfactory reply.

No one had seen anything of Helen Penraven, and as for Allan of the Glen, he had been seen to stagger away as if badly wounded in the very beginning of the fray.

Of Tom the waterman no one had seen or knew anything.

Rupert, sick at heart, turned away from the scene of strife.

After all this bloodshed what had been achieved?

Helen was, to all appearances, more lost to him than ever.

As he moved away with such feelings as these in his heart, his ghastly friend of the inn clapped him on the shoulder.

"Rupert Dreadnought," he said, "never give way to despair."

"There is nothing else before me," said our hero; "Helen is lost."

The stranger bent forward and whispered in his ear.

Rupert started; the rich blood flew to his cheeks, and he cried in a loud voice—

"Friends, this way! Follow me!"

With these words he hurried along the dark street, and made his way towards the banks of old Father Thames.

CHAPTER XXIII.

A STRANGE DISCOVERY.

As we are now approaching the event which formed the great crisis of this part of Rupert Dreadnought's life, we will return for a moment to Oscar Penraven and Alford, and see how they fared with Mr. Gregory Bramble.

Exactly at the hour named Alford and Oscar presented themselves at the office of the lawyer.

Alford's disguise was exactly as it had been the day before, and Oscar could not but admire the wondrous change he had also made in his manner.

He seemed altogether a different person.

Mr. Bramble advanced towards Alford when he entered, and shook him with such cordiality by the hand that Oscar Penraven was taken quite aback.

"I am glad to see you, Sir Richard," cried the man of law, "*very* glad to see you! We had all given you up for dead."

"Yes, it was so reported," replied Alford. "The wish was father to the thought in many cases. But you see I *have* survived in spite of all."

"Yes, yes, I see, Sir Richard. Sit down, and I will explain what is to be done."

And the fussy little lawyer took his way back to the fire.

This conversation caused a strange sensation in the mind of Oscar.

The impostor, whom *he* himself was introducing, was spoken of as "Sir Richard."

In other words, he was helping another to step into his titles!

Strange to say, this thought had never before entered his mind.

But the fear it brought with it was only momentary.

What mattered it?

The money once secured, Alford was Alford again, and all would be well.

The story of the death could be reiterated, a clever impostor would be supposed to have carried off the cash, and so Sir Oscar would be Sir Oscar once more.

The lawyer and the supposed Richard Penraven had a very earnest consultation for some time.

This consultation surprised Oscar more than anything.

In every little detail of Richard's life Alford was well posted up.

He remembered his school days, his boyish pranks; his parting with Sir Robert, his father; his journey to India.

"He is a clever rogue," thought Oscar.

As for the lawyer, he expressed himself quite satisfied, mentioning only that two persons present at his birth would be forthcoming in a few days, and that they would end the matter.

"You are about as good an impostor as could possibly be manufactured," said Oscar, as they quitted the house, and walked in the direction of Alford's dwelling.

"You think so?" said the latter, with his quaint smile.

"Yes, I do, indeed; but how will you contrive about the birth mark?"

"I can arrange for that," he said, quietly. "You can have little faith in my cleverness if you fancy I cannot settle *all* the little details. However, there *is* one thing which is rather awkward—far more awkward than the finding of the birth mark."

"And what is that?"

"About the title."

"What about it?"

"How are you to arrange to recover it? I shall be called Sir Richard, no matter where I go."

"Ah! but we must make up some account of your death. That can be easily done, and then I shall be Sir Oscar again."

Alford smiled.

"Ah! I see you have thought of all likely difficulties. Very well; directly Bramble sends for me again I will let you know."

The coolness of Alford discomposed greatly the mind of Oscar Penraven.

He could not for the life of him determine its meaning, except that in some way or another he meant to act the part of a traitor.

One thing, however, he consoled himself with.

The loss of money by Alford's treachery would not fall upon him but upon the Society, and the task of punishing him would also be the task of others.

On the second day after his interview with Alford and Bramble he received a letter from the former.

It was short and to the purpose:—

"MY DEAR COUSIN,—Please do me the favour of calling on me to-morrow at one, as I have affairs of importance to communicate to you.

"Yours sincerely,

"RICHARD PENRAVEN."

"Richard Penraven! confound the fellow," exclaimed Oscar; "but I suppose he must act thus to keep up the character."

Oscar was in no good humour.

News had reached him in regard to Rupert's doings at the old house which had roused his anger, the more so that he was unable at present to do anything against him.

He was eager, therefore, to rid himself of the business now on hand, which was of so little advantage to himself, and at exactly the appointed hour he made his appearance at the house of Alford.

He found that worthy sitting by the fire smoking, and still wearing the disguise which he had adopted since the commencement of the drama in which he seemed to play so willing and so capital a part.

"Good morning, cousin Oscar," he said, as young Penraven entered.

Oscar reddened.

"A truce to folly when we are together," he said. "I came anxious to know all the details of this business, for I have matters which will take me away shortly."

Alford pointed to a chair.

"Sit down, Oscar Penraven," he said, sternly, "and I will give you the details you require. They may perhaps surprise you."

Oscar sat down.

From Alford's manner he expected some strange revelation.

"In the first place," said he, "I have succeeded beyond all my expectations. The money is absolutely in my hands. I have so thoroughly proved to Mr. Bramble that I *am* the proper person that he has delivered over to me the entire control of the

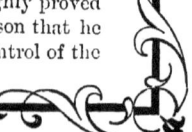

hundred thousand pounds which would have been my sister Helen's."

"Curse the fellow's impudence," thought Oscar. "His sister, indeed!"

But he did not interrupt him.

He was too anxious to hear more to do that.

So he merely said—

"Well, then, nothing remains to be done but to hand over to the Society ninety thousand pounds, reserving ten for yourself. This money would have been mine, but I regret it not since by adhering to our rules a greater fortune still is mine."

"Stay," said Alford, "the Society will not have a farthing from me."

"Not a farthing! And pray why?"

"For a simple reason, because I do not feel disposed to part with what is my own!"

Oscar sprang up.

"This passes all bearing," he said; "you must be mad to think I would countenance such folly. If you intend to carry out this imposture thus shamefully for your own benefit, I shall so inform our Chief, and a terrible vengeance will be taken upon you."

Before Oscar could proceed to the door, Alford had sprung up, and, locking the door, put the key in his pocket.

His manner was cool and determined.

"Sit down, Oscar Penraven," he said. "You have not yet heard all, nor do you know yet the only terms upon which I shall permit you to quit this room. Waste no more time, but listen."

Oscar, lost in wonder, and seeing the uselessness of resistance, did as he was directed.

"Go on," he said; "play the farce out."

"You will find it anything but a farce," answered Alford. "The way I have disposed of my money is this (for I have already disposed of it); I keep fifty thousand myself, the other fifty I give to Helen Penraven. As long as she is *not* with you, or does not marry you, the interest of this money is at her command. If she marries Rupert Dreadnought, or any other person of whom I approve, she will have the entire fifty then, and in her own hands."

"And why, pray, have you made this arrangement, and why do you refuse to give up the money to those who have enabled you to obtain it?"

"Because of many things," returned Alford; "but first of all, *because I am in very truth Richard Penraven, your cousin!*"

Oscar fell back in his chair in utter amazement.

The manner in which the words were spoken was so impressive and so truthful that he could make no answer.

Was it indeed true?

Had this man been biding his time, and had they unwittingly helped the rightful heir to his property?

"Yes," continued Alford, "I came from India under a ban. I knew nothing of my father's will; I fancied that he deemed me dead, and that I must live a disguised and forgotten existence. I joined the Poisoners to watch you, not to betray or aid the Society. Now I relinquish it: my birthright is proved by your aid undoubtedly. My birth mark, known to many, has settled all in my favour. I *am* your cousin, Oscar, but from you and your friends I will defend my sister."

"Are you mad, or do you in truth mean me to believe you?" said Oscar, in wonder — half in fear.

"I speak the truth. I defy you to disprove it," said Alford (I must continue for the present to call him so).

"I shall so endeavour," returned Penraven. "I will not run the risk of death—a traitor's death, too—for your sake. I shall at once inform the Chief of the Poisoners of the failure of their scheme, and your imposture, and leave them to deal with you."

Terrible, indeed, he intended in his own heart the punishment to be.

To permit Alford to live now would destroy all his hopes in regard to Helen.

Real brother or not he had been recognised and welcomed by those who would certainly be taken as judges in the matter, and he would therefore have far more voice than he in the guardianship of Helen.

"Stay," cried Alford, "there is one thing more I have to tell you."

And as he spoke he walked to the locked door, and put his back against it.

"You are aware, Oscar Penraven," he said, "that I am a good shot?"

"I am."

"Well," he added, taking from his pocket a double-barrelled weapon, "you have your sword; but one step towards me, until I give you permission, seals your doom. You must swear to me, ere you quit this room, that for four days you will keep the truth from this Society. Refuse, and you die!"

"And think you," said Oscar, "that there is no punishment for such an open murder?"

Alford smiled.

"I should provide against that," he said; "when you were dead I should wound myself in the arm, and place your blood-stained sword by your side. I should then tell every one that you had treacherously tried to assassinate me, and that I shot you in self-defence."

Oscar was in a complete trap.

There was no use in thinking of drawing his sword and rushing at his enemy.

Ere he could reach him the ball would have sped.

For once Oscar felt himself completely beaten.

"You have conquered by main force," he said. "I *must* make the promise."

"It is no promise," said Alford, sternly, "no such light thing that I require of you. You know the oath—the terrible oath you took when you bound yourself to the Society of Poisoners. You must take an oath quite as binding—quite as terrible. Repeat it after me."

Slowly and methodically Alford enunciated the words of an oath, from the breaking of which even a demon would have shrunk, and Oscar clearly and distinctly spoke them after him.

"Curse you!" he said, as Alford concluded, "curse you! I will yet be revenged for this."

"You may be," returned Alford, "but not in the way you are proposing to yourself. I have never betrayed the Society. I shall request permission to withdraw, and you will see how little then your anger will avail against me."

Oscar rose.

"I desire to hear no more," he said, "for four days you are safe. Now let me go, but remember my undying hatred will follow you for ever."

Alford unlocked the door and suffered him to go.

A smile of hateful anger and triumph wreathed itself over Oscar's pale lips, as he issued out into the street.

"I have promised," he said, "not to betray you to the Society. I have not promised *not to kill you with my own hand!*"

Then, shaking his fist savagely at the house, he departed.

CHAPTER XXIV.

ON THE TRACK OF THE CAPTIVE.

My readers must by this time be anxious to know what has become of Helen Penraven, who so mysteriously disappeared on the night of the attack of Rupert Dreadnought and his friends upon Oscar's house.

Rupert, as may be imagined, was in a state of intense excitement and dismay upon discovering the disappearance of his beloved Helen, and the probable disaster which had befallen his two faithful servitors, Allan of the Glen and Tom the waterman.

All search for them in the vicinity of the old house was quite useless, for not a single clue could be found to their whereabouts.

So Rupert and his other friends returned dispirited and wondering towards Rupert's house.

As they approached, they saw that the large windows were full of light.

"Who can there be at my house?" said Rupert. "Since my father died the house has not been lit up so brilliantly."

"Let us hasten on and see," said Stanley Sherrington. "You seem so thoroughly surrounded by spies and enemies, that anything unusual seems to portend evil."

Hurrying on, they reached the door, and rang violently.

The servant who opened the door greeted his master with a glad smile.

"Allan is upstairs," he said, "with Mistress Penraven.

"Mistress Penraven!"

Rupert did not pause to ask another question.

These two words were quite enough to prove that all his hopes had been realised, and that Helen Penraven was safe, at any rate, for the time being.

Both Allan of the Glen and Tom the waterman were there, but although he saw this at one glance his eyes were only for his beloved.

At one bound he sprang to the side of Helen, and in an instant they were clasped in each other's arms.

Over this scene we draw a veil.

We need not describe the tears of joy that were shed, and the words of eternal fidelity exchanged, but we can say that the hearts of Tom and Allan were rejoiced to see the reunion.

At length Rupert Dreadnought remembered the friends who had brought about the happy event.

He sprang to his feet.

"Allan, and you, Tom," he said, grasping them both by the hand, "think me not ungrateful that I have not thanked you before. Tell me now, friends, are you wounded?"

"But slightly," said Allan, "and Tom has escaped unhurt."

"I was told that you were wounded, and staggered helpless out of the old house in the middle of the affray," said Rupert Dreadnought, "when the house was fired. I feared that both you and Tom and my dear Helen had perished. But tell me how did you effect her escape? It seems truly miraculous."

From Allan's brief story it appeared that seeing the slow progress of the contest in the entry of the house and the smoke which told of the coming conflagration, they made a pretence of being wounded so as to avoid pursuit.

Hastening, then, to the ruin next door they made their way over the rickety wall, and, knowing how necessary haste was now, they both clambered over at once and commenced an attack upon the bars with the axe which had proved of such assistance in forcing the outer door.

He found that the masonry crumbled beneath his heavy strokes, and it was not long before he was enabled to drag one of the bars from its place.

Two more quickly followed, and a third had but just shared the fate of the others, and been flung down the dark abyss below, when the burly ruffian whom Rupert Dreadnought had seen there before made his way into the room.

In an instant Allan had sprung through the window, and confronted him.

Seeing Tom follow, the fellow was completely discomfited.

To resist was useless.

Fancying of necessity that he had only to deal with a lady, the man had sheathed his sword, and Allan's strong hand had clutched his throat before he had time to redraw his weapon.

"Yield!" cried Allan, with his sword at the man's throat. "If you permit us to bind you quietly no harm shall befall you; if you resist death is your fate. Quick! there is no time to lose."

RUPERT; OR THE DREADNOUGHT. THE SECRETS OF THE IRON CHEST

"HE IS DEAD; THE ASSASSIN'S KNIFE HAS STRUCK SURELY," SAID THE MAN.

Under circumstances such as these, what could the man reply, but that he would do as they wished.

So he was at once bound, and in a few minutes the dangerous task of rescuing Helen was commenced.

It was indeed a perilous undertaking.

Even when one person was making his way over

the wall it staggered and shivered beneath the weight of him, and now it would have to sustain that of three persons.

Helen Penraven, however, was not one to risk the lives of others unnecessarily, and as soon, therefore, as they had succeeded in helping her out of the window, she passed along the wall by herself, grasping firmly the broad belt of the Scotch youth.

On reaching the street they were unable to find any trace of Rupert, and so they had at once made their way to his house.

The next thing to be done, now that Helen had been rescued, was to keep her in safety, and it was resolved that on the next day Helen should be taken to the house of Lady Claremont, a near relation, whose house was a kind of castellated mansion in a quiet suburb.

This plan was accordingly carried out.

On the following day the lovers, therefore, again parted, and Helen, whose departure from Rupert's house had not, apparently, been watched, was, for the time, at any rate, in safety.

According to the arrangements, and the injunctions given him by his father, he was empowered now to open the first compartment of the IRON CHEST.

But, eager as he was to do this; anxious as he was to unravel the strange mystery, he was resolved not to risk the failure of this mission by being too precipitate.

He resolved, at any rate, to wait a few weeks in order to see if his enemies had watched his proceedings, and were in a position to take Helen once more from her concealment.

Then, if all went well, he would commence at once his mission of vengeance, and discover the FIRST SECRET OF THE IRON CHEST!

CHAPTER XXV.

MURDER!

RUPERT knew little what a strange chain of events was preparing to drag asunder all his cherished schemes.

He had truly a strong band of honest and earnest friends, but he had enemies against him in still larger numbers, unscrupulous, desperate, hungering after gold; seeming to love crime for crime's sake, and far more, therefore, to be dreaded in their doings than honest men.

It is in the track of these enemies we must now tread again.

More especially in the track of Oscar Penraven, whose first idea was the destruction of Alford, or, as he felt him to be, his supposed lost cousin Richard.

To permit him to live now was to risk ruin, disgrace, even death.

He could not return to the Chief of the Dread Society with such a disjointed story as alone he could now unfold, kept as he was within a narrow limit by the fearful oath he had taken.

Strange was it, indeed, that this man who looked so calmly on death should hesitate at perjury!

The first thing which he did upon quitting Alford's house was to proceed to the house of the Poisoners in order to procure a disguise.

There was in the great mansion a room in which disguises of every conceivable kind were kept, and here he soon obtained one which exactly suited his purpose.

It was the disguise of an old beggar.

No one could possibly (no matter how clever he might have been) have recognised the dashing though stern-faced Oscar Penraven in the crouching, bent form that quitted the abode of the Poisoners.

Long, ragged locks fell over his shoulders; his features were unrecognisable in consequence of paint and false wrinkles, and heavy, jagged eyebrows, beard, and moustaches.

A long cloak full of holes hung in a slovenly manner from his shoulders, and his feet were almost shoeless.

His whole appearance was that of a wretched, decrepid, poverty-hunted old man.

Beneath this guise was a wrist of iron, an arm of steel, a hate as black as that of a demon, while beneath the wretched garments were weapons to destroy human life.

Confident that in such a guise as this it would be quite a matter of impossibility to recognise him, he made his way at once towards the street in which Alford resided, and hung about its skirts until evening.

He guessed that under present circumstances Alford would not go out much in the daytime, and that when he *did* go he'd be likely to try and quit the country.

Slowly the hours went by, and the assassin had nearly began to doubt that he should be able to clutch his prey, when the door opened and Alford stealthily made his appearance.

He glanced up and down the street, as if suspecting that his arch enemy would be on the look out to destroy him.

The poor old beggar who emerged from the darkness and began shambling along the street, did not even attract a passing glance, and seeing that there was no one else near at hand, Alford at once emerged from the doorway and hurried away along the street.

Our readers must remember that no gas or even brilliant lamps of any kind were in the streets at this time to light the wayfarer.

It was a very easy matter, therefore, for the supposed beggar to make his way after his victim; and he was enabled also to go as quickly, the shadows of the high houses completely veiling him.

It many times occurred to him to rush across the street, and at once accomplish his revenge by plunging a dagger into the back of his unsuspecting enemy.

But there was the risk of failure and of discovery.

A loud cry at that early hour might rouse the neighbours, and he would either have to fly, perhaps, with his revenge half accomplished, or would remain to be seized and made prisoner.

So he waited patiently until at last at the angle of the street Alford halted.

There were three streets joining here, and he glanced anxiously up each.

Then seeing no one approach, he made his way across the street to a spot where a glowing light, looking merry and cheerful in the darkness, showed the point where a tavern offered its hospitable shelter to the tired and thirsty traveller.

Here he entered, and after speaking to the landlord, passed into an inner room.

Oscar remained outside.

Many persons paused and looked at him.

But not one suspected him.

His disguise was complete, and not a few who departed from the house of entertainment slipped alms into his outstretched hand.

Alford, meanwhile, when he entered the inner chamber, found in it but one man, who greeted him cordially.

This stranger was dark and swarthy, and both by his dark skin and his peculiar features seemed to speak of Indian blood.

"Well, Richard, or rather, Sir Richard, I should say," he cried, with a smile, "you have come at last. I had begun to think that some untoward event had occurred to keep you back."

"Not so," said Alford. "I have delayed in order that my doings may not be watched by my enemies."

"And are you sure you have not been observed now?"

"Certain."

"That is good. And now sit down, have some wine, and tell me what are our plans."

"I shall not remain long," replied Alford, as he sat down by the fire, "for I have much to see to; and to-night I wish to see my lovely Lesbia.

The half-caste smiled.

"You still love her then," he said, "and yet she is a poisoner."

"By name only," returned Alford. "She was inveigled into the Society, and she has never in any way aided it."

"There you are wrong," said the other, "she is present at their balls, at all their meetings; she knows well who they are and what is their mission, yet she is friendly with all. Ah! Penraven, you see with the eyes of love, or rather love blinds you."

"No; I understand her better than you," said Alford; "but never mind; every man has his infatuation. I have mine, and that is Lesbia. But come, we will drop her name and speak of our plans. You were always a cynic in love matters, Najid, and so it's of no use trying to persuade you of anything."

Najid laughed as he poured out some wine.

"Call me what you like," he said, "but you'll find me right in the end. But as you say, we'll talk of business. When do you propose starting?"

"To-morrow."

"And have you arranged the money safely?"

"I have. Everything is arranged in such a manner that as far as my fifty thousand pounds is concerned no one can touch it without my sanction."

"And Helen Penraven—your half-sister, what of her?"

"Her money is so settled that if she is forced into a marriage against her will, it cannot be touched by her husband. And feeling sure, therefore, that all my wishes will be carried out as I wish, I shall leave London with greater pleasure. To-morrow we will quit this country together, and at Paris I shall remain a month. By that time a letter will have left England, addressed to my old enemy, warning him of my presence in England. At the end of the month, therefore, I shall start for India and we shall pass him on the road."

"And shall I meet you here to-morrow night?"

"Yes, Najid; at the same hour as I came to-night horses shall be ready at the door for both of us. We will then lose no time in reaching the coast, and proceeding as secretly as possible across the channel."

Other little arrangements were entered into, a few more glasses of wine indulged in, and then the two friends parted.

It was getting late now.

The tavern was just closing as Alford left, and the streets were empty and dark.

The pretended beggar, too, was nowhere to be seen, but in reality he was not far off.

Under the shadow of the opposite houses, however, he still lurked, and when Alford moved away, he followed.

Now the time was approaching.

Alford was now nearing a part of the town which was but thinly inhabited, and unless he soon entered a house he would, in the course of a few minutes, be out in the open country, a dark, dismal part, too, where murder would very easily be accomplished.

So on went the victim, and on crept the assassin, noiselessly, surely, in his steps.

Presently the houses became fewer, and the trees more frequent, and after a time the road merged into a country lane.

Now was the moment.

With almost noiseless, cat-like steps the murderer crept on.

Alford, wrapped in dreams of bliss with Lesbia, heard nothing, for the assassin made his way along the soft ground, and only a slight rustling and crushing of leaves betokened the presence of anyone or anything near Alford.

The latter noticed this not, for the wind was sighing round him, and boughs were creaking, and leaves from evergreens falling and tapping on the crisp ground.

In an instant, in the hushing dark, the assassin was upon his victim.

The bright blade gleamed aloft, and descended like a lightning flash upon Alford's back, crashing in between the shoulder blades, and drawing from the unfortunate being one loud, prolonged shriek of agony.

Just as this terrible cry awoke the stillness of the night, and the murderer was kneeling to make sure of his victim, there was a shrill voice near at hand.

It sounded like the hooting of a night bird, but it was evidently only a good imitation of such.

As Oscar felt the pulseless heart, the cry was answered by another as shrill, and then two men sprang from out the hedge.

One of these was Stanley Sherrington.

Oscar waited not to give a second blow, but darted away ere the new comers caught sight of him, and rushed rapidly in the direction of the city.

They had heard the cry of agony which had proceeded from the mouth of the wounded man, and Stanley's companion, drawing a dark lantern from his pocket, directed its rays full upon the spot where the body lay upon its back, just as the murderer had turned it over.

He knelt down, gently raised him, and placed his hand then upon the heart.

"He is dead," he said; "the assassin's knife has struck surely."

CHAPTER XXVI.

TOM THE WATERMAN ON THE TRACK.

THE escape of Helen Penraven from the old house by the river was well known now to Oscar, but the business which he had had in hand for the Chief of the Poisoners had so thoroughly taken him off the scent, that he had no conception as to her having been taken to the residence of Lady Claremont.

Having thus lost the clue, it became necessary for him now either to punish Rupert, or, by getting him and his friends into his power, wrest from them the secret of her whereabouts.

It may seem strange that one possessed of the black heart and evil mind of Oscar Penraven, could entertain such a resolute feeling of love for Helen.

But it was *not* love properly so called.

There was no pure affection in his soul.

It was a wild passion, heightened to greater intensity by Rupert's love for her, and his own determination that he of all men should not possess her.

He admired her beauty, but he also admired the beauty of Rosalie St. Aubyn.

From this latter he preserved as a profound secret, the knowledge of his love for Helen Penraven.

Rosalie, lovely and young as she was, had a fierce and terrible mind—an implacable spirit of revenge—a resolute will—and even if she had cared nothing for Oscar, would have been stung to madness by the idea that he was forsaking her for another.

Little did Oscar imagine what a terrible Angel of Retribution he was raising up!

In his own heart his plan was easy and definite.

He would snatch Helen from the arms of Rupert, even if her death was the consequence.

Better death for her, than happiness with his hated foe; and then there would be happiness for him with Rosalie.

A desperate game this, Oscar, to play with two women!

It was on the evening of a dark day, some three weeks after the attack on the house, and the murder of Alford, that Tom the waterman made his way towards the house of Rupert Dreadnought.

He had been sent by Rupert on a mission of trifling importance; and as with the answer he entered the old porch, he came face to face with a burly ruffian, whose face he seemed to recognise.

It was not a pleasant face by any means, or a pleasant-looking person altogether.

He was a stout, ill-dressed, swarthy, ragged-haired fellow, with a huge scar on his forehead, hardly concealed by the hat he wore slouched over his brow, and an animal, famishing look in his eyes.

A second glance convinced Tom where he had observed him before.

It was at Oscar's house.

He could be on no good errand, that was very certain, unless, indeed, he came, as was likely with a ruffian such as he, to betray his master.

However, as he had issued from the house quietly by the door, Tom did not accost him, but hurrying up the steps, knocked at the door.

"Who was he who just passed out?" he asked eagerly of the domestic who answered his summons.

"A messenger from Stanley Sherrington."

"And is Master Dreadnought at home?"

"He is not; he has gone to Master Sherrington's."

Tom waited for no more.

Without saying a word to the astonished servant, he dashed down the steps, and followed in the track of the ruffian.

The latter, who had either no necessity or desire to hurry himself, was soon overtaken.

Tom's wish, however, was to follow him until he reached a lonely spot.

There might, indeed, be no time to waste in delays; but it would be more dangerous still to be precipitate.

So he kept his quarry in view.

Presently the fellow dropped into an ale-house.

"Good," thought Tom; "this is all the better for me. If he drinks hard he will be more readily my prey."

Tom the waterman had, since a boy, been celebrated among his companions for his wonderful powers of imitation.

He could, after once being in the presence of a person, imitate the gait, the manner, the voice to a nicety, and he had often kept his friends in a roar by his peculiar skill.

This skill he had never yet put to any purpose save that of amusement.

Now he resolved to put it to good account in the unravelling of what he felt sure was a mystery affecting Rupert Dreadnought's safety.

The ruffian in pursuit of whom he was did not remain long in the ale-house.

In that time, however, he had imbibed sufficient to give an additional redness to his features and an unsteadiness to his gait.

Humming to himself the refrain of some Bacchanalian song, he now, at a more rapid pace, took his road into a lonely and dark portion of the city.

Here Tom followed him up closely, and at length as they neared a dead wall, he sprang forward.

The ruffian, however, had just caught the sound of his approach, and darting on one side he had time to draw his knife before Tom was upon him.

The face of young Braxley was strange to the villain.

"What want you with me?" he cried, loudly, and in a swaggering tone.

"A word or a blow—which you please," said Tom.

"The word first then."

"Good. You come from Oscar Penraven?"

"You lie," returned the bully; "but if it were so, what is it to you?"

"Much, as you will find to your cost," replied Tom. "I am the friend of Rupert Dreadnought, sworn to aid him and protect his interests. You have taken to him a letter purporting to be from Stanley Sherrington."

"Well?"

"It is not well," cried Tom, boldly; "it is a forgery!"

The bully laughed loudly.

"You have settled it so," he said, "therefore I will not gainsay you; but you have *not* seen the letter, and cannot, therefore, know what it contained."

"Enough," cried Tom. "I can waste no further time in bandying words with you. I know full well that no letter from Stanley Sherrington would come to Rupert Dreadnought through your hands. Tell me at once whence came you, and whither Rupert Dreadnought has gone, or I shall cut out your lying tongue!"

The ruffian laughed loudly.

"Ha, ha!" he said, "you boast well. Well, I refuse. Come—put your threat in practice!"

In an instant Tom rushed forward, and the two men were engaged in a fierce combat.

It was a desperate, deadly struggle—truly hand to hand.

There were no swords' lengths here; but knife to knife, stabbing, hacking at one another.

Both were adepts in the art, but Tom's head was cool, his arm strong, his footing sure, while the bully's brain was excited by drink, and, besides the fact that he was fighting for hire, his legs were far from being under his control.

It soon became evident both to attacker and attacked that the bully was losing ground.

Frequent wounds, too, although each slight in itself, told upon his strength, and as his blood flowed, and he grew weaker, Tom pressed him more hotly and more hotly until at length, staggering back quickly to avoid a stroke, the ruffian fell to the ground heavily.

Tom could now have easily dispatched him.

But his object was not to kill.

It was to gain the secret where Rupert had been inveigled, and to save him.

Instead, therefore, of at once stabbing his adversary to the heart, as he could have done had he felt disposed, Tom the waterman threw himself upon him, and knelt on his chest.

"Now," he cried, "tell me what I require or you die."

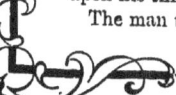

As he spoke, he pressed the point of the knife upon his throat.

The man uttered no sound.

STANLEY SHERRINGTON.

There seemed to be in his mind a sullen determination to resist.

"Speak, I say," cried Tom again; "speak or you die."

As he said this, he pressed the point so hard against the ruffian's throat that the steel entered the flesh.

Resolute as the man had been before, this changed entirely the state of his feelings.

"Stay!" he cried, as his blood began to flow afresh, "stay; I will tell you all. Suffer me only to rise."

The conqueror withdrew the point of the knife.

But he was not foolish enough to acquiesce in the request of the ruffian.

"No," he said; "you must remain as you are until I know all. Even then you will remain my prisoner. Quick! speak!"

The man, in spite of the helpless position he was in, muttered a curse between his teeth.

But he at once recognised his danger, and saw the peril of delay.

"I was sent by Oscar Penraven," he said, "to inveigle Rupert Dreadnought to his house."

"Which house?"

The man hesitated.

"Quick! tell me," said Tom, once more applying the sharp point of the dagger to his throat.

"I have to break a fearful oath," muttered the man; "but for the sake of dear life I suppose I must do it. Rupert Dreadnought is by this time in the hands of the Poisoners."

"Of whom?"

"The Poisoners, of whom Oscar Penraven is one."

"And where is their home?" asked Tom, as a new light dawned on him. "Quick! I have no time to enquire further now. Tell me, where is this house?"

Pressed thus, the man soon informed Tom of the exact spot where he could find the house, gave him the password, and full information of everything.

Having thus satisfied himself on the points upon which he was most concerned, Tom searched the ruffian, took from him everything which could in any way be converted into a weapon, and then, still holding him by the arm, rose to his feet.

"Now," he said, as he drew a pistol from his belt, "now, if you attempt to escape, or to excite the attention of any passer-by, I shall blow your brains out."

The whole affair had happened very quickly, and it was in a surprisingly short space of time that they stood at the door of a house where resided one of Tom's oldest friends.

He was a strange-looking customer this friend; short, thickset, and powerfully built.

We have met him before when the watermen had endeavoured to save Helen Penraven.

It was in fact Bill Flaxman.

In a few words Tom explained all.

It was indeed a matter of life and death.

The delay of half-an-hour might prove fatal to Rupert Dreadnought.

"But this fellow," said Flaxman, "what am I to do with him?"

"He is worthy of no consideration," he said. "I will tell you."

He leaned forward, and whispered in his friend's ear.

The latter started.

"It is a horrible punishment," he said.

"Not too horrible for a ruffian, such as this—a poisoner—an assassin. Quick! we have no time to lose."

Hurrying the wondering ruffian along a passage, they emerged in a back yard, and, crossing this, ascended a few steps, and entered an outhouse, which had the appearance of a disused stable.

Here they opened a dark lantern, and the prisoner guessed at once the doom to which—for a time at any rate—he would have to submit.

Fixed in the wall by powerful iron staples was a stout chain.

For whatever purpose it may have originally been placed there, it certainly had the appearance of one of those chains which are used to fasten murderers in the worst of prisons.

For an instant his glaring eyes were fixed upon his foes.

He was evidently measuring their strength and his own.

There was now no drunkenness left in him.

His desperate fight and his wounds had succeeded in thoroughly sobering him.

Suddenly, therefore, he dashed forward unarmed as he was.

But it was in vain.

It was but a sudden effort, and the two captors had him soon again upon the ground.

Here Tom held him with a pistol to his forehead, while his friend fetched the key of the great iron hoop which was to be fastened to his leg.

"There is one thing more," said Tom, "which I must know."

"What is it?" asked the man, who was now gasping for breath after his severe struggle.

"Your name?"

"Jack Gradley."

"Good," said Tom: "and now let me give you one warning. I am going, at the peril of my life, to release Rupert Dreadnought from the hands of Oscar Penraven. If I return not by to-morrow morning—if, in fact, through any false information of yours I should fall this night, my friend, who now approaches, will take his revenge upon you."

"I have told you all," said the man, who now seemed paralysed by a deadly fear, "I know not what they intend to do with them. You must enter the house privately with the key you took from my pocket, and wait in the large ante-room till Sir Oscar calls you. That is all I know."

It did not take long to fix the heavy fetters upon the leg of the prisoner, and in a few minutes he was chained to the wall.

He glared terribly with a mad stare at them as they left him in utter darkness.

Then he began to leap wildly—desperately about, in a way which threatened to drag the staple from the wall.

"Oh, if I could only escape now," he muttered as he gnashed his teeth and the white foam gathered on his lips, "I should have a splendid reward and a glorious revenge!"

CHAPTER XXVII.

THE DOOM OF RUPERT DREADNOUGHT.

The writing of Stanley Sherrington was far from being a peculiar one.

In fact, in those days writing had not become the art it is now, and there was a greater similarity than now exists between the writings of both rich and poor.

The wording was so exactly what would have been Stanley's under the circumstances, and the whole tone of the letter was so exactly what his writing would have been expected to be, that there could not reasonably arise in Rupert's mind any suspicion of foul play.

The appointment was made at the meeting house of the Mohocks; past events were spoken of and certain little matters alluded to which completely put Rupert off the scent of suspicion.

"Bring Allan of the Glen with you," said the letter, as it wound up, "as there may be tough work to do to-night."

As the letter contained this intimation, neither Rupert nor Allan, as may be imagined, forgot the precaution of being well armed.

As Stanley Sherrington had on so many occasions befriended them, both master and servitor imagined that he intended to ask of them a favour in return, and they went, therefore, prepared to grant it to the full.

The night was, as I have said, a very dark one, and just such a one as they might fancy Stanley Sherrington would choose for an adventure, either of gallantry or revenge, and they advanced along the streets, scarcely taking the precaution of looking out for enemies.

Before reaching the meeting place of the Mohocks they had to pass an awkward and perilous-looking spot.

There were no lights anywhere to be seen, and for several hundreds of yards a number of ruined edifices, relics of the old fire of London, raised their gloomy and jagged walls against the sky.

It was here that Oscar Penraven had prepared his trap.

Suddenly, when they least expected it, there was a rush of feet, and before they could understand what it all meant, and even see who or what were their assailants, a sense of insensibility came over them, and they knew no more.

When they recovered they were in a strange room, bound.

It was a place without any window, with a door which, apparently, had no lock.

Rupert Dreadnought was the first to wake from his unconsciousness.

His companion, Allan of the Glen, was seated in a large chair, with his head bent down over his chest.

Rupert himself was also seated in a chair of luxurious dimensions and make, from which he had no wish to move.

There was, in fact, a lassitude over him that prevented for the moment all idea of rising.

When, however, he did try to do so in order to endeavour to rouse Allan, he found that his feet were confined in such a manner that he could not move from the spot.

"Allan," he cried, as he once more relapsed into the seat, "Allan, awake!"

The Scotch boy started, and then sprang up.

He too, however, was confined safely by his legs, and fell back in his chair helplessly.

"Where are we, I wonder?" he said. "They seem to have left us our hands free, and our swords by our sides."

"That is in mere ridicule of our misfortunes," said Rupert. "These iron bands which confine our legs prove too certainly what deadly enemies surround us. For myself I trust in Heaven always, but we are nevertheless in a terrible predicament. I care less for myself than for you, who are only their enemy because you are my friend."

As he spoke there was the sound of feet approaching, and the door opened suddenly.

Oscar Penraven and Rupert Dreadnought met now for the first time face to face.

Behind him was the Chief of the Poisoners, with about a dozen armed attendants.

All, with the exception of Oscar, were masked.

The first impulse of Rupert Dreadnought was to spring to his feet and draw his sword.

But, as if he had anticipated this movement on his part, Oscar advanced quickly to the centre of the room, and pressed his foot violently and with a sudden jerk upon one of the planks of the flooring.

In an instant the chairs upon which both Rupert and Allan were seated became instinct with life.

A huge eagle's head rose as if by magic from the back of the chair, while from the sides rose talons, which seizing the unfortunate captives by the head and arms, kept them down with irresistible force, in such a position, that they could move neither to the right or the left.

When this had been effected, the Chief of the Poisoners advanced towards the captives.

"Rupert Dreadnought," he said, "in the name of Oscar Penraven and our great convention, established for the purpose of rescuing Society from wealthy reprobates—from the CURSE OF RICHES—I am about to ask you a few questions."

Rupert made no answer.

"In the first place," continued the Chief, "I demand to know where is Helen Penraven?"

A derisive smile crossed the features of Rupert Dreadnought.

"I refuse to answer," he said. "No matter what torture you put me to, I shall never consent to permit her to fall into your hands."

"There is worse still than that," continued the Chief; "but remember that we do not torture. Torture to a brave man is nothing. DEATH is the best punishment of all. DEATH, which cuts you off at once in the midst of youth. DEATH, which takes you from all you love. DEATH, which——"

"You need say no more," returned Rupert. "DEATH also re-unites us to friends—eases our sorrows—releases us from man's tyranny and cruelty. No fear of this will make me do anything you desire. I have no dread of death, or of your Society!"

"Your doom, then, will be a far more terrible one than you imagine," said the Chief of the Poisoners. "*By a subtle essence, which we shall administer to you, you will be deprived of all power of speech and motion. You will then be placed in a vault, where two men will watch you night and day. No food will be given you, and you will in two weeks cease to exist. During this time you will be asked, twice in each day, whether you consent to our terms. By your eyes you will be able to express 'yes' or 'no.' And now for the terms upon which your safety can be secured. In the first place, you must disclose the place of concealment of Helen Penraven; in the second place, you must deliver over to the Society two-thirds of the property left by your father; in the third place, you must swear that you will never, to any one, under any circumstances, reveal the proceedings of this night!*"

The Ccief paused.

His stern eyes were fixed upon the unfortunate prisoners.

On Allan's face was expressed nothing but astonishment.

His brave heart, like Rupert's, knew no fear.

On the face of Rupert there was the supremeness of contempt, mingled with the despair which no one could avoid feeling, under such circumstances.

"I refuse again," replied he. "Nothing will induce me to be a traitor, or to give up the mission which was left to me by my father. Helen Penraven was left to my guardianship. I will protect her, or I will die in the attempt. My fortune is hers, if I die; and as for betraying the proceedings of this evening, if Providence does aid my escape, I shall do my best in every way to make them known to every one, and to destroy your infamous companionship!"

A grim smile wreathed itself over the lips of the Chief.

"You will make one more martyr to human obstinacy," said he. "Oscar, sound the bell."

Oscar drew near the fire-place and pulled a rope.

A loud, gong-like sound resounded through the building.

Then the door opened, and six men appeared robed in black.

At the head of this sombre procession was a man dressed in exactly the garb in which the villain had been dressed who had brought the false letter to the house of Rupert Dreadnought.

In his hand he carried a black bottle.

A bottle of iron!

The object of this instrument was easily apparent.

Containing as it did the deadly liquid of which the Chief of the Poisoners had spoken, it could be introduced into the mouth of a victim by force and could not be broken.

"Advance," said the Chief of the Poisoners. "The prisoners are ready."

The man, scarred, dirty, with his ragged red hair, advanced towards Rupert Dreadnought in the first place.

Then he bent over the captive and placed the bottle near his lips.

"Villain," said Rupert, "you will repent this."

"Hush," whispered the man in an almost imperceptible tone. "I am a friend. It is I, Tom the waterman. I can say no more. Drink."

"What say you?" asked the Chief of the Poisoners.

"The prisoner spoke," replied Tom, in a voice which was a splendid mimicry of the dark-browed ruffian's tones. "I know not what he says, but I believe it to be something against the Society."

Rupert spoke no more.

He was wrapped in astonishment.

But still he believed the speaker.

Tom's natural voice was too much opposed to the surly tones of the other whom he represented, to permit him to be mistaken.

A whirlwind of thoughts rushed through Dreadnought's mind.

How had Tom entered the very heart of the Poisoners' citadel?

What was he doing there?

What chance had he among such a set of villains?

These, and a hundred more ideas, entered Rupert's brain, but he nevertheless recognised in this hour of danger the wonderful interposition of Providence and believing in Tom as he would have believed in a brother, he drank as directed.

Here Tom whispered, as he poured the liquid down the victim's throat—

"In ten minutes you must assume insensibility."

Then he moved to the side of Allan of the Glen.

"Drink," he said.

"You may force it down my throat," returned Allan, who, of course, had not heard Tom's words of warning, "but I will not drink willingly."

"Hush!" said Tom to him, as he had said to Rupert, "hush. I am Tom Braxley. Drink!"

Allan, who was not quite so convinced of Tom's fidelity as Rupert, glanced quickly at his master.

"Drink," said Rupert. "*I* have done so. Be as brave as I am, and be assured that those who *dread nought* can safely fight against the world."

The tone and the look were enough for Allan.

With an inward prayer that Providence would one day restore him to Mary Macpherson, he allowed the iron bottle to be placed between his lips, and drank!

"Farewell," said the Chief of the Poisoners, turning towards the door.

Then the gloomy procession once more moved towards the door, which opened as if of its own free will, and allowed them to pass like noiseless spirits out into the dark passage.

Oscar was the last, and the look he cast back ere he disappeared Rupert never forgot.

CHAPTER XXVIII.

THE APPOINTED HOUR.

TOM the waterman, in his new character of Jack Gradley, was, of course, compelled to quit the room at the same time as his new masters.

But his actions already were enough to show that bad as the position of our hero was, he had, notwithstanding, a good friend near.

It was but a shadowy hope of safety, however, even now, for how long Tom would be able to keep up the illusion it was a matter of difficulty to determine.

In a nest of villany such as he was now, where all around him moreover were strangers, what numberless chances there were of discovery!

"Allan," said Rupert, as soon as they were alone, "be careful what you say. No doubt there are plenty of means by which spies can overhear our conversation; so mention nothing which can harm us or our friends. We shall be saved."

"I believe it," said Allan, "though, to tell you the truth, Master Dreadnought, I feel strangely bewildered by all that is passing round me."

"Ah! what is that?" exclaimed Rupert, suddenly.

Well he might ask.

As Allan had uttered his last words, the whole room shook violently, and gradually but surely the flooring of the room had begun to sink.

Rupert had heard of such things as these, but in such modern times it seemed truly a romantic idea to believe them possible.

However, there was now no doubting that such things were.

The windows, and then the high edging of the floor sank out of view, and still they descended.

This descent was almost noiseless.

Down—down went the flooring, with only the slight jarring of a chain to show by what agency it moved.

A colder air was soon diffused around the captives, showing that they were gradually approaching underground regions, and then the descent stopped.

Around them now were dark stone walls, humid and gloomy, while a barred window was seen close by one of the dark arches, which supported the walls.

While they were wondering what next would occur, and whether the carpeted floor would remain there with the vast expanse of emptiness above them—they saw a trap-door opened, and three men appear.

Now was the critical moment!

Neither of those who appeared was Tom the waterman.

These were paid ruffians; and both Rupert and Allan saw that they had a difficult part to play.

The ten minutes mentioned by Tom the waterman had now elapsed, and they must, therefore, pretend to be insensible.

When, therefore, the men approached, they permitted them to remove their bonds, without moving either to the right or the left, and without even moving their eyes.

The ruffians, who were under the influence of drink, would scarcely have been able to notice them even had they been less expert in their acting.

Rudely undoing the bands which confined them, they first raised Rupert and then Allan, and carried them through the trap-door, down a short staircase into the room below.

This was their place of doom.

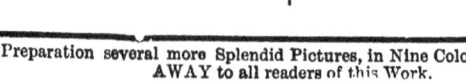

RUPERT DREADNOUGHT; OR THE SECRETS OF THE IRON CHEST!

THE LIVING TOMB.

As soon as they were both at the bottom of the steps, the floor upon which they had descended once more began to ascend, and, when it had risen into its former position, they found that they were in a chamber whose only furniture was a table, two chairs, and a long, tressel-like apparatus, like that which is used to support coffins.

Upon this now were a mattress, a blanket, and a velvet pall edged with white.

The only thing which gave any shadow of comfort

to the room was a large fire, which blazed merrily up a broad and ample chimney.

As soon as the movable ceiling had settled into its place, the men raised Rupert and Allan, and placed them side by side on the tressels.

Over them they then placed the blanket and the velvet pall, and, this done, they took from the cupboard a number of altar candles, and, lighting them, placed them in rows on both sides of the bier.

This was, of course, to enhance the horrors of the situation; and to any one who had no shadow of hope—who had no friend near, the appearance of the whole place was certainly enough to rouse horror and dismay.

As it was, however, although thus buried in the bowels of the earth, neither of the prisoners despaired.

They remained quite still, while one of the men quitted the chamber, and left the others sitting by the fire.

One of these presently went off into a sleep, as could be told by his loud snoring, leaving his companion to watch.

It was now that the first suspicion of foul play entered the minds of the captives.

A drowsiness irresistible came over them, and in spite of all they could do they were unable to keep open their eyes.

Even now they were afraid to destroy the plan of their unknown friend by speaking, and so silently they lapsed into sleep.

CHAPTER XXIX.

THE MYSTERY.

When they awoke again, a dark form was bending over them.

This was Tom the waterman, still in his disguise.

"You have deceived me," said Rupert Dreadnought. "You told me to assume insensibility, while in fact you produced it."

"I did so for a good purpose, Master Dreadnought, as you will soon know. It was necessary for you to be silent for two days. I did not desire you to be put to such a terrible test as that of having to keep silence for such a time."

"And have we been here two days?"

"Yes, two days and two nights," replied Tom. "It was necessary that you should remain so until I became one of the watchers, in order that you might learn from me the only method of escape. Here is wine; quick, drink it."

Eagerly the two prisoners drank up the generous liquid.

Then Tom bent over Rupert, and detailed to him his plan.

This plan, strange, mysterious, perilous as it was, we shall not detail here.

The workings of it will be seen throughout our true but wonderful history.

Suffice it to say that the prisoners joyfully listened, and acceded to it, and when Tom departed they had little doubt of their escape.

About the fall of night one of the watchers approached them.

He held in his hand a lamp, which he raised high above the head of the two captives.

"Do you consent?" he said, as Rupert fixed his eye firmly on him.

There was no reply.

To answer verbally would be, as Rupert well knew, to destroy entirely the great plan which Tom the waterman had concocted.

"If you consent, close your eyes," said the man again.

But the eyes remained open.

"Well, well," said he, as he removed the light and returned to his seat, "these mad people will die like the others, I suppose. It's no business of mine."

But it *was* the business of the other watcher, who was no other than Tom the waterman.

He kept his eyes closed, but he slept not.

His thoughts were too busy to permit him to slumber.

He kept a careful watch not over the prisoners, but over his companion, now and then pretending to move uneasily in his sleep and casting an eye upon the man.

He was waiting his time.

As soon as the other began to show signs of drowsiness, nodding in his chair, and jumping up suddenly as if to rouse himself, Tom pretended to wake from a heavy slumber, and said, yawningly—

"You can have your turn now. I've been dreaming ugly things, and don't care about sleeping again."

"No wonder *you* dream ugly things," said the other; "with all the blood *you* have on your soul, I wonder you can bear to sleep at all!"

Tom smiled.

He had, he knew, taken upon himself the similitude of a ruffian, but he was unaware till now that this ruffian was one who was unpopular among his fellows.

However, he did not make any reply.

It might have been dangerous so to do, and he therefore held his peace.

His companion, meanwhile, having delivered himself of his sentiments, appeared satisfied, and coiling himself up, so to speak, before the fire, lapsed, in a very few minutes, into a heavy slumber.

Tom waited until he was sure of his man, and then rose.

Approaching a cupboard he took from it some viands and some wine, and drawing near the strange bier, he whispered—

"Here is food. Quick, eat, you will have need of it."

The two strangely imprisoned men rose from their recumbent positions, and eagerly devoured the somewhat scanty meal which Tom the waterman was enabled to provide for them.

This they did with all the haste possible, and then resumed their former positions.

They had stronger hope now.

Yet, what a mystery came next!

* * * * *

The appointed time passed.

The hour came—the final hour when Rupert Dreadnought and Allan of the Glen had to give in their adhesion to the wishes of the dread Society in whose power they were or die a quiet, yet terrible death.

In the room in which upon a former occasion they had assembled to try Gascoigne the traitor, the terrible tribunal were assembled.

Around the table were gathered masked men whose eyes, the only visible sign of life, glanced eagerly and wonderingly at their Chief.

There were some there who had never assisted at a similar ceremonial; but all were aware that something extraordinary was about to happen.

When all had assembled and the doors were closed, the Chief of the Poisoners rose, and commanding silence by a wave of the hand, said:—

"As we must expect in all great ventures, we have met with a signal failure.

"At least, if we have not already failed, I expect every moment to hear that we have done so.

"Both Rupert Dreadnought and his retainer remain obstinate.

"They seem to prefer death to yielding to us the property which by right of victors belongs to us."

As he spoke there was a knock at the door, the announcement that a messenger desired to be admitted to the august tribunal.

"Enter," said the Chief, in a solemn voice.

The door opened and one of the watchers entered.

"What news bring you?" asked Oscar.

"They are dead!"

"Dead!" exclaimed all present in tones of astonishment.

"Yes," said the man, "their forms are not only cold and rigid, but show already signs of decay. They must have been dead some time."

A frown gathered on the brow of the stern Chief.

"Who has been watching?" he asked; "those who had the care of the prisoners should have been able to tell when the awful change came."

"They watched zealously," returned the man, "but as the prisoners could not speak, they had no means of ascertaining when death came."

The Chief thought a moment.

Then he rose again.

"Friends," he said, "let us descend and gaze upon our enemies."

The masks rose at once, and, preceded by their chief, filed out of the room, and entered the chamber where stood the two spring chairs.

At a signal the floor began once more to descend, and when it had reached the bottom they passed through the trap-door down into the dark vault.

All there was very still and solemn as the moveable ceiling returned to its place.

The high altar candles burned around the bier with a dim light, and on the bier lay TWO DEAD BODIES! their faces partially concealed by a heavy cloth.

There was no doubting the fact that they were dead.

The glassy eyes, the changed complexions, the ghastly pallor, the rigidity, the whole air and manner of them proclaimed too thoroughly the fact of dissolution.

One glance the Chief gave at them, and then he turned to Oscar Penraven, who stood next to him, and whispered some words in his ear.

Oscar, after one more glance at the inanimate forms, quitted the Chamber of Death; and, after a few moments, the side of the vault opened as it were like one large wall.

Four men then advanced to the bier, and raising it on their shoulders, bore it quickly away.

The whole of the masked men followed until they arrived in a huge vault.

Here they halted; the altar candles were placed in niches round the walls, and the bier having once more been laid down, the men proceeded to raise some of the huge flagstones of which the flooring was composed.

There seemed very little difficulty in this, for the stones were lifted rapidly, as if they had been accustomed so to be raised often.

When about six had been taken up, there appeared a black surface, which soon proved to be an iron slab, with a huge keyhole at one end.

To this the Chief of the Poisoners, who seemed anxious to keep up the solemnity of the occasion (although the impression was to be made upon his friends, and not his enemies), advanced, with measured tread, and taking from his pocket a large key, opened the lock of the mysterious slab, which fell downwards with a dull sound that echoed through a large black vault below.

A stifling vapour ascended hence.

The vapour of death!

Who could gaze down into this dark abyss of crime without a shudder?

It looked what it was.

A receptacle for hidden villanies!

The men now, at a sign from the Chief of the Poisoners, raised the bodies one by one, and descended the steps which led down into the gloomy abyss.

Then, with no funeral service read over them, the dead were placed in niches in the wall—coffinless, uncovered, save by their own clothes, with their swords by their side, and their daggers in their girdles.

After this the black slab resumed its place, and the Chief of the Poisoners, raising his hand, said—

"So PERISH THE ENEMIES OF THE CONVENTION!"

A smile of satisfied hate crossed the lips of Oscar Penraven, as they turned away.

"They are dead," he said. "My uncle's wrongs are avenged. I no longer live for vengeance, but for myself."

He forgot that if his enemies were dead, there were Avengers who would demand from him a terrible account.

END OF BOOK I.

BOOK II.

THE FIRST SECRET OF THE IRON CHEST.

CHAPTER I.

THE STRANGE MASTER—THE MYSTERIOUS MEETINGS —THE OLD HOUSE IN NEW HANDS.

It was about a month after the strange and horrible events narrated in our last chapter that a change of great importance took place in Rupert Dreadnought's house.

One day there was extraordinary bustle.

A man arrived in a carriage—entered the house, though a stranger, with the air of one in authority, and in the course of a few hours the servants began to quit the place.

Before evening the place was empty, the shutters were closed, and no signs of life were visible in any part of it.

So it remained for a week, though it was evident that people were eagerly watching it, for relays of patrols passed to and fro incessantly.

As the darkness of the seventh night, however, fell over the city of London, a carriage again drew up to the door of the old house.

From this descended four men and a woman.

The former were all masked, the latter deeply veiled.

They entered hurriedly, by means of a key—the door closed—the carriage drove off—and all was once more as still and sombre as before.

On the next day, however, the windows were all opened, and the house resumed something of its former appearance.

A new batch of servants made their appearance—all strong, hearty fellows, as able to wield a sword as to perform menial offices—and it was currently reported in the neighbourhood that the old house had got a new, brave master, though every one regretted the departure and strange disappearance of the last Scion of the House of Dreadnought.

The new-comer, that is to say, the one who took possession of the house, was a dark-skinned man, apparently about thirty years of age, with a heavy moustache and beard.

His figure was tall and commanding, his face noble and expressive; his air and carriage altogether that of one used to command, or, at least, one who considered himself to have a right to command.

There was a certain sternness about him which did not detract from the general amiability of his manner, but which showed that his life had a solemn purpose in it.

On the evening of the second day all the inmates of the house—retainers and others—were gathered in the banqueting hall of the old mansion.

At the head of the table sat the stranger.

On the board near him were those who had come with him—the three men and the veiled lady.

Two of the four men were strange-looking beings—ghastly, scarred—seeming as life's struggle had been with them a hard and a terrible one.

The others strong, hale, and hearty.

The lady, veiled as she was and dressed in deep mourning, was yet one easily recognisable.

It was Helen Penraven!

The retainers, if so we may term them who stood round, were, as I have said, all good, stout fellows, and seemed to take a lively interest in the proceedings about to commence.

When all were gathered together, and the doors closed, the one who sat at the head of the table rose.

"Friends," he said, "we have met here for a sacred purpose.

"Combinations have been made against us, and these combinations we must meet by others.

"We are here then, to vow Eternal Enmity and vengeance against the foes of Rupert Dreadnought, and to swear moreover to carry out to the best of our power the mission left him by his father, and which we have before this engaged to carry out.

"Will you all, without reserve, swear to devote every energy of mind and body to this task?"

"We will," replied all.

"Then," continued the speaker, "repeat these words after me. '*We swear, in the sight of Heaven, to devote all energies of mind and body to the task of destroying Oscar Penraven and the hideous Society with which he is connected; to risk life willingly for this purpose; to follow implicitly the instructions of our leader in this and in the unravelling of the strange secrets of the Iron Chest. And as we fulfil faithfully our vow, so may Heaven have mercy upon us.*'"

Slowly and solemnly the speaker enunciated these words, and slowly and solemnly all those present repeated them after him; Helen Penraven rising and speaking with the rest, her sad face beaming with the glow of enthusiasm.

When this was over, the strange speaker again addressed them,

"And now, friends," he said, "since you have taken this all-important oath, let me ask you another question. Are you satisfied with the leader you have had? are you content that I should continue to hold my position as your chief?"

"Yes, yes," was the answer on all sides, "we desire none better."

The speaker bowed.

"Good," he said; "then I will endeavour to fulfil faithfully—as I will at the peril of my life—the task imposed upon me. This day week meet me here again and I will lay before you all I know in regard to the strange and mysterious secret contained in the first compartment of the Iron Chest. Now, for the time, farewell."

The assembly, including Helen Penraven, then quitted the room, and the master of the house remained alone.

When they had all gone he rose and stood by the fire for a few moments, wrapped in deep thought.

Then he raised his hands, took from his head the wig which covered his own natural hair, threw back the flowing locks to their original position, and stood there, though darkened artificially in complexion, the same Rupert Dreadnought that had dared, and had sworn to dare in the future, a thousand dangers to perform the mission left to him by his father!

"Time will yet prove," he said, "that the small but brave and willing band that surround me will prove more than a match for the combination of villains who meditated giving to me and mine so hideous a doom. Now, courage, Rupert—the FIRST SECRET OF THE IRON CHEST MUST BE REVEALED!"

CHAPTER II.

THE FIRST SECRET.

IT required some degree of courage on the part of even Rupert Dreadnought to begin the unravelment of the complicated mystery which was his legacy.

It was of course the first step in the weaving of a strange web of destiny that he was about to take.

Yet it was not exactly a feeling of alarm that invaded his heart.

It was a sensation of awe.

Respectful awe, at thus once more opening up the secrets of the beloved, though stern old father who was now gathered to his ancestors.

It seemed like opening a vault to open that old bedchamber once more.

Since the day of the funeral the door had never once been unlocked.

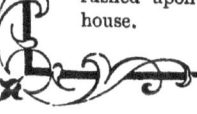

And now as, lamp in hand, he turned the key in the lock and pushed open the portal, the cold air rushed upon him as from the depths of a charnel house.

The light waved as he held it up, and threw quivering and fantastic shadows on the walls.

But Rupert's heart failed not, even though the bed stood there white and cold just as it had been when the grand old earl drew his last breath of life.

Advancing boldly, he closed the door behind him, and, locking it, placed the lamp on the table, lit the tall wax candles which were fixed in candelabras depending from the walls, and in a few moments a bright and comfortable light was diffused over the apartment.

Then taking the key from his pocket, the key which in the early part of the evening he had dug up from its mysterious receptacle in the old vault, and advancing to the rose-bedecked pillar and counting carefully, he found out the centre flower.

LESBIA.

Pressing this hard, he was soon rewarded by the sight of a wide panel, which opened swiftly, and revealed a dark interior.

He then—ere he trusted himself to a darkness which might launch him to the same doom as that which had attended the midnight robber—returned to the table, and taking the lamp, carefully examined the opening.

It was no illusion that greeted his eyes,

It was not this time an apparent fathomless abyss, but a large closet, in the centre of which was the IRON CHEST.

Gloomy and mysterious it looked, with its black sides unrelieved either by glittering fastenings or brass nails.

As far as was possible with an inanimate object it seemed to tell you that it was the repository of strange and sacred mysteries.

With a beating heart, Rupert Dreadnought knelt down, and, putting the key in the lock, turned it eagerly.

The contents of the chest was covered with a red cloth, and, on removing this, he exposed to view two rusty swords, lying cross wise over each other.

On the point where they crossed lay a skeleton hand, grasping a roll of paper, while in one corner was a cambric handkerchief, which had once evidently been steeped in blood.

After gazing for an instant in awe and wonder at the sight before him, he took the skeleton hand, and, removing from it the roll of paper, he unfolded it.

The manuscript was in the handwriting of the old earl, and ran as follows—

"MY DEAR BOY,—You already know my story, and I shall not, therefore, need to remind you of any of the circumstances which formed the curse of my young days.

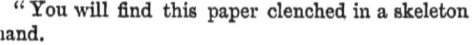

"You will find this paper clenched in a skeleton hand.

"This hand belonged once to the murderer of a dear friend of mine.

"This friend had always doubted the sincerity of Richard Penraven, and once had the courage to say so in public.

"This was when I was away from England, and when Robert Penraven began to circulate the report of my death.

"He boldly asserted that Penraven lied.

"This he did before a number of Penraven's friends.

"The companion of the villain who knew all the truth, was at first confounded, fearing no doubt that my poor friend, Henry Fortescue, had proofs of my being alive.

"Finding, however, that it was not from proof but simply from conviction that my friend spoke, Penraven's friend, Robert Redlock, renewed his swagger, and openly ridiculed the idea.

"'I tell you,' said Fortescue, fiercely, 'that you lie. Dreadnought lives.'

"In an instant there was an uproar, and urged on more by the eagerness of his friends than his own wishes, Redlock challenged him.

"There was talk of a meeting in the early morning.

"But friends made up in clamour what was wanting in real impatience; and the morning was voted accordingly too far distant.

"'Now, now is the time.'

"'There's no time like the present.'

"So a space was cleared, the doors were locked, and the two angry men faced one another.

"There was no chance of foul play on the part of Redlock and his friends, and numerous friends of Fortescue were present who would soon have stopped anything of the kind.

"I need not describe the duel.

"It will suffice to say that Henry Fortescue was no mean swordsman, and that as he ran his sword in, it caught his adversary's wrist, and severed it completely from his arm.

"You will observe it is the left hand.

"Nevertheless, the duel was over.

"Redlock could no longer engage in any combat, disabled as he was, and accordingly Fortescue was declared the conqueror, and carried away as soon as possible by his friends.

"Months passed.

"During this time Fortescue had heard nothing of the man who had lost his hand in the foolish encounter, and who undoubtedly had acted in all he had done at the instigation of Penraven.

"During the sixth month, however, there was a change.

"Without absolutely seeing anything, Fortescue felt himself watched.

"Wherever he went there seemed a shadow by his side.

"And at length this shadow took substance.

"Fortescue was walking with me (after my return to England, and my discovery of Penraven's treachery), when the darkness overcame us just in a suburban lane.

"It had been very stormy all day, and now a heavy mass of grey cloud obscured all glimpse even of the setting splendour of the sun.

"What came, came so suddenly as to be almost indistinguishable.

"There was a sudden cry, Fortescue fell forward, and I saw a man, *whose left hand was gone*, rushing away with a long and dripping knife clutched in his right.

"I just caught a glimpse of his face; but as I was about to fly towards him, Fortescue caught my cloak, and I tripped.

"'Don't leave me,' he said; 'I feel I am dying, and have but few words to say. It is Redlock who has murdered me. Avenge me!'

"He grasped my hand, glanced once with a look of wondrous friendship in my face, and then—all was over.

"I carried his body to the nearest house, and then made an attempt to trace the assassin.

"It was in vain.

"I have never seen him since, though I know he lives.

"He will be, when you read this, about five and forty years of age, with a long hooked nose, piercing small black eyes, a broad-built, heavy frame, a thick, repulsive mouth, and *remember he has but one hand!*

"The task of destroying this man I leave as a heritage to you.

"Unless you discover certain proofs of his death, remember that you must never cease from the search.

"REMEMBER YOUR VOW!"

"I will accomplish it," said Rupert, "so help me Heaven!"

And on that day week, when his friends assembled, the same vow again ascended to Heaven!

CHAPTER III.

RED LIGHTS ON THE DARK RIVER.

IT was about a week after this that Tom the waterman rowed across the river a man who was wrapped in a cloak, and whose features, although he wore no mask, were quite undistinguishable in consequence of his hat being slouched down over his eyes.

What he could see of the stranger's face was white and ghastly, and his eyes glared fiend-like from beneath beetling brows.

The few words he said, however, were of kindly import, and he paid liberally when he reached his destination.

He had taken Master Tom's boat from the stairs close to the house of the Poisoners.

Of this circumstance, however, the young waterman had taken no notice, although when he returned he cast a look of inquiry and hatred as he remembered the fearful scenes through which—in its gloomy depths—Rupert had been subjected.

He was just meditating thus, when he fancied he saw a red light flickering in one of the windows.

For a moment he took no further notice; but presently his attention was irresistibly drawn to it, for this time a crimson glow pervaded the chamber, and shed its light far over the waters.

Tom's heart leaped joyfully.

"The place is on fire," he said, "and the villanous brood will at length be destroyed."

He resolved in his own heart that nothing should be done by him to render any assistance to the hideous crew who were the scourge of London, and he accordingly simply rested on his oars, and gazed at the strange scene before him.

It was not long before greater indications of a terrible conflagration were apparent.

The red glow which had only shown at intervals, now became a steady light, and lurid flames thrust their forked tongues upwards towards the sky.

Out of the casements they came, mingled with smoke and steam, and soon the entire building was wrapped in the consuming element.

Nothing for a long time could be seen but the fierce tongues of fire.

Clouds of sparks, like red snow-flakes mounting heavenwards; huge beams, swaying about in fiery tangles; windows crashing out; old pictures shrivelling to destruction; cold statues, warmed, as it were, into life by the hot embraces of the Fire God!

Soon, however, the scene changed.

A fire is always attractive.

In these days it is pre-eminently so.

In those days it was more so still.

Remembering the terrific conflagration which, but a few years, as it were, had devastated a great portion of London, the citizens flocked eagerly to the scene of such a fire as this.

Soon, therefore, in every available corner in the streets adjoining, and in the large open space before the building, an immense crowd was assembled, and, little knowing what a villanous crew they were helping, they began exerting themselves to the utmost to save the inmates.

The latter, strangely enough, had not yet shown themselves.

All seemed tired of life.

"This is a queer affair," said one man to another, as they hurried up with a ladder; "there doesn't seem any one in the place."

"Oh, that can't be," returned his companion, "for it was a short time since, passing by this house, I saw numberless figures at the windows, and heard the sounds of revelry."

Seeing the crowd, and rightly imagining that he might learn something, and see something which would be of service to his master, Tom the waterman landed, and made his way in among the throng.

As he landed there was a sudden outburst, a sudden roar from the huge assemblage.

Well it might be so.

At three of the windows appeared some human beings, who at first, in the glare and the smoke, were unrecognisable as male or female.

In a few minutes more, however, two of them were seen to be women.

In the eyes of a crowd women in danger are, of course, terrible objects of interest; and for a few moments all present were paralysed with fear.

The very desire to aid them seemed to interfere with their power to aid.

Then, with a sudden cheer, they burst away, and within a short time three long ladders were brought up to the spot.

It was just at this moment that three horsemen appeared on the scene, who, though disguised in cloaks and masks, were still recognised by Tom the waterman, who at once advanced towards them.

"Master Dreadnought," said he, in a low tone, as he approached, "the nest which has harboured our enemies so long will at length be destroyed."

"Aye, Tom, but the evil brood, may yet escape. They have, perhaps, by this time, escaped by the river gate."

"There are some yonder," said Tom, as he pointed upwards.

Rupert glanced in the direction which the young waterman indicated, and, as his eyes fell upon the forms of the women standing in the glare of the furnace within, he uttered a cry of wonder, alarm, and anger, as it were.

What was to be done?

Was he, known and appreciated as he was by all his friends for bravery, was he to stand by and see the destruction of two women, who might be innocent of all knowledge of the brutal traffic of the Poisoners?

He strained his eyes upwards, but their features were, of course, utterly undistinguishable amid the smoke.

As he gazed, the ladders were placed in position.

They had been taken at random, however, and they were now found to be short.

A man dashed forward with a shorter one.

"Who will mount and carry this up?" he cried. "They can be saved by this."

The man stood still as he spoke, not offering to work himself.

This was more than Rupert could stand.

"Come," he said, to Tom the waterman, as he leaped off his horse, "come, let us ascend. If we err in saving them, we know how and when to retrieve the mistake."

In a few moments—sooner, indeed, than it takes to write these lines—the brave young earl had seized the ladder and was mounting the long one, with Tom the waterman close behind him.

On reaching the top spoke of the ladder he fixed the small one securely so that the other end touched the window sill.

"Now, then, Tom," he said, "hold this with all your strength. I will ascend."

He had no sooner done this, however, than the man who was the third of the group seized one of the females in his arms and rapidly descended.

The woman whom he left behind was evidently insensible, lying in her ball dress helplessly, with her head upon the window sill.

As soon, therefore, as the first couple had descended, Rupert Dreadnought rushed upwards and seized the fainting female in his arms.

He had no time or opportunity of observing her features now.

Whoever she was she was at any rate a woman, and he had come to save her, so, folding her gently though firmly to his breast with his left arm, he began steadily to descend, amid the loud cheers of the multitude.

The descent was by no means an easy one.

Flames red and threatening were bursting from

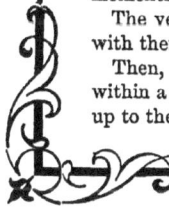

the lower windows, and almost completely enveloped the ladder and those who descended.

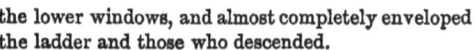

Bravely, as on a former occasion Allan of the Glen had borne Helen Penraven from the old house, did Rupert Dreadnought now pass through the fire with his burden, precious to him because of its being of the sex of the one he loved.

As soon as, amid deafening plaudits, he brought her to the ground in safety, he bore her away from the crowd towards a hostelry close at hand.

Here he quitted the press of curious people, and bore the woman he had saved, at the peril of his own life, up into a room, whither Tom the waterman accompanied him.

"Quick," said Rupert, to the waiter, "quick, some brandy. The heat and the fright has cast her into a dead faint."

"She is very beautiful, very beautiful," said Tom, as he gazed upon her.

Truly she was.

Dressed as she was in the costume of the ball, all her lovely shoulders and her round, dimpled arms were bare; deadly white now, like her bosom, where rose-buds nestled upon mounds of snow.

Her eyes were closed; but her pretty mouth, her rounded cheeks, her long, drooping lashes, her lustrous hair, gave promise that when they did open two orbs of dazzling beauty would be revealed.

Yet Rupert Dreadnought did not for a moment answer Tom's words of admiration.

His eyes, truly, were fixed upon the lovely vision before him.

Yet he appeared not to see it.

At length, just as the waiter entered with the brandy, he said—

"This lovely creature can never be a poisoner. I know the face well. Where have I seen it? Ha! I know it now; it was she whom I rescued from the hands of the Mohocks. She was at the boarding-school; she has no doubt been lured in some manner into this den of iniquity."

As he finished speaking, the eyes of the lovely being, who had taken some of the invigorating draught, slightly opened.

It was, indeed, Rosalie St. Aubyn who lay before him!

She gazed for a moment wonderingly at the masked stranger who leaned over her, and then her eyes closed again.

For a few moments she remained thus, and then a shudddering sigh shook her soft bosom, her eyes once more opened, and she slightly raised herself, while a sweet blush as of maiden modesty overspread her face.

"Where am I?" she said, in a sweet voice, then she added, rising with a pretty start, and with an admirable assumption of terror, "am I free from those horrid wretches who inveigled me to that house?"

"Yes, fair lady," said Rupert, "you have escaped from them. With the aid of this brave fellow I contrived to rescue you from the flames, and I will, if you desire it, see you safely home."

The lustrous voluptuous eyes of the beauty were fixed upon the speaker as he said these words.

"We have met before," she said

'We have," he said, feeling, as she looked at him, the same glow of excitement, the same apprehension of coming evil that he had experienced before. "I remember your face well."

"And I, strange to say, remember your voice," she said; "this is the second time that you have saved my life; may I not know the name of my preserver?"

"Not at present," said Rupert; "I have my reasons for keeping it secret for the present. Some day, no doubt, we *may* meet under other circumstances, and then my name shall no longer be kept from you. But now, fair lady, shall I conduct you to your own home?"

Rosalie thought a moment.

He had asked an awkward question.

"No," she said, "I think if they can accommodate me here I will sleep here to-night. Will you kindly ask them? In this guise I should scarcely dare to return at this hour."

The thought, now for the first time, struck Rupert, how was it that in such a place as the Home of the Poisoners she should have been attired in all the voluptuous undress of the ball room?

"How was it," he asked, "that I found you in such a house dressed for a ball?"

"That is easily explained," she said. "I was in the very heat of the dance, when, feeling faint, I asked my partner to lead me into the conservatory.

"No sooner had we entered the moonlit house of flowers than I felt him press something over my face. I lost consciousness, or rather the power to cry out and resist, and in a few moments I found myself in a carriage being whirled away towards London.

"I then quite lost my senses, and I knew no more what happened to me until I found myself in a room with a number of masked men.

"There was apparently to be some kind of trial, but what it was I never had the opportunity of knowing.

"Before scarcely a word was spoken there was a loud outcry, and a man bursting into the room proclaimed the fact that the building was on fire.

"In an instant all was confusion.

"The masked men sprang from their seats, and in a few moments I found myself alone.

"They knew the means of escape.

"It was not so with me.

"The building and everything in it was perfectly unknown to me; and, when I fled from the room, I found myself at the top of a staircase, up which the smoke and flames were rolling in thick volumes.

"Naturally I fled upwards; but, when I reached the room where you found me, I was enveloped still more in the fire, and I swooned."

Rupert believed to a certain extent this strange story. But he received it with reservation.

He had been so utterly deceived in so many things, that he was not only resolved to be cautious, but he also felt an instinctive drawing back as it were, a disinclination to believe as he had been accustomed to believe.

"You know, of course, the person who so treacherously inveigled you from the ball-room?" he said.

"Yes, well; his name is——"

Given away with No. 3 of "Rupert Dreadnought." "Boys of England" edition.

"'FORWARD, LADS,' CRIED TOM THE WATERMAN, BEATING DOWN THE SWORD OPPOSED TO HIM."

(See an early number.)

RUPERT; OR, THE DREADNOUGHT. SECRETS OF THE IRON CHEST!

"THE MOHOCKS DASHED MADLY AT THE TWO FRIENDS.

Rosalie stopped suddenly.

This time there was no acting. She really had been upon the point of committing an error.

She turned her look of blank dismay into one of arch pleasantry in an instant, with the skill of an accomplished actress.

"You forget one thing," she said, while a smile wreathed itself over her pouting lips.

"And what is that?" asked Rupert Dreadnought.

"You reserve your name from me—I must be equally reserved with you," replied the lovely deceiver; "but pray ascertain now for me if I can remain here for the night."

Rupert descended to speak to mine host, and in a few minutes returned with the news that the best room would be got ready for her reception.

"And now," he said, "I must quit you, I have other work to do ere I retire to rest. Farewell."

He bowed over her hand, as he took it gently.

She gazed at him earnestly; her eyes gleamed; her bosom rose and fell in soft undulations with the violence of her emotions.

"We shall meet again," she murmured, this time in genuine agitation.

"Assuredly," said Rupert, "though when it would be difficult to say."

"Well," added Rosalie, "since you have not disclosed your name, and my name also is unknown to you, let us at least have some password by which we may recognise each other again. I have it. It is for your ear alone."

Rupert bent down, and her little hot lips were placed close to his ear.

"The password shall be 'Love and Night.'"

Rupert laughed lightly.

"Good," he said, "I will keep it secret, though, doubtless, ere long you may meet me unmasked, when you will recognise me without its aid. And now, fair lady, adieu once more."

He pressed her hand slightly again, and then quitted the room.

"That lady's in love with you," said Tom the waterman, as they descended the stairs.

"Her manner seems truly strange," said Rupert Dreadnought; "but I do not fancy that it is love by which she is actuated."

He was wrong, and Tom was right.

Strangely enough Rupert Dreadnought had raised in the bosom of this evil-hearted woman a devouring passion, which utterly obliterated all thoughts of Oscar Penraven.

When Rupert had quitted the room she sank back upon the couch, pressing her hand over her heaving breast, and murmuring in low, but resolute tones—

"I love him—I love him! He must be mine!"

CHAPTER IV.

THE FIRST GLIMPSE OF THE ENEMY.

On leaving the tavern where he had placed Rosalie St. Aubyn, Rupert at once hastened back to the scene of the fire.

The conflagration was now at its height, and out on the river the waves rolled like blood.

The flames were ascending eagerly and triumphantly now with a roaring sound, as if proclaiming their victory; and, as the great crowd gazed at the scene, the roof fell in, and a myriad of sparks of fire floated upwards towards the starlit heavens.

It was quite impossible to render any assistance in extinguishing the flames in the building itself, for they had far too firm a hold; but it was possible to prevent its spreading to any alarming extent, and workmen were employed now in pulling down an old, half-ruined edifice that joined it at one end.

At this point, where the noise of the hammers and the picks could be heard even above the roar of the fire, the largest and most eager crowd was now collected, for the fire had not yet reached this point, and it became a matter of interest to see which could work quickest, the workmen or the devouring element, which, in spite of the jets of water continually cast upon it, was gradually but surely approaching the spct.

Among the crowd here, too, were to be seen many well-dressed men, who conversed eagerly together in low tones, and who seemed most eager to watch the result of the conflagration.

Near these Rupert and Tom (their other companions having ridden off) placed themselves.

Instinctively our hero felt that these were in some way connected with the Society of Poisoners who had attempted his death, and from whom he and Allan had so miraculously escaped by placing the dead bodies of the two keepers in their places.

"Tom," he said, in a low tone, "I feel certain that these men who are talking so eagerly here have something to do with the Society of Poisoners."

"They seem very much interested in all that is going on," said Tom; "they little think how near them stand the men who killed their keepers, and deceived them into burying the wrong men."

"Hush!" said Rupert, "let them not hear our voices. Ah! what is that?"

As one of the men in front of them raised his arm to point out something to his companion, something gleamed brightly in the light of the fire.

It was not a sword point, neither was it a dagger.

It looked rather like a hook of steel, such a hook as is placed at the end of an arm *from which the hand has been cut off.*

A thrill passed through the frame of Rupert Dreadnought.

The man of whom he was in search had lost his left hand.

Here was one whom he already suspected to be one of the Poisoners.

Could this be the man?

Could this be his enemy, brought thus almost miraculously before him?

His blood coursed more quickly through his veins, and he resolved at once to discover the truth.

Moving forward, he suddenly, as if by an accident, pushed up against the man, who turned round quickly, so that the full glow of the firelight was on his face.

"Your name is Redlock!" cried Rupert, in an instant, as he seized him, and gazed full into the features, which, through his father's description, he now recognised fully.

The man glanced at him in wonder and some alarm.

"Who are you?" he cried; "and why do you thus madly assail me?"

"I am Rupert Dreadnought, son of the old earl," said our hero, "and the avenger of Fortescue. Come quickly with me."

A shudder passed through the stranger's frame, and he attempted to wrench himself from the grasp of his assailant.

"You are insane," he said, "thus to assault a stranger in the street. My name is not Redlock, and I know nothing of you or those of whom you speak."

A fierce fire glowed in Rupert's eyes.

"Come with me," he said, in a stern undertone; "I have something most essential to speak about to you. Come!"

At this moment a shrill, wild cry arose from a hundred throats.

"Run for your lives! Save yourselves!" were the words which could be distinguished, amid the hoarse shouts of men, and the shrill screams of women.

And then a huge rafter, balancing itself for a moment warningly on the summit of the wall, toppled over into the space which had so lately been filled by an excited and bustling crowd.

As it was, they were not all able to escape, and the end of the beam just caught the tail of the flying crowd, crushing down two or three as they sought vainly to struggle through the mass of humanity before them.

In an instant, Rupert felt himself wrenched violently away from the man he so longed to attack, and when the beam had fallen, and the crowd had flowed back as it were, into its former position, Redlock, if indeed it was he, was no longer to be seen.

"Dastard!" muttered Rupert, angrily, to himself; "but he shall not escape me. I have seen his face now, and it is more than ever vividly engraven on my memory. Strange that he should thus be thrust in my way only to escape once more, as if to show me how difficult is the path marked out for me. Never mind. The vow I have sworn I will carry out, and the more willingly when I think of Helen, the lovely prize I shall win in the end."

As these thoughts found vent in a low whisper to himself, as it were, he felt a hand suddenly clapped upon his shoulder, and turning round he beheld Allan of the Glen standing near him with a flush of excitement upon his handsome face.

CHAPTER V.

THE NIGHT DUEL IN THE STREETS OF LONDON.

"QUICK, quick, this way, Master Dreadnought," said Allan, in a tone of intense agitation.

"Why, what is the matter, Allan?" asked Rupert; "you seem out of breath."

"Stanley Sherrington is awaiting you. Oscar Penraven is near at hand, and you have a chance now of meeting your enemy face to face."

Rupert's heart leaped in his bosom at these words.

He had indeed met Oscar face to face.

But it had been when he had been helpless either to avenge the past or to defend himself in the present.

Eagerly, therefore, he turned to Tom the waterman.

"Come," he said, "let us hasten. My enemy awaits me, and while I contend against him, you and my other friends must watch and see fair play. Quick, come."

With flushed cheeks and eager steps Rupert Dreadnought followed the steps of Allan of the Glen, and in a few minutes they had emerged from the dense crowd and reached a spot where even the blaze and roar of the conflagration could no longer be seen or heard.

Here Allan led them into a tavern, where they found Stanley Sherrington and another awaiting them.

"Allan tells me Oscar is near at hand," said Rupert Dreadnought.

"He is," replied Stanley Sherrington; "he is in this very building. He and a number of those who have escaped the destruction of the old house are at the present moment making merry in an upper room, little dreaming that we are here. We must watch their departure and destroy him."

"There must be a fair fight," returned Rupert Dreadnought. "Villain as he is, I will not have it said that the assassin's knife put an end to his infamous life. No, my own good sword, backed by my good cause, will be enough for me. But are you sure they are still here?"

"I am."

"And in which room are they?"

"That above us."

"Good; then we can watch their movements, and they cannot well escape."

They had not long to wait.

They had scarcely finished their second glass of wine, when they heard the sounds of steps descending, and going to the door, they beheld Oscar and his friends pass out.

"Now, then," said Rupert Dreadnought, "let us follow at once."

Within a few moments they had sallied forth, and as they did so, the bright glare of a lamp at the corner of a street showed to them the friends separating and going different ways.

Oscar and one friend then passed down a street, and Rupert's mind was at once made up.

"Sherrington," he said, "you accompany me. This duel to the death shall be a fair one. Oscar Penraven has one friend only with him, so also will I. You, Allan and Tom, can return home. Come, Stanley, let us hasten onward."

There was no time for much consultation, so they advanced at once, and after following their enemies until they reached a spot somewhat more secluded than ordinary, they advanced quickly and challenged their enemies.

Oscar and his friend turned quickly.

He had been during months past the victim of such constant mishaps and attacks, that it was with some alarm now that he heard the challenge given in a strange voice.

When he turned to face the stranger who had shouted "Stand there, on your life!" in so resolute a tone, he failed entirely to recognise his adversary.

He had no conception that Rupert Dreadnought lived.

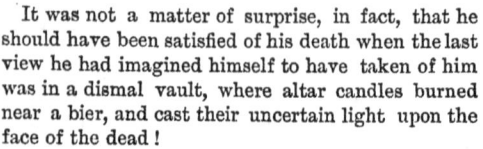

It was not a matter of surprise, in fact, that he should have been satisfied of his death when the last view he had imagined himself to have taken of him was in a dismal vault, where altar candles burned near a bier, and cast their uncertain light upon the face of the dead!

"Who are you?" he asked, boldly.

"I am one you little expect to see," returned Rupert Dreadnought. "I have met you now face to face. You have a friend with you; so also have I. We have time and opportunity. Old scores, therefore, can be paid, and the vengeance I have long sworn against you and yours can now be accomplished!"

Confident as Oscar Penraven was that Rupert Dreadnought was numbered with the dead, the words of the stranger were utter riddles to him.

"I know not what you mean?" he said. I know not your face—your form—your voice. You are following some shadow."

"Oscar Penraven," said Rupert, in a stern voice, "think not so to avoid a meeting with me. No doubt after the murderous efforts you have made against me and my friends, it will astound you to know that we are living; but fortune has favoured me—Heaven has protected me. Behold, Oscar Penraven, your sworn enemy, Rupert, Earl of Dreadnought!"

Oscar started back in utter amazement as our hero uttered these words.

"Cast aside your disguise," he said, "and let me see your face. You ask me to treat you as an honourable man. Let me do so, as I am willing; but let me know with whom I am fighting."

"I have already told you," replied our hero; "I am Rupert Dreadnought, does not that suffice?"

"Show, then, your face. Rupert Dreadnought is dead. I saw his dead face; I was present at his burial."

"You lie!" exclaimed Rupert, "I live."

And as he spoke he flung aside the hat that covered so completely his features and disclosed the well-known though darker countenance of Oscar's foe.

Oscar was no coward.

We have before seen this.

When Gascoigne the spy had been left to him to destroy, he had not shrunk from his fearful task.

So he eyed his enemy boldly, though his heart leaped and his face turned deadly pale from mere astonishment.

"Strange, indeed, this," he said; "you must have risen from the dead! But fear not; I will fight you. This is too dark here for you or for me. Let us go on to yonder square; or stay rather. Yonder come two watchmen. We will enlist their services."

His voice was free from all fear.

He spoke boldly and coolly.

"Good," thought Rupert, "he will not shirk his duty. I shall soon obtain my revenge."

The watch seeing four men evidently bent upon fighting, thought it a good opportunity for a little bluster.

"What is this? What have we here, gentlemen?" cried a fat, fussy, little party with a red nose. "We can have no combats and blood-shedding in the streets."

Rupert seized him by the arm as he spoke.

"How far are we from the watch-house?" he asked sternly.

"Some mile and a half," said the Charlie; "but come, young sir——"

"A truce to folly," exclaimed Rupert Dreadnought, "open your lanterns; stand yonder and raise them aloft, so that we can see to fight. Quick, we have no time to lose."

The watchmen looked from one to the other in utter wonderment.

"But indeed, sir," exclaimed the one who had not yet spoken, "this is against the law; we really must——"

"Hold your tongue," said Oscar, "or you may chance to have it cut out. I will now stand in line, so that will do. Now then, Rupert Dreadnought, I am ready."

The watchmen saw that all resistance on their part would be simply folly.

So they yielded gracefully.

Their lamps were opened and raised on high.

The bright swords of the deadly enemies were drawn and crossed, and in the middle of the dark street the duel began.

Duels with swords have been so often described that it would be useless again to enter into every detail.

But this was a curious one in every way.

Besides the fact that it was taking place between the heirs of two deadly enemies, the circumstances which surrounded it were strange.

The fact of its being fought boldly in the open street where all such meetings were strictly forbidden—the fact of the very custodians of the public peace being compelled to be unwilling aiders and abettors in the transaction, made the whole matter out of the way and unusual.

Neither of the combatants, however, seemed influenced by the peculiarities of the scene.

They thought of nothing but attack and defence.

The one was thirsting for revenge.

The other was resolved now, once for all, to rid himself of a foe who was continually dogging his footsteps, and rendering every hour of his life a terror and a misery.

So every lunge was deadly: every parry was given and watched with eager eyes.

Both of them had been brought up with a purpose.

One to avenge, the other to destroy.

Both, therefore, were good swordsmen, and for a long time there was little perceptible difference in their positions.

Presently, however, both warmed to their work.

Their blades flashed brightly in the light of the lamps, and they advanced and retired rapidly and eagerly, while spots of blood upon the pavement showed that wounds had been given and received on both sides.

Seeing his adversary's blood flowing, Rupert Dreadnought became more desperate, and attacked him fiercely, never for one moment, however, losing his presence of mind, or suffering his hand to become unsteady.

Gradually now Oscar began to yield ground, and as he did so, the face of his second became dark, and he half drew his sword from his scabbard.

Stanley Sherrington was eagerly watching his movements, and as he saw him thus preparing for an attack, he advanced towards him.

"Stay," he said, "stay. We came here to be witnesses of a fair fight. If you interfere, I have a sword, and can interfere also."

The other eyed him for a moment angrily, but after reflection returned his sword to its scabbard.

"No," he said, "we will not fight now. Whatever happens we will be but spectators, and can settle our quarrels after."

While they had been speaking, the battle between Oscar and Rupert had waxed fast and furious.

Huge drops of perspiration fell from the faces of the combatants, while their shirt-sleeves were stained heavily and darkly with blood.

Their eyes gleamed savagely.

Their swords writhed like gleaming serpents.

Then they stood closer to one another.

All danger was forgotten.

All they thought of was that they were deadly foes, and that their business was to destroy each other or perish in the attempt.

To the wondering eyes of the two watchmen it seemed at length more like a stabbing-match than a duel, so quickly did the blades dart to and fro.

Then at length there was a brilliant pass, a sharp cry, and the contest stopped.

RICHARD PENRAVEN.

Rupert Dreadnought stood firm, while his adversary fell back into the arms of his second, the blood pouring from a large wound in his chest.

Rupert was drawing his sword back to give a final thrust, when the second raised his hand deprecatingly.

"It is not needed," he said. "He is dead!"

Whatever Rupert's intentions were, now he was utterly unable to carry them into effect.

There was suddenly a wild and unearthly yell—a crowd of dark figures came dashing round the corner, and in an instant the Charlies were on their backs, and their lamps extinguished, while Rupert and Stanley Sherrington found themselves surrounded by a shrieking mob of bacchanalian revellers.

The new-comers were no other than the Mohocks.

"What have we here?" shouted one, in a drunken voice of solemnity. "A duel in the streets of London! This cannot be."

And ere Rupert was aware of it, a bag of flour was dashed in his eyes, and one of the maddened drunkards rushed head foremost at him.

Eluding this drunken imitation of a battering-ram, Rupert leaped aside, while his would-be assailant catching his head against a post, fell stunned and bleeding to the ground.

This was the signal for a desperate outcry on the part of the Mohocks.

They were unused to find themselves worsted in these mad scenes, and to see one of their number stretched apparently lifeless on the pavement drove them in their state of inebriation to a state bordering really on madness.

Wild cries filled the air—unearthly shrieks, like those of some savage tribe.

Swords were drawn, and, regardless of all else but their determination to avenge themselves for the discomfiture of their comrade, they dashed at the two friends.

Stanley Sherrington, as we know, was a member of the Mohocks, and again and again he strove by shouting their war-cry to attract their attention, and let them know that he was one of their friends.

But it was in vain.

They were thoroughly exasperated, and would listen to no reason.

Wild cries resounded around the open space.

"Death to the Night Prowlers!"

"At them—at them!"

"Blood for blood!"

"Down with them!"

"The Mohocks for ever!"

This last cry was fatal to their chances of success.

People had looked out from their windows when the other duel was proceeding, but they had taken no notice.

They were used to such scenes as this; but, when they heard the name of Mohocks shouted out, they recognised a common enemy.

In a few moments, therefore, doors were opened, and men, with swords drawn, were seen rushing from their houses in their knee breeches and shirts.

They were only just in time.

Drunk as they were, they were still more than a match for the two friends, one of whom was tired already with the severe struggle with Oscar Penraven, and though they had their backs to the wall, they were becoming thoroughly exhausted.

The wounded Oscar and his friends had, during the fray, disappeared entirely from the scene, for when the lanterns of the Charlies had been extinguished the open space was enveloped in utter darkness.

It may be imagined, therefore, what difficulty there was in distinguishing friends from foes; but those who issued from the houses being all in their shirt sleeves, were at length enabled to range themselves on the side of Rupert and Sherrington, and then the tide of battle turned.

Those who had so suddenly and opportunely appeared on the scene were nothing but citizens, unused to the use of swords, but the name of Mohock seemed suddenly to turn them into soldiers.

They had all grievances against these prowlers of the night.

Some had been brutally attacked, some had wives and sisters who had been insulted, and they had now an opportunity of revenging their wrongs.

The Mohocks were taken utterly by surprise. Drunk as they were, they yet saw that they had fallen among the Philistines, and they gathered themselves as it were together.

But they were no use against their more sober assailants.

Gradually they were compelled to give way, and at length the shrill note of warning from their chief warned them that they were to disperse.

They made now but a feeble resistance, just making one stand and then breaking away, as they had done upon the night when Rupert and his friends had saved from their clutches Rosalie St. Aubyn and the other young ladies from Primrose Academy.

Their enemies, when they had defeated them, did not think it worth while to pursue, but suffered them to escape, while a shout of derision followed them.

The result of the enemy's proceedings were eminently unsatisfactory.

He had indeed seen the wounded Oscar fall back into his friend's arms with the blood pouring copiously from his breast.

Yet he had had sufficient experience in the manner in which even from the most deadly scrapes clever men could escape, that he was far from being satisfied that even now Oscar Penraven was safely disposed of.

He himself had made his way out of the very jaws of death as it were, from the very grave over which his enemies had rejoiced, and it was therefore unsafe for him to believe in the destruction of an enemy upon whom he had not seen the evidences of decay surely creeping.

"We have yet more work to do," said he to Stanley Sherrington, as they thanked their strange friends, and sheathing their swords made their way from the scene. "I believe not in Oscar's death until I have seen his utter destruction."

"The past justifies you in saying so truly," said Sherrington; "but if we follow up this night's adventure we may yet carry out our design before we had hoped to do so. To-morrow we will pay a visit to the old ruin and see if there is any clue to be there discovered."

CHAPTER VI.

A STRANGE VISIT.

Among those who exhibited most interest in the events of the past evening, where, on returning home, Rupert Dreadnought narrated them to his friends, was one whose red wig and peculiar caste of appearance altogether denoted a disguise.

The most interesting portion of the evening's proceedings to him, however, seemed that in which Rosalie St. Aubyn was concerned.

At the mention of her name he started, and an unwonted fire gleamed in his eyes, which seemed all the more fiery in comparison with his ghastly face.

"You call her beautiful?" he said, as Rupert finished speaking.

"I do, indeed," said Rupert. "Perhaps, if we except Helen Penraven, I never saw so loveable a face."

The other smiled.

"Ah," he said, "no doubt you are right. Her face is lovely, but I have learned to fear beauty. And has she succeeded in her desire?"

"What desire?"

"The desire to make you love her."

"No, indeed," said Rupert; "though, were I inclined to be conceited, I should say she had conceived a strange passion for me. No, no, the woman does not live who can wean my affections from Helen Penraven."

Soon after, the one who had taken so great an interest in the conversation, rose, quitted the room, and, arming himself, issued forth into the street.

Meanwhile, Rosalie St. Aubyn retired to rest almost immediately Rupert Dreadnought quitted her presence.

At three o'clock that morning we find her fast asleep in the bed.

She looked most beautiful now, for her eyes were closed in a calm and pleasant sleep, and their evil gleaming could no longer be seen.

The heat of the weather had caused her to throw off some of the bed-clothes, and her white shoulders and rounded arms, therefore, were visible as they had been when she had first appeared to Rupert Dreadnought in her ball-dress.

A beautiful flush was upon her cheeks, her parted lips disclosed two rows of pearly teeth, while her lustrous hair fell in wild profusion over her heaving bosom.

She was lying thus when her window suddenly begun to be opened from without.

The new-comer had evidently no desire to be detected, for he proceeded to his work slowly, gently, and methodically.

Gradually, therefore, the sash was raised, and presently a man peered in.

He was masked, but the little that could be seen of his features showed that it was the pale man who had suddenly quitted Rupert Dreadnought's house not long before.

He glanced eagerly round the room, which was enveloped in partial gloom, a lamp, half turned down, on the table in the centre of the chamber, casting but a feeble radiance over the objects around.

Then his eyes were rivetted for a moment on the figure that occupied the bed.

A gleam as of fire appeared then to shoot from his distended orbs.

It was the fire of revenge!

There were no gleams of love or passion in them.

It was the flame of fierce hate and cruel vengeance that lit them up, and made him more quickly and with less caution make his way into the room.

Then he closed the casement by which he had entered, turned the lamp up to its full height, and approached the bed.

Here he stood, and gazed for a moment at the picture of beauty before him.

"Beautiful demon," he murmured; "no wonder is it that people are deceived by you; no wonder that your lovely form has led men on to their destruction. No more shall it be so; no more shall you revel in the belief that you are far beyond the reach of the avenger's arm. You shall know and tremble as you know who is on your track."

As he spoke, he laid his hand on the fair sleeper's shoulder, and shook her gently.

She shuddered slightly, and then her eyes opened, and she gazed wildly round the chamber.

In another instant she had sprung up in the bed, and a scream was about to issue from her lips, when the new-comer placed his hand over her mouth, saying sternly—

"One word and your life is forfeit."

"What want you here?" she cried, in a tremulous voice, as he removed his hand, still not daring to scream in face of the gleaming knife which he held close to her throat.

"I have come to speak with you, and to warn you," he said.

"To warn me! How came you here, then, and who admitted you?"

"I admitted myself through yonder window," he said; "what I have to say must be said in secret, and I desired no one to know of my coming."

"Your purpose cannot be a good one," she said, "or you would not come through the window like a thief in the night. But whatever you have to say, say quickly, for I have no desire that you should be found in my chamber at this hour of the night."

"Who more right than I?" he answered.

Then he added aloud—

"You are luring another into your deadly coils. This night I have discovered it."

"Of whom speak you?" she said, while her features became deadly pale.

"I speak of Rupert Dreadnought," he answered.

"And who spoke to you of him in connection with me?"

"He himself."

"And does he love me then, and are you a woman that you are jealous?"

She said this eagerly and then sneeringly.

A smile wreathed itself over his lips.

"He loves you not," he answered, "he loves another; but tell me, you know Alford?"

"I do. He is dead."

"He is not."

"You are wrong. He was killed by Oscar Penraven."

"So Oscar thought. He was wrong. He lives still. I am he."

So saying, he withdrew his mask, and revealed the pale and ghastly features of the man whom Stanley Sherrington had taken for dead.

The features of Rosaline St. Aubyn underwent pleasureable change as he did this.

"Why do you come thus mysteriously," she said, "since you are one of us, and since you and I have always been friends?"

"We are friends no longer," he said, sternly; "I will not kill you as you deserve—I will not cast shame on your name, as I could, by opening this door and calling in the people of the house. I will only enjoy the great triumph of telling you all I know, and how utterly and miserably your plans will fail in the future."

Rosalie St. Aubyn gazed at him now in real amazement.

He had always been on terms of friendship with her.

What could have made this change?

She was a vain woman, full of the consciousness of her glorious beauty, and she did not remain for many moments in doubt.

He loved her; he was jealous of her passion for Dreadnought.

"What has changed you thus?" she asked, as her eyes assumed a softened expression.

"I will tell you my reasons afterwards," he said; "now listen while I crush your hopes one by one. In the first place, you have cherished a mad hope that Oscar Penraven will make you his wife."

"He has sworn it."

"He means it not," returned Alford, "he loves Helen Penraven, and is pledged heart and soul to her. He means no marriage to you."

A flush of anger and irritation crossed the face of the lovely woman.

But she betrayed no further her emotion.

"He is welcome to wed whom he pleases," she said, "I love another. This is no sorrow to me."

"Be it so," said Alford, "though I believe it not. In the second place, your name is not Rosalie St. Aubyn, but Lady Richard Penraven."

It was now that the first evidence of intense agitation betrayed itself.

The woman's body became, as it were, convulsed; her mouth opened, and she clutched the bed on both sides of her, sitting up erect and staring at Alford with wildly glancing eyes.

"Madman!" she murmured after a moment, "what fool's tale is this you repeat?"

"What makes your heart palpitate with dread—what makes you turn sick with fear—what crushes your hopes for ever?" said Alford, triumphantly. "I am Rupert Dreadnought's friend. I know, and he knows your story, although he does not as yet know your identity with Lady Penraven, or rather, the Mrs. Richard Penraven of the scandal."

"And you are going to tell him, I suppose? You are going to enlighten him when it *can* be no interest to you to ruin me," said Rosalie St. Aubyn, bitterly.

"Excuse me, you are wrong," returned Alford; "I am *not* going to tell him."

"Then, what *do* you mean?" she said. "I confess myself at a loss to understand you."

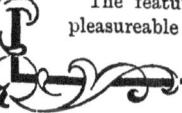

"I will let your passion for him increase; I will even, if I can succeed in doing so, induce Rupert Dreadnought to lose his fealty to his real mistress, and love you. Then will my moment of triumph come," he cried, raising his hand aloft. "Then, when you imagine your best hopes realized, I will disclose the whole story of your infamy; how your husband——aye, madam, interrupt me not—I *will* speak; how your husband rescued you at the early age of sixteen from the companionship of villains; how he married you; how you fled from him after a long period of devotion; how he met your betrayer; how he shot him to the heart, and how you left India for England to seek out another victim to deceive and destroy. And he can also tell more."

"What mean you, most sapient historian?" said Rosalie, who had by this time recovered, by a violent effort, all her composure.

"He can tell how the husband, who was said to have destroyed himself by casting himself into one of the deep and swiftly-running rivers of India, followed his wife to England; how he watched all her movements; how he saw her on the point of inveigling his friends; how, at the last moment, he met her face to face, and, taking off his disguises one by one, thus, and thus, cried, 'Behold the one you thought dead—the one who lives to punish and avenge!'"

As he suited the action to the word, and threw his wig and false moustache and beard on the floor, the fair demon, as he had termed her, uttered a cry of fear.

No wonder was it.

The one whom she had wronged and fondly imagined dead and out of her way, had suddenly reappeared to thwart all her plans.

She seemed thoroughly paralysed.

"You are mad," she said. "Who are you who thus take the semblance of the dead to extort from me money or a confession?"

"Rose Allerton," returned Alford, sternly. "You know me well, your husband Richard Penraven. You guess your future from the fact of my reappearance."

There was now a moment of intense silence, during which the husband and wife, long separated, gazed at each other in silence.

Then there was a sudden start, a dash forward, and Alford staggered back, pressing his hand to his brow.

Then as he essayed to utter a cry, he gasped for breath and fell heavily on the floor.

What had happened?

CHAPTER VII.

THE SECRET CONCLAVE—THE CHAINED MADMAN—THE TERRIBLE FIGHT.

Before continuing Alford's adventure in the tavern where he had so adventurously entered in search of Rosalie St. Aubyn, we must return to Oscar Penraven and narrate the circumstances which followed his duel with Rupert Dreadnought.

The wound he had received at the hands of our hero was a most severe one.

It had passed through his shoulder, the fleshy portion of which it had torn open; but nevertheless it had not passed through such a portion of his body as to render the injury a mortal one.

His second carried away the wounded man to the nearest tavern, where he was soon in the hands of a skilful doctor.

His swoon lasted a long time; but towards morning he opened his eyes and glanced round him in surprise.

He naturally had expected when the cold steel had plunged through his body that he should never again open his eyes upon this world, and now that he found himself in bed in a dark room he naturally reckoned upon finding himself in the hands of his foes.

"Where am I?" he said, in the loudest voice he could assume.

A man crept up to the bed.

It was his second—Mark Forrester.

"Ah! Mark," said Oscar, "are you there? This is indeed a surprise. I had reckoned myself with the dead."

"You are worth many dead ones," said Mark, with a cheering laugh, "your luck is too good to give them a chance of disposing of you."

He was right.

A strange destiny seemed to watch over the young reprobate.

It seemed, truly, as if fortune were assisting in the exact development of the mission given him by the old earl, as if young Rupert's sword was fated to destroy Redlock ere it could succeed in doing more than wound any other.

It would be useless to describe minutely the convalescence of Oscar Penraven.

It will suffice to say that it was a somewhat long and tedious matter, but at the end of the time care and fresh air restored himself entirely to his old vigor.

His hatred now redoubled against Rupert Dreadnought, and he left his sick room vowing unceasing vengeance against his hereditary foe.

During his illness the Poisoners had not been idle.

Their residence in the very heart of the city of London had certainly possessed great advantages, but it had also its disadvantages.

It was in the centre of action, but then also it was capable of being unceasingly watched.

It was resolved, therefore, to move entirely from the metropolis, and, as they had plenty of agents at command, they were not long before they pitched upon a suitable locality.

It was some distance down the river, on the Essex coast, close to the river. It was always convenient to be near the swift flowing waters of the river, as it enabled them to bear away their booty—to carry the bodies of murdered victims and cast them into the centre of the stream, as well as to go and come without attracting notice.

While they had been in search of their new domicile, they had many secret meetings in the vaults of the old building, which had not been touched by the devouring element that had otherwise destroyed the abode of crime.

They came under cover of the dark night, and were thus unnoticed by any.

Again and again they had endeavoured to ascertain the cause of the calamity which had so utterly destroyed their old place of concealment.

But in vain.

Whoever was their enemy he had taken his measures well, and had left behind him not the slightest clue to his whereabouts.

RUPERT
OR THE
DREADNOUGHT
SECRETS OF THE IRON CHEST

"STAND BACK!", CRIED LESBIA, "THE FIRST MAN WHO APPROACHES DIES."

It was in the dark vault where they held their meetings prior to making their way to the old house on the Essex side of the river that Oscar Penraven made his first appearance after his illness.

He was welcomed with acclamations by all as kind of martyr to the cause, and was raised by general accord to the position of one of the council of the Society.

The office of the council was far above that of the other portions of this hideous community.

They had power over all the others, were able to send them upon any mission, and were entitled, moreover, to a larger share in the disposal of the riches acquired by murder and crimes of every hue.

The failure of the scheme in regard to Alford, did not detract from Oscar's reputation.

He had fought well for them, he had done his best, and if he had failed he had done only what others had done before him, and had spilled his blood in their behalf.

It was with utter astonishment that they learned from him the fact of Rupert having escaped from the deadly trap that had been laid for him.

How he had done so was indeed to them a perfect mystery; but this mystery they determined at once, if possible, to unravel.

"Let us open the Death Vault," said the Chief of the Poisoners, "and see who lies in their places. There must have been murder done, if no treachery was afloat."

The vault in which the two friends had been supposed to have been buried after their long and ghastly imprisonment had not been touched by the fire.

They adjourned, therefore, in a body to the place where they had seen the last of their enemy, and Allan of the Glen, and proceeded to raise the stone.

There beneath the slab were two bodies enveloped in their winding sheets.

Their faces could not at first be distinguished, but on removing the clothes from their features, they started back in astonishment.

The faces they saw were not those of Rupert and Allan, but those of the two men who had been set to watch them.

How they had been placed in the vault, and how they had been killed, was still a matter of mystery.

But one thing was still evident.

There had been a traitor in the camp.

"There will be another fearful ordeal for some one to go through," said the Chief of the Poisoners. "If our present terrible rules do not keep our Society from treachery then we must invent some torture more terrible and desperate still, which will wring with horror the heart of him who is seduced into treacherous actions. Come, let these men rest in peace; they died in the execution of their duty. We will return to our place of meeting."

They had not again taken their seats more than a few minutes, when there was a rushing noise along the passage, and then a rattling as of iron being dashed again and again along stone pavement.

Accompanying this was a sound as of successive shrieks and groans from some one in mortal agony, and then a heavy substance came dashing up against the door.

One of the assemblage at once opened the door when a strange object presented itself; a man with long matted red hair, wild eyes, and haggard face; a man attenuated by long illness or long confinement in an unwholesome atmosphere; a man whose clothes were torn, and to whose limbs a long chain was attached.

His eyes had a ravenous look in them like those of a wild animal, and as he entered the council chamber he cast a look of idiotic savageness around.

Then he broke into a maniacal laugh, and with a wild bound mounted on the table.

Here he danced and screamed like one bereft of his senses, and madly flung his arms about.

It was some time before they could recognise the strange being.

But at length Oscar Penraven cried,

"It is Jack Gradley, one of our keepers. What can this mean?"

"Gradley," said the Chief, "whence come you?"

The madman glanced at him vacantly for a moment, and then broke into a wild laugh.

"Ha, ha!" he cried, "hell is around me now! The demons surround me—the wild shrieks of the fiends ring in my ears. Avoid thee—avoid thee, satan!"

As he said these words with frantic emphasis, he swung the heavy chain round his head and struck out madly at those around him.

Then he remained stiff and motionless as a statue, with eyes starting from his head like one lost.

"This man is the one, and the only one who can elucidate the great mystery," said the Chief of the Poisoners, "and he is mad. What is to be done?"

"I will speak to him," said Oscar. "Let us approach him. Draw your swords, and let me have room to escape from his mad efforts, should he be roused again to his insane condition."

The assembled men did as he desired, and formed in a circle round the table where the infuriated wretch crouched as still and as mute as an image.

It seemed absurd to take precautions against such a being.

He seemed now in a state of harmless idiotcy.

But Oscar knew that he was not to be trusted.

Drawing his sword, he approached stealthily and warily.

As he did so the poor maniac drew back a foot, uttering a noise like the growl of a wild beast.

"Fear not," said Oscar Penraven, "I desire not to harm you. Answer me, Jack Gradley, do you know me?"

The man shook his head.

Evidently he had no recollection of him whatever, and yet on a dark night he had found his way to the old house of the Poisoners.

"Where have you been?" asked Oscar.

The maniac grinned.

"Ha, ha!" he shouted, "ha, ha! I have escaped. Oh, it was a fearful place! cold, very cold. The sun never shining. All wind—chill wind, and no sunshine. Rats to keep you company, and men to mock you! Oh, it was horrible—horrible!"

"The poor devil has suffered much," said the Chief of the Poisoners. "This Rupert Dreadnought and his friends, who set up for humanity, have allowed a fine specimen of it to escape. Speak to him again, Penraven."

"Gradley," said Penraven again, "speak to me. How came you to leave us? Tell me, I am your friend."

As he spoke he held out his hand.

The maniac misunderstood the motion.

To him it seemed the movement of an enemy, and in an instant he darted back, raising his chain above his head, and uttering a sharp, hissing noise like a monkey in a rage.

The chain was a formidable weapon with heavy links, and the madman raised them apparently without any difficulty, and in an instant commenced his attack.

He gazed round savagely upon all, but Oscar Penraven was his special mark.

He appeared to see in him a likeness to one of his keepers, and he darted at him with fearful malevolence.

"Ha! ha!" he shouted, as he swung the rusty iron links round his head, "ha! ha! once I feared *you*, now I am free; it is you who fear me!"

The sword which Penraven carried was no use in parrying blows from such an awkward, and at the same time heavy, weapon as that used by the maniac, and the only way, therefore, in which he contrived to elude the fierce swinging blows was by stooping suddenly.

"He must die!" said the Chief of the Poisoners. "It were better for him to quit life than to live on; and, moreover, if we allow him to depart he may partially recover his senses and betray us. At him my friends, cut him down!"

The poor wretch seemed to understand in some degree the cruel hands into which he had fallen, and drew back into a corner gibbering like a wild beast.

Oscar Penraven, who was nearest to him, commenced the attack, and was seconded by many others.

But for a long time the mad man held his own.

It was really difficult for the men, numerous as they were, to get near him while he remained in a corner.

But his discretion did not last long.

Suddenly seeing, as he fancied, an opportunity, he rushed forward, and, swinging the chain savagely round his head, dashed one of the poisoners to the ground deluged in blood.

It was this moment that Oscar Penraven chose to settle the matter.

Drawing his sword back he grasped the hilt firmly and drove it through the madman's heart!

With a wild shriek the poor wretch fell back—his eyes glazed and then he staggered dead upon the floor.

"There is another victim to our enemies," said the Chief of the Poisoners; "more than ever now will our vengeance follow our destroyers. Friends, we will bury this wretched being, and let that be our last action in this house. We will leave it this night for ever. In future it will be as a spot accursed—a memory only of our wrongs."

Wrongs!

The direst villain of the age—the curse of London, preached to his hideous flock about his wrongs!

Within half an hour a grave had been dug, and the remains of the unfortunate maniac had been deposited therein.

Then the ghastly assemblage broke up, and the old house was deserted by them for ever!

CHAPTER VIII.

THE SUBTLE ESSENCE.

When Alford fell to the ground in the room where Rosalie St. Aubyn had been carrried by Rupert Dreadnought, she sprang out of bed, and after slipping on a few articles of clothing, stood and gazed at him.

"He thought to triumph over me," she murmured, 'but he is conquered. He should have known what it was to raise up the demon in me."

Then a strange and inexplicable change came over her.

She looked down upon his haggard visage—his ghastly features—his attenuated form, and a feeling of compassion entered her heart.

She remembered him as the love of her youth—the man who, in the prime of his manly beauty, had won her heart—who in the old times had been the admired of all.

And there he lay now, poor fellow, stricken by her misdeeds—helpless through her wickedness—at her mercy!

What advantage should she take of him?

Should she not rather try to persuade him?

Should she not rather try to make him remember old times, and forgive her for the great love she once bore him.

Foolish woman!

She forgot that the greater the love the greater the hate!

It was well, however, for him that she did not indulge in such thoughts.

It saved his life.

Going to the bell-rope, she pulled violently and the chambermaid appeared after a moment.

"What is the matter, my lady?" she said, starting in wonder as she saw the lady standing in partial undress with her hair falling wildly over her white shoulders and her features expressing the intensity of her agitation, while lying on the floor was Alford still pale and motionless.

"My husband here, pursued by ruffians, has entered my room by the back window," said Rosalie. "He seems dying. What hour is it?"

"It is now five in the morning," replied the maid-servant.

"Good," said Rosalie, "then let a carriage be fetched at once for us, and we will return to our own house."

The girl stared at her in wonder.

"Had I not better fetch a doctor?" she said.

Rosalie frowned.

"Do as you are bid," she said; "I understand my husband better than you. He is suffering from faintness and weakness, that is all. By the time you obtain the coach he will recover."

What she could not do by force she had resolved to do by stratagem.

The girl said no more, but retired slowly from the room.

Well she might wonder.

The whole affair was a mystery.

When she had assisted in undressing Rosalie St. Aubyn, the latter had told her that she had resolved to remain all night, and perhaps the following day.

Now she was going suddenly, and more than this there was now in her room a strange man who seemed to be in the last agonies of death.

The girl was of an inquisitive turn of mind, and she resolved therefore to see if she could discover anything by a little eavesdropping.

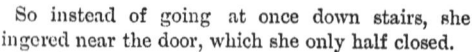

So instead of going at once down stairs, she lingered near the door, which she only half closed.

Peering through, she saw the strange woman kneel down, draw something from her bosom—a small bottle, apparently—and pour a liquid into the mouth of the insensible man.

The effect was magical.

It seemed scarcely to touch his lips before he opened his eyes and stared round him.

It was a wild, half-maddened stare.

Then he closed them again, and murmured, in a low voice—

"Where am I?"

The strange woman stooped down and pressed her lips to his brow.

"Poor Richard!" she murmured.

Then she said, in a louder tone—

"You are with friends—fear not."

The girl, on seeing this, and hearing these words, considered that there was no immediate necessity for her interference, and moved away.

In about a quarter of an hour she returned, and knocked gently at the door.

As she entered the room Alford was seated in a chair, apparently sensible, for his eyes were open wide, and his colour somewhat restored.

Rosalie St. Aubyn was standing by his side, as if she had been tending him carefully.

A sweet smile played over Rosalie's face as the young girl entered.

It was, indeed, no guide to the fierce passion which was agitating her breast.

"If you can oblige me with a cloak to wrap around my shoulders," she said, "I will pay you well for it."

"I will do so," said the girl, who, like others of her class, was by no means averse to making money, "I will do so. The carriage is ready, and I will procure it for you at once."

The promise of reward having enlivened her footsteps, she soon returned, bearing a heavy travelling-cloak, and, Rosalie having given her a handsome gratuity, she led the way down to the coach.

Alford appeared to the unsophisticated girl to be quite recovered from his swoon.

His eyes were open; his colour, as I have said, was restored, and he walked without much difficulty as he leaned upon the arm of his fair companion.

But she little knew the subtle essence which had instilled this seeming life into his otherwise senseless body.

It was the deadly poison which the Poisoners' Society alone knew of.

Like the *Aqua Tofana* of old Rome, it was an indefinable essence, only that while the one killed the other annihilated reason only; made the brain, in fact, stagnant, while the rest of the body preserved its power of motion.

They passed slowly down the stairs, and entered the carriage.

Rosalie waited for a moment until the door of the tavern was shut, and then leaning out of the carriage window, she said to the coachman,

"To Granville House, Putney."

The coachman at once ascended the box, and drove hurriedly away in the direction indicated.

During the journey not a word was spoken.

Alford remained perfectly still, and, in fact, in the same position as when he entered the coach, until they reached their destination.

The carriage stopped at a house of dark and gloomy exterior, surrounded by heavy pine trees.

Rosalie assisted Alford out with every care and tenderness, and the man still walked on as in a dream.

A slight tap at the door was sufficient to obtain admission, and, as it opened, an elderly servant showed himself.

He expressed no surprise on seeing his mistress enter in so strange a garb, or with so strange a companion.

He simply bowed in a stolid kind of way, and at a sign from Rosalie, took Alford's arm, and led him up the stairs.

Here, had he been in the possession of his senses, he would have seen that he was in a large room, elegantly furnished, but with barred windows.

"See that he is put to rest and has all he wants, Martyn," said Rosalie to the man. "Although he is now like many before him, he is no enemy."

And so she left him.

Mad, foolish, wicked woman!

In her own hard, cruel heart, blackened by a purposed indifference to crime, she saw not the fearful injury she had done to him.

No enemy!

No savage tortured by another could have felt more terribly vengeful in his heart against his foe than was Richard Penraven against her.

CHAPTER IX.

A DEADLY CONFLICT.

On the following evening Rosalie St. Aubyn visited her prisoner.

He had recovered his senses partially during the morning.

The drug was of the same nature as that which had been administered to Rupert Dreadnought and Allan of the Glen by the conspirators, and he was only able, therefore, to move about in a dazed kind of way, able indeed to glance out of the barred windows, and move about the room.

Towards evening he was well enough to eat a meal, and, after he had partaken of a few glasses of wine, and some food, mechanically, as would an automaton, he sat by the fire, looking vacantly into it.

Now and then a gleam of consciousness seemed to come across him, and he would start and raise his hand to his brow.

But then the old gloom seemed to settle once more upon him, and he would sit still again, and gaze, like one distraught, into the flames.

Presently the door opened, and Rosalie St. Aubyn entered, her splendidly rounded form cased in a robe of black velvet, so tight as to show every outline of her superb contour.

She closed the door gently without taking the precaution of bolting it, and approached her prisoner.

She knew well he was in no condition to enable him to make his escape.

"Richard," she said, in a gentle voice, "do you know me now?"

He gazed vacantly at her a moment.

Then she held to his nostrils a bottle containing a strong aromatic liquid, and he seemed to revive from his lethargy, shivering violently and gasping for breath.

He glanced at her then in surprise and wonder.

"You here!" he said. "I thought I was dead. Where am I now?"

"You are in *my* house."

Alford shuddered.

"In your house!" he murmured. "Why did you not let me die while insensibility held me in its chains rather than bring me here to endure a long misery?"

"Such is not my wish," replied Rosalie St. Aubyn. "I desire not to torture you. You are wrong there—cruelly wrong. I want to make a compact with you."

"As to what?"

"As to our behaviour towards each other in the future."

"Well, and what want you?" said the helpless man, shivering. "I am cold; give me wine."

Rosalie rose, and, pouring out a large bumper of wine, gave it to him.

He drained it in a draught.

"Now," he said, "I am better. Answer me."

"Listen then," she murmured, "and I will explain. I married you, did I not, when I was a mere child?"

AGNES MAYLAND.

"Yes, if you call it childhood to be sixteen—to be a woman full of passions and daring enough to break hearts and laugh at the ruin you make."

"Stay, waste not the time in recriminations. I have much to say and much to do. Admitted, I was sixteen. I did not love you. You persuaded me into marriage against my will.

"For a long time I strove to be a good and true wife to you.

"But I could not.

"I saw others happier—I heard others more joyous—*you* led me into the society of men whose only enjoyment in life was to fascinate and destroy. I *was* fascinated—I *was* destroyed. You killed my destroyer. I hated you for it then—I thank you for it now."

"Well, and what now?" asked Alford as Rosalie St. Aubyn paused for a moment.

"I love another."

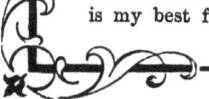

"I know it—Rupert Dreadnought—but it is useless. I have sworn to be his friend; no matter who may be the one who endeavours to injure him, I have sworn to befriend him. Never shall he who is my best friend—who has been instrumental in saving my life—be induced for a moment to fall into such a deadly snare as that you desire to set for him."

Rosalie eyed him with a hateful look in her eyes, as she answered—

"Cannot you forget the past? Can you not, at least if you *will* remember, think that your own folly in marrying me so young was an excuse for my mad folly also? Cannot you think of me as a stranger, and let me go my own way unmolested; I know you love another; I will place no obstacle in the way of your marrying Lesbia Howard; but on that condition I must act as I please with Rupert Dreadnought."

"Never!" said Alford, "never! Though here helpless, in your power, I will never consent to degrade myself by such a compact. Were you a stranger to us it would be just the same— I should think it my duty to warn Rupert against you."

The gleaming hate in Rosalie's eyes became more intense as he spoke.

"Is this your resolve?" she hissed, as she leaned her beautiful form over him.

"It is—in the face of all dangers—yes."

"Then you must die," she said, and again the fatal handkerchief was pressed to his nostrils.

This time it did not take so great effect as it had done at the tavern.

He lapsed into helpless immobility, but he had still the power of hearing and seeing.

He was, in fact, in the same condition as Rupert and Allan of the Glen had been, in the old house by the river.

As soon as she saw the condition into which he had passed, she moved towards a secretaire, and drew from it a small dagger, fine at the point like a needle.

With this she approached Alford.

"Now," she said, "I will give you one more chance. You cannot speak, I know, but you can express yes or no by your eyes. What I wish you to express is this—that you swear never to molest me again, no matter under what circumstances—never to interfere between me and Rupert Dreadnought - never, in fact, to treat me otherwise than as a stranger. Promise this, and you are free on the instant—refuse, and you die now. If you wish to say 'yes,' close your eyes."

But the brave man was not dismayed.

He looked her boldly in the face.

Not a sign was there of yielding.

"Good!" said Rosalie. "You have sealed your own fate."

And, as she spoke, she began slowly unfastening

the doublet of the helpless man, so as to be certain that the fatal instrument would reach his heart.

But Providence still watched over him.

Just as the wretch was about to plunge the knife into his heart, the door was burst violently open, and a woman entered.

A deep veil obscured her features, but this was at once thrown aside, and disclosed the features of Lesbia Howard, radiant with triumph.

The knife dropped from Rosalie's hand.

"Ah!" cried Lesbia. "I am just in time, wretched woman!"

"How came you here?" cried Rosalie, white with rage.

"I heard that Alford was in your power."

"Where?"

"I tracked you to the tavern. They told me of the strange man whom you had claimed as your husband, and with whom you had gone away—he in a helpless state. I knew well who it was by description, and I readily guessed that your country house would be the place to which you would take your victim."

"What right then have you here?" [said Rosalie, defiantly. "This man *is* my husband!"

For an instant Lesbia was staggered.

This man her husband!

If this were true, then she was the infamous, faithless woman who had crushed Richard Penraven's life.

The woman, who really loved him, recovered herself, however, in a moment.

"If it be so," she said, "I should, if I were you, be ashamed to own it. But, nevertheless, husband or no husband, you have no right to murder him, and here I take my stand to defend him."

As she spoke she took from her bosom a pair of small, finely-chased pistols.

A look of scorn passed over the lips of Rosalie St. Aubyn.

"What care I for your threats?" she said. "In an instant I can call to my aid a dozen servants, who will turn you from my doors or destroy you at my bidding."

Lesbia's courage did not for a moment give way.

The man who was more to her then all the world besides, was lying there helpless in the power of his greatest enemy, and if she was unable to deliver him it mattered not to her whether she lived or died.

Rosalie St. Aubyn was unprepared for any display of desperate courage on the part of her antagonist, and Lesbia's next speech took her completely by surprise.

"I fear you not," said Lesbia; "the man whom you have yonder helpless in you power is the only being in the world whom I love. If you slay him, you take from me all my happiness in life. As, therefore, I know that if I leave him in your power you will kill him, I will swear this that if you attempt to cry out I will fire."

The resolute woman, as she spoke, held one of her pistols in a direct line with the head of her enemy.

There was no mistaking the courage which beamed from her eyes, and was evident, in fact, in her every attitude.

"What want you, then?" asked Rosalie.

"You have the courage to murder, have also the courage to defend yourself. Take that pistol, while I retain this, and let us fight."

"You are mad!" said Rosalie. "Duels are for men—not women."

"Nevertheless," said Lesbia, "I am determined that it shall be so. Accept my terms, or you will die like a dog."

Rosalie gazed once more at the woman who addressed her thus with all the boldness and resolution of a man.

She saw in the face of her adversary not a sign of relenting, and she reluctantly, therefore, took up the pistol.

As usual, her heart was full of treachery, and she, therefore, resolved if possible to take a base advantage of her brave enemy.

"Well, then, since you are resolved," she said, "I must agree."

Then, suddenly, when Lesbia least expected it, she raised her pistol and fired.

Fortunately for Lesbia, Rosalie, in her trembling eagerness for murder, took but an unsteady aim, and the ball which was intended for her heart passed harmlessly by.

A deadly whiteness passed over Lesbia's face, her eyes shot fire, and, with a quick, but steady hand, she raised her pistol and fired.

Rosalie St. Aubyn had no time to avoid the shot, and, as the smoke cleared away, Lesbia Howard saw her enemy falling back, with blood spurting from her bosom.

As she fell back, the door was dashed open, and a man rushed in.

A man about five-and-forty, with blue eyes and fair hair, and with but one arm!

"Oh! Redlock," murmured Rosalie St. Aubyn, as she sank down upon the couch, "I am dying!"

"What does this mean?" he cried, rushing forward, and catching his mistress in his arms. "This is murder!"

"No murder," said Lesbia, proudly; "see the pistol still in her clenched hand. On my part, at least, it was a fair duel."

"Let her not escape," said Rosalie, in a faint voice, as Redlock handed her some wine. "Let her be confined in a barred room, and see that this man has no access to her."

"Fear not!" said Lesbia, as Redlock rushed to the door, after seeing that his mistress was safe on the sofa, "fear not! I shall attempt no escape. I came to save that man, and if I cannot do so I care not for life. Do with me as you will!"

Redlock passed out to call the servants, and send one of them for a doctor.

In an instant Lesbia sprang up—rushed to Rosalie—snatched the pistol from her grasp, and then approached Alford quickly, loading the two weapons meanwhile.

"Alford—Alford!" she said, shaking him, "wake—wake! Have you no strength to rise and aid in your own deliverance? Rise—rise! I entreat you. I am here to save you! It is Lesbia, your own Lesbia, who speaks!"

It was in vain she tried this.

He was powerless to rise, and she might as well, in fact, have appealed to a stone statue.

The man who had not been awakened by the report of the two pistols could not be roused by the mere voice of the one he loved.

She had hoped, wildly, for a moment that she could have awakened him—placed in his hand a loaded pistol, and that they could thus have fought their way out of the house.

But this hope was nipped in the bud as Alford looked at her, wistfully, without being able to speak to her, and make her understand by any gestures his utter helplessness. Her bosom heaved, and the tears flew to her eyes.

But she quickly dashed these aside.

This was a time for courage, not for tears.

Thrusting the pistols into her breast, she raised the attenuated form of Alford in her arms, and, approaching the door, was about to pass out when Redlock appeared, followed by several men.

Drawing one of her weapons again, she stood before them blazing with fierce anger and resolution.

"Stand back," she cried, "stand back! The first man who approaches dies!"

There was a momentary hesitation on the part of the men.

There was no doubt in their minds as to one fact.

One, at least, of their number would fall before that pistol held so steadily by that little white hand.

However, this hesitation did not last long.

"Come on, my men," cried Redlock. "Let us not be startled thus by a woman. The pistol has been discharged; fear not."

The men at this made a dash forward, and Lesbia, aiming at Redlock, fired.

The ball missed him, but took deadly effect upon a man behind him, who fell with a loud shriek into the arms of his comrades.

The diversion caused by this bold act gave the brave woman time to draw the other pistol from her bosom and again confront them.

Redlock himself was staggered by this display of courage and precision.

But he was, nevertheless, a determined and resolute man.

When Rupert had accosted him in the street the name of "Dreadnought" had for a moment paralysed his strength, but here there was no such cause.

"Come," he said, "come on, my men; let us make another attempt. On all at once as I bid you."

They quickly and bravely did as they were bidden, and again the fatal report rang out, the bullet sped, and another of the attacking party fell.

She made a dash forward now in the frantic hope of escaping amid the confusion.

But it was all in vain.

She was but one against many, and she had the weight of a man in her arms.

Her courage, kept up to this moment, now at length gave way, a deadly sickness invaded her heart, and had it not been for those around her, Alford would have been dashed down the steep staircase.

"You will be punished terribly for this," said Redlock, as he seized her, and bore her back into the room; "you will be denounced to the Society."

Whatever idea this presented to the mind of the listener, it was evidently one of horror, for a shudder passed through her frame, and she sank down into the chair nearest her.

"I care not," she said, in a low voice; "if he is in your power, I have nothing to live for. What have they done with him?"

"Ask not; he will die; but you, you will, as I have said, be denounced to the Society; and you know what terrible doom will follow that."

Again the shudder came, and the chill at her heart, and she sat still, saying nothing.

In a few more moments Rosalie faintly opened her eyes, and asked Redlock to approach.

He at once approached her.

"Take her away to the fifth chamber," she said; "let her not remain here while the doctor is here. Quick, I feel very faint; more wine, more wine."

Whatever position Redlock held in the household of Rosalie St. Aubyn, he seemed very eager to obey the behests of the wounded lady, and he obeyed with the utmost alacrity.

He brought her the wine, assisted her while she drank it, and then approaching Lesbia, said—

"Now then, follow me."

His voice was harsh and stern.

From him she knew she could expect no pity.

So she rose slowly.

One glance again she gave at Alford, helpless, motionless, all but his wistful eyes.

"And will you not tell me what you are going to do with him?" she asked again.

"I have answered you once," replied Redlock. "I can say no more."

She saw it was utterly useless to ask more, and so in silence she followed her conductor.

He led her up two flights of stairs, and emerging upon a broad landing unlocked the door of a room into which he motioned her.

Resistance being utterly useless, she entered.

It was a place over whose portal should have been written, as over the Hell described by Dante in his "Inferno,"

"Abandon hope all ye that enter here."

It was a dark, gloomy chamber, to which the light only came through a small barred window.

The walls were of a colour which appeared black, and there was no fire-place in which the cheerful companionship of a bright blaze could be secured.

She made no remark, however, but passed in and took her seat upon a chair.

She had not been in this gloomy abode more than a few moments when a wild cry of agony assailed her ears.

The sound reached her, not through the doorway nor the window, but from some other opening in one of the walls behind her.

Glancing round her, she saw a recess covered over by a black curtain.

She at once rose, and, approaching the spot, drew aside the curtain, and beheld a sight which filled her with astonishment.

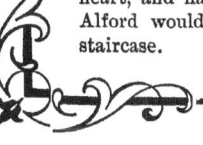

Sloping down from the room in which she sat, was a wide, smooth shaft of wood, and up this came the agonizing cries of a man.

She soon recognized the voice, and trembled to her heart's core as she listened.

It was Alford who spoke.

"Oh, great Heaven!" he was saying, in a half-suffocating voice, "why not have left me as I was in a state of insensibility, and not have roused me into life again that I might suffer thus!"

Then there was a stifled shriek, and all was still again as death.

In vain she listened for further sign of life, and, at length, weary, dispirited, and fearing she knew not what, she seated herself by the little barred window.

CHAPTER X.

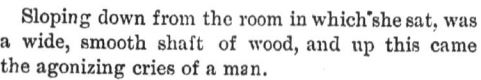

THE MYSTERIOUS VISITOR.

We must leave Alford and Rosalie St. Aubyn for a time, and return to other personages in our story.

Allan of the Glen, as has been shown, was one of the most active friends of whom Rupert Dreadnought could boast.

While Alford and the other mysterious man who was now one of Rupert's friends, worked their ends by intrigue and subtlety, he and Tom the waterman and Allan fought against their enemies by sheer pluck and strength, combined with the use of ordinary common sense.

It is of Allan of the Glen that we must now turn more particularly.

He, of course, as one of the most persistent and energetic champions of the young Earl, was now marked out by the Poisoners for destruction.

He knew, of course, to a certain extent, in what a perilous position he stood.

But no thought of danger made him swerve from the path which he had marked out for himself—the path of unswerving devotion to the man who had saved his life.

It was with confidence the most implicit that Rupert Dreadnought left his house in charge of Allan whenever he had occasion to go abroad alone.

It was one evening that Rupert Dreadnought had gone out with Tom the waterman that Allan remained in Rupert's bed-chamber, according to his master's directions.

It had been a bright day, and the evening had dwindled gradually away from twilight to darkness, so gradually that Allan scarcely noticed the change, but sat there by the glowing embers, never even troubling to light his lamp.

He was sitting thus, when the door opened, and a servant entered, bearing a letter.

"This is for Mr. Dreadnought," said he; "see that he has it, Allan."

"Leave it there; it will be quite safe," said Allan of the Glen. "I shall remain here awake until he returns."

"Shall I light the lamp?"

"Yes; but turn it down," said Allan. "I like this twilight; it brings back old memories."

He sat here for another half-hour thinking of the Hidden People, of his lost Mary Macpherson, of the strange father who had so mysteriously taken him from friends only again to desert him, when he fancied he heard the door open.

He listened and looked, but saw nothing.

Satisfied that the sound was no delusion, he rose, and going to the door found it slightly open.

But that was all.

Everything outside was still.

Along the broad old corridor, moonlight streamed in in ghastly bands, and lay quivering on the waxed floor.

Gentle breezes rushed in from a half open window, but that was the only sound.

Satisfied now that he had made a mistake, he returned to his seat, closed the door, and walked back towards his seat.

As he did so, he turned up the lamp and glanced at the superscription of the letter.

It was in a pretty female hand, one that Allan had often seen before, the hand of Mistress Helen Penraven.

A sigh escaped his lips as he thought of his own lost love, and then he reseated himself before the fire, and once more relapsed into his reveries.

Thinking of bonnie Scotland and his bonnie lassie he at length lapsed into a refreshing sleep.

He dreamed a strange dream.

Dreams, be it said, are always strange, always wild and mysterious.

This was no more so, perhaps, than dreams usually are, but throughout its entire length it was Rupert Dreadnought who was in danger.

No matter in what position Allan himself was in this wild vision, a dark cloud seemed to hang over and shadow the fortunes of Rupert.

It was while dreaming thus that he awoke with a start.

He rubbed his eyes, looked around him, saw that the lamp was burning low, and that the fire was nearly out.

Scarcely had he come to the full consciousness that he had been dreaming, when a shadowy form left the dark gloom behind the head of the bedstead, and darted towards the door, which Allan now saw was half open.

Seizing the first weapon he could see, which happened to be a short dirk, and casting aside, as it were, his drowsiness, he dashed after the intruder.

But he was too late.

Quick though he was, the fugitive was quicker.

Guilt, and a desire to preserve a strict incognito, lent wings to his feet, and ere Allan was within three yards of the window, he had swung himself out, dropped into the darkly-wooded garden, and disappeared.

RUPERT OR THE DREADNOUGHT
SECRETS OF THE IRON CHEST

"AS THE UNKNOWN FLED, ALLAN STAGGERED BACK IN TERROR!"

Allan was not slow to follow his example.

But it was all in vain.

The gardens, even in those days, were not very large in that part of the city, and Allan had soon explored every portion of them.

The fugitive, whatever his errand had been, had disappeared, and Allan of the Glen was compelled to return, baffled and angry, to his chamber.

As he did so, his first idea was to see if the letter was safe.

It was in its former position.

He took it up, and in an instant he saw that some villany had been at work.

The handwriting was still that of a lady, but it was *not* Helen's, though it was an excellent imitation of it.

For a long time Allan thought and pondered.

What new trap was this?

Into what fresh snare did Rupert's enemies design to drag him?

He felt certain that the letter now in his hand was *not* from Helen Penraven, and yet he hesitated to open it.

If it contained any appointment which was on the face of it a trap to ensnare his master, he had resolved to act as Tom had done, adopt a disguise, and foil his enemies with their own weapons.

He could personate Rupert, dress himself in his clothes, and incur the risk, whatever it might be, to save the one who had saved him.

Still it was not the act of an honourable man to break open a letter, no matter what he suspected to be in it, and at length he cast it down on the table again, and with a sigh resumed his seat.

Honour prevented his aiding his master.

He was saved from much debate upon the subject by the entrance of Rupert himself.

Eagerly he seized the letter, but Allan of the Glen detained him.

"Stay, Master Dreadnought," he said, "that letter is an imposture if it seems to you to come from Mistress Penraven. I have a story to unfold—a confession to make, too, for I have slept at my post."

Rupert smiled.

"My friend," he said, "you cannot be expected to watch at all hours. But quick; tell me the story, for I am all impatience to see what this letter contains."

Briefly Allan told his tale.

"Curses on this midnight intruder!" cried Rupert. "He has taken Helen's letter, then, and in that, no doubt, she has mentioned her address."

As he spoke he opened the letter.

Well might he start with astonishment as he read its strange contents.

It ran as follows:—

"One who loves you and has your interest at heart begs of you not to disregard the request made in this letter. At ten o'clock to-morrow night a man will await you on the second arch of London Bridge. You know him not, but do not fear to meet him; his desire, as mine is, is to save your life. Remember the watchword, 'Love and Night.'"

It was, then, from Rosalie St. Aubyn.

Knowing not her name, he yet well remembered the password.

Could it be that the woman whose life he had saved at the peril of his own was now endeavouring to betray him?

No; he could not believe it.

"I shall keep the appointment," he murmured, and as he he said so, his eye caught a postscript, hurriedly added, in a fainter ink:—

"I know well your story. I know that you have repeatedly been the victim of conspiracies and attempts upon your life. Still, keep this appointment. You will perhaps give greater credence to my words when I tell you—when I openly confess to you that the man whom you are to meet holds a high position in the terrible Society which has so long been a scourge to London!"

Rupert Dreadnought started in astonishment.

The confession before him was indeed a strange and unexpected one, coming as it did from the lips of so fair a being.

That she *was* the writer there could not be much doubt, for no one but himself and she knew the password.

"Pray do not go," said Allan of the Glen, as his master told him of the contents of the missive. "Let either I or Tom, or both together, go instead of you, and learn from the lips of this stranger what he requires of you."

"No, no," said Rupert. "I have good reason to believe that this appointment is not a snare, but one that I ought to keep. I shall go."

"You will at least allow us, or me, at any rate, to accompany you?"

"Yes," said Rupert, "*you* can accompany me if you please. That will be quite sufficient."

"You may think so," thought Allan, as he quitted his master's presence, "but *I* will see that you are not deceived."

In the wonder excited by the strange epistle, Rupert Dreadnought had forgotten one thing.

Helen Penraven's letter was in the hands of Rosalie St. Aubyn's messenger, and in that letter her address was given!

CHAPTER XI.

THE MEETING ON OLD LONDON BRIDGE.

On the following night, at half-past nine, Rupert Dreadnought and Allan of the Glen quitted the old house, and made their way slowly towards the place of meeting.

They watched carefully to see if any spies were about, but not a soul was in the street.

Evidently those who expected them, friends or enemies as they might be, made sure of their coming.

It was a somewhat cloudy night, though the moon showed itself at intervals, and when they at length reached the bridge, it was veiled in heavy darkness.

"Now," said Rupert, "you must leave the rest to me, Allan; fear not, if he attempts any treachery I will at once put you on the alert."

So saying he walked rapidly onwards, followed by Allan, who, though keeping at some distance, watched his every movement, and had his sword well loosened in his scabbard.

The person who awaited the arrival of Rupert Dreadnought had been there some time when the young earl approached, and at once advanced to meet him.

To any one who had seen him once before, he could easily have been recognisable.

He was none other than the man with the red gleaming eyes who had so alarmed Rosalie St. Aubyn at the meeting which I described in the first chapter of my story.

He was wrapped now in a large cloak, but he had no farther disguise.

"You have then come to time," said he, as he advanced so suddenly as to startle our hero.

"I always keep my appointments," said Rupert Dreadnought. "This is truly a strange one; but tell me what is its object?"

"We are unobserved," said the stranger; "therefore we can speak freely. You are aware who I am?"

"Yes; the letter disclosed to me the terrible fact of your connection with that society of monsters which has been the scourge and terror of London."

The stranger's brow darkened.

"I have come here," he said, "as a friend, and, therefore, I have a right to demand some courtesy. I have come here to save your life."

"You expect me to believe you when I know that my father fell a victim to your hideous fraternity?"

"I do expect your belief in me," returned the stranger, "for one simple reason."

"And that is——"

"Because I have a debt of gratitude to pay you—a deep debt of gratitude."

The stranger's voice trembled as he said the words.

"Gratitude to me!" exclaimed Rupert Dreadnough. "What mean you? I know you not!"

"You do not, but I know *you* well," returned the other. "You met one evening, not very long since, a youth who was being beset by enemies. You saved his life at the peril of your own, and he is now in your service. That youth has noble blood in his veins, and his father—were he alive—would invoke blessings on your head for rescuing his child from the daggers of low and cruel assassins."

"Of whom do you speak?" said Rupert.

"Of Allan of the Glen!"

Rupert started.

Well he remembered the story which the young Scotch boy had told of the strange father who had rescued him from the dominion of friends only to discard him, and place him under the care of highland robbers and outlaws.

What connection had this man with him or with them?

That was the question he desired at once to solve.

"Who are you, then?" he asked.

The stranger smiled.

"It is not for me yet," he said, "to disclose that secret to you. Time may come when I may consider it safe to do so. But it is sufficient now that I tell you *why* I desire to save your life."

"Yes; tell me quickly now how my life is in danger, and how you propose to save me from it."

"I will. The Society of the Poisoners," said the man, as he drew Rupert Dreadnought further into the shadow, "reckons among its numbers no more respected member than Oscar Penraven."

"He is just the villain to suit them," said Rupert. "It was he who incited them to the murder of my father."

"You have twice laid your father's death at the door of our convention," said the stranger. "It is false. He died by a natural death; at any rate as far as Oscar and the Society are concerned. We had no hand in it. This I can swear. But to resume, Oscar Penraven is your bitterest foe."

"He is, as I am his."

"True. Then it follows that in Oscar Penraven you have an enemy to be feared."

"No, not to be feared; an enemy to be watched and punished."

"We waste time in choosing words," said the stranger. "Let me proceed, for my moments are precious. There is no doubt that within a month you *must* fall a victim to the Poisoners. They are all to a man sworn to destroy you."

"They tried once," said Rupert Dreadnought, "and I was rescued out of the very jaws of death."

"Yes, but that time they had a reason for deferring your death, and they consequently aided in their own defeat. This time they will adopt the means, sure and undiscoverable, by which all their other victims have fallen."

"Granted that I recognise the danger," said Rupert. "What is the remedy?"

"You must join our Society. You must——"

"Never!" exclaimed Dreadnought, impetuously.

"Stay, stay. Ere you speak rashly, listen to all I say. I ask you not (and recollect that in asking you I am acting entirely for myself and the fair lady who loves you), I ask you not to join the Convention in any active way. I simply ask you to take the oaths, to swear not to betray the secrets of the Society, to become a member of it in name only, and I will then give you a password which will be your protection everywhere."

The man's manner was so earnest and sincere that not for a moment did Rupert Dreadnought doubt that his hideous proposition was made to benefit him.

It was a madman's idea of rewarding an honest man, but it was proferred in that form.

"I thank you," said Rupert; "no doubt you have made this proposition to me in all sincerity, but I cannot and will not accept it. No matter to how little extent I was implicated in the doings of your Society, I should still consider myself culpable. I should be tacitly aiding by the mere fact of not betraying. No; I thank you for your wish to serve me, but I cannot accede to your plan."

The stranger heaved a deep sigh.

"I regret this the more," he said, "because another whom I wish to serve is included in the fatal list."

"And who is that?"

"You call him Allan of the Glen."

As he spoke the stranger's voice faltered.

"Ah! he is my faithful servant. I have more, it seems, than myself to defend."

"He was with you when you so miraculously made your escape from the vaults of the old house by the river."

"He was."

"He also then knows our secrets. Can you wonder that he *is* included? But mark you," and as he spoke the stranger pressed Rupert's arm. "I am, or, rather, was, his father's friend, and though I *am* one of the Convention, I wish to save him. Give me, at least, the chance of trying whether he, too, is as obstinate as you are."

"He is here, not many yards distant from this spot," said Rupert.

"He his here!" exclaimed the stranger, excitedly. "Let me then see him."

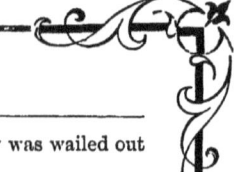

"You can do so," said Rupert. "Here, Allan?"

His clear voice had scarcely rang out over the waters of the dark river when Allan of the Glen sprang forward, sword in hand.

Hearing Rupert's voice, he naturally supposed that danger was near, and rushed forward as for a rescue.

"Nay, Allan, there is no danger," said Rupert Dreadnought; "I called you simply because my strange friend here desired to see you."

"To see me!" said Allan of the Glen. "Whom, then, have I offended?"

The stranger gazed at him for a few moments fixedly.

There was a dreamy, far-off look in his face as he did so.

He seemed to be recalling old memories long buried.

"Young man," he said, "you have, as you are aware, offended the Convention."

"I know of no Convention," he said.

"He alludes to the Poisoners," said Rupert Dreadnought, "those whom, by almost a miracle, we were enabled to escape from."

"How, then, have I offended them?"

"By the simple act of escaping. But listen: this person has a strange and momentous question to put to you."

"And, mark you," said the man, "I ask you to permit him to give me an answer without in any way biassing his opinion."

"Good," said Rupert; "I will not interfere with him. Speak on."

The tall, commanding figure of the stranger moved nearer to Allan, and took his hand.

"Young man," he said, in a voice which betrayed some emotion, "I was the friend of one who, if he had been here now, you would have obeyed—I mean your father. In his name, therefore, I conjure you to give credence to what I have to say."

He then briefly, but with emphasis, made to Allan the same offer that he had made to Rupert Dreadnought.

But it had the same result.

The young man, staunch and true as the young Earl, refused at once.

"Horrid as the proposition you make me is," he said, "I believe you make it out of true friendship; but I must decline it."

A great struggle seemed taking place in the other's breast.

He made no reply.

"Why do you not yourself leave the terrible Convention," said Allan, "you could then aid both me and my master?"

A look of horror overspread the stranger's features, and he raised his hands shudderingly.

"Talk not of it—it is impossible," he said; "nothing but death can release me from a convention to which I am pledged, not only by terrible oaths, but by being implicated in awful deeds. No—no—if this is the only way in which I can serve you, I cannot serve you at all. But oh! Allan, consider—consider the danger you are in."

"Providence and my good sword will protect me," said Allan; "I can make no compacts with the devil."

At this moment a long, shrill cry was wailed out over the river.

The stranger, over whose face a cloud had passed as Allan spoke, started as he heard this cry repeated.

Then, as if acting under the influence of a sudden impulse, he darted forward, and whispered four words in the ear of the astonished youth.

Then he fled away, and Allan of the Glen, as he saw him disappear amid the shadows, staggered against the wall of the bridge, saying in hollow accents—

"My father! My father!"

Seeing the condition of his companion, and hearing words which, under the circumstances, were of such fearful import, Rupert Dreadnought darted after the flying figure of the stranger.

But it was quite in vain.

The irregularly-built old houses on the bridge precluded any moonlight from descending to the thoroughfare; and, indeed, from the manner in which the unknown had departed, it seemed as if he had disappeared into one of these.

Which of them, however, Rupert could not tell.

After a few minutes' fruitless search, therefore, Rupert Dreadnought returned to the side of his companion, who had now to a certain extent recovered himself.

"What ailed you but now, Allan?" he asked.

"A dreadful discovery, Master Dreadnought," returned Allan of the Glen, in a hollow voice, "that man—one of the Chiefs of the Poisoners—declares himself to be my long-lost father!"

CHAPTER XII.

REDLOCK, THE ONE-HANDED.

We must leave Rupert and Allan to make their way home from London Bridge, while we return to Lesbia and Alford.

It will be remembered that when my readers last saw them, a wild and piercing shriek of agony had resounded through Lesbia's room, and that then Alford's voice was heard from below pleading for mercy.

Naturally enough it occurred to Lesbia that it must be something grave in the extreme which would wring from a strong man's lips the cry she had heard, as well as the plea for mercy.

She was correct in her surmise.

They had released him from the influence of the fatal draught, only apparently to increase his misery and suffering.

As soon as the doctor had appeared, and had attended to the wound inflicted upon Rosalie St. Aubyn by Lesbia's pistol, and she had received stimulants which somewhat revived her, she sent for Redlock.

The man of medicine had ordered that she was not for some time to be moved, and coverings were laid over her, therefore, upon the sofa where she had been first placed.

"Bring Alford's chair near to me," she said; "then make him drink a reviving draught. I wish to speak to him."

"If I do so he will escape," said Redlock.

"Not so; see that his arms and legs are well secured ere he drinks," said Rosalie.

For some reason or another Redlock performed her every bidding with the most abject show of haste and obedience.

He seemed a perfect slave to her will, and hastened to quit the room, and return with cords, as if he were bent upon doing a favour to himself.

Though the chair in which Alford had been replaced by Lesbia after her ineffectual attempt to save him was in no respect similar to that in which Rupert had been seized by lion's claws, it was of such a shape that when his arms and legs were tied, it was quite impossible to move.

But a few moments was required to render him a helpless prisoner.

Then the draught was given him and in an instant a tremor, a strange thrill passed through his frame, and opening his eyes he gazed earnestly around him.

REDLOCK, THE ONE-HANDED.

Rosalie motioned Redlock then to depart, and he quitted the room at once without hesitation.

"Richard," said Rosalie, "the one you love has been here."

"I have seen her, I know all," returned Alford, "she tried to save me."

"She did; and she is now in my power," returned Rosalie, with a vindictive smile.

A smile crossed Alford's face also.

"You dare not harm her," he said; "she is, you, one of the Society. Your oath precludes you from harming either me or her."

"And yet she has harmed me. You rave," she said, sneeringly, "the Society does not protect one more than another. Lesbia Howard assailed me. I can show the wound she inflicted upon me."

"Yes, in a fair duel."

"Oh, duels between women are not recognised," returned Rosalie; "at any rate I can end this discussion readily. The Convention may not recognise the right of one member to punish another in private; but supposing that, that one is helplessly in my power. Suppose the Society knows nothing of it, and suppose the heavy clay encloses the dead body of a victim destroyed in secret. What then? Who is to tell the Society?"

"I acknowledge that you can do murder," said Alford, "but you cannot do it single-handed, and there are traitors everywhere who will afterwards betray you."

"True; but remember that Lesbia Howard is no real member of the Convention. She was forced into it; under fear of death she was compelled to take the oath. She hates all there save you. I can denounce her to the Society as a traitor."

For the first time emotion was visible in Alford's face. His pallor increased to a perfect ghastliness, and he bit his blue lips.

"I have moved you, I see," returned Rosalie. "Now I am going to renew our conversation. Lesbia, in one way or another, is absolutely and entirely in my power, and in that way, if in no other, perhaps I can find a way to your heart."

"Of what, then, do you wish to speak?" said Alford, coldly.

"Of Rupert Dreadnought," she answered.

And then, as before, she spoke of her intense passion for the young earl, and besought Alford never to reveal to him her follies and her crimes.

It would be waste of time to repeat her arguments here.

What she said was an impassioned repetition of what she had said before at the tavern where Alford had paid his midnight visit.

But it took as little effect.

He listened to her in silence, with a sneering smile upon his lips, and, when she had finished speaking, he was as stony as before.

Well," she said, her heart feeling a freezing sensation within itself as she gazed upon the man sitting there immovable as a statue, "well, have you nothing to say?"

"Nothing but what I said before—that I refuse," returned Alford, severely. "The oath that I made when I was left by you for another I will keep, in spite of the world."

Again there was a passionate appeal.

She would have thrown herself on her knees had she been able, but her wound prevented her, and she could only look her anguish and her eagerness.

But it was all in vain.

Alford was resolute.

He was determined not to yield, even in the face of the utmost peril, and in his stern face Rosalie read the hopelessness of further persuasion.

Her brow grew dark as night.

Then she raised her hand feebly and pulled a bell-rope.

After the delay of a few minutes, Redlock reappeared.

This delay was necessary to him to enable him to calm himself, to smooth down his features, to change the intonation of his voice.

Unseen by either of them he had been the witness of all that had taken place; he had eagerly drank in the words of both, and his brow had grown dark as night as he had listened.

"What," he murmured, as he heard Rosalie's avowal of her love for Rupert Dreadnought, "what!

after all this striving, after all this slavish obedience shall I lose my prize at last? No, no! Rosalie St. Aubyn shall be mine, or she shall be no man's. I will spoil her pretty scheme."

When he entered the room, however, not a sign of emotion was visible upon his face.

"I find this man obstinate—utterly so," said Rosalie; "place him in the vault."

Redlock bowed, and, re-approaching the door, called for the attendants, who, to the number of six, entered the room.

They then unbound Alford from the chair, leaving his hands and ankles still tied, and then lifting him in their arms bore him from the room.

They carried him at once to the basement floor, then down a murky, damp-smelling staircase of stone, and then halted at the door of the vault.

This they opened, and, ere he had any notice, hurled him, with jeering laughter, into what seemed a black abyss.

It was at this moment that the wild cry escaped him as he found himself, bound and helpless, falling among jagged stones.

Redlock turned fiercely towards the half-drunken crew as they closed the door of the vault.

"Fools!" he cried, "did you receive instructions to act thus?"

"No," said one of the men, in a swaggering tone, "no. But we know right well that when anyone is placed in the vaults it matters little whether he comes forth alive or dead."

"You lie!" said Redlock, angrily, "and have, moreover, exceeded your duty. Enter again, and see that no evil befals him."

As the somewhat disconcerted men turned to do as they were bidden, he retraced his steps, and made his way towards Rosalie's room.

He was madly eager to tell her all he had heard, and to learn his fate.

CHAPTER XIII.

IN WHICH REDLOCK RECEIVES AN UNEXPECTED CHECK.

ROSALIE ST. AUBYN'S wound was a serious one, and it may well be imagined that it was with no degree of pleasure that she saw Redlock again entering her room.

The loss of blood, and the sudden shock, moreover, had severely tried her nerves, and she was just lapsing into a state of slumber when he came in.

She looked up somewhat startled, and, seeing who it was, she frowned.

"What want you now, Redlock?" she said. "Have my orders been carried out?"

"They have," he answered, closing the door, and approaching her. "I have, in fact, more than fulfilled your instructions."

"You have not killed him?" she cried.

A peculiar smile flitted over Redlock's face as she said this.

"No," he said, "as regards Alford your orders have been obeyed. I spoke in regard to myself. I have been playing the eavesdropper."

Whatever colour had been left in Rosalie's cheeks faded away at this announcement, given as it was in a tone of deep meaning.

"And pray, sir," she said, "pray what have you gained by your treachery?"

"You use a wrong term," he said, "it is *not* treachery. Were I desirous of betraying you I should not come to you with a confession of what I had done. But as to *what* I learned it was knowledge that will be of the utmost use to me. In the first place Alford, or rather Richard Penraven, is, it appears, your husband."

"Well."

Redlock's eyes gleamed fiercely.

"You confess it boldly, then?"

"Of what use is it to deny it? You heard all."

"How then—" he began; then he interrupted himself saying, "yet stay, I will first say that I heard also your declaration that you loved Rupert Dreadnought. How does this tally with the hope which you have alway held out to me?"

The eyes of the young girl as he spoke naturally took in the whole appearance of this man who set himself up as Rupert Dreadnought's rival.

Redlock was a man of some five and forty years, and looking older.

His figure, broad and set; his face, here and there, seamed with scars; his whole demeanour that of a coarse and brutal person; while, on the other hand, there was the vision in her mind of Rupert, young, handsome, elegant.

Redlock, though he kept his features under control, saw her action, and readily guessed her meaning; but he awaited in silence her reply.

"It does not affect anything I have said or promised," she said, sullenly, "Rupert Dreadnought is, you *know*, an enemy to the Society; by inducing him to love me I can lead him into a trap and destroy him. You are too impatient, how can I be your wife while Alford lives?"

"Then, if I destroy him, will you swear to be mine at once?"

The girl thought a moment.

"I do not wish him destroyed," she said, musingly. "I wish him to release me from the bond that connects us, and set me free to marry whomsoever I please."

"You love him still then?"

"No, no; but I remember that I owe him much; that he was a friend as well as husband, and that I betrayed him—outraged his best feelings—trampled on his honour, and I will not fill up the catalogue of my evil doings by shedding his blood. No, no. We will compel him to yield all claim to me—to leave England, and then I can be yours; but not till you have assisted me in snaring Rupert Dreadnought. Had you no other proof of my love for Rupert being assumed, you should know that no woman ever loves where she is despised as he despises me."

This, in spite of her weakness, was said with some degree of energy.

But her manner did not deceive Redlock.

He saw at once that it was put on, and he resolved to deceive her, as she was deceiving him.

Madly—passionately in love with her as he was, this man of many crimes only saw one way of securing her to himself.

His plan, which flashed with lightning speed through his brain, was one of duplicity and crime.

He would free Alford, that he might proceed at once to Rupert Dreadnought, and inform him of the schemes of Rosalie; he would then dispose of Alford also, by murder or otherwise, and through this crime wade his fearful way to the love of the one who now regarded him with contempt.

"Good," said he, concealing his real feelings, "you may depend upon my assistance, but I cannot see why you should wish to spare Alford."

"I have told you."

"Yes, but in this case he is your worst enemy. It is incomprehensible."

"Not to me," said Rosalie, shuddering. "I have committed many crimes, but I shrink from this. I remember the time when I loved him, and I cannot —will not—consent to his death until nothing else will avail me."

"Good," said Redlock, taking her unwilling hand, and raising it to his lips, "good—we will work together in this, and as soon as all is accomplished you will be mine?"

"Yes; I have promised."

And ere the words were scarcely formed, or, rather, ere their echo died away, she had formed in her own mind the resolution.

"This Redlock becomes importunate. When he has aided me in bringing Rupert Dreadnought to my feet, *he must die!*"

On quitting the room of the woman with whom he was so madly infatuated, Redlock, who had constituted himself a kind of *major domo* in this mysterious house, proceeded to every part to see that all was safe—that all the doors were locked, and that no prying retainers were about.

Then, in pursuance of his plan, he proceeded first to the room in which Lesbia Howard had been imprisoned.

Here he tapped gently at the door.

Lesbia was not asleep.

In such a house she feared to sleep, and, even if she had under other circumstances been inclined to do so, the cry of despair which Alford had uttered still rang with a dismal echo in her ears as to preclude all idea of rest.

Naturally enough, she feared to open her door at Redlock's summons.

"Who is there?" she asked, timidly, as she approached the door.

"It is I, Redlock."

"What want you?"

"I desire to speak with you a moment. Quick! open, it is important!" he cried, in a tone of eagerness.

The key without was useless to him, for she had shot a bolt within.

What was she to do?

She was safe apparently until morning.

Why not remain so?

"Speak as you are," said Lesbia. "I fear to open the door, knowing you to be my worst enemy—knowing how I tried but now to take your life."

"Fear not," whispered Redlock. "I come to save you; I swear it."

There was silence, and he continued—

"I give you five minutes to consider. I cannot say more here. If you will not trust me I shall go and leave you to your fate."

Lesbia thought a moment.

If this man really was there for an evil purpose; if he came there, in fact, as the emissary of Rosalie St. Aubyn, he could burst open the door.

So, after a few instants' reflection, she turned the key in the lock.

Redlock glanced round him, and entering with stealthy steps closed the door behind him.

"I do not wonder at your hesitation to open the door," he said. "It was simply natural. But when I tell you that I come to save Alford, you will doubt no longer."

Lesbia gazed earnestly into his face.

"To save him?" she said, eagerly. "Oh, could I think this true!"

"It *is* true," answered Redlock. "I will save you both. But on one condition only."

"And that is——?"

"That neither you nor Alford disclose to a living soul the manner in which you contrived your flight. You must swear this."

"Yes; I will swear it," answered Lesbia. There *can* be no harm in such a promise."

"Indeed, no," responded Redlock. "I have my reasons for acting as I do; what they are, matters not to any one, but I have no harm in store either for you or the one you love."

"I swear it, then," repeated Lesbia; "never to a living soul will I divulge this secret."

"Good," said Redlock, as he motioned to her to approach the spot where the mysterious shaft descended. "You see this sloping shaft?"

"I do," said Lesbia; "and from the bottom of it I heard Alford's voice raised in pain."

"Yes, the brutal fellows cast him in headlong upon the jagged stones. I am now about to descend to the vault where he is concealed, and explain to him what I have explained to you. Then, when I call to you, descend the shaft fearlessly. It is of polished wood, and you will descend quickly and safely."

One glance of doubt overspread the features of Lesbia Howard.

Was this a trap to induce her quietly to descend into the living tomb that contained Alford?

Redlock understood her meaning at once.

"You still doubt," he said. "You tell me that even from this place you could recognise Alford's voice?"

"Yes, at once."

"He then shall bid you descend when all is ready," said Redlock; "he would never lead you into danger. And now, for the moment, adieu. Remain here and listen for a voice."

Redlock then stealthily opened the door, and closed it after him, while Lesbia crouched down near the opening of the shaft, and listened.

CHAPTER XIV.

THE VAULT—THE COMPACT—THE CONFLICT AT THE DARK GATE.

When Redlock descended to the door of the vault in which Alford was confined, he found that two

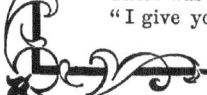

men (whether or not ordered there by Rosalie St. Aubyn he knew not) were seated, or, rather, half-lying near it.

One of them was already in a deep slumber, but the other was making pretence to be on the watch, in spite of his numerous potations.

When, therefore, Redlock approached the vault door, the custodian caught him by the leg.

"What have we here?" he cried, as he turned the light of his lantern upon Redlock's figure. "Ha! Redlock."

"Yes, Redlock," said the one-armed man. "What then? Give me the lantern. I have a message from Mistress St. Aubyn to our prisoner."

The man hesitated, but after a moment delivered up the light without a word.

Then, as Redlock entered and closed and bolted the door after him, he shook his companion rudely until he woke him.

"Rouse up, Jack," he said, in a hurried whisper, "rouse up. There's some devilment up here, I think. Quick! follow me."

"Why, what's the matter think you, Bob?" growled the other, who was in no way pleased at being thus roused from his sleep.

"Mistress St. Aubyn has been for some time in a sound sleep," returned the other, addressed as Bob, "and Redlock, I verily believe, is prowling about for his own purposes. She will pay well if we thwart any secret design of his. Come, let us hasten away. I'll show you where to watch."

Thus incited, the man rose from his recumbent position and hurried away with his companion, who, in spite of the drink that was in him, had had the shrewdness to detect in Redlock's face the signs of some hidden purpose.

When the latter entered the vault and allowed the full light of the lantern to play upon the walls of the subterranean apartment, it disclosed a strange scene.

The place looked more like some underground spot beneath an old abbey or church than a room under an ordinary house.

There were huge, rough-edged stones about, and here and there among them grinned the skull of some victim whose other bones helped to aid in the confusion of the various portions of the vault.

It looked like a dead-house or an adjunct to a dissecting-room, rather than what it was, and the ghastly figure that now presided over it gave to it a more than ever unearthly and hideous aspect.

When Alford had been so hastily and brutally cast in by the myrmidons of the Fair Demon of the place, he had fallen face forward upon the jagged stones, and both his hands and his features were besmeared with blood.

He was now seated on a huge stone amid a pile of human bones and rubbish, and, as the light of the lantern fell upon his gory features, Redlock started at the sight.

Hastily, however, he recovered himself, and approached the prisoner.

"Alford," he said, in a low tone, as he drew from his pocket a flask of brandy, "Alford, I am come to save you. Drink."

Alford made a gesture of repugnance.

"No, no," he said, in a low and painful voice; "I have already had enough experience of your drinks. What want you with me?"

"I am come to save you," repeated Redlock. "Listen, and I will tell you how."

He then briefly explained to him the same which he had explained to Lesbia.

Alford listened with greater incredulity than even Lesbia had done.

He knew nothing of the shaft, or the proximity of the one he loved,

"Your's is a specious tale," he said; "how can I be certain that you are not deceiving me?"

"Ask Lesbia Howard herself. See here. Call to her up this shaft, and she will descend to you. I desire to be revenged upon Rosalie St. Aubyn: is not that enough to persuade you that I am in earnest?"

Alford, without further delay, rose in spite of his great weakness, and, approaching the shaft, called loudly the name of Lesbia.

She instantly recognised the voice.

"I will come," she whispered down the shaft, and in another moment the sound of some one descending was heard.

Another moment again, and she was clasped in Alford's arms.

"Now," said Redlock, "have I deceived you?"

"At present—no," answered Alford; "but until I breathe the free fresh air of Heaven, I cannot be expected to believe you. However, give me the brandy; I am too weak to do anything without some kind of stimulant."

He took the flask, and drank a deep draught.

"And now," he said, "where is my sword?"

"You shall have mine," returned Redlock, as he unbuckled his leather belt, and handed Alford the weapon. "Now hear me. I shall now lead you by a subterranean passage to a spot where you will find yourself on the verge of the high road. Having done so much I can do no more. There may be spies watching you, but I cannot aid you, for to allow Rosalie St. Aubyn to know that I aided your escape would be to bring ruin on all my plans. You have a good sword, and you have one with you who has the courage of a man. You can safely trust to her. See, Mistress Howard, here is a pistol. I am aware that you know how to use it."

"Aye, I know well how to use it," returned Lesbia, meaningly, "and if treachery be intended, I shall willingly risk my life in a conflict."

Redlock then placed in her hand a large chased pistol, and saying—

"Now follow me,"

Led the way to a corner of the vault which was immersed in the deepest darkness.

RUPERT; OR, THE DREADNOUGHT SECRETS OF THE IRON CHEST!

"YOUR WILL IS LAW," REPLIED OSCAR BOWING.

Here he raised himself upon a large stone, and pulled an iron handle, which one unused to the place would never have discovered.

As he did so, a large doorway, coloured similarly to the rest of the stonework, swung noiselessly upon one side, and disclosed a dark and gloomy passage.

At the extreme end of this, a searching glance could discover a faint glimmering of light.

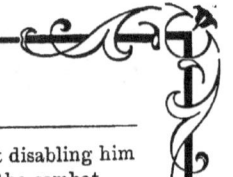

"See yonder," said Redlock; "there is the spot towards which you must make your way. Draw your sword, and keep yourselves on the alert, for you know not what spies Mistress St. Aubyn pays to watch her residence."

Redlock held the door open until the fugitives had passed through.

Then it noiselessly slid into its place again, and they were alone.

They paused not to utter a sound now, but quickly hurried on towards the spot where the glimmer of light gave token of an opening into the free air.

After a few minutes' walking along a sloping ground they reached it.

"Now then," said Alford, "we must be careful!"

The opening was covered with densely growing twigs and undergrowth, and the keen edge of Redlock's sword had to be used to cut this away.

He did this as noiselessly as he could, and in a few moments they were standing on the outside—free!

But Redlock had told them the truth.

There was danger lurking near at hand.

No sooner had they issued from the gloom of the subterranean way than there was a scuffling of feet, and two men rushed forward from behind the shadow of the heavy trees that here overshaded the high-road.

These were the men who had been watching at the door, and had seen Redlock enter the vault.

"Stand and surrender!" cried the man who had been called Bob.

A mocking laugh escaped Alford's lips.

"Escape thus far, and then yield!" he said; "no, no, you must be mad. Never will I yield. Death may overcome me, but if that does not overtake me, never will I submit to be a prisoner again in yonder house of crime! Stand aside there and let us pass."

As he spoke he advanced boldly, sword in hand, and Lesbia also, levelling her pistol, followed bravely by his side.

There was not a moment of hesitation on the part of the men.

They had a grudge against Redlock, who was, as may be imagined, no gentle master, and they knew well that the discovery by Rosalie St. Aubyn of any treachery on his part would be the signal for his ruin.

With this incitement, as well as the expectation of a handsome reward, it may be imagined that they thought not of danger.

Lesbia, who had already seen two men drop before her death-dealing weapon when endeavouring to save Alford from Rosalie, was loth again to shed blood, and as her adversary advanced she held her pistol straight towards him, but did not fire.

"Back," she said, "or death will be your portion."

But the man was not to be alarmed even by such boldness as this.

He advanced steadily and suddenly; making a lunge with his sword he endeavoured—not to wound his fair adversary—but to dash aside her weapon.

In this, however, he failed, and the leaden messenger of death sped on its way.

Not fatally this time, however.

It took effect in his left shoulder, wringing from him a cry of pain, but otherwise not disabling him so far as to prevent a continuance of the combat.

The ball being now spent, Lesbia clubbed her pistol, and awaited thus the arrival of her adversary.

But she was not sufficiently used to conflicts to render her courage of any further avail; and in the space of but a few minutes she was on her knees at his mercy.

He had no desire to kill.

His object was to bind her, and carry her back into the house a helpless prisoner.

Meanwhile, Alford had by far the best of the battle.

Added to his brilliant skill as a swordsman, there was his determination to escape, and gradually but surely he drove back his enemy, wounded and dispirited, towards the open highway.

The minions of the Fair Demon were making a final effort when there was a rush of feet along the subterranean passage as well as the sound of horses' feet along the high road.

A reinforcement of four ruffians came leaping out of the underground way, and at once fiercely attacked Alford, who found himself now sorely beset on all sides.

But there were friends as well as enemies in sight.

No sooner had the villanous crew issued forth into the night than the horsemen, whoever they were, drew nearer, a dark form leaped up towards the villain who was assailing Lesbia, and, with a loud cry of agony, he fell prostrate upon the ground.

A long knife had been, with unerring certainty, plunged into his back.

A dark face peered down over his form, and, after a moment's scrutiny, the friend who had arrived so opportunely raised Lesbia from the ground, and untied the bonds which already confined her legs and arms.

Then Alford saw who it was.

It was his Hindoo friend, Najid.

In a moment after the liberation of the young girl, he was in the middle of the fray, which had not progressed long before the horsemen whom they had before heard arrived upon the scene.

Comprehending instantly the state of affairs, the newcomers, who were two in number, at once leaped from their saddles, and drawing their swords, ranged themselves on Alford's side.

The men who thus had so opportunely arrived were Rupert Dreadnought and Allan of the Glen.

Alford's heart leaped as he gazed upon the noble countenances of these two youths beaming with enthusiasm.

There seemed no doubt as to the issue of the conflict now that their stalwart arms were ranged upon his side; and seeing that Lesbia had now fled out of danger, he redoubled his efforts.

In the midst of the affray he had remembered the promise he had made to Redlock, and saw that if either of the men who had first attacked him were allowed to escape, they would be certain to betray him to Rosalie.

Glad enough, therefore, was he to see the first villain dispatched by the ready knife of Najid, and he with eagerness sought to destroy the second.

He was saved the trouble.

Allan of the Glen saw at once that Alford's adversary was no mean swordsman; and as he leaped from his horse, he thrust his gleaming blade through the back of the man, who fell to the earth with a loud cry of despair.

"Mount," cried Rupert, as he still pressed onward, "and we will place the lady before you. There is no need of your aid to thrash these cowardly miscreants."

Alford, for Lesbia's sake, could have acted on the suggestion, but he had no idea of leaving his brave preservers to punish his enemies alone.

He, therefore, ran to Lesbia, bade her mount one of the horses and be ready to accompany him, and then he rushed back to the scene of conflict.

It was soon apparent, however, that the myrmidons of the Convention had had enough.

Seeing the fate of their comrades, they gradually withdrew towards the mouth of the subterranean passage, and then turning, fled at full speed into the house.

For a few moments Rupert hesitated.

"I have a good mind to remain and set fire to the house," he said; "these dens of iniquity should be rooted out of the land."

Lesbia clasped her hands, and cried with a shudder.

"Oh, no, no," she said, "not that, anything but that. You know not—"

A hard grasp upon her arm restrained her from further speech.

"You forget," whispered Alford, as he leaped upon the crupper of the horse, "you forget that what you were about to say would amount to a forfeiture of your promise to Redlock. We have promised, and, though he is a villain, we must keep that promise, or we cannot hope to succeed. Come, Dreadnought, let us hasten away. I am faint and ill; and eager, moreover, to save Lesbia. We know not how soon we may be beset by larger numbers."

After a moment's hesitation, Rupert Dreadnought and Allan mounted their horses, the latter taking Najid up behind him, and they were soon speeding away on the road to London.

And (the two villains being dead) no one through all this suspected Redlock of any complicity in the escape of the prisoners.

CHAPTER XV.

IN WHICH OSCAR PENRAVEN IS ENABLED TO DO HELEN A SERVICE.

Lady Claremont, at whose house Helen Penraven had been left by Rupert Dreadnought, was a lady of high aristocratic blood, and among the lower orders was no favourite.

The Claremonts had fought at Marston Moor against the friends of the Commonwealth, and among those who still retained a slight tinge of the old Puritan blood, she was, as may well be imagined, anything but a favourite.

There was not a few of these Puritanical people in England, and more especially in London at this time.

As London is now the centre of liberalism, it was then the centre of Republicanism; and many a time did the Lady Claremont, now a widow, hear deep groans and hisses as she entered her rich carriage.

Her husband had been a fervent believer in the rights of the Stuarts, and in her they saw his representative, though truth to tell, it mattered not to her whether George or the Stuarts were on the throne.

At the time of which we are writing the spring had come in chill and damp, and provisions were terribly dear.

Angry words had been spoken; remembrances of the old civil war were brought forward; once more the "accursed" name of "aristocrat" was whispered low, as in Paris some seventy years later.

The authorities took little notice of it.

They regarded the riotous cries they heard as only the result of hunger, and disdained to regard them as implying anything serious.

Hunger was the creator of a terrific Revolution, and a twenty years' war not long after; but the distress in London never approached in its dimensions that in Paris in 1789, nor were the English aristocracy to blame, as were the French.

It was on the evening of a cold, miserable day that Helen Penraven and Lady Claremont were seated in the drawing-room of Claremont House.

Lady Claremont, a lady on the verge of fifty years, was reclining near the window.

They were talking of Rupert Dreadnought, whose arrival they momentarily expected, when suddenly Helen started.

"Hark!" she cried. "What is that?"

Lady Claremont ceased speaking, and both listened.

At first the sound that met their ears was like the far-distant murmuring of the sea; then it swelled in volume as it came nearer and took the form of the loud and hoarse voices of men raised in anger.

"What can it mean?" said Lady Claremont, shudderingly. "And see that red light—what is that?"

They both sprang up, and, approaching the window, gazed out.

A red light was certainly glowing in the sky.

It was the fiercely flickering light of a huge conflagration.

The mob had risen, the riots had begun! They were setting fire to the houses!

Helen Penraven had, in her early childhood, heard rumours of terrible doings in the times not so very far removed from those in which she lived—doings which presaged the downfall of the Stuart dynasty and the rise of daring old Noll.

No wonder, then, that she experienced a deadly chill of the heart as she saw the red flames lapping up towards the sky and heard the mutterings of the angry populace.

"What are they going to do?" she said, turning to Lady Claremont—"what does it all mean?"

"They are hungry and unreasonable," said Lady Claremont. "They will, no doubt, in their mad fury, attack the houses of every one whom they consider to be their enemies. We must prepare for them."

So saying, she rang the bell, and, in a few moments, a man servant appeared, looking white and scared.

"What is it, my lady?" he said.

"The populace has risen for some mad purpose," answered Lady Claremont; "see that the iron shutters are closed, and every preparation made for defence. Be quick, that there may be no chance of the wretches entering."

The man bowed, and hastened away, without speaking, to obey the orders of his mistress, and in a short time the house was in a state of defence, which it would have been difficult for a crowd to have forced in unless they had persevered for hours together.

The preparations were not made too soon.

Hardly had the great chains and bolts been shot into their places, than the roaring, yelling crowd rushed into the open space in front of Claremont House, and began anew their game of pillage.

"See! here is the house of old Claremont!"

"Down with the Claremonts!"

"Down with the robbers of the poor!"

Such cries, and others more terrible still, were yelled out by the hoarse throats of the crowd, and, within a few moments of the time when they entered the open space, the attack had begun in real earnest.

In order the better to see during their hideous work of destruction and revenge upon an innocent woman for the fault of her forefathers, they lit a huge bonfire in the front of the house, made of the straw, and hay, and furniture, which they had dragged from the bakers and corn-shops, and soon, through the cracks in the iron shutters, could be seen the reflection of the ruddy light.

Then came showers of stones, and the heavy blows of sledge-hammers on the door.

The women clung to one another in terror, as well they might.

The yells and mad rage of the crowd without showed plainly what destruction, reckless destruction, was in their thoughts.

Helen Penraven herself was unknown to the mob, but the very fact of her being a friend to Lady Claremont would, she knew well, be enough to condemn her.

"Bread! bread! Give us bread!" shouted the mob.

And then, some of them, more desperate than the rest, came rushing with a huge scaffolding-pole, which they used as a kind of battering-ram against the door, which soon began to give way.

It was at the moment when it was just yielding, and when the women were giving themselves up for lost, that the door opened, and Oscar Penraven entered.

In an instant a wrong view of the case entered Helen's mind.

She seemed now to appreciate the whole of the desperate scene.

The mob were but blind instruments in the hands of her worst enemy.

The place seemed to swim round with her; she faintly murmured Rupert's name, and, overcome by the terror of the situation, she swooned away.

Oscar Penraven rushed forward and caught her in his arms.

"I will save her," he said, as he bore her towards the door.

Lady Claremont had never set eyes on him before.

"Stay!" she cried. "Who are you?"

"Oh! there's no time for babble," he cried; "it is enough that she is in danger, and that at the peril of my life I am here to save her."

And without deigning further words, he rushed away.

Hurrying down the stairs, he made his way to the rear of the premises, and through the little gate in the garden.

Here his carriage was waiting.

To hail the driver, open the door, and deposit the form of his fair and inanimate burden within was the work of an instant; and, giving the man some hasty directions, he entered, and the coachman hastening his horses into a gallop, turned the corner just as Lady Claremont, led by a man-servant, reached the corner of the avenue.

"It won't do to stand here, my lady," said the man, as he caught sight of the fast receding carriage; "that stranger has got away with Mistress Penraven safe enough, and now we must take care of ourselves. If they get hold of me or you, they may kill us. I know a hiding place."

Starting off with him, Lady Claremont soon found herself standing outside a building which was in the course of construction, not far off.

Standing outside until some of his fellow-servants came up, he assisted her into the area, and in another moment they had, luckily unobserved, found a safe refuge, for a time at least, in the cellar, between a pile of timber.

Meanwhile, Rupert Dreadnought had heard of the desperate scene that had been enacted, and, with Stanley Sherrington and a small number of friends and retainers well armed, came gallantly on towards the house—the mob giving way before them—and succeeded in reaching within fifty yards of it just as the door gave way before the continued battering of the beam, and the thronging crew began pushing and crowding in.

There was no time for hesitation.

The watchmen had long been disposed of by the populace, the soldiers had not yet arrived, and so, getting his men into line, Rupert ordered the mob to fall back.

His orders were laughed at, and a volley of stones followed the derisive yells and cries which greeted him.

"All right, friends," he said, "we will fire on them. That will bring them to reason. Fire!"

A volley was immediately poured in among the crowd, from long horse pistols, shooting down several of the foremost rioters.

"On them, boys! Drive them back! Charge!" shouted Rupert, and, waving his sword, he rushed forward, followed by his men.

Stones, bricks, and every sort of flying missiles came hailing down upon them, and one of Rupert's men fell.

But the rest still pressed boldly on, encouraged by the cheers and gallant words of their bold leader, by whose side Allan of the Glen and Tom the waterman were conspicuous for their determined bravery.

They gained ground step by step until they had nearly reached the house, when the mob, now desperate, made a determined stand, having been reinforced by a number of men armed with muskets which they had stolen from neighbouring gun-smiths.

Rupert's position was now critical in the extreme.

It was impossible for his handful of men, plucky as they had proved themselves to be, to stay long against such odds, and he began to fear lest he should be obliged to retreat and leave Helen in her danger, when he heard a loud shout behind him.

Turning quickly round he beheld to his delight a large body of soldiery charging through the streets.

Again facing the mob he shouted,

"Once more, men! Charge them home! down with them! Follow me!"

A volley of fire-arms, stones, &c., were hurled in defiance, but none of his men were hit, and with renewed energy they pushed onward, while the soldiers now coming up, the mob gave way at last and took to their heels in a panic.

By this time flames were issuing from the top of Claremont House, and scores of people, men and women, were in the lower part engaged in carrying off the valuables and wantonly destroying what they could not take away.

As soon as he could, Rupert mounted the steps, and, with his friends, rushed into the house, forcing aside the mad crowd within in a wild search for Helen.

But it was in vain.

Neither Lady Claremont nor Helen Penraven were there, nor was there one to tell how and whither they had gone.

THE ATTACK ON CLAREMONT HOUSE.

CHAPTER XVI.

HELEN IN DANGER.

HELEN for some time remained in a state of unconsciousness upon the carriage-cushion where Oscar Penraven had placed her, and, as soon as all danger of pursuit had passed, Oscar turned to her and raising her from her recumbent position, seated himself by her side, and taking her hand in his commenced gently chafing it, in the hope of restoring her to consciousness.

As he looked into her face, whose loveliness seemed rather heightened than diminished by the deadly pallor which pervaded it, the feeling which had so long animated him assumed its sway in a greater degree than ever.

He had intended to have tried, by restoring her to her friends, to endeavour to do away with the evil impression he had before inspired, but now his old evil wishes predominated again.

Fate having thrown her once more into his hands, he would be losing a golden opportunity should he restore her.

He had rescued her from a dreadful fate; should he, now that the object of his mad passion was in his possession, run the risk of again relinquishing her?

No!

He would not!

Fate had given her to him, and his should she be!

Having arrived at this conclusion, and made up his mind what course to pursue, he leaned from the open window of the carriage, and spoke hurriedly to the driver.

The man, without a word, increased the already rapid speed at which they were going, and altered his course, while Oscar, drawing down the silken blinds of the coach, supported Helen in his arms, and gave himself up to planning the details of the scheme by which he hoped to secure his object.

Within a few moments, however, Helen began to show signs of returning consciousness.

She heaved a deep sigh, the colour began to return slowly to her lips and cheeks, and the lovely blue of her eyes was becoming visible through their partly opened lids.

Oscar started when he witnessed these indications.

He knew well that should she awaken, she would never consent to continue the journey which he contemplated.

Another moment, and she would be once more herself.

In possession of her senses she would listen to nothing from his lips.

What was to be done?

For an instant an expression of disappointment flitted over Oscar's face.

Then, suddenly, as if struck by a bright idea, he brightened at once, and, quickly placing his hand upon his breast, he smiled with satisfaction, as it pressed against some hard object concealed in the inside pocket of his coat.

Quick as lightning he drew forth a small phial containing a colourless liquid, and, drawing the cork with his teeth, he poured a portion of the contents upon his handkerchief, and placing it against Helen's face, allowed it to remain there until she had inhaled the fumes of the liquid for some minutes.

He then gently withdrew it, and gazed anxiously into her face.

The colour had partially returned to her cheeks, tinting them with a flush as delicate as the first faint streakings of dawn.

Her eyes were once more closed, her bosom rose and fell with her gentle breathings, and her features wore an expression of calm and tranquil repose.

Oscar saw this with the most intense gratification.

His rapt gaze remained rivetted upon her pure, unconscious loveliness, until his whole frame became agitated by the intensity of the feelings which filled his being.

Her lovely head lay pillowed on his arm, which half encircled her, and, with eyes aglow and flushed cheek, he stooped his head towards her face and pressed his lips passionately to hers.

"Never," he said, aloud, as he raised his head, "never shall Rupert Dreadnought possess so much loveliness as lies here now in my arms."

The carriage rolled swiftly and smoothly along until it arrived at a plain, rustic gate which stood at the entrance of a long but narrow avenue, shaded on either side by rows of majestic willows, whose drooping branches met overhead and formed an arch of brightest green.

Along this avenue they proceeded until they arrived at a broad lawn, around which a wider road, also shaded with willows, led to a large, old-fashioned house, before the wide porch of which the carriage stopped.

Before Oscar could alight an old female servant made her appearance at the head of the broad flight of stone steps.

"Here," said Oscar, as he opened the carriage door, "here, come and help me to take this lady out."

"A lady!" cried the woman. "Lord sakes! so there is, and as pretty as a picter. Why, she's fainted clean away."

"Yes, she has been in great danger and much frightened," said Oscar. "Let us get her in at once."

Helen was soon carried in and upstairs into a large and elegantly furnished room in the front of the building, where they laid her on a sofa, and after some little time she returned to consciousness.

Pressing her hand to her throbbing brow, she gazed around her distractedly, and said softly—

"Where am I?"

Then, ere the old woman could reply, the dull heavy expression of her eyes left them, and, starting suddenly up, she exclaimed,

"How came I here? Now I remember. The mob—the yells—the oaths—the thunderings at the door—the dreadful fear that overcame me. But who brought me here? Where is Lady Claremont?"

"Don't look so scared, child," said the old woman. "Master Oscar Penraven brought you here in a coach, and told me to take good care of you as you'd been in danger."

"Master Penraven! And where is Lady Claremont?" asked Helen.

"I don't know," said the woman; "only when you came here you had fainted clear away."

Helen rose, and approaching the window, gazed out, and started in surprise as her eyes fell upon the broad lawn, the tall trees, and the artificial lake—a scene which plainly told her that she was far from the crowded city.

She stood a moment as if in doubt whether what she saw was real.

Then turning, she said—

"What place is this?"

"It is the Willow House."

"Whose is it?"

"Master Penraven's."

"Where is he? Let me go to him at once," said Helen, angrily. "This conduct is shameful."

"Well, I'll lead you to him in a moment," said the woman; "but just take a glance at the mirror, and see how disordered your things are."

Helen did, and seeing that her radiant curls had escaped from their confinement, and fallen in heavy masses over her shoulders, she opened a dressing-case standing on the table in search of a comb.

As she did so, she saw a small phial containing a red liquid.

Instinctively she clutched it, and raising it, read the one word on the label—

Poison!

Glancing in the mirror, and seeing that the woman was not watching her, she quickly concealed the phial in her bosom, and having gathered up her tresses, was about to quit the room, when a knock came at the door, and after a moment Oscar Penraven entered, and beckoned to the woman to quit the room.

"I am glad to see you recovered," he said.

"Where is Lady Claremont, and why am I alone?" returned Helen, without noticing his words.

"Because I could only save *you*, and I brought you thus far that you might be out of the way of the furious mob. When I looked behind for Lady Claremont she was beyond my reach, and not a moment was to be lost. If I had left you to save her you would have been sacrificed. Let us hope her servants succeeded in saving her."

"Again I say why am I here? Was there not, in all the vast city, any place where I should have been as free from danger as here?"

"No: the excitement was widespread," said Oscar. "The mob infested a dozen different positions of the town, and no one could tell where its fury might fall. No place was safe, and so I brought you here. Fear nothing! I have sent already for Lady Claremont."

"Then, till she comes, leave me," said Helen, firmly.

"Your will is law to me," he answered; "but you have little faith in my honour."

"I shall have more faith in it if you withdraw at once from this chamber, and leave me to myself," said Helen.

Oscar hesitated but a moment.

Then he bowed deeply.

"As I have said, your will is law," he answered. "Farewell, then, until Lady Claremont arrives!"

"Or until you send me safely to her care," replied Helen.

Penraven made no reply, but, turning away, quitted the chamber.

CHAPTER XVII.

THE MIDNIGHT INTRUDER.

As soon as Oscar had left her, Helen flew to the door, and after securely locking and bolting it, threw herself upon the sofa and gave way to the grief and tears she could no longer controul.

She had no faith whatever in the assurances Oscar had given her of Lady Claremont's safety, and the fears, too, she entertained in regard to herself by no means abated her excitement.

She could not but see in all Oscar's actions a design to force her into the hateful marriage with himself which had long been her horror.

Why else had he brought her so far?

Why to this lonely place, where there were none but his own servants, the willing slaves of his will, no doubt?

As these thoughts filled her mind, her tears abated, and her grief gave place to a wild, uncontrollable longing to fly and make her way somehow back to the city, and seek to end the suspense she felt, no matter what danger she risked.

She rose, and paced the room with heaving bosom and distracted looks.

The night had now fallen, and, as she stepped from the room out upon the wide balcony that surrounded the house on three sides, and looked towards the city with longing eyes, she saw the sky lit up with a red, lurid glow, and ever and anon could catch the distant sounds of bells, and a dull, heavy roar, which came borne to her ear across the country by the wind, showing that the riots were still going on, and that the work of robbery, destruction, and perhaps murder, was not yet complete.

Turning at length from the contemplation of this scene, with all its terrible and sickening suggestions, she once more entered the room, where her ears were startled by a tapping at the door.

She made no response at first, but at length the tappings increased to loud knocks, and she heard the old woman's voice calling—

"Here, mistress, open the door. I bring you a lamp and some supper. It is only me, I assure you."

Thus assured, Helen undid the fastenings of the door, and the old woman entered bearing two lighted wax candles and a tray, upon which was set out various articles of refreshment.

"Now, my dear lady," she said, in a coaxing voice, as she sat the tray down upon the table, "now, my dear lady, you must be faint and hungry, do try and eat."

"No, thank you, I require nothing," replied Helen Penraven.

"What, not eat!" cried the woman. "I never heard tell of such a thing. You needn't be frightened to taste them. I cooked everything myself. Just look at that boiled chicken!"

"You're very kind," said Helen, smiling, "but I require nothing."

"What! can't I do anything for you?"

"Yes, one thing," said Helen, seizing her eagerly by the hand.

"What's that? I'll do it if I can."

"Assist me to leave this place," said Helen—"show me some way of escape from this house."

"Why, Lord a' mercy, my lady!" exclaimed the old servant, "why do you want to get away? Nobody'll hurt you here. Where do you want to go to?"

"To London."

"Oh! my lady, that's not possible. It is a long way off; the roads are as dark as pitch, and full of rioters. You'd be running right into the lion's mouth. Never fear, no harm shall come to you while I'm here, I'll promise. Come, do eat something; you'll be ill."

"Thank you for your kindness," said Helen, "but it is not possible. I could not force myself to eat; but I see the dangers you speak of, and shall remain."

"Well, then, I'll lead you to your bedroom," said the old woman, taking a lamp from the table.

"No, no," said Helen; "I will not leave this room. I feel safer here. Good night. I would rather be alone."

"Good night, then," said the servant, and in a few minutes she had quitted the apartment, and Helen Penraven was once more left to her own thoughts.

The words of the woman had to a certain extent re-assured Helen, so far as any danger she might have feared for herself was concerned, for she felt as though in any emergency she might rely upon such poor protection as she could offer.

With heavy heart, however, she once more sought the balcony, and turned her longing eyes towards London.

Once the thought entered her mind that she could succeed in stealing out of the house unobserved, and fly from the place.

But where could she go, and what other grave dangers might she not encounter in her flight?

She knew not the road by which she had come.

There was no other human habitation visible to her sight, and the high-road was, as the old woman had said, teeming with rioters, who, no doubt, were by this time in a state of insolent drunkenness.

What insults and shame might she not be exposed to on such a journey, on a dark night such as that which now spread its mantle over the country?

She, therefore, reluctantly was compelled to give up all idea of flight, at any rate for the present.

If Oscar Penraven really did intend to inform Lady Claremont of her whereabouts, there would at any rate be a change for the better within a few hours.

At last, worn out with grief and care and the

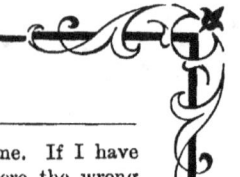

anxiety she had gone through, she re-entered the room, and closing the windows as well as she could and securely fastening the door, she threw herself on the sofa, and exhausted nature yielding, she fell into a fitful sleep.

From this she was awakened by the sound of some one cautiously opening the window at the further end of the room.

She started up at once into a sitting posture, and gazing in the direction from which the sound proceeded, saw by the faint light of the candle the figure of a man emerging from the balcony.

Thrusting her hand into her bosom, she grasped the phial she had concealed there, and rising to her feet, exclaimed—

"Who is there?"

"Do not be alarmed, it is I," a voice responded, which she recognised as that of Oscar Penraven, who now moved towards her with rapid steps.

"Begone!" she exclaimed, "leave me on the moment, for I swear that if you advance a single step further I will drain this phial, which contains a deadly poison, to the very dregs. I am in earnest. If you would not have murder on your soul, stand back!"

Penraven, who had advanced within a few paces of her, paused instantly.

Helen stood with one hand extended towards him, as if to waive him away, while with the other she raised the poison towards her lips.

There was a pause for a few moments, during which Oscar gazed on her with mingled fear, surprise, and admiration; but at last recovering from the shock her words and actions had given him, he exclaimed—

"In heaven's name hold your hand! You are mad. I come not to harm you."

"Then why are you here at all?" cried Helen. "Why do you steal upon my seclusion, in the dead of night, like a thief, if you mean no harm? Your words and acts are at strange variance."

"Because I am mad!" replied Oscar, who, if he was able to entertain no other pure feeling, was at least sincere in his love for Helen; "because I could not resist the temptation to be near you, even while you slept unconscious of my presence!"

"I will hear no more!" she cried, sternly. "Begone!"

"Nay, listen to me!" he exclaimed. "Do not turn from me or drive me hence, but hear me."

"I will *not* hear you!" she exclaimed. "What can you say that will excuse your cowardly act in dragging me here—separating me from those I love, and whose life is far more precious to me than my own—under the false pretence of saving my life, only to doom me to a fate worse, ten thousand times, than death itself? I know well that you will do anything to force me into a marriage with you. But you do not know me! My life is nothing to me, and if you dare attempt to come near me but one single step, I will keep my word, and end it at once! The sin be on your head, not mine."

"By Heaven!" he cried, "you do me wrong! No thought of wrong has entered my heart. If you would but listen to me—if I could but picture to you the pure and holy feeling with which your beauty, purity, and virtue have inspired me, you would be more ready to pity than condemn me. If I have done you wrong in bringing you here, the wrong ended with that act. You have misjudged me. You have mistaken the truest and purest love man ever felt for woman, for base passion! I brought you here that I might tell you of that love—that I might kneel at your feet and beseech you to bless it with your own!"

"You confess this," said Helen, "and yet tell me that your love is pure! Do you pretend to forget that I am the betrothed wife of your greatest enemy? Do you not know that I have sworn never to be your wife? I will not listen to another word, for every one you utter is an insult. I feel myself as much the wife of Rupert Dreadnought as if the ceremony had already been gone through. Once more I bid you leave me. Your carelessness has given me a weapon in this little phial, which makes you powerless to harm me!"

"Do you refuse to listen to me in my own defence," cried Oscar, "and thus condemn me unheard?"

"Yes: when I cannot listen to you without dishonour."

"But you may. Even if you were Rupert's wife, you are free."

"What mean you?"

"That Rupert Dreadnought is dead!"

"Dead!"

"Aye, dead! While you were his betrothed wife, you would have deemed each word I spoke an insult, and would have driven me from your presence with scorn and contumely. Now you are no longer bound, and I am free to declare my deep—my lasting—my unconquerable love!"

"You have invented the story of his death to deceive me," cried Helen, "thinking, in your vanity, that if I believed it I should listen to your vows, and be willing to rush into your arms. But I believe you not. Rupert Dreadnought is *not* dead! My heart tells me so!"

"I tell you he *is* dead. He was killed when the crowd burst into the house."

"I believe you not! Leave me!"

"Oh, woman!—angel!" cried Oscar, with outstretched hands, "you know not the feelings with which you inspire me! My love is free from every taint of grossness—it pervades my inmost soul. It is not force of impulse, it is the offspring of respect. It springs from admiration of your mind—your soul—which gives loveliness to your form. It is not wild and transient, but firm and lasting, and will live upon the slighest hope. Oh! deign to say one word of hope for the future. I will imperil my life by breaking terrible vows I have made. I will leave all and follow you. Only speak to me!"

RUPERT THE DREADNOUGHT

OR THE SECRETS OF THE IRON CHEST

"DISMOUNT, AND FIGHT FOR YOUR LIFE," CRIED RUPERT.

As he spoke with all the fervour of his warm nature, he had kept his eyes fixed on Helen, who, as she listened, so far forgot the fear which until now had prompted her to watch his movements, that she allowed her hands to fall by her side, and removing her gaze from his face, suffered her eyes to search the ground.

Oscar saw this, and quick as lightning he rushed

forward, threw himself at her feet, and seizing the hand which held the poison, grasped the phial and cast it behind him to the furthest end of the room, where it was shivered against the wall.

Helen started back in sore affright, and would have fled, but Oscar held her hand so tightly in his own that she could not withdraw it, when in a voice of tremulous fear, she cried—

"Unhand me, or I will alarm the house!"

"Nay," exclaimed Oscar, producing a pistol from his breast, and forcing it into her hand, "here is another weapon more powerful for your defence. That poison you could but have used against yourself; this you can turn upon my heart if by word or deed I give you cause to fear, or but offend you with a look. See, I am entirely—absolutely, at your mercy. Decide my fate—you cannot misjudge my purpose now. I am kneeling at your feet—my very life at your disposal, imploring you to accept my love—to be my wife if Heaven has removed the barrier between us."

He paused, and Helen stood gazing at him with heaving bosom and wondering eyes.

At length she was about to speak and bid him rise, when the sound of voices and footsteps fell upon her ears, and with a bound she sprang towards the door, which was shaken violently from without, while a voice demanded admittance in loud and agitated tones.

CHAPTER XVIII.

FLIGHT.

In Helen's mind the loud clammering at the door announced the arrival of friends.

To Oscar's calmer brain it was only a premonition of danger.

"Who is there?" he demanded, in a loud voice, at the same time gently preventing Helen from withdrawing the bolts of the door.

"It is Redlock," said a voice. "I have important news."

"Quick, Helen," said Oscar, in a low tone, "retire behind those curtains where no one can see you. These men must not know you are here."

"No; I will remain and demand their protection," returned the young girl, standing resolutely before him.

"For Heaven's sake be not so mad!" cried Oscar. "These are ruffians employed by a society to which I am bound by terrible oaths. They must not see you here; you run the risk of insult."

"Quick! quick!" cried Redlock, in a tone almost of anger. "What delays you?"

"He is Rupert Dreadnought's deadliest enemy—Redlock the One-Handed," said Oscar, sternly, as he began to unbolt the door. "Whatever happens is your fault, not mine."

These words were so evidently dictated by sincerity that Helen no longer hesitated.

She heard without the tramp and oaths of a number of men, and, hurrying across the room, she concealed herself behind the heavy curtains near the casement of the balcony.

Then the door was thrown open by Oscar, and Redlock rushed in, followed by a crowd of men eager and excited.

"What on earth ails you, Redlock?" cried Oscar, as he gazed on the white and ghastly features of the one-handed man. "You look, truly, as if you had seen a ghost."

"This is no time for jesting, Sir Oscar," returned Redlock; "if I am white, it is because I and my fellows here, too, have rushed hither in such eager haste."

"And what ails you, then?"

"I come to apprise you that Rupert Dreadnought and his men are on your track, and——"

A smothered exclamation of delight from behind the curtain restrained him.

"What was that?" he said. "There's some one in the room!"

"No, no," returned Oscar, hurriedly, "it was the wind that stirred the casement. Proceed."

"Well, it is no matter of mine if there are listeners as long as you vouch for their truth," continued the one-handed. "Well, as I was about to tell you, Rupert Dreadnought and a large number of men are on their way hither. Those among the crowd who have refrained from drink, have eagerly enrolled themselves under his banner, for he has denounced you as a poisoner—one of the Chiefs of the Poisoners—and the mob have commenced to shout out—'Death to the Poisoners! they have robbed us of our money and our bread! death to the enemies of the poor!'"

"And how know they their way hither?" asked Oscar; "this house belongs not to the Poisoners; this is my private house."

"I saw how that was done," returned Redlock. "When Rupert and his men, with the aid of the soldiery, drove the mob out of the house of Lady Claremont, and had, in vain, searched for Helen Penraven, a man from the crowd sprang forward, and seized the bridle of the horse upon which Dreadnought rode.

"Rupert at once imagined that it was the first signal of a general attack, and was about to cut him down.

"The man, however, held up his unarmed hand, crying—

"'Hold! You seek Mistress Penraven?'

"'I do,' said Rupert, lowering his sword.

"'Then follow me," returned the man. 'I know where she is confined. She is in the hands of Oscar Penraven, one of the Chiefs of the Poisoners.'"

"Curse him!" murmured Oscar Penraven. "He must be some traitor. Could you not see his face?"

"Yes, I saw his face, and should know it again at once," said Redlock; "but it is not one which is familiar to me. However, the words he spoke were caught up by the crowd, and the cries I have before told you of were yelled from a hundred mouths."

"'Do you swear you are not deceiving me?' asked Rupert.

"'I do swear!' replied the man.

"'Then lead on. Let us at once advance!'

"Then Rupert, with his own friends, and nearly a hundred of the rioters, started on their road hither."

"A hundred, say you?"

"Yes, full that number, and, excited by the recent events as they are, they are no mean adversaries."

Oscar remained for some minutes deep in thought.

What was to be done?

He had in his house only a handful of men, and these were ill armed.

He had no conception of being able to withstand any attack.

The house was a private one, and only known to a few persons as in any way belonging to him.

"We cannot withstand any attack here," said Oscar. "They will destroy us like rabbits in their holes. How far distant are they now?"

"Not far. If you go out on the balcony you can see the lights of their torches and hear the shouts of the rioters," replied Redlock.

Oscar moved hastily across the room and gazed out towards London.

Redlock was right.

The advancing crowd were not more than a quarter of a mile distant.

He could hear the confused murmur of their loud voices, like the far-off murmur of the sea, and see the flickering of their torches.

"Curse them!" he said, as he brushed by the curtains behind which was standing Helen Penraven with a bosom heaving with a fervent hope of rescue. "They will be here before we can make good our retreat, if we go not at once."

"And whither do you propose to fly?" asked Redlock, in surprise.

"To the ruins of the old Abbey—Cronmess Abbey. Go quickly below, see that the postern is opened, and return instantly. I may then have something in which you can assist me."

Redlock saw the necessity of haste, and, though somewhat curious to know for what mysterious purpose Oscar desired to be alone in this hour of danger, he hastened away and closed the door after him.

Oscar then immediately drew back the curtains and bade Helen come forth.

"You have heard all," he said, sternly, as he saw by the bright light in her eyes and the tremulous motion of her breast how full of eager hope of rescue she was.

"I have," she said. "Yes, I have heard that Rupert is coming. Let me stay to meet him. You told me he was dead, and if you mean truly to give me up to Lady Claremont, you will not detain me longer."

"Helen Penraven," said Oscar, quickly, "this is no time for argument. Every moment my enemies are drawing near. Into Rupert's hands you shall not fall again; sooner would I see you stretched dead before me. You have only one minute to decide. Either consent to go with me this instant peacefully, or suffer the indignity of being bound and borne forcibly away."

Delay was everything to Helen.

Already she could hear the sounds of the approaching crowd.

If she could but hold out, Rupert would soon be there. So she determined to brave all risks.

"I will not go quietly," she said.

"Very well," said Oscar, "then you will have to be bound with ropes. You have, while you have been with me, been treated with every respect; now if you submit yourself to the rudeness of strange hands, and oblige me to have you forcibly bound, it is your fault, not mine."

Helen had no idea that he would proceed to that extremity, and still refused to yield.

"I care not," she said. "Do as you please."

With a muttered curse, Oscar quitted her side, and, proceeding towards the door, shouted for Redlock.

In a few moments the one-handed ruffian made his appearance.

"Is all ready?" he asked. "For there is no time to lose. Ah! a lady! I had thought so."

"Yes, all is ready, save one thing," said Oscar. "She refuses to go quietly. Bring up some rope and tell Lambert to come up with you. She must be bound and borne away in the next few moments, or we shall be too late."

"You are right," said Redlock. "Already the crowd is within a stone's throw of this house."

And with that he sped away.

Not yet did Helen Penraven yield.

Oscar had placed in her hand a pistol, and she resolved to brave it out as long as she could.

"You have armed me against yourself," she said, as she raised the weapon; "the first one who lays a finger on me dies."

A cruel smile played over the features of Oscar as she spoke.

"You have a weapon truly, but it is harmless," he answered. "Think you that I would have trusted in your hands a weapon with which you could have destroyed all my long-conceived plans? No; you are in my power. I have behaved towards you like an honourable man, and yet you will not trust me further."

One glance at the pistol told her how she had been deceived.

There was no flint in it.

With a cry of anguish she flung the weapon down, and sinking into a chair, cried—

"Oh! villain, villain—perjured villain!"

At this moment Redlock appeared, accompanied by the man whom Oscar had sent for.

"Now, then," he said, "be quick. Our enemies are at the door; quick, bind her, and follow me."

The sight of the man as he advanced towards her at once altered Helen's resolution.

She could not dream of struggling in the arms of two such ruffians.

So she rose with dignity.

"I am conquered by your villany," she said; "I must yield, and will go with you. But remember that your conduct now is so thoroughly distinct from your professions but a few moments ago, that I shall always hereafter know how to estimate the value of your words."

As she moved towards the door there was a roar of many voices, and a loud knocking at the outer gate.

One wistful glance Helen cast towards the open window.

Then she prepared to yield to her fate, and, with a bosom heaving with sorrowful emotion, she followed Oscar.

The villain was only just in time.

As he descended the stairs and made his way through the stone court to the postern, the summons at the front gate was repeated still more loudly, and loud and angry voices demanded admittance.

CHAPTER XIX.

THE FORCED MARRIAGE.

"Now," said Oscar, as they hurried through the postern, and made their way through the wooded country at the back, "now I shall be able to prove to you that all my seeming harshness is only the result of my love. Before to-morrow night *I* myself will deliver you into the hands of Lady Claremont."

"I cannot believe," said Helen, who was now in tears; "this is only some fresh phase in your villany. I will believe nothing."

"My actions, then, shall prove it," said Oscar. "Come, give me your hand, it is dark, and the road is new to you."

Oh! how bitter where the young girl's reflections, as they passed along that dark path.

Here she was being hurried away by the one whom, of all others, she hated, while only a few yards from her, as it were, was the one to whose bosom she longed to be clasped.

But it was no use repining.

The only thing now to be done was to dissemble and try her utmost to escape.

The Abbey ruins were soon reached.

They were undistinguishable in the dark night, except as a mass of rugged masonry; but Oscar seemed to know his way well, and they were soon descending some rough stone steps leading to an underground vault.

Here Oscar showed Helen a rough, rude bench, gave her his cloak, and bade her sleep while he watched.

This command she resolved not to obey; but tired Nature was too much for her, and she at length relapsed into slumber.

About eight in the morning they were joined by Redlock, who narrated to Oscar and to Helen, who awoke at his entrance, the events of the preceding night.

Rupert Dreadnought and his men had entered the house, in spite of all protest, and searched everywhere.

They were utterly astounded on finding that the bird had flown.

They resolved, however, to keep watch for some time, and see that no communication was had with any one.

After some hours, however, they went away, thoroughly convinced that they were on the wrong scent, and vowing vengeance against the man who had led them there.

This Redlock had heard from another.

He had concealed himself in the woods, and had not ventured near the house until he knew for certain that all were safe out of it.

"But," he added, when he had concluded his tale, "it is not safe to remain here, or to return to the Willow House. Why do you not——"

Helen heard no more.

The rest of the sentence was whispered so gently as to be inaudible.

Whatever it was, however, that Redlock said, it caused Oscar to start and glance at Helen, with a peculiar look which made her tremble.

"Yes, yes," he said, "I will take your advice. This evening we will quit this place, and proceed to the house of Sir Houlston Redclyffe. You, in the meantime, must proceed to London and endeavour to discover where Lady Claremont is, in order at once to request her to join Mistress Penraven. Return now to the Willow House, procure some refreshments for us, and give instructions that a carriage is to be waiting at eight o'clock on the highway yonder near the gate."

At eight o'clock the carriage came round as arranged, and, reluctantly, Helen took her place in it while Oscar took his place by her side, and directed the coachman to drive on rapidly.

It had grown very dark, and they were proceeding at a rapid pace, when the driver suddenly slackened speed, and, opening the little window in the front of the carriage, said, in a voice of alarm,

"We are pursued!"

Oscar listened.

The sound of horses' feet was plainly distinguishable.

"Turn to the left," cried he, "and drive at full speed."

The window was once more closed, and, obeying his master's instructions, the man turned sharply to the left, and drove away at a headlong rate.

Farm-houses, villages, they passed, never once stopping until the steam from the horses obscured the glass of the windows, and the people, as they gazed, thought the horses were running away.

Helen's heart turned faint, and she grasped his arm, tightly.

Her face was absolutely ghastly as she turned and gazed at him.

"You are deceiving me," she said.

"In what way?"

"This is *not* the road to London; you promised me, when we left the Abbey ruins, that you would take me somewhere near London, where I should soon be with Lady Claremont."

"It is true; we *are* still going in the direction I indicated, but, as you yourself heard, we are pursued, and I have been compelled, therefore, to make a detour to the left."

As he spoke they turned again to the right, and up an avenue of lofty elms leading to an old house.

Helen could not see where they were until they were close up to the door of the building.

Then, however, when she looked out, her idea of treachery was confirmed, and her heart beat wildly with emotion.

As Oscar leaped out of the carriage, and bade her alight, she cried in a voice which trembled with mingled fear and anger—

"Oscar Penraven, you are again acting the part of a villain. What place is this?"

"A house where I must hide for a short time—say an hour—until I can baffle my pursuers. Come, let us enter quickly."

"I shall not enter here," said Helen, firmly.

Oscar waited for nothing further.

Seizing her in his arms, before she was aware of his intention, he bore her from the carriage, hurried up the steps, and entered a room in the rear of the building.

There was now no longer any room for doubt.

She had been entrapped once more.

"Sir," she cried, as, panting from her vain struggles, her every limb palpitating with her efforts, she sank upon a chair, "what am I to understand from this?"

Oscar smiled.

"That by a clever ruse, Helen, I have again secured you," he said.

"Wretch, perjured wretch!" she murmured.

"I can afford, Helen, to bear your compliments for a time," he answered; "I trust, however, that time will change you. In two days I shall return to London, taking you with me as my wife."

Helen eyed him contemptuously.

"That can never be," she said.

"To-morrow morning a priest will be in attendance here, and unite us in the bonds of marriage. On the following morning we will return to London. For the present, farewell; the room next to this is your bed-chamber; you will find all you require, for I gave strict instructions that your comfort should be attended to, and a supper be prepared for you. Adieu, fair one, adieu for the present."

So saying he bowed and quitted the room, locking the door on the outside.

When he had gone Helen rose to reconnoitre.

The chamber in which she had been placed was fitted up as an elegant sitting-room, and the bed-room into which it opened was equally luxurious.

Yet the prospect which met her eyes as she gazed out of the casement was anything but inviting.

Nor did it accord in any way with the luxury of the interior.

The moon was shining now with unwonted brilliancy, and as she gazed out she could trace the outline of a ruined wall, and the shattered relics of what seemed a chapel.

"In the morning," she thought, "I shall be able to discover the features of the place before he comes."

She partook sparingly of the delicate viands provided for her, and then threw herself on the bed without undressing, and after carefully locking the bed-room door, to snatch, if possible, a few hours repose.

It was quite evident to her that Oscar did not anticipate any very determined resistance on her part, or else on his next visit he did not purpose coming alone.

On the table, where her supper had been spread, knives had been placed.

THE RETREAT OF THE POISONERS.

One of these, a long-bladed one, with a sharp point, she secreted about her person, and then lying down, as I have said, she slept until the first rays of morning burst into her room.

She then rose eagerly and looked out.

On one side rose the ruins of an old chapel, next to which was the house in which she was, and which appeared to be coeval with it.

Around them the grass grew in wild luxuriance.

Evidently the place had long been uninhabited.

But what struck Helen with some degree of wonder was the fact that beneath her window she could see a deep stone passage, or, rather, the commencement of a series of stone passages resembling cloisters.

Why the idea occurred to her she knew not; but unconsciously she seemed to connect these cloisters with the hope of escape.

How she was to reach them she knew not.

The window was far above the level of the ground, and to reach the intended place of concealment seemed impossible.

Yet she could not banish the idea from her mind that amid these dark and gloomy passages, which seemed to wind and twist around house and chapel, she should find her safety.

As she turned from the window she started back in surprise.

All vestiges of the supper had disappeared, and a breakfast was ready. No knives, however, were on the table.

This time they had evidently thought of the imprudence of supplying her with weapons of defence, and had, perhaps, missed the knife she had secreted about her person.

She searched round and round the rooms, but could find no outlet.

Yet the doors were still locked, and no one had evidently tampered with them, as the bolts were still there.

No one appeared till ten in the morning, nor, indeed, did she hear the slightest sound in the house.

As a neighbouring clock struck the hour, a loud knock was heard at the door.

"Who is there?" cried Helen.

"It is I," replied Oscar.

"I shall not undo the door."

He had locked it on the outside, but she had shot the bolts.

Oscar laughed.

"It is vain for you to endeavour to keep me out,

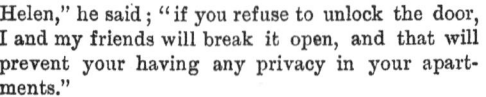

Helen," he said; "if you refuse to unlock the door, I and my friends will break it open, and that will prevent your having any privacy in your apartments."

Helen saw it was in vain to resist.

She unlocked the door.

Oscar entered, followed by five gentlemen, or, rather, men dressed in the garb which is supposed to be the attire of gentlemen.

When they had entered, Oscar relocked the door.

"Allow me, Helen," he said, with a nonchalant impertinence which was infinitely provoking, "allow me to introduce you to the Reverend Edward Tyrell. He has attended at this hour and place for the purpose of uniting me to you in the holy bonds of matrimony."

The Reverend Edward Tyrell was a man about the medium height, with large, bland eyes, a bland smile—a bland style of manner and appearance altogether.

He smirked benevolently at Helen, placed his hand on his heart, and after a low bow turned to Oscar.

"Sir Oscar," he said, "I trust you have with you the licence."

Oscar drew from his pocket the requisite document.

"Here is a special licence, Mr. Tyrell," he said; "read it, and then commence the ceremony at once."

The clergymen took the paper, and read it.

While he was doing so, Helen rushed up to his side.

"Oh, good sir!" she said, "if you are indeed what you seem to be, save me from these men. This perjured wretch—the chief of a society of assassins—is one whom I loathe and hate. I will never be his wife. I am here by force. You dare not perform a ceremony which would be a mockery and a sacrilege."

Mr. Tyrell's pale face grew a trifle paler as he turned to Oscar.

"Sir Oscar," he said, "this is quite a new feature in the case. I cannot perform such a ceremony as this. I cannot marry that young lady to you against her will."

Helen murmured her thanks, and clung to him as if for protection.

Oscar frowned, and pointed to the licence.

"Is that licence in due form?" he asked, sternly.

"Yes, quite; but then—"

"What you now say is quite sufficient," interrupted Reginald, "that licence directs you to marry the persons named in it at any hour and place. Is it not so?"

"It is; but—"

"Do your duty then."

Tyrell handed him back the licence.

"I refuse to proceed," cried he, firmly.

Oscar drew from his breast a loaded pistol.

"I will have no trifling," he said, fiercely, "I have not brought you here to make a fool of me. Proceed, therefore, or I will blow your brains out."

The savage tone in which these words were uttered left no doubt on the mind of the unfortunate man that Oscar would carry out his threat.

What was he to do?

He was surrounded by five men, all evidently bent upon carrying out this compulsory marriage.

He turned to Helen.

"My dear child," he said, "I have a family dependent on me, I cannot, for their sakes, afford to die thus unprepared. You must forgive me if I am forced to read the marriage service."

Helen saw that all was now over.

She sank down and wept bitterly.

"Heaven protect me," she murmured, as the clergyman began to read the service.

And so it proceeded.

Oscar gave the responses, while Helen still knelt and wept, her whole person convulsed with agitation.

As he finished a triumphant smile passed over the face of Oscar Penraven.

"Mine at last!" he whispered in her ear, as he raised her from the ground.

She made no reply, but shrank from him and sat down in a chair by the window.

The clergyman followed her.

"My dear child," he said, "my name is Tyrell, I live at the rectory about a mile from this. Trust in me. I have done a wrong action to save my life. I will sacrifice my benefice if necessary to undo the evil."

"Now," cried Oscar, "let us have the certificate."

"I have no form with me," returned the priest.

Oscar uttered an oath.

"You must make out one on paper then," he said; "I warrant me no attempt will be made to dispute the marriage."

The clergyman did as he was desired, but Helen refused to append her name to it.

Oscar was about to drag her to the table when, springing up, she drew from her bosom the long, sharp knife, exclaiming—

"Come not near me, or I will bury this knife in my breast."

"No matter," he said, "it is as well as it is. The hour will come when you will be glad not to have this marriage disputed."

He then whispered a few words to his friends and turned to Tyrell.

"You must remain here awhile," he said, "It would be unsafe for me to trust you abroad, I should have the neighbourhood about my ears. To-morrow you shall be released, until then I assign you a room in my house."

The clergyman turned pale.

But he made no reply.

He saw, in fact, the utter uselessness of resistance.

Oscar then approached the door and said—

"Follow me."

Then, as if he had forgotten something, he approached Helen and whispered in her ear—

"Expect me, my dear bride, early this evening."

These words produced the most sickening feeling in her breast.

She had just strength to stagger across the room, as Oscar and the five men left it and locked the door; then everything seemed to rise and swim around her.

The furniture, the floor itself, appeared rolling like the billows of the sea.

After this all consciousness left her, and she fell on the floor in a dead faint.

How long she remained in this condition she knew not.

When she recovered she was lying on the bed in the adjoining room, while on the table were preparations for dinner.

As she rose, she caught sight of a piece of paper on one of the plates.

She snatched it up eagerly.

It was a rough scrawl, evidently in a female hand, and ran as follows,

"The gentleman who married you to Sir Oscar Penraven this morning, says that if you escape, you are to go to the rectory. On the left side of the bed is a brass knob, which——"

Here the note broke off.

Evidently the writer had been disturbed.

Eagerly Helen ran to the place indicated.

There *was* a brass knob, but it seemed fixed in the solid wall.

She pressed and tried to turn it, but all without avail.

Then, at length, when she was about to give up the attempt in despair, it slid on one side, a door opened, and she almost fell into a dark abyss.

She looked up and down on either side, but she could see nothing but darkness.

Was this an attempt at murder, and, if so, who was the would-be assassin?

CHAPTER XX.

ON THE TRACK OF THE GUILTY.

To depict the feelings of Rupert Dreadnought when he found Oscar's house empty, and, in spite of the numbers at his back, could do nothing to save Helen Penraven from her worst enemy, would, indeed, be a difficult task.

He was, as it were, thrown back upon himself.

While Helen was in danger, he was precluded from following up the clue to Redlock's whereabouts, and the work of vengeance was indefinitely postponed.

His marriage with Helen, moreover, (even if she could be saved from Oscar) could never take place until after he had fulfilled the five missions which formed the substance of his life work.

The possession of this beautiful creature was what he lived for.

What would his feelings have been could he have known that she had been absolutely united to Oscar Penraven in the bonds of wedlock!

On the evening following the attack on Lady Claremont's house—that is, the evening when Oscar inveigled Helen away with him in the carriage—London had resumed somewhat of its former quiet aspect.

The authorities had taken prompt measures.

Soldiers patrolled the streets, and the people, who, on the night previous had relieved their anger, had been supplied with something to supply their appetites, and relieve their hunger.

On this evening Rupert was sitting writing, when a servant entered with a letter.

The superscription and the contents were both written in a strange hand, and the letter ran as follows:—

"I am aware, of course, that you regard as a traitor and deceiver the man who led you from Lady Claremont's house to that of Oscar Penraven. You are wrong. I am that man, and I acted for the best. Oscar Penraven *was* the one who took Helen from Lady Claremont's, and it was to his house in the country that he bore her. He escaped with her that night when he found you at his door clamouring for admittance; but whither he has gone now, I know not. I did not present myself with this for two reasons; I have no desire to be known, and, moreover, I have no doubt you would assail me as a traitor. However, to prove to you I am not, I will give you a second piece of information that will be useful to you. You are in search of one named Redlock. Go to-night or to-morrow night at ten to the sign of the 'Three Neighbours' in Crane Street, and you will see him. He will come forth a little after ten *alone*. I need say no more."

There was no signature; and the handwriting was very strange.

Rupert placed it on the table before him, and, for a time, gave himself up to thought.

Was this a genuine friend who wrote to him in this strange way?

It was evident that, whoever it was, he knew exactly the state of his feelings in regard to Redlock.

Should he trust him?

He took but a short time to consider.

Yes; the case was desperate: he *would* trust him.

The time now, however, was nearly the appointed hour; eager, therefore, as he was to encounter the one who was specially marked out by his father for vengeance, he resolved to defer all attempts until the following night.

The hour soon arrived, and without insinuating to any one whither he was going, he buckled on his sword—*the* sword which the IRON CHEST had yielded up to him as the instrument of revenge—and sallied forth into the night.

He went out so quietly that no one knew of his departure, or, in spite of his marked reticence, Allan of the Glen would have followed him.

Allan had sworn never to desert him in danger, and he was resolved to keep his vow.

On this occasion, however, he had not the opportunity given him, for when he knocked at Rupert's door, and, receiving no answer, entered, he found the room deserted, and a few lines hurriedly written on a slip of paper on the table.

"Do not be alarmed at my absence; I am upon a special mission. If I meet an enemy it will be but one, and you need, therefore, fear nothing. I shall probably be home ere morning."

Meanwhile, Rupert made the best of his way towards Crane Street, and arrived there just before the clock struck ten.

The "Three Neighbours," where he was told to watch for Redlock, was an old-fashioned inn with a solitary lamp swinging over the doorway and diffusing only a dim light around.

Opposite was an archway leading to some outbuildings, and here, accordingly, Rupert Dreadnought posted himself.

He had not long to wait.

Redlock, a few moments after the hour had tolled, appeared with a friend at the doorway.

Here they paused to speak a few words, the friend then went in and Redlock passed away alone.

A thrill passed through Rupert's heart as he saw him depart.

"Now, then," he said to himself, "the beginning of the end approaches."

Then he loosened his sword—THE SWORD OF VENGEANCE—in its scabbard, and followed in the wake of his enemy.

Redlock was so thoroughly immersed in his own thoughts that he would not have noticed the approach of a more clumsy pursuer than Rupert.

The latter, however, kept steadily on his way, never once making a false step or permitting his shadow to fall where it could be observed by his enemy.

As luck, or, to him, ill luck would have it, Redlock had a desire that night to visit Rosalie St. Aubyn, who was now certainly well recovered from her wound, and was able to move about.

Redlock, however, had been so engaged in other ways that he had had no time to pay her a visit, and he, on this evening, resolved to do so.

His way, therefore, led not through the crowded streets of London, but through country roads, for Rosalie was still residing at her country house.

He, therefore, soon after quitting the sign of the "Three Neighbours," passed into the courtyard of another inn, rang a bell, and within a very few moments was supplied with a horse.

It was now a desperate game.

If Rupert permitted this man to quit the place on horseback, he would certainly lose him for the time.

He resolved therefore to chance it.

Drawing his hat down over his brows, and raising the collar of his cloak, he rang the bell, crying in a loud but altered voice—

"Ostler."

Redlock's horse was already being saddled.

Another ostler bustled out.

"I want a horse," said Rupert, in an undertone; "I want one saddled instantly in order to follow yonder gentleman."

"You are a stranger to us," said the man; "you will, of course, leave money."

"Yes, yes," said Rupert, quickly; "here is a purse of gold, only be quick."

The word "gold" acted magically.

The man hastened in to count the money, but not before he had given orders to a man to hasten the saddling of a second steed, which was ready just as Redlock mounted and rode out of the yard.

It was not Rupert's policy now to seem too eager, and he, therefore, allowed his arch-enemy to ride out of the place before he made any attempt to approach his horse.

When, however, he had ridden for some yards down the street, Rupert leaped into the saddle and followed.

Redlock soon saw that some one was on his track, but perhaps from the same reasons which actuated Dreadnought, he did not attempt to come to an open rupture in the street.

He kept on, therefore, at a moderate pace until they passed out into a more open part of the country, when he put spurs to his steed and began galloping rapidly.

Rupert followed at the same pace, and they soon found themselves in the open high-road, fringed by the budding trees.

Now came the trial.

Redlock had no wish to be overtaken, and finding now that he was really pursued, he gave the reins to his horse, and dashed away at a headlong rate.

Rupert was, of course, not slow in following his example, and at once a tight race ensued.

Both horses were of good mettle considering that they were hired, and for a long time it would have been a matter of difficulty to know which had the best of it.

Presently, however, Rupert began to overhaul his adversary, and that too pretty visibly.

It was no very great distance now to the house of Rosalie St. Aubyn, and Redlock, therefore, who was determined not to be overtaken, made now the most frantic efforts to escape.

But it proved in vain.

After rattling over Driftwood Bridge, and reaching a wider part of the highway, they came alongside, and Rupert cried in a loud and resolute voice—

"Halt! or I fire."

Reluctantly Redlock drew rein.

"Who are you," he said, "who thus stop people on the high road? If your object be robbery, you have stopped the wrong person."

"My object is *not* robbery," answered Rupert Dreadnought, sternly, "it is vengeance."

"Who, then, are you?" exclaimed Redlock, in wonder.

"I am the son of him whose friend you murdered," replied Rupert, raising his pistol, and presenting it at Redlock. "I am Rupert Dreadnought, son of Earl Dreadnought, the avenger of Henry Fortescue. In my father's chest—nay, interrupt me not—I found a skeleton hand—*your* hand; I found also the sword with which you murdered Fortescue. That sword I wear now to avenge him. Dismount and fight for your life!"

The words were uttered in a stern voice that left no doubt as to the determination of the speaker to carry them out to their full meaning.

"This is no fair duel; this is an attempt at assassination," said Redlock. "Why not appoint a time and place where we can meet with seconds and settle this matter properly?"

"*You waited for no seconds when you murdered Henry Fortescue,*" returned Rupert sternly; "therefore, do as I desire or die."

Prize J Ticket.

"IN AN INSTANT REDLOCK WAS AT HIS MERCY."

Redlock saw now that there was no use in delay.

"Good," he said, "since you insist upon this combat, I agree to it. We will fasten our horses to yonder tree and try the issue."

In an instant both had dismounted, and passing over the velvet sward which at the side of the road divided the highway from the hedge-row, they fastened their horses by the bridle to a tree that overhung the path, and returning to the centre of the opening, crossed swords.

"Now then for justice and for vengeance!" cried Rupert, as the sword of Redlock crossed the blade which had entered the heart of poor murdered Fortescue.

The moon, which shed its pale brilliance on the scene of strife, perhaps never shone upon two faces more lit up by fierce passion—the one the passion of anger and fear, the other the passion of resolute justice and revenge!

It was a fight to the death!

Both were eager for each other's destruction.

Any one could have seen this from the fierce and angry glare of their eyes, and the muttered exclamations which escaped their lips.

At length it was evident that Rupert was gaining the advantage.

This was no sooner observed by Redlock than he brought a peculiar mode of conflict into play.

He parried the blows with his iron hook, while he contended with his right, and began sorely to perplex his young adversary. But not for long.

Rupert Dreadnought soon got used to his peculiar mode of behaviour, and aimed to disable the left arm of his foe.

In doing this, at length his sword got entangled for an instant in the iron hook and sleeve, and, suddenly wrenching it on one side, he seized his enemy's sword-arm in his left.

In an instant Redlock was at his mercy, and his sword was drawn back to deal the death blow, when the one-handed man cried—

"Hold! You would save Helen Penraven. If I die the secret shall die with me!"

The magic name of Helen stayed the hand of our hero.

"Drop your sword," he said, "and I will release you. If I find you are deceiving me I will take no unfair advantage of it, but will fight this fight over again."

Somewhat amazed at this proposition, the one-handed man dropped his sword, and, in an instant, Rupert Dreadnought released his hold upon his wrist.

"Now then, speak," he said, sternly, "and to the purpose."

"As I said before," returned Redlock, "you desire to save Helen Penraven?"

"I do."

"Shall I tell you more? Your father instructed you to destroy me, no doubt, but he also said that you were to attempt nothing while Helen was in danger. Is it not so?"

"You are right," said Rupert Dreadnought; "but how did you receive this knowledge?"

"That is a secret which I shall keep to myself," returned Redlock; "but I know this, that by this time, if I am not mistaken, Helen Penraven is the wife of Sir Oscar."

"The wife!" gasped Rupert.

"Aye!—in name at least. I know well his plan—believe me, or believe me not, as you please."

Rupert now was full of intense emotion.

He sheathed his sword.

"Quick—quick!" he said, "tell me where she is concealed."

"Excuse me," said Redlock, "that is my only safeguard. I will conduct you thither, but rather than reveal the place to you now I will renew the fight."

A hundred thoughts rushed through Rupert's mind at once.

What should he do?

He had sworn to slay this man—the sword of vengeance was even now at his side, and yet if he were to slay him he should, perhaps, lose for ever the chance of saving Helen.

Yet was he but trifling with him? was he but leading him into some ambush?

"Redlock," he said, "how do I know you are not betraying me?"

"I can only reiterate what I have said," returned Redlock. "I can only swear that I know Oscar's plan. His scheme was to take her to a certain place, obtain a special licence, induce a clergyman to perform the marriage ceremony, and return to London on the following morning. Whether you believe me or not, I cannot help it. I only say that I can lead you to the place where they are—you may take as many persons with you as you please, but all I advise you to do is to be quick, for, by this time, if Oscar's plans have been carried out, Helen Penraven is his wife!"

"Quick, then!" said Rupert; "let us mount the horses, and start at once."

This was soon done, and in another moment they were speeding away along the road to London.

CHAPTER XXI.

THE CHARNEL-HOUSE.

We must now return to Oscar's house.

There appeared, as I have said, no outlet to the room in which Helen Penraven was immured.

In the dark chasm which opened before her, when she pressed the brass knob in the wall, there seemed no staircase or means of exit whatever.

Did the person who wrote the mysterious note desire to destroy her?

The tone of it precluded the idea.

And then, again, it appeared certain that this was the only method by which the attendant who brought her her meals could enter.

She crouched low on the floor, and glanced down.

Her eyes had deceived her.

What she had thought to be an abyss of darkness was merely a landing, surmounted by a black door.

When she had become accustomed to the dim light she observed a handle.

Turning this she pushed the door open and found herself at the top of a flight of steps.

Hastily closing both the doors, she hastened down, and was soon among the cloisters.

Dark and gloomy enough they appeared, but yet not dark enough.

In the twilight she ran the risk of being discovered.

Where should she hide?

After tremblingly glancing around her she saw beneath one of the archways a door, and resolving to enter here at all hazards, she tried to push it open.

It yielded to her touch.

But the sight that met her eyes was one which would have appalled any one engaged in a less important enterprise.

Heaps of bones lay around.

Bones of every shape and size.

Here a skull—here an arm—here a thighbone—here a rib.

Such a place would scarcely have been selected by any one under any circumstances, and, though running from a fearful peril, Helen felt a creeping horror in her limbs, and retreated.

But then what could she do?

Was not her danger great?

Was she not alone in the house—alone, indeed, as regarded friends?

Would she not, in a few hours, receive a visit from one who now claimed to be her husband, and who was aided by unprincipled men?

Would she not, by returning to that room, or showing herself in the cloisters, where she might be dragged back, be sacrificing for ever her hopes of happiness?

The sound of approaching footsteps determined her.

She entered hastily.

The only fastening to the door was a hasp for a padlock, but the padlock had long ago been taken away.

Seizing one of the small bones, she hastily placed it in the hasp, and concealed herself by crouching behind a huge heap of bones.

But the sound died away in the distance, and no one came.

Then a new idea struck her.

Might there not be some other outlet?

Eagerly she sought round the damp and dirty vault.

No sign of a door was visible, and a long and weary search ended in her being compelled to sit down, breathless and discomfited, upon the stones.

A gloomy afternoon had passed into grey twilight, the grey twilight had passed into a dark night, when Helen, trembling with cold, and tormented, too, by the pangs of a hunger she could not appease, heard angry voices without.

They were the voices of Oscar Penraven and Lambert.

The thought immediately occurred to her that, as the door was not closed before, and there was no visible mode of egress, the fact of its being now shut might excite suspicion in their minds.

Quickly, then, she arose, rushed to the door, and took out the piece of bone.

Then she regained her corner.

The voices became more distinct.

"How can she have fled," said Oscar, as they halted near the door, "is a mystery. She cannot have found the brass knob, and the window was unopened."

"Have you searched both rooms well?" said Lambert.

Oscar replied impatiently—

"Yes, yes; there is not a corner in either chamber I have not ransacked. She must be out here somewhere."

Lambert laughed drily.

"Perhaps she's in the bone-house," he said; "let's go in."

"No, it is not likely she's there; the sight of the hideous relics would alarm her."

"Not in such a case as this," returned Lambert. "She's evidently resolute against having anything to do with you, and would, I think, gladly accept death if she had to choose between it and you."

Oscar took no heed of the bad compliment thus paid him.

"Well, then," he said, "we will begin with the bone-house, as it is the first of the vaults. *We can close them up as we proceed and thus make sure of her!*"

Close them up!

What words of horror were these?

Words implying nothing less than a long, lingering, terrible death by starvation!

Death but a few feet underground beneath the hum and busy life of the world!

Death, when those who loved her were seeking her, and might walk unheeded over her living tomb!

Death, just as life was young and hopes were brightest!

They approached.

She feared no longer the dead, but the living.

Down over her, therefore, she dragged the huge pile of bones until they covered her everywhere, and the relics of mortality touched her very lips.

The first horror gone, they alarmed her no longer.

Poor remnants of lives long lost, why should she fear them?

The hearts which had once beaten within those frames, what had they not suffered! What anguish had they not endured before they shuffled off this mortal coil, and fled away to other realms of existence!

The two men of crime entered.

In Lambert's hand was a lantern.

The bright light from the bull's eye flashed hither and thither over the dark and murky walls like a jack-o'-lantern, showing here a furrow made by decay in the old walls—here a brick displaced—here a skull, grinning alone in a corner—here a skeleton lying in grim silence on the oozy and uneven ground.

Lambert laughed coarsely.

"This is a pretty place for a bride to hide in on her wedding night," he cried. "I doubt very much if we shall find our bird here."

Even Oscar shuddered.

A terrible dread invaded his heart at the thought that to avoid him the girl he had so much outraged had hidden herself among those grinning skulls.

"You are right," he said, "quite right. Helen would never conceal herself in such a place as this. Come away!"

Lambert drew him back as he was moving off.

"We are less likely to be overheard here than anywhere else," he said, "so let me ask you one or two questions. Depend on it those skeletons, of which you seem so much afraid, will not resume their flesh to attack you."

"Speak on!" said the young man, impatiently.

"You speak your own thoughts, not mine, when you talk of fear."

"In the first place, then," said Lambert, "what about this parson?"

"I do not understand you."

"What are you going to do with him?"

"Leave him here."

"What, to die?"

"No; he will find some means of escape. But before we go we will slip beneath the door the key of his room. He will find it in the morning, and, by that time, all will be well. But come—let us be going. While we remain here the girl may escape. Let me but find her now," he added, with a muttered curse, "and she will have but a sorry wooing of it."

They then quitted the bone-house and secured the door without by fastening the bolts.

Helen's heart sank within her.

"Heaven help me!" she said, as she disengaged herself from the skeletons and emerged from her terrible hiding-place; "Heaven help me and guide me from this place."

There was, indeed, but a dreary prospect before her.

On the one side starvation, on the other the love of Oscar Penraven.

Of these two she greatly preferred the former.

CHAPTER XXII.

AN UNEXPECTED DELIVERER.

ANOTHER day passed.

On the night following the evening of her escape, Helen Penraven, wearied and faint, fell asleep.

She awoke in the morning racked with the terrible torments of a fierce hunger, to find not far from her side a jug of milk and a piece of bread.

Some one, then, had discovered her hiding-place.

Whether it was friend or foe she could not tell, but it certainly seemed unlikely to be the latter.

Any companion or parasite of Oscar Penraven would have dragged her forth into the light of day to a doom more terrible than death.

After satisfying the cravings of her appetite, she rose and approached the door.

It was still fastened, and the bone she had replaced before retiring to rest had not been touched.

There was a mystery here.

There seemed no outlet, and yet some one had not only seen her but had entered and supplied her with food.

But the very mystery seemed to console her.

The same unaccountable secrecy had hovered over her dwelling in the old house.

So, as I have said, another day had passed away.

Night once more veiled everything, and deeply veiled it too.

Helen could see the light through the chinks of the door, and so as evening closed over her, she knew it by the fading away of even the muffled light within her dismal cell.

During the day, and more especially the afternoon, she had heard voices without, and among them she seemed to recognise the voice of Oscar Penraven.

In the old house, too, there were murmuring sounds as of people hurrying to and fro, and discussions in angry tones.

But as night closed in, there was a lull over everything, and the place appeared to be deserted.

It was about nine o'clock, and Helen was in that state of dreamy reverie that she might almost have imagined herself to be asleep, when she heard a noise above her head, which caused her to start and look up.

It was difficult, indeed, to distinguish objects in the darkness, but as far as she could tell it seemed to her that a face was peering down at her through the muffled light.

Suddenly a swinging lamp of peculiar construction was let down to the ground by a string.

Then she could see two feet and a pair of legs, which she could just distinguish as those of a female.

Then appeared the body, and a girl of some nineteen years of age dropped to the ground.

She was a pretty girl, with a pleasant, happy face.

It was Agnes Mayland, Tom the waterman's sweetheart.

She smiled sweetly as she entered.

Then she gathered together a pile of skulls and bones, so as to form a seat, and sat down.

"Well, here I am," she said.

"Yes, I see," said Helen, smiling, in spite of herself, "and tell me why?"

"I am come to save you. Do you see that hole up there where I came through? Do you think you could scramble up there?"

Helen looked up, and saw that there was a rope hanging down.

"Yes," she said, "I think I can climb up."

"Well, you can take your time," responded Agnes, "they are all gone."

"Are you certain?"

"Yes—yes—they are gone—every one of them, and if you follow me I'll save you."

So saying, she, without further parley, clambered up the rope, and in a moment after Helen followed her.

Though not quite so active as Agnes Mayland, she was soon at the top, for the girl was there to aid her ascent.

As soon as she had squeezed herself through the narrow opening she rose to look around her.

It was a strange place in which she found herself, the interior of an ancient church.

Around her, jagged and decaying, were the walls of some edifice, in which, at one time, hymns of praise had risen to heaven.

Above her, the eternal skies, forming for a time its roof, smiled down, as it were, upon the relics of man's frail creation.

And the still night air told her of the liberty she inhaled at every breath.

On the cold stones she knelt and prayed earnestly for a few moments; then she turned to Agnes Mayland.

"And who are you," she said, "who have done me this unexpected kindness?"

"I am Agnes Mayland, the cousin of Tom the Waterman. Master Dreadnought knows him well."

"Yes—yes," said Helen, "I know him well, too. Many a time his brave arm has been raised against my enemies. But how, in the name of wonder, did you come here?"

"Well, returned Agnes, smiling, "it is a curious story. I was staying with some friends at a farm-house near, when I heard that a gentleman of the name of Penraven had taken this old house, which for some time had been untenanted; I heard, too, that he was going to be married, and wanted a maid-servant. One of the girls at the farm wished to go, but I was determined to find out the mystery, and so, by a little gratuity, I was enabled to go as the young girl's substitute. It was I who wrote you the note, but I was interrupted and could not say more. Now let us hasten, for fear any one should be on the watch."

They had soon set out on the high road, and after showing to Helen the way to Mr. Tyrrel's house, Agnes kissed her warmly, and returned towards the farm-house.

Mr. Tyrrel's house was situated about half-a-mile beyond the old ruin which Oscar Penraven had rented.

The Ruins, as this place was called in the neighbourhood, had not been inhabited for years, and when Lambert made so sudden an offer for it, it was at once accepted.

The edifice had originally been a Catholic church, and the house adjoining it had been set aside for the residence of the priests.

Both, however, had been nearly destroyed by fire, and had never been restored.

Mr. Tyrrel, as I have said, was a married man, and he was under the thumb of his wife.

What Mrs. Tyrrel said was right, and had to be done, no matter how much it affected the reverend gentleman in purse or feelings.

Equally, it may be imagined, that what Mrs. Tyrrel did not like, Mr. Tyrrel dared not do.

When, therefore, Helen arrived at the door of the rectory, she was ushered at once into the presence of Mrs. Tyrrel, who sat be-ringleted and be-ringed in her arm-chair, which, for want of a better, was her throne.

She surveyed with much mental disturbance the face and form of the beautiful girl, both begrimed with dust.

"Who are you?" she said, sternly.

She always disliked pretty girls.

Helen told her story.

Mistress Tyrrel eyed her superciliously.

Such was a rule; she, in fact, delighted in saying that she was a check on her husband's rash charity.

When Helen had finished, she waited a moment and then said—

"And do you expect me to believe this most extraordinary story?"

Helen flushed crimson.

"Certainly," she said, with quiet dignity, "I claim your belief."

Mistress Tyrrel smiled.

"My husband," she answered, "has just left for London. He would certainly have mentioned the case to me if it had been a deserving one. I must beg you, therefore, to excuse me if I decline to have anything to say in the matter."

"MY MISSION IS FULFILLED," SAID RUPERT.

Faint and weary, Helen turned from the door.

What could it mean?

Had the clergyman, who had seemed so kind to her, deserted her at the last moment?

What was she to do?

She had not a penny, not an idea of the road, not a conception of the distance she would be compelled to walk before she reached London.

Nevertheless, weary as she was, and dark as was the night, she resolved to make inquiries at the nearest house, and commenced her journey at once.

As she had so resolved, she heard footsteps approaching, and fearing every one now, she turned in alarm.

It was a woman with a baby slung at her back.

Helen waited for her to come up.

"Which is the way to London?" she asked.

The woman gazed at her in wonder.

"London did you say, mistress?" she asked.

"Yes."

"Well, then, you're coming straight away from it. But it's a long way; you can't be going to walk it."

Helen smiled sadly.

"Yes, indeed I am," she answered; "I'm obliged to do so. I've no money—no friends here, and until I get to London I've small hope of getting either."

"I'm going part of the way," said the woman, "I'll put you on the road."

So they plodded on together.

She need not have blamed Master Tyrrel for anything that had happened.

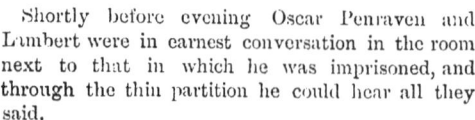

Shortly before evening Oscar Penraven and Lambert were in earnest conversation in the room next to that in which he was imprisoned, and through the thin partition he could hear all they said.

"There is no doubt," said Oscar, in a tone of vexation, "that Helen has somehow or another escaped."

"Certainly she is gone," said Lambert; "that girl, Master Penraven, was never meant for you. She has escaped you in every way. It has all been your own fault, however, for you have had her in your power half-a-dozen times."

"I'm not such a villain as you are," said Oscar Penraven; "besides, I love her truly, and took no advantage of opportunities. However, she is no doubt by this time in London. We must follow. Go and see if all is ready."

They were, of course, utterly unconscious that the clergyman could hear what they said.

He heard all.

He heard, too, a stealthy step creeping along the passage and stopping before the door.

A chill pervaded his form.

What did this mean?

Did they intend to murder him?

His suspense was of short duration.

There was a rustle on the floor, and then his eager eyes caught the glistening of a key.

He seized it eagerly.

"They are going away," he thought, "and are leaving me the means of escape. Heaven be praised."

He listened again.

He heard them depart; he heard their voices lessen in the distance and their carriage roll away along the hard road.

Then all was still.

Only a short time he waited to be certain he would not be discovered.

Then he unlocked the door, and went out softly.

There was no need for precaution.

It was quite evident that the house was entirely deserted, at any rate for the time; the doors were wide open; the outer door ajar; everything denoted a hurried departure.

With a heart full of gratitude for his own escape, and the signal failure of Oscar Penraven's schemes to ruin for ever the happiness of Helen Penraven, Tyrrel issued from the house, and made his way home.

He was satisfied, from the conversation which he had overheard between Lambert and Oscar, that the young girl had escaped, and was now on her way to London, or perhaps at his house.

When, therefore, he arrived at the rectory, he merely asked—

"Has any one been here?"

"No one, sir," said the servant.

Then he entered the presence of his august wife, listening calmly to her reproaches for his conduct in remaining absent a whole night (he a minister of the gospel, too); and then stating quietly that business of an important nature demanded his immediate presence in London.

To London, therefore, he proceeded at once, with the intention of handing over to justice, if possible, those estimable friends, Lambert and Oscar Penraven, and also to discover what proceedings were necessary to annul the marriage, such as it was, between Oscar and Helen.

Meanwhile, Helen plodded on.

The woman who was with her had come many miles, and when they reached Sainton, a little village some four miles from the ruins, she entered an ale-house to have some refreshment.

Helen hung back.

"Why don't you come in?" said the woman.

"I've no money," returned Helen, in a low voice.

The woman laughed.

"It ain't to be supposed you have any," she said, "after going through all you have told me. Come in, and share with me what I have."

So they went on together until late at night, when they slept in a barn.

In the morning they parted.

"My husband is working at Exham," said the woman, as she left her companion, "and I'm on the tramp to meet him. Here's shilling, if that'll help you."

She placed it in Helen's hand, and made off before Mistress Penraven could make any comment.

Helen watched along the road—watched her until she faded away and disappeared in the distance, just as she must now fade and disappear for eve from our story.

Then once more she went on her lonely way, thinking how hard the world must be when she, innocent and pursued by deadly enemies, could find no help.

But so it was.

Against her claims to aid, the hearts of all seemed closed.

Some sneered, some laughed at her, some insulted, none helped.

No one cared, as it appeared, to waste upon her a kind word, much less a kind action.

Some looked from her pretty face to her torn and dirt-stained clothes, and regarded her as the authoress of her own misfortunes.

Some shut their doors rudely in her face—others scouted her.

All combined to drive her well nigh to despair.

Yet she went resolutely on.

On—on! though the weather was cold and the wind howled dismally, and the storm clouds gathered over her head.

On—on! though her legs trembled beneath her, and her tongue clove to the roof of her mouth and her heart was faint and weary!

On—on! without food—without a word of kindness—almost without hope.

On—on! until passing from the high road along a bridle path, she found herself suddenly in a churchyard.

The church itself was ruined, but the tombstones still clustered round it.

It was a dreary place to stop in, but she could go no further.

Fainting with cold and hunger, and almost too desperate to know what she was doing, she sank down upon a mound, and lost all consciousness.

Picture her to yourselves, fair readers, whose

homes in these courting days are lit by the smiles of husbands, or fathers, or brothers!

Picture her to yourselves as she plodded on through starless nights and sunless days; and then think what were the feelings of her desolate heart when she lay down to die upon that churchyard mound beneath a black and stormy sky!

CHAPTER XXIII.

ON THE WRONG SCENT.

It will not surprise those of our readers who are acquainted with the character of Redlock, the one-handed, to know that in his heart of hearts he intended to deceive Rupert Dreadnought.

There was a curious mixture of feelings in his mind.

In the first place, Rupert Dreadnought was, as he himself declared, his natural enemy—his hereditary foe.

In the next place, he had a wish for him to be taken out of the way of Rosalie St. Aubyn, either by fair means or foul.

Loving Rosalie as he did, the assassin of Henry Fortescue saw, of course, in Rupert a formidable rival in his affections.

And yet to destroy him would take him out of the path of Oscar Penraven, who was another rival.

Better was it, then, to permit Rupert to discover Helen, and marry her; or if Oscar *had* married her, to wait and ascertain the fact before destroying Rupert.

In this, however, he did not see his way clearly.

To lead Rupert Dreadnought to the house which Oscar had chosen as the scene of the false marriage, would be to permit Oscar to know of his treachery, and this would, therefore, be courting destruction for himself.

What, then, was he to do?

The traitor soon decided.

He would lead Rupert to London, suggest the propriety of procuring the assistance of his friends, and then, while he was arranging matters, he could make good his escape.

"We must hasten on," he said, as he rode along by the side of his companion, "or we shall be too late. This evening was the time fixed by Oscar Penraven for the solemnization of the marriage ceremony; and, unless some strange accident has occurred to assist her, Helen Penraven is by this time his wife."

A thrill of terror and mad rage ran through the person of Rupert Dreadnought as Redlock spoke.

"By heavens!" he cried, "if she *is* forced into this union with a man whom she hates, there is no punishment that I shall consider too terrible for him. On—on! let us spur forward!"

"You had better seek the assistance of your friends," suggested Redlock, as they sped onwards at a still more rapid rate; "*he* will not be there single-handed to meet you, and it will be of no avail for you to proceed thither alone. You understand, of course, how far our compact extends. I'll lead you to the house, but my sword will not be drawn against my friends."

"Good," said Rupert, "I will take your advice most certainly. Oscar will find that there are bright swords and strong arms always ready to defend me and mine."

After a rapid ride they reached Rupert's house, the bell of which our hero rang hastily and loudly.

No one in the house had expected the return of the young earl before morning, and it was, therefore, with some degree of surprise that the servant who put his head out of window saw Rupert standing at the gate.

In a few minutes after the gate was opened, and our hero and his father's foe entered together.

It may seem strange that Redlock should thus deliberately put his head in the lion's mouth, but the truth was that from all he had heard of Rupert's character he felt not the slightest fear of treachery.

Dreadnought might be a terrible and uncompromising enemy, but he was also an honourable man.

In a few moments Allan of the Glen and four of Rupert's servants were dressed and ready to start, while, within a quarter of an hour, all were equipped and mounted.

A sharp look-out had been kept on Redlock, and when all were ready he was placed in the centre.

Then he gave the word, as a direction which way they were to go, and off they started.

My readers already know how Helen Penraven escaped from the hands of Oscar Penraven, and that by the time Rupert was on his way she was already beyond his reach.

We will not, therefore, linger too long on the details of this journey.

Suffice it to say that the golden streaks of morning were inundating the country side as Rupert and his friends, with their captive guide in the midst, drew up for refreshment at a roadside inn.

"Are we far now from our journey's end?" said our hero, turning to Redlock, as they drew rein.

"We are not," replied the one-handed. "Yonder, among the trees, some mile distant, is the spot."

As he pointed to a place where the bright rays of morning were tipping the summits of the trees, a bright thought suddenly struck him.

He would deceive Rupert, and so avoid, also, the consequences of what he most dreaded, the anger of Oscar Penraven.

He knew that near the house which had been selected by Oscar for his nefarious purpose was another inhabited by two old maids.

He would point *this* out to Rupert as the one in which Helen had been confined, and he trusted to his own cleverness to entirely deceive him.

"I am all impatience," cried Rupert, as his friends were quaffing eagerly the ale, so cool and refreshing after their long ride. "It is but a mile more; let us ride as for our lives."

So on again they dashed.

In a very few moments they reached the house.

"Now then," said Redlock, in a voice of sincerity, "now then, I beg that I may be acquitted of all blame. *This* is the house, but I know nothing of how many men Oscar Penraven has with him. As to that you must, of course, accept the responsibility."

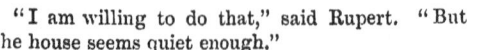

"I am willing to do that," said Rupert. "But the house seems quiet enough."

"That, of course, is on purpose to throw you off the scent," said Redlock. "Two old women are there who pretend to be owners of the house, and who will deny all knowledge of the matter. You, of course, understand how to dispose of them."

"Yes, yes," said Rupert. "Now then, Allan, follow me."

A loud knock at the door brought to an upper window an old lady, who poked out her head enveloped in a frilled nightcap.

"What do you want, master?" she asked, in a trembling voice, as her eyes fell upon the group of mounted and armed men.

"Instant admittance," cried Rupert. "Open the door, or we shall break it down."

"Certainly, certainly, you shall be admitted, gentlemen," said the old lady, who, of course, having nothing whatever to do with Oscar or Helen, was in a state of utter bewilderment, and closing the window, she hurried down.

In the few minutes which elapsed, however, two things had been done.

In the first place, a boy whom the old maids kept to do odd jobs was dispatched by a back way across the fields to the parish constables.

In the second place, a couple of huge bloodhounds, which were kept for the defence of the old ladies and their property, were let loose in the hall.

It was a rather dangerous experiment thus to act, for the old women knew nothing of the errand upon which Rupert and his men were paying them so early a morning visit.

But the looks of the party were so fierce, that they had put them down at once as highwaymen.

Presently the door opened a few inches, a chain being kept up, but the aperture being sufficient to show just the faces of the two desperate bloodhounds.

"Now, gentlemen," said the old lady, in as firm a voice as she could command, "now, gentlemen, what is it you require?"

"I desire to see Sir Oscar Penraven," returned Rupert Dreadnought; "I have come here for the purpose of rescuing from his clutches the young lady whom he is holding here by force."

"You are talking to me in riddles," returned the old lady, eyeing him in intense surprise; "I know of no such people."

"I anticipated that such would be your answer," returned Rupert Dreadnought, "but it will not suit me. Open the door; I intend to search the house. And, if you set any value on the lives of those dogs of yours, remove them, or they will be shot."

The parish constable's house was not very far distant from the house in which the old ladies resided, and they, therefore, resolved to make as much resistance as possible and delay, so that there would be a chance of a rescue.

"You must either be mad, or you must intend to rob my house," replied the old lady. "I shall, therefore, refuse to open the door. Burst it open if you please, but do not expect that I am going to yield without a struggle."

Then, in an instant the door was flung to, and they were once more on the outside.

In an instant Rupert dismounted, as did the rest of the troop.

One man was left with Redlock, to see that he did not effect his escape, and the others immediately commenced an attack upon the door.

Allan had brought his hatchet with him, and, as he had done once before, he soon began to make an impression upon the woodwork.

The deep growls of the bloodhounds could be heard as the work proceeded.

But they were undismayed.

Again and again, taking it in turn, they drove the sharp steel into the woodwork, and soon they had made a hole sufficiently large to allow a man's hand to be inserted and the bolts withdrawn.

The old ladies had not counted on this.

They began, seeing the daring way in which the assault was being made, to suspect that really some mistake was being made, and one of them—the younger of the two—once more approached the door.

"Gentlemen," she said, "I feel certain that you are making some error. If there was a man in the house, do you suppose he could be such a coward as to leave us here helpless? He would come to our assistance."

"Believe not a word they say," whispered Redlock.

"You may be telling the truth in this respect," replied Rupert Dreadnought, "there may now be no man in the house, but that is no reason why Helen Penraven should not be here. I have reason to know that she *is* here, and I *will* release her or destroy the place."

"I solemnly declare," said the ancient dame, "that we know not what you mean."

There was such an air of sincerity in her voice and manner as she said this, that she, for the moment, convinced Rupert.

He turned to Redlock.

"Are you certain that we are at the right place," he asked, "or are you deceiving me?"

"Considering," replied the one-handed traitor, "that I never came here with Oscar, I cannot swear that he came to this spot at all. All I know is, that this was the place he told me—this was the place he hired—this was the place to which he ordered his coachman to drive when he carried off Helen Penraven. More I cannot tell you. I am not deceiving you, but if you believe so I am in your power, and you can act as you please. I think I should indeed be mad to attempt it under present circumstances. Search the house and see for yourselves."

RUPERT

OR THE DREADNOUGHT

SECRETS OF THE IRON CHEST!

"THE LANDLORD, SEEING THE LADY, IMMEDIATELY OPENED THE DOOR."

Urged on thus by the traitor's plausible words, Rupert returned to the shattered doorway and drew from his belt a double-barrelled pistol.

This he levelled at the dogs, who were now baying savagely and leaping up at the aperture.

There were two reports, and then the two faithful creatures were stretched dead on the floor.

To undo the bolts within was now no difficult matter, and in a few minutes the party of besiegers stood within the hall.

In spite now of the tears and remonstrances of the old ladies, who were nearly terrified out of their lives, they were seized and bound, and left in a room in the basement while a vigorous search was made throughout the building.

"You'll be punished for this," sobbed one of the poor old creatures, as Rupert quitted the room. "I've sent for the parish constable."

"Good," said Rupert; "we must then be all the more rapid in our movements."

Every nook and corner of the place was soon searched.

But, of course, nothing was found.

Not a trace was to be seen of any female inhabitant, save the old ladies, and not the slightest sign, moreover, of any secret doors or passages.

"I have been deceived or *you* have," said Rupert to Redlock, as he descended to the hall; "but what have we here?"

"It is, I suppose, the parish constable and his friends," said Redlock; "I saw them hurrying along the road. We had better mount and ride away. If there has been any mistake, it might prove a somewhat awkward affair."

There was no doubting the wisdom of these words.

Deceived or not, there was no use in remaining, and the idea of being arrested and locked up in a country gaol was infinitely revolting to Rupert's mind.

Besides, what time would not be lost before he could prove the truth of his story?

"Mount, my friends," he said, pointing to the crowd, who were now not many yards from the front gate. "Mount, and let us be off."

"But the two old ladies," suggested Allan.

Rupert smiled.

"We will leave the parish constable the task of seeing to their comforts," he said. "At present freedom is everything to us, and yonder crowd seem evidently inclined to dispute it with us."

It was a strange rabble that the parish constable had brought with him.

Having an idea that one of the most daring bands of highwaymen then known in England had gathered round the house of the old ladies—feloniously and murderously intent—he had not deemed it prudent to rush to the scene of action with the aid only of his two assistants.

He wisely imagined that any daring knight of the road would simply laugh at them.

He had, therefore, enlisted the sympathies as well as the persons of a number of valiant citizens, who now, to the number of at least fifty, were approaching, armed with sticks, and old muskets, and pitchforks, and divers other weapons.

Rupert and his friends had but time to mount and reach the front gate, when the throng of people surrounded it.

"Now, then," cried he; "I fear we have made an error, and we must not be taken. Do not, however, hurt these people unnecessarily. Strike with the flat of the sword, and ride them down, but do not kill."

Drawing their swords, they struck the spurs into their horses' flanks, and dashed forward.

But they were met with a most vigorous resistance.

"Sieze the thieves! Capture the highway robbers and murderers!" cried the parish constable, flourishing his sword, but wisely keeping in the background.

Those who were behind and safe, therefore, pushed and pressed on those in front, so that the points of some of the pitchforks entered the horses' chests, and made them plunge and heave like mad things.

"Now, then," cried Rupert, and with the flat of his sword he struck the foremost man on the side of the head, and sent him sprawling on the ground.

His fall was the signal for the utter defeat of the rabble.

Upon him fell several others, among them the parish constable, and, putting spurs to his horse, Dreadnought leaped clear over the fallen group.

His friends were not slow to follow his example, and, amid the yells and screams of the disappointed crew, they were seen cresting the hill, and dashing away on their return journey.

CHAPTER XXIV.

SAVED.

BEFORE following any further the fortunes of Rupert and his friends, we must introduce our readers to a man who is hurrying along the road towards Essex from London.

As the moon breaks from behind a cloud just as he enters St. Luke's churchyard, a short cut to the high road, and inundates the ruins of the edifice destroyed by a recent fire, we see Tom the waterman.

As he passed beneath the ruins of the church, he saw something in the moonlight lying on a mound—the mound of a newly-made grave.

He stopped still and gazed at it.

It seemed like the form of a woman.

He approached therefore and spoke.

"My good woman," he said, "tell me what is the matter."

There was no answer, and kneeling down, therefore, he took her hand.

It was cold and clammy.

He raised her up then and the moonbeams fell full upon her face.

"Great heavens!" he cried, "it is Helen Penraven, and she is dead."

She did, indeed, seem dead.

A livid pallor had overspread her features and her, limbs appeared rigid.

But heaven had ordained it otherwise, and saved her for many more trials.

Her eyes slowly opened, glanced at Tom, and then with a shudder she closed them once more as if to shut out a dream of horror.

The scene was scarcely one calculated to reassure her.

The sky was grey and monotonous.

On one side rose the ruins of the church, shattered by a conflagration and blackened by smoke.

Round them were the tombs, white and grey with

time, and here and there leaving a slant from the subsidence of the earth.

In the darkness she did not recognise Tom.

"I am Tom the waterman, don't you know me?" he said.

A faint smile passed over her lips, and her eyes again opened.

"I am cold and hungry," she said, "I feel as if I were dying."

Her words were uttered in a whisper—a low whisper, like the voice of one in the last stage of life.

Gently he raised her up, and set her up with her back against a tombstone.

Then, drawing a flask from his pocket, he poured some brandy down her throat.

This had the desired effect of reviving her, and she staggered to her feet.

"I will try and walk now," she said.

"It is quite useless," replied Tom; "I will carry you to the nearest inn, where you can obtain refreshment, and repose also for the night."

He took her up in his strong arms as he would have done a child, and bore her away through the tombs.

Many times during that strange journey he stopped and listened, and hid himself and his charge in shadowy corners.

He thought, naturally enough, that treacherous enemies might have pursued her, and be even now on the watch.

The noises which alarmed him, however, were but the voices of the night; the sighing of the wind; the swaying of the trees; the creaking of the branches.

At length the welcome light of an inn appeared in view.

This was the spot where Tom had originally intended to rest for the night before pursuing his journey by the stage coach towards the very spot where Rupert and his men had so recently been, though with a far different purpose.

He was on the road to join Agnes Mayland, his sweetheart, at the farm, where, as we have said, she had been stopping with some friends.

Now, however, all his plans were changed.

Pledged as he was to aid Rupert in all his plans, his duty to Helen Penraven demanded that he should abandon his journey for the present, at any rate, until he had placed her safely in the hands of her friends.

The inn was closed when he reached it, for Helen was a weighty burden to carry so far, but the landlord seeing him bearing the form of a lady, apparently insensible, immediately opened the door.

"An accident, sir?" he inquired, in a kindly tone, as Tom entered and sat down on a bench.

Tom placed Helen by the side of him on the bench, and said—

"No, not an accident exactly. This lady, the betrothed wife of a gentleman I know, has lost her way, and is cold and hungry. Let her have a hot supper and a warm bed, and *I* will pay."

"Good!" said the Boniface, as he closed the door. "There is a large fire in the parlour yonder. Take the lady in there, and I will rouse up my wife."

Tom gently helped Helen into the parlour, which though roughly and uncouthly furnished, was at any rate warm.

A cheerful fire blazed in the grate, and, seated by this, Helen narrated the events which had brought her to this sorry pass.

"Cheer up, Mistress Penraven," said Tom, as the landlady appeared, bearing some hot soup, and some other warm comestibles. "To-morrow I'll take you to Dreadnought House."

"But the marriage—the marriage!" said Helen, shudderingly. "Oh, how I dread to see Rupert."

"The marriage!—a fig for it!" said Tom. "Don't distress yourself about that. It's no marriage at all, and can be set aside directly. Eat your supper, mistress, and get to bed, or you'll be tired to death by the morning."

"Yes, I will try and eat if you will join me," said Helen, with a pleasant smile.

"With pleasure," said Tom, "for I'm very hungry, too, I can assure you."

And so Tom the waterman and the daughter of the baronet sat down together to their meal, after which the landlady took her to a bedroom, where a nicely warmed bed was provided for her accommodation.

But any hopes as to her speedy recovery were destined to be nipped in the bud.

The morning found her in a low fever, unable to raise her head.

She was feverish and helpless, and sometimes even incoherent in her talk.

Poor Tom felt quite in a dilemma.

"What am I to do?" asked the brave, simple fellow of the landlady.

"Well, you can't do anything," said that worthy lady, with a smile; "if you know her friends you'd better go and tell them at onne. She *must* stay here."

"That *will* be the best," said Tom. "I'll start for London at once. You have a horse, I suppose, to let me?"

"Yes, my master'll let you have his own nag," said the woman; "and, meanwhile, I'll send for the doctor."

"Thank you, thank you many times for your kindness," said Tom, as he turned to seek the landlord. "Master Dreadnought will reward you handsomely."

Then a sudden thought struck him.

"Stay," he said, "I have forgotten one thing. Whoever comes to see her *without me* (except, of course, the doctor) don't you admit him. She has just escaped great danger at the hands of lawless men, and they are most probably in pursuit of her."

"Never fear," said the landlady. "I see you're kind to the lady, and she knows you. I won't let any one else come near her."

Within three hours Helen, who had fallen into a heavy slumber, awoke to find Rupert and Lady Claremont sitting by the side of her bed.

About this part of my story I will not linger.

It will suffice to say that it took but a short time to restore Helen to health, and that it was not long before she was enabled to return to London.

The question then came where would she be most safe?

Lady Claremont's home was certainly not the spot which could be chosen as a place of refuge; and it was suggested by Tom the waterman that she should adopt a disguise, dress herself in humble habiliments; in fact, assume the position for a time of Agnes Mayland, and remain in quiet seclusion at his mother's house.

This, as a most sensible solution of the difficulty, was at once accepted by Rupert Dreadnought.

"But," said Tom, "there's a much easier way out of this, Master Dreadnought."

"And what is that?"

"You love Mistress Penraven, and she loves you. Why not marry her at once?"

Rupert smiled.

"Tom," he said, "your solution of the difficulty is one which I would gladly accept. But it is impossible."

"And why?"

"Can you ask me when I have explained to you that at my father's deathbed I took a solemn vow never to marry Helen until I had fulfilled every mission left for my fulfilment in the Iron Chest. The very first of the five missions is not yet accomplished."

"Ah, well," said Tom, "of course it's not *my* place to advise you; but if it were *my* case, and Agnes Mayland, my cousin, were the one in danger, I'd marry her first, and fulfil the missions afterwards."

Helen was, on the very evening of her return to London, transferred to her new quarters.

Willingly, indeed, she went, although to such a humble home.

After all she had been made to suffer, it seemed to her a palace.

Another matter also came to light as soon as Helen was restored to health.

Rupert then learned how utterly he had been deceived by Redlock, and he at once dispatched Allan of the Glen to the house of the old ladies with a handsome compensation for all injuries received, accompanied by such apologies that the ancient dames were compelled to receive the matter agreeably.

These matters having been settled, the hour approached for vengeance upon Redlock.

The one-handed was still a prisoner in Rupert's house; and on the evening after Helen's removal to Mrs. Braxley's, Rupert resolved to bring matters to an issue.

CHAPTER XXV.

IN WHICH REDLOCK FIGHTS HIS LAST BATTLE.

It was in the large banqueting hall of Dreadnought House that Rupert awaited the entrance of Redlock, the man with whom he had now to fight a duel to the death.

Redlock entered with a pale face, but yet not one in which any emotion or fear was visible.

When the door closed behind him, and he found himself alone with Rupert Dreadnought, Allan of the Glen, and Tom the waterman, he folded his arms, and, looking round with a sneering smile, said—

"Well, am I brought hither for execution?"

"You know well that you are not," replied Rupert Dreadnought. "You are come here to fight a fair duel, although, considering that not many days ago I held your life absolutely at my mercy and gave you but a reprieve, I might commence from the point where I held my sword at your throat."

"And pray where are my seconds?" said Redlock. "Is it fair that you in case of need should have two friends here to aid you and I be alone, to die, perhaps, unnoticed? What is my guarantee that if I get the best of the fight I shall have fair play?"

"I told you upon a former occasion," returned Rupert, sternly, "that you waited not for seconds when you murdered Fortescue. However, I will not be hard upon you to such an extent. If I can have any proofs that my messenger will not fall into any ambush, I will send to some friend of yours and let him be present."

For an instant the face of Redlock brightened.

But only for an instant.

In this concession there was only hope of justice, no hope of safety.

"Well," he said, "send for my friend. I will give you the address now. But it is some distance hence."

Rupert saw through this ruse at once.

It was a pretext for delay.

"If you have no friend near at hand," he said, "I shall not send. This night must decide between us. I can see in your suggestion a plan for deceiving me, and, after the manner in which you betrayed me in regard to Helen Penraven, it is not likely I shall trust you."

"Be it as you please then," replied Redlock, "I have no friends near save those who would come rushing here in a body. Promise me two things First, if I succeed in destroying you, I may go scot-free."

"I promise; and the second demand," said Rupert Dreadnought.

"Is, that if I die, my friends may be allowed to know how I fell. If yours is a just cause, you should not be ashamed to tell the vengeance you have taken."

"Be it so then," said Rupert; "write upon a piece of paper the name and address of the person, and give it to Allan yonder. Then both he and my other friend there will retire and leave us alone with locked door. The odds will then be even."

Redlock advanced to the table where stood the materials for writing, and hastily wrote out a name and address.

Then he placed the paper in the hand of Allan of the Glen, and turning faced Rupert, sword in hand.

"Now," he said, in as firm a voice as he could command, "I am at your service."

Allan of the Glen and Tom the waterman then retired from the room, and Rupert proceeded to the door to lock it.

As he did so his back was turned towards Redlock.

In an instant the treacherous villain conceived an idea worthy of his antecedents.

If he could thus, unawares, slay Rupert, there were no witnesses to know whether it was in fair fight or not.

Suddenly darting forward, therefore, he made a

lunge just as Rupert Dreadnought had turned the key in the lock.

He missed his aim, however.

The sword only grazed Rupert's left arm slightly.

"Treacherous villain," cried our hero, starting round and eyeing his adversary fiercely. "Well do you carry out your murderous character. But, by heavens, you have committed your last assassination. I feel within me the strength and determination to destroy you. This sword I hold in my hand was once red with the blood of Henry Fortescue, my father's friend—you will now see how, whetted with the blood of the murdered, it will find the heart of the murderer! Come, cross swords. My brain is on fire. I can brook no further delay."

His words but expressed his looks.

Disgusted beyond endurance by this last attempt at treachery on the part of Redlock, his eyes shot fire, his features assumed a deadly pallor, and his lips, too, were white and quivering.

He was in a fierce passion, but yet his hand trembled not.

His nerves were firm for the battle.

Redlock seemed to read his own fate in the eyes of his adversary as they crossed their swords.

Still he resolved to fight to the death.

A strange fortune had saved him from destruction before in the lane.

Some accident might occur again.

It was no duel this.

There was but a momentary pause, a measurement of distances, and then Rupert's blade was uplifted, and the fight began.

Even now Dreadnought showed his strict adherence to justice.

Redlock had but one available arm, and was, therefore, to a certain extent at a disadvantage.

He accordingly drew his left arm behind him, and displayed only the right, filled, as it was, with the *sword of vengeance*.

I cannot describe this duel at any very great length, as in its general details it would be but a recapitulation of many others I have described before.

After many desperate lunges had passed, however, Rupert's sword traversed the fleshy part of Redlock's right shoulder, and at the same time Redlock's sword wounded Rupert in the left.

Both staggered back badly wounded, but Rupert had, of course, the advantage.

His one-handed foe saw this, and redoubled his efforts, knowing that after a short time the wound would stiffen his right arm, and entirely disable him from further useful exertion.

Rupert's sword seemed, however, to flash hither and thither like lightning.

His style was far too brilliant to enable his adversary to wound him, and Redlock was compelled to keep on the defensive.

As this idea penetrated his brain, he trembled.

There was Death in the thought!

Delay was useless.

To act on the defensive was simply to prolong the fight, for out of that room Rupert Dreadnought had sworn that both should not pass alive!

HELEN SEEKS REST IN THE CHURCHYARD.

Nerved to desperate and reckless exertion at this, Redlock began to fight like a madman, his strength every moment becoming less and less.

Suddenly the sight of something inspired him with fresh energy.

In backing from one of Rupert's rapid lunges, his eye fell upon a pistol lying upon a table in a corner of the room.

To a treacherous mind such as his the idea at once occurred—

"Here is life and liberty. I will shoot him before he can have the chance of finding me at his mercy."

So when Rupert rushed forward and made his next pass, Redlock withdrew, and dashing back, seized the pistol, and cocking it, levelled it at Rupert's head.

All this was done so quickly that Rupert had no chance of preventing him, and the report and the crash of glass behind him was the almost instantaneous sound which followed.

The ball had whizzed by his ear, and crashed through the lofty mirror behind him!

Redlock stood aghast at his failure, the exploded pistol still in his hand.

Slowly Rupert put his hand to his belt, his eye still on his enemy.

Then for the first time Redlock saw that he had pistols in his belt.

"Murderer!" cried Dreadnought, in a voice of thunder, "I have given you every fair chance; I have treated you as an honest foe when you have acted the part of an assassin! Now die the death of a dog!"

He raised his pistol as he spoke, took deliberate aim, and ere the trembling villain could speak, the weapon belched forth its flame, and the ball went crashing through his skull.

Rupert paused not to look at him, but unlocked the door, and admitted Allan and Tom, and, drawing them to the body which lay prone upon its face, he said solemnly—

"MY FRIENDS, YOU ARE WITNESSES! MY FIRST MISSION IS FULFILLED!!"

END OF BOOK II.

BOOK III.

THE SECOND SECRET OF THE IRON CHEST.

CHAPTER I.

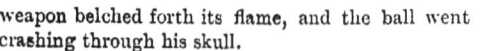

IT was with a feeling akin to awe that Rupert Dreadnought looked forward to the opening of the second compartment of the Iron Chest.

The terrible punishment which his father had caused him to inflict upon Redlock, made him fear lest the second mission might be of the same nature.

However, whatever it might be, he was bound to perform it.

He had sworn to carry out whatever behests his father might give him.

So a week after the death of Redlock—after, in fact, the body of the traitor had been buried—Rupert once more made his way to the room in which was the IRON CHEST.

With a tremor at the heart, he placed the key in the lock, and opened the strange receptacle of secrets.

The second compartment having been arrived at, he found lying before him a large parchment, tied with red silk, and directed to himself.

Opening it with eager hands, he read as follows:—

"MY DEAR SON,—Again the sword of vengeance must be drawn.

"Fear not that I shall ask you to shed blood without due cause.

"A vow which I took myself, and had not time to carry out, I have left to you, and by all your hopes of salvation you are bound to carry it out."

Rupert paused a moment.

A tremor invaded his limbs.

What dreadful thing was coming that the old earl thought it necessary to remind him of his vow again?

But the vow had been taken, and he was bound to fulfil it.

So, summoning up his courage, he proceeded.

"In the second vault, on the left-hand side of the subterranean passage beneath the church of St. Andrew's, Chichester, you will find an empty stone coffin.

"In that stone coffin one of my dearest friends, a cousin, was murdered.

"Lured there by his younger brother to search for a pretended treasure, he was suddenly attacked, and, after receiving a heavy blow from a mallet, was forced by his unnatural companion into the coffin.

"There he died of suffocation, and his younger brother, and the man he had brought with him to aid him in his hideous work, locked the vault and left him.

"The younger son, who was at least twenty years the junior of the other, now, of course, inherited the estates, for after a few days the vault was unlocked, and in the search the body was found.

"How he got into the coffin was, of course, a mystery, but, at any rate, the desired end was attained.

"He was dead, and the next heir was, of course, a wealthy man.

"The death-bed confession of the minor villain made me acquainted with the horrid deed, and it was then I heard that, as he was being forced into the stone coffin, he uttered my name.

"I at once considered that he had appointed me his avenger, and for twenty years I have sought the assassin in vain.

"His name is Hugh Dalrymple, and you will know him, perhaps, by the following description:—

"He is very tall, over six feet, and broadly-built.

"His eyes are black and piercing, his voice harsh and dissonant, and his hair is generally worn in tangled masses over his shoulders.

"An aquiline nose gives a peculiar character to his face, while across the right cheek is the deeply-marked scar I gave him when we had our only combat.

"He is now about eight and thirty.

"I have sworn that he shall be laid in the coffin where his murdered brother was suffocated by his unnatural hands, and that in that very vault he shall meet his doom.

"This oath you have now inherited from me. See that it is performed to the letter.

"R., EARL OF DREADNOUGHT.

"6 Oct., 1712."

"Thirty-eight in 1712, and it is now 1714," murmured Rupert Dreadnought, as he threw down the parchment, and leaned back in his chair; "he is at the present time, then, forty."

Then he remained for some time lost in deep reverie.

Here was another vengeance to accomplish—another life to take!

A bitter sigh escaped his lips as he thought of these sad tasks which were left to him to fulfil.*

* My readers may, perhaps, be inclined to think that this part of my story is exaggerated. But it is not so. In Corsica and Sicily *vendettas* of far more terrible extent are frequent, and considered perfectly legitimate and even necessary.

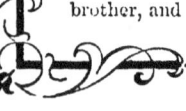

But there was no chance of escaping the evil.

He had sworn, and his vow must be kept.

As on a former occasion, he, on the following day, collected his friends together, and narrated to them the discovery he had made.

Allan of the Glen was the most attentive listener of all; and when Rupert Dreadnought had completed his account, he sprang to his feet.

"Master Dreadnought," he said, excitedly, "I will take the responsibility of this mission from your shoulders."

"What mean you?" asked Rupert Dreadnought, in surprise.

"I know this man. I am certain, from the description you have given of his voice and appearance, that he is one whom I met in the streets not many nights since—who insulted and struck me, and was carried off by his friends before I could resent the affront. Leave this task to me. Your sword has already drank too much blood."

"True, true," said Rupert, with a slight shudder at the words which so expressed his own feelings; "but I have sworn with my own hand to accomplish this vow, and I must give it to no one else. I will accept your assistance as ever, but that is all."

To this Allan of the Glen was bound to yield, at any rate in appearance.

It was only in appearance, however.

Inwardly he resolved that if he could contrive to obtain the time and the opportunity, his own sword should reach the dastard heart of the man who had struck him and fled.

CHAPTER II.

ON THE TRACK OF THE GUILTY.

NOT far from London, on the road that leads from Finchley, stood a building which was more a castle than an ordinary mansion.

It stood on the edge of the high road, with a broad deep ditch running like a moat round it—a wide bridge of planks spanning this, and being capable of being withdrawn if required.

The windows on the basement were mere loopholes, like those of a prison, while those above were barred so as to prevent any escape or entrance.

Round the summit of this mansion, which was flat, ran a stone balustrade, built like ramparts, and here on the evening on which I introduce the spot to my readers were walking two ladies.

The one was about five-and thirty, tall, finely-moulded and well preserved, the other about eighteen.

The former was the mistress of the house, the latter her handmaid.

There was a striking contrast between the two.

The one, as I have said, was tall and well preserved, with a fine sweep of limb, a stately walk, dark eyes, dark hair, and a proud air of superiority about her—the consciousness of wealth and station, perhaps, too evident.

The other was fair and rosy, with blue eyes, golden hair, and an exquisitely-proportioned figure, just indicating the budding bust and the pretty, rounded shoulders of sweet maidenhood.

"Mary," said the lady, as she leaned languidly over the balustrade, "he is long in coming. The evening shades are falling fast, and yet all along the road from London I can see no sign of his horse. Fetch me a chair."

The girl at once obeyed, and in a few moments she had placed her mistress in a chair, settled a shawl around her shoulders, and was standing silently by as she gazed out over the changing landscape. Presently she turned.

"Mary," she said, "I doubt if he will return to-night. I will remain here till dark; but before I rest to-night I desire to see Lady Clanberris."

"There is danger in that, my lady," said Mary. "Suppose my master were to return and find her here; you know how he would storm and rave."

"Ah, yes; but I will run the risk, Mary," returned her mistress. "I have waited too long already. My heart is longing to hear news of——"

She stopped, and a bright blush overspread her features.

But the maiden had seen it, and interpreted it aright, although the lady had not mentioned the name for whom her heart was longing.

Who it was our story will explain in due course.

"It is a lonely path to Clanberris House," said Mary, with a shudder, "but I will go."

This hint did not take any effect upon the lady, who was evidently deeply wrapped in the thoughts of the intended visit of Lady Clanberris and the news she would bring her of some one whose name she could not utter.

There was a far-off look in her eyes as she gazed out over the hushing landscape, and she turned suddenly round to Mary, as if she had not heard her words.

"Be sure," she said, "to be careful. If my husband has not returned I will leave the flag flying on yonder staff. The moon will be bright to-night; if you are late, and if you see no flag flying, you must return. Go quickly, Mary, and that necklace you so coveted yesterday shall be yours."

A bright flush surmounted the girl's cheeks at these words, but it gave place to a pallor and a moisture of the eyes as she turned away.

Alas! the thought occurred to her,

"Of what use are ornaments to me who have none to love me?"

The road to Clanberris House was truly, as she had said, a most lonely one, leading along a narrow, rocky pathway, and over a heather-covered heath, where very few pedestrians were ever seen.

However, she had traversed it on many occasions before, and though now she felt a kind of presentiment that something unusual was about to happen, she went on courageously.

Hurrying along, she reached Clanberris House ere the dusk had much deepened, and was soon admitted into the presence of the lady whom her mistress was so eager to see.

This lady, thought also beautiful, offered a marked contrast to both Mary and her mistress.

She was about thirty years of age, neither blonde nor brunette, having blue eyes and dark brown hair, with a good, though scarcely fair complexion.

"Well, Mary," she said, "what brings you hither over the lonely moor to-night?"

"It is over that lonely moor that I wish your

ladyship to accompany me," returned the maiden. "My mistress wishes urgently to see you."

"Is your master from home, then?" said Lady Clanberris, in surprise.

"Yes, and she does not expect him to return to-night. The flag on the flag-staff on the summit of ur house will be flying as long as he is absent. So there is no danger of our making an error."

"Good," said Lady Clanberris. "We will go at once then. I have important news for her, and no doubt she is eagerly expecting me."

In a very few minutes, Lady Clanberris had seen her husband, and, muffled in a heavy cloak, had passed out into the dusky night with the young maiden, who, still impressed with the idea that something unusual was about to occur, was glad enough of a companion.

The shades of evening had now begun to fall more heavily upon the already sombre heath, and objects were not plainly visible.

Hedgerows and trees looked like misty rows of men, while over the short heather a white fog began to rise.

Mary clutched at her companion's arm tightly, regardless of all distinctions of rank, and the two women hurried on like frightened things.

Half-way was an old wooden bridge spanning a narrow stream, and they had just began to ascend the slight incline which led to it, when two men rushed from behind a hedge, and stood before them.

They were broadly-built, burly, ragged ruffians, evidently intent on plunder, and their appearance, armed, as they were, to the teeth, was certainly not such as to reassure two terrified women.

"Now, then, my pretty ones," said one of them, addressing both unceremoniously; "now, then, my pretty ones, let us have all your money and jewels, and be sharp about it."

Lady Clanberris was equal to the emergency.

She saw at once the utter uselessness of resistance.

They were wholly in the power of those lawless men, and to resist would only be wilfully subjecting themselves to indignity.

So, without a word, she divested herself of all her ornaments, and took from her pocket a tolerably well-filled purse.

"Here," she said, "take these; my companion is but a servant, and has no money or jewels with her. Take this, and let us go in peace."

As she spoke, the men rushed forward, and seizing each of them round the waist, dragged them apart.

"We don't want any of your nonsense," said one; "it's only a game to save your money. But it won't do for us. She doesn't look like a servant."

While both gave vent to the most piercing screams of distress, the men began to search them roughly.

But not for long.

The shrill cries for help prevented them hearing the sound of horse's feet, deadened as it was by the turf, on which the steed was proceeding rapidly, and before they were aware of it a horseman dashed up and sprang from his saddle.

"Ha! now then, villains!" cried a loud voice, as he darted on them, sword in hand, and wounded one of them severely. "What mean you thus molesting ladies on the high road? Stand, cowards, and defend yourselves!"

But they were not, by any means, disposed to act on the defensive.

Bullies, as they had proved themselves towards women, they were cowards now even before a single brave man, and, releasing their victims, they darted through the hedge and dashed away at full speed in the darkness.

As they did so, Mary, alarmed beyond her power of endurance by the scene through which she had passed, fainted, and would have fallen to the earth had not the new-comer caught her in his arms.

"Here, madam," he said, addressing Lady Clanberris, "here is a lantern in my belt. Open it and throw the light upon this lady's face while I administer to her a little brandy."

The lady was not slow in obeying his behests, and in a moment the bright light of the lantern was turned full upon the pale features of Mary.

As it did so a wild cry of delight escaped the lips of the young man.

"By heavens!" he said, "it is Mary Macpherson, my long-lost Mary!"

Allan of the Glen and his mountain-love were once more united.

The brandy which he administered in a few moments restored her to herself, but when she opened her eyes and beheld the features of her lover, she shuddered and closed them again, as if she imagined herself in the realms of spirits.

"Fear not!" said Allan, upon whom the movement was not lost; "fear not. It is, indeed, Allan, your own Allan; tell me, tell me, do yon love me still?"

Then the beautiful eyes were opened again, and the soft arms were flung around his neck, and Allan and Mary were now clasped to each other's breasts.

Allan was the first to realise the fact that the situation was in no way interesting to Lady Clanberris.

He quietly disengaged Mary's arms from around him.

"Mary," he said, "whither are you going? I will see you safely to your destination."

"Not very far from this," she said, "we have only to reach Dalrymple House."

Allan started.

"Dalrymple House!" he said, "to whom does it belong?"

"To Sir Hugh Dalrymple," replied Lady Clanberris. "But now, my noble preserver, let us hurry forward, for the night is coming on apace."

To describe the effect produced upon Allan of the Glen by her words would be impossible.

"ALLAN STAGGERED FORWARD WITH A GROAN!"

It seemed truly as if the age of miracles had returned.

It was but a few days, as it were, before this meeting, that Rupert Dreadnought had learned the second mission which his father imposed upon him; and now—unless there was a strange coincidence of names—Allan had already discovered the lair of his enemy.

The heart of the young Scotch boy beat high with joy.

He had asked Rupert to be allowed to take upon himself the fulfilment of this mission, and had been refused.

Rupert could not blame him if, having his enemy, as it were, in his clutches, he did his best to destroy him.

Smothering as well as he could, therefore, the emotion which stirred his heart, he answered—

"Let me precede you. The way is very dark and lonely, and those ruffians may yet be inclined to return. Or stay: if you and Mary mount the horse I will lead him."

This suggestion was at once put into execution; and, having assisted them to the saddle, Allan of the Glen, still sword in hand, led the way, under their directions, towards Dalrymple House.

Presently they came in sight of the gloomy old building.

"We are safe," cried Lady Clanberris. "See, the flag is waving in the breeze. Sir Hugh is absent. Let us press forward."

The horse accordingly was allowed to trot along the now even road, and in a few minutes the wooden drawbridge was reached.

"Now, my preserver," said Lady Clanberris, "I must leave you. I am compelled to enter this house by stealth. You cannot enter!"

"Cannot enter!" echoed Allan.

Knowing, of course, nothing of the circumstances, he had anticipated naturally that he would be received into the house as the preserver of the lady and her companion, and that he would thus be able to learn important particulars regarding Rupert's enemy.

As he echoed Lady Clanberris's words, therefore, he turned towards Mary Macpherson.

"Allan," she said, "it is now too late to explain anything. Believe me, she is not ungrateful, but every moment she remains here is fraught with danger to her. To-morrow evening at eight meet me by yonder oak tree, and I will explain all. For my sake, Allan, ask no more now."

He could not, of course, refuse anything to her, and so, kissing her ripe, red lips, he bowed to Lady Clanberris, and leaping on his horse sped away.

He was disappointed; and yet he had, in very truth, no reason to be so.

He had truly not been permitted to enter the house, but he had most unexpectedly discovered the whereabouts of his master's new enemy.

With this, therefore, he was tolerably satisfied, and looking forward to the following evening, when he should meet alone the one he loved, he put spurs to his horse, and hastened onwards on his journey.

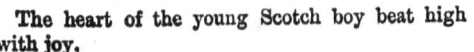

CHAPTER III.

LOVE'S MYSTERY.

As soon as the forms of Allan of the Glen and his horse had faded away in the distance, Mary Macpherson took the hand of her companion, and led her along a narrow path which skirted the moat.

For a short distance this path was open enough, but it presently led beneath tall and heavily foliaged trees.

Only a few yards along this part did Mary proceed, before she stopped at a spot where the earth had been cast into the moat, and dammed its waters.

Here, across a narrow wall, as it were, of hardened clay, they passed, and found themselves at a small gate.

No need was there to knock or ring here, for Mary Macpherson had left it ajar when she started from the old house.

They were soon, therefore, within the precincts of the old house itself.

"Hist!" said Mary, as they reached the bottom of the spiral staircase which formed a kind of secret mode of entrance to the chamber of Lady Dalrymple, "we must be very careful now, for we may be watched. *My* absence may have been observed, and from that other things may have been suspected. You know that Lady Dalrymple is watched—has treacherous spies in her house, and any one who is known to be friendly to her is subject to the same suspicion."

Lady Clanberris made no reply, but clasping the young girl's hand firmly as in acquiescence, followed her up the stairs.

In a few moments they had reached the apartments of Lady Dalrymple, apparently unobserved.

It was only apparently, however.

As they passed up the dark stairs, an old and long disused door had been stealthily opened and a pair of gleaming eyes watched them.

Only for an instant did they show.

One glance apparently was enough.

The door was closed noiselessly, and the two women passed up, imagining themselves to be unobserved and unsuspected.

Lady Dalrymple greeted her visitor eagerly.

Throwing her arms round her neck she kissed her fondly, saying—

"How good—how kind of you to come and see me so late. Have you news for me?"

"Yes, great news," returned Lady Clanberris; "are we quite safe from intrusion?"

"Yes," said Lady Dalrymple, who was now evidently under the influence of intense excitement, "yes. Look once more, Mary, to see that all is closed, and then we can talk."

The two ladies sat down in the centre of the room on a broad ottoman, while the young Scotch girl went to the door, tried it, and even peered out.

All was still.

"It is quite safe, my lady," she said, returning.

"Good," said Lady Dalrymple; "and now, dear Alice, *do* begin."

"Quite safe?"

She had on many occasions heard strange things said of Dalrymple House.

Rumours of terrible deeds had floated about for years.

Memories of past horrors had been kept alive by strange and mysterious events in the present.

She knew not, therefore, how many secret doors were in that old mansion, or how many methods of entrance her husband and his myrmidons had both to the house itself and its various chambers.

There *was* danger, though they knew it not.

The same pair of gleaming eyes which had glared at them as they ascended the stairs now glanced at them from behind the tapestry, where a panel had noiselessly slided upon well-greased grooves and admitted a dark figure.

However, as I have said, they knew nothing of this.

"Well," said Lady Dalrymple, "tell me all you have heard."

Lady Clanberris took her friend's hand and pressed it.

"My dear Margaret," she said, "I have heard from abroad—from my brother. You guessed this.'

A crimson flush overspread the features of Lady Dalrymple.

"Yes, yes," she said, in a tremulous voice; "yes, yes; I guessed it. And is he well?"

"Yes, well, and coming home."

"Coming home!"

The flush was succeeded by a deadly pallor as she repeated these words, and her bosom heaved violently.

"Yes: are you sorry?" asked Lady Clanberris, smiling.

"What would you have me do; what would you have me say?" returned Lady Dalrymple, in a low voice. "How *can* I welcome him; how *can* I be glad to hear of his return? True, I was forced into a marriage with this man whom I hate; true, I was compelled to quit Henry without a word; but I *am* the wife of Sir Hugh Dalrymple, and, as such, I understand how to conduct myself. Not a shadow of suspicion must fall on my good name."

Tears stood in her eyes as she spoke, and Lady Clanberris pressed her hand warmly.

"Cheer up, my dear Margaret," she said; "who knows what the future may have in store for you? Henry Clanberris, be it remembered, is not one who would run even the slightest risk of compromising one whom he loved. He would wish to see you once and that is all."

Lady Dalrymple withdrew her hand, and pressed it convulsively over her eyes, as if striving to collect her thoughts, or at least to gain courage.

Then she withdrew them with a sudden start.

"Alice," she said, "this *must* not be—I cannot see him. I *will* not. It would be wrong!"

Lady Clanberris smiled.

"And yet," she said, "yet you were so eager to hear of him."

"Oh, Alice!" returned Lady Dalrymple, passionately. "You know not how I loved him, or you would understand that I know not what I *do* wish sometimes. But I can explain all. I wish to hear of him; I wish to know that he is happy; I wish to know that he is well and fortunate, but that is all."

"Good," returned Lady Clanberris, "he *is* well, he *is* fortunate, wealth has been showered upon him. Whatever he has touched has seemed to turn to gold. I tell you all this—but you say you wish also to know whether he is happy—shall I tell you that he will bring home with him a wife?"

A deadly pallor overspread the features of Lady Dalrymple.

These words seemed to chill her very heart.

She bowed her head, and half averted her face.

"You are cruel," she murmured, "and yet scarcely know what you say. Is it so?"

"No," murmured Lady Clanberris, "it is *not* so. He is *not* wed. He loved you too well to permit another to take the place he destined for you. He wishes to see you to tell you that his heart is still yours."

"Ellen, I *cannot* see him—I cannot see him," said Lady Dalrymple; "tell him what you know of me when he *does* come—tell him how I have cherished his memory, but say that duty forbids my seeing him again. Never—never must we meet again."

Lady Clanberris rose sadly.

"Well," she said "*I* have no right to dictate other feelings to you. It would be wrong, I know. But I dread to see Henry."

"Let his cousin, your husband, then, tell him for you. He might break it better to him than *you* can. I cannot—will not see him."

Lady Clanberris rose.

She was evidently somewhat disconcerted.

"Well, well," she said, "perhaps you are right—It might lead to no good results. Good bye, dear, I will try to do the best for you. And now I will go while we are safe."

They indulged then in a loving kiss, and Lady Clanberris was led out of the room by Mary Macpherson, and down the stairs.

"You need not return to my chamber to-night, Mary," said Lady Dalrymple, as she closed the door. "I would rather be alone."

Then, when Mary and Lady Clanberris had gone, she flung herself down upon the ottoman and burst into a flood of tears.

For some quarter of an hour she remained thus.

When she roused herself, she saw sitting opposite to her, with the back of the chair in front of him, a coarse, ill-looking fellow, who was dressed like an Alsatian bully.

CHAPTER IV.

THE TRAITOR.

THE man laughed coarsely as he saw the alarm so plainly depicted on the face of Lady Dalrymple.

"You didn't expect to see me here, did you?" he said.

Lady Dalrymple sprang from her seat, and rushed to the bell-rope.

But something peculiar in the manner of the man restrained her.

"Hold a moment," he said, "before you destroy yourself."

"Destroy myself!"

"Aye, destroy is the word," said the man, "destroy is the word."

"And why? What right have you here? Do you suppose I am going to permit you to remain?"

"Of that I am not aware," answered the man; "but it will be against your interest to expel me. I am come, not to do you any harm, but to inform you of something which is to your interest."

"It cannot be. I will not listen," returned Lady Dalrymple; "leave my chamber at once or I will alarm the house."

The man rose at once.

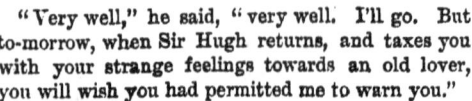

"Very well," he said, "very well. I'll go. But to-morrow, when Sir Hugh returns, and taxes you with your strange feelings towards an old lover, you will wish you had permitted me to warn you."

With these words he turned to quit the chamber.

Very slowly, however.

He knew well that he had touched the right chord.

"Stay!" cried Lady Dalrymple, "if you have anything to communicate speak, and speak quickly."

The man laughed a short, dry laugh, and reseated himself.

"My name's Barton," he said; "I'm one of Sir Hugh's men. You might have seen me if you had taken the trouble, for I've been in and about Dalrymple House a long while. Well, I've amused myself, when Sir Hugh has not required me, by finding out what I could about the house. It's a queer old place as I've found out, and I've found among other things a private door to this room."

"Well, is this all?"

"No, no. You are impatient," returned the fellow. "I have been here some time, and I have heard all that has passed."

She had almost expected this, yet the announcement came to her, notwithstanding, with terrible force."

Though she paled slightly, however, and her bosom trembled with the sudden leaping of her heart, she did not delay her reply.

"Well," she answered, "if you have heard all, you know also that I have acted in such a way that I care for no one."

"So you think, madam," returned the man, "but you are wrong. Suppose I repeat the conversation differently."

"Villain, I have witnesses," cried Lady Dalrymple indignantly.

"Witnesses!" repeated the fellow, sneeringly, "a bosom friend and a confidential servant. I have myself—the jealousy of Sir Hugh, and the fact that your lover is positively on his way to England, aye, may be here now for aught I know. These things are evidences; but in addition there is the knowledge in your own heart that if he *does* return you *will* see him, in spite of all you have said!"

"A crimson flush of shame and anger overspread the features of Lady Dalrymple as he spoke.

"Wretch!" she cried, "how dare you insult me thus? What is it you want of me, that you use these taunting words?"

"Ah! now you are coming to the point," said he. "I want money."

"How much?—tell me quickly," she answered.

"Oh—I don't want much now," he said; "a little now and a little again will suit me better than having a lump of cash, which I should spend all at once. You can give me ten pounds now, and when I want some more I'll ask."

Lady Dalrymple shuddered at the very thought of the answer she felt obliged to make.

"I will let you have what you require, and if I do you swear to be silent?"

"I swear," replied the man, with a chuckle.

Foolish woman!

If she had boldly told her husband the truth, she could have saved herself from calumny, though she might have endangered the freedom of her position.

Now, by placing herself in this fellow's power, she was destroying her last chance of liberty!

This view of the case, however, never occurred to her.

All she thought of was her husband's violent temper, and the danger there was of a hostile meeting between him and Henry Clanberris, her old lover.

So she rose, approached her secretaire, and took from it the gold which was to buy the fellow's silence.

With a shudder she placed it in his coarse hand.

"There," she said, "*I* have fulfilled my promise; see that you fulfil yours. Circumstances have not as yet drawn me into stern action; but I know that if you betray me I am capable of taking a terrible vengeance."

For an instant, as she glanced at him, the ruffian quailed before her.

There was a strange gleaming in her eyes, which meant more than in her own heart she felt herself capable of.

"Be assured," he said; "I will keep my word; and now I will depart."

"When does Sir Hugh return?" she asked, as his hand was placed upon the panel to slide it into its place.

"By midnight to-morrow he will be here," said the man.

The next moment he had gone, while Lady Dalrymple sank upon her knees, and burst into a passionate fit of weeping.

CHAPTER V.

IN THE LION'S DEN.

As may be supposed, Allan of the Glen waited with the utmost impatience the arrival of the hour which was appointed for his meeting with Mary Macpherson, whom he had naturally supposed lost to him for ever at the time of the dispersion of the Hidden People.

The night, fortunately, was a somewhat dark one, and when he reached the old tree, therefore, which she had pointed out to him, he was enabled to conceal his horse behind some heavily-growing bushes.

Mary Macpherson was punctual to her appointment.

As the clock of the old house tolled out the hour she tripped lightly up from the postern and met him.

I will not describe their joy as they met.

Those of my readers who know what it is to be separated any length of time from one dearly loved can imagine to themselves the scene.

I must hurry on, therefore, to the development of my story.

"And now, dear Mary," he said, after awhile, "I have a favour to ask."

"And what is that?"

"I want to enter Dalrymple House secretly."

"Oh, you cannot—you cannot," she said; "it would be death to you."

Allan smiled.

"I must chance that," he said. "I have lived a strange life, one in which I have had to dare many dangers worse than this. I must see him in private. Will you uot manage this for me?"

Mary thought awhile.

"Does he know you?" she asked.

"No, but he has seen me once before," replied Allan; "but that would not matter. I wish to see him on business."

Mary smiled up into his face.

"You are deceiving me somewhat," she said; "I am sure you are. You do *not* know him, and you have some mysterious reason for desiring to see him now."

"Mary," said Allan, reproachfully, "have you not sufficient trust in me to believe that I am on no bad errand. You know your master to be a bad man."

"Yes; but I am his trusted servant," said Mary.

"Or rather the trusted servant of his wife," returned Allan. "But never fear; I will not compromise you. I will return to London, and seek out one who knows him, if that is necessary to my introduction to him. However, for our love's sake, Mary, I had thought you would aid me in this."

"Do you know any of his friends then?" said the young girl.

"I do not. Name one or two."

The Scotch maiden thought a moment.

"There is Sir Oscar Penraven, for one," she said. "Do you know him?"

The question staggered Allan of the Glen for a moment.

Oscar Penraven one of Sir Hugh Dalrymple's friends! How everything seemed working in a circle of crime.

"I do," he said. "I know him well. He is an assassin, a murderer, a poisoner; a villain who has oft and oft attempted the life of my greatest benefactor—the one who saved me from ruin and death when I first reached London. Believe me, Mary, you will do right in admitting me. Your master is a murderer and an associate of murderers. Come now, dear one, after our long separation grant me this favour."

Then, without awaiting for her reply, he told her, under pledge of secrecy, the whole story; the mysteries which surrounded Rupert Dreadnought's life, and the hideous crime which had given to Sir Hugh Dalrymple his wealth and his power.

"THE GLEAMING EYES WERE ON THE WATCH."

Whatever scruples Mary Macpherson might have entertained in regard to permitting Allan of the Glen to enter Dalrymple House were now entirely overcome.

Her love for him prevented her from criticising too closely the motives which made him anxious to enter secretly; and so it was arranged that, on the following night, he should be admitted.

Then, with a tender embrace, the two parted.

It may be imagined that Allan of the Glen awaited with intense impatience the arrival of the following night, which would find him face to face with the man whom Rupert Dreadnought was sworn to destroy, but whose destruction he had resolved to accomplish for himself.

At length, though not soon enough for his anxious spirit, the time arrived, and as darkness spread itself over the scene, the fair form of Mary Macpherson quitted Dalrymple House, and approached him.

"You have come at last then," cried the ardent lover, as he clasped her to his breast. "Is Sir Hugh at home?"

"Yes, he is; in his study," replied the young girl: "and if you enter at once, you will be able to enter unperceived."

Even love was forgotten at this speech.

"Let us lose no time, then," he said. "I am eager to see him."

"Come, then, Allan," said the maiden; "though I fear that in going you run a risk which you will not confess to me."

"Fear not," he said, as he kissed her once more. "He will greet me far differently to what you expect."

In a few minutes the postern had been reached, and they were ascending the dark stairs, where, a few evenings before, Lady Clanberris had been seen by the spy.

"Shall I knock at his door and announce you?" asked Mary, as they reached the door of Sir Hugh's apartment.

"No; I will enter alone. Fear not, my love," he added, seeing the frightened look upon her face; "I mean no harm to him, and he shall do no harm to me."

He kissed her fondly again, and then made his way quickly towards the door which led into the chamber of Sir Hugh Dalrymple.

Turning the handle quietly, he entered noiselessly, and advanced towards the table without being perceived by the master of the house, who sat by a table with his head buried in his hands, engaged evidently in deep thought.

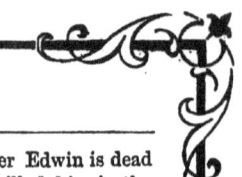

Had Allan of the Glen been of the assassin type, how ready to his hand now was his victim.

One raising of the knife, one strong blow, and Rupert Dreadnought's second mission would be over.

But such a consummation would not have suited the noble heart that beat within the bosom of the Scotch boy.

Yet he paused a moment.

He had truly succeeded in entering the presence of the man whom he desired to punish, yet even now how could it be done?

Was he not absolutely in the lion's den?

What excuse could he give for his presence?

He saw plainly now that his youthful enthusiasm had led him into an error; but he was gone too far to recede, and, indeed, the idea of doing so never occurred to him.

Drawing a pistol from his belt, he suddenly placed his hand upon Sir Hugh Dalrymple's shoulder.

The latter was instantly roused from his reverie, and started back in his chair with undisguised wonder not unmingled with alarm.

His features, however, when he carefully scanned Allan's form and face, were far more expressive of astonishment than fear.

He rose.

"Pray, young sir, and who may you be, and how dare you thus intrude yourself upon my presence unannounced?"

"I have dared," answered Allan, playing with his pistol, "because I know I can defend myself. I have desired the interview in order to explain certain matters to you, and after the explanation to kill you."

"Well, Master Scot," replied Sir Hugh, with a smile, "you must be either a madman or a robber, and an insolent one too. But, since you hold in your hand so conclusive an argument, I must e'en listen to you. Tell me what is it that you desire to explain?"

"Simply this," returned Allan. "I will be brief, since delay is useless to either. You had a brother, Edwin? He is dead. *You* murdered him!"

Sir Hugh's features assumed a ghastly pallor, and his hand naturally was placed upon the hilt of his sword."

"Insolent madman!" he said, "you shall suffer for this."

"Stay," returned Allan, coolly, "when I have told you all, I will place my pistol in my belt and fight you fairly. If, however, you attempt to attack me before I have time to give an explanation, or if you alarm the house, I shall fire!"

The determined manner in which the youth uttered these words was enough to prove to Sir Hugh Dalrymple that he was not to be trifled with, and inwardly he could not avoid feeling a kind of respect and reverence for the bold young Scotchman who thus dared him on his own hearth.

"Good. Speak on then," returned Sir Hugh Dalrymple, "and quickly, for I have much to settle to-night."

"You have," said Allan of the Glen, significantly. "Well, as I said before, your brother Edwin is dead and you are his murderer. You killed him in the vaults of St. Andrew's church, Chichester, that you might inherit his fortune. A friend of his has sworn to avenge him; but *I* take the duty off his hands. Do you not know my face?"

Sir Hugh Dalrymple scanned keenly the bold features of the handsome Scotch boy.

But he really failed to recognise him.

"No," he said, "I know you not."

"Not long ago when you were in London," replied Allan, "you came out of the 'Golden Sun' in Eastchepe with other roysterers, who rudely pushed the crowd hither and thither. Among that crowd was I, and when I resisted your intemperate haste you called me insolent Scot and struck me in the face. I drew my sword to avenge the insult, when the crowd carried me away and we were separated. Since then I have been burning to avenge the insult, and the opportunity has at length arrived. My friend's vengeance devolves on me, and here am I to take it."

"Foolish boy!" cried Sir Hugh, contemptuously, "why, if I chose, I could call my servants and have you cast forth into the road, or thrown into a dungeon. I like you for your courage. Go while you are in safety."

The eyes of Allan of the Glen flashed fire.

It was insult to his mind to be addressed thus.

"I defy you," he cried, "I defy you to execute your threat. While I hold in my hand this pistol you dare not do as you say. Let us talk no longer—let us fight."

"Good," returned Sir Hugh, with a malignant smile, "good—then since you *will*, I suppose that I must consent. Let me first lock the door, however, that I may be sure that we shall not be interrupted. I would not have my servants see me bearded in my own house by such a boy!"

So saying, he drew his sword, as if to convince Allan that he really intended fighting, and then walked slowly towards the door.

Then occurred what seemed like a miracle.

Sir Hugh stood still for a moment, and then stamped on the floor.

In an instant a panelling shot away and hid him from view.

Allan sprang forward, sword in hand.

But all was in vain.

He was completely hemmed in.

"A prisoner! by heavens!" he cried; "he has duped me after all."

He had scarcely uttered the words when the panelling slid back into its place.

The door was open now, and within it stood several armed men.

"Seize him!" cried the stern voice of Sir Hugh Dalrymple, "seize him, and bear him to the dungeons."

In an instant the place was invaded by about seven or eight armed men.

They were all dark-looking, rough-featured fellows, evidently not the ordinary servants of the house, but men whom he could hire upon any occasion to perform deeds of robbery or bloodshed.

As all my readers are aware, Allan of the Glen was a brave and resolute character.

Young though he was, he had gone through so many scenes of peril, that even in this extremity he felt no sinking of the heart.

But for the moment he was taken so aback that though standing in the middle of the room, with his sword drawn, he made no effort to defend himself.

But in another instant he recovered his presence of mind.

He glanced around him quickly.

Behind was an open window.

An idea of escape at once occurred to him.

Driven to bay as he was, there was not the slightest use in attempting the execution of his original plan.

He saw now the folly of his attempting the enterprise alone.

But what could he do?

There was no use in trying to defend himself.

He must fly.

Turning suddenly, therefore, he made a rush towards the window.

But it was of no avail.

Below him was a terrible depth.

The darkness, also, was so intense, that it was impossible to see where he would fall.

There was not a single shrub or tree within reach.

He felt he was indeed trapped.

He turned round savagely.

To his bold young heart there was something astounding—impossible, as it were—in the thought that he could be thus caged against his will.

His blood boiled within him, and forgetful of the fact that he was in the nest of enemies, he rushed madly at the crowd of murderous villains, whose numbers he did not pause to count.

Had he done so, perhaps he would have seen the madness of what he attempted.

There were at least ten ruffians in the room, each one of whom regarded murder as a matter of business.

But the Scotch youth thought not of this.

Whirling his sword round his head, he sprang into the midst of them just as they were about to close round him, and ere he knew what he had done, one of his enemies had fallen, bathed in blood, upon the floor.

Full of fire and energy, now, he swung his weapon round his head, and brought it down with terrible force upon another of his foes, who fell pierced through the shoulder, while *he* remained unscathed.

For a minute the foe seemed paralysed.

The fiery young Scotch boy standing before them with gleaming eyes and panting frame, caused them for a moment to fall back.

But only for a moment.

In another moment their energies returned, and they dashed upon him in a body with revengeful features and fierce shouts.

The sight of their comrades—one dead, one dying—on the ground might well have inflamed their worst passions.

But, demons as they were, they were compelled to restrain their feelings.

They were not to kill.

Such were the instructions of Sir Hugh Dalrymple.

So, although they assaulted with determined energy, they sought only to wound him so far that he might be easily overcome.

This was easily effected.

Treachery did what fair and open fight would not.

One of the men, clubbing his pistol, rushed in upon him from behind and struck him violently on the head.

He staggered forward.

His sword described a wild circuit in the air and then he fell prone upon his face.

"Good," said one of the men; "he is nigh a dead 'un now. Take him up and bear him to the dungeon. He'll rot there for all I'll do for him. See poor Lomax there, he's dead; and Bill Locksby don't look much as if he'd ever recover."

While the fellow was thus grumbling, they raised the inanimate form of Allan of the Glen in their arms in by no means a tender manner and bore him from the room.

Passing along the dark corridor, they approached the stairs where Allan had ascended, and, passing through the little secret door where the head of the treacherous fellow had protruded on the night of Lady Clanberris's visit, descended another flight where the cold, chill atmosphere betrayed the fact that they were going beneath the earth.

The cold and chill air increased in its chilliness and coldness, as they descended, and a suffocating moisture, like that or a charnel house, invaded their nostrils.

To Allan, had he been in possession of his senses, it would truly have seemed as if he were entering his last home—as if he were being placed in a living tomb; but, of course, senseless as he was, he knew nothing.

Pausing when they had descended some depth, they entered a dark dungeon, where now, at night, not a ray of light was visible, and which in the day time was only illumined by a few feeble beams struggling through the bars of a diminutive window, high up in the murky wall.

Entering here, they placed Allan against the wall, and fastened him by an iron chain to it.

Then one of them fetched some dry straw, and placed him upon it.

After this one of them administered to the stunned man some liquid which seemed to revive him, and when the first signs of reanimation were observable, they left him to himself.

The door clanged to with a woeful sound, and Allan was alone and a prisoner!

CHAPTER VI.

ANOTHER TRAITOR.

Sir Hugh Dalrymple sat in his room, waiting nervously for the arrival of the news of Allan's discomfiture and capture.

He desired not his death.

To kill him would be to destroy for ever his chance of obtaining from him the secret of his mysterious visit, and his more mysterious knowledge of his history.

Sir Hugh felt greatly disturbed in spirit.

The secret of his cowardly murder of his brother

had been buried so many years, that it seemed strange, indeed, that it should now be revived.

The Phantom of his Crime truly had ever stalked at his side, save when his brain was clouded with drink.

It had stood by the altar; it had stood in his nuptial chamber; it had followed the tracks of his prosperity.

But it had appeared only to his own vision.

To others he had imagined his evil deed to be dead and forgotten!

By his side now, as he sat near a blazing fire, shivering with an inward cold, stood a youth of some nineteen summers.

He was dressed in the costume of a page, and stood before his master in an attitude of respect.

But though he stood thus, his features expressed anything but a meek and gentle disposition.

There was that in his eye and in the lines of his mouth which was expressive of stern determination and a cold resolve to make his own way in the world irrespective of the wishes or the good of others.

"They are a long time, Colin," said Sir Hugh, addressing the page; "a very long time."

The page smiled.

"Your wishes speed quicker, maybe, than their swords, Sir Hugh," he said; "but from all you have told me of this youth, he is most brave, and mayhap may give them some trouble."

"True; but no one man, however brave, can stand against such odds as those that have surrounded *him*. Hark! they come!"

Sir Hugh turned eagerly towards the door, through which in another moment one of the ruffians entered.

"Well," he asked impatiently, "is all right?"

"Yes; he is in the dungeon," returned the man: "but he gave us immense trouble. Lomax is dead, and Locksby is nearly so."

"Curses on him! but he is safe now. And is he wounded?"

"Yes, slightly. He has a shoulder scratch and has been stunned by a severe blow on the head."

"Ah, well, I will see that he is well taken care of," said Sir Hugh Dalrymple. "You can leave me now. See to Locksby, and then go down into the hall; you will find there something to cheer you after the battle. Your reward will be bestowed to-morrow."

The man bowed and left the room, and Sir Hugh turned to his page.

"Colin," he said, "proceed to the dungeon where this upstart Scotch youth is confined, and see to his wounds. I know you are dexterous at such things, since you saved my life at Worcester."

"Why wish to save his life, Sir Hugh?" returned the youth. "He came here to beard you in your own house, and I cannot tell why he should not lie where he is and rot."

The eager way in which the page said this appeared somewhat to surprise his master.

He turned and glanced at him fixedly for a moment.

"Ah," he said, "you understand not what you say. He has a secret of mine which I had imagined none else knew, and I must know how far his knowledge extends and whence he derived his information. I have more foes somewhere than I knew of, and I desire to discover them."

The page bowed.

He had guessed as much.

"Very good, master," he said; "I will see that your commands are obeyed."

Then he turned and quitted the room.

"A strange but faithful youth," said Sir Hugh, as he went.

He would have thought differently had he looked into Colin's heart.

"I must find out this secret for myself," was the thought of the "faithful" servant.

He had not proceeded far along the corridor when a figure glided out from behind a statue, which cast its shadow heavily across the passage.

It was Mary Macpherson.

Her face was ghastly pale; her bosom heaved violently; and her whole person, in fact, was tremulous with emotion.

"Colin," she said, "a word with you."

The youth smiled and tapped her under the chin, with a kind of insolent familiarity.

"Yes, pretty one, a dozen if you please," he answered; "what can I serve you in, my sweetheart?"

"Oh! this is no time for love-making," she said, in a voice expressive of intense irritation; "I wish to speak of the prisoner."

The page's smiles vanished at once at this.

"What of him?" he asked quickly.

"He is a countryman of mine, and in danger," she answered, hurriedly.

"And how know you he is here, and in danger?" he asked. "Are you the traitor, then, who admitted him to the house?"

Mary trembled.

But her love for Allan of the Glen kept her from much display of emotion.

"You speak riddles to me," she said; "I heard from the men who are drinking and carousing below that a Scotch youth who has been here to see Sir Hugh has offended him—has killed one of his retainers, and is now confined in a dungeon. They say he is wounded and in need of help. Suffer *me* to go to him in your stead."

"Impossible," returned Colin; "you would be watched, and they would know well that Sir Hugh would not send a woman down to succour one of his prisoners."

"I know it," replied Mary, "and in my own mind I have provided against that. You must lend me your clothes. I will tend him, and in return for your kindness——"

"You will give me what I am dying for," said Colin; "your promise to be mine?"

RUPERT
OR THE
DREADNOUGHT
SECRETS OF THE IRON CHEST!

"THE SHRIEKING CROWD FOLLOWED HIM MADLY!"

"No; in return for your kindness I will go with you next Thursday to Calswell Fair," returned Mary.

"Good," returned Colin, who saw in this a nearer approach to what he wished, the hand of Mary Macpherson, "good; I will agree. Wait here a few moments, and I will bring you what you desire."

"I will await you at the door of my room," returned the young girl, whose heart was now bounding eagerly in her bosom.

Within ten minutes Colin had changed his clothes, and handed them to Mary, who was soon indued into them, her rounded and supple limbs and elastic figure showing to good advantage within them.

Colin glanced at her with undisguised admiration as she once more emerged from her chamber.

"You look so well in them," he cried, "that you ought never to leave them off."

"There, don't keep me," she said, blushing; "remember, the poor prisoner is now waiting for me. Give me the key and whatever you intended to take him."

The page handed to her a flask of spirits, some soft linen to bind up Allan's wounds, and a lantern, and then the young girl hurried away.

The door of the dungeon was soon reached, and Mary entered.

In the dim light of the cell she could scarcely at first see anything, but, as soon as the mask of the lantern was removed, she saw Allan seated on his wretched heap of straw, and his head bowed down upon his breast.

He was apparently asleep.

Carefully closing the door behind her, Mary Macpherson approached her unconscious lover, and discovered then that he was insensible.

The pain of his shoulder wounded had evidently caused him to faint.

Taking his head tenderly, and drawing it down upon her bosom, she poured some brandy down his throat, and bathed his brow, too, with some of the liquid.

In a few moments he opened his eyes, and seeing some one kneeling by him in the costume of a page, he drew back in surprise and some alarm.

But the voice of the one he loved soon reassured him.

"Allan dear, it is I," she said. "I am here in disguise."

He took one glance at her face as she raised the lantern so that the light might fall upon her face, and in another instant the two lovers were clasped in each other's arms.

"Dear Allan," said Mary, sobbing, "did I not tell you that you were throwing yourself into the midst of danger? Why did you persist in perilling your life?"

"It was my duty," answered Allan, "and that I never shirk. But is there any chance of escape hence?"

"Not this night," said Mary. "But come, while I am here let me bind up your wounds. As I am doing so, try and explain to me whether I can go to seek your friends, and bring them to your assistance."

As clearly as he could, Allan of the Glen explained to her the position of Rupert Dreadnought's house.

"Do you think you can safely find your way alone," he asked, "or have you any one that you can trust?"

Mary shook her head.

"No," she said, "there's no one I can trust here. I'll go myself. In this dress no one will know me."

Allan glanced at her, and smiled, as he thought how little her round and pretty limbs were disguised by her male attire.

"You had better wear a long cloak and a sword," he said, "although if it comes to hard knocks I doubt if your use of a sword would not betray you more than anything else. I should know you to be a woman anywhere."

Mary blushed, as her lover's eyes scanned her pretty figure.

"I shall go on horseback," she said, "and wear a cloak as you say. But as for the use of a sword, I am not so ignorant of it as you fancy. I have practiced in jest, and when the Hidden People were discovered I defended myself with a claymore against two Lowlanders. But I must go now, or I shall be suspected."

"And when do you start for London?"

"This night."

"So that you will see Rupert Dreadnought by morning. 'Tis well—ere to-morrow's sun declines in the west, Sir Hugh Dalrymple perhaps may regret the steps he has taken."

Then there followed another loving embrace, and leaving the brandy flask by Allan's side, Mary Macpherson moved away, and passing through the door, closed it after her as quietly as possible, and crept up the stairs.

Colin, of course, expected that as soon as she returned from her visit to the prisoner she would divest herself of her male clothing and return it to him.

But she had no such intention, as we have seen, and this was evident enough to him as she came up.

So he resolved to watch.

He was mad with jealousy.

He had made up his mind, in spite of entire absence of encouragement, that she should be his wife; and now a suspicion had entered his mind that the stranger whom he had in the heat of the moment permitted her to see, was, perhaps, after all, some favoured lover.

He had followed her to the door of the cell, and had listened.

But all in vain.

Not a sound could be heard through its thick platings of iron.

So he had retired thence discomfited.

Now, however, he resolved to watch, as I have said.

Mary Macpherson entered her room, and remained there a few moments.

Then she came forth, still wearing her male costume, and proceeded towards Colin's door.

Here she knocked twice.

"This is curious," thought the page. "I will keep my eye on her proceedings here, too."

But what followed surprised him more.

When she came out again she wore his plumed hat and cloak.

He ground his teeth with rage.

"She is deceiving me," he muttered. "Never mind; I will not betray myself, but watch."

She glanced round her rapidly, but, seeing no

one, made off as swiftly as possible towards the public staircase.

This she descended at a run, and was soon outside the house.

Her make-up was now so exactly like that of Colin, that she was unchallenged until she arrived at the stables, where she admitted herself, and procured a fine horse.

With a joyous smile now she leaped into the saddle, and was soon careering along the high road to London.

She knew not that, at no great distance, a horseman was following her.

This was Colin !

CHAPTER VII.

THE FIGHT AT THE INN.

WATCHED, but not knowing what was impending over her, happy in the idea that she was about to save her lover, Mary Macpherson rode on, and by dint of many inquiries, found little difficulty in finding the house of Rupert Dreadnought.

Rupert had not risen when she arrived, but in a few minutes he had dressed himself, and was standing before her in surprise.

He had certainly remarked upon the unaccountable absence of Allan of the Glen, but he had never dreamed that anything was wrong ; and now that he saw before him the handsome form of the disguised page, he could in no way understand the meaning of the first words that were uttered.

He could plainly see from the rounded contour of the person before him that it was a woman in disguise.

"You come from Allan of the Glen ?" he said, in surprise.

"Yes, he is in danger—in peril," said the young girl, feeling no degree of bashfulness in the presence of the noble-hearted young hero. "I come to you, as his only friend, to save him."

"Be quick, then," said Rupert Dreadnought, "and explain all, that we may go to his rescue."

It was in a few words that Mary Macpherson explained the position of her lover.

"So you, then, are his mountain love ?" said Rupert Dreadnought. "Strange, indeed, that you should meet him thus. And what say you is the name of his enemy ?"

"Sir Hugh Dalrymple."

I have before described the effect that was made upon Allan of the Glen when he first heard these words.

Upon Rupert Dreadnought the effect was still greater.

His frame quivered, his lips trembled, his eyes were ablaze with excitement.

"Sir Hugh Dalrymple !" he repeated ; "by heavens, my mortal enemy !"

Then he paused for awhile overcome by the intensity of his emotion.

Mary Macpherson did not disturb him.

She saw the fulfilment of the mystery at which her lover had hinted, and she was anxious to see the result.

After a few moments Rupert Dreadnought recovered his presence of mind.

"We must start at once," he said ; "but it will not be well to attempt anything before nightfall. How far reckon you it from London ?"

"Eight miles."

"Good ; then there is no hurry. An adventure such as this would be destroyed in its effect by being prosecuted in the daylight. I will send my men on before me, and you and I will follow."

"I will do just as you please," replied Mary Macpherson. "I know you are Allan's friend and will act for the best."

In the space of two hours Tom the waterman had been summoned, and together with the retainers of the house, had started for their destination.

They were told to dispose themselves in the wood near at hand and watch the place, and if Allan of the Glen was removed from his prison they were to capture him if they were strong enough, or follow and see where he went, if the other party were too strong.

Towards dusk Rupert started with Mary Macpherson.

They had no sooner left the door on horseback when a figure emerged from its hiding-place opposite.

This was Colin.

He came from his hiding-place so stealthily, however, that neither of those he followed perceived him, and they accordingly proceeded on without suspicion.

His purpose, however, was not to follow them.

He knew well which road they would take, and what places they would have to pass, and he therefore turned his horse's head another way, and proceeded at full speed across country.

Arriving at the half-way inn, he tied up his horse to an old tree, and called for refreshment.

The half-way inn was the last tavern on the road before you reached Dalrymple House, and as the next house of entertainment lay at some considerable distance, it was generally crowded with visitors of all grades.

The public room was at this moment full of men and women eating and drinking, and Colin, as he elbowed his way through them, assumed an air of great gravity.

"You look serious, young sir," said a jovial-looking farmer, as the youth took his position near the fire.

This was just what the page wanted.

He would now put in practice his cowardly scheme.

"You would look serious too did you know what villany is afloat," returned Colin.

"Of what do you speak ?" asked the sturdy farmer.

"Of highwaymen."

"Highwaymen !" echoed several voices, "have we any hereabouts, then ?"

"You will have shortly," said Colin, "and, unless there be those among you who will aid me in arresting them, the mail coach will be robbed this night, and murder will be done !"

The landlord had heard a few words of the conversation, and he now pressed forward.

"What does all this mean ?" he cried, "speak less in enigmas, boy, and tell us all about it."

Thus pressed, Colin at once commenced his story, a tissue, of course, of most atrocious falsehoods.

"I was in London not long since," he said, "and on my way to Dalrymple House, when I chanced to overhear a few words that proved some villany was afloat.

"An attack, in fact, is meditated upon the mail coach, which will pass here in an hour.

"The villains who are to assist in the attack have gone on before.

"But their leader is on his way now."

"Is he alone?" asked the sturdy farmer.

"No; but his only companion is his mistress—a young girl of some eighteen years, who is disguised as a page."

"They must be secured," said the farmer, valiantly, now that he knew that there was only one man and a girl to contend with. "We must organise an attack."

Colin smiled.

"There'll not be much trouble I should imagine," he answered, "in effecting their capture with all those who are here; but there will not be much time for organization; if what I heard was correct they will be here in an hour's time."

"And will he pull up here for refreshment?" asked Boniface.

"Yes, such is my belief."

"And how shall we know him? Is he a villanous-looking fellow?"

"Oh, I shall be able to point him out," replied Colin; "but he is by no means what you would suppose him. He is a young and handsome man, and she who accompanies him is fair and graceful. I will go now to the door and watch, that they may not elude us. A goodly reward will, no doubt, be ours if we seize them."

So saying, the young traitor moved towards the entry, and took his station at a point where he could command the high road, leaving the yokels within to wonder and make many boasts as to their intentions.

It was not long before he saw approaching along the highway two figures on horseback.

His heart beat high within his bosom as he beheld them.

His cowardly vengeance was now about to commence.

Rushing back into the room, he announced to the anxious crowd that the daring highwayman was approaching, and bade them conceal themselves in a yard at the side of the inn, where they could rush out upon him unawares.

They accordingly passed out by a side door and waited.

Rupert, of course, had no idea of danger, and reining up at the door of the inn called for some ale.

"Egad!" murmured the landlord, when he had observed him, and his eyes had taken in all the details of the form of the pretty girl at his side, "egad! if that's a highwayman and his mistress, I can only say that he's a fine fellow, and *she* seems a lady. However, there's a deal of deception about, and there's no use in going by appearances."

So he brought out the ale and received the money, for he was a prudent man, and Rupert, having drank it, prepared to go.

Then it was that it seemed as if a very Babel had been let loose.

The door of the yard was flung open, and a crowd of men and women rushed forth, armed with every imaginable kind of weapon.

Clubs, sticks, swords, pitchforks, were flourished just as it had been at the old house where Rupert had been led by Redlock in search of Helen.

For an instant Rupert was paralyzed with surprise.

What did it mean?

What treacherous villain had betrayed him?

He soon saw, however, that there was no time for reflection.

If surrounded by this yelling crew, what could he say if taken to the constabulary?

"You had better fly, Mary," he said, addressing the girl who was with him; "fly, and make your way into Dalrymple House."

"But you! what will you do?" she answered.

She already felt a deep interest in the handsome fellow at her side.

"I will cut my way through," he answered; "fear not for me—fly to Allan, and tell him I am coming to his rescue."

The young girl glanced round her.

Not an instant was to be lost.

They were even now prancing and careering in the middle of the crowd.

So, putting her spurs into her horse's flanks, and pressing her legs against his sides, so as to secure herself in the saddle, she suddenly wheeled him round and darted away, overturning Colin as she did so, and inflicting a severe gash upon his forehead.

She did not observe him, however.

It was the last thing in her thoughts that he would make his appearance in such a scene.

Though she knew him to be her lover, she did not suspect him of treachery.

So, thinking merely that she had overturned one of the rustics, she darted on, and was soon plunging away swiftly across the open country towards Dalrymple House.

She must not for this be accused of cowardice, or of leaving her best friend in the hour of need.

It must be remembered that her own betrothed was in danger.

It must be remembered also that Rupert Dreadnought had sent on before him a number of fellows to aid him in the rescue of Allan of the Glen, and it occurred to her at once that perhaps she would be able to meet with these, and send them back to aid Rupert.

So away, as I have said, she went at full speed, while the yelling crowd, having now only one to deal with, became more courageous and determined.

They struck the horse, tore at the rider, endeavoured to drag the bridle from his hand, and were cast down to the ground every moment by the kicking out of the terrified animal, and the blows which Rupert freely gave with the flat of his sword.

Then suddenly Rupert drew his right rein violently, caused his horse to perform a complete pirouette, and then suddenly, as the yelling throng fell and stumbled back, he dashed away.

The shrieking crowd followed him madly, some

with sticks, and others with pitchforks, the women crying at the top of their voices—

"Stop the highwayman!"

"Seize the robber!"

"Kill him—kill him!"

But, seeing that he had not attempted to shed any blood, there was no one in the crowd courageous enough to fire, although the landlord had supplied several of them with pistols.

So, with a loud shout of defiance, Rupert Dreadnought dashed away, and the discomfited throng could only gaze and wonder at his energy, and their own folly in permitting him to escape.

CHAPTER VIII.

A STRANGE MODE OF LOVE-MAKING.

HAVING started across country, instead of taking the direct route along the high-road, Mary Macpherson had to proceed a far greater distance than Rupert, or any one going by the ordinary way.

When, therefore, Colin recovered from the blow which her horse's foot had given him, he darted away eagerly along the highway.

His face was, of course, entirely unknown to Rupert Dreadnought, and he therefore regarded him simply as one of the crowd flying from the scene through cowardice.

He was bent on quite another errand, however.

He was longing for vengeance.

True he loved Mary.

But she had duped him.

He now saw how thoroughly he had been deceived.

The stranger who was languishing in the dungeon was evidently a dearly-loved friend, and the young girl had risked all to save him.

The demon of jealousy and hate had now possession of Colin's heart.

He would revenge himself terribly.

He would cause his death, and she should witness the disaster. So he dashed eagerly on.

It was now getting on towards night, but he could, nevertheless, see for some time the graceful figure of Mary Macpherson bending over the horse as he advanced at full speed over hill and dale.

But though she rode so rapidly, he gained on her, for the road he took was not half the distance, and all even ground.

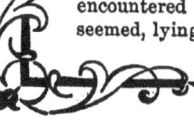

As he passed along, running at full speed, he encountered a number of men who were, as it seemed, lying in ambush by the roadside.

ALONE IN A LIVING TOMB.

They knew nothing of him, however, and they took, therefore, no notice of him, and away he ran towards the old house.

As he reached the postern, the thick twilight had deepened, and he could not see anyone approaching.

It enabled, however, the traitor to conceal himself and wait.

He had not to do so long.

In a very few minutes the sound of a horse's hoofs was heard, and then the figure of Mary Macpherson was seen approaching.

She leaped off her horse, and was about to lead him to the stable when she was seized suddenly in Colin's arms.

She uttered a cry of alarm, but upon seeing who it was her fear subsided.

She had no idea of his treachery.

"Ah, Colin," she cried, "this is no time for love-making. Let me go. I have something most important to do."

She tried to disengage herself gently from his embrace, but she could not.

Then she saw with wonder the fierce glitter in his eye. His words, however, soon explained his meaning.

"Love-making!" he cried. "It is not for that I detain you. Did you not see me in the crowd at the inn when your horse kicked me and inflicted this gash upon my face."

"*You* in the crowd, Colin?" she said. "I saw you not. What did you there?"

"I know all," said Colin; "how you have duped me for another, how you disguised yourself with my cloak, and took my sword, and rode my horse to London; I know how you have brought a friend with you to rescue Allan of the Glen, as he is called, and now you will see how I intend to spoil all your plans."

Then, suddenly, before she knew what he was going to do, he tied a thick handkerchief over her mouth; then he secured her wrists, and forcibly tied her legs together.

"Now," he cried, as he lifted her in his arms and bore her towards the little gate, "now you will see how I will foil you. You are my prisoner, and nothing but your promise to be my wife will obtain your release."

What emotions were in the young girl's heart as she heard these words and felt herself being borne away in the arms of the man she disliked, and who had now discovered himself to be a dupe, I shall not nowpause to describe.

In vain she struggled.

Her limbs were so strongly confined that all her efforts were useless, and, as they entered the dark passage of the old house, she subsided into a faint yielding.

In a very short space of time, therefore—less time, in fact, than it takes to describe it, she found herself occupying a chamber, or, rather, a dungeon not far from that in which Allan of the Glen was confined.

Here he hurriedly unfastened, or, rather, loosened her bonds, and darted from the room.

He had no fear now.

Scream as she might no one would hear her.

So, closing the door of communication between the cells and the house itself, he hurried up again to the postern.

He had a good plan in his mind now.

He was dressed in clothes almost identical with those of Mary Macpherson.

In the dark Rupert Dreadnought would not know him.

He would deceive him, therefore, and lead him into an ambush.

He was just in time.

Rupert rode up upon his panting horse just as Colin emerged into the dim light that the rising moon shed over the precincts of the postern.

"Are you there, Mary?" said Rupert.

"Yes," answered Colin, in a feigned whisper, "yes. Where are your friends?"

"Among yonder trees."

"Be quick, then," continued the traitor, still in the disguised whisper. "Call your men and enter quickly."

"How shall I know when all is ready?"

"You will hear the shrill cry of an owl," replied Colin; "then enter one by one, and I will lead them to their places."

He said this at random.

He knew not, of course, what arrangements had been made by Rupert and Mary.

"Do you remember my instructions?" said Rupert.

"Yes; I know their import," replied Colin, "but you may as well repeat them. You wish, of course, to see Sir Hugh Dalrymple secretly."

"I do," replied Rupert Dreadnought; "we must seize upon him, and then, at the sword's point, force him to yield his prisoner to us. Now then, I will go and fetch my men. No time must be lost."

He then turned his horse's head and rode away, while Colin rushed eagerly into the dark passage.

Now was the time for action.

He knew the nearest cut towards what might truly be called the guard-room, where he could always make sure of finding a number of rough fellows.

In a minute he had made his way in, and found himself in the midst of a rough, rollicking set of drinkers, who burst into a loud laugh as he made his appearance.

"Have you seen a 'ghost, Colin," said one, "that you look so eager and scared?"

"No, no; but I have work for you," he said.

"What work—is it work that will pay?" cried one brawny ruffian.

"Yes, yes; only listen," replied Colin, "there is no time to lose. There is a plan to surprise the house, to seize Sir Hugh and release the prisoner. You must follow me, and before Sir Hugh knows anything of the matter we shall have trapped and secured them. You know well the secret gate on the stairs?"

"Yes."

"Well, then, that must be opened, and they must be allowed to enter there and descend towards the dungeons. Then the gate must be closed and Sir Hugh must be apprised of the capture."

"But whom will they trust who will admit them?"

"I shall. They believe me to be some one else—they believe me to be helping them. The man who leads them is Sir Hugh Dalrymple's greatest enemy, and a rich reward will be ours if we capture him. Come."

The men rose, as if by a natural instinct, and buckled on their swords.

"I can't see why Sir Hugh should not be told of this," said the leader, as he proceeded to the door.

"There is no time, delay would spoil all," returned Colin; "besides, when the deed is done, his pleasure and our reward will be all the greater."

The young traitor had an aptitude, apparently, for command, and, turning as he spoke, as if the matter was settled, he led the way down the staircase.

Arrived close to the secret gate, he pointed out to his followers the positions they were to occupy, and having seen that they were so placed as to be entirely screened from observation, he hurried to the entrance, and uttered the shrill cry which had been agreed upon as the signal.

Within a minute Rupert and his men, leaving their horses in the shadow of the trees, under the care of one of their number, had approached Dalrymple House, and advanced to the edge of the moat.

"Now, then," said Colin, in a low and somewhat tremulous voice, "now, then, enter quickly one by one. Follow me, and I will show you the secret door which leads to the cells in one of which Allan of the Glen is confined."

Rupert Dreadnought was thoroughly trapped.

How *could* he suspect that this page, who was dressed like Mary Macpherson, and spoke, too, like her, was a traitor, and that the pretty companion of his ride was a prisoner?

Advancing boldly, therefore, he reached the secret gate.

"Descend," whispered Colin; "your men must enter one by one."

Within five minutes Rupert and his companions were safely within the passage.

Then the door clanged to, and they found themselves in utter darkness.

Colin had trapped them without having need of his friends.

They were caged without the shedding of a single drop of blood.

For a few moments complete silence reigned.

Then finding that no one spoke, and that there was a sound of whispering outside the door, he said—

"Mary, where are you?"

"Here I am," said a voice which sounded strangely through the closed door.

"Are we to remain here in the dark, then?" asked Dreadnought.

"Yes; but only for a time; keep still while I go up and procure the keys of the dungeon."

So Rupert and his men waited while the cunning traitor darted up the stairs, and proceeded towards the room of Sir Hugh Dalrymple.

Sir Hugh was surprised to see him enter.

In fact, there was a strange look of sternness on his face.

"Where have you been?" he asked.

"On your business, Sir Hugh," he said.

And then as briefly as possible he told his story, omitting the capture of Mary Macpherson and her confinement in one of the dungeons.

"This is some of Lady Dalrymple's treachery," muttered Sir Hugh, when Colin had told all; "Mary Macpherson is her companion. Where is this treacherous maiden?"

"I know not," said Colin, "she fled from the attack at the inn, and I have seen nothing of her since. In fact, I saw not which way she went, for the blow her horse's hoof gave me, nearly deprived me of consciousness."

"And you say now that you have caged his friends?"

"I have; they are now in the dark subterranean passage, over which, as you know, runs the open gallery."

"Good; and what is the name of the leader of these fellows?"

"Rupert Dreadnought."

Sir Hugh Dalrymple staggered back in surprise.

Had a thunderbolt crashed through the ceiling and dashed through the flooring, he could not have been more utterly overwhelmed for the moment.

"Dreadnought!" he said, "well do I remember that name—the name of my old enemy—my brother's friend. I can see now the network that is being woven round me. He must die, and his friends too. Good fortune has delivered them into my hands. Colin, where are the men?"

"They have returned to the guard-room," replied the page, "and are awaiting your orders."

"You must go and lead them to the secret gallery, then," said Sir Hugh, excitedly. "Let each be provided with a flambeau so that at a given signal the whole corridor may be lit up. Then we can fire down upon them without their being able to make any resistance."

Colin's heart leaped with a savage joy as he heard these words.

Such a massacre would indeed be a terrible excitement.

And then, also, could he not include in it his rival?

"And this Scotch boy," he said. "Shall I let him out of his dungeon so that we can destroy him as well?"

Sir Hugh pondered a moment.

"Well," he said, "I kept him only that he might reveal to me secrets which would now be of no use to me. Yes, let him join his friends. But have a care, they might suspect you."

"Not they," said the cunning young traitor. "I can deceive them. I will just explain to the men their orders, then I will proceed down the stairs, and release Allan, after which I will rejoin you."

He hurried towards the door, but there he halted a moment.

"And I suppose you will grant me a reward for this?" he said.

"What do you ask?"

"Liberty to marry Mary Macpherson, and a present such as you think proper."

"Liberty to marry Mary Macpherson, the traitress who has brought about all this misery—who has nearly cost me my life! Why, are you mad, boy?"

"I can explain all," said Colin. "Still what I ask we will not discuss now; there is no time. I will at once away, and see to our caged birds."

And then, with an exulting smile—a smile of diabolical triumph and zest, he turned from his master's presence.

"A thorough-paced young villain," said his master, musingly, as he quitted. "Had I been—ah! well, memories will not now avail. I must to work. Ghastly work it is truly, but it must be done."

He turned to a cupboard near, drew out a bottle, and drank off a large glassful of raw spirits.

Then he took from a drawer a pair of long and finely-chased pistols, and placing them in his belt, awaited Colin's return.

CHAPTER IX.

THE MASSACRE.

The young traitor at once proceeded, according to his instructions and his own eager wishes, towards the guard-room, and gave to the men Sir Hugh Dalrymple's orders.

Though grumbling at being thus disturbed as it seemed for nothing, they drank off the tankards of foaming ale before them, and having seen to their muskets prepared to follow their leader, for such, indeed, Colin seemed for the time to have constituted himself.

The place to which they were led was a strange one, in truth, if we consider the age in which the events occurred.

The passage in which Rupert and his men were waiting was, as my readers, are aware, a subterranean one, much below the level of the house itself.

Round it, at a distance of some twelve feet from the ground, ran a gallery which thoroughly commanded it, and yet was quite inaccessible to any one below.

Into this gallery, therefore, it was that the men were to be led, so that leaning over the balustrades of the gallery they could fire down upon the helpless prisoners beneath.

Rupert Dreadnought and those with him could not of course imagine what a hideous tragedy was contemplated.

It certainly seemed odd that they should be left thus to wait in the darkness; but, when the door was once more opened and Colin appeared, even the slightest suspicion that might have arisen in the minds of any was banished.

"Here," said the young traitor, in a low voice, "here is the key which opens your friends dungeon. Quickly release him. See where yonder light glimmers; that is his place of confinement. I will be with you directly, and perhaps without any bloodshed you may be enabled to carry him away with you."

"But why do you hurry away?" asked Rupert Dreadnought.

"I shall be missed—besides, I do not wish to be seen in this attire," replied the assumed maiden; "I will return in a few moments, when I have seen my mistress, and let you once more out."

"But why need you lock this door?" asked Tom the waterman, in a tone of suspicion.

"I will not lock it, then," returned Colin; "but if you take my advice you will make no attempt to go out until I return; you do not know your way sufficiently, and may fall into a trap. However, I am but a poor weak girl, I cannot pretend to know so well as you, so you must judge for yourselves."

There was something in the words and the manner in which they were said which might have struck Rupert on another occasion as extremely unlike those of a young girl.

But if it had struck him, he had but little time for thought.

The youthful betrayer darted away at once.

The door was closed, and they were once more alone—locked in, too, for the key had been turned noiselessly.

The faint glimmer of light which had been pointed out by Colin came from a grating opposite the little window where the moonlight struggled through into Allan's cell.

Towards this they now made their way, and in a few moments reached it.

Eagerly they inserted a key in the lock, and turned it.

Then a pitiable sight met their eyes.

Allan, chained and helpless, lay upon his bed of loose straw.

"Who is there?" he cried, as one of the men drew from his pocket a dark lantern, and cast its light upon him.

"Rupert Dreadnought and Tom the waterman," said the one who carried the lantern. "We have come to save you. Be still, and we will soon release you."

Mary Macpherson had informed them that her lover was chained to the wall, and they had, therefore, brought with them the implements necessary to release him, and in a few minutes they had succeeded in filing through his fetters.

A few words sufficed to explain to the Scotch boy the state of affairs, and they at once hurried out into the open space.

As they did so, a plaintive cry struck their ears.

It seemed like the groaning of one in deep distress and pain.

They stood still, and listened.

Again the cry.

This time they were enabled to tell that it issued from some chamber at the far end of the corridor, and thither, forgetful of their own danger, they at once rushed.

They guessed that some one else was in confinement and peril, and, whoever it might be, they resolved to release him.

On arriving at the end of the passage, it was a matter of no difficulty to discover whence the sounds proceeded, and they found, to their great joy, that the key given them by Colin fitted the lock.

In another moment the door was flung open, and the light of the lantern revealed to them the form of the real Mary Macpherson, lying on the ground, with a pile of fallen bricks upon one of her legs.

Allan rushed forward distractedly, crying, as he pressed his lips to her cheek—

"She is cold—quite cold! She is dead—lost to me for ever!"

"And we," cried Rupert, "are trapped and betrayed!"

The fact of Mary Macpherson being found lying in such a place proved that some one in disguise had been misleading them.

Who it was no one was able to say.

Colin was not known to any.

His voice had seemed that of a woman.

At any rate, they *had* been deceived, and all recognised the necessity of immediate action.

The first thing to be done, however, was to extricate Mary Macpherson from her perilous position beneath the fallen masonry.

The ready hands of all were soon at work, and, before many minutes, the bricks had been removed.

Then a little brandy was poured down her throat.

Presently her sweet eyes opened.

She gazed in wonder around, and then recognizing her lover flung herself into his arms.

The injury she had received was, after all, only a terrible series of bruises on her limbs, and, after a few minutes she was enabled to stand.

Then occurred what caused them to stand still with astonishment.

The place was inundated with roseate light.

Into the gallery filed eight men, bearing torches.

These they stuck in the walls, so as to illuminate the whole place.

Then they raised their guns and waited.

This was the preparation for the massacre.

"What can this mean?" said Rupert Dreadnought, breathlessly.

Allan shook his head.

"I know not," he said, "but it seems like the commencement of some hideous treachery. Let us stand to our arms, and be ready to act instantly!"

"IN VAIN RUPERT WAVED HIS HAT."

It was quite evident that some horrid scheme of treachery was on foot, though it might reasonably be considered a difficult task to guess at its extent.

They were not left long in doubt.

The men in the gallery, acting on an order given by their leader in an undertone, raised their guns and fired.

Whether it was the peculiarly cowardly mode of warfare which displeased them or made them nervous, or whether the glare of light was too much near them, and the darkness below too intense, I cannot say.

At any rate this first volley took no offect.

The balls rattled against the stone walls, but no one was injured.

In an instant there came a response.

The pistols of the little party, cooped up as they were in the narrow passage, were raised as in one body, and the reports were followed by groans of agony.

This rendered Sir Hugh furious.

"Take better aim, and fire coolly," he cried. "Now, altogether."

At this moment, however, a figure sprang from the side of the gallery, and flung itself before the guns of the retainers.

It was Colin.

"Hold! hold!" he cried, "see there!"

And he pointed wildly to a form which stood within range of one of the muskets.

He had recognised, even in the semi-darkness, the form of the disguised Mary Macpherson.

"What means this folly?" cried Sir Hugh Dalrymple, angrily. "Out of the way, mad boy, and let the men do their duty."

"No, no, Sir Hugh," exclaimed Colin; "that page yonder is the one of whom I spoke. Spare her, if not the others."

"She is the traitress; let her then die!" returned Dalrymple.

The young traitor was for an instant dumbfounded by the words of the elder traitor, who was his master.

Then he recovered his senses suddenly.

Dashing up the levelled guns, he suddenly sprang over the balustrade, and, regardless of the depth, dropped into the darkness below.

He was saved from any injury, however, by those below, who caught him in their arms.

"This way," exclaimed he, as he landed safely on *terra firma*, "for *her* sake I will save you all follow me."

With these words he led the way to a corner of the passage, opposite that where they had entered, and hastily touching a spring, disclosed a small doorway.

Through this the men dashed furiously, and succeeded in passing through just as a discharge of musketry rang through the subterranean corridors.

Not a shot, however, took effect, for they were far beyond the reach of any, and as the little gate closed they could hear a shout of disappointed vengeance.

"Now," said Rupert, as they halted in utter darkness, knowing not, of course, how to proceed, "now where are we?"

"We are at the bottom of a flight of stairs which winds round and round until it reaches a high and isolated terrace at the summit of the castle. When you arrive there you will be able to enter a chamber, where you must remain for a time."

"But this man will discover and destroy us by some treacherous means," returned Allan. "Is there no method of reaching the free, fresh air?"

"Not yet—the wing of the castle in which I am leading you is isolated from the rest of the building, and there is but one door of communication, which is the one by which we have just entered. You and your friends could defend the stairs against a host of foes. But you will not be called upon to do so. Master, though he is, of this place, Sir Hugh Dalrymple knows not of this door, he will fancy that you have escaped by the other gate, and will not even seek you here. Follow me."

There was no choice.

Colin had shown himself to be a thorough traitor, and there might even now be a doubt as to his sincerity.

But there was just a hope that the manner in which Sir Hugh had proposed to destroy the one he loved would lead him to act really in this as he had promised.

So, without full faith—keeping, that is to say, a thorough look-out—Rupert and his friends decided to follow their strange guide.

"Lead on," said Dreadnought, "and we will proceed after you. But how can we see in this utter darkness?"

"You have a lantern, have you not?"

"Yes; but is it safe to use it?"

"Quite," replied Colin; "through this door no ray of light can be seen. Come."

Tom the waterman at once turned on the light of his lantern, and it was then easy to see that they were at the bottom of a well staircase, leading up so far that they could see nothing of its summit.

Colin at once singled out the form of the one he loved.

"Follow me, Mary," he said.

Allan made a gesture as if to start forward.

But Mary Macpherson restrained him by a whisper.

"Keep back," she said; "arouse not his jealousy, or he might betray us all."

Then, with the speed and grace of a fawn, she sprang forward, and followed her would-be lover.

CHAPTER X.

THE ASCENT—THE ISOLATED TERRACE—THE MYSTERIOUS SUITE OF APARTMENTS — COLIN'S RETURN—THE IMPROMPTU BANQUET.

A LONG and wearisome ascent brought them to a small doorway, which yielded readily to a gentle push from Colin, and admitted a fresh and welcome current of air.

Then they stepped out upon a wide terrace overlooking the country for miles round.

"This way," said Colin.

Crossing the terrace, he proceeded through a French window into a large and richly furnished apartment.

Gorgeous as it might be, however, there was that in it which sent a chill to the heart.

It had a close, musty smell about it, as if it had been long disused.

A damp, unhealthy atmosphere pervaded it, as if it were but a gilded sepulchre.

However, for the time, it was a place of safety, and the tired band were glad to avail themselves of it.

They could see but little of its details, for their

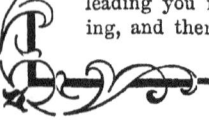

only light was that given by the lantern which Tom the waterman had produced.

"I will bring a lamp and some provisions before morning dawns," said Colin, "so I will leave you now."

"But are you not afraid of being discovered and seized?" asked Rupert, doubtingly.

"Not I; I know too well the secrets of this old place," returned the page. "I will bring what I promise ere dawn."

"And," whispered Mary Macpherson, "bring me my own clothes. I have no wish to preserve longer this masquerading attire."

"Which you only assumed to dupe me," replied Colin, in an undertone. "However, I have now risked my life for you and your friends, and I hope you will be grateful."

Then he hurried away, and disappeared once more through the little doorway.

"Let us explore this new place," said Rupert to Tom the waterman; "you others had best remain where you are to watch and also to guard this lady."

So saying he took the lantern, and sword in hand he passed through a little door at the further end of the chamber.

He now found himself in a bedroom, which seemed, by its atmosphere and its appearance, to have been more recently used than the other they had just left.

This, again, led into a third, and there the suite of rooms stopped on this side.

On the other side there were two rooms also, and no more.

"This is, indeed, a strange place," said Rupert, as they returned to the centre one, where the men were sitting round dozing on the chairs while Allan of the Glen and Mary Macpherson were talking sweet nothings in a corner.

"Yes, it is strange," replied Tom the waterman, "but it is just the thing for us."

"How so?"

"We can remain here until we have a chance of descending and punishing our treacherous enemy."

"Yes," replied Rupert, "if Colin remains true to us. Upon that everything depends, and that is but a poor thing to trust to. A man who has once betrayed you can never be believed in."

The night wore away but slowly.

Everything without the castle was very still and solemn, while within the conversation soon flagged, and, save those whose duty it was to keep watch, all dozed off into a sleep more or less sound.

Just as the first golden streaks of light began to shoot up from the eastern horizon the little door on the terrace opened, and Colin made his appearance, bearing a large bundle and a basket of provisions.

These he carried in triumph into the room.

"Here," he said, "are enough provisions to last you the day. To-night I will bring more, and a lamp as well."

"To-night!" exclaimed Rupert, in astonishment; "why then I hope we can leave this place for good. I must meet Dalrymple face to face ere I quit the castle."

Colin gazed at him in amazement.

"What," he said, "thrust yourself once more into the lion's den?"

"Yes, for what else did I come here?" said Dreadnought. "Did I not come to avenge a friend, to punish an assassin?"

"Yes, and were caught instantly in your own trap. Of what use was it my saving you, if you are going to return to his power?"

"I am bound by an oath," said Rupert Dreadnought, "and from that oath I cannot depart. However, if this night will not be convenient to your plans, we will stop for the next, but see him I must ere I go."

"To-morrow night he quits this castle," replied Colin, "and to-night he has a large concourse of people—a ball to all the neighbouring gentry—on neither, therefore, can you see him. At dawn, however, when all the guests have departed, I will lead you to him; but you will surely not compromise the safety of all for the sake of carrying out a whim."

"It is no whim, but a sacred duty," replied Rupert Dreadnought. "However, since it is more suitable to you, I will await your coming. Do you remain here?"

"No, I will return this evening," replied Colin; "meanwhile, keep as quiet as possible, and do not show yourself on the terrace."

He then departed.

Mary Macpherson lost no time now in taking off her male attire, and donning her own.

She came into the room, looking so pretty and so different to what she had seemed in the disordered and unaccustomed dress of the page Colin, that she excited the admiration of all.

She was like a sunbeam among them, and soon had made a difference in the appearance of the room.

The meal was spread on the centre table, and there, in the very lion's den, the men whom Sir Hugh Dalrymple had designed to murder, sat down to feast upon his good things.

CHAPTER XI.

SIR HUGH DALRYMPLE'S RAGE—THE UNEXPECTED MEETING—AN OLD SORROW, AND AN OLD LOVE—THE BALL—THE MOONLIT TERRACE—THE DECLARATION OF A MAD PASSION—THE FIRE!

When the page had leaped, as I described, from the balustrade of the subterranean gallery, and rushed in among the ranks of the very men he had betrayed, Sir Hugh Dalrymple had been for the moment struck dumb with amazement.

Then, in a fit of fury, he had ordered his men to fire.

This proving useless, he had dashed down to the little door by the winding staircase, and searched everywhere for the second little gate.

But in vain.

Not knowing anything of the secret spring by which Colin had admitted himself and his companions, he merely spent his time uselessly, and retired, breathing vengeance upon the youth who had so quickly destroyed all his plans of revenge.

The retainers were nothing loth to avoid the massacre, which, savage ruffians as they were, was quite against their usual manner of business.

The whole night having passed without any sign

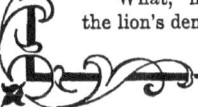

whatever of those who had mysteriously disappeared, Sir Hugh concluded on the following day that they had really made good their escape, and cast the matter for the time from his mind.

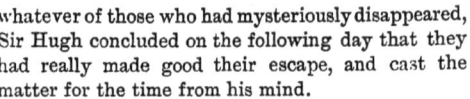

The next evening he proceeded to his wife's boudoir, and found her there dressing for the ball.

"You have not forgotten what to-night is then," he said. "I wish you to look your best. I have a friend coming—in fact, I believe he is here already—to whom I desire to introduce you; he has just returned from abroad. His is quite a romantic story, I believe, and he worships fair women."

Lady Dalrymple smiled languidly.

She was so weary. It all mattered so little.

So, with a little shiver, she proceeded with her toilet, and, soon after her husband's departure, she was ready to descend to the reception room.

As she entered it a young man, who had been standing near the window, advanced to meet her.

He was tall, fair, and pale, and as he gazed upon the beautiful vision that confronted him, he grew yet more ghastly.

They stood looking at one another.

No sound came from either.

Could it be possible that her husband had brought *him* there?

Was she going mad, or was it Henry Clanberris that stood before her?

"Oh! Henry—Henry!"

The voice, hoarse and broken, came forth in gasps from the parched lips.

"Oh! Margaret, my darling—my Maggie!"

And then she was clasped in his arms, his hot breath upon her cheek, his passionate kisses on her brow!

Was this trembling, sobbing woman, the cold, calm Lady Dalrymple?

All was forgotten in that first embrace—all the past long years, the pain, the weariness, her husband, honour, all.

There was a step in the corridor at this moment, and Sir Hugh entered.

The pair had left each other now. Lady Dalrymple was seated on the ottoman, and Henry Clanberris was standing once more by the fire-place, more deadly pale than ever.

"Why, Rolliston, you look more ill than I've seen you before," cried Sir Hugh. "Come with me and taste my wine. That will revive you, I'll warrant me!"

This was enough.

Sir Hugh Dalrymple had addressed him as Rolliston.

He had come there purposely, therefore, under an assumed name.

The assassin's punishment was truly commencing in earnest!

* * * * *

Lights gleamed that night on smiling faces and graceful forms; on rainbow-hued silks and foam-like lace; on wreathing flowers and gleaming jewels.

Fairest among the fair, peerless among the beautiful, reigned Margaret Dalrymple.

Her beauty had only required animation to make it perfect.

To-night those eyes, which had usually been so hard in their cold brilliancy, beamed with the softening light of intense happiness.

A deep flush crimsoned the pale cheek.

The delicate features had lost their stony expression.

The marble statue had become a living woman!

All eyes followed her.

By her side, gloomy, pale, abstracted, stood Henry Clanberris.

His very soul was bitter within him.

More selfish than she—as men are ever more selfish than women—he had loved her as deeply as his nature would permit; but never with the purity that distinguished her affection.

He had been left for dead upon a battle-field, but had only been wounded.

During years of captivity that followed, the memory of the fair English face had haunted him.

The tones of the clear rich voice rang in his ears day and night.

Had his love followed on tranquilly, perhaps he might have forgotten her, or only remembered his love for her as a pleasant episode in his life.

But with thoughts of her fresh in his mind trouble had come upon him.

With nothing to distract his attention he had dreamed of her continually.

Now he returned to find her the wife of another; and that other one who had been forced upon her by friends, and who bore a character by no means loveable or even upright.

And as he gazed upon her perfect loveliness, he swore in his heart that she should be his.

The rich strains of music were now sinking into a sobbing sigh, now swelling into a burst of wild exultant melody, as Henry Clanberris led her from the heated room out upon the moonlit terrace.

It was a calm and lovely night, and the silver moon had shed its brightest mantle over the hushing country.

For a few moments they stood in silence.

Never school-girl with her first love blushed and trembled more than did the haughty Lady Dalrymple.

Henry gazed in unrestrained admiration upon the delicate profile, half turned from him; the exquisitely graceful fall of her snowy velvet draperies; great coils of hair of living gold wreathing the small head; even the diamonds sparkling amid her tresses, and the blood-red rubies nestling on her white bosom.

Then he spoke.

"Maggie," he said, "it was on such a night as this I left you. Do you remember the moonlight in the long avenue at the Grange? But no; you have forgotten all now. Many and many a time, when weary and sick at heart, I have thought of you. But for the memory of your love I could not have lived those long years of captivity. I might have expected to find you changed, but *not* another man's wife."

The great violet eyes filled with tears, but she never spoke.

So he went on.

"Tell me you have not quite forgotten me, Maggie. I once thought that time, absence, nay, even death itself, would not kill our love. Oh! darling, I have loved you so dearly—how could you cast me off? I would sooner have believed that the sun would fall from Heaven, than that you would be faithless to me. You never loved me—tell me that you never loved me, and I will leave you, and never look upon your face again."

"Oh, spare me, Henry!" she cried, "spare me—have pity. I have suffered so terribly."

"Suffered!" he cried, "and have I not *too* suffered? Do I not suffer? You are as cold as stone—a true woman, fickle as the wind. Oh! love, forgive me, I know not what I say. My beautiful Margaret, say you once loved me—only tell me that."

"I never loved any one in the world but you," she murmured.

And Henry Clanberris, with triumph beaming in his dark eyes, bent over her, whispering—

"Nothing will then persuade me that we shall be parted for ever. I shall wait, and——"

Then he drew her once more towards him, and imprinted a long and fervent kiss upon her lips.

She drew herself gently away.

"Enough," she said: "this is wrong—very wrong, Henry. We will wait, and hope if we will; but such meetings like this must not take place."

Henry did not attempt to detain her.

Gladly would he have whispered of flight—of instant departure from the power of one she did not love.

But he saw how she would receive it—loved her the more for her purity, and resolved in his heart of hearts that if ever the chance occurred she should be his wife.

He might, truly, have years to wait, but meanwhile no other woman should claim one moment of his thoughts!

Again his arm encircled her elastic waist in the dance; again the voluptuous music filled the air, when suddenly some affrighted servants sprang into the ball-room, while at the same moment a cloud of hot smoke came whirling in at the open door.

"The castle is on fire!" cried the domestics, in frantic accents.

Sir Hugh Dalrymple stood for an instant as if paralysed, while all his guests gathered round him in a huddled group as if they could find security near him.

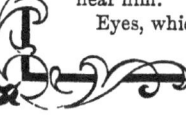

Eyes, which, a moment before, had been gazing tenderly into those of loving partners, now glanced in horror and dismay at the master of the castle.

There were no means near for extinguishing the fire.

In those days fires were attacked by means of a little parish engine, which it would have been an absurdity to have used against a huge building such as that which was the home of the Dalrymples.

So the only thing to think of was escape.

"This way, my friends," cried Sir Hugh, pointing to the great doorway, and leading the way, at the same time taking his wife's arm, and running rapidly towards the great hall.

But there he found that he had miscalculated distances.

They were met by a wall of fire!

SIR HUGH DALRYMPLE.

CHAPTER XII.

THE CONFLAGRATION REACHES THE PRISONERS—MARY'S TERROR—THE FRIGHTENED VILLAGERS—COLIN'S SCHEME OF SAFETY—THE DESCENT FROM THE WINDOW—THE MYSTERIOUS SPIES—ALLAN'S DESCENT—THE PUNISHMENT OF THE TRAITOR.

MEANWHILE, before pausing to describe how they fared in this unexpected and fearful emergency, we must return to the prisoners who were cooped up as it were at the top of the burning castle.

The smoke, rolling over the top of the building, was the first intimation to them that the conflagration had commenced, and then Colin rushed up frantically.

"Be still," he said; "do not give way to fear; I shall soon be able to release you. Do you remain here, Master Dreadnought, and watch the open space yonder while your men assist me. Mayhap the villagers may flock to the rescue with their ladders. If not, in ten minutes we shall have broken through into another part of the castle, whence we can descend easily by a rope."

So saying, he rushed excitedly away.

Rupert Dreadnought remained standing on the terrace.

He was not, however, left long alone, for he had not been standing more than about a few minutes before Mary Macpherson rushed out of the chamber dressed in a long white robe.

Her eyes were ablaze with terror, and she ran towards Rupert, crying—

"Oh, save me! save me!"

She had awoke to find her room filled with dense

curling smoke, and, despite the assurances of Allan, whom she met at her door, she could not believe that escape was possible.

"Keep up your courage," said Rupert, as the terrified girl clung to him. "See yonder, they are coming to our assistance."

As he spoke, he pointed to the open space before the castle, where a crowd of excited villagers were gazing up at the blazing edifice.

In vain, however, Rupert waved his hat; in vain Mary Macpherson frantically fluttered her handkerchief in the breeze.

"Oh! they come not; we are lost!" she cried.

"Nay, then," said Rupert Dreadnought, as he passed his arm comfortingly round her waist, while he still raised his hat on high, "this is but one mode of safety. Colin will save us."

But though he spoke thus bravely, his heart somewhat misgave him.

The fire was evidently gaining ground upon them.

The smoke curled above them in huge wreaths.

The flames roared and flickered near, and their heat could be felt distinctly now.

Even the tips of the tongues of fire now and then glinted out through the crevices of the little doorway.

If Colin failed to find the passage he sought, how *could* they escape, cooped up as they were?

However, as the terrified girl clung to him, and waved her hand to the villagers alternately, he whispered words of comfort.

"You have here brave and willing hearts to aid you," he said; "do not give way to fear; that will aid in destroying our chances of escape."

Mary Macpherson looked up inquiringly, fixedly, at the face of the strong man by her side.

"Do you fear, or, rather, have you any hope?" she asked, eagerly.

"Yes," he said, firmly; "I believe we shall be saved from this."

"Then," she answered, standing up as determinedly as she could, "I will hope too."

She had scarcely uttered these words, when the voice of Colin was heard calling them.

In another instant he burst through the French windows, and appeared before them full of excitement.

"This way, this way!" he shouted, eagerly; "lose no time!"

Then, without leaving Rupert Dreadnought the chance, he seized Mary Macpherson in his arms, and hurried away with her into the large room.

Passing from this into the sleeping chamber, where she had rested, he entered the small anteroom beyond, where, to Rupert's astonishment, he found his friends standing near a large hole in the wall which they had battered through.

Smoke was to be seen issuing slightly from the other portion of the building which was thus laid bare, but only as if it were oozing from some fissure.

"Where are we?" cried Rupert. "Are you about to lead me to Sir Hugh Dalrymple?"

"By this time," replied Colin, "he has doubtless escaped, and taken refuge in one of the neighbours' houses. No, this would not be the way to find him. Quick! let us lose no time in talking. Follow me."

He had now released Mary Macpherson, who by her struggles plainly told him that his assistance was not only not required, but was disagreeable; and so, with a growing hate at his heart, which made him invent another treachery, he led the way towards a room, where a narrow window overlooked a wooded garden, which emerged gradually into the large wood beyond.

"Here," he said, "is a stout rope, which, if doubly twisted, will bear the weight of two. Mary here cannot descend unassisted. Will you, Master Dreadnought, bear her down while we assist you? We can follow."

There was no time to deliberate.

Leaping on the sill of the window, therefore, Rupert securely seized the rope, and Mary Macpherson, who was now trembling with intense agitation and alarm, was raised against her own will into his arms.

It was a terrible and perilous descent.

The rope, truly, was a stout one, but it had never been intended to bear two persons, and, moreover, the distance from the window to the ground was full thirty feet.

However, those above adopted the best plan to prevent an excessive strain.

All those in the room held the rope, and let it run down as swiftly as was consistent with the safety of those descending.

Allan of the Glen was the one who had handed Mary Macpherson to Rupert Dreadnought, and he therefore remained at the window, and eagerly and without the slightest tinge of jealousy watched Rupert as he held the young Scotch girl in his strong arms.

To *him* he was grateful.

In the case of Colin he would have felt a bitter burning at the heart.

As Allan watched them descending, his eye suddenly caught a sight which was lost upon Rupert, engaged as he was with his fair and precious burden.

Two men in masks, and with swords drawn, were standing beneath the shadow of the trees.

They were evidently on the watch for Rupert and his charge.

There was no mode, however, by which Allan of the Glen could apprise him of the danger, as he was now near the ground.

The only possible way to aid him was to rush down the rope immediately that his master and Mary Macpherson reached *terra firma*.

This spoiled entirely the plans which Colin had framed for himself.

He had hoped that when Allan descended he would be able by some manœuvre to cause his fall upon the hard ground below.

But in this he was foiled.

Directly that Rupert and his fair burden had reached *terra firma*, the young Scotch boy cried aloud to his companions—

"Hold fast, my friends."

Then, without giving them further intimation of what he was going to do, he seized the rope and ran down it with the nimble steps of a wild animal.

The men, who had been watching below, saw his movement.

They understood that he had seen them, and that for the present their plans, whatever they might be, were foiled.

So, ere the active young Scot had sprang to earth, they had disappeared.

Where, it was impossible to say.

There seemed truly no place where they could have concealed themselves.

Yet that they had done so was evident.

They had not had time to clear out of the grounds, and yet when Allan reached the ground they were nowhere to be seen.

"You have saved what I hold dearer than life itself," cried Allan to Rupert, as they met. "How can I ever repay you?"

Rupert smiled.

"You forget," he said, "your own services to me. But come, let us not neglect our friends. See, they are even now waiting our aid."

They accordingly seized the end of the rope and steadied it.

Then one by one the men came rushing downwards.

Colin came last.

He was thoroughly disappointed.

He had seen in this perilous descent the means of killing Allan of the Glen, and to hide his anger he now remained behind all the others.

The result was disastrous.

He had tied the double rope to the heavy furniture in the room ere the last three descended, and it had by this time been grated continually and heavily against the sharp stones.

When, therefore, he began his descent, he rushed down now as quickly as the others.

For two reasons he did this.

In the first plaoe, the flames were beginning to belch out from the casement immediately below the one from which he had to emerge.

In the second place, he desired to take Mary Macpherson from the hands of his fortunate but hated rival.

Dashing down, therefore, as he did, he paid no attention to the fact that the rope had been so frequently and roughly used before, and in a very few moments he found it was visibly giving way.

There was no help for it now, however.

To ascend was to risk as much danger as to descend, and he kept on, therefore, quickly though cautiously.

After a few moments of deadly suspense, the crisis came.

It was unexpected below, and those who witnessed it were far more surprised than the horror-stricken victim.

Suddenly, without any previous notice, the rope snapped asunder, and Colin, clutching wildly at the air, was flung headlong down upon the rough stones beneath.

CHAPTER XIII.

THE BALL-ROOM AGAIN—WILD THOUGHTS OF LOVE—THE ESCAPE—THE DESTRUCTION OF THE CASTLE.

We left the dancers in the ball-room of the castle, huddling together in dismay when the affrighted domestics entered with the news that the place was on fire.

No sooner had they passed out—it will be remembered, Sir Hugh Dalrymple leading the way with his wife—than they were met by a wall of fire, and in the confusion and delay that ensued, Henry Clanberris rushed to her side.

"Can I do anything to aid you?" he cried, nervously, yet bravely, thinking only of the safety of the one he loved—ignoring the presence of her husband—ignoring the flames that lapped up near them—only hoping, wishing that he could do something *for her*.

Up to this moment Sir Hugh Dalrymple had been entirely unsuspicious.

He saw now in his manner nothing but earnest friendship to himself.

"Yes," he cried, "you can. Take care of my wife while I rouse the servants to their duties. I know of but one chance of egress from this place, and that will have to be forced open.

So saying he placed the arm of Lady Dalrymple in that of Henry.

She clung to him now in terror, overwhelmed in fact by a multiplicity of feelings.

What a terrible meeting this was!

The first for so many years.

And now they were facing death together.

"Oh, Henry!" she murmured, as the huddling crowd thronged round her, "is this to be the end of all?"

He pressed her arm warmly.

"No, no," he whispered, "no, no. You will be saved—saved by me. Wait and hope, remember our motto. You will be saved for the future. Fear not, the past is but a trial."

She trembled as he spoke.

Not with fear.

Death was before—behind—around them—everywhere.

Yet no dread invaded her heart.

She trembled at the words and the voice of the one whom fortune had compelled her to discard.

She then knew how much she loved him.

She then brought to mind the words of the treacherous villain who had overheard the conversation she had had with Lady Clanberris, and who had threatened to betray her.

Was he not right?

He had prophecied her feelings towards her absent lover.

Were not her feelings just as he had predicted?

In the midst of this danger, a perilous idea suggested itself to Henry Clanberris.

Perilous to her peace of mind—perilous also to his own.

Could they not escape together in this hour of terrible danger?

Could she not be his now?

Could she not allow it to be supposed that she had perished in the conflagration, and thus forsake her husband for ever?

His love for her was so pure that, under other circumstances, the idea would never have suggested itself.

But, looking down upon her lovely form, and seeing the devouring flames surrounding her, contemplating her utter loss, he began to regard things recklessly, and be ready for any desperate action.

"Oh! Margaret," he whispered, "in the face of this awful peril, tell me do you love me still."

The soft arm of the unfortunate wife trembled in his.

"Oh! Henry," she said, "do not ask me again. I have already said too much to you."

He was about to say more—to beg of her to fly with him—to speak words which would have caused him to curse himself on the morrow, when Sir Hugh Dalrymple returned excitedly to the terrified group.

"This way, my friends, this way," he cried, and, flinging open wide the door by which he had entered, he showed the entrance to a broad staircase leading to a subterranean corridor.

Down this dark and unwholesome-smelling place the terrified guests were hurried. Just in time.

They had, as I have said, been met by a wall of fire, which, for the time, had confined itself to one spot; but now the lurid tongues of fire began to spring in spiral columns, and lick the ceilings, and thrust themselves along the floors.

One spark flung out from among them, and falling amid the lightly-dressed throng, would have set the whole place in a blaze—the whole crowd on fire—and death to every one would have been the result.

So it may be imagined that the throng of merry pleasure-seekers dashed madly after the master of the castle, and Lady Dalrymple, as if conscious that in her own heart she was wronging him, was the first to leap to his side.

She knew nothing of his desperate villany.

She knew not that he was the assassin of his brother.

She knew not that he had projected the cool and deliberate massacre of innocent men, and had only been prevented by an accident.

Otherwise, wrong as it now appeared to her, she would have still shrunk from him, and clung to her lover.

As it was, thinking him only a tyrant—looking upon him unlovingly only as the one who had been forced upon her by her friends, she took his arm, and with him headed the escaping throng.

Thanks to their good luck Sir Hugh Dalrymple was soon in the open air.

Here he, and all his guests and servants, were in safety at least.

But this was all that could be said.

The castle, that had been his pride, its grand pictures and its wondrous secrets, were now all things of the past.

Nothing on earth could save them.

A neighbour's house, as Colin had surmised, sheltered him for the night—the morning dawned to find him once more on the track of revenge!

CHAPTER XIV.

THE TRAITOR ONCE MORE—THE SCENE IN THE FOREST—THE CONSULTATION—THE TWO WATCHERS—MARY MACPHERSON AT THE INN—THE VILLAINS EFFECT AN ENTRANCE—THE ABDUCTION.

MANY persons who had suffered as much as Rupert Dreadnought and his friends in the pursuit of Sir Hugh Dalrymple, would have certainly felt inclined to abandon the affair altogether.

But our hero was not to be so deterred.

He had sworn to carry out the mission entrusted to him by his father, and he resolved therefore to remain in the vicinity of the castle until an opportunity occurred once more to come face to face with his foe.

Towards his punishment he had resolved now that Colin should be made to assist.

The unfortunate youth, victim of his own treacherous hatred, had not been killed instantaneously by his fall from the window.

He had broken both his legs and otherwise desperately maimed himself, but he was still breathing when the men raised him from the ground, and bore him away among the trees to the spot where Rupert had led Mary Macpherson.

The wretched creature opened his eyes and gazed painfully and wildly round him, and as his eyes fell upon the lovely form of the Scotch girl bending over him, it seemed to soothe his agony.

When restoratives had been applied to him by Rupert, who knew nothing, of course, of the hateful feelings he entertained towards Allan of the Glen, a litter was hastily made, and in accordance with his own wishes he was borne away to the house of the village surgeon.

When the men returned, a consultation was hastily held, and it was decided that Mary Macpherson, under the care of Allan of the Glen, should proceed to London, and placed in charge of Helen Penraven.

Allan was then to return with two more of Rupert Dreadnought's retainers, and two friends of Tom the waterman.

After taking leave of her preservers, therefore, Mary Macpherson leaped up before her lover, and they dashed rapidly away.

Not unnoticed, however.

The two men who had watched the night escape from the old castle, saw their departure, and followed in their track.

There being not sufficient hurry to warrant Allan in risking the health of Mary Macpherson by a fierce and desperate ride to London when she had neither sleep nor rest, he resolved to stay for a few hours at the first inn he came to, and give her refreshment and an opportunity for sleep.

Dressed as she was, moreover, it would have attracted some little attention had he borne her along in the daylight in the streets of London; and he wished if possible, therefore, to procure for her some more suitable habiliments.

Not far from Dalrymple House, it will be remembered, stood the inn where the attack had been made upon Rupert a night or so before.

To this, therefore, he at once made his way.

Arriving there he found, as he expected, that the people had all turned out to see the fire, whose lurid flames were still leaping up towards the sky, and illumining the country for miles around.

"RUPERT'S SWORD PINNED HIS ARM TO THE TREE!"

It was nothing strange, therefore, for him to ride up in hot haste with a lady half dressed in his arms.

The crowd at the inn door who had been so anxious to seize and drag to justice the supposed highwaymen, now made way at once for the lady in distress, and Allan found it a matter of no difficulty to reach the door, and assist Mary Macpherson into the inn.

"This lady has been just saved from the fire at Dalrymple House," he said to the landlady who came bustling out, "I want her to have a bed and refreshment and by to-morrow afternoon some clothes, for which I will pay you well."

"Certainly, certainly," cried the worthy woman, whose good nature was brightened by the promise of good money, "come this way, my dear. I will see that you have everything you wish. And you, master, you will require a bed and some refreshment also?"

"Yes; and the sooner the latter is brought, the better."

And so saying he walked into the room.

Presently the landlady returned, bringing with her the materials for a substantial meal, as well as Mary Macpherson dressed in some of her daughter's clothes, which, scarcely a good fit, were at any rate more fit for travelling than the undress she had been compelled to quit the castle in.

The meal was not long in being dispatched, and then after an affectionate embrace the lovers parted, and went to their respective chambers.

During all this time they had not been unwatched.

The two mysterious men who had, as I have said, seen the escape, had followed them, and had during the whole period of their supper been near them, though unnoticed either by Allan of the Glen or his mistress.

In fact, so many persons went in and out during the progress of their meal, that they did not observe any one in particular.

Had Mary Macpherson done so, she would have noticed the faces of two of Sir Hugh Dalrymple's retainers.

They were cunning rascals.

They had no desire to risk an open rupture even with one man, and, whatever their errand was, they appeared bent upon performing it by stratagem.

They had their ale, listened to Allan's arrangements, and then quitted the inn.

They had, in fact, heard enough.

The young girl and her lover were to sleep there, and, whatever their design was, they knew the time in which they had to perform it.

The sky was still rosy with the tremendous conflagration, and they soon beheld the room in which the young girl had retired to rest.

Having satisfied themselves of this fact, they concealed themselves among the bushes and quietly waited.

It was not more than an hour before the throng quietly dispersed, tired of looking at the same monotonous flames, the inn was once more closed, and the inmates retired to catch a few hours of repose before being compelled to open again.

When everything was quiet, the two mysterious watchers left their covert and looked around them.

It was evident now what they were after.

They halted below Mary Macpherson's window, and then one of them, raising himself upon the shoulders of his companion, drove, as noiselessly as possible, a long nail in the wall.

When this was firmly imbedded, he raised himself up by it, and, steadying himself upon it, grasped the window-sill.

After this he drew from his pocket what seemed to be a coil of strong though slender rope, but which, when shaken out, proved to be a rope-ladder.

At the end of this, which the man held in his hand, was a spring of iron, so formed as to close on the window-sill, and sustain itself the more firmly the greater the weight imposed upon it.

Having fixed this, he stepped upon it, and commenced the work of opening the window, which he found no difficult task.

Having opened it, he passed into the room, and called to his companion, who, having fixed in the earth the long spikes which were at the other end of the ladder, at once climbed up.

"Look," said the one who had first entered; "we're in luck. She's never undressed herself."

He was right.

Mary Macpherson was lying fast asleep upon the bed fully dressed.

The men approached the lovely sleeper with cautious steps.

Then suddenly one of them drew a handkerchief from his pocket, and pressed it to her face.

A slight quiver passed through her limbs; there was a slight clenching of the hands, and the sleeper slept on.

It was the sleep now, however, of insensibility.

They lost no time.

One of them raised the senseless girl in his arms, while the other hurried back to the window, and getting out, stood on the ladder ready to receive her form.

To bear her to the ground was a matter of no difficulty.

Rupert Dreadnought had done so with the aid only of a single rope, while they had a rope ladder.

They were soon on *terra firma* once more, the window closed, the rope ladder removed, and everything left as it had been.

The kidnappers' horses were close at hand in the wood, and in a few minutes they were dashing back towards Dalrymple House.

When she awoke, she found herself in the bed-chamber, and supported in the arms of Lady Dalrymple.

"Oh! madam," she said, "why have you done this?"

"Alas! my child," said Lady Dalrymple, in tears, "I, too, am a prisoner."

CHAPTER XV.

ALLAN'S MAD SORROW—HE RETURNS TO THE FOREST—THE STRANGER—THE QUARREL—THE DUEL, AND THE STRANGE DISCLOSURE THAT RESULTED.

THE rage and terror of Allan of the Glen can well be imagined when the landlady, pale with affright, informed him of the disappearance of Mary Macpherson.

It was indeed a terrible disappointment to him.

He had so suddenly and unexpectedly met her after so long and weary an absence; and now, after going through unheard-of perils to save her, she was lost to him again.

At first he felt inclined to blame the people of the house.

Certainly it *did* seem strange.

The bed had not been slept in.

The impression of her person was on it certainly, but that was all.

The window was closed, but the door, being locked on the *inside*, precluded at last any notion of attaching blame to the landlady or landlord.

How she had gone was a mystery.

But not a moment did he doubt her love for him.

Not a moment did he imagine that she had fled of her own free will.

The tender words whispered to him when her soft warm arms were round his neck in the room at Dalrymple House were quite enough to prove this.

Discording all foolish feelings of jealousy, he also discarded any notion of proceeding to London upon Rupert Dreadnought's business before returning to the neighbourhood of Dalrymple House, and informing his master of the misfortune which had occurred to him.

So, leaping on the horse he had ridden there on the night preceding, he paid the landlady for her kindness and trouble, and rode away towards the wood which abutted on the old house.

Here he had not much difficulty in finding Rupert and his friends.

During his absence they had made themselves as comfortable as they could in a little inn which abutted on the forest; and now as the dawn overspread the land, they had once more taken up their station at a point where they could overlook the approaches to the castle.

It was with the utmost surprise that Rupert beheld Allan approaching.

"What ails you, Allan?" he cried, seeing his wild and disordered looks: "have you been to London and back in this time?"

"No; I have not attempted to go," replied Allan, almost impatiently. "I am distracted—mad! I have been robbed of her I love best in life. Think not I am neglectful of your interests, for I desire as eagerly as you do to avenge myself on Sir Hugh Dalrymple, but I could not rest till I had told you all and asked you to aid me in recovering the one I prize so dearly."

Hurriedly he told his story.

Rupert Dreadnought listened attentively, and at once a light broke in upon his mind.

"Allan," he said, "this is the work of Sir Hugh Dalrymple."

"Why so? What spite *can* he have against her?"

"It is easily to be seen," returned Rupert, "why he should have an enmity against her, and what use he hopes to make of her."

"In what way?"

"In the first place that arch traitor, Colin, consented to our death. Was it not so?"

"It was."

"Well had it not been for his love for Mary Macpherson, we should have all been sacrificed. It was the sight of her among those to be massacred that made Colin leap from the balustrade of that subterranean gallery, and form our escape. There is not the slightest doubt that Sir Hugh Dalrymple has inveigled her away in some manner, and expects to learn from her our numbers, our purpose, and our whereabouts."

Allan's countenance fell at this.

In the power of Sir Hugh Dalrymple!

If Colin recovered then he would be able easily to communicate with her.

"You will, I hope, keep a good watch on Colin," he said, "*he* will be the one who will be best informed of her whereabouts."

Rupert thought a moment.

"You had better remain, Allan," he said. "I fancy, now that we have no ladies in the company, we can do with the force we have."

It was on the next morning, that, while Allan and Tom the waterman were keeping watch at the entrance of the wood, they saw approaching them a tall gentleman dressed in semi-military costume, with a beard and moustache which reminded him of Sir Hugh Dalrymple.

He at once acquainted Tom the waterman with his surmise.

"What are we to do?" asked Tom.

"Follow him," said Allan, "and when we have him far away from the highroad accuse him."

"And if we make an error?" asked Tom.

"We must chance that," said Allan. "I feel sure it is he. If not, it is some one whom I have seen in his house. Come, be not afraid. I am not," he added, with a smile; "I am not going to ask you to assist in murdering him."

Tom at once followed Allan, and they hurried after the stranger into the forest.

As luck would have it, whatever errand he was on, led him towards the spot where Rupert and his men had located themselves; and as he entered the glade where they were seated, a shrill whistle from Allan apprized them of the approach of a stranger.

In an instant they all sprang up.

"Who are you?" demanded Rupert, who guessed, from Allan's warning, that his enemy was at hand.

The new comer started back haughtily.

"What have we here?" he cried. "Have I found myself in the lair of a new Robin Hood? What want you?"

"Your name," replied Rupert.

"I refuse it, then," returned the stranger. "You have no right to ask."

Rupert's eyes flashed fire, and he drew his sword from its scabbard.

"Your words assure me that I *have* a right," he cried. "You are Sir Hugh Dalrymple."

The stranger laughed derisively.

"I see now that you are thieves and robbers," he answered, "who want a specious pretence for your villany. Tell me what money you require and let me pass."

"Not so," replied Rupert. "I refuse. Tell me who are you?"

"I refuse again," said the haughty stranger.

"Then, with my sword will I compel you to speak!" cried Rupert Dreadnought. "If you are a man draw and fight."

"You are assassins as well as thieves, I see," exclaimed the stranger. "Nevertheless, since you compel it I suppose I must fight."

"We are neither assassins nor thieves," answered Rupert; "but since you disbelieve us we will adjourn hence. I will appoint one of these two to be your second. Yonder Scotch youth shall be mine. Fear not, you will have fair play."

To this proposition the new comer, who imagined these proceedings to be only the prelude to some deed of villany, felt himself compelled to assent; and, passing into a woodland glade near at hand, they prepared for action.

Before swords were crossed, Rupert Dreadnought once more gave his antagonist a chance of avoiding the contest.

"If you tell me your name, and prove it to be correct," he said, "I will no longer delay you, unless, indeed, you be the Sir Hugh Dalrymple I seek."

"I again tell you I am not he," returned the stranger; "but I shall, nevertheless, refuse to disclose my name. I have reasons for keeping it secret: and how do I know you may not be in league with the very men from which most I would keep the knowledge?"

There was no further parley.

Rupert Dreadnought was determined that the stranger should speak.

Both he and Allan suspected that it was, indeed, Sir Hugh Dalrymple that stood before them.

The only way, therefore, to force the secret from him was at the sword's point.

CHAPTER XVI.

AT THE SWORD'S POINT.

THE manner in which the two strangely-matched opponents stood, was enough to show that they both knew well the use of the sword.

Their eyes gleamed brightly, but with far different feelings.

The one with resolution, the other with anger at being thus forced into a contest.

The duel waxed warm.

Several times Tom the waterman, who had been appointed the stranger's second, expected to see him pierced through, while, on the other hand, Allan felt his master to be in constant danger from the brilliant swordsmanship of his adversary.

As they fought they grew eager and more eager.

They became less careful in their passes, and their hot breath steamed in the chill air.

They forgot what they were fighting for in fact, and finding before him an enemy who was nearly his match, Rupert Dreadnought felt as if it were indeed his enemy that confronted him.

Presently the stranger, becoming inflamed with anger, made a desperate lunge, and Rupert, parrying his stroke just as he backed against a tree, passed his sword right through his arm, and pinned him to the trunk.

The sword fell from the stranger's hand, and involuntarily he uttered a cry of pain.

He was completely at the mercy of Rupert Dreadnought.

But the latter had no wish to take an unfair advantage of his position.

"Now, then," he cried, "I have you in my power completely. Tell me who you are. I seek Sir Hugh Dalrymple, a dastardly ruffian and assassin; a villain whom I am hunting down for the murder of his own brother. If you are he expect no mercy at my hands. If you are *not* he, prove to me that you are not his friend, and you shall go free."

The manner in which Rupert Dreadnought said these words was enough to prove his sincerity, and a most wonderful change came over the face of the stranger as he spoke.

"Had I known what you said before to be true," he cried, "I should not have refused to reply to your inquiry. As it is, the pain of my wound is great. Release me, and, while my second here binds it up, I will explain who I am. In the first place, however, I am not Sir Hugh Dalrymple, but Henry Clanberris."

The name had in it a familiar ring for Rupert.

Allan of the Glen had heard from Mary Macpherson many particulars in regard to the love of Lady Dalrymple for an absent one, and now eagerly withdrawing his sword, he offered him a drink of brandy and bade Tom at once bind up his wound.

Briefly then Henry Clanberris told him his story.

He said very little of Lady Dalrymple; not a word in regard to her love for him.

He spoke bitterly, however, of the forced marriage and his own blighted hopes; expressed his belief in the unhappiness of Lady Dalrymple, and honestly declared that if Sir Hugh Dalrymple *was* the villain that Rupert represented him to be, he would gladly aid in his destruction.

Rupert saw at once that he had to do with no impostor.

He therefore briefly recapitulated the reasons for his invasion of the Dalrymple mansion; the cause of Sir Hugh's not daring to call in the assistance of the authorities; and wound up by explaining his own name and station.

"Well," said Clanberris, "I am here also in a position of difficulty. Time has changed me. Sir Hugh Dalrymple does not see in me the hated Henry Clanberris of old; he only knows me by the name of Rolliston. Despairing of being able otherwise to see Lady Dalrymple, the love of my youth, I assumed this name, obtained an introduction to him, and was received at his house. The result you know. It remains now to sieze upon this man, drag him to the place where the murder was committed, and where you have sworn to punish him, and there force from his lips a confession of his crime."

"Such is our course. But where am I to find him?" said Rupert.

"*I* will see to that," replied Clanberris, who mingled with his sense of justice could not help recollecting that the destruction of Sir Hugh Dalrymple would mean happiness for himself and Lady Dalrymple. "I am now proceeding to see my sister. When I return this evening I will arrange with you as to how this villain is to be secured."

Having arranged matters thus far, and settled the time of meeting, he then quitted them, and in spite of his wound passed on with alacrity towards Clanberris House.

The wound, in fact, had far more pleasure than pain in it.

It was a token that he was on the road to success.

It was a sure sign by which he might remember how the happiness he had so longed for might be obtained.

Visions of bliss floated through his mind.

He should now ere long be enabled to possess the one for whom he had so long waited.

How glad was he now that his half-framed words had never left his lips; how glad that the terrible fire had not resulted in his asking her what she would have refused perhaps in tears, perhaps in anger!

Rupert Dreadnought had made no stipulation with him as regarded informing Lady Clanberris of what had happened.

He told her all, therefore.

She had, as we have seen, pleaded his cause to Lady Dalrymple on a former occasion, and she was happy enough, therefore, to see a chance of his being able at least to make her happy.

"Say nothing of all this to Margaret."

Such was her advice.

"I will not even see her," replied Henry. "It would be wrong to do so."

He was resolute now. He would not give himself the chance of giving way.

At the appointed hour in the evening he met Rupert in the wood once more.

The latter was awaiting him with anxiety.

"You have come then," he cried. "I am all eagerness to commence and bring to a successful conclusion my work."

MARY MACPHERSON.

"Well," returned Henry Clanberris, "I have been thinking over the matter, and I come to this conclusion. I have entered Sir Hugh Dalrymple's house by stealth and under a false name, and I will not so far continue my treachery as to betray him into the hands of those whose bounden *duty* is to kill him."

Rupert started.

The angry blood flew to his cheek.

"You wish to back out of your bargain now, then, I presume?" he said, with a frown.

"No, no," he said; "what I meant I, perhaps, did not express very clearly. I mean this; I will proceed to his house, I will enter, and at a certain hour I will place a light in a window. When you see this, you will understand that a certain little gate, which I shall show to you, is open. You will enter there, and ascend to the top of the staircase, where you will find me, most probably with sword drawn against Sir Hugh."

"Why so?"

"Because, as I have said, I will no longer sail under false colours," replied Henry Clanberris, "I will tell him all and leave you to do the rest. But stay; I have not yet explained myself. I told you I would not betray him to men whose duty it was to kill him."

"Well."

"You must, if I place him in your hands, consent to permit him to fight fairly for his life."

"It shall be so."

"And when and where he likes."

Rupert shook his head.

"No," he said, "I cannot concede that."

"Why not?"

"You forget my vow," replied Dreadnought, "I have sworn that when I have captured him, I shall bear him to the old church—place him in the vault—kill him and bury him in the same stone coffin as contains the bones of the brother he murdered."

"True, true, I had forgotten," replied Henry Clanberris, "nevertheless you can give him his sword, and I, if you like, will be his second in that dismal fight."

"Agreed," said Rupert; "in such a cause I shall feel my arm doubly nerved for the fight, though in very truth I am sorely tired of blood. But come—let us go. You wish me to accompany you, I believe, as far as the house?"

"Yes; but we must be cautious," said Henry Clanberris; "if we are watched I must explain to you from afar the locality of the little door; come, let us hasten."

Bidding Allan and his other friends await him in the wood, at the same spot, and be ready to rush after him at a given signal, Rupert Dreadnought then passed away with Henry Clanberris, and they were not long before they reached the corner of the wood, which abutted, as it were, upon the house where Sir Hugh Dalrymple had taken temporary refuge.

"Yonder," said Henry, as they paused here, "yonder is the house in question. At the side you observe a willow tree, whose branches hang almost to the ground. Behind that natural screen you will find the little door of which I speak. As soon as you see the light hurry in with your men, for it may chance that I am in danger, and in need of your aid."

Having settled these preliminaries, they parted,

and Henry Clanberris knocked boldly at the door of his enemy's house.

"Is Sir Hugh alone?" he asked of the man who admitted him.

"Yes," he said. "Shall I tell him you desire to see him?"

"No," replied Henry, "I will go up to his study; I know my way."

The man made no objection.

He knew him as a friend of his master's, and could have no suspicion of his mysterious errand.

Henry Clanberris, therefore, quickly ascended the stairs.

On arriving near the door of the study where Sir Hugh Dalrymple was sitting, he halted a moment, and then, instead of proceeding straight on, turned sharply to the right.

This led him at once to the top landing of a narrow staircase, which conducted to the small postern to which he had alluded in speaking to Rupert Dreadnought.

Noiselessly he descended.

Then he cautiously withdrew the bolts and left the door open to the extent of an inch.

Then as noiselessly he ascended the staircase, and knocked lightly at the door of the study.

"Come in," said Sir Hugh, languidly.

Henry drew a long breath, and, making his way in, locked the door behind him.

Sir Hugh gazed at him in surprise.

"Ah, Rolliston," he said, "you have something very private to tell me I expect, since you close the door so carefully."

Henry eyed him sternly.

"I have," he said, "something most private. It was not until to-night that I discovered that I was in the house of an assassin and a parricide."

For an instant this sudden blow paralysed the efforts of Sir Hugh Dalrymple.

A greenish pallor overspread his features, and he gazed at the speaker in wonder.

Then he sprang to his feet.

"Madman!" he said, "do you come to beard me here since you dared not in my own house?"

"This house is yours for the time," returned Henry, coolly, "therefore you're master as much here as at Dalrymple House."

"At any rate I will not suffer this insolence," cried Sir Hugh, furiously; "quit my presence at once."

"I refuse," replied Henry, "for two reasons. In the first place——"

"I will not listen," cried Sir Hugh, drawing his sword. "Leave this apartment, or I will call my servants to eject you."

"I have prepared myself for that," said Henry Clanberris.

And drawing a pistol from his breast, he levelled it at Sir Hugh.

"Coward!" cried Sir Hugh, as he sank back in his chair. "Say on, say quickly what you have to say, and quit my presence."

"In the first place, then," said his strange guest, "my name is not Rolliston; it is Clanberris."

"Clanberris!" exclaimed Dalrymple, his face blanching again.

"Aye, the one whose fair name you aspersed—the one who's bride you stole. But never mind that. I would not put you to the shame of this knowledge before. Now that I know you for what you are, I care not—I glory in it. But speak not. Listen. You are, as I have said, an assassin and a parricide. I am about to deliver you into the hands of those who have sworn to punish you."

"Traitor!" cried Sir Hugh Dalrymple, quivering with rage.

"Not so," replied Henry Clanberris, "not so. When I first came into your house, I imagined you certainly to be a slanderer and a deceiver, but I knew not that you were a murderer. Had I done so I would have proclaimed it aloud before your guests. At any rate, I consider myself to be acting conscientiously. No matter what I do, therefore, beware of calling out, or I shall fire and take upon myself the responsibility of judging you."

A cold sweat now invaded the limbs of the parricide.

He saw before him the quick approach of his punishment.

"You are in a hurry, indeed, to commit your dastardly crime," he said, with a ghastly effort at being satirical. "Might it not occur to you that I may have things to arrange before I am dragged away to certain death by assassination?"

"Your words are but a ruse," he said, "you cannot deceive me. If you have made a will, well and good. If you have not, your next heir will receive all."

"And leave my wife destitute," said Sir Hugh, catching at this as a drowning man catches at a straw.

Henry's eyes gleamed with a strange meaning.

"Fear not for your wife," he said, "*she* will want for nothing."

"Curse you!" muttered Sir Hugh Dalrymple, "if I escape from this enemy's trap your punishment shall be such as shall make you shudder to contemplate it."

"You will not escape," said Henry Clanberris, solemnly, and taking the lamp from the table in his left hand, he moved with it towards the window, still keeping the pistol ready in his right.

Having placed it on the window, he approached the door, still proceeding carefully backwards, and, unlocking it, left it a little a-jar.

He listened awhile.

But no sound came.

In fact, he was a little before his time.

He had forgotten to give Rupert Dreadnought sufficient time to go back to the forest glade and return with his men.

He sat down therefore and waited.

It was now growing dark and Rupert Dreadnought therefore could not be long.

Black clouds began to roll along the sky, and the wind began to rise and howl around the house, and shake the few walls which still remained of the burnt castle.

The two men sat silently watching one another.

Presently there was the tramp of approaching feet.

"They come," said Henry Clanberris.

A tremor invaded the heart of Sir Hugh Dalrymple, in spite of all his daring courage.

He was absolutely surrounded by unavoidable peril.

The tramp of feet came nearer, and then the lower door was cast violently open.

A violent gust of wind roared up the staircase, and flung open the door of the room.

In an instant the lamp that stood in the open window was dashed out into the road, and the room was left in total darkness.

The report of a pistol followed instantly.

Determined that the parricide should not escape if he could by any means prevent it, Henry Clanberris had fired the shot, and then rushed eagerly forward.

But it was of no avail.

In the darkness it was impossible to tell with precision where the person was whom he wished to attack, and the ball took no effect.

As Henry Clanberris rushed upon his adversary, therefore, he received a violent wound with a sword, and fell backwards heavily to the ground.

In another instant Sir Hugh Dalrymple had dashed out of the window and was gone just as Rupert Dreadnought and his men burst into the room.

CHAPTER XVII.

THE ESCAPE—THE INNOCENT WIFE AND THE REMORSELESS HUSBAND—THE QUARREL—THE SUPPOSED ILLNESS—THE RIDE TO CHICHESTER—THE FOLLOWING PHANTOMS—ALONE WITH THE MURDERED DEAD!

SIR HUGH DALRYMPLE knew well that, with such a host of enemies on his track, it would be utterly useless to attempt any real escape from the vicinity that night.

All his pride was gone now.

All he thought of was dear life.

He saw himself helplessly in the toils.

What he must do now was to remove all evidences of his crime, and if he could not then brave it out fly to the continent.

But first he must see his wife.

She was near, in a friend's house—her residence known only to himself and the two willing ruffians who had abducted Mary Macpherson.

At her place, therefore, he would find the best safety.

And, more than this, he would have the demoniacal triumph of punishing her for her fault—a fault not her own!

How could she avoid being loved by one who has been her childhood's friend, and who had been her heart's desire until Sir Hugh Dalrymple had appeared like an evil genius upon the scene?

Dropping from the window, at the peril of life and limb, he rushed towards the house where Lady Dalrymple was, so to speak, confined.

She had told Mary Macpherson she was a prisoner.

This was literally true.

A few vague words dropped by a guest had set his mind in a flame, and he had rigorously concealed her.

Now he felt more than ever the justice of what he had done.

And yet there was no necessity!

The clock was warning the ninth hour, she was just preparing to go to her lonely couch, and with a weary heart she rose to leave her room.

Softly she opened the door and glided down the dimly-lighted corridor, thinking of the past—of her present almost forlorn condition, and—of Henry Clanberris.

No wonder, thinking of him, that she started back.

Who stands before her with set, haggard face and blazing eyes?

No words escaped his pallid lips as he passed his arm round her shivering form, and carried her through the dressing-room into the bedchamber beyond.

As she sank trembling upon the couch, her heart quailed with deadly terror as she looked upon the face of the husband whom she hated.

"Where were you going, Margaret?" he asked, in a stern voice.

"To bed. Where else, since all here is drear and lonely?" she replied, almost angrily.

"Are you sure you were not trying to leave the house by stealth?"

She clenched her hands tightly and gazed at him boldly.

"Why should you think so?" she said. "Why should you dream of such a thing? Do you know that I am justified in desiring to escape your tyranny that you speak thus?"

Sir Hugh Dalrymple saw he had gone too far.

He assumed, therefore, a sanctimonious air, if we may so express it; and said, in low, hoarse tones—

"I know all, Margaret; you wish to leave me, but *I* can prevent that. You will live to thank me for saving you from being the vilest thing on God's earth. You need not fear. I shall not harm you, and I shall not expose you. *Your* honour is *mine*. But never again shall you occupy the place of wife. You shall be as dead to the world as though you slept in your grave. Never shall you have the opportunity of disgracing me. My mother, thank Heaven, was a good woman; and one who has sinned, even in thought, shall never take her place!"

He thought that all this would be very terrible to her.

It was not so.

She merely smiled.

"I fear you not," she said: "neither do I pay heed to your menaces or your insults. I am your faithful wife, and I have ever behaved as such; treat me as you will, you can never drag from me a confession of anything that is wrong. *You* know that you stole me from one who loved me; that I was forced into a marriage with you when I hated the idea. But in the face of all this you know how I have behaved; how devoted I have been; how I have striven to conquer my aversion. But there; I will not attempt to defend myself when I am guilty of nothing. Read your own heart, wretched man, and if it accuses me, say so"

He had no time to reply.

Before he could utter a syllable, there was a loud and impatient knocking at the door.

Sir Hugh turned ghastly pale.

He was not only foiled again, but these might be enemies.

If they were, he stood the chance of losing his wife also.

"Margaret," he said, solemnly, "will you swear to me that you are not in league with the men who this night have made a dastardly attack upon me?"

"I know nothing of it," replied Margaret, earnestly, "to this I swear. I know not even what you mean."

"Good; then understand me," said her husband, "this knocking at the door portends danger to us both. Take this pistol; go into that inner room and lock the door. If any one threatens to molest you, fire!"

Gazing at his beautiful wife—seeing his own danger—knowing that her old lover, Henry Clanberris, was the leader of his enemies, he was determined that she should not fall into their hands.

In giving her the pistol he had a deep design.

He hoped that Henry Clanberris would force his way into the room in the darkness, and that her own hand would take her lover's life.

She took the pistol, and he gently led her into the adjoining chamber.

The door of this she locked, and then drawing his sword, Sir Hugh Dalrymple advanced to open the door.

There had been a repetition of loud and impatient knocking during the short conversation which had ensued between Sir Hugh Dalrymple and his wife.

But it was not as he had anticipated.

The person who had given the summons at the door was not an enemy, but one of the servants.

He looked pale and scared.

"What ails you?" cried Sir Hugh. "Quick! speak!"

"I know not what it means," replied the man, "but there is some devilment about."

Sir Hugh frowned.

"Explain yourself," he said. "This is no time for folly. Quick, say—what is it you mean?"

"Well, Sir Hugh," said the man, who still trembled violently, "I was leaning out of one of the back windows when I saw a crowd of men approaching from the direction of the house which had been given up for your reception. They stopped in the highway opposite this, and one of them, who was dressed in a Scotch dress, advanced and pointed out this place."

"Well?" said Sir Hugh, impatiently.

"Well, Sir Hugh, they then proceeded in different directions, and I thought I had seen the last of them for the time—but no!"

"Are they there now, then?" asked Sir Hugh.

"No, Sir Hugh. I will tell you. I kept looking still out of the window when I thought I saw one of the bushes move.

"It was not fancy.

"They were now in the gardens.

"I could see their forms moving about, and ——"

"Where are they now?"

"Here," cried a voice, and, as it spoke, Rupert Dreadnought and Henry Clanberris, followed by their men, burst into the room.

Too late now Sir Hugh Dalrymple saw the truth.

He had been betrayed by one of his own retainers.

The conversation which the man had held with him had been only a pretext for delay.

"Cowards!" cried the parricide, now really at bay. "Cowards! is it thus you attack one man?"

Rupert Dreadnought advanced towards him.

"We come not here to attack you," he said.

"Why thus in arms, then?" cried the other.

"Because we come to arrest you, and are prepared for resistance," replied Rupert. "I come in conformity with the vow which I have made, and the particulars of which have been given you by Henry Clanberris, who stands beside me. I come not to assassinate you as *you* assassinated your brother. I come to take you to the spot where that foul murder was committed, and there, with my own arm and my own sword, to punish you for that deed or perish. You will have fair play, doubt not."

A sneering smile passed over the lips of Sir Hugh Dalrymple.

He pointed to his drawn sword.

"I am armed," he said, "and ready. Why not fight now?"

"Because," returned Rupert Dreadnought, "that is not according to my vow. It is of no avail to keep it unless I keep it thoroughly. Come, sir, sheathe your sword and go quietly. Resistance is utterly useless."

Sir Hugh did as he was bidden.

"Providence," he said, with an affectation of solemnity, "will watch over me. You are either murderers or madmen. But stay," he added, as a sudden thought occurred to him, "may I take leave of my wife?"

It was a simple request.

They knew not its deep meaning.

Rupert, of course, could not refuse him such a thing as this, and, under guard, he was allowed to enter.

He had thought he could have a chance of escape, but he was wrong.

Within half an hour he was mounted on a horse and on his way to St. Andrew's, Chichester.

This was the place where his terrible retribution was to take place.

Given away with No. 6 of "Rupert Dreadnought."

"Boys of England" edition.

"RUPERT STOOD FIRM AS HIS OPPONENT FELL BACKWARDS."

(See an early number.)

RUPERT OR THE DREADNOUGHT SECRETS OF THE IRON CHEST

"THE BULLET, SENT WITH A TRUER AIM, SOON LAID HIS ADVERSARY IN THE DUST."

After a short journey Sir Hugh Dalrymple was removed from horseback and placed within a close carriage.

This expedient was adopted in order to preclude the possibility of his crying out and attracting the notice of passers by.

It was none of Rupert Dreadnought's plans to follow the carriage which contained the prisoner.

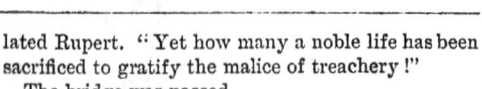

He knew well that so large a concourse of persons guarding a prisoner would excite suspicion.

So he placed the party in the hands of Tom the waterman.

"Be careful," he said, "to guard him, but do not let him be seen more than is absolutely requisite."

"I will not let him leave the carriage. We will travel post. He cannot cry out bound and gagged as he is, and there is, therefore, no fear of detection. And where, tell me, is the place of rendezvous?"

Rupert thought a moment.

"At the 'Chequers,' near Chichester. Opposite that inn there is a dense wood, in that you can place the carriage and its prisoner, and await my arrival.

"Good," said Tom; "but will these men obey me?"

Rupert turned to the men who were on guard round the carriage.

"Remember," he said, "Tom Braxley is going upon a mission which involves a subject very dear to my heart, so obey him as you would me, and doubt not that I will amply reward you."

A murmur of approbation and consent passed through all as he turned towards the spot where his horse was standing.

CHAPTER XVIII.

PERILS BY LAND.

"Adieu, then, my comrades! Bear in mind the instructions I have given you, and all will be well."

So said Rupert, as he vaulted to the back of his gallant steed, and waved his hat to his companions.

"Now, away! away!" he continued, patting the noble animal's neck, and slightly touching his flanks with his glittering spurs.

How wonderful is the attachment which sometimes exists between the noblest types of human and brute creation. The noble horse knew his master's voice, and, obeying the word of command, started off at a rapid pace.

The numerous steeples and turrets dotting the smoky horizon, grew larger and larger in his vision, as he neared the great city.

Rupert would have avoided London had he not been pressed for time.

It was necessary that his journey should be performed quickly as well as secretly; so, as he rode on, he held mental debate with himself.

Unless he reached his destination within a given time, his journey would be, to a certain extent, useless.

So he resolved to brave the chances of recognition in the streets of London rather than journey by a roundabout route.

Still, as he rode through the streets of London, he glanced cautiously about him to be certain that he was not watched.

At length he saw before him the frowning gateway of Old London Bridge, and he cast a shuddering glance at the ghastly relics of mortality which grinned above the gateway.

"Pray Heaven mine may never be there," ejaculated Rupert. "Yet how many a noble life has been sacrificed to gratify the malice of treachery!"

The bridge was passed.

Rupert felt more at ease, for he fancied that now his greatest dangers had been encountered.

Little did he dream that the quiet, shady lanes in which he soon found himself contained far more perils than the busy haunts of men.

A few miles more and the perspiration reeking from the sides of his gallant horse told him that it was time to rest.

He looked about him somewhat anxiously for a glimpse of a human habitation.

Some little distance ahead was a clump of trees, from which arose a column of blue smoke.

A nearer view revealed to him a small wayside inn.

"The very place for me," thought Rupert. "Here, at all events, I can rest awhile without fear of being disturbed."

He rode up to the door.

"Ho, there, landlord!" he shouted.

For some moments there was no response.

He shouted again, and a voice was heard replying.

"Coming, good sir," it cried; "curb your impatience for a few minutes."

Rupert dismounted.

"A strange-looking place this," he said to himself; "but one in which I shall not be likely to meet any acquaintance."

The landlord appeared at the door.

He was a stalwart man, in the prime of life; and Rupert noticed, as he stood uncovered by the side of his horse, that his head was bald, and bore the traces of a deep wound.

"What is it you want, sir?" he asked, gazing in the face of the traveller.

"Food and drink for myself and horse," replied Rupert.

The landlord answered by leading the steed to the stable, pointing at the same time to the doorway.

Rupert strolled up the sanded passage, and entered a little room on the right.

In a few moments the landlord joined him.

"I have attended to your beast," said the man; "now what shall I have the honour of serving you with?"

"A bottle of your best wine, and any food that you can place on the table within the space of five minutes."

The host of the roadside tavern gave the necessary instructions to his buxom spouse, and in a very short space of time Rupert was seated before a flask of Burgundy, a loaf of brown bread, and a substantial joint of roast beef.

"This is the best I can give you," said the landlady, as she dropped a curtsey, and lingered in the room a few moments to see whether the handsome young stranger had any commands.

But Rupert's modest wants were satisfied, and he politely intimated that he could dispense with the good woman's presence.

As soon as his simple meal was ended, Rupert strolled up to the window, and looked forth.

"Would that I could end my days in such a scene

as this," thought he, as he gazed at the green fields and the waving cornfields, from which came no sounds save the hum of insects and the song of birds.

All seemed peace, yet near him was fearful danger.

Behind the hedgerow which skirted the road lurked a man.

That man had seen Rupert enter the inn, and was now waiting anxiously for his re-appearance.

"The bill, mine host," cried Rupert.

The young traveller threw a piece of gold upon the table, and ordered his horse to be brought to the door.

"One glass with me, good sir," said the host, when Rupert was once more fairly in his saddle; "it is not usual for my guests to refuse the stirrup cup at parting."

A glass was brought, and Rupert raised it to his lips.

"A pleasant journey to you, good sir," said the host.

"Amen!" returned Rupert.

"Ha! ha! ha!" laughed a hoarse, discordant voice.

Rupert glanced round.

A man's face had for a moment appeared among the bushes near.

But he was now gone.

No one was in sight save the host, and thinking that his ears had deceived him, he resumed his journey.

But his ears had not deceived him.

The man who had laughed rushed away into the wooded country near, and in a few moments was dashing after him on a splendid horse.

CHAPTER XIX.

THE APPARITION.

It was some minutes before Rupert knew that he was pursued.

At length he heard the sound of other hoofs besides those of his own horse.

He turned to see who was coming.

He did not recognise the face of the stranger, and at first thought that he was some peaceful traveller on the king's highway.

But as time passed on, and the unknown still persistently dogged his path, he began to think that it was time to inquire his business.

He turned his horse's head and halted.

The stranger did the same, and the two men remained facing each other.

"Who are you, and why do you follow me?" demanded Rupert, sternly.

The stranger at first made no reply.

Rupert repeated the question, giving his words additional emphasis by laying his hand on the hilt of his sword.

"It matters not who I am," replied the stranger, "but my business is with you."

"With me?"

"Aye."

"What do you desire to know?"

"Whither you go and your object in going."

"You are insolent, sir," responded Rupert. "Begone, rascal, nor dare annoy me again."

The stranger suddenly drew a pistol from his belt, and levelled it at Rupert's head.

"Ha, traitor!" thundered Rupert, as he imitated the example of his adversary.

The pistol held by the unknown stranger exploded with a loud report; but Rupert was quicker, and his bullet, sent with truer aim, laid his adversary in the dust.

In an instant our hero dismounted, and gazed well into the features of his fallen foe.

"Why did he foil me thus?" he mentally remarked.

There was no solution to this question.

Our hero searched the pockets of the dead man, but there was no document of any kind to prove his identity or give a reason for his strange conduct.

He pondered for a few minutes.

"I must give information," he thought, "or some poor fellow who chances to pass by this way will be arrested for murder."

So he reluctantly rode back towards the inn.

But ere he had traversed half the distance, a strange unaccountable feeling came upon him, filling his mind with vague doubts and gloomy presentiment of coming evil.

His head felt heavy, his eyes became dim.

He reeled in the saddle, and with great difficulty, reached a little brook that crossed the road, dismounted, thinking that a draught of the cold water would refresh him.

But he was mistaken, for, as he knelt down to drink, he fell senseless.

* * * * *

An hour afterwards two peasants returning home from their labours saw a dark object lying on the moonlit road by the side of the brook.

It was Rupert.

His faithful steed was bending over him, endeavouring to call back life to the senseless form of his beloved master, rubbing his nose against his face, and caressing him in a hundred different ways.

The peasants were startled.

They feared that a murder had been committed, and trembled lest they themselves might be accused of the crime.

After a short consultation they decided upon a plan.

Rupert was laid across the back of his horse, and so conveyed to the inn.

A sleeping apartment was hastily got ready for him, and a surgeon who had just arrived volunteered his services.

"He will soon recover," said the medical man. "Aid me in pouring this effervescing draught down his throat and the unnatural slumber will quickly terminate."

These orders were obeyed, and the patient was then left to himself.

It was nearly midnight when Rupert awoke.

He felt confused, and for some time was unable to clearly account for his presence in a strange place.

At length, when he could clearly recollect all that

had taken place up till the time he became unconscious, he endeavoured to rise.

But bodily weakness had succeeded mental oblivion.

His limbs refused to fulfil their office, and much as he wished to rise and continue his journey, he was compelled to remain recumbent till his strength had returned.

The moon's light shining through the lattice window enabled him to see pretty clearly the various objects in the room.

On the table by his bedside was a bottle.

Rupert seized it, and tasted its contents, which he found to be good wine.

A moment after a rustling sound in the room attracted his attention.

"Who is there?" he asked. "Is it you, mine host?"

There was no response.

The draught of wine had reinvigorated Rupert's frame.

He sat up on the bed, and glancing towards the window, saw a strange sight.

There was a tall ghost-like figure, clad in garments of the orthodox spiritual hue, being draped in a long white cloak or mantle.

Rupert grasped his sword, which had been left by his bedside, and sprang up.

The figure in white saw the movement and disappeared through the open window.

Rupert followed; but ere he reached the ground the unknown was lost to sight behind the stables by the side of the inn.

A thought struck Rupert's mind as he followed in pursuit.

He had caught a glimpse of the face of his ghostly visitor, and he felt certain that the features were those of the man whom he had left for dead on the road three hours before.

"Then I did not kill him," thought he; and at that moment, as if to strengthen his conviction that the man still lived, he heard sounds resembling the galloping of a horse over the adjacent meadows.

Our hero was now thoroughly roused.

He hastened back to the stables, opened the door, and saddled his steed.

Two courses were before him: either to follow the strange intruder or continue his journey towards Chichester. He decided on the latter.

First carefully loading his pistols and seeing that his sword was loose in its sheath, he led his horse out of the stables and mounted.

He cared not now for any danger he might encounter, for he was prepared.

The night was very dark, and objects were not plainly visible.

Yet, now and then, it seemed to Rupert that some one was following him.

That he should be followed thus was, of course, no matter of wonder.

The mission he had in hand was one of stupendous importance, and of a nature unsanctioned absolutely by law.

It was not to be wondered at, therefore, if many persons connected intimately with the man whom he was forcing to his doom should attempt to destroy him.

However, he thought little of it.

He was engaged upon a good errand.

Providence had hitherto watched over him with care.

Why should he doubt now that it would cease its protection?

So on he rode.

On the road the mysterious apparition never once made his appearance, and he arrived at the appointed place with no further interruptions.

CHAPTER XX.

IN WHICH SIR HUGH DALRYMPLE ACTS A NEW PART.

We must now follow for awhile the fortunes of the one whom Rupert's friends were carrying to his just doom.

When Rupert arrived at the inn, he found that his friends truly were there, but the prisoner was gone!

Here was a mystery.

But he *had* gone!

They had never once ceased to watch him, but he had slipped away during the journey.

There was, in fact, a traitor among them.

He had pretended to be the most zealous of the party, and during the slow passage of the carriage along a rough portion of the road, he had opened the carriage door and let him escape.

Sir Hugh, who knew well the destination to which he was going, was more mad than sane as he rushed away, and conceived the idea of destroying the church where lay his murdered brother and papers which implicated him.

So he proceeded to the house of the old sexton, who knew him well, and who was somewhat startled by his haggard appearance.

"Go, old Thomas," he said, "and fetch me your friend Langton. I have work to do this night."

There was the glitter of madness in Sir Hugh's eyes.

The old sexton feared him.

But he *had* been a friend to him in times gone by.

So he resolved to obey him.

"Good," he said, as he slipped on his heavy cloak. "Be careful with the place."

A presentiment that he was being deceived made him speak thus, but Sir Hugh only nodded, and, as he passed out, sat down moodily.

For some time after the departure of old Thomas, Sir Hugh Dalrymple sat very still gazing at the flames.

Then the fire grew dead, and he became cold, and rising, searched the cottage for fuel.

In this search he discovered certain objects which made his eyes gleam, and his heart leap in his breast.

Once before he had sought for them when his mind was still strong and healthy within him.

Now, amid the ruin of his health, both bodily and mental, they suggested to him a wild and terrible idea.

And what were they?

The keys of St. Andrew's church.

He took them down from the nail behind the door, and eyed them curiously.

Had he been quite sane the idea might have suggested itself to him that he had acted foolishly in hiding documents in a coffin, and that it would be well for him to destroy them even now.

But he was cold, and the idea of a fire suggested itself naturally to him.

A grim smile stole over his lips.

A demoniacal smile it was, as if he appreciated and enjoyed beforehand the huge and terrible conflagration which would hide among its ashes relics of family mysteries, and registers of births, marriages, and deaths—registers upon which depended the hopes and fortunes of many a house.

He walked to the door, and looked out.

The sky had been very dark, and threatening snow.

Now the mist, which had spread itself over the country, was dispelled, however, and here and there the heavens were visible.

Not a mouse stirred.

All was hushed, as if in expectancy of something.

Sir Hugh cautiously closed the door behind him, and walked calmly towards the church, quickly, boldly, in the dim light, as if he were afraid of no man.

He passed into the church, shut the heavy door behind him with a slam, and made his way to the vestry.

As luck or ill luck would have it, two men were returning about this time from a friendly gathering at an inn a little above the church, and as they passed they noticed an unusual light in the building.

There was a flicker on the windows, a dull glare among the pilasters of the belfry, and then a pane of glass cracked.

After standing in wonder a moment, they rushed to the "Chequers," and gave the news.

Rupert and his friends at once hurried out, and rushing to the spot pulled the bell of the churchyard.

Receiving no answer, they leaped the low paling, and knocked at the cottage door.

There being no reply here, they pushed the door open, and looked in.

The room was empty, and the fire was nearly out.

"We'd best go up to the church," said one of them, "and see for ourselves."

They went up.

"A MAN'S HEAD APPEARED AMONG THE BUSHES."

There was a strange smell—a crackling and a snapping noise.

The door was hot.

The vestry was on fire.

They thought, too, they heard a moaning, wailing cry within, but of this they were not sure.

"Master Dreadnought," cried Tom, "I will run to the village and tell the people to come up. You stop here; you may, perhaps, see something."

Without waiting to explain his meaning, he ran off and left Rupert alone.

What he saw then, no one believed, when he told them, until he had solemnly assured them of the truth of his words.

He drew himself up by his hands to the sill of a window, and then gradually stood up, and forcing in the ventilator, gazed in.

The church was alight in a dozen places.

The altar, the pulpit, the pews, the vestry, and everything inflammable, in fact, were slowly burning.

And here and there, in every part of the church, now in the black of the choking smoke, now in the red of the fearful glare, he saw flitting to and fro the form of a man.

Who he was he knew not.

He had never seen, to his recollection, his face before, and could not see it now plainly.

As far as he could make out the features, they were set in a face of a wild and unearthly mould, a pale, ghastly, spectre-like face, such as few have seen and few would care to see again.

In vain Rupert endeavoured to force his way into the edifice.

The framework of the windows was of stone, and the part where the glass was, was too narrow to allow of his squeezing his body through.

And so, without being able to raise his hand to help, he gazed hard at the form of the madman, now at the road, where the expected help was to arrive.

There was a strange smoke ascending from a door near the altar, and the horrible conviction forced itself into the watcher's mind that the bodies and their coffins were burning below.

He shouted to Sir Hugh Dalrymple, whom, in the fearful light, he did not recognize.

But amid the roaring of the flames, and the crackling of the wood, and the splitting of the glass, the madman heard him not.

The heat was now becoming so excessive that Rupert Dreadnought could bear it no longer, and leaping over he looked eagerly towards the village to see if help was coming.

The fire could now be seen for miles around.

The huge lurid flames shot up in horrid tongues towards the heavens, through window and roof and skylight, and vacant places, where huge beams had been, were soon filled by a red-hot glare.

Up from the town streamed the crowding population.

Round the church they gathered, standing awe-struck, amid the tenements of the quiet dead, wondering how the place could be saved, yet not one suggesting the means.

Then while they were considering, a huge piece of blazing timber fell from the belfry, and dashed down upon the ground.

A myriad fiery particles floated through the air like flakes of red snow, and whirling in through the open door of the cottage, set that also in a blaze.

It was now that a whisper ran through the crowd that there was a man in the burning edifice.

No one could see him, for the place was all aglow, and in the white heat no objects could be distinguished.

But Rupert had told them what he had seen, and they had heard a moaning cry ever and anon ascending through the crackling of the timbers and the roaring of the flames.

So they began to break open the door.

Again and again they attacked it with pickaxes and spades and strong shoulders, and, at length, the hinges, yielding from the burning wood, gave way and a heavy body wavered and fell in among them.

It was a man's form.

He uttered a hollow groan as they seized him in their arms, and, placing him on a shutter, bore him away towards the village.

As they did so, he uttered a few disjointed sentences about the cold and "Sir Hugh Dalrymple."

Rupert heard the name and sprang forward.

"A moment!" he cried. "What name was that he spoke?"

The bearers stopped at once, and Rupert ran to the man's side.

"Lower him a little," he said, and the suffering man was at once lowered.

"What name was that you spoke?" asked Rupert.

"Sir Hugh Dalrymple," whispered the man, in tremulous accents of great pain. "The sexton is a friend of his; don't trust him."

At the very moment he was speaking, Sir Hugh Dalrymple, who had escaped from the church by a side door, had hurriedly crept up to where the sexton was standing watching eagerly the attempts made to save his cottage; attempts, be it said, which turned out to be successful.

"Say not a word," whispered the villain, "say not a word. The vault is unharmed. See that it is locked and that no one touches it. Here are the keys. I will return to-morrow night at ten and meet you at the 'Chequers Inn;' a good reward shall be yours."

Then he turned and fled away into the night.

It is not necessary to speak of how the cottage was saved sufficiently to enable the old sexton to resume his dwelling in it, or how St. Andrew's church was almost levelled to the earth.

Suffice it to say that the whole population of the suburb of St. Andrew's, Chichester, was unable to fight against the huge conflagration, and that it was almost morning before they returned to their homes.

CHAPTER XXI.

THE OLD SEXTON MAKES AN ERROR.

On the following night old Thomas, who generally spent his whole time at the "Chequers," remained at home, in spite of the admonition of Sir Hugh Dalrymple.

Over his glass, and with his welcome pipe, he sat by his wood fire, which blazed and crackled merrily up the chimney.

He was thinking of the strange events of the night before.

The quiet around was deathlike.

But Thomas was used to this.

His cottage was near the large gate, with its quaint awning, and its bell to ring in the dead.

And yet he lived amid a cluster of tombstones.

The early inhabitants of St. Andrew had not reckoned that posterity would die as well as they, and the burying ground was so small that it was necessary to encroach upon what had been a kind of ornamental ground, around the sexton's dwelling.

Old Thomas had made no objection.

As long as he could remember he had been accustomed to death.

Death had been his companion, his employer, and it had no terror for him.

Yet a little sound from some object without startled him.

A deeper shade on the wall—a rustle as of gliding footsteps on a marble floor, and it was gone.

He was unused to the slightest noise in that lone spot, except a chance vehicle along the road; and now he had not noticed even a footfall.

Had any one approached, he felt sure he must have heard his coming, for the night was frosty, the ground hard, and in that deathly silence a pin-fall might have been detected.

He rose and looked out.

All was still.

The moon was high in a blue, clear sky studded with stars.

The tombs looked white, weird, unearthly.

There a plain, stone slab; here an iron-nailed block of wood; here a tall pilaster standing in bold relief against the cold sky; here a mound of turf-covered earth to show how the head that rested there was humble while it lived, to show, too, how man strives to keep up after death the hollow distinctions of life.

Clear away the headstones, break up your marble monuments, dig down two feet below, and level the ground.

Who, then, in searching shall distinguish noble from peasant, king from subject?

What are these headstones but tributes to regret—monuments to our own littleness.

Do we not place them there in sorrow because our life is so brief?

Do we not place them in fear lest the world should pass by in its wanderings and forget us for ever?

So old Thomas stood at his door, and looked out.

But he could see nothing—hear nothing.

"Ah!" he said, "I must have made a mistake. However, I'll leave the door ajar, and listen."

He half closed it, and then, returning to his seat by the fire, resumed his pipe.

Whether it was the soothing effect of the fragrant tobacco, or the cool night air, I cannot say, but certainly the old man closed his eyes, and dozed.

From this he was roused by the rustle of feet once more, and, as he started, he caught sight of the shadow of a man's form in the doorway—deep, clear, unmistakable, as it fell between it and the moonlight.

Alarmed, and full of superstitious awe, Thomas sprang up, and rushed out into the night.

There was nothing to be seen.

All was again still, hushed as usual.

The sexton trembled.

"This is very dreadful," he murmured, as he wiped the cold drops of perspiration from his brow. "Me an old man, too, and all alone. I don't half like it, and I wish I had gone to the inn."

He looked fearfully around him.

"Yet I don't know," he went on, "as anybody would harm me. There ain't no good to be got by it. An old man here like me what has nothing to be robbed of, and has done no harm to no one. Put on your hat, Thomas, and go and see what it is, that's what I say."

So talking and murmuring to keep his courage up, the old man re-entered the cottage, took his hat and a stout stick, and walked out along the broad path towards the church, never dreaming that danger was before him.

Meanwhile, Sir Hugh Dalrymple, who had no idea of trusting the sexton at all, had approached the cottage at the very hour which he had appointed to meet Thomas at the "Chequers Inn."

Clambering over the churchyard railings, he went to the sexton's door.

Here he listened.

Old Thomas was talking to himself, and through the keyhole Sir Hugh Dalrymple saw him rise and approach the entrance.

Sir Hugh drew back, and hid himself among the tombstones.

"Hang the old fool," he muttered; "at this moment I made certain that he was at the 'Chequers Inn.'"

When the sexton, therefore, left the door open, and started at the sound of rustling feet, it was Sir Hugh who had entered and purloined from behind the door the heavy keys admitting to the vaults of the destroyed church.

Making his way, then, swiftly towards the ruins, he found the staircase leading to the vault of the Dalrymples.

This he descended quickly, and was soon in a stone chamber with ledges round it, upon which were stowed away the ancestors of the family in stone coffins.

Placing his dark lantern on a ledge, he took from his pocket a short piece of iron, and prepared to force open the lid of one of the coffins.

It was that marked—

"Horace Dalrymple."

CHAPTER XXII.

THE FIGHT IN THE DEATH VAULT.

Any one less bold, or rather, any one less under the influence of semi-madness than Sir Hugh Dalrymple, would have trembled at the task he had set himself.

His idea, however, was to destroy the papers he had foolishly concealed in the coffin of his murdered brother, and to destroy also the skeleton upon whose fractured skull still rested the evidences of guilt.

So he resolutely worked away, driving back the feelings which every now and then sent a tremulous fear to his heart.

The coffin had originally had a key by which to open it.

This key, however, was now in the possession of Rupert Dreadnought, and nothing could, therefore, be done but wrench it open.

Sir Hugh Dalrymple was so intent upon his terrible work that he noticed nothing else.

With all his force he wrenched away at the stone-work, which presently yielded with a crash and split in several places.

For a moment Sir Hugh stood still, his chest heaving with intense agitation.

Then he placed down the piece of iron, and with an almost superhuman effort raised the lid.

Then he stood petrified.

The skin of the murdered corpse was still upon the face, while the head of the grinning skull was bare, and showed the fracture.

He gazed at this sight in horror, and his thoughts were just wandering back to the fearful night when he had committed the terrible deed, when a loud voice exclaimed—

"Sir Hugh Dalrymple, you have come to your own judgment."

Had a thunderbolt suddenly crashed through the ruins of the old church and riven the ground at his feet, it could not have taken a greater effect upon Sir Hugh than did these words.

He started back and clasped his hands.

A greenish pallor overspread his face.

His whole person trembled with emotion, and he raised his eyes slowly towards the spot where the sound proceeded.

What he saw proclaimed to him his doom.

There, standing on the stone steps, was Rupert Dreadnought.

With him were Allan of the Glen, Tom the waterman, and Henry Clanberris.

In an instant his madness appeared to leave him.

It fell from him like a film from his eyes.

Resolutely he spoke.

"What want you here, gentlemen?"

"You need no information on that score," replied Rupert Dreadnought. "This gentleman, Henry Clanberris, whose life you attempted, told you long since the reason of your appearance here. You are now about to be punished for the murder of your brother. If you wish to make your peace with Heaven, make it now."

A bitter smile crossed the lips of the man thus brought to bay.

He turned to Henry Clanberris.

"It is as I said," he cried; "it is no fair fight. It is assassination."

Clanberris would have answered, but Rupert interrupted him.

"You have been told that you are to have the free use of your sword to combat me," he cried. "Nevertheless, I feel my arm nerved to the combat —strengthened by justice; and, though Henry Clanberris is to be your second, I see before you no chance of avoiding the just punishment of your sins. Come, gentlemen, close that door, and let us at once to work."

Sir Hugh Dalrymple saw death staring him in the face.

But he was resolved that the papers he desired to destroy or save from others, should never fall into the hands of his foes.

With a sudden dash, therefore, he seized the documents which were lying near the dead man's side, and rushing to the flame of the open lantern thrust them in.

To attempt to save them was useless.

Brittle and dry with age, they flashed up into a flame at once, and evaporated in fire and smoke long before any one could reach out their hands to prevent the catastrophe.

"What papers are those you have just burned?" cried Rupert, angrily.

"Papers which I desired should not fall into your hands," replied Sir Hugh Dalrymple. "What they are will never be known either to you or your friends. Secrets whose knowledge would be useful to those who hate me I will never betray. Come, I am ready for this ordeal."

He said these words with considerable courage.

He had recognised the uselessness of resistance, and had strung up his nerves to meet his fate, or, if possible, to gain the combat.

Some men would have given up the case as useless, and have begged and implored for mercy.

But Sir Hugh Dalrymple, though regarding Rupert as an implacable foe, still recognised in him one who would keep his word.

If he could kill Rupert, therefore, he was free.

So the two antagonists placed themselves into position.

Tom the waterman sat on the staircase to prevent escape or to warn of the approach of any one.

Allan of the Glen ranged himself on the side of Rupert, while Henry Clanberris, according to his promise, took his position as the second of Sir Hugh Dalrymple.

"Now, then, my friends," said Rupert, ere the swords crossed, "listen to me. I am not carrying out any quarrel of my own, I am but fulfilling a mission which by a vow I have taken upon myself to perform. So let there be no interference. Let me alone take the brunt of this affair. If I fail, I must die."

Then he turned towards his antagonist.

"Now then," he said, "now then I am ready."

The contest was but similar to all those through which our hero had passed, but it was rendered somewhat different by the peculiar surroundings of the place.

The gloomy vault, the coffins, the stone sarcophagus holding the bones of the murdered man, all were illumined only by the weird light of the torch which Tom the waterman held in his hand, and the feeble rays emitted by the lantern which Sir Hugh Dalrymple had brought with him.

It was a most unpleasant place to choose for a combat of any kind.

The smell of the recent conflagration was not yet gone, the heat had not quite dried up the dankness of the place, but had settled it in steam upon the walls and the ceiling.

There was an unpleasant smell, consequently; a kind of misty atmosphere, which penetrated the nostrils and raised a kind of dimness before the vision.

Nevertheless, despite all difficulties, they fought on; both very calmly and deliberately, without any false moves, looking in each other's eyes to avoid any unskilful movements.

Such a conflict became at length only a question of endurance.

He who first felt his wrist becoming weakened was the one who must first succumb.

In stature Rupert Dreadnought was quite a match for his antagonist.

But not in bodily build.

Sir Hugh Dalrymple, both from his age and the wild adventurous life he had led, was a stouter and heavier man.

But he was unable to keep his temper as well.

The thought that he was there alone with three men, all of whom desired his death, no matter how honest and straightforward might be their actions, seemed to enrage him.

He consequently rapidly lost command over himself, and made frequent and angry dashes at his adversary.

Rupert Dreadnought received all these coolly.

He did not care for delay.

There was no immediate necessity for hurry.

He took no notice of his adversary's lunges than was required to 'parry them, and to watch for a favourable opportunity to drive his sword home.

At length the opportunity presented itself.

A false step brought Sir Hugh Dalrymple within such an easy distance of Rupert's sword that it entered the fleshy part of his arm.

This enraged the fratricide, and, with a yell, he sprang forward—forgetting all principles of fencing —and whirling his sword round his head to deal a savage downward blow.

This Rupert Dreadnought, however, easily parried, and had just the chance he required.

Rushing in, ere Sir Hugh could recover himself, he dashed in rapidly, and his keen blade flashed through the yielding flesh.

RUPERT; OR, THE DREADNOUGHT SECRETS OF THE IRON CHEST

"SEE—SEE! HE COMES!" CRIED MARY MACPHERSON.

There was a cry of horror and pain from the stricken man.

Then his sword fell from his grasp, he staggered backwards a few paces, and fell heavily to the ground.

He was not quite dead when he fell.

But his game was over.

It was easy to see that.

His hands clutched at the yielding earth beneath him.

His glazing eyes rolled hither and thither as if for aid, and, when his second approached, he leaned his head heavily on his knee.

"It is all over with me," he murmured. "Heaven have mercy on me."

This was all he said.

The power of speech was gone.

One glassy stare more !

One shiver of the convulsed limbs !

Then all was over.

"Now," said Rupert, pointing to the stone coffin, "now, my friends, we must raise this skeleton, and place the parricide at the bottom of the coffin. So will my vow be fulfilled."

Taking out as gently as they could the bones of the murdered dead, they deposited them on the ground.

Then they raised the still warm but lifeless body of Sir Hugh Dalrymple, and placed him within the stone coffin.

After this the bones were replaced, and the coffin lid let down.

Upon the lid was then carved in rude but easily distinguishable characters, the words—

"Murderer and murdered lie side by side. See the retribution of Heaven !"

Rupert was much moved.

"Come, my friends," he said, in a hoarse voice. "Come, let us leave this place. The air of it now oppresses me. There is an atmosphere of blood within it which, in spite of my eagerness to carry out my vow, is far from agreeable to me."

Without further words, he began the ascent of the staircase, and passed through the door which Tom the waterman had opened for him.

The air was very cool, the sky dark, and Rupert, overwhelmed with sad thoughts, walked slowly and solemnly among the tombs.

"My friends," he said, when they had reached the high-road, "my friends, you have seen that I have fulfilled my mission, and for your assistance in it I thank and shall reward you. But now I would be alone. This constant bloodshed weighs upon my mind."

"Whither go you, then?" asked Allan of the Glen.

"To London."

"And I?"

"Can go whither you please. It will be some weeks before I open the Third Compartment of the Iron Chest, for I fear lest some deadly vengeance may not be again exacted at my hands."

"I shall gladly, then, take advantage of your leave," said Allan of the Glen, "to find my mistress."

"In that case," said Rupert, "you had better all travel by separate routes. I go to London."

"And I to Finchley by London."

"Our roads are the same, our destination the same, then," said Henry Clanberris. "We could have gone together, but Master Dreadnought's wishes shall be obeyed."

It was not long before, after a warm leave-taking, the leaders and retainers started *en route*.

We must follow now the fortunes of Allan of the Glen.

CHAPTER XXIII.

IN WHICH ALLAN OF THE GLEN PROCEEDS IN SEARCH OF MARY MACPHERSON.

Allan of the Glen was nothing loth to have such a leave of absence as that now granted him by Rupert Dreadnought.

For his master he felt the utmost friendship and gratitude.

He had been the first to offer him a helping hand.

Ever since he had treated him like a friend, when he might have treated him like a master.

However, even the gentle rein held by Rupert had prevented him from carrying out any object of his own, and he felt now a sensation of release.

The horse which he procured at the nearest inn was the gallant steed which had brought him to the town of Chichester.

He was fresh now from his temporary release from work, and as soon as he felt his master on his back he went prancing away at a splendid rate on the road to London.

On his road he passed a horseman riding very slowly.

He seemed absorbed in his own thoughts, and did not even observe Allan of the Glen as he passed.

But Allan knew him.

It was Rupert Dreadnought.

Knowing well that the latter had no desire to be disturbed, and in fact might be angered by his joining company with him after his decided prohibition, Allan rode swiftly by without even a word or a bow of recognition.

The country near Chichester was very lonely, and as soon as practicable, therefore, Allan of the Glen put up at an inn.

It was not many miles from the spot where he had passed Rupert, and ere he retired to rest he gazed from his window and saw the muffled form of his friend and master riding slowly by.

His journey to London would be very uninteresting.

We must hurry him across Old London Bridge, therefore, and introduce him again to our readers when we find him riding once more into the wood near the house where Lady Clanberris was waiting impatiently news of her husband's death or safety.

It was early morning.

The dew was just drying beneath the warmth of the morning sun.

It was, of course, too early to commence anything like a search, or to ask any question in the neighbourhood.

So he resolved to rest awhile.

First he fastened to a tree his faithful steed.

It had borne him many miles that night and was as fatigued as himself.

Then he took off his plaid, spread it on the ground and laid himself down beneath the shadow of a tree.

He was used to this.

In his life he had roughed it greatly.

A sleep in the wild woods, therefore, was far more to his taste than a slumber between the sheets of a civilised bed.

So in a few moments he was fast asleep.

It was now that something happened, which proved that he had not been very observant on the journey.

No sooner was it absolutely certain that he *was* fast locked in slumber than some stealthy forms emerged from among the trees.

Slowly they approached him.

One of them was a man who belonged evidently to the higher class. This one was masked.

The others were burly ruffians of the lowest stamp, who had no compunction in showing their brutal features to the bright light of day.

They approached their victim with rapid steps.

But they were noiseless on the soft dewy grass.

The leader stood somewhat aloof while one approached to see if the sleeper were really so far locked in slumber as they imagined.

This man bent over him, saw by his hard breathing that he was quite unconscious of all things around, and, pointing to his recumbent body, beckoned his companions to approach.

This they did in a body.

Suddenly surrounding him, they seized him before he had time to put his hand to his sword, and in a few moments he was a helpless prisoner.

The leader then approached, and kneeling down by the side of the captive, bent over him and slightly removed his mask.

Allan knew the features at once.

They were those of Oscar Penraven.

"The vengeance is about to begin," said Oscar, "you have escaped us long, but now we shall crush you beneath our feet. Where is your master?"

"Do you mean Rupert Dreadnought?"

"Yes."

"I know not."

"And where is Sir Hugh Dalrymple?"

"That villain, then, is a friend of yours?" exclaimed Allan of the Glen.

Oscar frowned.

"I am not here to be questioned," he said; "I am here to ask questions. Where is Sir Hugh Dalrymple?" I repeat.

"And I can say nothing but that I believe him to be dead."

"By whose hand, then, did he fall?" said Oscar Penraven.

"That," said Allan of the Glen, "is a secret, and shall remain so. I know by whose hand he died, but I shall keep the knowledge for ever to myself."

Oscar Penraven might have proceeded with his questioning, but the stern resolution visible on Allan's face proved how little use it would be.

He sprang to his feet.

"Off with him, my men," he said; "you understand the spot. When night falls he can easily and safely be removed."

The men at once raised him in their arms, and bore him away, one of their number having first gagged him, lest his cries for help might rouse the few passers-by.

They did not go far.

They simply bore him to a denser part of the forest, and into a kind of alcove formed by interwoven bushes.

Here, after a time, food was brought to him, and here he remained until evening.

As soon as it grew dark, Oscar Penraven once more made his appearance.

He made some mysterious communication to his men.

Then Allan of the Glen was once more gagged, seized, and borne away.

The appearance of the place to which he was carried when they reached the high-road appeared to him strangely familiar.

It seemed, in fact, just similar to the house where Sir Hugh Dalrymple had been seized, and where Rupert had allowed him a last interview with his wife.

Here, then, a kind of hope entered the bosom of the young Scotch boy.

Even if he had been ungagged, however, he would have made no remark, but waited on events.

CHAPTER XXIV.

MARY MACPHERSON TO THE RESCUE.

ARRIVED at the gate of the house where Lady Dalrymple resided for the time, Allan was passed in by the postern, and led into a room at the summit of the house—a room with a window strengthened by iron bars.

Here his chains were removed, and his gag removed.

"You will have to remain here until the council has decided what to do with you," replied one of the men to a question put to him by the Scotch boy.

"What council?" demanded Allan, in surprise.

"The dread tribunal which you so often have had cause to fear, which pursues to this moment your master, Rupert Dreadnought, and whose vengeance will fall upon all who aid him," returned the man, solemnly.

Allan smiled jeeringly.

"You allude to the Poisoners, I presume," he said, "the infamous crew who have so long been a scourge to London. I fear them not."

"Have a care of insolence," returned the man. "You are in their power."

"I defy them."

"They could order you now to be put to death."

"Nevertheless I say again I defy them. Providence will deliver me out of their hands," returned Allan of the Glen, resolutely; "but, since it is the desire of the council that I should be kept a certain time waiting for their decision, perhaps you will be kind enough to send me food and wine, for I am hungry."

"One of the attendants shall at once bring you in some refreshment," said the man, pompously; and so saying, he made a sign to his men, and they all filed out of the room.

As soon as they had departed, Allan had time to look about him.

The room he was in was not *very* small, but it was one in which no degree of comfort was apparent.

The window, in the first place, was barred, as I have said.

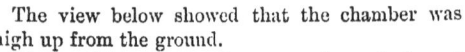

The view below showed that the chamber was high up from the ground.

The walls were of plaster, and cracked and dirty.

A plain wooden table, a plain wooden chair, and a bench completed the furniture, with the exception of *one* thing.

This was a picture.

A terrible picture for a prisoner to continually gaze at!

It represented a scaffold.

Upon the block a victim had laid his head, and above it was uplifted the gleaming axe of the headsman.

In this cheerful abode Allan had not remained long when the door opened, and a female form made its appearance.

The room was illumined only by the feeble rays of a grimy lamp suspended in one corner.

But Allan of the Glen recognised at once the face and figure.

They were the face and figure of Mary Macpherson.

She placed her finger on her lips as she approached.

"Speak not," she said: "to speak would be dangerous until I have been in a second time. Wait and hope till morning."

In spite of this warning, Allan of the Glen could not resist pressing her warm, rich lips as she bent down to place the comestibles on the table.

Mary blushed and smiled, and lovingly returned the pressure, whispering—

"Dear Allan, fear nothing; you will be saved."

Then she tripped away, and left him once more alone.

But he was not devoid of hope now.

He knew Lady Dalrymple to be the friend of Mary, and she would, therefore, of necessity, be a friend to him.

After partaking of the good and substantial meal set before him, without paying any attention to the fact that the viands might be poisoned, Allan accordingly stretched himself fearlessly on the wooden bench and, soldier like, was soon asleep.

When morning dawned, he anxiously awaited the arrival of Mary Macpherson.

Time seemed to pass by on leaden wings, but at length the tramp of feet was heard, and the key was once more turned in the lock.

He glanced eagerly towards it, grasping his sword, which, with unaccountable negligence, they had left to him.

But he had no cause of fear.

The new comer was Mary Macpherson.

She closed the door gently behind her, and approached her lover.

Allan drew her down upon his knee, and kissed her fondly.

"Prison is *no* prison where *you* are," he said, tenderly.

"Ah! but of what use is love in such a place as this," she answered. "*I* pine for freedom, *I* who am no captive. I long for my native hills—my free mountain air. How must *you* feel who fancy yourself in a prison?"

Allan smiled.

"Fancy!" he said; "I fear it is no fancy."

"Yes; it *is* but fancy after all," returned Mary Macpherson, in a whisper.

"How *can* it be so?" asked Allan, in amazement.

"Oscar Penraven," continued Mary, whose whispers were drowned almost to others from the fact that she was so closely nestling on her lover's breast, "Oscar Penraven has no conception that Sir Hugh Dalrymple is unloved by his wife. He fancies that she would gladly join in punishing those who have destroyed him. He knows nothing, moreover, of the fact that I am your betrothed wife."

"Well."

"He has explained his plan fully to Lady Dalrymple, and she advised him at once to place you in safe custody here."

"And does he suspect anything?"

"Nothing."

"Why, then, can I not escape at once?" asked Allan.

"Simply because at the present moment there are several of his men in the house," said Mary Macpherson. "We heard him give them instructions; all save one to quit the place in three hours upon some expedition, of what nature I know not. At any rate, there will be but one person in the house to guard you."

"And then I can escape, and you will fly with me to London," said Allan, eagerly.

He pressed her still more warmly to his heart as he spoke.

Mary blushed deeply.

"Yes, yes," she said; "both I and Lady Dalrymple will fly to London. She is very kind to me, and I wish to remain with her. In a few minutes I expect Henry Clanberris to arrive."

"He is her lover!"

"Yes, long and devotedly he has loved. Hark! what is that?"

She sprang from his knee, and gazed out of window.

"See, see," she cried, pointing through the casement towards a horseman who was dashing along at full speed. "See, here he comes."

Allan had risen, and now stood beside her, leaning on his sword.

As they stood thus, they observed not a slight noise near them. But so it was.

The door opened gently, *almost* noiselessly behind them.

Then a face peered in.

They still stood unobservant.

"Ah!" thought the new-comer, "I will enter and listen."

The one who now entered was a young girl of some seventeen years, tall and finely formed.

But her face spoiled her.

It was the face of a traitress!

Small eyes, a sharp, thin nose, sharp, thin lips, cadaverous coloured skin.

Such was the picture.

She had always hated Mary Macpherson.

Her beauty and her goodness raised spite and malice in her evil heart.

Now there seemed a chance of taking her revenge.

She had heard as yet nothing.

The thickness and closeness of the door had precluded that.

But she had suspected something in consequence of the protracted visit of Mary Macpherson to the prisoner.

Now when she opened the door and beheld the Scotch youth with his arm round Mary's waist—when she saw her pointing eagerly out over the landscape, she guessed that there was something on foot and listened anxiously.

"See!" pursued Mary Macpherson, "see yonder horseman, who hastens hither with such speed."

"Yes, yes," said Allan, "I both see and recognise him. It is Henry Clanberris, I am then safe."

"Not so safe as you imagine, my young friend," murmured the traitress to herself, "So this is your lover, Mary Macpherson; he shall suffer for the hate I bear *you*."

"Talk not so loud," cried Mary Macpherson, looking round nervously, "ah! great heavens! we are watched, see there is Rose Afford, my enemy! What do you here?"

The girl's countenance betrayed no sign of emotion.

"I come to fetch you," she replied, "you are wanted."

Mary Macpherson eyed her contemptuously.

"I hate mean spirits who listen at doorways," she said; "you could have knocked and announced your presence. As it is I shall come as soon as required, and now quit the room."

The girl smiled—a ghastly smile.

She knew she had her rival in her power.

"I have no wish to remain," she said; "no wish to disturb you. I will tell my mistress you are engaged."

"Not so," replied Mary Macpherson; "I am not engaged. I am coming now. I fear you not, believe me. I know your cowardly, treacherous nature—I know all you would do had you the power. You can do nothing. This gentleman, who is a prisoner here, demands the sympathy of all. He *has* mine, and I am not ashamed to own it."

She then turned to Allan.

Stretching out her little white hand, she said, lovingly—

"Adieu, Allan; fear not, remember you have good friends."

She did not shun the embrace which, despite the presence of the girl, he freely offered. On the contrary, she pressed her lips warmly to his, murmuring—

"This treacherous one has no power to harm you."

Alas!

She knew not, could not guess to what an extent treachery can injure the innocent!

After these words, she quitted his embrace and joined Rose in the passage.

When the door was locked, she seized the spy by the arm.

"Rose," she said, "listen."

THE MAN BENT OVER HIM AND BECKONED.

"I do."

"Beware, then, of me!"

The girl laughed.

"Why?" she asked. "Why should I fear you?"

"Because you are trying your utmost to betray me."

There was a laugh again.

"Well, and what then; how can you harm me?" she said, tauntingly.

"You will see," returned Mary Macpherson, "you will see. I shall not threaten, I shall act!"

So saying she swept by her rival and hastened towards the room in which Lady Dalrymple was awaiting her.

As she did so she did not observe that she was again watched.

This time by a strange object indeed.

A shrunken form, a shrunken face, blood-stained features, gleaming, staring eyes.

These eyes followed her with the glare of a demon.

Well she might have trembled had she been able to see them.

They looked anything but human.

But she could have recognised them at once.

They were the eyes, the malignant eyes, of her would-be lover.

Colin was not yet dead!

He had fallen, as I have described, from a terrible height.

Bruised and shaken well-nigh unto death, he had, as I have before said, been conveyed away upon hurdles to the house where Sir Hugh had resided after the fire.

Here he had been nursed by the traitress Rose Afford.

She liked this office.

Her affections, indeed, were set upon the handsome page.

And all through his nights of delirious frenzy what misery she had to endure.

One cry was on his lips—

"Mary, where are you?"

He was ever thinking of the one who hated his very sight.

Now she was in his arms, and he tenderly kissed her, pressing her form to his, and expatiating upon its beauty.

In these times he could fancy that his nurse was the one he loved, and she would lie upon his breast for hours, submitting to the caresses which he meant for another—anything only to be in his arms.

Then he would thrust her from him and cry aloud in anger—

"Traitress! who *are* you? *You* are not Mary Macpherson!"

Then the woman, who loved him as the tigress loves her mate, would cling to him, saying—

"Push me not from you; let me be with you. I am caring for you; I am nursing you; I love you!"

Then he would soften again, and gather her up into his arms, and she would lie sobbing on his bosom.

"Do you love me?" she whispered once.

"Yes, yes," he said; "is *he* dead?"

He spoke of Allan.

"No. If I killed him for you, would you love me for ever?"

He clutched her arm, and glared wildly into her face.

"Who are you?" he asked, more sanely than he had spoken for a long time.

"I am Rose Afford," replied the girl, half afraid to record the truth.

"I thought so," said Colin, in a wandering way; "I thought *she* would not nurse me. But you spoke of killing Allan; what do you propose to do?"

"I will tell you. He is here; now in this very house."

"In this house!" exclaimed Colin, springing up in spite of his wounds.

"Aye; brought here by Oscar Penraven."

"I know him well," said Colin; "I know him well. If he is his captor, his days are numbered. And where is he? Is he anywhere where he can be brought into my power?"

Rose thought a moment.

An infernal thought occurred to her.

Could she not invent some method by which Colin should be so inflamed by jealousy that he would destroy even the one he loved?

"You know Mary Macpherson?" she whispered.

A shudder ran through the frame of the wounded man.

He was now thoroughly roused from his delirium

"Yes, yes," he said; "I know her well. I love her, as you are aware, at least, I did love her, though I know not what feelings are now creeping into my mind. I feel, indeed, as if my love were turned to hate."

A dull sensation of hideous pleasure sprang up in the mind of Rose.

Here was her chance.

Colin's heart was being weaned from his old love.

"Yes," she murmured, "she loves you not. In a few moments she will be in the prisoner's room. I will follow her and listen to all that passes. But stay, are you strong enough to rise?"

"Yes," said Colin, with a hideous smile, "yes. Hate makes me strong!"

He rose by a great effort, and ghastly and blood-stained as he was, tottered to the door.

"Come," he said, "you see I can stand; what do you wish me to do?"

"Follow me and hide behind the pedestal of Diana. Come!"

She led the tottering form of the man she loved up the broad staircase and placed him where she had said, behind the pedestal which supported the lovely form of the goddess.

What a contrast was there!

The blood-stained, savage, relentless face of the cowardly traitor, and the ripe, rich beauty of the pure-faced statue, sublime in the nakedness which formed its innocence!

It was hence then that the gleaming eyes of the page, old in his very villany, saw Mary Macpherson as she advanced upstairs towards her mistress's room.

Oh! how his heart pulsed.

He felt now he hated her.

She had a smile upon her face, upon those lips yet dewy with the kisses of young and ardent love.

Kisses from him whom he hated.

She had almost forgotten Rose and her treachery when she ascended the staircase.

Her mind was full of Allan and the chance she saw now of escape.

When she had passed into Lady Dalrymple's room, the wounded page emerged from behind the statue of Diana.

He grasped the arm of Rose tightly.

"You have conquered," he said; "aid me to kill him and her, and I will love you—marry you!"

The girl grasped his hand.

"You swear this?" she said.

"Yes; I swear it."

"Good; I have a subtle poison," hissed the traitress, "that will soon dispose of him. As for her, I ask not *her* destruction. It will be punishment enough for her to know that the one *she* loves is dead!"

Then the guilty pair, having made their hideous love compact, glided down the stairs once more, and entered the room of the wounded man.

CHAPTER XXV.

IN WHICH HENRY CLANBERRIS IS ABLE TO SPEAK OUT HIS MIND.

The horseman whom Mary Macpherson had pointed out to Allan of the Glen afar off was, indeed, Henry Clanberris.

It may be considered wrong on his part to think of visiting the widow of Sir Hugh Dalrymple so soon after his terrible death.

But in such a case as his, an action of this kind may, perhaps, be considered excusable.

He had loved her for years.

He had been deprived of her by a man whom she hated.

He had seen *her* sorrow and *his* crime, and knew well, too, how she loved him.

He regarded her husband solely as a hateful obstacle, which Heaven's justice had removed.

So on he sped on the wings of love, and though arriving many hours after Allan of the Glen, he had yet hardly rested on his way.

Rupert had especially enjoined upon them that they were all to proceed by different routes, and they had obeyed his instructions.

Henry Clanberris, therefore, had come by a longer route, and, having arrived so soon after Allan, he was tired and travel-stained.

But who shall restrain the impatience of love?

Casting his rein to the man who came to the door, he was about to dash upstairs, when the latter said—

"Master Clanberris have a care."

"Of what?"

"Of your enemies."

"There are none here."

The man approached near.

"You know one Oscar Penraven?"

"I know him well. But what of him? He knows not that I am here—he knows not, or if he *does* know, he is an enemy of Lady Dalrymple."

"He *is*," whispered the man; "but he is not aware of the fact that she knows him to be a foe. He knows only that Sir Hugh Dalrymple was a friend, and he fancies that his widow would desire to avenge him. Now, does this man know you by sight?"

"He does not."

"Then take my advice; disguise yourself as one of the retainers, and let the tide of events roll on."

Henry Clanberris stared.

This was, indeed, a strange kind of servant.

He spoke as one far above him in station.

Yet, disguised or not, he looked like an ordinary retainer.

"You *are* not what you seem," said Henry Clanberris. "You may, for aught I know, be a traitor. Stay! take no offence. Even now you were warning me against treachery. Why should I not suspect you?"

The man smiled.

It was an honest smile—the smile of a true man!

"You speak truly," he said; "why should you not suspect me? I can give *no* answer, except to say that I must leave all to you. I know that I am acting for the good of you and yours, and if you cannot trust me I cannot blame you."

Henry Clanberris took his hand.

"I believe you to be honest," he said; "I read it in your eyes; but tell me, you *are* disguised—you are *no* servant."

"There you are right," said the man; "I am an old friend of Henry Clanberris; I need say no more. So now come in with me, and we will choose a disguise."

They entered together, and the man at once led Henry Clanberris into a side room, where there were a number of clothes and strange costumes of all sorts.

Some of them were the last relics of the fire.

Saved from old store-rooms promiscuously, and hurried to friend's houses.

"Now," said the mysterious man, the strange friend of Henry Clanberris, "now, if you will but follow my advice, you are safe."

Henry Clanberris would have taken any advice so that he was enabled quickly to see the one he loved.

"What *is* your advice, then?" he said.

"You see yonder costume?"

"Yes."

"It is that of the retainers of Sir Hugh Dalrymple."

"Well?"

"You are not too proud to take the character for a while."

"I am not. Quick. Say what do you desire me to do."

"Dress yourself in that costume as rapidly as you can, then await the time of Oscar Penraven's departure, and then—"

"Well then?"

"You are at liberty to act as you please," returned the man.

"Good," replied Henry Clanberris, "I will do as you wish, although I like not anything which keeps me so long from her."

"Never mind," returned the other, as he busied himself in preparing the clothes for Henry Clanberris's wearing, "never mind. It is better to see her safely than to rush precipitately into danger. When Oscar Penraven is gone, you can fly at once."

Henry Clanberris, eager as he was to clasp to his heart the form of the one he adored, saw of course the reasonableness of this argument, and quickly moved himself into the clothes.

Then he quitted the room and followed his mysterious friend into another, where he sat down by a fire with a book he pretended to read.

Time went slowly by.

People flitted in and out the room.

But no one observed him.

If they spoke he shammed sleep.

It was but two hours' delay, which he had to endure.

It seemed a week.

At length a familiar voice spoke.

"Now, then, Master Clanberris, are you ready?"

It was the voice of his mysterious friend that uttered these words.

He started up eagerly.

"Yes," he said, "I am ready."

"Follow me, then."

"Is Oscar Penraven gone?"

"Yes; he has just left with all but one retainer. Come."

Eagerly Henry Clanberris ascended the stairs, and entered the room where Lady Dalrymple was sitting.

For an instant she did not recognise him in his disguise.

Then she rose with a strange smile, saying—

"I am glad you have come, Henry."

The words were said oddly and slowly, as if she knew the position to be an awkward one.

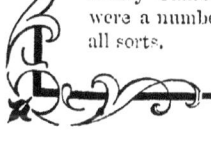

Henry Clanberris fondly clasped the hand extended to him, and raised it to his lips.

"Yes, dearest Margaret," he said; "I am here to save you. You are now a widow, and to the widow of such a man I need not mind speaking, even so soon after her husband's death. I come to save you, as I have said, but I came also because I love you."

Lady Dalrymple blushed.

"Oh, speak not now of that," she said.

"And why?"

"Because my brain is in a whirl; I know not what I am doing; you can forgive me for it I know; but when all is over, when my mind is in a state of quiescence, I may then find courage to say, 'I love you too, dear Henry.'"

He took no notice of her words, but advancing towards her, clasped her in his arms, and imprinted a passionate kiss upon her lips.

Her resolution now gave way, and she sank impassive into his arms.

"You love me?" he whispered, as he pressed her still closer to his breast.

"Yes, yes," she said, "I do; I confess it. But ask me no more now. Tell me what are your plans?"

"I wish to go to London at once. You are not safe here."

"Yes; I will go," she said; "that is our best place. I have those here who will watch me because they deem me unable to guard myself against the world; in other words, because they imagine me to have been instrumental in my husband's death. God knows I am innocent of that, and can even regret that he died so suddenly and so unprepared."

"Is it true," said Henry Clanberris, who desired to change the subject, "is it true that Allan of the Glen is here?"

"Yes, he is below."

She rose from the sofa to which he had drawn her, and rang the bell.

In a moment the mysterious friend made his appearance.

"What is your ladyship's wish?" he asked, with all humility.

"Is Oscar Penraven completely out of the way?" asked Lady Dalrymple, eagerly.

"Yes; his form passed over the hills long since. I watched him and his men from our topmost window, and, unless they fly, they cannot return under half an hour.

"And his retainer?"

"He is below in the room."

"Does he suspect anything?"

"Nothing."

"Well, then, we must to work at once. Mary Macpherson has the key of his cell; *she* will release him."

At this moment there was a gentle tap at the door.

"Come in," said Lady Dalrymple.

Her voice trembled.

She feared lest even now some unknown danger might be threatening her.

The door now opened and Mary Macpherson entered.

Her face was very pale, and her bosom heaved with intense agitation.

"There is danger afloat," she said.

"Where?"

"In this very house," replied the girl. "Rose Alford, my enemy, is concocting a scheme of villany between herself and Colin, who is the worst enemy that Allan of the Glen has in the world."

"How know you this?" asked Lady Dalrymple.

"I overheard their villanous conversation," returned the agitated girl.

"And is their plan to betray us?"

"No, it is to poison Allan and myself, and for this treacherous act Rose Alford has the promise of being made Colin's wife."

Lady Dalrymple smiled.

"We can foil their plans then easily," she said. "Do you," she added to the mysterious friend of Henry Clanberris, "proceed directly with Master Clanberris, and gag and bind the retainer which Oscar Penraven has left here on the watch."

"But Colin?" urged Mary Macpherson.

"You will then proceed to the cell of Allan of the Glen and release him. Then we will quit this house together, and leave Rose Alford and Colin alone."

"But in regard to their pursuit of us. They can release the retainer from his bonds, and put him on our track."

"True, both of them had best be bound also," said Henry Clanberris. "We will leave word (when we have two miles start) at the inn on the roadside that there are prisoners in the house. They will then be released when it is far too late to pursue us."

This scheme was at once put into execution.

Henry Clanberris at once descended with his mysterious assistant, and gently entered the room where Oscar Penraven's man was waiting.

He was nodding in his chair.

Never, therefore, observing their entrance, he started both in surprise and anger when he found his arms seized.

His hand flew naturally to his sword.

But it was of no avail.

Henry Clanberris was binding his arms, while the other was pressing the cold barrel of a pistol to his forehead.

"Who are you, and what want you?" he cried.

He had never seen either of them before.

"We are no enemies of yours, and desire to save you trouble," said Henry Clanberris. "You are the retainer of Oscar Penraven, who is our greatest enemy. We shall not harm you so that you do not resist."

The man saw that they meant him no harm.

Besides, he saw the impossibility of resistance.

RUPERT
OR THE DREADNOUGHT
OR THE SECRETS OF THE IRON CHEST!

" THE STRANGER FELL HEADLONG TO THE FLOOR."

So he remained quite still while they gagged and bound him.

Then they secured him in a chair, so that it was quite impossible for him to move, and proceeded to dispose of those who were more easily managed.

They imagined, of course, that they would find Colin in his room of sickness with the traitress Rose

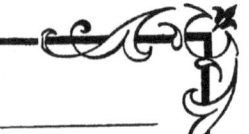

Afford by his side. In this, however, they were disappointed.

When they entered the apartment where they expected to find the conspirators they were not there.

A chill invaded their hearts.

Perhaps they were even now too late.

The wretches might already be carrying out their nefarious design.

Rushing down towards Allan's place of confinement they quickly opened the door and entered.

As they did so they beheld a sight which quite carried out the suspicions of Mary Macpherson, but at the same time assured them that there was no immediate fear.

Rose Afford was engaged in laying out upon the table a tempting repast, while Colin, even then hovering at Death's door, was endeavouring to prove to Allan of the Glen the sincerity of his friendship.

The words, however, which he had heard fall from the lips of Mary Macpherson, when Rose Afford had entered the room on a former occasion, were sufficient to prove to him how little faith he could place in their professions, let them be ever so plausible.

Colin was just pouring out a glass of wine for Allan, when Henry Clanberris and his mysterious friend entered the cell.

Clanberris rushed forward.

"Hold, Allan!" he cried, "there is death in the cup, drink not!"

The guilty pair turned towards the speaker in as much astonishment as fear and anger.

It seemed truly astounding that their secret plans should thus publicly be known to their enemies.

Allan sprang up.

He was about to dash the wine in Colin's face when Henry Clanberris restrained him.

"Stay," he said, as he quietly locked the door on the inside, and advanced towards the table, "stay, I have a better way of disposing of that wine than the one *you* propose. Colin—I know you by no other name—and you, Rose Afford, is it true that, failing to destroy Allan of the Glen here by any other means, you formed the project of poisoning him?"

Rose raised her hand aloft in token of her surprise and horror.

Colin concealed *his* emotion under the semblance of extreme and sudden pain from his recent wounds.

"Poison!" cried the girl, with well-assumed disgust and abhorrence. "We never dreamed of such a thing. I don't know the gentleman, and why then should I wish to kill him?"

"You love Colin here?"

"Yes."

"*He* hates Allan of the Glen?"

"I don't know. That's got nothing to do with me."

"It has. You are speaking falsely. We know, from good authority, your infamous compact. You have consented to aid Colin here in the destruction of Allan of the Glen, on the condition that as soon as he is well he will marry you."

"It is false—a base, treacherous lie!" cried the girl, wringing her hands.

Her courage was now beginning gradually but surely to desert her.

She saw that she was discovered.

She had, in fact, seen this from the very beginning of the scene.

She now saw more.

The stern, implacable faces of Henry Clanberris and his companion told her what mercy she and her base lover could expect.

"Good," returned Clanberris, "you deny it all."

"We do, we do," said the girl and Colin, as with one breath.

Clanberris turned to his companions with a strange smile.

"We may be wrong," he said, "but it is easy of proof, and I should be very sorry to punish persons unjustly. Since the wine and the food you have brought here is not poisoned, pledge the health of the prisoner whom we are about to release. Here, Colin, is the wine which you intended for Allan. Drink."

The traitor had expected that something of this kind would be demanded of him.

Yet the order came upon him with a crushing weight.

A ghastly pallor overspread his blood-stained and haggard features.

"I drink no wine," he said; "in my wounded state such drinks are suicidal. I will eat, but not drink."

A stern, terrible determination was visible on the face of Henry Clanberris.

"Colin," he said, "I am for the moment your judge. If I left you here when I fled from the place, I should leave you free to escape within a few hours. No one would know the fearful and cowardly crime you intended, and you would escape for ever the retribution due to your crime. Now, however, as both you and your companion here have been discovered in a base attempt to destroy a friend of mine, I constitute myself your judge. If this wine is not poisoned you can suffer no harm; if it *be* poisoned, a just death is yours. Time presses; drink."

Colin glanced round him.

There was no hope.

He and Rose Afford, his treacherous accomplice, were in the hands of three strong and resolute men.

What could he do?

He took the glass.

Rose knew it would be her turn next, and fell upon her knees.

"I drink to your Eternal Destruction. Curses on you here and hereafter," cried the traitor.

Then he hesitated.

"Give me a sword," he said, "and let me fight for my life."

"No," replied Clanberris; "your refusal to drink condemns you as poisoners. Into your own trap you have fallen. Die, then, by the potion you prepared for the innocent. Drink!"

There was now no further use in delay.

Perfect silence reigned everywhere.

Oscar Penraven had gone to London; was now many miles distant, and had no intention of returning for two days.

There was nothing for it but to yield.

Death in its cruellest form had overtaken the traitor.

Better death then at his own hands, than death forced upon him by his enemies.

"The curses of a dying man light upon you then," he cried, as he raised his glass to his lips. "Courage, Rose; it is but an instant and all is over."

Then casting a look of intense hatred at his self-appointed judges, the wretched poisoner drained the glass to the dregs.

Having done this, he replaced the glass on the table and sat down.

The deadly liquid was not long in taking its effect.

The eyes quickly became glassy—the lips turned of a blueish tint—the hue of death overspread the whole features, and then with a grasp and a gurgle the traitor gave up the ghost.

His hands clenched, his limbs quivered, and his head fell forward upon the table.

"Our task is half ended," said Henry Clanberris, solemnly. "Now, Rose Afford, you have seen the fate of your companion in guilt. Prepare to share it at once."

The girl, still on her knees, threw her head back, clasped her hands, and glanced at her judges in wild entreaty.

"Oh, mercy, mercy!" she cried, "as you hope for mercy grant it."

"There is *no* mercy for murderers," answered Henry Clanberris. "Drink."

And he proferred her a glass of the rich red wine so bright and so deceptive.

"No, no! I cannot—I will not!" she shrieked, wildly. "Oh! mercy!—no, no!—will no one help me? I cannot—I will not drink!"

And she grovelled upon the ground in a shapeless heap.

Henry Clanberris made a sign to his friends.

In a moment they stooped down, and, despite her struggles, raised her from the ground, and placed her in a chair, where her head sank upon her breast.

"Rose Afford," said Henry Clanberris, "were we to leave you to be dealt with by the laws of your country, you would escape punishment, because, for certain reasons, we should not wish to come forward to denounce you. We know your crime—we know you to be guilty, and we are resolved that you shall die by the poison you intended for another. One more strong willed than you has been compelled to yield. See, he sits dead beside you! Drink!"

The girl was now roused to madness by the utter impossibility of escape.

Seeing the bottle of poisoned wine before her, she dashed it wildly to the ground in the hope of destroying it, and thus effectually preventing the enforcement of Henry Clanberris's threat. But this was useless.

The glass of wine—enough to harrow up her vitals—was already poured out, and was in the hand of Henry Clanberris.

"Curses on you, villains—cowards!" she shrieked. "Heaven will punish you for this!"

"Drink," said Clanberris.

He suffered her not to touch the glass.

He guessed at once what would be the result if he did so.

While the mysterious friend who accompanied him, therefore, kept down her hands, Henry Clanberris held her head and pressed the glass to her lips.

With bubbling curses the wretched creature then swallowed the draught, and when she had done so fell back in hysterics on the floor.

From these she never recovered.

Justice was soon appeased, for swiftly the bright, deceitful eyes closed, the red lips whitened, the pretty limbs stiffened, and Rose Afford had passed from this world to join the traitor who had planned with her the dastardly attack on Allan's life!

"A sad scene," said Allan, as he raised the body of the wretched woman, and placed it on a chair by the side of Colin. "Would that we could have been more tender hearted."

A sneer passed over the lips of Henry Clanberris.

"Tenderness of heart towards criminals is an incitement to crime," he said. "No, no; the world is well rid of such wretches, no matter what sternness is required to accomplish it. Come, let us leave them here, and quit as soon as possible this scene of infamy and horror."

Nothing loth, Allan and the other left the chamber with Clanberris, and hurried up to the apartment where Lady Dalrymple and Mary Macpherson were awaiting them with all anxiety.

"Ah! my young preserver," cried Lady Dalrymple, as Allan approached her, "you are, then, safe?"

"Yes, madam, though my friends came but just in time to save me. Another moment and they would have been too late."

A brief explanation, which sent a thrill of horror through the breasts both of Lady Dalrymple and Mary Macpherson, was then given, and then all haste was made to the stables.

Here they procured four horses, and within ten minutes they were galloping away at full spee along the high-road to London.

Here Lady Dalrymple and Mary Macpherson took refuge in the house of a friend, and the two couples parted in greater happiness than had been theirs for many a long day.

END OF BOOK III.

BOOK IV.

THE THIRD COMPARTMENT OF THE IRON CHEST.

CHAPTER I.

IN WHICH AN OLD FRIEND IS INTRODUCED, AND SEES A PHANTOM, WHICH TURNS OUT TO BE TOO SUBSTANTIAL AFTER ALL.

I HAVE no doubt that there are few of my readers who have not recognised in the pale, ghastly-looking man, who on several occasions befriended Rupert Dreadnought, Gascoigne, the police-spy, whose death had been apparently consummated by Oscar Penraven, at the command of the Chief of the Poisoners.

It was he who had so materially assisted on the night when, at the old house near the river, Rupert Dreadnought had rescued Helen Penraven from the hands of her villanous cousin.

He had escaped the attack made upon him by Oscar Penraven in a most miraculous manner.

The wound inflicted was, of course, a most deadly one, and he had fainted from the effects of it.

But he was not dead.

When the Chief of the Poisoners and the others entered, therefore, and, opening the trap-door, flung him from the room down a seemingly fathomless abyss, the plunge into the cold water revived him, and, with the strong instinct of self-preservation, he struck out.

The water in the usual course of events was very deep in the pit that yawned for the victims of the hideous crew.

But on this occasion there had been a very low tide, and consequently the part where the waters of the river entered was almost exposed to view.

When the body of Gascoigne fell, therefore, it dived far down and ascended outside among the rushing waters of the River Thames.

Here a few feeble strokes brought him to some floating pieces of timber.

Upon these he crawled.

His strength sufficed him so far and no farther, and, clinging on with the grim grasp of a dying man, he lost consciousness.

He awoke to find himself in bed and well cared for, and, when fully restored to health, he swore a terrible oath to be avenged upon the Society.

He would drop his identity and fight them as they fought the world—in the dark.

In the recent adventures in which Rupert Dreadnought had been engaged Gascoigne had not figured.

He had, in fact, been engaged in a twofold manner.

He had been gathering health in the first place.

In the second place he had been steadily and secretly on the watch.

He had discovered many things during this interval of quiet.

He had found out the new retreat of the Poisoners, a pleasant country spot in Essex on the banks of the river, as before described.

He had seen them going to and fro, and among those most frequent in their visits were Rosalie St. Aubyn, the man with the red gleaming eyes who had claimed to be Allan's father, and Oscar Penraven.

Gascoigne knew well from Alford (or Richard Penraven, as we might properly call him) the whole of her infamous career, and, somehow or another, he connected the assault on him by Oscar Penraven with the influence of this beautiful demon.

We have not seen anything of her since; through the instrumentality of Redlock, Alford and Lesbia escaped from her house.

She had now quite recovered from the wound inflicted upon her by Lesbia Howard, and had, as I have said, resumed actively her connection with the Poisoners.

What Gascoigne noticed as being so peculiar was that on her return from the house of the Poisoners she was always accompanied by a gentleman—never the same one.

These persons went with her to her house, but they never returned.

He watched once for days, but all he saw was that the victims (for such he believed them to be) entered and never departed.

He resolved, therefore, at the peril of his life, to enter the house, and discover its hideous secrets.

He waited one evening until the shades had fallen, and he had seen the fair demon take her way from the house.

Then he crept over into the grounds, and made his way to a point where he had particularly observed an open window.

It was always open up to a certain hour, as if to serve as a signal for some one.

Near it grew a poplar, whose lithe trunk swayed almost into it.

Up this tree the active man clambered until he came opposite the casement.

Then he took from his pocket a rope with a noose at the end of it like a lasso.

This he adroitly threw over the post of a bedstead within, and then, dropping himself, came with a bump against the wall.

Undismayed by danger, and the bruises he had

received, he clambered up once more and was soon within the room.

The chamber in which he now found himself was very small.

It was, in fact, nothing but a servant's bedroom.

But the door was open and Gascoigne knew well how to proceed.

He was just about to pass out into the corridor when he heard footsteps approaching, and he had hardly time to conceal himself beneath the bed when a young female domestic entered, and going up to the window closed it.

"Just in time," thought Gascoigne; "another moment and I should have been too late."

The girl did not remain long, and after a few minutes of suspense Gascoigne was once more alone.

He waited until her footsteps died away in the distance, and then he quitted the room and passed down the corridor to a staircase which seemed to lead to the grand apartments.

Here he boldly entered one of the chambers and ensconced himself in a recess behind some deep folds of heavy tapestry.

It might be supposed that being thus in the house of an enemy—in the very den of a cruel and blood-thirsty murderess—he would have experienced a tremulous feeling at the heart, and would have watched eagerly hour after hour.

It was not so.

Drawing his cloak tightly round him, he drank some of the brandy he had brought with him, and leaning back against the recess of the window he suffered himself to fall into a sound slumber.

He knew well that, under ordinary circumstances, Rosalie St. Aubyn would not return from the Retreat of the Poisoners until nearly midnight.

His sleep, he reckoned, would be over by that time at any rate.

He was wrong.

He was visited by hideous nightmares, by awful visions, by phantoms that pursued him with spectral and blood-stained hands.

Yet they did not wake him.

They seemed, indeed, to chain him all the more tightly in his slumber, and he slept on for hours till he awoke at last to hear the sound of voices near him.

He listened intently, and then found the sounds came from beyond the room.

He crossed the saloon with a hasty step, and went out of the door which opened on a corridor communicating with the staircase of the right wing.

The wax light in his hand burned dimly, and flickered as the draught from the closing door caught it.

The light showed Gascoigne he was not alone.

From the far end of the corridor, to the centre of which he he had emerged, something came towards him.

Something which chilled his blood and made his heart stand still.

Something in human shape, which yet seemed not human.

"ROSE FELL UPON HER KNEES."

It seemed the form of a beautiful woman, yet not a woman.

An awful phantom, with a shadowy face as of a woman with brown, bright eyes, and rich brown hair heaped up from the broad brow, and falling on bare, polished shoulders, majestic, yet terrible, for the form seemed to have no earthly substance.

The phantom came towards him, walking with an onward sweep of the limbs unlike anything he fancied himself to have seen before.

It was clothed in garments of rich trailing brown satin; the robe was held aside with one little hand, showing a small but pretty foot, which glided almost noiselessly along, gleaming with diamond buckles.

In one hand was a pistol.

This showed at once to him who watched that what he had taken for a phantom, was, after all, no vision, but a reality.

He stood up as near to the wall as he could while she passed.

But it was evident, from the manner of the person whom he now in passing recognised as Rosalie St. Aubyn, that she was too much occupied by her own thoughts to observe him.

She was evidently upon the eve of some great trial.

The way she swept by, noiselessly gliding, with set features, and pistol firmly clenched, proved this.

"Whither can she be going?" thought Gascoigne.

The sounds of merriment he had heard accorded ill with the firmly clenched pistol.

But this was soon remembered by Rosalie St. Aubyn.

When she reached the door, she appeared to rouse herself suddenly from a reverie.

Thrusting the pistol into her bosom with a start, she changed the expression of her face swiftly.

A smile crossed her features.

A sweet smile.

Yet how deceptive!

When she quitted the corridor, she looked sweet and loveable as an angel.

"I will follow her," thought Gascoigne.

At the peril of his life, he resolved to do this, for he knew well that if he discovered no immediate mystery which would be of benefit to him, he would, at least, be enabled to see the meaning of these constant visits to her house of gentlemen who never returned.

CHAPTER II.

THE NOISELESS MURDER.

At the extreme end of the corridor Rosalie St. Aubyn turned to the left, and pushing aside a heavy curtain, disappeared.

As she did this, a flood of light inundated the gallery.

But as the curtain dropped, all was again veiled in semi-darkness.

Gascoigne crept on.

In a few moments he was safely ensconced behind the folds of the heavy tapestry, where he could see and hear all.

In the centre of an elegantly furnished room was a large table, on which were spread delicious viands, fruits, and wines.

At this table sat a man not over thirty years of age.

He was handsome, noble-looking, and had features which were perfectly strange to Gascoigne.

This was, in fact, part of the mystery.

All he had seen with her had been utter strangers, and he began now naturally to suspect that, like Margaret of Burgundy, she was engaged in some foul conspiracy to decoy persons to her house, and then destroy them.

The young stranger turned upon Rosalie St. Aubyn as she entered a look of intense admiration.

It was the look of one who was under the influence of a fatal fascination.

"Ah! sweet one, you have returned," he said, as he took her hand, and drew her down beside him on the couch where he was sitting.

"Yes; have I been so long, then?" she said, gliding her arm round his neck.

"It has seemed an age, dearest," he said; "but now you can stop."

"Oh, yes, I will remain, now, and take some refreshment. I feel faint and weary."

In a few moments the fair demon and her companion were engaged in disposing of some of the delicate viands.

Scarcely any conversation passed during this time.

Ardent looks and kisses, and sweet whispers were exchanged, and that was all.

When the viands and the fruit were disposed of, however, and they lapsed into drinking wine, the conversation began afresh.

"Now, then, pretty one," said the handsome stranger, "you must tell me what it is you wish me to do."

"Yes, certainly," replied Rosalie. You see I am somewhat of a politician."

"Yes."

"I am one in a tremendous conspiracy, which is formed for the purpose of bringing back to the throne the Pretender—Charles Edward!"

The stranger started.

"Restore the Stuarts!" he cried.

"Yes. Are you their foe?"

"Foe! No. It is and has been always my dearest dream to see the restoration of that dynasty," cried the young stranger. "But you astonish me."

These words were said with no spirit.

Gascoigne saw he was acting.

So also did Rosalie St. Aubyn.

"In that case," she said, as her warm arms still treacherously encircled his neck, "you will not refuse to aid the cause?"

"In what way? by my sword?" asked her companion, nervously.

"No, no, not by your sword," said Rosalie; "you shall not waste your precious blood; you can aid by money. Money buys soldiers."

As she spoke, she drew him fondly to her, and imprinted a kiss upon his lips, looking full into his wondering eyes with her ardent ones.

"What want you?" he asked. "If I can aid in money I will; but I must not—cannot have my name mentioned in the matter."

"You are rich," said the temptress; "five thousand pounds will not harm you. I will get you pen and ink—you can afford me that."

Five thousand pounds!

To aid in a cause he secretly abhorred to win a smile from this fair demon!

But he was in the toils.

She rose, brought the pen, and ink, and paper, and kissed him lovingly again.

Then she placed the paper before him, and put the pen in his hand.

The stranger hesitated but a moment.

One look at the fair being by his side, and he heaved a sigh and wrote quickly.

The fair demon allowed not her face to be seen by the stranger while the order was being written.

But Gascoigne saw it.

There was on it a look of triumphant malignity which sickened him as he gazed.

When the victim had completed his task, Rosalie St. Aubyn took up the paper and placed it in her bosom.

It was now expected by Gascoigne that the unfortunate man whom the temptress had got so completely entangled in her toils, would fall into a slumber, and die off from the effects of some deadly narcotic.

But it was not so.

For some reason or another Rosalie had no recourse to poison.

"Now," she said, when she had placed the order in her breast, "now, if you will take that lamp and light me on my way I will retire to my boudoir; I am tired and ill to-night."

The flush upon her cheek and the gleam in her

eye spoke rather of madness than illness, or of some fell purpose just about to be fulfilled.

Her companion saw in her brilliant orbs, her heaving bosom, and flushed face, only the natural results of the wine, and rising from his chair he took the lamp, as she had desired him, and preceded her towards the corridor.

Gascoigne at once concealed himself still further back among the shadows.

As the stranger passed by him how he wished that he were able to warn him!

But he knew it to be vain to do so.

If he showed himself he would, of course, put off the execution of her fell design, and claim the protection of her guest.

So he was compelled to see him walking to his death.

Why, he knew not.

But he felt sure murder was at hand.

He seemed to feel a chill of dread as he had felt before when he had looked on her as a phantom.

She seemed to be walking along in an atmosphere of horror, and as the two entered the gallery, the stranger in front, he involuntarily held his breath.

The fair demon permitted her victim to precede her some yards, and then, quickly presenting her pistol, she fired.

There was a flash, and the stranger fell headlong to the floor.

But there was no report.

The ammunition, whatever it was, was thoroughly noiseless, and not a single trace remained of the fatal deed but the motionless body on the floor and the shattered candelabra by its side.

The beautiful devil moved the victim with her foot.

"Quite dead!" she murmured, and clutching her pistol she moved away.

The natural impulse in the mind of Gascoigne was to rush forward and seize the murderess.

But he restrained himself.

To have acted thus would have been to destroy all chance of discovering the secret he longed to know.

To avenge *one* man's death he might fail in finding a clue to the disappearance of hundreds of others.

So he waited until she had disappeared.

Then he hurried forward.

Kneeling down, he leaned over the prostrate form of the guest.

There was no doubting the truth.

He was stone dead.

The only mercy in his death was that it must have been instantaneous.

Hardly had he ascertained this fact, when a rustle of approaching feet was heard, and he had hardly time to conceal himself when Rosalie St. Aubyn and four attendants entered.

"There he lies," she said, in a somewhat hoarse tone, "carry him to the vaults, and place him with the others. Follow me."

"*With the others!*" thought Gascoigne. "I, too, will accompany her. Now is my time for discovering the extent of her hideous villany."

CHAPTER III.

LOVE AND HATE.

Before describing how Gascoigne succeeded in his efforts to discover the secret of the death vaults of Rosalie St. Aubyn's house, I must return for awhile to Helen Penraven and Rupert Dreadnought.

The latter had resolved, as I have said, to give himself a short cessation from the labours which his father had so rigorously imposed upon him.

There was no specified time in which he was forced to accomplish his vow.

The only thing from which he was debarred by his vow was his marriage with Helen Penraven.

Even this, however, scarcely offered sufficient inducement to him to throw himself at once into another terrible conflict—to embrue his hands in fresh blood.

He had already sickened of the task.

Although he had trodden in the strict path of stern Justice, he often wished that his stern old father had never exacted from him such a terrific task.

The only time when he felt free from his sterner life was when he was in the companionship of Helen Penraven, and to her now he flew in his grief.

She had, as my readers will remember, taken refuge in the house of Tom the waterman, and, with Mrs. Braxley and Agnes Mayland, she had passed a very happy time.

The disguise she had assumed, as one on an equality in position with those with whom she lived, had not been penetrated.

Introduced to friends as the daughter of a relation in the country, she was spoken of as possessing most distinguished manners.

But that was all.

Her beauty was nothing.

Loveliness exists as much in the lower classes as in the higher.

For this then she was not noticed, except that people said when she walked out with Agnes Mayland—

"What a pretty pair!"

It was a novel life for her, and its very novelty succeeded in preventing the regret which would have come sooner or later, regret for the grand old house and the society of polished people.

She was glad enough to see the face of Rupert Dreadnought appear one morning at the door, and in the fervent embrace that followed there seemed to be concentrated a lifetime of bliss.

He speedily told her his plans.

After the stirring adventures through which he had passed, he desired a short time of rest before embarking in the accomplishment of the third task imposed upon him by his father.

Under these circumstances, he wished her to proceed to the house which Lady Dalrymple had taken for herself a short distance from London.

He was going to remain there with her a short time, and there was no danger, therefore, of any attempts on the part of Oscar Penraven.

At least so he thought.

No steps had been taken as yet in regard to the marriage into which Helen Penraven had been forced.

Oscar knew well the impossibility of enforcing the contract.

Rupert knew well, on the other hand, that it was absolutely invalid.

Neither, therefore, cared for the present to take any active steps in the matter.

The matter of the visit was soon arranged, and, taking leave of those who had been so kind to her, she quitted Tom the waterman's house, and proceeded westward with Rupert Dreadnought to the charming retreat which the widow of the parricide had selected for her home.

I will not pause to describe it, for I must hurry on to stirring scenes.

There is one part of it, however, which I *must* mention, because it was there that occurred an event which tended materially to urge our hero on to the quick accomplishment of his mission.

This was a terrace, wide, and overhung with trees, which overlooked a beautiful tract of country, for, in the days of which I write, bricks and mortar had not entirely destroyed the picturesqueness of the suburbs of London.

Close up to this terrace were thick bushes and plants, too, which clambered over the parapet, thus completely obscuring the view of that part of the garden immediately beneath.

It was here, on the third evening after their arrival, that Helen Penraven and Rupert Dreadnought strolled out just as the sun was shedding its last golden rays over the landscape.

It was a lovely evening, cool but not chilly—a genial warmth pervading the atmosphere—a light zephyr stirring the leaves.

Another set of lovers were in the verandah of the house.

These were Henry Clanberris and Lady Dalrymple.

They had now yielded to the force of love, and made a mutual confession of their passion, and their marriage was to take place in a few weeks.

Helen Penraven and Rupert Dreadnought sat down side by side on the broad marble bench which stood on the terrace.

"Dearest Helen," said the young lover, as he passed his arm round her waist, and in that sweet seclusion fearlessly kissed her ruby lips, "does it not seem hard that my father's will keeps me from making you my wife?"

The young girl smiled and kissed him in return, while a rosy hue overspread her pretty cheeks.

There was no shrinking away, no false modesty with her now.

She was his betrothed wife; she knew well that he loved her and that she loved him, and she clung to him in innocent purity.

"Yes, it *is* hard, Rupert," she said; "I feel it hard myself. I seem lost now, with no protector, no one who has the right to guard me."

So they went on in sweet converse, saying the sweet nothings that lovers will say.

They little knew who was near them.

They little knew what danger was near.

A deadly peril, however, was at hand.

When they first emerged from the house, a man concealed among the bushes had beheld them.

A chuckle had escaped him as he saw them sit down, and observed how closely they were engaged in conversation.

When they had been seated some moments, he glided out from behind the bushes.

When the light of the dying sun fell upon his face it was easy to recognise him.

He was one of the bullies who had aided Oscar Penraven when Rupert had made his attack upon the old house on the Surrey side of the Thames to save Helen.

Slowly he glided on towards the happy couple, knife in hand.

A demoniacal smile overspread his face.

For two reasons.

He liked the reward which he had been promised by his employer.

In the second place, he liked the shedding of blood for its own sake.

His object was to stab Rupert in the back, and then make his escape ere Helen could succeed in alarming the house.

His features expressed a deadly triumph.

His face and Helen's presented, in fact, a perfect picture of "Love and Hate."

On, on, stealthily he came.

But he was not destined to fulfil his hideous mission.

Just as he rose—just as his gleaming knife was raised on high, there was the report of a pistol, and Rupert sprang up to see the villain sink, knife in hand, weltering in his blood.

Helen clung to him in horror.

"What does this mean?" she murmured in accents tremulous with fear.

"I cannot tell," said Rupert, "it is a mystery. This fellow, who lies there still grasping his knife, was apparently on some murderous errand. But whence came the shot that stopped his hand?"

As if for answer there was a crashing among the bushes which separated the garden from the high road, and a man, booted and spurred, stood before them.

It was easy to recognise him.

He was no other, in fact, than Stanley Sherrington.

He advanced towards Rupert Dreadnought with a cheery smile, and grasped his hand.

"It was you then who shot this fellow," cried Rupert. "You arrived just in time."

"No. That shot," replied Stanley Sherrington, "was the result of much deliberation. I arrived just at the moment when the villain was crawling out from behind the bushes. I guessed at once he was on no good errand, and I resolved to watch. I did so, and saw then two things which decided me. He had that knife in his hand, and he was gliding towards you stealthily. I knew then that he was on no good errand, and, as he raised his hand to strike, I fired. Ah! he's moving; he must be questioned."

With No. 20 was given away a Splendid Coloured Picture, representing

"LOVE AND HATE."

OTHER SPLENDID PICTURES TO FOLLOW.

RUPERT OR THE DREADNOUGHT; OR, THE SECRETS OF THE IRON CHEST

"THEN THE FAIR DEMON GLIDED MAJESTICALLY AWAY."

As he spoke he leaned down, and raised the head of the would-be assassin, who was bleeding from a deep wound in his chest.

The man slowly opened his eyes, and uttered a groan of pain. As his glance fell upon Stanley Sherrington, a scowl of hate overspread his features. He seemed to recognise in him the one who had stayed his murderous hand.

"Who are you?" asked Stanley Sherrington, "and who sent you hither?"

The man muttered something between his teeth which sounded like an oath.

Then he said—

"I am dying, I feel it. My secret shall go with me. To betray my master would be to take from me my only chance of revenge. You shall never know who sent me."

The exertion required to say these words appeared to paralyse all further efforts.

He gasped for breath; blood now oozed from his mouth, and he sank back exhausted.

Then his eyes glazed, and with a last convulsive shudder he fell dead.

During this scene Helen Penraven had hidden her face on Rupert's shoulder.

She could not bear to look upon so fearful a death.

Stanley Sherrington, as soon as all was over, searched the pockets of the man.

But all was in vain. Not a clue could be found to the person from whom he had come.

While this was going on, however, Henry Clanberris hurried out, and making his way to the group, inquired what was the matter.

One glance at the man's face seemed to settle the question in his mind.

"That," he said, "is one of Oscar Penraven's friends or retainers. I met him and Oscar on the road to London after his visit to Lady Dalrymple."

"You can be certain of that," returned Stanley Sherrington; "it is of him that I come to speak. There is some conspiracy afloat against you in London."

"How know you that?"

"Men have been watching your house day and night," replied Stanley, "and last night as I and some friends were passing we were only in time to prevent three ruffians from entering by a window."

Rupert Dreadnought glanced at him in wonder.

"Where are my retainers," he said, "surely they ought to be better on the alert than that? Did you knock and inform them of the attempt?"

"We did," replied Stanley Sherrington, "but with no effect."

"They would give no answer?"

"None; we knocked again and again, but with no effect. They seemed deaf to all our demands. No doubt they had been alarmed, and, perhaps, deceived by others who had made similiar attempts at entrance, and thought it prudent not to come to the door."

Rupert shook his head.

"I fear you are wrong," he said; "my men could never permit a person to go away without at least challenging them through a window. There has been, in my opinion, foul play somewhere!"

Then he turned to Helen.

"You see, dearest," he said, "it is quite useless for me to attempt to remain with you for any length of time until my enemies have been swept from the face of the land. I must return to London this night. My retainers have been, perhaps, foully murdered. Come, let us enter the house. I must take a hurried farewell of Lady Dalrymple, and start for London at once."

So saying, he gently drew her arm within his, and hastened into the house.

Then, having taken leave of his hostess, and left her in charge of his young and beautiful betrothed, eh mounted his horse, and with Henry Clanberris and Stanley Sherrington started at full speed for the metropolis.

His heart was full of care, for he felt that he was about to discover some fresh and hideous crime.

CHAPTER IV.

THE DEAD WATCHER.

They reached London just as night had folded its wings over the city, and without delaying a moment pressed on towards Rupert Dreadnought's house.

It was suggested by Henry Clanberris that, in order to guard against accidents, it would be better to call in the assistance of Tom the waterman or one other of his friends, but Rupert was far too impatient to reach his home.

"We are strong enough at any rate," he said, "to discover what is the matter. If we find the place invaded by our enemies we can then send for our friends.

"When they arrived at the door they knocked quickly and imperatively.

But—no answer came.

Not a light was in any window.

It was like an uninhabited house.

Again and again they knocked still more loudly than ever.

Only the same success attended this.

There was no reply.

A sickness invaded Rupert's heart.

"I fear the worst," he said.

"What mean you?" asked Stanley Sherrington.

"I believe," returned Rupert Dreadnought, "that they have been murdered."

"Let us break the door down," said Henry Clanberris, "let us begin at once."

No sooner said than done.

The three young men, each possessed of great strength, drove their shoulders against the woodwork of the door.

Then they forced their knives between the door and the lintel, and one of them rushed at it with all his force.

After several efforts they succeeded in forcing it open.

Not without attracting the notice of the passersby, who were somewhat numerous, and collected in a wondering crowd round the door.

But Rupert Dreadnought paid no attention.

He simply pushed aside the persons who opposed him—pushed them aside as one who had authority, and entering the passage with his friends placed a heavy chair against the door and descended to the servants' hall.

There they found that Rupert's worst suspicions were not exaggerated.

On the ground lay the bodies of six men, stiff in death.

Their faces were ghastly blue; decomposition had, in fact, already begun.

Their death had evidently been by poison.

Not a sound was to be heard anywhere in the place.

All was as still as the tomb.

"You see," said Rupert Dreadnought, turning sternly to Henry Clanberris, "my words were true. There has been foul murder here."

"Yes," replied Henry Clanberris, "you are right. But are these all the servants you left here?"

"No; there are three more. Let us ascend to the upper chambers and see what other hideous scenes are prepared for us."

With Rupert leading the way they accordingly proceeded upwards until they reached Rupert's chamber.

In this room a man lay on Rupert's bed.

He, too, was stone dead!

In another a faithful retainer was also stretched a corpse.

They then descended once more until they reached the chamber where was the closet containing the Iron Chest.

Here a strange sight presented itself.

Propped up against the secret panel, with his back firmly set against it, and one hand clutching a chair near, as if for support, was the last of the retainers.

In his other hand was a pistol, and his eyes were fixed with a glassy stare upon the door.

"He has died doing his duty," said Rupert, with emotion. "This is, indeed, a strange and hideous crime!"

"What do you propose doing now?" asked Stanley Sherrington.

Rupert paced the room a moment.

"I will tell you," he said; "the door below shows only by the lock that it has been forced open."

"True; well?"

"We will fix the door so that there shall be no evidence of our entrance, then we will leave the window slightly open and watch."

"And then supposing that they come in large numbers?" said Henry Clanberris.

"We must chance that," said Rupert Dreadnought. "If we found ourselves being overpowered we could easily call in the assistance of our neighbours. But I do not believe that there will *be* any necessity."

"And why?"

"Because, as they have poisoned all my servants, they will not expect any resistance, and will not come in force."

"You are right, I believe," said Henry Clanberris. "We will at once see to the door, and then we will find hiding places."

The door was soon secured.

Then the three friends returned to the room where the Iron Chest was concealed.

The dead man was left as they had found him, staring with his glassy eyes at the door, and the three watchers hid themselves away behind the tapestry.

It was the Iron Chest itself that Rupert Dreadnought expected to be the object of interest to his enemies.

CHAPTER V.

THE WATCHER—THE DEATH-VAULTS—THE SILENT COHORT—A COURAGEOUS ACT—THE SECRET ENTRANCE—THE GROANS OF THE DYING—SAVED FOR A SECOND DEATH—THE DEPARTURE OF THE WATCHER.

In order properly to follow the sequence of events and prevent the necessity of retrospection, I must return to the point where Gascoigne was following in the wake of Rosalie St. Aubyn.

The attendants were far too engaged to observe him, and in the semi-darkness he contrived to glide behind tapestries, and from pillar to pillar, until they reached a black and winding staircase.

Here they descended cautiously until they reached a vault, whose ceiling was supported by pillars spreading wide at the top.

It was easy here to glide behind one of these, and Gascoigne, who had now taken the precaution to place upon his face a black mask, passed at once into a position where he was concealed entirely from view.

Rosalie St. Aubyn had, up to this moment, led the way.

She now, however, quitted her position as guide, and halting, pointed to the door, which was of massive oak, and studded with heavy iron nails.

"There," she said, "you know your duty now. Place him with the rest, and leave him."

Then the fair demon glided majestically away.

"Is it possible that Heaven's lightning will spare this woman?" muttered Gascoigne, as he watched her myrmidons bearing the body away.

As soon as the door was open he glided in with the rest.

It was a brave deed.

Brave almost to recklessness.

But he had a good and necessary purpose to serve, and he was resolved not to flinch from his duty.

The men did not observe him.

They were far too much occupied in their fearful work to do so.

So, when he entered the vault, he ensconced himself in a corner behind a pillar and waited.

He watched carefully the spot where they deposited the dead body of the lately murdered man.

Then he thought only of his concealment, and watched no more.

The men were not long in doing their work, and presently the great iron-bound door was clanged to with a sound that resounded through the Vaults of Death.

Gascoigne waited until the echoes of their footsteps had died away.

Then he stepped forth into the open space.

Here he drew from his pocket a dark lantern, and raised it high above his head so as to reconnoitre.

The sight that met his eyes was truly appalling.

On every side were piles of dead bodies.

At least a hundred.

They were not in coffins, but placed each on a plank which served as a shelf.

Their faces truly were veiled from view.

But the knowledge that they were all dead—*all murdered*—imparted a feeling of terrific horror to the mind.

A suffocating atmosphere, moreover, pervaded the place.

Many of those, of course, who lay there in the still majesty of death had been dead a long time, and I need say no more than that scarcely any means of ventilation existed.

With a shudder Gascoigne proceeded to the spot where he had seen the retainers place the body of the newly-murdered man.

He soon found the spot.

The young stranger was placed upon his back on one of the shelves.

His face was very calm, like the face of one in sleep.

But from the wound in his chest welled the blood which told of the murder.

In every pocket Gascoigne searched to see if he could find the slightest clue to his identity.

In his pockets, however, there were no papers of any kind.

In fact, the only thing he found was a portrait.

The portrait of a beautiful, fair-haired girl—a perfect stranger to Gascoigne.

"So far so good," thought Gascoigne.

But now came the question—how was he to make good his escape?

Having discovered this receptacle of wholesale murder, how was he to leave it?

To say that this idea had never occurred to him before would be false.

But he had risked the chance.

Convinced that another murder would be perpetrated on the following night, he was resolved to wait patiently and quit the place when the retainers brought in another victim.

Sleep, of course, was an utter impossibility.

Even if drowsiness began to overcome him he would not have yielded to it, for how could he have brought himself to lie down with the dead?

Drawing from his pocket a flask of spirits, he drank a good draught, and was about to commence a further exploration of the place when a strange sound startled him.

It sounded like a groan.

Naturally, in such a place, it roused his astonishment.

The man who had just been brought into the vault was most certainly dead.

He had ascertained that ere he quitted the gallery where the deed had been committed.

Who, then, could it be?

He raised his lantern and once more glanced round the huge vault.

But nothing moved.

"I must have been mistaken," he murmured, "nevertheless, I will listen and see if the sound is repeated."

So he stood motionless, listening.

He was not long kept in suspense.

Presently the groan was repeated—louder still than ever.

It seemed to come from behind the ledge where the newly-murdered man had been laid.

He immediately rushed to the spot.

The idea at once occurred to him that the victim of the evening before might not be yet dead, and that he would naturally be found near the victim of that night.

Drawing away the body of the handsome stranger, who had but a few hours before been sitting at supper with his murderess and clasping her fondly round the neck, and thrilling to the magic of her gleaming eyes, Gascoigne glanced eagerly behind.

He then quickly saw whence the sounds proceeded.

The next body moved slightly.

Reaching out his hands he drew it gently towards him.

As he did so he felt a slight warmth; and a tremour, too, ran through the frame of the still man.

Gascoigne poured a small quantity of spirits down his throat.

Then the eyes of the man opened slowly, and glared round with a glassy stare.

"Where am I?" he said, in a whisper. "Oh, ah, I see. In the tomb—in the tomb!"

The face of the speaker betokened a man of about thirty years.

The voice was that of a man of sixty.

"No," said Gascoigne, "this is not the tomb. I am a friend. I am here to save you from this dismal vault. Do you know where you are now?"

The man rose slightly, and glanced around him eagerly.

Then he pressed his hand to his brow.

"Yes, yes," he said, faintly; "I fancy I can remember now. Am I not in the house of Rosalie St. Aubyn?"

"You are," said Gascoigne.

The man shuddered.

"Ah!" he said, in a voice which was full of despair; "then *you*, I suppose, are one of her myrmidons? Could you not let me die in peace, or has that monster in human form ordered me fresh tortures?"

"No," returned Gascoigne, "I am no myrmidon of hers. I hate her as strongly as ever *you* can. I was a witness—an unseen witness—of her hideous crimes this night. I saw yonder man fall beneath her weapon, and I followed hither to see the number of her victims, and the place where they were deposited. You must escape with me. The next thing to be done is to discover the means of exit."

The man, who had once more partaken of some spirits, felt somewhat revived now, and could speak far more freely.

"I see now," he cried, as he glanced round at the bodies, "that I am not the only victim."

"The only one!" exclaimed Gascoigne, "not by a hundred. This place is a very den of murder. But come, we will not waste time in talking. I will see if by chance there is any mode of egress. Fear not," he added, as he saw the man's eyes turned wistfully upon him, "fear not. I will return."

So saying, he once more took up his lamp, and passed quickly towards the extreme end of the vault.

Here he found a door, or rather, an open archway, leading into another vault of dimensions quite equal to the other.

There were no dead bodies here, but there were shelves ready to receive them, just as if the murders were intended to be continued wholesale.

From this vault there appeared to be egress by means of a small doorway at one end.

To this Gascoigne made his way eagerly, and pushed hard against it.

It did not yield at once, but it was evident, from the way in which it gave, that to force it would be a matter of no difficulty.

Exerting all his strength, therefore, Gascoigne pushed against it, and presently, to his intense satisfaction, he felt the fastenings giving way.

One more strong push, one more strenuous effort, and away it went, bolts and all, into the darkness beyond.

Gascoigne was thrown to the ground, and was so shaken and bruised by the fall, that he could not rise, nor could he tell where he was.

What he had fallen on was soft earth, but his head had come in contact with some brickwork.

When he had recovered sufficiently to enable him to stand up, however, he soon discovered that he was in some place where he was open to the free winds of heaven.

He could feel the cool air rushing upon his forehead, and having stood still a moment to ascertain in which way the current came, he advanced slowly and carefully towards the welcome spot.

He fancied he was in some subterranean passage of very narrow dimensions, so narrow, indeed, that he could touch both sides with his hands as he walked.

Though sincerely hoping and believing that he had discovered some secret means of egress with the outer world, he was yet very careful lest he might come upon a pitfall.

However, he met with no accidents.

After a tedious journey of only a few minutes — but appearing twice the length—he reached an opening which led through some dense bushes to the highroad.

The passage through which he had come was, in point of fact, the one through which Alford and Lesbia had been led by Redlock on the evening when Lesbia and Rosalie had had the encounter.

He gazed around in delight at the free country round him.

"By heavens!" he cried, "I have tracked the murderess to her lair, and more than that, I have found the means of destroying her."

After a few moments inhaling of the fresh air, which was infinitely delightful after the close and fetid atmosphere of the death vaults, he turned back and made his way more easily and rapidly back.

He was aided, in fact, in his return by the twinkling of a small ray of light from the vault, for he had left the lantern with the resuscitated victim of Rosalie's treachery.

Resuscitated, alas! but for a moment.

When Gascoigne returned he found him lying back stark dead, with the lantern grasped tightly in his death clasp.

The sudden awakening in such a place—and, perhaps, the spirits also—had been too much for him; and his spirit had this time fled from misery for ever.

This was, of course, a great loss of evidence against Rosalie St. Aubyn.

But there was no use in despairing.

Moreover, the presence of this vast number of corpses in the vaults of a private house would be enough to bring down the anger of the law upon her.

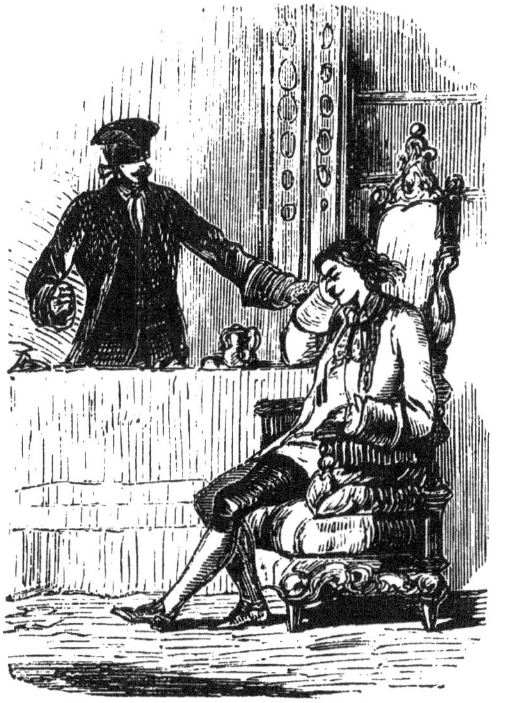

"A HAND WAS SUDDENLY PLACED ON HIS SHOULDER."

With a sigh, he replaced the body in the place where he had first found it, having unsucessfully searched every pocket to discover some papers which would throw a light upon the name and vocation of the victim he had hoped to save.

Then, placing the lost victim exactly where he had found him, he proceeded towards the secret passage.

Here he replaced the door as well as he could, shooting the bolts into their places, and filling, with the soft soil of the passage, the holes which he had made by forcing them out.

Then, closing his lantern, he passed out into the night, and made all haste in the direction of the inn where he had left his horse.

He felt truly like one in a dream.

The adventures and horrors he had endured during the past few hours were truly enough for a lifetime.

In all his experience he had never come across so terrible a mystery—never seen a demon invested in so fair a human shape.

However, he lost not much time in thought.

What he desired was to hasten as quickly as possible to London, and see Rupert Dreadnought, whom of all others he regarded as the best able to aid him in his enterprise.

As may be supposed, the night was far advanced, and, in fact, morning was already beginning to break when he started.

But he heeded this not.

In spite of the fatigue both body and mind had gone through, he was resolved not to delay.

Life and revenge were involved in the accomplishment of his enterprise.

CHAPTER VI.

THE FIGHT FOR THE IRON CHEST.

I MUST now return to Rupert Dreadnought and his friends, who, in the still old house, were waiting eagerly the arrival of those who had, in so dastardly a manner, poisoned the domestics.

They waited fully an hour, exchanging only whispered words now and then.

At the expiration of this time they heard a slight jarring noise at the window.

Then it was gently raised, while a man's form showed up darkly against the sky.

When the casement had been opened more widely, the man, who was closely masked, entered, and fixed a rope ladder to a heavy piece of furniture within the bed-chamber.

Then he gave a cry like that of a screech-owl, and waited a few moments.

The cry was soon answered from some little distance, and after another short delay four more men entered the room.

Then the window was fastened down, and the masked strangers struck a light and lit the lamp which stood on the centre table.

A loud, coarse laugh escaped the lips of the one who appeared to be the leader as his eyes fell upon the figure of the domestic sitting propped up against the door with the pistol grasped in his hand.

"Ha, ha, old fellow! your days for fighting are over," cried he. "You look very solemn, but your fidelity has cost you your life."

The cruel insolence of this speech was almost enough to make Rupert spring from his hiding place and rush at the speaker.

But he restrained his anger for the moment for a reason.

He wished to see what was the object of the new-comers, and also how far their knowledge extended.

The voice of the man who had spoken had told him nothing.

It was that of a perfect stranger.

The leader now dragged away the body from before the doorway, and then felt everywhere for the spring by which to open the panel.

"They are at fault there," thought Rupert.

He was right.

Although they knew the existence of the IRON CHEST, and the place where it was stowed away, it was quite evident that they were far from being aware of the secret spring by which they could reach the receptacle of the mysteries of Rupert's life.

"Here, Frank," cried the leader, addressing one of the men, "bring your crowbar here and wrench this panel open."

When he uttered these words, both Henry Clanberris and Stanley Sherrington imagined that Rupert Dreadnought would spring to his feet, and give the word to them to rush on the foe.

But he made no sign, evidently desiring to see how far they would go.

The man whom the masked intruder had addressed as Frank advanced at once to the wall with a long iron bar.

He was a broad-shouldered, tall young fellow, of Herculean mould, and a few blows, given with all his force, soon told their tale upon the woodwork, which splintered up, and quickly left a wide opening.

After about five minutes' work, the others, with their hands, tore away the broken panelling, and it was not long before the IRON CHEST stood revealed to the eager eyes of the five men.

"Quick!" said the leader, in a voice full of emotion; "drag it out into the light. We will first see what secrets it contains, and then we will destroy it. There will be an end then of the bloodthirsty mission of Rupert Dreadnought."

Scarcely had the man advanced to lay his hand upon the iron handle of the box, when there was a sharp report, and he fell prone upon his face—dead!

Then Rupert sprang to his feet, and shouted in a loud voice,

"At them, my friends! No quarter for the robbers and assassins!"

My readers can well imagine to themselves the utter astonishment of the intruders when the shot was fired, and the three friends rose from behind the tapestry.

But the latter did not give them much time for thought.

Rushing at them at full speed, with sword in hand, they took them quite by surprise, and had them by the throat ere they had time to draw their weapons.

The leader, however, contrived to seize his knife and stabbed Rupert in the arm, compelling him for an instant to draw back.

Between them, therefore, there was a fierce encounter with swords.

With the others the fight resolved itself into a hand to hand struggle, in which they rolled hither and thither in a fierce wrestle for the mastery.

The one whom Rupert attacked was a good master of fence, and, though only armed with a short knife against a long and keen-bladed sword, he contrived for a long time to keep his antagonist at bay.

Then suddenly he performed a feat which placed him on equal terms with Rupert.

Seizing his opportunity, he dashed suddenly into the dark recess where stood the IRON CHEST.

Here in the shadows he was enabled to draw his sword, and in an instant he was on an equality with Rupert Dreadnought.

Our hero was in no way discouraged by this change of tactics on the part of his antagonist.

But he staid his hand a moment.

"You are a brave man, and can be no personal enemy of mine, since we are utter strangers," he said; "tell me who are you, and why you are here, for I feel certain that you are acting under some misconception."

The other laughed scornfully.

"You fear me now we are on equal terms," he cried. "See, my men hold their own! No matter who I am, you will find that my sword is as keen as yours, and the arm that wields it is as strong."

"You shall see I fear you not," exclaimed Rupert. "When my sword is at your throat, and you are craving for mercy, then you will see that I will force from you the knowledge of who you are."

So saying, he attacked his antagonist with greater fury than ever.

The stranger, whoever he was, was right when he said that his men were holding their own.

Being built on the same herculean mould as the one named Frank, who had fallen a victim to Rupert's pistol shot, they were more than a match for Henry Clanberris and Stanley Sherrington.

Three men are always more than a match for two in a struggle, and they found it as much as they could possibly do to prevent themselves from being wounded in the struggle.

Presently, however, there was a change for the better.

One of the men rolling over, Henry Clanberris contrived to drive his knife home, and left them with but one adversary each.

Meanwhile, Rupert and his adversary attacked one another furiously.

There was no fear of interruption.

The windows were tightly closed.

Heavy curtains obscured the glass, while the doors were tightly closed, and not a sound crossed from the chamber into the street below.

As I have said before, Rupert's antagonist was quite his equal in the art of defence, and it seemed as if in that confined space he had the advantage.

Rupert found himself, in fact, on several occasions driven back, and obliged to drop the offensive and act on the defensive.

To the mind of our hero fear was a thing unknown.

Yet he regarded the doubtful nature of the contest with a feeling of exasperation.

He felt certain that the man with whom he was contending was a stranger to him, and he had also an idea, a conviction, in fact, that he could not shake off, that he was acting throughout under misapprehension, both of his character and the motives which actuated him in the course of his strange and varied adventures.

If, therefore, any accident should occur to him which should delay the fulfilment of his last vow, he would never forgive himself for having delayed its commencement.

Again, as he began to regain his position, he demanded of his adversary—

"Who and what are you?"

He received no reply.

The stranger seemed resolved to preserve his incognito at all hazards.

This seemed to nerve Rupert's arm with fresh strength.

Pausing a moment to gain breath, and acting for the time only on the defensive, he looked his antagonist straight in the eye, and then rushed at him.

It was a sudden rush.

The stranger, taken off his guard, was obliged to fall back, and in parrying Rupert's sword, his own weapon snapped some inches from the point.

Still he refused to give in.

Planting his back against the wall, he seemed still determined to do battle *à l'outrance.*

Meanwhile, Henry Clanberris and Stanley Sherrington were fiercely engaged with their foes.

It was, as I have said, a hand-to-hand struggle, and no one for the time could use their knives or weapons of any kind.

But all men tire, no matter how eager they may be for victory.

After a time, just about the moment when Rupert and his masked adversary paused, the four wrestlers stopped also.

Then, as with one accord, they sprang to their feet and glared at each other.

Savagely they glared like wild beasts.

But even now they had no time to spare in which to draw swords.

Their knives, however, were quickly raised, and for a moment it would have been difficult to say who meditated the attack and who were the aggressors in the fight.

"Hold," cried Henry Clanberris, addressing them, "you are but the servants of yonder man. Why fight you? Let them decide the battle. We have no wish to shed the blood of retainers."

The men laughed scornfully.

They mistook his words, or pretended to mistake them, for evidences of cowardice.

"Retainers or not, we fight when our master fight," they cried, as with one voice; "we surrender when he surrenders."

There was something in their manner which seemed scarcely to belong to retainers.

They spoke haughtily, and as people used to good society.

"Your blood be on your own heads, then," cried Stanley Sherrington.

"Or yours on yours, insolent," shouted one of the antagonists, as he made a rush at the speaker.

On all sides the battle now was waged in desperate earnest.

The struggle between Rupert Dreadnought and the masked stranger was fierce enough.

But that between the others looked the most deadly, as the struggle took place with knives.

I will not unnecessarily prolong this scene.

Suffice it to say, that the superior skill and resolute courage of Henry Clanberris and Stanley Sherrington at length prevailed.

The two men fell, desperately wounded, to the ground, and thus the two friends were free to assist Rupert.

Rupert saw this.

He determined to take advantage of it at once.

His object was to wound or disable his adversary in some way—not to kill.

To do the latter would be to lose, perhaps, all clue as to the identity of the stranger himself, as well as to the person who had sent him on his errand.

"Help, here!" he cried.

The stranger burst into a loud laugh.

"So, ho! Master Dread-*nought,*" he shouted, "you need help against *one* man."

"I wish to save your life, madman," returned Rupert, angrily. "I want your secret not your blood! Seize him, my friends."

Both Henry Clanberris and Stanley Sherrington dashed at once forward, and drawing their swords, menaced him on both sides.

But even now he would not yield.

He seemed resolved to die before he dreamed of yielding.

But three were too strong for him.

Just as he made a desperate lunge at Rupert Dreadnought, Henry Clanberris dashed forward and seized him.

This was the end of the fight.

He made a feeble struggle.

But it was of no use.

Stanley Sherrington seized his other arm, and in a few moments the stalwart stranger was helpless on the floor.

"Now, then," said Rupert, as they disarmed him, "you see we are not cowards. We sought not your life. Your friends yonder have suffered terrible injury, if not death, through their obstinacy. *You* ran the same risk, but your good luck saved you. Clanberris, get something with which to bind our prisoner. In the room yonder you will, I think, find some rope."

In a few moments Henry Clanberris returned with the required coil of rope.

The stranger spoke not while he was being bound.

He seemed resolved to be obstinate to the very last.

But there was one thing he could not avoid.

That was, a search throughout his pockets.

This was very successful.

In this case there had been no suspicion that Rupert or his friends would return so opportunely.

The stranger consequently did not take the precaution to destroy any documents which he had about his person.

The first paper which Rupert came across was a letter from Oscar Penraven :—

"DEAR FLAXMAN,—Be sure and procure for me the men of whom I spoke. I have reason to believe them to be trustworthy and brave.

"The IRON CHEST is to be found in the chamber adjoining Sir Rupert Dreadnought's bedroom.

"You will find it behind a panel in the wall on the left hand side of the door.

"I cannot tell you where the spring opening it is concealed, but if you have any difficulty break through the panelling, which you will find very light.

"I am supposing, of course, that you have disposed first of the domestics in the manner we arranged.

"As soon as you have taken from the IRON CHEST all its documents, destroy the rest of its contents, and leave the empty chest in the room.

"OSCAR PENRAVEN."

"A somewhat imperative missive," said Rupert Dreadnought, "but one which proves that he knows more than I wish him. We must see to this."

A further search revealed still further secrets.

All except the identity of the stranger.

There were letters and memoranda proving his intimacy with Oscar Penraven.

But that was all.

His name, Flaxman, led to nothing.

When unmasked he presented the features of a handsome, well-looking man of about thirty.

But no one had seen his face before.

"This is enough for our purpose," said Rupert Dreadnought; "as the search has proved his connection with and employment by Oscar Penraven, I have learned enough !"

"You will then suffer him to go ?" asked Henry Clanberris.

"Yes ; his companions are all dead. See, there they lie. I will send him back to his employer with my last words. Raise him up and unbind him when you have placed all weapons beyond his reach, then place him near the window."

Rupert's orders were soon obeyed.

The stranger stood with folded arms, stern and defiant.

"Master Flaxman," said Rupert, "I know not who or what you are. But I have discovered who it is for whom you risk your life. It is Oscar Penraven."

"Well ?"

"He is a poisoner—an assassin. He has misrepresented me to you," continued Rupert. "I am pledged to certain missions by a vow to my father on his death-bed. You call them bloodthirsty. They may apppear so to *you*, but each one devoted to destruction is an assassin or a parricide. Go, tell Oscar Penraven I have discovered his schemes. Tell him I fear him not. Say that there is an Evil Genius hovering over him and all the guilty, which will lead them into the snare at last, no matter through what rosy scenes it may conduct him at first. Go now, and give him this message. Let me not see you again, for remember wherever I meet with you, I shall run my sword through your body. Go !"

As he spoke, he opened the casement, and pointed to the rope ladder which still depended from it.

The stranger hesitated a moment.

But only for a moment.

To have resisted now would have been utter madness.

With an angry scowl, therefore, he turned impatiently away, and as quickly as possible descended into the street, which was now devoid of all passers.

"Now," said Rupert, "we have a sickening task before us. We must bear the bodies into yonder—or rather, they can remain here, and I will retire to my bed-room. Aid me to place the IRON CHEST back into yonder closet, and then let me beg of you to make my house your own, and choose a bed for the night."

The IRON CHEST was soon replaced.

Then another panel was slid aside, and some choice wines were disposed of by the tired combatants.

They then retired to one of the upper chambers, while Rupert, entering his own, placed a tankard of wine before him, and sank into a deep reverie.

He was deep in thought, when a hand was laid suddenly upon his shoulder.

Glancing up, and half starting from his chair, he saw a masked man standing beside him.

"Who are you ?" he cried, drawing his sword, "and how came you here ?"

"LYING ON HER SIDE UPON THE WOODEN CORNER OF THE WELL WAS A FEMALE FORM."

CHAPTER VII.

THE THIRD SECRET.

"FEAR not, I am a friend," said a voice.

Then he threw off his mask and disclosed the features of Gascoigne.

"I meet you in a house of death," he added; "I stumbled over dead bodies enough on my way to this room. Egad! with the piles of corpses I have seen elsewhere this night, I thought I had had enough dealings with the Arch Destroyer for once."

"You surprised, me, indeed," said Rupert, as, re-sheathing his sword, he sat down once more. "How, in the name of wonder, did you enter?"

"I found the street door open," replied Gascoigne. "the wind had blown it easily in, for the locks and bolts were wrenched off. I secured it as well as I could, and then coming up the stairs I entered your room. I never, as you know, gave over my plan of bearing with me a dark lantern, and this I at once turned on to find myself once more in the presence of Death by Violence!"

"Once more you say!" exclaimed Rupert. "Pray explain yourself."

"I will," said Gascoigne; "but if you will allow me I will take a draught of that wine. I have suffered much, and ridden long and rapidly."

Having taken a goodly draught Gascoigne told his story.

Rupert listened in wonder.

It seemed to him, as it had seemed to Gascoigne, a mystery that such terrible villany should exist in so lovely a body.

"This is no longer for us to deal with," replied he, when Gascoigne had concluded his narration; "we cannot deal with such wholesale enormity. We must inform the authorities."

"May not that interfere with your fulfilment of your vow to your father?" asked Gascoigne.

Rupert thought a moment.

"Perhaps you are right," he said. "I am afraid I have too long delayed the reading of the third mystery. I am resolved this night to investigate it, and I have been resting after my labors ere I opened the Iron Chest once more."

"But you have not told me yet," said Gascoigne, "what adventure has happened to you this night."

Rupert briefly told him.

Gascoigne listened intently.

"This is certainly becoming too perilous," he said. "Action at once—that must now be your motto. Shall I accompany you into yonder chamber of death?"

Rupert rose.

"No," he said. "I alone must touch that repository of dread secrets. Remain here, and rest awhile while I search for my next dread task."

It was evident to Rupert Dreadnought now that he must lose no time in investigating the further secrets of the Iron Chest.

It was for this reason he had desired his friend to remain where he was.

He wished to be alone.

Much as he had desired to avoid immediate action, it was now plain that neither his own life nor the lives of those he loved, were safe until his foes were disposed of.

He could not doubt that, among those who now pursued him, there were many who were connected in some way or another with the mysterious bequest of his father, and he resolved now, in the stillness of the night, to unfold the third mystery.

He accordingly passed—not without some heaviness at heart—into the next room, and approached the dark closet where the Iron Chest stood.

With a heavy sigh he placed the key in the lock, turned it, raised the lid, and bent down to search with eager and wondering eyes for the Third Secret.

The instructions which the old earl had left were very brief.

They were written on a piece of parchment, in which was enclosed a Diamond Cross.

The third enemy which Rupert Dreadnought had to clear from his path, was none other than Dr. Henzollern, the Chief of the Poisoners!

This name was but an assumed title.

His real name was Ishmael Hasser; he was, in fact, none other than the gipsy chief mentioned in our first number as the friend of Robert Penraven, and the grandfather of Oscar.

When Ishmael Hasser had aided Robert and his brother to seize Alice, the latter had fallen in love with the gipsy's daughter; and, after first endeavouring to induce her to fly with him, he was forced into a marriage.

The gipsy had been a terrible enemy to the old earl; he had been the instrument used to work out all the dastardly designs of the Penravens; he had dyed his hands in the blood of the earl's best friends.

"Therefore," concluded the writing on the parchment, "either destroy him yourself, or give him over to the authorities. I care not which.

"The fact of his being at the present moment at the head of a great conspiracy (for what purpose formed I know not) will, of course, render it a matter of difficulty for you to approach him.

"When you suspect yourself to be in his presence, however, the diamond cross will reveal to you his identity.

"Say to him 'The Cross and the day.'

"If he then refuses to acknowlege his identity, say 'The Vaults and the 15th January.'"

Then followed an elaborate description of him, chief among the specialities of which was a scar extending across his left cheek.

It needed not the description to enable Rupert Dreadnought to guess who it was that was meant by his father.

The chief of the great conspiracy was, of course, no other than Dr. Henzollern, the leader of the Poisoners!

Gascoigne was the first person whom he consulted. His advice was good.

"The new retreat of the Poisoners is in Essex on the river's bank," he said. "The best thing to do is to proceed to that neighbourhood, and establish yourself in a house close to it. There you can be on the watch."

"Had we not better at once give notice to the authorities," said Rupert, "and let the runners seize upon him and his villanous crew? You see my father gives me such permission in his instructions."

Gascoigne smiled.

"Take my advice," he said, "and give no such information. I have been a Bow Street runner myself, and know how you will find it if you act as you suggest. Do you suppose for one moment that among a vast conspiracy such as that of the Poisoners there will be no secret agents, avowedly in the pay of the government, but really in the pay of the Terrible Band? If you let the runners know, information will at once be given to your enemies, and all your efforts will be in vain."

Rupert saw plainly the force of this argument.

Gascoigne had too much experience in the workings of the secret spy system to make it advisable to disregard his counsel.

"I will do as you advise," he said. "After we have disposed of the dead bodies of my faithful domestics, and obtained the services of some one who can take charge of this house, we will proceed in the search for a suitable habitation."

"Or better still," said Gascoigne, "*I* will set out to-morrow, and seek a place for you, while you are making your arrangements in London."

CHAPTER VIII.

ON THE TRAIL.

It did not take long to settle what little matters Rupert Dreadnought had to arrange.

The unfortunate men who had died in defending their master's interests were duly interred, and Mrs. Braxley, Agnes Mayland, and Tom the waterman were installed as guardians of the old house, while Gascoigne gave strict injunctions to the watch to keep a good look-out upon it day and night.

Gascoigne had meanwhile discovered a pleasant rural retreat not half a mile from the house occupied by the Poisoners, and to this, as soon as convenient, our hero removed.

The position of this place was doubly pleasant to him.

It was so close to the retreat of his enemies that he could be constantly watching his foes; and, in the second place, it was at no great distance from Brentwood, where Henry Clanberris had bought a beautiful residence, which he named after himself.

Lady Dalrymple had no reason to pretend any deep feeling of sorrow at the death of Sir Hugh.

She had hated him before marriage, and patiently borne with him after, and now that she was free to marry the love of her heart, she no longer saw cause to hesitate.

When, therefore, he urged on an early marriage, she no longer hesitated, but consented at once; and one bright morning she became his bride.

They had now removed to Clanberris House, and Helen Penraven had gone with them.

He would thus, therefore, be able not only to be on the watch, but to visit constantly the one he loved.

About a week after his arrival at the house which Gascoigne had obtained for him, the latter had proceeded on a voyage of discovery to the house of the Poisoners.

Rupert, being thus left alone, started upon a lonely walk through the wooded grounds which almost entirely surrounded the beautiful retreat.

He was proceeding along leisurely among the dense trees, thinking over the past, when a loud cry aroused him from his reverie.

At first he was doubtful whether it was the cry of some bird, or that of some human being in distress.

So he stopped still.

For a few moments all remained quiet as the tomb.

Then there arose a second cry, more shrill and despairing than the first.

"Help! help!"

There was no mistaking it now.

It was the voice of a woman in distress.

"Help is near!" shouted Rupert at the top of his voice, and drawing his sword he plunged through the brushwood towards the place whence the cries proceeded.

By the aid of the moonlight he found his way to a spot where there was an incline, and where some rough steps descended towards a disused well.

Here he beheld a strange sight.

Lying on her side upon the wooden corner of the well was a female form.

It was that of a beautiful woman about nineteen, dressed in the extreme of fashion.

She was quite insensible now, but no one was near.

Rushing down, Rupert knelt by her side, and raised the beautiful head upon his knee.

He did not recognise the features of any one he knew, but it was one whose name was well known to him, but whom he had never seen.

It was, in fact, Lesbia Howard.

A goodly draught from his flask of spirits revived the unconscious beauty, who, as her eyes opened, smiled sweetly upon her preserver.

"You arrived just in time," she whispered faintly, "in another minute I should have been hurled to the bottom of this well."

"By whom? and why?" asked Rupert, eagerly.

"By Dr. Henzollern, the Chief of the terrible Society whose crimes are decimating London."

This was enough.

Anxiously Rupert inquired her history, and listened with wonder as she recounted her adventures—her love for Alford, and the reasons of her entering the dread Society.

She had been denounced at last, as threatened by Rosalie St. Aubyn, and the President himself had received the task of destroying her.

He had inveigled her into the wood by representing that they were being watched, and there, at the well, he had told her how she had been denounced as a traitress, and that the hour of death had at length arrived.

"And where is this villain now?" said Rupert, as he tenderly aided her to quit the dense wood.

"I know not; having failed in obtaining his end, he will not return to the Retreat; but I can tell you where you will find him in three days hence."

"And where is that?"

"At Brentwood, among the throngs of gipsies. He has work before him that requires the aid of his old friends and relations, and he goes disguised among them."

For the time being Lesbia Howard resolved to accompany Rupert to the house he had taken, and, arrived there, she heard with surprise and pleasure into whose hands she had fallen.

She gave him full directions in regard to the future movements of Dr. Henzollern, and Rupert determined at once to take advantage of her information, and proceed to Clanberris House.

This accordingly he did, and the next day saw him at their destination.

At the time of my story Brentwood was a quiet but thrifty village.

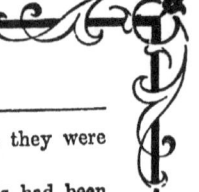

Since the advent of railroads, it has assumed grander dimensions.

But in the days of which I speak, the only time when there was an air of life and activity about the place was when the country agricultural fairs were held there.

Within the limits of this, there was a race-course, which, at certain seasons of the year, brought together a motley crowd, the major part of which was composed of characters not the most reputable.

As may readily be imagined, there was not that good order preserved, nor were they governed by those wholesome regulations which characterise the race-courses of the present day.

Drinking and gambling booths abounded, cards and dice met you at every turn, and drink flowed freely.

As a matter of course license and misrule prevailed almost unchecked.

There was a sprinkling here and there of the better classes, and that was all.

The gathering this time was larger than usual, and Brentwood was crowded with people.

Among them was the usual collection of noisy brawlers, flash gentlemen and gamblers; but among all, as Rupert Dreadnought and Henry Clanberris strolled through the crowd in search of the one he was so eager to find, there were two who particularly attracted their attention.

They put up at the inn where Rupert had stopped on the previous night.

They were dressed in tawdry finery, and bore a very sinister expression.

One of them, the most talkative, had a slight cast in his eyes, which impressed you at once unfavourably.

He was evidently a shrewd fellow, and knew his way in life too well—the criminal way be it said.

The other had more of the bull-dog in his disposition, and was in every respect a surly brute.

A scar on his left cheek-bone and a nose battered out of shape, did not add to his good looks.

One could see, at a glance, that they were desperate characters—men who would stick at nothing to accomplish their ends.

They seemed to have plenty of money, and spent it freely, but were unusually quiet in their manners.

Rupert noticed that they had no acquaintances among the crowd, or if they had they did not recognise any; and, although attending the race-course, they appeared to take very little interest in the proceedings.

They wandered about apparently without any special purpose.

There was that about them, in fact, which excited the suspicion of both Rupert and Henry Clanberris, and they accordingly watched their movements closely.

From the first moment they saw them, in fact, they seemed to connect the strangers with themselves, as if they meditated a personal injury to one or the other, or to one in whom they were interested.

If either Rupert or Henry Clanberris had been asked to say why he thus felt, he would have found it impossible to tell.

Neither was more than naturally suspicious, neither was superstitious, yet they both suspected the two men, and had a vague foreboding of impending evil.

We have all of us, I daresay, at some time or another in the course of our lives, been subject to similar impressions—shadowy premonitions of some calamity awaiting us.

We may array reason against them, we may ridicule them; but reason or ridicule as we will, we cannot dislodge them.

There they remain, clinging pertinaciously in spite of all our efforts to loosen their grasp.

It is one of the mysteries of our nature which we have not yet fathomed.

As a general thing, the ladies in those days did not frequent the race ground.

Sometimes a few would gather in the outskirts away from the vicinity of the crowd.

It was among these Rupert saw that the two men were usually to be found, idly sauntering about without apparent object.

But a close scrutiny would have detected, notwithstanding their nonchalant manner, that they were very busy with their eyes, casting quick, furtive glances among the ladies, which rested, as was natural, on those who were the most attractive.

There was nothing offensive in all this, and yet their was a something in their look which created a feeling of uneasiness for the time.

Henry Clanberris had always been an ardent admirer of horses, and Lady Margaret, too, was a skilful rider, and cherished her favourite pet in the stalls.

On the third day of the race there was to be a trial of some noted horses, and Henry Clanberris, Lady Margaret, and Helen Penraven were on the ground in an open carriage.

Rupert was on horseback by them, and had been holding a brief conversation with them when he noticed the two strangers standing a little apart, gazing fixedly on Helen.

As he turned towards them, a meaning look was exchanged between them, and, dropping their heads, they slowly shuffled their way through the throng.

There was nothing in the look that Rupert would have noticed, had it not been that his curiosity and suspicion had been aroused by his previous observation of the strangers.

As it was, it affected most unpleasantly the mind of my hero.

The beauty of Helen was so prominent that one would not be satisfied with a casual glance at her brilliant features and graceful form, therefore it was not strange that she should attract more than ordinary notice.

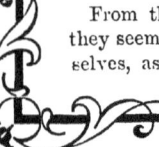

But there was a brutal admiration expressed in the stare of the two men that grated on Rupert's feelings.

Helen did not observe it, or after her many adventures she would have feared some terrible consequences.

During the race the same two men hovered in the vicinity of the carriage, and when the sports were over, they contrived to ascertain which direction the carriage took.

All this Rupert observed narrowly.

And why?

What occasion was there for uneasiness?

What reasons had he for suspecting these strangers of evil intentions, and what harm could now befall Helen when under the protection of such friends?

"What folly this is," thought Rupert, "to permit my mind to be distracted from my great purpose by such suspicions!"

Yet, though he said this to himself, he found himself instinctively forming plans to thwart them!

At last the races were over, the booths were cleared away, and quiet reigned once more.

Rupert had seen nothing of his gipsy foe.

But he still remained in the neighbourhood, making an excuse to stay at the inn to sleep instead of at Clanberris House.

Late the next night, as he sat down in the public room to take a glass of spirits before retiring, he was surprised to see the two strangers enter.

Once more suspicion leaped into his breast.

Why had they remained?

"Very fine country about here?" said the one having the cast in his eye, as he sipped his grog.

Rupert nodded assent.

"Some beautiful spots I have observed in my rambles round," pursued the other. "Are you a resident here?"

"No," returned Rupert.

"Still perhaps you can tell me who owns that lovely place a little out of the village to the south."

"His name is Clanberris," said Rupert.

"Indeed! a good name. He is very wealthy, I believe," replied the other.

"He is reputed to be," said Rupert.

"Won't you join us in a glass of something?" added the other.

Rupert declined, and presently they parted company for the night.

"THE TWO MEN SLUNK HASTILY AWAY."

CHAPTER IX.

THE ABDUCTION.

THOUGH nothing of any consequence had as yet transpired, it was strange how the feeling haunted Rupert Dreadnought that Helen in some way was in danger.

Try as he could, he could not shake it off, and when morning came he found himself in such a state of excitement that he was compelled to enter an apothecary's shop to obtain something to allay his nervous irritation.

As he entered he observed that the atmosphere was strongly impregnated with ether, and he remarked upon it.

"Yes," returned the apothecary, "I have just put up a quantity for some customers, and accidentally spilled a part. I sold it to two strange-looking persons who are at the 'Arundel Arms,' I believe."

Rupert started.

"How long since?" he asked, hastily.

"About two hours ago. They wanted it, they said, to bathe the limbs of their horses."

Rupert waited to hear no more, but hastily quitted the shop.

A terrible thought had flashed into his mind.

Hastening to the tavern he inquired for the strangers.

They had been gone about an hour and a half, and had departed in a dark-covered waggon they had brought there that morning.

They had gone directly out of the village, taking the western road.

This was all the information he could gleam, and for a moment he was irresolute how to act, that terrible thought brooding, brooding continually, giving him no peace.

Clanberris House was about three quarters of a mile from Brentwood—that is from the heart of the village, and lay towards the south-east.

A strong impulse led Rupert on to hasten thither and see if Helen was at home.

Ordering his horse, therefore, he put spurs to it and hurried away, never thinking of any excuse he could make for making his appearance so suddenly and in such evident alarm if Helen herself were there.

His eager haste soon brought him to his destination, and arriving there he at once rushed in.

Helen was out.

That his first question elicited.

"Good Heaven!" cried Henry Clanberris, as he saw his pale and agitated features, "surely nothing has happened to her?"

There was no room or reason for holding back the truth.

Rupert told him briefly his suspicion, and then, without waiting to ask him to accompany him on the journey, put his horse to his utmost speed down the gravelly road, leaving Henry Clanberris in a state of great alarm.

He felt that the moments were far too precious to be wasted in explanations.

Rupert's brain was in a whirl as he dashed through the village and out on the western road.

Up and down the inequalities of the road he urged his swift-footed horse, keeping a sharp look out for Helen.

He had gone a mile or more without a sign of her, when at the bottom of a slight descent, in a hollow, he descried something white fluttering by the road-side.

He reined in his horse, jumped down, and picked it up.

It was a lace handkerchief, and in the corner were the initials "Helen Penraven."

He cast a hurried glance around the spot.

There were footprints leading to the side of the road, and others, near the middle, huddled in that confused manner which plainly indicated that a struggle had taken place there.

It needed not these, the handkerchief was enough to confirm his worst suspicions.

Presently he reached a gentle eminence where he could see a turnpike.

Towards this he galloped.

Here there might at last be a clue.

"Have you seen a lady pass by this way?" he asked, as he drew up his steaming horse, and accosted the keeper of the gate.

"Yes; a lady passed through here, and returned again about an hour ago. You ought to have passed her on the road if you come from Brentwood."

"Has any vehicle passed since?"

"Yes; a dark-covered waggon not long after coming from the village, and driven as if the old boy was after them."

Rupert hardly heard the man out, but putting spurs to his horse, started away at full gallop, leaving the keeper of the gate gazing after him in bewilderment.

His horse flew over the ground with the speed of a bird.

He was a mettlesome animal, and he was now put to his utmost effort.

Not an idea of the existence of danger entered Rupert's mind.

His sole object was to overtake the waggon when he felt quite equal to cope with both the villains single-handed.

He passed over three or four miles without slackening his speed.

Not a single person did he meet on the way.

Here a dilemma threatened to upset everything.

He noticed that, not a great distance ahead of him, the road forked, one branch running off to the north-east the other to the west.

Which should he take?

It was as puzzling as it was all-important.

He thought that, perhaps, the wheel-tracks might guide him, for all along the road he had observed them.

But even this guide was quickly lost, for suddenly they disappeared.

While cogitating upon this matter, he came upon a small farm-house standing a little back from the highway, just beyond which was a barn, with its doors open wide.

A casual glance revealed a dark-covered waggon inside.

Turning at once into the little lane that ran up to the house, Rupert accosted a man who stood near.

"Is that your waggon?" he asked, as he drew rein.

"Yes, master."

"Has it been out to-day?"

Yes; he had lent it that morning to two men to go to Brentwood.

"When did they return it?"

"Well," said the man, "what I'm going to say may seem strange, but they didn't return it at all. The horse came back of its own accord, and pretty well done up he was too, all smothered in foam. It was a cruel shame to serve the dumb creature so."

The horse, it seemed, had returned about three quarters of an hour before Rupert's arrival.

At some distance from the farm, and over some rising ground, was an old disused road leading into the highway to London, and close by the junction was a large inn where post-horses could be obtained.

Rupert could see the place at a glance.

They would carry the insensible girl to the place, say she was ill, and hire post-horses to take her to her "friends" in London.

It did not take long for Rupert to reach the tavern alluded to.

It had happened just as he had anticipated; she had been carried there as an invalid, and they had engaged a post-chaise to carry her to London in safety.

Borrowing a fresh horse, and leaving his own, Rupert once more dashed away.

Burning as he was with desire to save his mistress, and to avenge the outrage which had been put upon her, he yet saw the necessity of caution.

He must be cool and calculating.

One rash move might defeat all his purpose.

He this time was in reality unaware who his enemies were.

The idea of Helen, the pure, angel-hearted girl, being in the power of those two ruffians, in a large city, surrounded by their creatures, helpless and hopeless, would intrude upon his mind.

The question, "Was it for money or for a fouler purpose that she had been carried off?" would also come up in spite of all his efforts.

Such thoughts as these made him shudder, and he strove to throw them off—to close his mind against them, for they made him almost frantic.

After a time he mastered his feelings and recovered in a measure his equanimity.

As he galloped on, the fresh air cleared his brain,

and all his thoughts were bent on the means to be employed to rescue Helen.

In those days the telegraph, that nimble thief-catcher, was not known, or it would have been a far easier affair to catch the scoundrels.

Click, click, click! and all the detectives of London would have been on the alert.

It would be needless waste of time to speak of the torture he endured on his passage towards the city.

All the love that was in his heart was quickened into immediate action for the imperilled girl, every fine feeling was on the throb.

She had been dear enough before, she was still dearer now.

CHAPTER X.

A DETECTIVE OF THE OLDEN TIME.

It was late in the evening when Rupert arrived in London.

Rupert had obtained some little information as to a posting house, which might possibly be the one where the postboy would stop, and here he found that a carriage *had* stopped there.

It contained two men, and a woman, who appeared to be a great invalid, as she had to be lifted from *one* carriage to the other.

Rupert was thus absolutely defeated.

The people of the inn had entertained no suspicions, and, of course, therefore, had not followed the party.

He himself had merely the vaguest suspicion as to the person who had given directions for the outrage, and it was utterly useless, therefore, to act upon his own ideas, or without the assistance of the law.

With this, therefore, he resolved at once to proceed to the house of Robert Lavarette, a "*runner*," or detective, as we call them now, of the most acknowledged ability.

It was not long before he stood in the office of that worthy, who eyed him with a keen and scrutinising glance.

"Take a seat, Master ——," he said, hesitating at the name.

"Lord Rupert Dreadnought," replied our hero, "though for reasons of my own I desire rather to be called plain Master Dreadnought."

The name seemed to take an electrical effect upon the wiry, parchmenty individual who had so great a reputation as a thief-taker.

Without much preface, Rupert detailed all the circumstances connected with the two men, from his first meeting them to his arrival in London.

He heard Rupert in silence.

When he concluded, he said—

"I hope you were not too particular in your inquiries at the inn in regard to the carriage and the way it took?"

"No; I thought you could manage that best," answered Rupert.

"A very judicious conclusion, my lord," returned the other. "It might have occasioned remark. Now please repeat the description of the men."

He did so as accurately as he could.

"Did you hear any names mentioned?"

"Yes; in the room where they were drinking their grog I heard one call the other 'Cozens.'"

"Ah!" said the detective, eagerly, "Cozens was the one with the broken nose and scarred face."

"You know him then?"

"Yes, I fancy I do," replied the detective, "as one of the most desperate characters in London. His companion is as bad, if not worse. We shall have to go about this matter cautiously."

"They must be employed by my private enemies, or I cannot see their object," said Rupert.

"Oh! money, that's their object. The lady is wealthy and *you* are wealthy, and they may hope for a great reward. But they may yet have another object. You say the lady is young and beautiful. Beauty commands a high price in London, especially when combined with youth and freshness. You shrink at my remark, my lord, but you must know it is the truth, and we may as well face truth first as last."

He rang a bell as he concluded, and the summons was answered by a young man.

"Philip," he said, "send in Nos. 8 and 9."

The young man left, and presently two men entered whose appearance somewhat astonished our hero.

You could have sworn at a glance that they had lived all their lives in the precincts of Alsatia—rough, brutal-looking fellows in tawdry finery.

Very few words passed.

"Have you seen Red Brampton and Bully Cozens lately?" he asked.

"No; they have been missing four days," said No. 9.

"Well, they returned to London this evening in a post chaise," said the detective. "I want you to get up on their track. It is an important case, understand—a very important case. They have abducted a young lady in the country under the influence of ether, seemingly an invalid. These are the main points. Be off immediately, and report whatever you discover as soon as possible."

"Aye, aye, master," was the brief rejoinder, and the men started on their mission.

When they had gone, the detective rubbed his hands genially, and said—

"My lord, what kind of job does this promise to be?"

Rupert was pleased with the man's candour.

"Rest assured that you will be well rewarded," he said. "The lady is more to *me* than life itself."

"Well, that is enough. I will take your word, my lord. Where are you stopping?"

"Oh, now I am in London, I shall remain at my own house," said Rupert Dreadnought; "but cannot something be done to-night?"

"Believe me, my lord," replied the detective, in a kindly tone, "I fully appreciate your feelings; rest assured there shall be no delay on my part. I have already put two of my best men on the scent, and I shall set others to work immediately. I promise you that all that can be done shall be done. It is a very complicated machine that I have to take charge of, but I will not fail. Good-night, and keep up your spirits."

Upon this hint Rupert left.

There was nothing now, in fact, but to wait the issue of events.

He was satisfied, by the prompt action of the

detective, that the matter was in good hands, and he returned home to pass the night as best he could.

It may well be imagined that it was a restless one.

He did not court sleep by seeking his bed even.

Racked as his mind was with thoughts of Helen, Rupert knew it to be useless.

In vain he endeavoured to vanish his dread.

Her terrible position haunted him continually; alone, exposed to insult—to a fate compared to which death was a blessed boon.

In such torture he passed the night, counting wearily the hours as they were pealed away heavily from a neighbouring clock tower.

In all his life he had never passed such a night.

He thought it would never come to an end.

But the morning came at last.

About the middle of the forenoon Lavarette made his appearance.

Rupert almost feared to ask him a question.

He could read nothing in his face, encouraging or disencouraging, as he entered the room.

"Well, I am here at last," he said, "somewhat later than I intended, but the fact is I did not get to bed before daylight. But I see you are impatient for news. Everything is working favourably. I have picked up a thread or two which may help us to unravel the scheme. No. 9 has got Red Brampton in hand. The latter is a sly dog, and close as an oyster when sober; but he has a weakness for spirits, which is pretty sure to loosen his tongue. Enough has already been gleaned to assure us that no personal violence has yet been offered the lady."

"Thank Heaven!" murmured Rupert, "you have lifted a weight from my heart."

"As I remarked at our first interview," proceeded the detective, "money is undoubtedly their object."

"Then, in Heaven's name," exclaimed Rupert, "get at their terms at once. Let them name th amount, and it is ready for them."

"Not so fast, my lord," said the cool detective; "if money is to be freely dispensed, I am for its falling into honest hands. Besides, I desire to dispense justice as well as golden coins. Now, I will let you into a little secret. In our business, you know, we have to work with all sorts of tools. No. 9 and Red Brampton are old friends, and have robbed together, and may do so now for all *I* can tell to the contrary. Yet I have the utmost faith in the man. *But*, to make *sure* of him, a little money is necessary."

"Name the amount!" cried Rupert, eagerly.

"Well, say a hundred pounds."

"You can have the money at once," said Rupert.

"Very good. I will not mind telling you why I want it. No. 9 has made a bet with Red Brampton that he is only romancing about kidnapping the girl, and will not be convinced of the fact until he has ocular demonstration. When he has seen her he will forfeit the stakes, and not before. So it is arranged for him to see her this afternoon. Once made acquainted with her place of concealment, I will take good care that she is not spirited away."

"Cannot your man contrive to convey a note to the lady?"

"Perhaps so. What is it you wish to write?"

Rupert at once took pen and ink and wrote—

"DEAREST HELEN,—Keep up a good heart. I am at work to rescue you.

"R."

The detective took Rupert's slip of paper, and, having received the money, and made an appointment for the afternoon, he departed.

Rupert now felt like a new man.

A great stone had been rolled away from his heart.

That calamity which he had shuddered to contemplate had not befallen Helen.

It was true she was yet in peril, that as yet her deliverance was not sure, but as they were really on the right track there was now every cause to hope.

Late in the afternoon Rupert proceeded to the house of the detective, according to agreement.

He had not long been there, when No. 9 entered.

"Well," said his employer, addressing him, "how are matters progressing at Exborough Street?"

The man gave a start of surprise.

"You have been dogging me?" he said, in a tone and with a look of reproach.

"No; upon my honour, I have not," returned Robert Lavarette. "I received my information from quite another quarter this morning. But then, you know, she might have been removed. It seems she has not been, and I must rely upon you for a description of the interior and the room she occupies. Did you give her the note?"

"Yes; and it seemed to have a wonderful effect upon her. I am glad," he continued, "that you learned about the house from other parties, for I hated the idea of peaching upon Red Brampton. Has the gentleman agreed to our arrangement?"

"My man and Red Brampton, a great many years ago, my lord," said the detective, with a look which Rupert understood, "were great friends, and for old acquaintance sake he does not like to be the means of bringing him to harm. The arrangement he speaks of is, that we shall not arrest Brampton, or if we do, we will let him slip through our fingers. Bully Cozens, in fact, has been the prime mover in the business, and Brampton a mere tool. Now, Cozens I have got in a tight place, where conviction is sure, and I am bound he shall not escape me. As to Brampton, he is of no account and always accessible. Do you consent to the arrangement?"

"One word first, excuse me," said the man, whose confused appearance attracted Rupert's attention; "that story of my betting with Brampton was all a sham."

RUPERT DREADNOUGHT OR THE SECRETS OF THE IRON CHEST

"HE WAS GAZING ON HIM FIXEDLY, PISTOL IN HAND."

"So I supposed," said the chief, with cool assurance, although I doubted if the thought had ever occurred to him; "the pretended stake was, in fact, a bribe. That showed your shrewdness."

"That's it," said the man, brightening up, as if relieved from something embarrassing. "I said to Brampton, 'Bully Cozens is only using you as a catspaw. If a reward is offered for the girl—that's what they're looking for, of course—he will take the lion's share, and put you off with scarcely anything.' So I took the liberty of offering him the hundred pounds, with a promise that he should come to no harm, if he only made the coast clear for us, and he's done it. It's the honest truth I'm telling you, my lord. I don't care a rush what becomes of the other fellow, but you'll give Red Brampton the go-by ?"

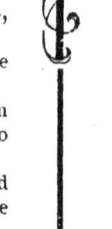

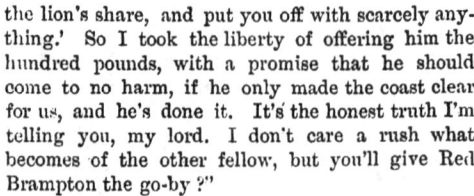

The last remark, of course, was addressed to Rupert Dreadnought.

"Certainly," he answered.

Of necessity, he was willing to agree to any arrangement that Lavarette saw fit to make.

With him the paramount object was the release of Helen Penraven.

That once accomplished, the end of justice might be considered.

"Let Red Brampton go, by all means, if he helps us in our work," said Rupert. "Place the lady under my protection, and after that you can do as you like."

This matter settled, it was arranged that the detective should call for Rupert at his house, after dark, and that there they would take a carriage for the scene of action.

"You had better come fully armed," said the detective, as Rupert left, "you may find it very necessary."

CHAPTER XI

THE SPIDER IS CAUGHT AND THE FLY IS RELEASED.

AGAIN, with eager impatience, Rupert Dreadnought waited for the arrival of the hour of action.

Between eight and nine o'clock in the evening the detective came.

According to agreement, Rupert had a carriage waiting at the door, and they at once entered and drove to Exborough Street.

There, a short distance from the house, they found No. 9 waiting.

"All right," he said, in a low tone, "Red Brampton will let us in. The other fellow he says is with the lady, and he thinks he is up to some devilry. You had better hurry. Remember, it's the third door on the right from the head of the second flight. I and Brampton will remain at the outer door; you two can manage him."

Rupert and the detective were cautiously admitted into the hall.

A dim light revealed their way.

Rupert's heart beat with great throbs as he ascended the stairs, and he could hardly curb his impatience.

Hurrying on he reached the head of the second flight, when he heard the noise of a struggle going on in the third room, followed by a piercing shriek of—

"Help! help!"

Darting forward he reached the door.

It was locked.

He made but one effort, and it flew from its fastenings.

The spectacle that met his eyes within the chamber wrought him up to the highest pitch of excitement.

Pale and terror-stricken, Helen was on her knees, senseless, in the ruffian clutch of Bully Cozens.

Rupert sprang forward and grasped him by the throat.

He was a powerful man, but he was a child in the hands of our hero, whose excitement seemed to endow him with supernatural power.

He held him until he grew black in the face, and then shook him off as he would a viper, and the ruffian measured his length on the floor.

Helen started up, gazed in bewilderment for a moment, and then, springing forward, clung to her lover for protection, crying hysterically—

"Safe! safe! Thank Heaven! thank Heaven!"

Rupert folded the trembling girl to his breast in a warm embrace.

Turning his head he saw that the scoundrel had regained his feet, and was in the act of springing on him.

He was gazing on him fixedly, pistol in hand.

Disengaging himself from the embrace of Helen, which impeded his actions, he drew from his breast pocket a pistol.

"One step forward, and you are a dead man!" he said, in a calm, determined voice, as he covered him with his weapon.

He stood still, glaring at Rupert like some wild beast brought to bay.

"Two can play at that game," he shouted at last, with a horrid oath, and a formidable pistol was levelled directly at Dreadnought's head, not two paces distant.

Before he could press the trigger, his arm was stricken down, a slight scuffle followed, and the man was a helpless, handcuffed prisoner in the hands of the detective.

"Let us leave this horrid place," said Helen, in a weak voice, again clinging to her lover, as if with him was her only safety.

A malignant, fiendish look was bent on her by the fettered culprit, as they passed by him and quitted the room.

Rupert had to support Helen down stairs, for she was nerveless in every limb.

As they came out two men were standing on the side of the road.

One of them said—

"Here, Brampton, you have fairly earned it. I will see you at the old place to-night. Now be off."

This was the last Helen saw of Red Brampton.

They at once drove off towards Rupert's house, and Helen was for the time again in safety.

When he had made such arrangements as seemed necessary for her comfort and safety, Rupert made the best of his way to the house of the detective.

Here they had taken Bully Cozens.

Much against his inclination, the Bow Street runner had been persuaded by Rupert not to give the scoundrel up to the law until he had been questioned.

So, bound and gagged, he remained seated in the detective's room until Rupert made his appearance.

Then the gag was removed from his mouth, and he was permitted to speak.

"Curse you," he said. "Who are you, and where am I? If I am not before my judges, why am I a prisoner?"

"You will be a prisoner no longer if you confess the truth," said Rupert. "Who was your employer in this outrage?"

"I refuse to tell," returned the man, doggedly.

"It matters not," said the detective, with a quick glance at Rupert, "we asked but to try you. Red Brampton will disclose to us all we want without your assistance, and we shall deliver *you* up to the authorities."

The cool way in which the detective spoke had the effect of convincing the villain.

"Well, if you're going to let me off Scot free, I'll tell you all I know," he said.

"You have been told," said Rupert, "that you *are* to be free to go. Is not that enough?"

"Yes, I'll take your word. We were employed by Dr. Henzollern."

Both Rupert and the detective started at the mention of this name.

"I had thought," said the former, "that it was the work of Oscar Penraven."

"In this case the Chief acted for one of his subordinates," said the man; "it was for Oscar Penraven that he engaged us. We understood that the lady was Sir Oscar Penraven's wife."

"Why, then, if she is his wife does he not claim her openly?" said Rupert.

"I don't know anything about that," said the man; "but such was what he told us. At any rate it was the doctor who employed us."

"And pray," said Rupert, sternly, "what was the meaning of the cries of distress which we heard issuing from the room? Did Sir Oscar Penraven, fancying that she was his wife by law, give you authority to use violence to her?"

"No; but when I told her that the time had arrived for taking her to her husband's house, she began making such a violent resistance that I had to threaten her. It was then that I seized her, and at the very moment *you* burst into the room."

"Yes, and you may thank your good luck that at the present moment you are here at all," said Rupert, with anger evident in his tones: "however, I will keep my word with you. Answer me my questions to the best of your knowledge, and I will set you free—not at once, remember, because that might ruin all our plans again; but you shall have your life spared, you shall not be delivered up to the authorities, and after a few days you shall be at liberty to go where you please. Now, in the first place, where is this Dr. Henzollern to be found?"

The man hesitated.

"Speak," said Rupert, "your life depends upon your speech."

The man saw he was in the hands of resolute men.

But even now he did not know *how* far he would have to proceed in his tale.

"Do you know the retreat of the Society to which Dr. Henzollern and Oscar Penraven belong?" he asked.

"We do," responded Rupert.

"He is there," said the man; "I can tell you no more."

"You can," replied Rupert, "and that, too, something far more *apropos*. What is the sign and countersign, and the password?"

The ruffian at these words turned deadly pale.

"I know the password," he said, "but that I dare not tell."

"You must and *shall*," replied Rupert. "You are here helpless in our power, and if you refuse to disclose all we ask, or give us false information, your life will be forfeited. Now speak."

"I know not what to do," replied the man, who was evidently under the influence of strong fear. "If I refuse to tell you I am threatened with death. If I tell you I incur death at the hands of the Society, and break a terrible oath."

"That has nothing to do with us," said Rupert; "we have you here, and you are the only one through whom we can ascertain what we require. As you are in our power, you must be made to answer our purpose. Speak or die!"

The cold rim of a pistol applied to the head of the man was a convincing proof that he was with those who did not intend half measures; and, in spite of his terror at the idea of what he was about to do, he saw that he *must* succumb.

Death was *present* in the hands of Rupert and the detective, while, as regards the Society, there was at least a chance of its being deferred.

"Well," he said, "since you *insist* upon my telling you, I *must*; but you will, at least, promise not to betray me?"

"Of course we shall not betray you," said Rupert. "Speak quickly."

The man shuddered, as if about to do some terrible thing.

Then, with an effort, he said.

"You must knock three times at the door faintly. Then, when the man who opens the door appears, you must say, before he speaks, 'Companions of the Fourth Order.' 'By what sign?' he will ask; and you must answer, 'By the sign of the Silver Cross.' You must go masked, and dressed in black velvet. You are not required to unmask unless they suspect traitors to be present, and then *all* would have to show their faces."

"Why should they suspect if you have told us the truth?" said the detective.

"I know not. They have spies everywhere," returned the man. "You yourself may be one for anything I know to the contrary. There are, how. ever, only a certain number of persons admitted to the meetings, which take place every Thursday evening—one hundred. If one hundred and two are counted at the door they know two strangers to be present. Then, again, all may not come."

"We will risk that," said Rupert, "and take strong measures for our safety. This is Wednesday. To-morrow, then, is the day. You can make arrangements for the safe custody of this man until then, I suppose?"

The detective, to whom Rupert addressed himself, smiled, as he replied—

"Yes; and for some of his friends, if you desire it. He will be well taken care of, and will have no reason to complain of his prison."

CHAPTER XII.

THE MEETING OF THE POISONERS.

The preparations which Rupert made for the following evening were somewhat elaborate.

He was resolved to penetrate the dark secrets of the order, and in the destruction of the Chief to involve the entire Society.

To makes themselves in any way a match for the hundred men of whom the man had spoken, he would certainly have had to call in the aid of the Government, and surround the place with an army of watchmen or soldiers.

But Bully Cozens had spoken the truth.

Perhaps among those very watchmen and soldiers there might be secret spies, if not positive members of the Society.

So it behoved them to be cautious.

Rupert therefore decided that his own friends, and their connections, should be the only ones to know of the scheme.

It was arranged, consequently, that Tom the waterman, Allan of the Glen, Stanley Sherrington, Henry Clanberris, and the retainers of the two latter, should be posted in a spot near at hand, ready to create a diversion at a given signal, and that Rupert and the detective should enter the den of infamy over which Dr. Henzollern presided.

It was dangerous work. But neither Rupert nor any of his friends shrank from it.

Fortune had hitherto favoured them in their attacks upon the villains, and they firmly trusted it would do so again.

When the little army of friends mustered in the grounds, Stanley Sherrington was found to have brought four men, Henry Clanberris five, the detective three, so that altogether they numbered eighteen persons.

Dressed all in black as they were, and masked, they looked a strange crew, and would certainly have been arrested as suspicious characters by any body of watchmen who came across them.

But the place was dark and wooded enough to have enabled them to conceal double the number, and they proceeded in twos and threes towards the place of concealment without meeting a soul.

At nine o'clock Rupert saw the members of the dread Society coming up one by one to the place of meeting, and entering after the usual challenge.

The time had now arrived for action.

His men were accordingly placed beneath a high and wide window, which was evidently that of the place of meeting.

At the sound of a pistol shot they were to rush to the door and burst it in, in order that the diversion thus caused would relieve Rupert and the detective from the danger of being discovered.

He had gained much useful information from Lesbia Howard in regard to the place.

Having been denounced, and having also been suspected for a long time, she had not been trusted with the password, but she gave them invaluable information in regard to the interior of the place, the way into the council chamber, and the position in which to stand to avoid observation.

Armed thus, they approached boldly, and tapped lightly on the doorway.

In a moment it was opened.

A tall, masked man stood before them.

As their informant had told them, he remained quite silent.

"Companion of the Fourth Order," said Rupert, in a disguised voice.

The detective uttered the same words.

"By what sign?"

"By the sign of the Silver Cross," said Rupert.

"Good," said the man; "enter."

Then they passed in, and the door clanged with an ominous sound behind them.

It was well that Lesbia Howard had given them some information in regard to the interior of the house, for among the winding staircases they would certainly have been lost.

However, through her they were enabled to reach the large council chamber in safety, and entered without further question.

They were surprised greatly by the appearance of the interior, and the style in which matters were conducted.

To a stranger it would have seemed but natural that a settled gloom would have been upon every one, and that a mock solemnity, at any rate, would have presided over everything.

It was not so.

As in the revel, the description of which began my story, there was more joviality than gloom.

Instead of a chamber draped in black, and bare of all comfort, they were ushered into a large room, brilliantly lighted, where numbers of persons were standing in groups, or sitting by a large table, at which were preparations for a banquet.

In order to avoid observation, Rupert and Robert Lavarette seated themselves at the table, and helped themselves to some of the wine, conversing meanwhile but very little.

They were eager to see how the proceedings would commence.

They had not long to wait.

The door after a very few moments opened, and a tall man entered, one who was evidently in authority, and who was well known in spite of his mask.

He was greeted with cheers.

"That is the Chief," said Rupert Dreadnought, to his companion.

"Aye," said a voice behind them, "and a good chief he is. He doesn't stick at trifles. I wonder who is the one he is going to propose to take his place while he is absent?"

"It is to be hoped that it will be one as energetic as Dr. Henzollern," said Lavarette.

"Yes, indeed," replied the other; "but we shall not know until after the banquet, and we may as well, therefore, wait patiently and enjoy ourselves."

The Chief now took his position at the head of the table.

Then doors were opened, and men entered bearing dishes of all kinds.

The company at a certain signal fell to work on these with a right good will, and never in the slightest disturbed by the thought of the hideous manner in which their money was obtained, continued feasting until they had satisfied themselves and then the Chief rose.

"Brothers," he said, "I intimated to you upon a

former occasion that I was about to quit you for a time.

"Important business connected with our Society takes me to Scotland.

"There, among the members of that powerful branch of our convention which has established itself in Edinburgh, I go to learn secrets which will be useful to us.

"Thence I proceed to Germany.

"This journey will occupy me about two months.

"During this time I trust you will not be idle, but persevere in the stupendous work you have commenced.

"And now, as it is necessary for you to have a leader, we will proceed to elect a deputy in my place.

"I know well that you have the power of selecting whom you like, but I beg to suggest one who would, in *my* opinion, be a firm and staunch supporter of the cause.

"I allude to Oscar Penraven."

At the mention of this name there were loud plaudits.

Evidently among this convival assemblage Oscar Penraven was a favourite.

"I see," said Dr. Henzollern, "that you receive this name with pleasure. Shall we proceed to his election, or shall we consider him elected? It will be best to hold up your hands if you agree with what I say."

"'SPEAK, OR YOU DIE!'" CRIED HE.

The meeting was unanimous.

Every hand was held up.

Rupert and Robert Lavarette naturally thought that if they kept their hands down a question as to their reasons for doing so might arise.

They therefore acted with the rest.

"I am glad to see you approve of my appointment," said the Chief. "Oscar Penraven is present, no doubt, and will return you his thanks when I have reported to you our proceedings during the last week.

"You know, of course, that our purpose is to continue our work until every member is possessed of twenty thousand pounds, exclusive of what he has expended during the time of labour.

"Matters are progressing well.

"We have now in hand sufficient to pay to each member ten thousand pounds.

"Sister Rosalie has brought to the Society, within two months, no less than forty thousand pounds, and *every victim is dead.*

"Sir Roland Compton, whose death brings to us a hundred thousand pounds, died yesterday by our secret poison, and the nurse who attended him is dead also.

"Lady Caroline Manvers, whose death will contribute twenty thousand more, will die to-night, and those whom I seek in Scotland and Germany will, I trust, contribute two hundred thousand more.

"You see, therefore, that our matters are proceeding better than you might have expected."

It was with a shudder that Rupert and Robert Lavarette heard these words.

How many persons must have suffered at the hands of the Terrible Society before they could have amassed sufficient to give ten thousand pounds a piece to more than a hundred members, besides the extravagant outlay which was necessary to keep up their Death Banquets!

The others in the room were evidently delighted at the way affairs were progressing.

It is difficult to imagine how so many fiends in human shape could be found banded together.

But, scum of the earth, detestable wretches, of all grades, they appeared to read in the horrible work which was enacting there; and wine was poured out and the Chief's health was drank, as was also that of the fair demon, Rosalie St. Aubyn.

After this, Dr. Henzollern raised his hand to enjoin silence once more, and the Poisoners at once reseated themselves.

"Friends!" he said, in a solemn voice, "having told you good news, I must now turn to a less pleasant duty.

"*We have traitors among us!*"

Every man started, and glanced at his neighbour in suspicion.

The hearts of Rupert and Robert Lavarette beat high with excitement. But it was a false alarm.

It was not to them that on the present occasion the Chief alluded.

"Yes," he continued, "Lesbia Howard, Alford, and Lionel Armer, have all of them been discovered to be conspiring with our enemies, and have been denounced.

"You know well, therefore, how to act.

"Whenever you meet them the knife or poison must do its work.

"Lesbia Howard, I myself undertook to destroy, but she escaped me.

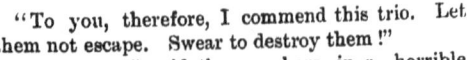

"To you, therefore, I commend this trio. Let them not escape. Swear to destroy them!"

"We swear!" said the members, in a horrible chorus.

Just as the words left the lips of the terrible throng, there was a rush of feet in the passage without.

The door then was thrown violently open, and the keeper of the outer gate appeared.

"To arms, gentlemen!" he cried; "there are traitors here!"

In an instant the whole of the Poisoners had risen to their feet, and drawn their swords.

"Close the door!" cried the President, in a voice of thunder. "If there are traitors among us, they leave not this room alive!"

The order was at once obeyed.

Then the Chief removed his mask.

"Friends," he said, "I have just spoken of three traitors—you see that we have more—our Society is disorganised, demoralised. Speak, man, what is it you mean?"

"There should be," returned the keeper of the door, "one hundred gentlemen present."

"Yes."

"There are at present in this room one hundred and two."

A dead silence followed.

Every man again looked at his neighbour.

But all being masked, none could recognise the other.

"Explain," said the Chief, "how found you this out?"

"I will, and briefly," replied the keeper of the door. "I, you may be sure, have not left my post, and yet the news of this treachery comes from the streets of Brentwood.

"My brother, who, as you know, is an active servant in the cause, was proceeding round the corner of a street when he heard two men in earnest conversation. He heard the word 'Poisoners,' and he halted to listen.

"'Twas well he did.

"In a few moments he heard words which induced him to think that the Society was being betrayed, and that to-night, unknown to you, strangers would be amongst us.

"He waited eagerly, therefore, until the two men were parted.

"They did so within a few minutes, and he at once followed the one who remained longest behind.

"There was no one near, and one blow on the back of his head stretched him upon the floor.

"He half raised himself at once, but the cold rim of a pistol was against his forehead and he saw the folly of attempting to make an alarm.

"'What is it you want with *me*,' he said; 'if it is money you are in error. I have none upon my person.'

"'No,' replied my brother, 'I require not your money. I have overheard your conversation with your friend. Tell me who is it who purposes visiting the retreat of the Society you spoke of? Quick, speak!'

"'I know not,' said the man.

"My brother pressed the pistol harder still against the man's forehead.

"'Speak, or you die,' said he.

"The man saw he was thoroughly in his power, and it was useless to attempt either to deceive or resist.

"'Robert Lavarette, the detective,' he said; 'he is going there, or rather, he is at the house now.'

"My brother wasted no more time, but rushed away, leaving the man on the ground."

The man paused.

"See," said the Chief, "dangers are threatening us. We must resort to extreme measures. I know well that it is a rule in our Society that we shall not be called upon to unmask. That rule I call upon you at once to cancel; let every man here who is not a traitor at once show his features!"

There was a momentary hesitation.

Some—dastardly poisoners though they were—did not care to exhibit their faces to their companions in iniquity.

During this instant of doubt Rupert formed his plans.

The room was lighted by one brilliant oil-lamp in the centre.

He had anticipated some grave dilemma, though not of this kind.

However, his former adventures had made him ready at any moment to conceive ideas of escape from terrible perils, and he at once conceived an idea of safety.

A pistol shot had been the signal agreed on by his friends.

Quickly drawing a pistol from his belt, he cried,

"Brothers, we cannot cancel thus our old law. There are those among us who are faithful members of the Society, but who desire not their names to be known, and whose identity will at once be discovered, should they show their features. I for one disapprove of the idea propounded by our Chief, and thus I, for the moment, at least, prevent its accomplishment."

Then before any one could prevent him, he raised his hand and fired at the lamp, which shivered in a hundred fragments, and left the room in utter darkness.

In the instant, as if they had risen from their place of concealment by magic, Rupert's friends dashed at the cellar door.

Within everything was in dire confusion before the knocking came at the door.

But now everything was different.

The thought of their having two traitors in their room had been astounding enough, but to find their sanctuary attacked publicly was worse.

"Brethren, we are betrayed!" cried the Chief, in a loud and resolute voice, "we must fight for our lives."

In the utter darkness it was, of course, impossible to distinguish friend from foe.

No attempt, moreover, could be made to re-light the lamp, whose shivered fragments lay upon the banquet table, and the only thing, therefore, to be done was to escape.

As soon as he had fired the shot which had so successfully deprived the Poisoners of all means of identifying their enemies, Rupert Dreadnought and Robert Lavarette remained perfectly still.

An attempt had been made by two persons near them to seize upon them and make them prisoners, but in the darkness it had failed utterly, and both of them, edging themselves through the crowd, pressed eagerly towards the door, through which the keeper of the gate had entered.

Their object now was escape, for though neither had spoken to the other, it was quite evident what was their proper scheme of action.

They had discovered the extent of the hideous villany by which the Poisoners were gathering their immense fortunes.

They had heard Oscar Penraven publicly named as Deputy Chief of the Society.

They had discovered the route by which Dr. Henzollern was about to proceed, and they were resolved to follow him, and foil his plans.

To do this, there must be no escape of the Poisoners.

They must remain within the house, and a cordon must be placed around it by Rupert and his friends.

In order to do this, it would be necessary to get close to the door, and rush away as soon as it was opened.

While they were doing this, the window of the large room was thrown open, and one of the Poisoners put his head out.

"What want you?" he cried.

"Admittance."

"For what reason?"

"That we will state when the doors are open," returned the voice which Rupert recognised as that of Henry Clanberris.

"Then you will remain there all night," replied the Poisoner, and the window was closed once more.

"How many are there of them?" asked the Chief.

"About a score or more."

"We can master them then," he returned. "Let us open."

"It will be dangerous to act so publicly when traitors are in our very midst," cried the voice of Oscar Penraven. "Let us rather escape by the secret way, and let the keeper of the door shoot the first man who lags behind."

"Very good," replied the Chief, "let it so be done."

But the besiegers gave them no time to perform this feat.

Scarcely had the words left his lips when there was a sound as of the dashing of heavy bodies against the woodwork of the door.

The assailants had begun their work now in real earnest.

A second dash, and with a crash the door yielded, and several dark bodies fell almost into the corridor.

Now was the time.

Darting out as with one will, Rupert and Robert Lavarette rushed into the midst of their friends.

They took all by surprise.

No one tried to stop them.

"Away!" cried Rupert, and with one accord the friends and their retainers had rushed away into the dark wood.

The Poisoners were confounded.

"Let us pursue them!" said Oscar Penraven, fiercely.

"No," said the Chief, "let us do nothing so rash; let us rather consult again what is to be done. I go to-morrow evening, and it will be better to decide at once what is to be done."

Returning accordingly to their banquetting hall after setting up the door as well as they could, they gathered once more round the board by the light of two candles, and, in the gloom of the semi-darkness, consulted what was to be done in the emergency which had overtaken them.

It was at length decided that all meetings should be suspended for a month.

The doorkeeper would remain and keep watch, and a secret meeting could take place in some other spot if his report was unfavourable.

"And now," said the Chief, "do *you* all of you proceed by the secret way, and depart to your homes."

"And you?" said Oscar Penraven.

"I shall remain here. I have some little preparations to make, and those I can best make here. Let the password on the next meeting night be, 'Death to the Traitors!' Remember those who are denounced—be watchful and resolute, and now farewell."

The Hundred Poisoners then filed out of the room, and by a subterranean way made their exit.

The Chief alone remained behind.

Little did he think how he was aiding Rupert Dreadnought and his friends and their designs by so doing.

CHAPTER XIII.

ON THE ROAD.

It was no difficult matter for Rupert to keep a good look-out upon the house of the Poisoners.

With seventeen watchers besides himself, it was an easy matter to have a relay of watchers, and Tom the waterman, Allan of the Glen, with four others, were left to watch till morning.

The subterranean passage which had been used as the exit of the Poisoners after they had received the last injunctions of their Chief, led a long way out under the high road, and the watchers saw nothing of their departure.

It was a most dangerous mode of exit.

The floor was composed of soft mud, where the water of the river had flowed in, and washed in surging tides almost up to the staircase by which they descended from the upper part of the building, and at some periods, when the tide was especially high, it was flooded to a perilous extent.

It was for this reason that they never used it as a means of entrance, and indeed on no occasion when they were not compelled, did they deem it necessary to wade through a foot of greasy mud.

The watchers, therefore, saw nothing of the departure of the hundred, and their report was, when they were asked in the morning, that no one had quitted the house.

The evening watch was taken by Rupert, Allan of the Glen, Henry Clanberris and Robert Lavarette.

The first two were to accompany one another on the journey to Scotland.

To any stranger they would have been quite unrecognizable.

All traces of the gentleman on one side and the Scotch youth on the other, had disappeared.

A red wig concealed Rupert's flowing locks, while his clothes mean, though not torn or dirty, proclaimed a kind of miserly lawyer.

To this was added a blue bag, and a clean shaven face, artificially coloured and adorned with well-made wrinkles.

Allan of the Glen looked like his assistant or clerk.

His legs were encased in tightly-fitting trousers too short for him, and displaying a pair of grey cotton stockings.

His face also was stained, and his whole appearance utterly changed.

Near at hand were two horses.

These two were curious specimens.

The one which was for Rupert was a tall, finely-made beast, capable of great work.

The other was a tall, raw-boned, ugly creature, who had been known to beat many a better-looking animal, but who was better suited to Allan's changed appearance than a better-shaped animal would have been.

Dr. Henzollern, not suspecting that he alone was the object of surveillance, would naturally not dash away at any great speed at first, and they would thus have abundant time to mount their steeds and follow.

They were waiting thus, when there was a rushing through the trees, and one of Robert Lavarette's men came up out of breath.

It was one from his house, and not one of those he had brought with him and Rupert.

"What ails you?" cried the detective; "you seem in a great state of alarm."

"No," said the man, "I am not in alarm. I am only wearied and scared by the rapidity of my journey. The man you left at home has escaped."

"Escaped!" repeated Rupert and Lavarette together.

"Yes; he was gone this morning," replied the man.

"And have you no clue to his whereabouts?"

"None; or, rather, we only know which road he has taken."

"Quick, then, speak!" said Robert Lavarette, who was labouring under great excitement.

"One of our men saw a person, corresponding with the appearance of the runaway, enter the 'Talbot Inn,' in Eastchepe. I at once hurried hither, and learned that a man, certainly answering his description, had borrowed a horse, saying that it must be a strong one, as he had a long distance to proceed along the North Road. He paid for the horse at once, and dashed away at great speed."

"We have the clue now," said Robert Lavarette. "He goes, of course, to meet Dr. Henzollern. But tell me, how did the villain escape? There must have been great neglect of duty somewhere."

"Well, it was not *my* fault, Master Lavarette," said the man; "one of the men remained in his room all night, and this morning we found him gagged and bound."

Lavarette's brow knitted, and his lips worked with passion.

"Who was this man who was found thus in the morning?" he asked.

"Richard Elphet."

"Good," said Robert Lavarette, "that will do. Here is a guinea for your trouble. Now rejoin the others."

When the man had thanked him and departed Lavarette turned to Rupert.

"This Richard Elphet is, of course, a traitor," he said; "he first removed the villain's bonds, and then suffered himself to be placed in his position. I see it all plainly now. But this fellow has made for the North Road to join his master. You must be wary."

"Yes," said Rupert Dreadnought, "fear not. But see, the door opens."

As he spoke the half-shattered door was pushed open, and Doctor Henzollern appeared.

He wore no mask now.

His features were plainly visible in the twilight, and Rupert recognised the man whom his father had so accurately described.

"I have made a vow to spoil his desperate plans of villany," murmured Rupert, "or I would at once challenge him to fight."

"No," said Lavarette, "do not allow headstrong passion to mislead you or draw you into rash conflicts. By following this terrible being you will be able to bring home to him some crime which will surely lead to his destruction and that of the accursed Society, of which he is chief."

"True, true," said Rupert, "I will restrain my passion. See! his horse is being brought round to him. We must prepare."

In a few moments Dr. Henzollern was mounted on a splendid roan, and at an easy pace was making his way along the high road.

In a few minutes after Rupert Dreadnought and Allan of the Glen were on his track, jogging on and taking apparently no notice of any one, the "clerk" following the "lawyer" at a respectful distance.

There was very little fear of their missing their quarry.

In these days what was called the North Road was the one invariably used by travellers to Scotland, and all that was necessary, consequently, was to push on to the first inn, and there await the coming of the enemy.

Even then it was not the intention of Rupert to accost him.

His wish was to unravel the thread of the mystery which attended the journey to Scotland, and even to follow him to Germany, if necessary.

RUPERT OR THE DREADNOUGHT; SECRETS OF THE IRON CHEST

"WHAT HAVE WE HERE?" CRIED STANLEY SHERRINGTON.

All that was requisite, therefore, was to keep his eye upon him.

As the doctor proceeded, at a very moderate pace, Rupert and Allan hurried on, and passing him without taking any notice of him, or attracting any, rode on towards the first inn.

At the first place they came to, they saw at once it was unnecessary to delay.

It was simply a small tavern, full of countrymen, and not the place where any one would dream of making a rendezvous.

So they pressed on to the next, which was five miles distant.

Here they at once saw that they had hit on the right vein.

Seated by a fire in the public room was the ruffian whom Rupert had first seen on Brentwood racecourse.

He glanced at them as they came in.

But he had evidently no suspicion of them.

Their identity was completely lost.

They took care, however, not to scrape acquaintance, but sitting apart, ordered refreshment.

They had been there some three quarters of an hour when the door was opened, and Dr. Henzollern entered.

He smiled as he saw the man.

"You have contrived to come, then?" he said.

"Yes," replied the other, "I have by dint of almost superhuman exertions. But I will explain all presently."

He gave a significant look at the supposed lawyer and his clerk, and Dr. Henzollern at once rang the bell.

"I am hungry," he said, as the landlord entered, "and so is my friend here. Let us have a good supper, and serve it in a private room, as we have business to transact."

The officious landlord bowed.

"Certainly, sir," he said; "you shall be accommodated with a nice room just above this. I will see that it is ready in a few minutes."

While Boniface was busying himself with his preparations, Dr. Henzollern and his companion discussed the ordinary topics of the day, the weather, and so on.

They had not long to wait, however.

In a few minutes the landlord returned to inform his guests that their room was ready and supper served, and, with a nod of politeness to the other travellers, the pair quitted the chamber.

"Now," said Rupert to Allan, "we *must* in some way hear this conversation. The question is how?"

"I will creep up to the door and listen."

"That would be dangerous."

"Bribe the landlord."

"That would be as bad. How do we know whether or not he is one of the foul conspiracy?"

Allan at this sprang up.

"I think I have an idea," he said. "I will return in half a minute."

So saying, he hastily quitted the room.

It was not long ere he returned.

"Pay the score, Master Dreadnought," he said. "There is a ladder in the yard by which we can ascend to a wooden terrace or balcony, upon which the window of their room opens. There we can hear all. There is no one out there to observe us."

Rupert at once paid the score, and passing out, they directed their course towards the high road, where they had tethered their horses

But no one was taking any notice of them, and returning quickly, therefore, they entered the yard, and made their way up the ladder into the terrace.

It was a somewhat warm night, though not a very bright one, and the window of the room in which sat the two Poisoners was partially open.

Through the aperture came clearly the voices of the conspirators.

The landlord was just bringing in some ale as our hero and Allan arrived at their place of concealment, and the conversation, consequently, had not yet begun.

When, however, Boniface had gone, Dr. Henzollern rose, locked the door, and then returning to his seat began at once—

"Now, you tell me, Ned Cozens, that you have a friend keeping a lonely inn, the 'McDonald Arms,' some miles from Edinburgh, near the banks of the Frith?"

"Yes, that is right."

"And this man will give up this place to you for a trifling consideration?"

"Yes; that is to say, you must pay him the full value of the place, or he can return when we ——"

"No, no," interrupted Dr. Henzollern; "if my plans are properly conducted and carried out, he cannot return. Enough of this—we can have the place, that suffices me. Now. listen to my story. It is a strange one."

"About two days after our arrival, there will reach Leith a young man named Francis Milroy.

"He comes to seek an earldom and a fortune, for his father's death leaves him sole heir to a magnificent estate.

"Now if this young man died, there is an uncle, one Robert Milroy, who would at once step into the property and title.

"This uncle is one of our sworn brothers, and it is his duty, therefore, to see that the fortune falls into the hands of the Society; but though the young earl, his nephew, has been many years abroad and has never seen his face, he fears that his great likeness to his father might betray him.

"This is *one* reason why he does not meet him himself; another is that I thought it better, as so immense a sum of money was at stake, to do all myself.

"He is, moreover, a distant relation of the Dreadnought family, and, should the uncle die by any means before he wills away the property, it would revert to my great enemy, Lord Rupert Dreadnought."

"My plan is this.

"He must receive a letter as soon as he lands, saying that a friend from London has arrived to greet him, and that he will find him at the 'McDonald Arms.'

"*You* must lead him to it, and there I will await him.

"I shall then plainly state the case, and if he refuses what I shall ask, why then—you may guess the rest.

"Now we must push on, for time is very precious. Your friend may not be so easily led as you imagine; but, nevertheless, you have full leave to make a good offer. You understand me, of course. You are to pay him what money he asks, and you are then to assume the position of landlord, turn away all servants or lodgers, and let us be alone in the house. We must have the place to ourselves to do *our* work properly."

"I will see that all is right," said Bully Cozens. "You yourself apparently do not wish to be seen in the affair until all is settled."

"Exactly so," replied Dr. Henzollern; "but, as I was never in Scotland before, you had better tell me exactly where the 'McDonald Arms' are situated."

"I will. It is about a mile from Leith, and stands in a lonely place, where the edge of the Frith is like a marsh, and the water laps dismally among nodding reeds. You will find it on the left hand of the highroad, and on the night in question I will so place three lights that they shall fall crossways along the road. You will not miss it. It is the only place of entertainment, and, indeed, the only habitable tenement of any kind for nearly half a mile."

"Good," said Dr. Henzollern, "we will travel on together as far as Edinburgh; there I will leave you, and you can arrange with your friend as you please. I shall assume that you succeed, and on the second night after I shall make my way towards the 'McDonald Arms.' Come now, let us do justice to this meal. Boniface has by no means been niggardly with his provisions."

The conversation between the two vile companions was now evidently at an end, and so, satisfied with what they had heard, Rupert and Allan quitted their post of observation, and, descending the ladder, proceeded to where they had left their horses, and rode off.

"*We* must be on the scene first," said Rupert, as they did so. "When we have reached Edinburgh we will resume our own style of dress. Come, let us put spurs to our steeds and away."

They had but one hour's start of those whom they were watching, however, and could not, therefore, expect to be far in advance.

Notwithstanding this, they did contrive to keep at a respectful distance, and they reached "Modern Athens" some time before anything was seen of Dr. Henzollern and Bully Cozens.

It now remained to them, of course, to change their dress, and find out at once the appearance and situation of the 'McDonald Arms,' which was intended by Dr. Henzollern evidently as the scene of a terrible tragedy.

They had not great trouble in finding it.

Passing as English travellers on the look-out for the picturesque, they soon obtained the services of a man to act as a kind of guide, and early on a bright morning they reached a point on the banks of the Frith of Forth where another inn, "The Pedlar's Rest," nodded over the water.

Here they dismissed their guide, stating it as their intention to remain there for some few days.

Sallying forth from this place, after partaking of a hearty meal, more relished by Allan of the Glen than by Rupert, they walked along a narrow pathway on the edge of the Frith for nearly a mile, when they beheld, not far from them, the "McDonald Arms."

The situation of the old inn was just as Bully Cozens had described it.

The beautiful flow of the broad tide was apparently close to it, as he had said, but when you came closer they could see the ledge and the reeds, the oozy slime and the dark trees, which at night made it so gloomy and murderous a looking spot.

One glance at it and its surroundings was enough for their present necessities.

To approach nearer would have been unsafe.

If Bully Cozens had already taken possession, he would, of course, recognise them, and at once spoil all their plans.

So, after noting everything as well as they could, they returned to the "Pedlar's Rest," and resolved there to await events.

The appointed evening came at last.

It came in dark and gloomy, and with clouds that threatened thunder, black banks of condensed rain, with great rifts of greyish light between.

In spite of the inclemency of the weather, however, a young man started, about ten o'clock, from the quai at Leith, and made his way towards the "McDonald Arms."

He was a tall, finely-proportioned young fellow, and walked with the erect and bold gait of one accustomed to command.

This was Francis Milroy, by the death of his father, Lord Milroy.

It might strike him as strange that he was asked to meet a stranger immediately on his arrival, and that the meeting was appointed to take place in such an out-of-the-way and gloomy spot.

But his life had been far from unchequered.

He had parted in anger with his father, and he knew not what family reasons there might be to render a secret interview in the first place necessary.

So, without fear of any such vile treachery as that preparing for him, he proceeded boldly and even jauntily on his way, and, undismayed by the gloomy aspect of the inn, knocked loudly at the door.

Bully Cozens was on the look-out, and in a moment, therefore, he made his appearance.

He was completely transformed now.

He looked quite the fawning, servile, "happy to see you" landlord.

None of the bully was left.

"Most happy to see you, sir," he said. "My place is but a humble one to receive such a traveller, but——"

"You do not know, then, of my appointment?" asked Milroy.

"Appointment! no indeed," replied Cozens, with a good show of surprise. "I was not aware that my poor domicile was so well known. But enter, pray enter."

He held the door open wide, and young Lord Milroy entered.

"He will doubtless be here shortly then; your friend, I mean."

"He will, I believe, since I had expected him here now," returned the young earl. "Let me have some refreshment."

The supposed landlord at once busied himself in seeing to the comforts of his guest, and in a few minutes a goodly meal and a huge tankard of ale stood before him.

He had done full justice to this, and had just begun to be on talking terms with Ned Cozens, when a loud knock at the door was heard, and, in another moment, Dr. Henzollern, well disguised, entered.

Before detailing this strange interview, however, I must return with my readers to London awhile, and see how matters fared with those in whose charge Rupert Dreadnought had left his house.

CHAPTER XIV.

THE SUBTERRANEAN CHAMBER.

LESBIA HOWARD, whom Rupert had so opportunely saved from the hands of Dr. Henzollern, removed with Stanley Sherrington and Tom the waterman to the London house of Rupert, where Helen Penraven soon joined them.

Henry Clanberris and his lovely wife were content to remain alone for a time.

Their mutual affection was quite sufficient to keep them happy, and Helen Penraven was ready at the first summons to help any friend of Rupert's.

Lesbia disguised none of her history.

She spoke of her love for Alford and of the connection she had formed for his sake with the dreaded Society.

Her words, however, were sufficient to prove that she was entirely innocent of any real participation in their horrid schemes of murder.

On the third evening Stanley Sherrington was sitting with the two ladies.

If he had not known that their affections were already secured elsewhere he might certainly have been induced to fall in love with one of the two.

Both were lovely.

Both were, in fact, exquisite in the extreme, and the dress of those days was such as to give a man a far better chance of judging female beauty than that of the present day.

Both had bright eyes, both had glossy, curling hair, both had creamy shoulders, and soft, delicate busts, both were full of the warmth and fervour of womanhood rather than girlhood.

"Rupert has given me a difficult task, ladies," he said, gallantly, as his eyes wandered over their features and forms in undisguised admiration.

"Why so?" asked Lesbia, with a charming smile.

"Because he has placed me in charge of such beauty that ere he returns I shall be in such a depth of love that I shall not be able to extricate myself," he returned, with an ardour which surprised even himself.

Helen laughed.

"Ah! Master Sherrington," she said, "we know you to be an accomplished gallant. What would you do for your fair ladies, for there are two you see, and we both claim you as our knight."

"I would do anything," returned Stanley Sherrington; "but I must keep my love-words silent, since that is treason to my friend. I have been wondering that our enemies have suffered us to remain here so quietly."

"Tis strange indeed they have not molested us before," returned Helen.

She knew not how at that very moment they were working against her and her beloved.

"Yes, it seems like a calm before a storm," returned Lesbia Howard. "They are always still like this when they are preparing for any deadly deed of villany."

As she spoke, there was a loud, rumbling noise in the house.

They all started to their feet.

Then followed a sound as of a pistol discharged either far away or deep in the bowels of the earth.

"What can this mean?" asked Helen Penraven, with pale lips.

"It means that the time of quiet is over," said Lesbia Howard, "and that our enemies are at work once more. Oh, Helen! this is far worse for me than for you; remember, I am denounced, and threatened with a terrible Doom!"

"Fear not," answered Stanley Sherrington, firmly, "we can protect you. Here, in the heart of London, they cannot attempt the same open outrage they might attempt in some out-of-the-way country place. But hark! that noise again! I must leave you one moment and ascertain what it means."

The noise this time was like the crashing of timber—the breaking in of some strong door.

The two young girls clung to him.

"Oh, do not leave us!" they cried; "you know not what mischief is brewing."

"Nay, there is no danger here," he answered, "and we know not what danger is elsewhere; let me go and see what has happened."

They still, however, clung to him, and he would certainly have been unable to quit them had not at this moment the door opened, and a serving-man entered.

"Tom Braxley wants to see you immediately, Master Sherrington," said the latter.

"And where is he?"

"He is below, master," replied the domestic; "he has found some traitor below and knows not what to do with him. Fear not, ladies, all danger is past."

"Are you sure?" asked Lesbia.

"Yes; he is already a prisoner."

"You see," said Stanley Sherrington, gently disengaging himself from the imprisonment of their soft arms, "you see there is no fear now, and I am required. I will return at once. Do you," he added to the man, "remain with the ladies until I come back. Where shall I find Tom?"

"At the very basement, at the foot of the last spiral staircase."

Stanley Sherrington waited to hear no more, but at once descended the stairs at full speed.

On reaching the basement, he heard Tom's voice crying aloud,

"This way, this way, Master Sherrington."

A dim light at the bottom of the stairs guided his steps.

In a few moments he came upon a curious scene.

The great door of one of the vaults was broken open, and lay upon one side.

In the centre of the vault stood Tom Braxley,

with his pistol aimed at the head of a man who was crouching up against a wall.

"What have we here?" cried Stanley Sherrington, as he entered.

"Once more a traitor," said Tom the Waterman. "See yonder."

As he spoke, he pointed towards a corner of the vault where a heap of newly-fallen masonry gave evidence of recent work.

"What means this?" asked Stanley, as he approached and examined the place. "Ah! I see; this is intended as some secret means of reaching the repository of Rupert Dreadnought's secrets. Fellow, rise, and give an account of yourself."

The man rose.

He had trembled before Tom the Waterman's pistol.

But he now put on a kind of braggart courage.

"Well," he said, "what do you wish me to say?"

"Your purpose here?"

"The same that has brought me here for seven nights running," replied the man, boldly.

"Insolent! And tell me quickly: what *is* this purpose?"

"To reach the Iron Chest, which is such a fruitful source of misery and murder."

"It is the fount of Justice, say rather," replied Stanley Sherrington; "but who is your employer?"

"I cannot tell."

"Do you pretend to be ignorant of his name?"

"THE YOUNG MAN SMILINGLY PLACED HIS FOOT UPON THE SWORD."

"I know it, but *will* not tell."

"Good; you refuse. Then we must find a method of forcing you."

The man smiled doggedly.

"Fear of death will not make me speak," he said. "If I betray my friends I risk death. I gain nothing by yielding to you, and have no greater danger to fear if I refuse to listen to you."

"Good," replied Stanley Sherrington, "if you are a brave man bound by a fearful vow, I can understand you. But we will try your courage. Here, Tom."

He beckoned to Tom, and whispered some significant words in his ear.

Tom at once quitted the vault, but after a few moments returned with several assistants.

"To the vault I named," said Stanley Sherrington, as they surrounded the prisoner, "and let him be secured by chains."

The man saw the uselessness of resistance.

But he was still resolute as to his refusal to confess.

"Once more," asked Stanley Sherrington, "will you name the man who sent you?"

"No, I refuse," replied the prisoner, boldly.

"Good," returned Stanley, "away with him."

In another moment he found himself the inmate of a dark vault, whose smell told him that it was far below the earth.

Of course, as our readers may suppose, the members of the League had no idea of being idle in the absence of their Chief.

Dr. Henzollern was a man of iron nerve, and had always kept them in a state of activity.

But in Oscar Penraven he had left an able deputy.

Influenced by far deeper personal motives; worked on by far greater malice and hate for Rupert Dreadnought and his friends, he resolved to use his short tenure of office—to use, in fact, the whole of the power of the Dread League for the furtherance of his designs against his own especial enemies.

By means, therefore, of spies chosen from men of all grades, he soon learned *two* things.

In the first place, he found that Rupert had quitted London, and left his house in care of Stanley Sherrington and Tom the Waterman.

In the second place, he learned that Rupert and Allan had discovered the destination of Dr. Henzollern, and were on their way to defeat his plans.

He at once conceived a double plan.

Calling together some trusty servants, he sent two away along the North Road.

These, he calculated, would arrive in Edinburgh two days after Rupert and Allan.

The third he commissioned to enter Rupert's house by stealth, and, by patient work, make his way to the shaft which led up from the vaults of the old house to the closet next to that containing the Iron Chest.

This Chest he regarded as the repository of secrets which would ultimately prove his ruin and that of his friends, and he wisely, therefore, directed all his attention to the easiest and quickest means of obtaining possession of it.

Two men had already lost their lives in endeavouring to seize it.

But this did not deter others from a similar task, and the reward promised being a heavy one, Oscar Penraven found no difficulty in obtaining the services of a brave man.

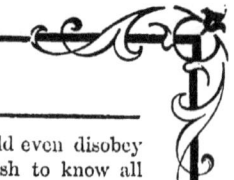

Such a one was he whom Tom Braxley had discovered in the vaults.

He had heard a strange rustling noise as he descended to the wine cellar, and had crept up and listened at a large wooden door which separated one vault from the other.

Here he distinctly heard the sound of a man hard at work.

"Who is there?" he demanded.

There was no reply, and having three times repeated the question, he fired through the woodwork.

A sharp cry of pain followed the splintering of the wood, and on bursting open the door, he had found the man crouching, wounded, by the wall."

The man was possessed, as I have said, of a courage worthy of a better cause.

He was quite undismayed by his imprisonment.

When he was left alone he glanced round the dark cell, and then felt in his belt.

"Ah!" he said, coolly, "they have left me my knife. I must escape."

CHAPTER XV.

IN WHICH THE CHIEF OF THE POISONERS MAKES A STRANGE PROPOSITION TO HIS SUPPOSED NEPHEW.

IN the meantime we return to the "McDonald Arms," on the Frith of Forth.

When the door opened to admit Dr. Henzollern, the young earl rose from his seat, and after a moment's scrutiny bowed to the stranger.

"I presume I have the honour of addressing my uncle, Lord Milroy," said the young traveller, as he quaffed off a glass of wine.

"No, my lord, no," replied Dr. Henzollern, "your uncle has not yet arrived. He will be detained in Edinburgh for an hour yet; but I am his bosom friend, his confidant in everything, and he has commissioned me to beg of you to be patient until his arrival. He has a most important secret, which I know, to reveal to you."

The genial manner which Dr. Henzollern had assumed, and his smiling countenance, had quite reassured Milroy, and, throwing off his cloak and hat, he drew his chair nearer to his supposed friend, and said—

"There is one thing which I should like to understand, and, since you are Lord Milroy's confidant, perhaps you can assist me. In the first place I cannot understand the meaning of his demanding this mysterious interview. The affectionate letters which I have received from him during the last three months have given me every disposition to submit myself to his wishes, since, next to my father, he is my nearest male relation. But, if after eight years of absence—if, after returning to England after a long and perilous voyage, I am to be prevented from at once seeing my mother, I cannot conceive the meaning of these letters. I have but one wish at this moment, and that is to understand the reason why Lord Milroy desires to delay this joyful meeting—this meeting to which I have looked forward with tears of gratitude. Tell me, I entreat of you, sir, what new misfortune threatens me—what fresh danger is there in my path? Not that I fear it, for I would even disobey Lord Milroy in this respect, but I wish to know all that I may be prepared."

A dark frown had settled on the brow of Dr. Henzollern as the nephew uttered these last words, but he quickly recovered his serenity and said—

"I will explain all, willingly; but in the first place I wish to ask you some questions."

"Which I will answer readily," replied Francis, settling himself to listen.

"You must allow me to assure you," said Dr. Henzollern, by way of introduction, "that it is solely in regard for your interests which induces me to ask you these questions, for I will not conceal from you the fact that your fate depends greatly at this moment upon the manner in which you answer me."

Lord Francis Milroy gazed at him in surprise.

"My fate depends upon my answers!" he exclaimed. "I understand you not."

Dr. Henzollern inclined his head gravely.

"Yes; your fate, your future, your very existence are in your own hands at this moment."

The young man became serious for an instant, muttering to himself—

"Ah! my presentiment, then, was not wrong; some danger does threaten me."

"A great danger," said Dr. Henzollern.

"And it's nature?"

"It depends entirely on yourself. Answer me now frankly. Remember, I am the confidant of your uncle. When you quitted Martinique, where you lived since your youth, and which you naturally regard as your native country, did you not experience a lively regret? I have read all the letters which you have addressed to your mother since the date when a question arose as to your return. In those letters it appeared to us that a sadness was mingled with your joy. You were ready, doubtless, to respond to your mother's appeal, and to take possession of the large fortune which awaited you, but yet we could perceive that there was an inward sorrow on leaving one happiness for another. Were we wrong?"

Lord Francis Milroy blushed slightly.

"You have asked me to be sincere," he said; "I will be so. It would, I fear, be useless to attempt concealment with one so versed in human nature as yourself. In the country you name I have left one whom I love passionately, and who loves me."

"And you desire to marry her?"

"Most certainly; Letitia Francorlet, though without fortune, is of good family, and worthy of anyone."

Dr. Henzollern had here an advantage, and he determined to avail himself of it.

The beauty, the frankness, the noble bearing of the young man impressed him. Why should he kill when he could save him?

"I am afraid," he said, as if with much concern, "I am afraid, then, that in leaving her you left her for ever."

The young man turned deadly pale.

"For ever! Why for ever?" he exclaimed. "I love her; she is beautiful; she is, I say, of good family; there can be no reason for objecting to our union?"

"Yes, indeed, one weighty reason," returned the other. "Your hand is promised to another."

The young man smiled ironically.

"I am of age," he said, "and can choose for myself."

"You are greatly mistaken in that respect," replied Dr. Henzollern. "Your return to England will not be a return to your mother's love, if you refuse her conditions. You must abandon all ideas of Letitia, and marry the young lady who is chosen for you, a lady of great beauty, let me tell you, and only eighteen."

The young man heaved a deep sigh, and answered not.

Doctor Henzollern grasped at the opportunity.

"What if I give you the means of escaping from this hateful marriage, and wedding the woman of your choice ?" he asked, leaning forward and taking him by the hand.

"The means! the means!" gasped the other, eagerly.

Dr. Henzollern appeared to hesitate.

"Your love for this girl must be very great to permit of such a sacrifice ?" he said, inquiringly.

"I love her before all the world," returned the young man, enthusiastically.

"This, then, is the proposal of your uncle," said Doctor Henzollern.

Milroy eyed him suspiciously.

"My uncle knew, then, the result of a conversation he had not heard ?" he exclaimed.

"He apprehended that result," continued Dr. Henzollern. "In order, then, to enable you to avoid an odious marriage, and marry the girl you love, he proposes that you should quit Edinburgh to-night."

"And then ?"

"In a few days you can be at Liverpool ; there your uncle will meet you, and, if you require, provide you with funds, and you will take ship to Martinique."

"And then ?"

"You can allow your letters to return unopened to England. Let your friends, whom you have never seen, suppose you dead, and your uncle will grant you any annual sum which you choose to name."

Earl Milroy grew slightly pale; then, bending forward, and placing his hand on his companion's shoulder, he said, quickly—

"And if I refuse this most noble and generous offer of my uncle's, and do not permit him to inherit my title and my property, what then ?"

"But you will not refuse."

"Stay ; supposing your anticipations deceive you ; supposing I do decline this very kind and obliging offer ?"

"Then," replied Dr. Henzollern, starting up from his chair, leaping towards the door, and placing his hand on his sword, "then you will die this night."

The young earl rose and faced his adversary.

The light in the room was very faint, yet each could see the countenance of the other.

There was a dread silence for a moment.

A thrill of horrible expectation rushed through the breast of Bully Cozens as he sat by the window and listened, gazing upon the features of those two men who eyed each other with such deadly hatred.

"So," said the young Earl Milroy, "you yourself are my brave and generous uncle ; you who have lured me into this ambush, you who desire to slay me that you may inherit my wealth and title. Why have you carried out this infamous comedy when you have already planned and resolved upon my death ?"

"I have not resolved upon it," cried his supposed uncle. "I offer you terms ; accept them, and you are free."

"Accept them ! never !" exclaimed the earl. "I have a sword and can defend myself. Let me pass."

And, so saying, he advanced upon his enemy.

But for an instant a silvery mist seemed to float into the room, and shut out his adversary from his sight.

And in that instant he saw two visions.

A young girl, over whose head but eighteen summers had passed, lay half reclining on an ottoman.

Dark locks, raven tresses, fell around her in wild profusion, drooping down, and wantoning over her bare alabaster shoulders, and almost reaching to her waist.

Her dress was of pure muslin, very low on the breast, and her white arms, naked from the shoulder, were cast languidly over her head, so as to display all the contours of her unconcealed bosom.

Near her stood a girl whose tawny skin proclaimed her a mulatto, fanning her gently, for the sun of a torrid clime was burning without, and the air was still and oppressive.

At her feet sat a young man, who, though his locks were dark and his features bronzed, was yet evidently of English blood.

He was gazing fondly upon the young girl, and evidently speaking to her of love, for his gestures were vehement, and his looks impassioned.

Then suddenly she started, a pallor as of death overspread her features, and tears stood trembling in her eyes.

The young man rose, raised her slightly and pressed her fondly to his heart.

Then he rushed from the room, and the one he had left sank inanimate on the couch.

Thus Lord Milroy had left his betrothed.

And then again he saw her, though the scene was changed.

She was in the dreary room of the lone inn where he now faced his mortal foe.

He was standing opposite his supposed uncle, and she was clasping his knees with one arm, while with the other was warding off from him a blow.

Her looks expressed earnest entreaty, and a dread too of the future.

Then the visions passed away, and Dr. Henzollern was there as before.

A cold chill struck the young earl's heart, a dreary and melancholy foreboding of an unavoidable calamity, a presentiment that in that dream he had seen his beloved for the last time.

"It is very dark," said Dr. Henzollern to Cozens, "let us have more light."

"You are then resolved on this meeting ?" said Milroy.

"I am. Come, Cozens, I am impatient."

Cozens seized a second lamp, and returning to the other end of the room, held one aloft in each hand.

The two men eyed each other menacingly as they crossed their swords in silence.

Dr. Henzollern stood on the defensive.

Knowing the fiery nature of his antagonist, he expected a first attack.

Rushing forward with the ferocity of a wild beast, the young earl attacked his dastardly foe.

The attempt was good—the pass a dangerous one.

But Dr. Henzollern was a noted fencer.

He had studied in the schools of London and Paris and was considered a match even for the masters who taught him.

He withdrew, therefore, from the lunge, and waved his hand in ironical approbation.

"Ah, ah! my lord," he said, "a good pass, by my faith. They fence, I see, in Martinique."

The only answer vouchsafed by the young earl was a second and more furious thrust, which his antagonist had considerable difficulty in parrying.

For some time it was continued.

All else was silent.

Nothing was audible but the thick, short breathings of the two men and the clash of their weapons.

Dr. Henzollern became angry and impatient.

He had underrated the strength and skill of his antagonist.

Losing, therefore, somewhat of his usual caution, he made a furious lunge, and slightly slipped.

In an instant his sword was twisted from his grasp and flung into the air, and Dr. Henzollern stood defenceless before the young earl.

The latter smiled, and placed his foot upon the weapon.

And where all this time were Rupert Dreadnought and Allan of the Glen, who had sworn to defend the proposed victim?

Why were they not at their posts?

Fate, alas! had ordered it otherwise; but what at that moment they were doing we must explain in a future chapter.

CHAPTER XVI.

THE ASSASSINATION.

Dr. Henzollern and the young earl had imagined themselves to be alone.

The Chief of the Poisoners had not chosen that drear and lonely inn on the banks of the dark Frith without fully reckoning his chances.

Bully Cozens was, as he had himself hinted, a man of utterly unscrupulous mind, whom he had met under peculiar circumstances, who had accompanied him through years of exile, and who knew, therefore, his most secret thoughts and been witness to his most secret actions.

Upon his secrecy, therefore, Dr. Henzollern could count, both from the fact that, villain as he was, he had some attachment to his master, and the knowledge, also, that one word from him would hurl the miserable wretch into the lowest depths of despair.

But there were other watchers besides him who saw and understood all.

At the first clash of the swords the inner door of the inn had been pushed ajar, and a head had been thrust through the opening.

This was the head of a young girl, beautiful, though pale as death.

"Heaven shield him!" thought she, as she beheld the sword of Dr. Henzollern fly from his hand to the ground, and the foot of the young earl placed upon it, "but if he is worsted, who will fly to his aid?"

Then she uttered a low cry of agony, and her head was drooped, and her face buried in her hands, that she might not see what followed.

She had stood without, her pale face pressed against the window pane, her form concealed in the dark shadows.

All through the threatening storm she had come, and all through its mutterings she had stood watching for the moment when the young earl should quit the inn and make his way towards Edinburgh.

As she had beheld the preparations for the fight, the drawn swords, the cold, cruel face of the supposed uncle, the calm, stern face of the young earl, she nerved herself for the trial, and supporting her throbbing form against the stone wall, gazed, with all her soul in the look, into the fatal room.

Now again, though for a moment she trembled, an unseen influence drove away her fear, and creeping back from the open door to the window, where she was less in danger of being observed, she gazed once more firmly in, though her heart beat still, and her blood stood still at the terrible spectacle she beheld.

"Are you satisfied?" said the young earl, as Dr. Henzollern stood before him, regarding him with a look of fury, "will you now demand pardon for your falsehoods? Will you swear to me, in fact, that you will not again cross my path? If so I will forget that I have spared you."

Dr. Henzollern bowed his head.

"My feelings towards you have not changed," he said.

The young man regarded him with a look of disgust and contempt.

For an instant, as his eye caught sight of the sword beneath his feet, he felt a desire to break it in pieces and dash it in the face of his enemy.

Then, as a new idea entered his breast, he stepped back, leaving the weapon where it was.

"Heaven knows," he cried, with emotion, "that I would willingly have spared you. I thirst not for your blood, but since you compel me——"

He said no more, for Dr. Henzollern had flown like a vulture upon his sword and attacked him with redoubled fury.

With No. 20 was given away a Splendid Coloured Picture, representing

"LOVE AND HATE."

RUPERT; OR, THE DREADNOUGHT. SECRETS OF THE IRON CHEST.

"THE COUNTESS STOOD ERECT, STERN AND IMPLACABLE."

For some time it was difficult to say who had the advantage.

Both fought with vigour and with caution.

Each displayed the utmost skill and address.

Suddenly, however, either from distraction or from fatigue, the earl gave a random plunge, and immediately taking advantage of the blunder, Dr. Henzollern twisted the sword from the grasp of the young man, and it fell between their feet.

Dr. Henzollern moved not.

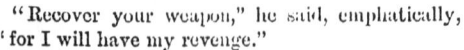

"Recover your weapon," he said, emphatically, "for I will have my revenge."

The young earl stooped to pick up his sword.

Hardly, however, had his hand touched the hilt, when the weapon of his treacherous foe was buried between his shoulders, and he fell with his face to the ground.

Bully Cozens uttered a cry of horror, and let drop from his hands the two lights, which were immediately extinguished.

By the uncertain light of the fire, however, the murderer could see the unhappy young man raise himself on one hand and turn his dying gaze towards the heavens.

Then murmuring "Letitia! mother!" he fell again upon his face and all was still.

Dr. Henzollern drew near and placed his hand over his heart.

"Dead!" he exclaimed, in accents of triumph.

"Dead!" groaned Cozens.

"Dead!" repeated a voice like an echo, behind the assassin and his accomplice.

Dr. Henzollern trembled violently as he grasped his companion by the arm in feverish terror.

"What was that?" he said, in a hoarse whisper.

Cozens answered not.

Fear had deprived him of the power of speech.

But Dr. Henzollern was not a man to be dismayed for a long time by any unusual circumstance.

Re-lighting one of the candles, therefore, he seized the young earl's sword, and, dashing open the inner door, scaled the stairs at one bound.

The door of the bedroom was partly open, and he peered in anxiously, while the trembling man behind him gazed with eyes half blinded with fear.

"There is no one here," cried Dr. Henzollern, when he had entered and searched throughout the room: "the chamber is deserted. Our ears must have deceived us."

"Both of us at one time," muttered Cozens; "that is odd, certainly."

"Odd, eh?" exclaimed his master, angrily. "Are you sure that you had no one in the house?"

"If I had had any one in the house, do you think I should have been mad enough not to tell you?" asked the man.

"Well, well, as I said before, our ears must have deceived us. It was an echo. This room is large, and sounds with every movement."

"It is, perhaps, then," suggested Cozens, "his spirit, which, in flying to the other world, is cursing us."

And he looked fearfully at the body of the poor young earl, which lay so still on the blood-stained floor.

"It was his own wish," said Dr. Henzollern, as he sat down.

"His own wish," muttered Cozens. "It strikes me it did not depend much on him."

"Did I not allow him to defend himself?" cried the Chief of the Poisoners.

"Yes, until the moment came when you thought fit to kill him."

Dr. Henzollern smiled disdainfully.

"Pooh! pooh! it was all fair," he said. "I wanted this man's riches for our Society. I have gained it the best way I could. Give me my sword."

"Your sword?"

"Yes, yes. Don't you understand me?"

And he pointed to the steel which was still buried in the body of young Milroy.

Bully Cozens raised his hands and shook his head.

"No—no, I cannot," he said, in a low voice.

"Fool," cried the other, as he rose and advanced towards the body, "you will have to help me presently to carry him out of this place."

"Whither?"

"To the river's bank; we cannot leave him here."

And so saying, he dragged the sword from the wound.

The effort, however, required strength.

The ground was slippery with the life-current of the murdered man, and Dr. Henzollern fell on his knees beside the corpse of his victim.

There was a moment of awful silence.

In spite of his cynicism, the murderer, on finding himself face to face with the dead man, and feeling the still warm blood upon his hands, turned deadly pale, and a cold sweat broke over his body.

Still, though his frame shook convulsively, he remained in the position where chance had thrown him, and fumbled in the pockets of the slain.

From these, at length, he drew forth a morocco pocket-book, containing a packet.

A packet of letters—letters from his mother—letters, too, from the loving uncle to the nephew.

Two miniatures, also, he found, one of his mother, one of his betrothed.

Dr. Henzollern, who seemed quite unstrung, trembled violently as his eyes met those of the portraits, which seemed to his bewildered vision to be endued with life, and to be gazing in reproachful anger at him.

"Burn this—burn this," he cried, as he handed the pocket-book to Cozens, and rose from his kneeling position to approach the window.

Just as a bright flame shot up the broad chimney, he threw open the casement.

"It is a night of storms," he said, as he leaned out, "we must lose no time."

The rain was descending in torrents, and though the lightning had ceased to flash, and the thunder had ceased to rattle, the clouds still hung heavily over the country.

The Frith, dark and dreary and deep, was rushing its tides towards the ocean, carrying in its still bosom the burden of many a dread and terrible secret.

The wind had risen but little, yet there was a faint murmuring sound as the water tinkled over the pebbles and the branches of lone trees swayed to and fro, and the reeds nodded and dipped in the waves.

It was a solemn scene.

Oh, how calmly terrible seemed the course of that silent highway, as Dr. Henzollern gazed out upon it from the chamber of death; but not so terrible as the fear which even then was gathering round his dark heart—dark as the current of the shadowy stream upon whose banks the slain one was about to rest in death!

"Come," he said, as he withdrew from the window, "come, let us hasten, it is growing late."

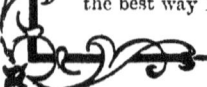

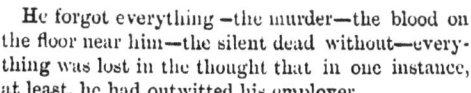

His voice was so choking and so hushed that Bully Cozens trembled as he spoke.

"What ails you?" he cried, in sudden alarm.

"Nothing, nothing," said the Chief of the Poisoners. "The night air is cold and damp and oppressive. Let us be quick and carry him out, that we may go to Edinburgh, where there's life around, and not this horrid silence."

And so they raised him from the ground, slipping in the blood under the weight of his heavy body and averting their gaze from the calm face which seemed as though it slept in peace.

Very fearful was it to see these men as they staggered out of the lone inn with their burden, glancing round them timorously lest any one should be near to behold their faces and bear witness of the bloody deed.

They carried him to the edge of the stream and laid him down among the reeds, with the willow branches waving his head, and the water lashing his cold and stony face.

They then fled back to the inn, and Dr. Henzollern sat down in fear and trembling in the dreary room to wait for his horse.

Eagerly he bounded upon it as it came prancing round to the entrance.

"And now, Cozens," he said, "remember what I told you. Burn this house—let no vestige remain of it."

"And you will think of me now that you have succeeded so well?" said the man. "You will not forget how I aided you?"

"No, no," said Dr. Henzollern, "I will not forget you. To-morrow I shall expect you at the 'New Inn' near the Cowgate, Edinburgh."

So saying, he put spurs to his horse, and leaning slightly over his head impelled it forward at its greatest speed.

He was glad, truly, to escape from the scene of that catastrophe which had given him the wealth he had sought.

Very dark and quiet was it when they had laid him down by the river, with his head amid the reeds on the soft, yielding earth and his dark eyes upturned towards the silent heavens.

But there was one who saw them as they carried him forth and buried him among the sedge; one whose heart was bursting as she saw his form droop down into the water; one who feared not to kneel by the dead and kiss his cold and clammy lips.

This one had seen, and watched, and prayed while the darkness was enveloping her and him she loved best in life; and now that all was over and the blow had been struck, and the shadow had descended, she gave to him this last and terrible embrace and fled away towards her home.

It was her shadow, as she rushed past the window, which made Bully Cozens tremble and cry out, and close the shutters ere he sat down to think.

CHAPTER XVII.

THE PORTRAIT.

THERE was no fear, however, on the face of the supposed landlord as he drew his chair to the fire and fumbled in his pocket.

He forgot everything—the murder—the blood on the floor near him—the silent dead without—everything was lost in the thought that in one instance, at least, he had outwitted his employer.

"And so," he cried, as he drew from his coat the morocco pocket-book, and holding it at arm's length, gazed at it affectionately, "and so, Dr. Henzollern thought I should be so mad as to burn this. No, no, I know the value of this. It will place us on far better terms—far more on an equality than you imagine. So, so, my worthy Dr. Henzollern," he continued to himself, "you have a secret by which you can crush me, yet you wish me to burn the only evidence I have of *your* guilt. No, no, that will not do; that is one-sided justice, my fine friend. I must keep these. I am such a shocking fellow for a hermit, I am so fond of company. Even if I swing, I will not swing alone."

A malicious, triumphant leer passed over the man's countenance as he uttered these words.

With trembling hands he undid the fastening of the pocket-book, and examined its contents.

The letters he passed over in silent indifference; the portraits he gazed at with much curiosity.

That of the earl's mother had been taken when she was very young.

There was a sad smile upon her face, which was pretty withal, but, though so lovely, his eyes did not dwell upon it.

They wandered with a kind of fascination to that of the young Creole, who had been the beloved mistress of him who lay in death without.

It was indeed a lovely picture, with her raven hair falling over her exquisitely-formed shoulders; the faint, rosy tint of life struggling everywhere through her dark skin; her large, almond-shaped eyes gazing in melancholy languor upon you; her beautiful figure attired in the very height of grace, the hot climate admitting of a garb which displayed to perfection her beautifully modelled breast, her whole person seeming impregnated with delicious warmth and grace.

Bully Cozens, however, thought not of her charms.

He regarded her not as a being of love and passion.

He looked upon her purely as one whose features, beaming forth, as it were, in that little miniature, brought back to him scenes and memories which had long since been hidden behind the ruins of his wrecked life.

He sat by the smouldering fire for a long time, grasping in one hand the light, and in the other, holding at arm's length, the portrait of the young girl.

Oh, those glorious eyes, that sunny smile!

What dreams of the past did they not conjure up before this man, to whom life was now but a desolate shore, laved by the waters of Eternity!

"Oh, my own one, my own one," he muttered, as he gazed at the face with eyes before which a thick mist was gathering. "How like, how like!"

Then he started and looked round, as if a voice had told him to watch.

"No, no; it cannot be, it cannot be!" he muttered, in a low tone, talking, as it were, to the portrait.

"It is like, that is all. No memories are there for me but of the dead and the lost!"

And he glanced, as he spoke the words, at the spot where the young earl had fallen—where the floor was still dark, and the blood lay thickening with the sand.

"No, no," he repeated, as he shook his matted head, and looked again at the portrait, and then again at the blood; "*that* is between me and the past, and the future has no way but one. I will not keep it. You have conquered, Dr. Henzollern. I will burn these evidences against you!"

And so saying, he placed the portrait and the letters back into the pocket-book, and rose to cast them into the flames.

But it was not to be.

The hours had fled rapidly, and the fire, unattended, had smouldered and gone out.

"It was ordered otherwise," philosophised Bully Cozens, as, with a sigh, he returned the things to his pocket. "Heigho! I need not use them because I have them, although, after all, they may bring me a fortune some day. And now for Edinburgh!"

As he spoke a crackling noise was heard near him. He started like a guilty thing.

"What is that?" he asked himself, with a shudder, as he advanced to the door and looked up the passage.

But there was nothing there.

The wind, perhaps, which was now rising, had moaned up the creaking stairs, and sighed through the half open door.

That was all.

So Bully Cozens made his way, not without much doubt and fear, up into his bedroom, where, remembering that in the inn that night would perish everything, he proceeded to adorn himself in the real landlord's best clothes.

Then he went to the drawer where he had placed the money which he had screwed out of the bargain with the real landlord.

But the key, which he found in the same place as usual, only served to prove to him the fact that every coin he had placed there had disappeared.

A goodly sum he had placed there in the morning, and they could not have gone without hands.

He remembered then that the only guests whom he had entertained had been left for a time alone in the house while he had seen to their horses.

"Thieves!" he cried, stamping his feet on the crackling floor in impotent fury. "Those fellows whom I left here alone; they robbed me and left their score on the table to insult me. Oh! if I catch them in Edinburgh."

And with clenched fist he made a gesture as if clutching an adversary by the throat.

It was evidently no novelty.

His hand clutched naturally round the bedpost, his fingers joining in an elegant grip on the other side.

"But come," he muttered, as he released his imaginary enemy, "it doesn't much matter. Dr. Henzollern and the League will supply me well as soon as I see them. I shall see *him*, I know, to-morrow. I have enough to procure me a night's lodging, so now for the inn."

So saying, he once more descended the stairs.

CHAPTER XVIII.

THE STRANGE GUEST.

BULLY COZENS looked quite a different person in his new clothes.

The slouch of the shoulders, the "humble servant" style of walk, the "most obedient" manner, appeared lost now that he had doffed the garb of the innkeeper.

But no change of garment, no fierce battle with his matted locks, could take away the expression of his face.

Bully had been written, as it were, on his face by Nature, and nothing he could have done would have obliterated it.

He now commenced his preparation for the destruction of the inn.

Gathering together all the faggots which had been accumulated for the winter in the cellars beneath, he piled them round the room and on the staircase, mingling them with straw, over which he sprinkled spirits with no niggard hand.

Then, after gazing round him with a look, as it were, of pity, he was about to set fire to the several piles, when again footsteps were heard without.

"The devil's in the place to-night," said he; "just because there is no need of customers, and the real landlord is absent, this obscure place is to be made a rendezvous."

It was past midnight.

Who could it be?

He listened again intently.

Had there been a witness to the murder, and was this the officer to arrest him?

There was no doubt about *one* thing.

Some one was coming over the pebbly path, and in another moment this person, friend or foe as it might be, knocked at the door.

How could he suffer anyone to enter with the blood still red upon the floor?

The knocking was repeated impatiently.

Bully Cozens seized a pile of wood, and dragged it over the spot where the young earl had fallen.

Then he approached the door.

"What is it you want?" cried he, in a loud voice; "it is too late now for respectable travellers to be abroad."

"I am cold, wet, and hungry," returned a voice; "admit me and I will pay well."

Bully Cozens thought a moment.

He had just discovered himself to be robbed. Would it not be better to take the money of any traveller who might present himself, and make sure of the means of subsistence for a night or so, without being compelled to apply to Dr. Henzollern?

The latter he knew well was in his power at any time.

He did not, however, care to be too eager in his demands.

By behaving in what he deemed a *modest* manner he hoped to be able, after a certain time, to obtain such a reward as would satisfy him for many years, and enable him to quit England for ever.

He little knew what reward was quickly in store for him.

So he approached nearer to the door and drew the bolts.

In the doorway stood a young man apparently, but what his features were like it would be impossible to say.

He wore a huge cloak, his hat was pressed over his brows, and nothing but the dim outline of a human form was visible.

"You are a long time opening your door, friend landlord," said he, as he entered. "I am wet and hungry, and I don't think, no matter what the hour may be, that it's a landlord's place to keep anyone out in the cold."

"No; but it is late, and late company is not always of the best," replied Bully Cozens. "What can I get you?"

"Well, I am hungry," said the new comer; "but I rather fancy also I have been followed—close the door well!"

The manner of the stranger was such as to remove all suspicion from Bully Cozens' mind as to being watched.

He took no further notice of the place than to draw his chair up, and grumble about the fire being out.

"No matter," he said: "there's plenty of wood here it seems, so that will enable us soon to have a blaze."

"If you'd come a few moments later there would have been a blaze and no mistake," thought Bully Cozens, as he threw a pile of wood in the chimney-place, and set light to it, and then busied himself in procuring some cold viands for the stranger's supper.

THE HOUSE BY THE RIVER.

As soon as the meat was laid on the table, the stranger, who persisted in wearing his hat, poured out a large glass of wine, and drank it off.

Then, turning to Bully Cozens, he cried—

"Sit down and help yourself. I'm fond of company."

The man had never any objection to make to wine, and without, therefore, waiting for further invitation, he sat down.

He sat opposite the stranger at the further end of the table.

When he was once seated, a wonderful change was observable in the manner of the stranger.

He pushed away the meat, and, drawing from his pocket a pistol, held it in a direct line with Bully Cozens' head.

The supposed innkeeper was about to spring from his seat.

But a motion of the stranger's stopped him.

"Remain seated," cried the unknown, "while I speak, or it will be the worse for you."

"Why, what is the matter?"

"Matter enough," cried the unknown, "when my feet nearly touch the stains of the blood of the young Earl of Milroy, murdered here in your presence by a villain. Nay, move not, or you die! If you believe me not, if you think I have no courage to act as I threaten, see now *why* you *must* believe."

So saying, the stranger removed his hat, from which fell masses of glossy hair, and revealed, too, a face of exquisite beauty.

It was the face of the girl who had watched the events of that night.

"Ah!" she cried, "you may well start and tremble. I am one he loved—one who waited for his return. I saw all the murder, but I was then unarmed and powerless, and could not interfere. It was I who cried 'Dead!' and startled your coward hearts when he fell upon the floor. I saw you carry him and place him among the sedge and the slime. Then I fled away to the 'Pedlar's Rest' to alarm those who might aid me. In this I failed, for the only persons who would have moved to save me were buried in an unnatural sleep. I told no one connected with the inn, because I knew they might betray me, but I procured male costume, and I return just in time to prevent your carrying out your favourite scheme of firing this place. You must not fire it; I require it as evidence against Dr. Henzollern, *your* friend, the Chief of the Poisoners!"

"By Heaven! this is too much," exclaimed Bully Cozens, moving as if to rise.

But he moved not far.

"Do you imagine that I am jesting?" she said. "I swear I am not. Unless you obey me in all things, you die! Be still, then, or you are a dead man. Ah! you have weapons there; place them on the table—so; and now that pistol—so. Ah! hark! they are coming; now, Master Cozens, the blood of the guiltless will be avenged!"

The sounds which so attracted the attention of the young girl were not very close to the inn when she first observed them, and she therefore rose and quietly possessed herself of the weapons which she had compelled Bully Cozens to yield up.

Then she said—

"Now, my worthy landlord, rise and open the door, that my friends may not be kept out in the stormy night."

Bully Cozens was quite in her power.

He was a sensible man, and he at once recognised the situation.

So rising with a muttered curse, he approached the door and opened it.

He did so just as two figures loomed out of the night air.

These were Rupert Dreadnought and Allan of the Glen.

CHAPTER XIX.

THE ESCAPE.

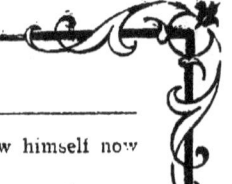

In order to explain how it was that our hero and his companion delayed so long their visit to the inn, I must beg my readers to return with me to the "Pedlar's Rest."

It was there, it will be remembered, that Rupert and Allan had put up, intending, of course, to proceed at the proper hour to the "McDonald Arms," and stay the hand of the murderer.

But it was not to be.

Evidently, as the young girl had hinted, the landlord of one place was in league with the landlord of the other, and when they attempted to snatch some temporary repose, they lapsed off into a slumber from which they found themselves unable to wake.

It was after the murder, as my readers already know, that the young girl, who had watched all the terrible proceedings, made her way to the "Pedlar's Rest."

Here she found them in so heavy a sleep that it was with the utmost difficulty she could awaken them. Even then they knew her not.

She simply appealed to them as an English girl in trouble.

Her first words, however, were sufficient to tell them that she was connected with the mystery which they were seeking to unravel.

It was with a lively sorrow that they learned how all their efforts had miscarried.

Rousing themselves, however, they procured her a male dress, and she rushed off in advance to prevent the firing of the inn.

When Bully Cozens saw them enter, he knew that, as far as the League and Dr. Henzollern were concerned, his game was up.

The only course open to him, therefore, was to make a clean breast of it, and side with those who had him in their power, if, indeed, the chance were left him.

So, when he had admitted the two friends, he sat sullenly down.

"Now," he said, in a gruff tone; "now what is it you want with me?"

"You must remain our prisoner," said Rupert, whose death-like pallor proclaimed how he had been awakened out of an unnatural sleep, "and you must lead us to the spot where we shall find Dr. Henzollern."

"And be denounced by the Society?"

"The law will protect you," said the young girl.

Bully Cozens curled his lip.

"The law," he said, sneeringly; "the law has no power to touch the League. It is far more powerful than the law."

Neither Rupert nor Allan felt inclined to reply to this.

What the man had said was in reality the truth.

The law, as yet, had proved itself powerless against the greatest offenders.

"We do not desire to waste time in quibbling," replied Rupert. "You are here in our power. To kill an assassin, or one who has aided an assassin, is a good deed, and one we shall not shrink from. So either agree to our terms, or make up your mind not to quit this place alive."

Bully Cozens, as I have said, saw himself now without hope of aid.

There could be no doubt that he was caged.

"I will do as you bid me," he said.

Well he might.

Not even on the countenance of the young girl was there a shadow of pity.

At heart, having seen the destruction of her lover, she was the most fierce and malignant of the three; and he well knew, from former experiences, of what Rupert Dreadnought was capable.

Having made up his mind, therefore, he turned to Rupert Dreadnought.

"Did I keep faith before?" he added.

"You did."

"And so I will again," continued Bully Cozens. "It will be useless for us to follow Dr. Henzollern to-night."

"Why?"

"Because I know not whither he is going; to-morrow night, I can lead you to the exact spot where he will be found."

Rupert eyed him strangely.

"It is strange," he said, "that he should have gone away and not left you his present place of abode. However, we will leave the matter till to-morrow, and meanwhile we will remain here. Let us have some refreshment."

"If I had thought who was coming," murmured Bully Cozens to himself, as he procured the liquor, "not one of you should ever have left this place alive after drinking these glasses."

But there was no help for it.

He had never dreamed of the arrival of the two enemies of the League, and so, for the time, he was compelled to be their willing slave.

When refreshment had been taken, they took it in turns to obtain a little rest.

But the young girl could not sleep.

Letitia, who had followed him unknown for so many miles, was far too wrapped in the contemplation of the horrid end of her love adventure.

All her mind was concentrated, as it were, upon one point.

That point was the destruction of Lord Francis Milroy's assassin.

Bully Cozens, heavy-brained ruffian that he was, slept calmly after awhile, and in the early watches of the morning, Letitia was the only one who remained awake.

The next day passed gloomily enough.

Naturally they might have expected that Dr. Henzollern would lurk round about to see if the man had done his duty, and burned the old place.

But though they watched eagerly, no one came in sight.

As for Letitia, her first pilgrimage was to the spot where the young earl lay in the still majesty of death among the reeds and the slime.

Here she knelt and kissed the pale brow, and renewed her vow of vengeance.

The cold, clammy corpse had no horrors for her.

It was the semblance, at least, of what had been her lover, and she loved it still.

As evening drew on, they were all excitement to be off.

As soon as the shadows began to fall, they started

along the road, and in due course arrived in the ancient city.

It will be remembered that Dr. Henzollern had desired Bully Cozens to meet him at the "New Inn," in the Cowgate.

To this, therefore, they directed their steps, and Bully Cozens found no difficulty in making his way towards the room where the Chief of the Poisoners had located himself.

The door was locked.

"Who is there?" asked the voice of the assassin.

"The Silver Cross," answered Bully Cozens.

"Are you alone?"

"Yes."

"You lie!" cried the doctor. "I saw you this moment talking to two strangers, who ascended with you. You have betrayed me, but I am not yet a prisoner. Remember, you will be denounced, and your doom sealed for ever."

At these words Bully Cozens trembled so violently that he could make no effort to force open the door.

Quickly Rupert pushed him on one side, and, with Allan, dashed at the door with all their strength.

The door shook and creaked under their united efforts.

Then suddenly it gave way. But their triumph was not even now achieved. The room was empty!

They rushed eagerly to the window, which was wide open. But they saw nothing.

All was dark and still without.

Below was a deep well as it were of darkness and gloom.

Certainly no indication of any place where a man could have made his escape.

"This is very strange," murmured Rupert, "he has escaped certainly, but how he has done so is a perfect mystery."

Allan, meanwhile, was walking round the room feeling the walls everywhere.

But th ere was no sign of any hollow place.

"Are you certain," asked Rupert, "that you gave him no intimation of our presence!"

"How could I? It would have been impossible."

"It seems so, certainly," returned Rupert; "but how can he have escaped!"

Bully Cozens smiled.

"You know little of him if you wonder at this," he said; "this is nothing. He is the very devil himself when he is in danger."

"He seems so indeed," said Rupert Dreadnought, "but, nevertheless, he can only escape us for a time. We will to horse, and if he has quitted Edinburgh by the North Road, we shall learn it."

CHAPTER XX.

THE HOUSE BY THE RIVER.

Horses were soon procured, and Letitia, who had often in her native island bestridden a horse in male costume, made no difficulty in accompanying them.

They soon found that Dr. Henzollern had not made his departure from the city by *that* route.

But they did not turn back.

Although Bully Cozens was ignorant of the whereabouts of the family of the young murdered earl, Letitia knew well, from his description, where it was, and they resolved, therefore, to pursue their journey onwards.

They did not require much consideration to tell them that the mother of the young earl was no party to his death, and to her, therefore, they determined to unmask the villany of the uncle and his ruffianly confidant, Dr. Henzollern.

There could be no doubt that the Chief of the Poisoners would now no longer remain in Scotland or pursue his intended voyage to Germany.

Having so quickly succeeded in his fell design, and having found, moreover, that Rupert Dreadnought and Allan of the Glen were on his track, he would probably think it best, before entertaining any other design, to state to the Society the success he had attained.

Of Bully Cozens they had now no fear.

There was no danger of his betraying them, for, after the terrible threat held out by Dr. Henzollern, there was little chance of his attempting to renew his connection with the Society.

Hurrying on to London, therefore, they met with little to relieve the monotony of their journey, until they put up at the "Rose and Sceptre," near Charing Cross.

Here they held a consultation, and it was resolved that Allan of the Glen and Letitia Francoilet should proceed to Milroy House and acquaint Lady Milroy of the assassination of her son by Dr. Henzollern, and with the connivance of his own uncle.

Rupert could then proceed home, and make preparations for the instant surrounding of the Poisoners' Retreat.

Milroy House, to which Letitia and Allan of the Glen set out that night, was a fine old English mansion on the banks of the river Thames, near Richmond.

Its two towers gave it somewhat the appearance of a church, and, standing as it did among clustering trees, it looked eminently picturesque.

It seemed so especially when seen from the river at night with its windows aglow, and casting their pleasant gleamings over the placid waters.

Within its time-worn walls there sat on that evening the widow of the old Earl Milroy.

She was a woman of some forty years of age, still retaining evidences of great beauty.

She had seen a somewhat stormy life it is true; but this had not marred that rich voluptuous elegance of form which is so much a characteristic of women of middle age.

Her face had about it a somewhat painful look, but the eyes were still bright, and the mouth still without hard lines.

Her dress, low in front, displayed to advantage a splendid bust, over which the black lace quivered.

She was sitting at the time we introduce her in a well-appointed room, gazing into the fire.

She was thinking of her son.

The uncle had been entreated by her to meet him, and she was anxiously awaiting the moment when she would be able to clasp to her heart her first and only child. Suddenly a maid-servant appeared.

"Two gentlemen desire to see you," she said.

Letitia had not, it will be remembered, discarded her male attire, and appeared in her disguise, therefore, as she had appeared at the lone inn.

"Two gentlemen!" cried the lady, springing up, and pressing her hand over her bosom; "oh, admit them at once."

"It is my son—my dear son!" she murmured, rapturously, as the domestic departed.

Her heart sank, however, when the door opened, and two complete strangers made their appearance.

They bowed respectfully as they advanced.

"You will excuse me, I am sure," said Allan, "for entering unannounced. We are both, however, utter strangers, and you would not have known our names."

"And whence came you?" asked the countess, motioning the courteous stranger to a seat.

"From Scotland, with a sad story," said Allan: "have you a brave heart to sustain a terrible blow?"

"From Scotland! terrible blow!" repeated Lady Milroy, with pale lips. "Oh!—my son—my son! pray Heaven no evil has befallen him."

"Alas! madam, it is of him we have to speak," answered Allan. "Will you listen if I unfold to you a dreadful secret?"

"Yes, yes, speak on," cried the lady, whose throbbing breast showed the violence of her emotion; "I will try to be brave."

So Allan told his tale.

The countess sat very still as she listened to the recital.

It was wonderful to see the command which she had over her feelings.

That heaving breast, those flashing eyes, told truly her emotion; but she did not rave or excite herself or her companions uselessly.

For some moments after Allan of the Glen had finished his recital, she sat without speaking.

Then she turned to Letitia.

Taking her head, she pressed it warmly.

"Oh, I thank you from my heart, brave girl," she said, "and you, too, sir," she added, turning to the Scotch youth; "would that you had arrived sooner, soon enough, at least, to prevent this terrible tragedy which will blight my heart for ever."

"Ah, would indeed," cried Letitia.

Then unable any longer to restrain her pent-up feelings, she flung her arms around the neck of the countess, and fairly sobbed upon her bosom.

For a few moments the two women gave way to their sorrow.

The countess was the first to rouse herself.

"Come, come," she cried, "we must live for vengeance."

At this moment a step was heard approaching.

Then a servant entered.

"Lord Robert Milroy desires to see you," said the domestic.

All sprang instinctively to their feet.

"He comes—not the assassin, but no less the murderer of my son," said the countess. "Conceal yourselves, my friends, behind yonder tapestry, and listen to the traitor's words."

They hurried to obey her.

Scarcely, however, had they time to do so, ere a man's heavy footsteps rang through the corridor.

The countess stood erect, stern and implacable as Medea.

In another moment the uncle of the murdered man entered.

He was a hard-looking man about forty; yet one withal who could evidently cringe and fawn.

He bowed with all seeming respect to the countess, who, resolved for a time to act a part, sank down listlessly into a chair as he entered.

"I trust I see you well, Lady Milroy," he said. "Any news from Lord Francis?"

"Accursed traitor!" thought the lady.

"Your best news of him would be that the ship containing him had gone down with all hands," she answered, "since you would then inherit both title and estates."

"Madam," cried he, with a look of injured honesty, "you are very severe on me to-night. But I can forgive you when I know your anxiety for your boy's welfare. Say, then, have you really any news of him?"

"I have."

"Is he well?"

"He is happy, I trust. He is dead!"

The words acted like an electric shock upon the villain.

He had had news from Dr. Henzollern.

But how had the mother discovered it?

"You surprise me," he cried. "I fear you are the victim of some terrible delusion."

The countess eyed him sternly.

"You did not know this?" she asked.

"I! How could I?"

"Shall I tell you how he died?"

Lord Milroy fairly trembled before her.

The cowardly traitor guessed that some dread revelation was coming.

He could plan a murder, but he could not face an injured and revengeful mother.

She felt that she had him now in her power.

"Lord Milroy," she said, freezingly, "Earl Milroy, through the death of my dear son, tell me have *you* had no news of him?"

"None."

"You lie, assassin!" cried Lady Milroy, unable any longer to restrain her passion. "He is dead, by the hands of the man who sent you, and this night how you had obtained your title. Dr. Henzollern, the Chief of the Poisoners, the wholesale murderer—*your* friend—he died by *your* connivance—through *your* inspiration. My son has died, forsooth, because you have leagued yourself with a band of villains whose hands desire to grasp your money. They shall never have it."

The man sat still—very still, as if carved out of stone, as the wretched mother spoke.

That she had heard much he could guess.

How much, was the question.

"I know not what you mean," he said.

"You lie—you lie again, base murderer!" returned Lady Milroy; "my child's blood cries from the earth against you! I have heard all! I know the story of the lone inn. I know how he was inveigled there—I know how a stab in the back dealt treacherously by Dr. Henzollern ended his life! I have proof positive as to the murderer, and you and he shall ascend the scaffold together!"

RUPERT THE DREADNOUGHT OR THE SECRETS OF THE IRON CHEST

"ROSALIE, THE POISONER, STOOD IN THE DOORWAY."

There was a solemnity in her words and her manner which fairly awed the craven heart of Lord Milroy.

He rose pale and haggard.

"You are mad," he said, "I will leave you for a time."

"No, miserable man," she said, "I am not mad I have witnesses, who will, in good time, prove my words. Where is your wretched accomplice, or, rather, the man who feared to trust you even on so simple an errand of murder?"

"I know not whom you mean," returned Lord Milroy.

"You do; but I will repeat the name. I allude to Dr. Henzollern."

"Madam, you speak in riddles," returned the earl. "I say again, I must leave you for the present. In a day or two I shall have proofs which I can lay before you to show how much in your anger you misjudge me."

He was making for the door when the lady touched a spring bell.

In an instant two servants appeared.

"Bar the door," she cried. "Allan of the Glen, appear!"

Both Allan of the Glen and Letitia at once sprang forward.

The coward turned pale.

"What does this mean?" he cried, as he laid his hand upon his sword.

"It means that you are a prisoner," replied the countess; "a prisoner in my house until I can think of means of punishing you. Radford, see that this man does not escape. Let him be placed in the Blue Room, and let sentinels be placed over him."

So saying, she turned away, still standing erect before him.

Lord Milroy eyed her with a glance of terrible hate.

He looked like a demon.

It seemed, indeed, as if, for the moment, the idea suggested itself to him to spring upon her and destroy her upon the spot.

But if such a conception was formed in his brain he soon abandoned it.

He had half drawn his sword.

He now resheathed it.

A contemptuous smile wreathed itself over his lips.

"No," he said, sneeringly; "to resist so silly a crew would scarcely be manly. I will abide this terrible fate with which I am threatened. Only, there is *one* thing, madame, I would wish to say."

"Speak," said the countess.

"Simply this," replied Lord Milroy, calmly; "that in your mad sorrow at losing your son you choose to believe me his murderer, or the one who ordered his death, and you are resolved to effect mine. Now I have friends who knew where I was going this night, and if I am not at my home by the morning they will know I have been dealt with treacherously, and will take a deadly revenge."

The countess made no reply.

Her heart was steeled against such appeals.

"Take him away, Radford," she said.

By this time several other servants had appeared upon the scene.

Lord Milroy was surrounded.

Resistance was useless.

"Good," he said, "lead on. It is you who have to fear, not me."

CHAPTER XXI.

LADY MILROY'S SORROW—THE THOUGHTS OF REVENGE—THE HOUR OF REST—THE TERRIBLE AWAKENING—THE DESCENT INTO THE VAULTS—THE CHAINED ASSASSIN—A FEARFUL DOOM!

As soon as his departing footsteps resounded along the corridor, Lady Milroy sank into a chair, and pressing her hand over her heaving bosom leaned her head upon her breast and wept.

Letitia's warm arms, as they crept around her neck, roused her from her dream of sorrow.

"Dearest lady," she said, "our sorrow is in common, is it not?"

"It is, indeed; *you* have lost a lover—the hope of your future years; *I* have lost my son, my only son!"

"Well, then," whispered Letitia, "what then? What is our course? Revenge!"

"You speak truly," replied the countess, "that is all now we have to exist for. But I would rather it were left to me. The vengeance *you* might consider enough would be to *me* nothing."

"But I will aid you."

The countess shook her head.

"No," she said, "you would shudder were I to propose to you half the torments I propose to inflict upon the murderer of my son!"

Letitia pressed her arm in a vigorous grasp.

"Shudder!" she cried, "you mistake me. I should shudder at nothing. This villain, the prime mover in the murder of the one I love best in life, is nought to me more than the merest worm that I might meet in my path. No tortures, however terrible that you might inflict upon him, would be thought too great by me. Let me aid you, that I may feel myself also satisfied of my revenge."

The countess raised her face and kissed the hot lips of the excited girl.

"Yes," she said, "since you have courage you shall aid me; but, mark me, if you fail me in the hour of peril my vengeance will then fall upon you!"

"I shall *not* fail you; but I must now leave you. It is late, and you have need of rest. When shall I see you again?"

"There is no need for you to leave me," returned Lady Milroy. "I have rooms in my house both for you and your companion. I will ring for some refreshment; and as the night is dark and the journey you have taken is long, you shall remain here for the night."

To this arrangement, tired as they were, neither Allan nor Letitia cared to demur.

After a few moments the countess rang a bell.

Radford appeared.

"Well," she said, "is he safely caged?"

"He is, my lady."

"Without possibility of escape?"

The man smiled.

"Aye," he said; "it would be strange if he escaped thence; the walls are too thick and there are no windows. I thought the Blue Room was not safe enough, so I placed him in the lower vault."

A grim smile overspread the features of the Countess Milroy.

"You have done well, Radford," she answered, "I

shall sleep more safely. And now bring me some refreshments for myself and my friends here, and tell Eleanor to prepare beds for both."

In a very short space of time an elegant supper was spread, at which the countess did the honours.

But little else but the choice wine was disposed of.

The minds of all were intent upon the scenes they had passed through.

Allan of the Glen, though only a mere acquaintance, as it were, of those who were in trouble, was yet influenced by the sorrows of others, and was very disinclined to be joyous.

The women, whose breasts were bursting with the desire for revenge, were little likely to desire refreshment, and they were glad, indeed, when the hour for retiring came and they were enabled for a time to be alone with their own thoughts.

Allan having retired first, the countess led Letitia to her room.

Then she left her, with a kiss upon her brow, and the young girl, secure in the custody of so good a guardian, undressed and retired to rest.

It was about midnight, just as she had lapsed off into dreams—dreams which could never now be realised—dreams of the one she had lost for ever, that she was suddenly roused.

She started up in terror.

But there was no cause for it.

The countess was standing by her side.

Her face was as pale as death, and she was tremulous with a fierce emotion.

"Letitia," she said, in a hoarse voice, "awake; I have something to tell you."

The young girl roused herself and sat up, drawing the clothes over her bosom, and glancing round her in a scared kind of way, her dream still mixed up with the reality.

"What is it?" she answered.

"You say you live for revenge?" said the countess.

"I do."

"Dress yourself, then," said Lady Milroy, "and you shall see how I have begun it."

"Now—at midnight!"

The girl feared her.

The glare in her eyes seemed that of an insane being.

"Not if you *do* not wish it," replied the countess: "but I could not sleep till I had told you of it. If your desire for revenge equals mine the sight you will see will make you happy. Come; fear nothing. Nay, do not tremble; no one in *my* house dare hurt a hair of your head."

Thus urged, the young girl emerged from her bed and dressed herself.

Then the countess, who had paced the room eagerly during this time, took up the lamp she had brought with her, and led the way into the still corridor.

Here she paused.

"Be very quiet," she said, "I wish none to know I am stirring. Even upon him I wish to come unawares. This way."

She hastened on again, and descending the broad staircase, and reaching the hall, she began the descent of a narrow spiral stair leading to the vaults.

It was easy for anyone to see whither they were going.

The cold, chill air was enough for this.

It was like descending into a tomb.

But Letitia did not fear.

The emotion visible in the face of Lady Milroy, and the eagerness with which she pressed forward, was sufficient to show that the one purpose had not left her mind, and that the young girl's own person was not to be the object of attack.

Presently they reached the bottom.

Here there was a long, subterranean passage.

Along this they hurried.

At length Lady Milroy paused with her finger on her lip.

"We approach him now," she whispered, bending low, so that her breath swept hot over the neck and bosom of the young girl. "Beware. Do not cry out. No matter what you see, do not cry out."

Shuddering, and expecting something terrible, the mistress of the young earl advanced after her strange guide.

After a few moments they reached a door, in the centre of which was a small, barred window.

"Look through and see the commencement of my revenge," said Lady Milroy; "'tis but the commencement. You will see the end!"

Letitia looked through.

Within there was a cell about eight feet square.

The damp floor was strewn thinly with straw.

The walls reeked with damp, and not a casement, save the one in the door, was there to admit a particle of light.

In the centre of the ceiling hung a lamp.

A murky, dismal thing.

Just enough to make the darkness visible.

On one side was a man—naked, with the exception of a pair of short drawers covering his loins.

His hands and feet were chained to the wall, so that he was compelled to maintain an upright position, and never strive even for rest, for the latter attempt would inevitably result in unendurable agony.

His face was white and ghastly.

Already the consciousness of an unerring vengeance was upon him.

He saw the Shadow of the Angel of Death, and heard plainly the flapping of its dismal wings above him.

"This is terrible!" murmured Letitia.

"But just!" said the countess. "To-morrow one of my servants will commence his torture. *You* shall be here to witness. Come, now let us go. You see, when I threaten, I act!"

Gladly Letitia retired.

Gladly she quitted the company of the terrible woman, and gladly she drew her pretty limbs beneath the snowy draperies of her couch.

Her heart also craved for vengeance.

But it was vengeance of a far different kind.

She expected naturally to see now the vengeance of a demon!

CHAPTER XXII.

THE EMISSARY OF THE POISONERS—THE ATTEMPTED ESCAPE — THE DISAPPOINTMENT — STARVATION!—CONQUERED BY HUNGER!

My readers will remember that when the man who had so mysteriously broken into Rupert Dreadnought's house was conveyed down into the vault beneath, his first thought, when he was left alone in the dismal place, was not "Despair," but "How shall I escape?"

The prospect was certainly not a cheerful one.

He was bound, and in almost utter darkness.

Yet he did not lose courage.

He had a bold heart, worthy of a better cause.

No sooner had his captors gone—no sooner, I mean, had the echoes of their footsteps died away in the distance—when he began active measures.

He was an adept.

It was easy to see that he had been in such scrapes before, and had escaped somehow or another from them.

Sitting down on the damp ground he began with his teeth to undo, or rather to bite through, the cord which bound him.

This was a matter, of course, of great difficulty, and required long patience.

But he knew well that if he did not escape by morning, there was every chance of his gaoler discovering that his bonds were useless.

What he had to endeavour to effect, then, was to make his escape ere morning dawned.

Steadily he worked; and in a few minutes one arm was free.

Then he felt for his knife.

This he found in the pocket of his waistcoat.

They had not thought of entirely disarming him, for, bound as he was, it naturally appeared impossible that he could in any way release himself from his bonds.

This found, he had no more work to do.

In a few moments he was a free man!

The first difficulty was over, truly.

The worst had to come.

What he had mastered was nothing but rope.

He had now to encounter *stone walls*.

His heart began to fail him, as, with nothing but his small knife, he began to essay the strength of the sides of his prison.

He had anticipated naturally that in a house, an ordinary private house like that of Rupert Dreadnought's, the walls would be made of simple brick or wood.

He was astounded to discover it solid stone.

The door was equally invulnerable.

It was *iron!*

There was no help for it now.

Sent thither by a powerful League as he had been, having within a few miles desperate men who would at the risk of their own lives save him, he was utterly helpless.

He was a prisoner in the hands of the worst and most determined enemy of the League, and all he had to do was to submit and escape by the first chance that offered.

Two or three efforts he made.

But it was all in vain, and, without even attempting to re-place his bonds, he laid himself down upon the straw, and endeavoured by sleep to forget the position he was in.

On the following morning, Stanley Sherrington, when he entered the cell, found the prisoner lying exhausted upon the straw.

He had done his best.

Again and again he had attempted to escape.

But, as I have said, the walls were of solid stone, and the little knife he carried was perfectly useless for any attempt at escape.

He sprang into an erect position when he, Stanley Sherrington, entered.

"Well," said Stanley, "you have contrived to unbind yourself, I see, but our walls are too thick to admit of escape."

"If you had thought so," returned the man, with a sneering smile, "you would not have bound me. Had I had but a dagger, I would have been ten miles distant by this time."

To this latter speech Sherrington made no reply.

"Good," he said, "you are here in captivity; if you desire liberty, you must earn it."

"How?"

"By revealing the secrets we desire to know in regard to your Society. In the first place, when does Dr. Henzollern return from Scotland?"

"I do not know."

"That is false. You are one of the hundred who were present at the meeting at the old house by the river. You heard the speech which your Chief made at parting. You heard Oscar Penraven placed in the position of Governor of the League for the time, and you know that he *has* gone upon a mission in its interests. What I desire to know is, is he going to Germany?"

The man shrugged his shoulders doggedly.

"I have told you," he said, "I know nothing."

"Very good," replied Sherrington, "we will see how long you will persist in this spirit."

The man at that moment would have laughed at the bare idea of yielding.

He knew not what the power of hunger was.

Stanley Sherrington made no further remark, but left him to himself.

During that day not a bit of food was served him or was a drop of drink given him.

He guessed then the trials to which he was to be subject to.

The next day passed.

Not a soul come near him.

On the third day he was very weak and faint.

His courage was beginning to evaporate.

That evening Stanley Sherrington came again.

"Now," he said, "has your memory revived? Can you tell me now where Dr. Henzollern is?"

"You have conquered," replied he; "but you are asking me to be a traitor. What is it you desire me to tell you?"

"I must know where he is before Rupert Dreadnought comes to London."

"He is not to return," said the man, "until he has reached Germany."

"And when does he start?"

"Immediately upon the completion of the business for which he visited Scotland."

Stanley Sherrington shuddered.

Knowingly or unknowingly the man spoke of murder as a business.

"Good, you shall have food now," said he; "but until Earl Dreadnought starts upon his mission in safety I cannot release you."

Then he quitted the cell, and the emissary of the Terrible League was once more alone underground.

CHAPTER XXIII.

AGAIN ON THE TRACK OF GUILT!—THE TENDER FAREWELL—THE FAIR DEMON ONCE MORE—ROSALIE ST. AUBYN ON THE WATCH—THE SECOND JOURNEY TO SCOTLAND—THE "PEDLAR'S REST"—THE COMPACT—THE SCOTCH SKIPPER—OUT ON THE SEA—THE CHASE—PURSUERS AND PURSUED—AT HAMBURG—ON THE ROAD TO THE OLD CASTLE.

Our readers, of course, remember that when Rupert Dreadnought and Allan of the Glen arrived in London with the unfortunate betrothed of the murdered earl, they parted on the road, and he returned to his own home, leaving them to break the terrible news to Lady Milroy.

The joy with which he was greeted by Helen may be imagined, but it was damped by the knowledge that he must almost immediately quit her side upon another and still more dangerous errand.

No time, moreover, could be lost.

Dr. Henzollern would probably quit Scotland at once, and in those days, as my readers may imagine, it would be a difficult matter to follow in his track to a foreign country.

"GENTLY THEY DREW HIM DOWN AGAIN INTO HIS CHAIR."

So, on the following day, as soon as Allan of the Glen had returned from his visit to Lady Milroy, he once more made preparations to go.

Helen clung to him eagerly when Allan had descended to the roadway where the horses were prancing impatiently.

"Take care of yourself for *my* sake, dearest Rupert," she murmured. "You are going upon a dangerous mission, and I feel a sad presentiment in my heart."

She would have felt a stronger and more terrible fear still could she have known by whom they were watched during the scene of tender parting.

Standing in the doorway was a woman.

A woman pale, ghastly, terrible!

Rosalie St. Aubyn the Poisoner!

My readers have not, of course, forgotten that at the first sight of Rupert she had conceived for him an insane passion.

It was an all-consuming passion.

Everything would be swept on one side by such a love.

Murder would not be too awful a method for casting to the earth an obstacle.

But she desired not her presence to be known.

How she had entered was a mystery.

But there she was as the lovers' lips met, listening to their tender words, and hearing too the plans of the young earl for the ruin of the League.

"I shall not return till he is my prisoner, or I have killed him," said Rupert. "I only blame myself for permitting him even to meet the young earl, whom he so basely murdered. But adieu, dear one; you have good friends here, and no harm will befal you."

Had he seen the pale figure that now glided away into the corridor he would not have used such words.

One more kiss—one more tender embrace, and they parted.

A chill of terror, or, rather, presentiment of evil, ran through the breast of Helen Penraven as she saw Rupert gallop off with his trusty friend, but she knew not yet what trial there was in store for her during his absence.

It is needless to describe the return journey of Rupert and Allan to Scotland.

It was entirely without adventures, and one dark evening they entered the good city of Edinburgh, after a monotonous changing and re-changing of horses.

The port of Leith was, of course, the one from which the Doctor would take his departure, and to this place, full as it was of terrible reminiscences, they quickly made their way, and put up at the "Pedlar's Rest."

The landlord knew them again at once, and remembering the hand he had had in the drugging of his guests on the former occasion, it is not to be wondered at if he felt somewhat doubtful as to the reception which would be accorded him.

But he was soon relieved from any fear on this score.

Rupert and Allan of the Glen were there to make discoveries, not to punish the insignificant.

Ordering a supper, they invited the landlord to join them at table.

He complied at once.

Not without fear be it said.

He had drugged them.

Might they not desire to poison him?

The viands having been disposed of, and the tankards replenished, Rupert Dreadnought spoke to the purpose.

"Your name is Andrew McAllister, is it not?" he asked.

"It is."

"Well then, Master Andrew," contined our hero, "you little know how very nearly you have run the risk of losing not only your means of subsistence but your life too."

The Scotchman turned pale, and sprang up from his chair.

Were his fears coming true?

"What mean you?" he cried. "Are you poisoning me?"

Rupert smiled, as he and Allan seized him, and with a gentle pressure, drew him down again into his chair.

"Fear not," said our hero. "I speak not of myself or my friend. I speak of those with whom you unfortunately were leagued in the commission of a foul and deliberate murder."

The Scotchman raised his hands aloft.

He was the very picture of terror.

With his white face and his hair erect, he presented such a comical appearance, that any one not knowing the serious part of the business would have fairly burst into uproarious laughter.

This was no time for merriment, however; and, moreover, Rupert saw plainly that the horror of the Scotchman was real and not feigned.

"Murder!" he muttered. "What now? You are doing this to frighten me."

"Not so," said Rupert; "we mean you no harm. I believe you really innocent of all participation in the crime, and I can promise you, therefore, a good reward if you aid me. But tell me first, are we safe here? Can we be overheard?"

"Not here. This is the best room in the house for that. Stay, I will lock the door so that we shall be free from all interruption."

He rose, opened it, glanced out, and listened.

No one was near.

Locking it, therefore, he returned to his seat and eagerly said—

"Now, then, gentlemen, I am all eagerness to know what great secret I am involved in, and what escape it is that I have had from justice."

"You remember our coming here?"

"I do."

"You remember helping to drug us?"

"Oh, Lord!" inwardly groaned the Scotchman "I thought it was coming."

"Well, gentlemen," he said, aloud, "well, you see, I was in fear of my life, and, when a man is in that state, why, you see——"

"That is enough; you confess it. Now, listen to me. During the time that we were lying here insensible, a young man was inveigled into the 'M'Donald Arms,' and there murdered!"

"Murdered!"

"Aye, treacherously murdered by the man who, for a time, put up at this place."

"What, the dark, gipsy-looking man, in high boots, who came from London?"

"The same!" cried Rupert, grasping the man's arm eagerly, "the same. You know him then?"

"I do; he was here but half a day since," replied he.

"Half a day since! then we have lost him but by a few hours," said Allan.

"No, I doubt if you have lost him," returned the landlord. "I can, I fancy, give you such information as will put you on the right scent. The vessel he was to sail in cannot be more than a few miles away, for it was not to start until six."

"And whither was it bound?"

"To Hamburg."

"Good; and its name?"

"The 'Vrow.'"

Rupert rose.

"Let us lose no time," he said. "Tell me where can we procure a vessel? Where is there one which will start soon for the same destination?"

The Scotchman thought a moment.

"Well," he said, "well, there is the 'Aberdeen,' she starts to-morrow morning. She's a fast sailer, and may be, if you made it worth his while, the skipper might sail before his time. Stay, I'll go with you."

"That will be best," said Rupert; "and, depend on it, you shall not lose by it."

In a few minutes the landlord had made all his arrangements.

His wife was left in charge of the house, and the three men were soon trudging along the rough road towards the harbour.

Drawn up as closely as possible to the landing-place was a fine schooner, over the bulwarks of which a man was leaning and smoking.

The landlord of the "Pedlar's Rest" at once hailed him.

"Hullo, Simon!" he cried, "is Captain Ludlam here on board?"

The man laughed.

"No," he said, "he's having his last drop before starting. We don't weigh anchor until dawn."

"Where can we find him?"

"At the 'Ship Tavern' yonder, where the green light hangs out over the water. Is it business you desire to see him upon?"

"It is."

"Then you'll see how he'll swear at you," said Simon.

"Not he," replied Andrew; "it's too good a bit of business for him to refuse to entertain it. Come, master, let us hasten."

Rupert Dreadnought required no inciting, but hurried on at the side of his companion, and it was not long before they reached the old tavern where the fishermen and sailors of the place always regaled themselves.

Here they were soon introduced into the company of the captain, a jolly, sunburnt, rubicund specimen of a tar, just the one to be trusted in a chase which had for its object the punishment of the guilty.

The old salt looked somewhat aghast at first at the idea of being so suddenly forced, as it were, into the transaction of business in the middle of his last scene of jollity.

But a whisper from Andrew changed his tone.

That whisper told him the sum which Rupert was prepared to give for his assistance.

At this he rose, quitted his companions, and, going to another room, had soon heard everything necessary.

When he had heard all, he struck his clenched fist upon the table till the glasses rang again.

"By all the saints!" he said, "we'll start at once, and if we don't overhaul that ship before she gets to Hamburg, my name isn't John Ludlam."

Preparations were soon made.

The ship was got trim, and, despite the grumblings of the seamen, who were unexpectedly roused out of their beds, the "Aberdeen" soon began to move slowly out of the harbour.

I am not going to describe this chase.

A chase at sea, although it has been so often and so excitingly described, is nothing in itself unless the vessels come to close quarters.

The ships go glidingly, slowly along as at any other time.

It is in the minds of the people on board only that the excitement exists.

The pursued, standing on the stern of the vessel, eye, with a terrible interest, the speck on the horizon as it gets bigger and bigger, or their hearts leap with joy as it recedes further and further, and is at length lost to view.

The pursuers, gathered on the prow—telescope in hand—think every moment too long that separates them from their prey.

It happened thus with the crews of the "Aberdeen" and the vessel it was following.

But swear and strive as Captain Ludlam might, there was no help for it.

He had misjudged entirely the speed of the vessel which was bearing away to Germany the assassin of young Earl Milroy, and when the shades of evening closed over the ocean the ship was nowhere to be seen.

They pressed, however, with all haste into the quaint old town of Hamburg, and, after rewarding the Scotch skipper as promised, Rupert and Allan of the Glen landed, and proceeded at once to make inquiries.

This was no difficult matter.

The ship in which the Chief of the Poisoners had sailed over had entered the harbour some four hours before, and was even now close up against the quay.

To go on board was the next thing, and in doing this also Rupert found no hindrance.

Whatever the manifold crimes of Dr. Henzollern, the captain of the ship that had brought him evidently knew nothing of them.

He answered all questions readily, and Rupert soon ascertained that he intended making no stay in Hamburg, but to push on at once to the Castle of Hendringing, which overhung a little lake some thirty miles distant.

With this knowledge Rupert was forced to be content.

The skipper could give him no information as to the manner in which the doctor intended travelling.

In fact, the Chief of the League had only been communicative to a certain extent.

He had spoken of friends in Germany.

He had said that his visit to the Castle of Hendringing was one of immense importance, and that he hoped to bring back with him things of great value.

But that was all.

What the valuables were he did not say.

The old Castle of Hendringing seemed well known to all.

At the first tavern Rupert received full directions, and, without waiting more than was necessary to take refreshment, the two young adventurers started forth on what may truly be called their perilous journey.

Before, however, we describe it, and the wonderful and terrible discoveries they made at its termination, we must return to London, and explain how it was that the first face they saw upon this journey was that of an old friend.

CHAPTER XXIV.

THE HOUSE OF GASCOIGNE—THE VENGEANCE OF THE LEAGUE AT WORK—THE GHASTLY ASSASSIN —THE STAINS OF BLOOD—THE CHOICE OF DEATH—DIAMOND CUT DIAMOND—THE BAFFLED POISONER—THE MURDER OF THE TWO DOMESTICS—THE CONFESSION—THE AGONY OF THE GUILTY—RETRIBUTION—THE END OF A MURDERER—THE VOYAGE TO GERMANY—AN UNEXPECTED MEETING.

GASCOIGNE, the detective, whose safety had now, for a long time, been a matter patent to the terrible Society of Poisoners, knew well that his life was in danger.

He took good precautions, therefore, to ensure himself against secret attack.

His house was like a fortified castle.

His windows were barred, his doors of iron, his servants (he had only two) old and trusty ones.

The one was a man whom Gascoigne had befriended when he was in the service of the government; the other was the man's wife.

With these two he felt safer than if he had a host of retainers, one of whom might turn out to be a traitor.

The Poisoners, however, knew well that, they could do nothing against him by force.

Indeed, as a body, they ignored entirely his existence.

Oscar Penraven it was who entertained so violent an antipathy against him.

In the absence of Dr. Henzollern, he had, as I have before said, resolved to use the Power of the Awful League for the destruction of his private enemies; and Gascoigne, the man he had once attempted to murder, was one of the first on the list.

Steadily, therefore, he laid his plans, and two evenings before the departure of Rupert for Germany, the scheme was considered to be ripe.

Gascoigne was sitting alone in his room.

Before him, on a table, were writing materials.

But he was not writing now.

Leaning his head upon his hands, he was involved in a deep reverie.

He was thinking of the past.

The past, when he was young and handsome and loved.

The past, in which the deepest wrong had been inflicted upon him by his enemies.

Suddenly a step was heard near him and a man entered the room.

A man, ghastly and horrid, with eyes glaring as if from the memory of some awful deed.

Gascoigne sprang up.

"What want you here?" he cried, in a loud, stern voice.

"I come to take your life!" returned the other, locking the door.

A smile of derision crossed the features of Gascoigne.

"And who has sent you, may I ask?" he said.

"I come from the League, who had supposed you dead. You know you are a denounced traitor. Therefore prepare to die."

It was now that, for the first time, Gascoigne noticed that the hands and clothes of the speaker were stained with blood.

Blood freshly spilled.

"Know you, mad assassin," he cried, "that one cry from me would bring my faithful servants to my rescue!"

The man smiled.

A horrid smile.

"They are dead!" he said.

"Dead!"

"Aye, by my hands: side by side they lie in their bed-chamber, stiff and cold."

The horrible solemnity with which the man spoke, showed that the deed he had done had taken strange effect upon his brain.

Presently his eyes fell upon a decanter of wine.

Seizing it, he applied the neck to his lips and took a long, deep draught.

Gascoigne watched him with a satisfaction which was very strange.

"Good," muttered the assassin, "that has given me strength. And now to business. I have here the usual weapons of the League, poison, the dagger and a pistol. Choose your mode of death!"

"I have been one of the League," answered Gascoigne, "and I have learned to fear nothing. Therefore, if you grant me five minutes' delay, I will accept the painless poison you have with you, and you will see I can die like a man."

The man pressed his hand to his brow.

He was evidently under some strange mysterious influence.

Presently he staggered.

"I feel ill," he muttered, "but yet I dare not let him see it. Come, sir, the time is up," he added, in louder tones. "Which mode of death have you chosen?"

A derisive laugh burst from the lips of Gascoigne.

"There is no death, I hope, for me," he said, "till I have had time for vengeance."

The man leaned faintly on the back of a chair.

"What mean you?" he cried.

"That *you* die, not I!" he answered. "I will tell you at once, that I may not keep you in suspense. The wine you have just drunk was full of deadly poison!"

The man opened wide his eyes and glared at the speaker.

"Poison!" he gasped.

"Yes, poison; the poison used by the League by which you are employed. This wine is some which I received from the Chief to give to unfortunate victims. This very night I have been using my best endeavours to analyse its contents, and discover if possible an antidote."

"And you have discovered it!" cried the wretched creature, with clutching hands.

"I have."

"You will save me?"

"That depends. If you answer all I wish to know I may do so."

"And if not?"

"I leave you to your fate."

"I will tell all," said the other, faintly; "but quick! quick! the antidote—I die!"

As he spoke, he fell backwards, and ere Gascoigne could aid him, fell, with the chair, to the ground.

Gascoigne eyed him with a grim smile as he fell.

"Ah!" he said, "how easily are the schemes of the wicked defeated. But, nevertheless, I must see to him, or the ecrets I desire to know die with him."

He drew from his pocket a small phial, and poured a few drops into a glass.

This he filled with water, and a milky liquid was produced.

Then he knelt down by the side of the assassin, and poured it between his lips.

The effect was not instantaneous.

Gascoigne knew that it would not be so.

"I must see what papers he has about him, and secure also his weapons," thought he.

He searched all his pockets.

The phial, the pistol, the dagger were there truly.

But as for papers, there were none.

"The League is too careful," muttered Gascoigne. "They know that failure is possible."

After putting in his pocket the weapons of offence, he unlocked the door, and proceeded upstairs, leaving the fellow still lying half insensible upon the carpet.

He knew well that it would be some quarter of an hour ere he recovered thoroughly the possession of his senses.

There was no hurry, therefore.

During this time he could explore the house and see how far the hideous confession of the blood-stained assassin was true.

Taking the lamp, he ascended the stairs noiselessly.

Awe was in his heart.

Everything was very still, and seemed to speak of death.

Up, up he went, to the top story.

It was here the old people slept.

At their door he halted a moment to take a long breath, and then, pushing it open, he slipt as he entered.

Blood was trickling along the floor.

He held up the lamp, shudderingly.

Blood was on the floor, truly, and on the bed-clothes, and splashed on the wall, while on the couch itself lay the bodies of the two faithful domestics, stabbed to the heart.

RUPERT OR THE DREADNOUGHT; SECRETS OF THE IRON CHEST!

"ONE MORE OF THE HIDEOUS CREW IS GONE," SAID GASCOIGNE.

Above them, in the ceiling, was a round hole, through which a man's body had forced its way from without.

Here was the mystery of the villain's entrance explained.

He had obtained some means of access to the roof, and had thence gradually made an entrance through the ceiling.

"Curses on the villain!" muttered Gascoigne, as he drew the clothes over the ghastly bodies, "curses on him! Who can blame me if I break my word with such a wretch?"

Then he quitted the room, locked the door, and descended once more to the room where he had left the Poisoner.

He found him sitting up.

A greenish pallor overspread his features.

"I am dying," he said; "you have deceived me—betrayed me."

Gascoigne frowned.

"I have seen your handiwork," he said; "death would be your proper portion."

"But you promised me an antidote."

"I did, and you have had it; otherwise you would, by this time, have been dead. Now, sit up in that chair and answer me my questions."

The man struggled up into his chair as best he could.

Gascoigne could not bring himself to touch him.

"Now, tell me," he said, "whither is Dr. Henzollern going?"

"To the Castle of Hendringing, near the town of Hamburg."

"Ah! I know well the name—it is the manufactory of poisons."

"The same," said the miserable man. "But how know you it?"

"Did I not tell you that I have been in the League? Have you forgotten that I was once considered one of its leading members?" returned Gascoigne. "When does he start?"

"I cannot tell the exact time. He is now on his way, I have no doubt."

"And will he remain long there?"

"That I am unable to say," replied the man.

"He goes to obtain a new stock of deadly poison?"

"He does."

"Good; that is enough. Stay, does he travel alone?"

"Yes; but pray give me some more stimulant. I feel fainting."

Gascoigne rose and approached the table.

Pouring out some water, he poured into it four drops from the phial which he had taken from the assassin.

This, also, became of a milky colour, like the antidote.

He handed it to the man, who drank it up eagerly.

In a few moments he became deadly faint, and still more ghastly than before.

Then he began to suspect that all could not be right.

"Villain!" he shouted, "you have deceived me—poisoned me!"

And he strove to rise.

He was far too weak to rise.

The poison was beginning again to work; but if it had not, the stern, calm, implacable face of Gascoigne, as he folded his arms and stood with his back to the fire-place, would have told its own tale.

"I *have* deceived you," returned Gascoigne. "You came here to assassinate me, and an accident only prevented you from attempting to put your threat into execution. You have already stained your hands with the blood of my two faithful domestics, and now you are dying, in punishment for your crimes. You are helpless; expect no aid—no mercy from me!"

The wretched man's agony of mind was terrible!

It was visible in his rolling eyes and quivering lips, as each moment the poison made him grow weaker.

"Oh, save me!" he murmured.

"Never!"

"Save me, and I will betray the entire League to the Government."

"I need not such promises. I know sufficient now."

"Oh, save me, in mercy!—save!—oh! save me!"

And then with a last gurgle, he clenched his teeth, his eyes rolled, and he fell back dead.

"One more of the hideous crew is gone. Now to punish the Chief of all!"

So saying, he quitted the room, taking the lamp with him, and carefully locking the door after him.

He had soon made what arrangements were necessary.

Taking his pistols and his sword, and donning his long cloak, he quitted the house of death, and proceeded to the head of the watch.

To him he told his tale, and delivered up the key of his house.

Any one less known than Gascoigne would, of course, have been detained.

His name, however, was enough to ensure freedom.

Besides, he was about to start on the track of a criminal.

So, without the least delay, he proceeded to his stables, and dashed away on his road to the spot where he expected to find a vessel bound for Hamburg.

In this he was fortunate, and he arrived in the town, and set out towards the Castle of Hendringing just two days before the arrival of Dr. Henzollern.

The castle was a strange and dreary old place.

It was surrounded on three sides by trees, on the other by a lake, on whose gloomy shores grew weeping willows and bushes, which seemed especially intended to conceal murders.

Its windows were small, and studded with iron bars.

And even these were seldom, if ever, lit up.

The only one in which a light seemed always to burn at night was a small casement in the topmost tower.

Not above a mile from the castle was a small inn.

Here Gascoigne, disguised as an English pedlar, put up.

He was, as we know, good at disguises, and no one in the establishment ever suspected him.

On the third morning after his arrival he took a stroll in the wood.

He was on the look-out for the doctor, and yet had missed him.

It was a cool and balmy morning, and scarcely a sound disturbed the quiet of the scene.

Presently, however, along the high road was heard the sound of horses' feet.

Gascoigne at once started forward.

"At last, perhaps," he thought, "my worst enemy approaches."

As my readers know, he was wrong in his surmise.

Dr. Henzollern had been at the castle some hours.

It was Allan of the Glen and Rupert who were approaching.

As they neared the spot where Gascoigne was lying in wait, they drew their horses into a trot, and he at once recognised them.

With a joyful cry he sprang out before them.

The two horsemen at once drew rein.

In his garb, and with his face disguised as it was with a dense beard, they did not recognise him.

"Who are you?" cried Rupert, placing his hand upon his pistols.

"Do you not know me?"

"Indeed no."

"It proves, then, how complete my disguise is," returned he. "I am Gascoigne."

"And why are you here?"

"I might ask *you* that question," replied Gascoigne. "I am here to find Dr. Henzollern, the Chief of the League of Poisoners. He is on his way from England to the yonder Castle of Hendringing, and I am on the look-out for him as he comes."

"Then you must have missed him," said Rupert. "We are on the track of the same man. but he preceeded us by some hours."

Gascoigne bit his lip.

Engaged as he had been for years in the vocation of a detective, he hated the idea of being discovered in the wrong.

"That is extremely awkward," he said: "if either of us could have seized him on the road we might not only have wrung his secrets from him, but we might also have punished him without the slightest fear of detection. Now, in yonder castle, it will be next to impossible to seize upon him."

"Your information, doubtless, is more precise than ours," said Rupert. "For what reason is he here?"

"The Castle of Hendringing is the chief manufactory of poisons," replied Gascoigne, "and he is here to obtain and to superintend the making of some more deadly materials for the Poisoners of London. It is a well-guarded place, and since he has entered it, it would be madness for us to think of anything now but to await his departure and endeavour to seize upon him when he is on his return to England."

"Good; but where can we wait?"

"Close to this spot."

"Are you acquainted with the locality, then?"

"I have never been here before; but I am at the sign of the 'Three Shepherds,' there you will find good entertainment for both you and your horses, and we can, moreover, by the exhibition of a little wealth, bribe the landlord to give us a little information."

"Let us on, then, at once," said Rupert. "I am all impatience."

There was that evening a grand scene of gaiety at the sign of the "Three Shepherds," which, as I have said, was within a mile of the Castle of Hendringing.

Situated on the highest point of the wood before mentioned, the place had a most melancholy aspect without; but in the interior it was well and even richly furnished.

Master Heinrich, the host, had two classes of customers.

He received hunters, trainers, police, citizens and their wives.

But when these were gone, the "Three Shepherds" was the rendezvous of the coryphees of the Hamburg Theatre and their admirers, who, after their little suppers, ran about in the woods in the costumes of dryads or nymphs pursued by their lovers, any one of the beauties being the property of the one who caught her, as in the Stag Park of Louis XV.

That evening, when Rupert, and Allan, and Gascoigne entered the public-room, they found it crowded with soldiers and others. the sergeant of the former being engaged in a game of cards with a young man who was dressed in the most singular fashion.

He had a bronzed face, with energetic, regular, and impassable features, large, sombre, and deeply set eyes, and black locks escaping from beneath a red velvet cap.

His ears were ornamented with long ear-rings of silver and pearl, and over his shoulders was thrown a kind of muleteer's cloak.

His nervous and strong legs were encased in large breeches, met at the knee by high boots of untanned leather.

The man with whom he was playing offered a striking contrast.

With his blue eyes, his long, light moustache, his aquiline nose, his smiling and sensual mouth, he was a pure type of the Gallic race.

He had gained several games, but, at length, as if the play did not amuse him, he threw himself back in his chair, crossed his arms and legs, and said, yawning,

"Ah! and so at present you are the doctor to the Count of Hendringing, eh, Master Kamril?"

"Yes; since I was sent for to cure the count of a bad wound he received in falling down the stone staircase," returned the other.

"And you cured him?"

"He was able to mount his horse a quarter of an hour after the operation."

"The devil! you perform miracles, you gipsies; let us hope the count gave you a good reward."

"Certainly," replied the gipsy; "he gave me and my friends one month to leave this place without being arrested and sent to the galleys; that was a good reward, by my faith."

The sergeant laughed.

"It is, by Jupiter!" he cried; "for the lieutenant of police is soon down upon vagabonds and unruly paupers."

"We are neither vagabonds nor unruly paupers," replied the gipsy.

And as he spoke his eyes shot forth flames of anger.

"I am quite sure of that. I know it well," replied the sergeant. "I have seen your mother, a superb woman."

"She is my mother," replied Kamril, "the queen who saved for Germany a good soldier."

"I know it," returned the sergeant, as he extended to him his hand; "but tell me what brings you to the 'Three Shepherds?'"

"I came," said the gipsy, "because it suited my convenience to come."

"Ah! well, I am glad it so suited you, since it has procured me the pleasure of meeting you and asking you to help me to empty this bottle of excellent wine."

"No thank you," said Kamril, rising.

"Come, then," returned the sergeant, "if you are not in a hurry to go in."

"I am not going," said the gipsy.

"Remain with us then," returned the other; "you will see something droll presently."

"What is that?"

"A duel between two fine fellows who are going to cut each other's throats under the trees."

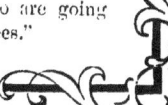

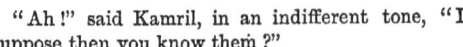

"Ah!" said Kamril, in an indifferent tone, "I suppose then you know them?"

"No; only my men and I are going to look on and see fair play, for one of the two combatants, who is a fine swordsman, is capable of attempting to draw his adversary into ambush."

"It is a good precaution," said the gipsy, "and I hope victory will declare itself on the side of right."

As he spoke, a metallic sound resounded through the room.

It was the landlord who struck the fender with a stick.

The sergeant whistled, and his men immediately came round him.

"Now, my friends," he said, "listen to me. You know well what is our work this night."

Then he turned to the gipsy, and took his arm.

"Come," he said; "you may be wanted, since you are a doctor. I have orders to leave none here save the landlord and his men."

"Very well," said Kamril; "since I must assist at this combat, I will go. I shall not interfere with your orders, then, and I *may* be useful."

As they turned to go, the sergeant caught sight of Rupert and his comrades.

They were in such a position that is was evident to the soldier that they had heard all that had passed.

"Gentlemen," he said, "permit me to request you to accompany us."

"Wherefore?" asked Rupert.

"Because I wish to secure fair play for my friend."

"And your friend is —"

"The enemy of the Count of Hendringing, although I appear to be on the other side."

Rupert at once rose.

"I will accompany you with pleasure," he said, "although I am an Englishman, a stranger in these parts, and therefore hardly authorized to interfere."

The sergeant bowed, and, without further words, they passed out.

In a few moments they were in the thick of the wood.

About a hundred paces on they came to a wide clearing.

The sergeant caused his men and companions to conceal themselves behind the dense brushwood, where they could see plainly all that passed in the centre of the clearing without being seen themselves.

They had not long to wait.

In about ten minutes, while they all remained silent and immoveable, a man of middle age was seen advancing from an avenue of trees, accompanied by a man in a long cloak, and followed, at no great distance, by a second couple.

The first man was about forty years of age, broad, well-built, strong.

The second comer was taller, but younger and slim.

"The first is the count," whispered the sergeant, to Rupert; "the other, in his hands, is as a child, though he is brave, and headstrong too."

The four men stopped in the centre of the clearing.

"I don't see any preparations for the amusement you spoke of," said the young man. "Where is the supper? Where are the nymphs of which you spoke?"

"You will see plenty of amusement presently," said the count, as he stuck the torch which he carried, in common with the rest, into the cleft of a tree. "You have not been brought here for nothing. You were told you would meet here the Count Hendringing."

"Well, and are we not at the rendezvous?"

"Certainly, and the count only waits your pleasure to offer you his most humble welcome, and to present you to some of his brave friends."

"I do not understand you," said the other, frowning sternly.

"You will soon understand," returned the comrade of the count, and he waved his torch aloft.

As he did so, Rupert and his companion saw his face.

It was that of the Chief of the Poisoners, Dr. Henzollern!

In an instant the sergeant and his men leaped to their feet and respectfully bowed to the young man.

Kamril, who had also sprang to his feet, now resumed his seat on the green sward.

"And now," said the count, taking off a black wig and his beard and throwing them on the ground, "allow me, my most noble sir, to introduce to you the Count Hendringing."

"You the count! you!" cried the other, turning pale as death.

"Yes; I am the true and redoubtable Count Hendringing, whom you desired, the other evening at the banquet, to have strangled, or in some other way put quickly out of the world."

The eyes of the young man darted fierce glances at the speaker.

He made a quick movement, and the barrel of a pistol glittered in his hand.

Dr. Henzollern darted forward just in time to push aside the weapon as the ball sped.

The bullet missed its aim and carried away a curl from the head of one of the soldiers.

"Well, I will not compliment you, Master Hans Horstacker," said the count; "if you love your mistress as well as you hate me you will make a good husband."

This remark, which made all the soldiers laugh, served te infuriate Horstacker (as the young man seemed to be called), and he made gigantic efforts to free himself from the hands of Dr. Henzollern and rush upon his enemy.

But Dr. Henzollern held him in an iron grasp.

"Come, come," said the count, as he undid the knot which held together two swords that he carried, "be a little calm. With the goodwill you have towards us now you could assassinate the whole fifteen of us."

"This is an infamous ambuscade," cried the other, bursting with rage; "you are bandits and cowards."

The soldiers began to swear and grumble at these words.

But the sergeant, by an imperious gesture, commanded silence.

"Evidently," whispered Rupert, to Allan, "these men do not know the character of the man they are protecting."

"Certainly not," said Gascoigne. "I know for a fact that the Count Hendringing is one of the most respected men in the country. We must be cautious."

"Come now, Master Horstacker," exclaimed Dr. Henzollern, "listen to me, you man of pistols. You have attempted to assassinate Count Hendringing, my best friend, and you now address as bandits and cowards these honest gentlemen, who are only here to assist at an honourable duel, and prevent any improper interference. I declare, if you try again, I shall take upon myself to settle the whole affair for you with this."

And he held up a long and formidable-looking knife.

Horstacker glanced round with a heavy stupor.

Then his eyes fell on Kamril, who was still seated on the ground with the coolest air in the world, and as if perfectly indifferent and strange to the scene going on before him.

A sigh of relief escaped the breast of Hans Horstacker.

He at once threw off his heavy cloak and his coat.

Then he turned to Dr. Henzollern.

"Give me a sword," he said.

"One moment," said Count Hendringing, after he had also cast aside his coat. "I think this really *is* the moment when you may justly be asked to tell me the reason of your hatred to me."

"THE TWO HORSEMEN AT ONCE DREW REIN."

The young man nodded.

Then he approached the other, and said, in a low voice—

"Count, you had a wife?"

"I have one now."

"But you had one long since in Spain?"

"Yes, but she is dead."

"'Tis false! she lives! *I* am her husband!"

Count Hendringing started back in utter stupefaction.

"Yes," continued Horstacker, "the husband of the woman whom you imagined to be dead in Spain, murdered by the gipsies."

The count burst into a loud fit of laughter.

"Well, well," he said, "I should never have interfered with your little arrangements, and I think it is absurd that we should have met together now, in this tragic way. By the way, have you any children?"

Horstacker was trembling with fury.

"I love Olivia with passion, with delirious love," he cried. "Do you understand now why I hate you, and desire your death?"

"And, *our* wife; does she approve of your ferocious wish?"

"Entirely."

"That does not astonish me," said the count. "But, come, I will give you another chance. If you do *not* kill me, which is very probable, and if I just give you a wound that you may prove to her that you have done your best, what will you do then? For my own part, I promise not to interfere with a couple so happy, and so well assorted."

"I swear, for my part," exclaimed Horstacker, "that if you refuse any longer to fight me, I will strike you in the face."

The count bowed.

"Many thanks for your frankness," he said, "I will endeavour, without any further delay, to send you to join your ancestors."

With these words he called upon Dr. Henzollern to present to his adversary one of the swords which he had brought on the ground with him.

The two combatants now placed themselves face to face.

Horstacker, more pale than a man going to execution, made desperate attacks on his foe.

But in vain.

The count maintained an imperturbable calmness.

Every now and then he launched forth terrible jokes.

But his eyes were always fixed upon his adversary.

The swords continued to flash for several minutes.

Then Horstacker made a pass far too low, and in an instant his foe took advantage of it.

His sword plunged completely through the chest of his foe.

Horstacker turned round and round in the air, and then flinging his arms up, fell prone on the ground on his face, vomiting blood.

The soldiers at once sprang forward to bear him away towards the inn, while the count resumed his coat, his wig, and his false beard.

"Is he dead?" asked Dr. Henzollern to the sergeant, as he saw him coming forth.

"No; but he does not seem to me to be much better."

"He must be bled at once," said the young gipsy, as he took from his pocket a small leathern case.

"Ah! I forgot you were a doctor. Come, quickly, Kamril."

Kamril at once followed him into the interior of the inn.

The count, who up to this time had taken no notice of the person who had been sitting during the duel quietly on the grass, turned sharply round, and made a movement of surprise, when he heard the gipsy declare that the wounded man must be immediately bled.

"Who is this Bohemian?" he asked, of Dr. Henzollern.

"What Bohemian?"

"The man in that peculiar dress."

"I know not," replied Dr. Henzollern; "but the sergeant yonder he seems to know him, since he spoke of him as a doctor."

"We had better mind what we are doing," whispered the count, drawing his hat over his brow; "this gipsy does not inspire me with confidence."

"Oh, the sergeant will see that we are posted with all that is doing," said the doctor," as he took his arm, and walked in the direction of the "Three Shepherds."

Arrived here, the Chief of the Poisoners ascended to the room where the wounded man had been taken, while the count remained below to give orders in regard to the horses which were in the stables.

The soldiers, meanwhile, gathered round the door, were discussing the brilliant sword thrust which had ended the combat.

After about ten minutes the sergeant came down into the public room.

"Well," asked the count, "has Horstacker recovered consciousness?"

"No; but he breathes well, and Kamril thinks that he will recover."

"So much the better," cried the count, "so much the better. I am sincerely glad to hear such good news of him. It would be a pity if Madame did not preserve one of her husbands."

As he spoke, he poured himself out an immense glass of wine, which he swallowed at one draught.

"Pardon, count," said the sergeant, "it is becoming late now. Have you any further orders?"

The count thought.

"No," he said, "I think not. Let your men go—after drinking my health. Ah! here comes my friend. We are going to walk, so Master Kenrich must send on the horses."

He then graciously shook hands with the sergeant, and linking his arm in that of Dr. Henzollern, sauntered away into the wood.

When they reached the clearing they halted.

"Now," said the count, as they sat down on a fallen tree in the dim moonlight, "we can talk."

CHAPTER XXV.

THE SECRET CONVERSATION—THE REAL FATE OF THE COUNTESS—THE PLOT—THE ADEPT—THE PRIVATE PASSWORD—THE SCHEME OF THE THREE COMPANIONS—THE AMBUSH—THE YOUNG GERMAN—THE TERRIBLE LOTTERY—THE CAPTURE.

BUT where, all this time, were the three companions, Rupert Dreadnought, Gascoigne, and Allan of the Glen? Not far distant.

During the combat and its exciting termination they had been unnoticed by those around them, and taking advantage of this they had slunk away in the darkness and taken up a position where they could lie hid among the brushwood and see without being seen.

Now, when Dr. Henzollern and the German count approached, they were just behind the speakers, and were enabled, therefore, to hear all that passed.

"What is this mystery with which you desire to make me familiar?" said the count.

"In the first place, why do you think your wife is dead?"

"I gave her in charge of some Spanish gipsies to carry to a convent."

"Well?"

"And on the road an attempt was made to rescue her."

"Yes."

"In that attempt I was told that a stray shot killed her."

"It *was* so."

"Yet this man says she lives, and that she is his wife."

"True; he says this to deceive you. Let me explain. When the gipsies, or bandits, whichever you please to call them, discovered they had lost a prize by her death, they took another woman to the convent and placed her in place of your wife. This other woman was the affianced bride of Horstacker, who was the leader of the band.

"She willed all her money to him and married him.

"He is here now to kill you that the money may be secure."

"Would that he *had* killed him," was the thought of those who listened.

They could see well that the villain had ordered her death.

The count laughed.

"He has missed his aim," he said, triumphantly.

"For the present he has," returned Dr. Henzollern; "but if you value your own life, he must be disposed of."

"True; I am not safe while such a man, with such a motive, is hovering near me. But tell me in regard to the matter of which I spoke to you."

"My memory fails me somewhat in regard to it," said Dr. Henzollern. "What is it you require?"

"I have lost one of my men. His mask was faulty in some particular, and he fell dead from the fumes of the poison," returned the count.

"You want another?"

"Aye; a trusty one. Can you tell me of such?"

"I can," said Doctor Henzollern. "On the second

night he shall be at the end of the little creek where the boat is."

"What shall his password be?"

"'NIGHT.'"

"And you will remember to tell him that not one word must pass his lips as he is being rowed over the lake."

"Yes; I shall not forget."

"And the terms."

"Yes; I know them. Now adieu. I have to go to Carlfad: and as the road is lonely, I will take advantage of the company of the soldiers."

The companions in crime then separated, and Dr. Henzollern hastened towards the inn.

He would have hastened all the more quickly had he known who was lying in wait for him.

We will not delay the progress of our story by narrating the events of the next two days, but hasten on to the point where the meeting was to take place between the new adept and the silent boatman.

It had been decided by lot between the three adventurers that one of them should take the place of the adept, and should run the risk of entering by stealth the precincts of the old castle.

The lot fell upon Rupert Dreadnought.

Their plan was very simple.

They were to lie in wait near the creek, and, as soon as they heard him approaching, the three were to seize him and gag him, while Rupert took his place, and went on into the jaws of the lion.

On arriving in the neighbourhood of the appointed spot, which they did some little time before the hour named, they found that the place was just the one to favour their design.

A long lane, as it were, ran between the trees, and led from the highway to the edge of the water.

Along this the adept would, of course, make his way, and the dense bushes on either side of it would enable them to remain safely concealed.

Behind a dense clump of brushwood, therefore, they placed themselves, and waited.

Presently the man came along, walking slowly.

Only the light of the moon was there to show them anything.

But this was enough to show them that the man was masked.

"Good!" thought Rupert: "this will answer well."

As soon as the man got in front of them they dashed forward.

He was so taken by surprise that he did not even cry out.

"Speak, and you are a dead man," said Rupert, in German.

The man saw that resistance would be worse than useless.

"I will not resist," he said. "But why is this attack?"

"I am going to take your place," replied Rupert. "Quick, give me your mask, and change clothes with me."

"You are going to certain death," said the young German, as he proceeded to undo his mask; "nevertheless, if you are resolved, it is nothing to do with me. But tell me, pray, what are your intentions as regards me?"

"You will personate me for a time," replied Rupert; "be treated in every way like a friend of these gentlemen. But if you attempt to escape you will die!"

"A pleasant arrangement," muttered the man: "but there's one comfort, you'll die in my place."

These words were certainly an enigma.

The man was talking of his death as a matter of course.

"What mean you?" asked Gascoigne; "you speak as if any one who entered the castle as you were to enter it *must* die."

The man's face was expressive of extreme emotion.

"I do mean it," he said; "but it was for my Gretchen's sake. During six months you are allowed to do as you please—send money to your friends, and hold a certain communication with those without; but," he added, with a visible shudder, "at the end of six months you die, and are no more heard of. The waters of yonder lake could tell strange stories if it chose."

"I see now how to work upon this man," thought Rupert.

"Friend," he said, "you knew, then, you were going to certain death?"

"I did."

"And your motive?"

"To save my mother and my beloved from ruin and starvation."

"I thought as much," said Rupert. "Now listen to me. You are an honest fellow, I believe. You know not for what you are going."

"I do not, except that it is some mysterious work."

"Good; then I will tell you. You were going there to manufacture deadly poisons, the very smell of which is death. Nay, start not, what I tell you is truth. Now, listen. Give me your mother's address and I will send her enough gold to keep her during the time that you are away. *I* shall not be long. Providence will watch over me and enable me to punish the guilty."

"Thank you, indeed, strange friend," replied the young man. "I will gladly give you my mother's address; and, believe me, you will never escape. Tell me, what is *your* motive?"

"Revenge!" said Rupert, solemnly; "the carrying out of a vow made at my father's death-bed."

"Then may Heaven aid you," said the young German, fervently.

They had now completed their exchange of clothing.

As fortune would have it, they were almost exactly the same height.

The mask which the workman was permitted to wear entirely concealed the features.

Even Rupert's friends would not have known him.

"You are going on a dangerous mission," said Gascoigne, earnestly.

"I know its danger."

Gascoigne pressed his hand.

"You did not know it in its entirety," he continued; "you are running a terrible risk. Remember those who await you in England; think of those who love you."

Rupert wrung his hand.

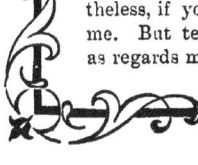

"Do not remind me of them," he said; "it might unnerve me, but never shake my resolution. We all know it to be a dangerous mission; we drew lots. I am the one chosen for the adventure, and I will not shirk my work. Now, then, listen to my last words. Take our German friend here to the inn with you, keep strict guard over him, and see that thirty guineas are sent to the address he will give you for the use of his mother and his betrothed. Now adieu, and may Heaven grant I may soon see you again."

He then shook hands with all, and walked boldly towards the lake.

"He is going to sure death!" murmured the German. "Once within these walls, only death will release him."

CHAPTER XXVI.

THE MYSTERIOUS CASTLE—THE SILENT GUIDE—THE FEAST—THE LABORATORY—THE STRANGE QUESTIONINGS—THE DEATH-LABOURS!

It would be difficult, indeed, to analyse the feelings of Rupert Dreadnought as he made his way with all speed towards the edge of the lake.

There was no doubt that he was advancing into the very teeth of a tremendous danger.

But he had accepted it willingly, and there was not in his heart the slightest sorrow or regret that he had done so.

Yet, as he advanced, thoughts *would* obtrude themselves.

Thoughts of home and of sweet Helen, his destined bride.

But he only felt, for her sake, the more nerved to exertion.

When he reached the little creek of which Dr. Henzollern had spoken, he found the boat already waiting for him, with a man sitting patiently in it.

The latter rose as Rupert Dreadnought advanced.

"The password," he said, in a slow, guttural tone.

"NIGHT," replied Rupert.

"Enter, then."

Rupert at once stepped in, and the silent rower began to row him over the silent lake.

In about ten minutes they reached the little door set deeply in the solid stonework.

Beneath the arch of this they halted, and the silent guide, leaving the boat, tapped three times distinctly on the door.

In an instant it was open.

A tall, mailed man in a black mask appeared.

"What is the password?" he demanded of Rupert.

"Night."

"Enter, then."

Rupert Dreadnought advanced boldly and passed in.

He found himself in a black, gloomy, stone corridor.

"A good beginning," thought he; "this place seems like the entrance of a tomb."

He dare not speak, however.

That had been one of his first injunctions.

So, when the tall, mailed man beckoned to him, he advanced up the broad staircase without a word.

They ascended some thirty steps, and then the guide said in a low tone—

"Remain here!"

The place where he was told to stop was a broad stone landing.

On one side was a recommencement of the stone staircase.

On the other was a heavy curtain, evidently concealing a doorway.

Pushing aside this curtain, the man passed behind it, a burst of silvery laughter breaking out as he did so.

This aroused naturally the curiosity of Rupert Dreadnought.

Chancing the danger, therefore, he pushed aside the curtains a few inches, and peeped in.

The sight he saw amazed him.

It was, indeed, a change from the gloom without.

Within, there was an immense apartment, brilliantly lighted.

Round it were couches and divans of the most luxurious kind, while in the centre was a table laden with choice fruits and wine.

On the walls hung paintings of the most voluptuous kind.

Reclining on couches drawn up to the well-laden table were the Count Hendringing and several ladies, the latter of whom were attired in the most daring undress, their eyes flashing and their cheeks burning from the effects of the sparkling wine.

"Ah!" thought Rupert Dreadnought, "this is a repetition of the terrible scenes enacted in London by the demons who constitute the League."

The women seemed annoyed at the entrance of the man.

But the count at once beckoned him to approach.

"What news? Has the adept arrived?" he asked, openly.

"He has. He now awaits orders from you, count," replied the man.

"Good; let him be taken to the small room next to my private laboratory, and let him there await my coming. I shall not be long."

The man bowed, and at once retired.

He was perfectly unmoved by such scenes as that before him.

He was too much accustomed to them to take notice of the flashing eyes, or the creamy shoulders of the syrens present, or the delicate fruits and delicious wines which perfumed the chamber.

He saw truly the bewitching picture there presented.

But he knew also the terrible skeleton beneath.

"Follow me," he said, as he rejoined Rupert, who had prudently retired from the vicinity of the door, and was leaning against the iron balustrade.

The masked guide now began the ascent of the second staircase.

It seemed truly as if this ascent would never be at an end.

Up, up, up they wound, the doors being many that they passed.

They were, in fact ascending to that little chamber where the light was always seen burning.

"Now," thought Rupert, "the secret will be revealed."

Given away with No. 16 of "Rupert Dreadnought."   "Boys of England" Edition.

THE NIGHT ESCAPE FROM THE OLD CASTLE. *See an early number.*

RUPERT; OR THE DREADNOUGHT SECRETS OF THE IRON CHEST

"DISGUISE IS USELESS," SAID GASCOIGNE. "I KNEW YOU AT ONCE!"

The windows of the other rooms—except diminutive casements, which looked like dots from without—were always closely shut with iron shutters when the lamps were lit.

The scenes within them were not such as men's eyes should look upon.

Up, up, up, until the air became cold, and then, pushing open a little door, the man ushered Rupert Dreadnought into a small chamber, in which burned a cheerful fire.

The man then opened a cupboard and brought out some wine and refreshment.

"Take your refreshment," said he. "The count will not be long."

Obeying his instructions to the letter, Rupert made no reply.

He merely bowed, and the guide, muttering something between his teeth, left him to himself.

There was now—at any rate, for the present—no fear of poison.

So, excited as he was by the astounding position in which he found himself, Rupert Dreadnought consumed some of the viands and drank some of the wine.

Then he glanced round him, and, observing a door, he rose to examine it.

Approaching it, he tried to push it open.

But it resisted all his efforts.

One thing, however, he could not fail to notice at once.

The atmosphere of the rest of the tower was cool, even chilly.

The very door (an iron door, by the way) of this inner room was warm.

There was no window of any kind to the chamber he was in.

The door, too, when he tried it, was firmly locked on the outside.

"If I am in a trap," said Rupert, "I am secure in it."

He had hardly any time left him to indulge in more reflections.

A heavy step was heard, the key turned in the lock, and the count entered.

He carefully closed the door behind him, and, without a word, advanced towards the entrance of the inner room.

Rupert's excitement was now wrought up to the highest pitch.

If he were recognised, instant death would, of course, be his portion.

More than this, if he were not recognised, he was about to be initiated in the mysteries of the strange castle—mysteries which, if told by him to others, might enable him to crush for ever, not only the manufacture of the deadly drugs, but annihilate also the terrible League that used them.

The count opened the door with a small key, and then turning waved Rupert to enter.

Rupert, without hesitation rose, from his seat and walked into the adjoining chamber.

It was a strange place, full of small tubes of glass and strange little phials and metal vessels.

Here and there were skeletons of animals, upon whom, no doubt, experiments of poison had been made, while interspersed with them were skulls of human beings of all ages and both sexes.

"Now, young man," said the count, as he sat down by the side of a small brick furnace, whose bright glow made the chamber to be so warm, "you have, I hope, kept to your instructions?"

"In what way?" asked Rupert.

"You have kept silence."

"I have—rigidly."

"That is good. Now, tell me, what is your name?"

This was an unexpected difficulty.

He had not learned the name of the young German whom he was now personating.

The count observed his hesitation, and said, immediately—

"Fear not; you need not tell me unless you please, though it can do no harm to do so."

"Well, then," returned Rupert, "I would rather not."

"You are not a German?" said the count, who, as a native, at once detected the difference of accent.

This was another difficulty, but Rupert soon surmounted it.

"Yes," he said, "I am; but I have been educated in England."

"Good," replied the other, "and now I will proceed to explain to you the terms under which you are here, and the work you have to perform."

Now was the critical moment.

The count spoke in low, solemn tones, as if what he had to tell was of unparalleled importance, and as if, moreover, he feared that there might even there in his *sanctum* be listeners.

"There is a drug," he said, "used in every part of the world expensive and difficult to make. Danger even attends its production, for while you are engaged in it you are compelled to wear a mask."

"So I have been told."

"Yes; the man in whose stead you come died through his own carelessness. It behoves all, therefore, to be careful. Well, I was going to observe that *my* establishment is the only one where this drug can be procured; consequently, as I alone possess the secret necessary to its manufacture, I am fast making a large fortune. I can afford, therefore, to pay those well who are faithful to me."

"Yes," thought Rupert Dreadnought, "and destroy them afterwards."

But he gave no vent to his thoughts.

He merely bowed in token of his belief in the count's kindness.

"Yes," continued the titled manufacturer of death drugs, "yes; now all I exact is this. You will do what you are bidden; you will preserve strict silence upon all matters; you will not talk to your companions."

"Stay," interrupted Rupert. "Do you mean that I am to be silent—absolutely silent for six months?"

"Nay, then; if you desire to speak, you can readily find opportunities," returned the count. "You can speak to me and to the head workman, but not to your confrères. That is forbidden."

"And at the end of six months?"

"You receive your liberty and a thousand crowns in gold."

"And death! Freedom truly," thought Rupert Dreadnought.

He only said, however—

"I have already, then, understood the terms, and I accept them willingly."

"Good," said the count. "Then you will take the oath?"

What this oath was it is unnecessary to state.

Suffice it that it was as terrible as any which bound the Poisoners together.

Rupert had not bargained for such a thing as this.

Oaths, as we have seen, he regarded as sacred: and this oath was one which bound him in no way to betray the secret of the Poisoners.

However, in his present position there was no help for it.

He took it, therefore, hoping that something would inevitably occur to enable him to evade it.

When the oath had been taken, the count held out his hand.

"You are one of us," he said.

Rupert seeing the action, pretended to be adjusting his mask, and the count, not suspecting or thinking it an immaterial matter, did not renew the offer but tinkled a small bell.

In a moment the armed attendant reappeared.

"Take the novice to his room," he said, "and to-morrow morning, let him be instructed in his duties!"

———

CHAPTER XXVII.

THE DUTIES OF THE NOVICE—THE SUBTERRANEAN WORKSHOPS—THE MYSTERIOUS OVERSEER—THE SECRET LETTER—THE OVERHEARD CONFERENCE—THE WARNING OF DANGER—ON THE WATCH.

HAVING bowed stiffly to the count, Rupert Dreadnought quitted the small laboratory, and followed the attendant down the steep staircase.

Half way down, not far, indeed, from the room where our hero had been an unseen witness of the voluptuous banquet, he halted and pressed a knob in the wall.

A door at once swung open, and Rupert being invited to pass through it, found himself in a small chamber, by no means uncomfortably furnished.

Here, without a word, the man left him, and the click of a spring, as the door closed, showed how completely he was isolated from the rest of the world.

It required good courage, as may be supposed, to act calmly under such circumstances.

But, young as he was, Rupert had had his nerves steeled by his many and perilous adventures, and instead of allowing his mind to dwell on the danger which surrounded him, he preferred to take his mind away from its contemplation by examining the details of his prison, as it might truly be called, a prison he had entered voluntarily.

As these details are most necessary to be understood by my readers, I will give them briefly.

It was, as I have said, a very small chamber.

In one corner was a bedstead fastened securely to the wall.

By this was a table similarly fixed, and a chair.

Round the wall were some pictures of various kinds, and in one corner was a set of shelves filled with books—mostly German books on medicine and philosophy—but some French works of a lighter nature.

The corner where the bedstead stood, it must be remembered, was that adjoining a small window, which was closely barred, and which, as Rupert soon found, overlooked the gloomy lake.

So far he took in the details that night, little dreaming how useful would ultimately be the knowledge.

Then, tired out, and convinced that, for the time at least, he was in safety, he threw himself, half-dressed upon the bed, and lapsed into slumber.

When he awoke the bright sun of morning was streaming in through the little window.

Rising, he glanced out of the diminutive casement, and beheld, plainly, the edge of the lake which he had crossed, the forest beyond, and the smoke rising from the little inn in its midst.

"I am near my friends," thought he, though not despondingly; "and yet—how far away."

About eight in the morning the grim attendant entered with breakfast.

"In half an hour you will be required," he said.

Then, without another word, he quitted the room.

Rupert had scarcely had time to do justice to the substantial meal set before him, when his chamber door again opened, and the man came in.

Without speaking, he beckoned Rupert to follow him; and they descended the steep staircase, passing the entrance hall, and making their way into subterranean depths.

Subterranean, though they were, however, there was a warmth and a glow about them which showed that fires were kept constantly alight.

When they had reached the bottom of the staircase the attendant threw open a doorway, which disclosed a curious scene.

In a large vault, extending under the principal part of the basement of the castle, and with a roof supported by huge stone pillars, numbers of men were working at innumerable small furnaces.

One furnace alone was untenanted.

This was the one destined for Rupert Dreadnought.

To this he was led by the attendant, and here he received his instructions.

These it is quite unnecessary for us to recapitulate here.

Suffice it to say that the details of the work were somewhat simple; that it was only necessary for safety's sake to keep on the mask, and that in his first experiment Rupert found that he could produce a liquid of exactly the same colour as the other without any poisonous effect except the appearance of a slight depression and languor.

Overlooking the establishment was a tall, bony man like a skeleton.

He was a negro.

His hands were as black as the mask which concealed his features, his voice was thick and guttural, his body hideous in his lankiness.

His bullet head projected forward at the end of a long, thin neck, and gave him the appearance of being always on the watch.

He never spoke.

Indeed no one spoke.

The work was carried on in total silence, save the roaring of the flames, and the chink of the vessels used, and now and then the faint humming of the refrain of some German air by the workers condemned to such unnatural quietude.

The day passed on quietly enough, and at length once more the night came round.

Then one by one the men were told off, and taken by the grim attendant to their respective rooms.

Rupert Dreadnought, as being the latest importation, was the last.

As he stood at the door of his chamber waiting for his turn to be admitted, peals of laughter were once more heard resounding from the room with the tapestried door.

It will be remembered that the banquet hall was near his bedroom.

Impelled once more by curiosity to brave danger, he approached and listened, peeping through the door as he did so.

The same voluptuous scene was being enacted, the only difference being that Dr. Henzollern was now one of the party.

"Do you think you can disguise yourself sufficiently to deceive so experienced a spy as Gascoigne?" asked the count.

"Gascoigne," thought Rupert; "they have then discovered our presence here."

"Yes," replied Dr. Henzollern, "I fancy I can

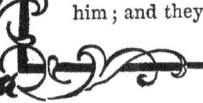

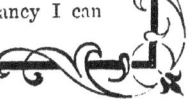

by the aid of a new dress, a new wig, and various minor details; at any rate I shall risk the trial in such a manner that I shall be able to make my escape should I be unfortunately discovered."

"Oh! that I could give Gascoigne notice of his coming," thought Rupert: "our prisoner would then be in our hands, and his punishment certain."

"Yes," continued Dr. Henzollern, when he had quaffed a glass of wine at the bidding of one of the sirens at his side, "yes. I shall then be able to discover whom he has with him, and tell you if my suspicions are correct. If they are it really matters very little."

The count laughed.

"As you say," he remarked, "it matters very little; for if he be a traitor he will never be able to carry away hence any information which will be useful to him. He will die!"

"They suspect me," murmured Rupert.

But he could hear no more.

The sound of feet approaching told him that the grim attendant was returning.

Once more, then, the door closed upon him, and he was in his voluntary prison.

He was about to dispose himself to sleep when something rattled against the window.

He approached and glanced out.

The water flowed beneath, and he knew, therefore, that no one could be there.

But still his friends without might wish to communicate with him.

So pushing open the little glass he waited, standing aside to allow the entrance of anything.

In a few moments something came whizzing into the room.

It was an arrow, and attached to it was a note.

Closing the casement, after first flinging the arrow into the lake, he opened the paper and read:—

"By this time you must, of course, be aware of the secrets connected with the old castle.

"It is not safe for you to remain too long.

"I fancy, from the manner in which men have been prowling about this inn, that both we here and you are suspected.

"Therefore, as soon as possible, begin to think of escape.

"In the corner of your room there is a fixed bedstead and a chair."

Rupert smiled.

"He knows the place well," said he, "although he has never entered it. Well, well, let me read on."

"You have abundance of time, and the fact of the bedstead being secured to the wall will prevent your masters from looking beneath them.

"Work here, therefore, and by degrees you will find that the old brickwork of the castle will yield to your efforts.

"You will thus be able to make a hole not only large enough to admit of your own departure, but the entrance of friends from without afterwards to seize upon the castle.

"I know from what Kamril, the gipsy, says, that you will be compelled to take a solemn oath not to betray the count.

"Your conscience surely will acquit you if you break such an oath as that.

"GASCOIGNE.

"N.B. The night before you intend to effect your escape place your lamp in the window for half an hour. Small as it is, we shall be enabled to see it. On the following night, at exactly the same hour, a boat will be beneath your room, and be ready to receive you."

"Well," said Rupert, when he had concluded and torn up into small pieces the letter, and burnt it carefully, "it is a mystery to me how they discovered this to be my room. At any rate, I shall take their advice. They evidently entertain suspicions as to my identity, and whether I am a foe or friend, I fear that treachery will be used against me. I may remain here, in any case, until the end of the six months, and then be murdered. This very night I will commence the trial of my escape."

CHAPTER XXVIII.

THE SCENE AT THE INN—THE ARRIVAL OF A STRANGER—AN UNEXPECTED RECOGNITION—THE PROPOSED DUEL.

DR. HENZOLLERN had expressed to Count Hendringing his resolve to visit the inn.

But the programme was altered.

News having reached the count that Hans Horstacker was recovered, he had a wish once more to see him.

Three efforts at disposing of him by stealth had failed.

So, leaving Dr. Henzollern in charge of the terrible manufactory, the count himself set forth for the "Three Shepherds."

At the inn there was a party of frolicsome roysterers, singing and laughing loudly.

Kamril was among the number, and Allan of the Glen and Gascoigne sat apart in a corner, looking on with some interest at the scene.

When the count entered, disguised in a manner similar to that which the Chief of the Poisoners had intended to use, there was some little stir among those present.

No one there seemed to recognise him; and when he had drank a tankard of ale, and sat himself down by the fire, as if to warm himself after a long journey, the merrymakers soon resumed their jollity, and began to sing and jest as loudly as before.

Presently, when he had succeeded in lulling all curiosity, he edged his chair towards that of Gascoigne.

The spy had apparently been taking no notice of him.

But in this he had been only acting a part.

He had in reality kept his eyes well on the alert.

"A cold and wintersome night," said he, as he neared Gascoigne, "and yet to hear these fellows no one would ever dream that they had long journeys to take in the cold."

"True," returned Gascoigne, "but they will have a good lining within."

Having thus initiated a conversation so as to take

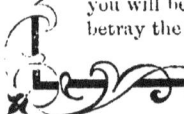

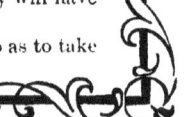

the notice of the company away from any future proceedings, the count suddenly bent forward.

"Sir," he said, "I would be glad of a word with you in private."

Gascoigne started in apparent surprise.

Yet it *was* only simulated.

He had guessed, when the count entered, that he had come on some peculiar mission.

"I have no objection—but you are an utter stranger," replied he.

"Not so great a stranger as you fancy—I know your name."

"What is it?"

"Gascoigne."

"And yours?"

"That I will tell presently. It is by deeds, not by name, you will know me!"

"Cannot we talk here?"

"No; it *must* be in private."

"Is it so very secret, then," persisted Gascoigne, whose eyes were meanwhile carefully scanning the speaker.

The count shrugged his shoulders.

"It matters not," he said, "if you have any fear of me—if you dread treachery, why we will say no more about the matter, and what I desire to say will remain unsaid."

THE BRIDGE OF FATE.

"No, I have no fear," said Gascoigne. "I will see that we have a private room to ourselves. Remain here awhile."

So saying he rose and spoke to the landlord, who at once quitted the public room.

In a few minutes after Gascoigne and the count were face to face with each other in the best apartment of the inn.

"It is an honour," said the count, bowing, "that one so humble as myself should be received by so distinguished a member of the detective service as Gascoigne."

Gascoigne quietly drew from his pocket a snuff-box and tapped it.

"Disguise is useless," he said. "I recognised you at once. You are the Count Hendringing!"

The count started back.

"Nay, then," he began.

Gascoigne interrupted him.

"Do not deny what I say," he cried, "for it only wastes time. Let us commence by understanding one another. I am Gascoigne and you are Count Hendringing. Now the question is, what do you want with me?"

This question was somewhat of a poser.

But the count was a man of ready wit.

"I will explain," he said, making a bold hit: "you are here with two friends."

"Their names?"

"Allan of the Glen and Rupert Dreadnought."

Gascoigne smiled.

"This guess is simply hazarded," he said. "You are wrong, however; Rupert is not here."

"Well, well," said the count, "that implies that Allan *is*. Now I know you as having been once one of the Great Society instituted in London to rid the world of pestilent money grubbers who grind down the poor."

He spoke thus of the Society of the Poisoners.

"Well," said Gascoigne, "I entered then to learn their secrets and betray them. In doing so I nearly lost my life, and would cheerfully do so again."

"You are a brave man; but I come to you upon this occasion for the very reason that you are *not* my friend."

"A strange reason."

"Not when I have explained all," returned the count. "Not long ago, a duel took place close by."

"I know it; I witnessed it."

"Good; now I wish to renew that fight."

"And what is that to me?"

"I wish *you* and your friends, if you have more than one with you, to be present as seconds to Hans Horstacker, my opponent."

"A strange proposition, truly," said Gascoigne. "And when, pray, is this duel to take place?"

"To-morrow night, if my foe will agree, at ten o'clock."

"Where?"

"At Linden Bridge; he will know it."

"And Kamril, the gipsy?"

"He may accompany you; you see you will be in numbers, and you need have no fear of foul play."

"I have no fear of that," said Gascoigne, a sudden thought occurring to him. "I will be there, if Kamril can take me to it."

"He can. Let Horstacker be at the place to-morrow night, and I will meet him fairly man to man."

"Agreed," said Gascoigne; "and may Heaven defend the right."

CHAPTER XXIX.

LINDEN BRIDGE—THE FATAL RENDEZVOUS—THE MEETING—PREPARATIONS AGAINST TREACHERY—THE DUEL—THE COUNT FINDS THAT THERE IS NO SUCH THING AS FATE AFTER ALL.

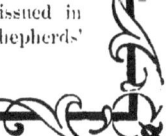

ON the following evening, ten people issued in couples from the door of the "Three Shepherds' Inn."

Among them were Gascoigne, Allan of the Glen, Kamril, and Hans Horstacker.

The others were strangers—strange-looking beings moreover.

They were no other than gipsies.

Not invited as may be surmised by the count, they came to guard against ambuscades.

The Linden Bridge, as Count Hendringing had named it, was a spot well known in the neighbourhood.

It was a plain bridge, built of stonework, to connect two roads, forming, in fact, a kind of viaduct over what had once been a stream.

The stream had now degenerated into an arid valley.

In the dry weather there was never a particle of water to be seen in it.

In winter the water from the hills sent a narrow rivulet through its centre.

But that was all.

The noble stream which tradition talked of, had long disappeared.

Strange rumours were connected with this bridge, and it was said that the lindens that gave to it its name would tell terrible stories of deeds of violence.

People who crossed it at midnight, were considered ever after to be unlucky.

People who made it a rendezvous were never afterwards seen.

To the Count Hendringing the place was, however, by no means a place of ill-omen.

He had fought twice beneath the its dark arch, and twice his adversary had bitten the dust.

To him the Bridge of Fate, as it was known to the peasantry, was a Bridge of good Fate.

Cheerily, therefore, he started from the castle with his friends.

Of these he had several.

Dr. Henzollern was not of the number.

As if fearing some evil, the count desired him to remain behind in his place, and took with him only the negro and some men whom he knew in the village near.

The soldiers, whose services he had secured on the occasion of the former duel, were not near, or he would have had them.

Hans Horstacker, who had gladly accepted the challenge, had not long to wait.

Along the road the forms of the count and *two* companions.

Both parties had hidden those whom they had brought to watch.

As soon as the count approached the bridge, he and his two friends swung themselves down by means of the lindens, and advanced towards the spot where Hans Horstacker and Kamril, Allan of the Glen, and Gascoigne stood.

"One moment, Hans Horstacker," cried the count, in a voice of suppressed rage; "one moment's speech with you ere we commence."

"With pleasure, count," returned Hans, with a decided sneer.

"Well, then, in the first place, you have lied to me."

"What mean you?"

"I mean that you stated—and acted your part so well that I believed you—that my wife had married again, and that *you* were her husband. You assumed a love for her and pretended that you desired my death that you might punish me for my behaviour to her. Now, my wife is dead; *your* wife is an impostor. My wife *was* slain in crossing the mountains, and you substituted in her place a gipsy girl. I know all, you see, but, lest your story *might* be too long, I come here to kill you, that I may make sure of the property, which is mine by right."

The gipsy kept calmly looking at him without a word or gesture as he spoke.

When he had concluded, he said—

"Well, since you know all, why should I deny anything? I am the leader of the gipsy band. Your wife *is* dead; my wife is *not* the one I represented her to be. But you are a thief and an impostor, an assassin and a villain, and I will kill you ere I leave this spot. Come, sir, my sword is trembling in my hand, more eager even than its master."

The count said no more.

He at once drew his sword, and in the bright moonlight they commenced the attack.

I have so recently described a duel that I will not occupy my space by describing this one.

Suffice it to say, that by a brilliant pass, Hendringing snapped his adversary's sword, and was about to run him through when he stumbled and fell forward, his sword also snapping off near the hilt.

Both antagonists were unarmed.

The count bowed.

"So far so good," he said. "Now we will take to our pistols."

A strange gleam shot from the eyes of Hans Horstacker at these words.

He took his stand with a firm and elastic tread.

There was no choice of places.

Both stood sidewise to the moonlight, so that neither had the advantage.

"Now, then," said Hans, "who will give the signal?"

"Let our English friend do so," said the count.

Gascoigne at once advanced.

"I will give the word, one, two, three," he said, "and then you will fire both together."

"Agreed," said both.

The space was measured duly, and all present waited anxiously.

Then rang out Gascoigne's voice clearly, distinctly in the night air—

"One!

"Two!

"Three!"

Then followed two rapid reports, and the smoke curled up blue towards the dark heavens.

Both antagonists stood for a moment firm.

Then the count threw up his hands and fell prostrate on his face.

They ran towards him, and cast the light of a lantern upon his face.

A round hole in his forehead told the tale.

He was dead, with a bullet through his skull.

Hans Horstacker was untouched!

The Bridge of Fate had proved the Doom of the Poisoner.

"A strange fatality," said Gascoigne, as they lifted him from the ground, and prepared to bear him away. "He seemed to have forced this death upon himself."

As he spoke, there was a hurrying of feet, and the men who had come out with the count hastened up to the spot where he was lying.

"Is the count dead?" cried the tall, gaunt negro in his guttural voice.

"Aye, dead enough," said one of Hendringing's friends; "let us bear him home."

So saying, he bowed shortly and stiffly to Gascoigne and his companions, and with the others began to bear the count towards the castle.

"This is a good beginning," said Allan of the Glen, as the bearers of the body disappeared along the dark road. "The master of the castle is dead, and Rupert, having discovered all he desires to know, will now have all the more opportunity of escape."

In a few minutes, as it were, after the echo of the fatal pistol shot had resounded among the hills, the Bridge of Fate was quiet as before, the blood had sunk into the oozy soil, and nothing was left to show where the deadly combat had taken place.

Leaving our friends here in Germany to fight out their adventures, we must return now for a time to London, and see how fared Helen Penraven with Rosalie St. Aubyn, and how Lord Milroy fared with those who had sworn to avenge the murder of the young earl.

CHAPTER XXX.

THE IMPRISONED MURDERER—THE PUNISHMENT—THE TERRIBLE ORDEAL—THE IMPLACABLE MOTHER—A JUST RETRIBUTION—LETITIA FINDS A TRUE FRIEND.

It was some time after the departure of Rupert Dreadnought for Germany that Rosalie St. Aubyn ventured to do anything active against her enemies.

Until she was quite satisfied that they had departed from the country, she feared to act.

She desired to have the punishment of her son's assassin entirely in her own hands.

But then again she wished not to commence a vengeance she could not finish.

A week passed before she went again to see the object of her hatred.

When she visited him, he was still in the same position.

His flesh was blue with the chill air of the vault.

The few days of confinement in so terrible a position had already had their effect, and the jaunty murderer who had entered the room of his victim's parent with such an air of self-possession now looked gaunt and famished.

"Well," said Lady Milroy, as she entered his cell, and stood near him, "do you *now* see how a mother can punish the assassin of her child?"

Lord Milroy uttered a groan.

"All mothers are not demons," he said.

"I *am*," returned Lady Milroy. "But you have not yet experienced all."

She then went to the door, and cried aloud—

"Radford."

In a moment a man appeared.

It was he to whom Lady Milroy had given the charge of Lord Milroy on the night when Allan of the Glen told his story.

"The hour of punishment has arrived," she said. "Let your men enter, and spare him not."

"His cries will alarm any stray passengers who may chance to be on the road," said the man, hesitating.

"Let him be well gagged, then," said the implacable countess, "and let him suffer in silence."

She then quitted the cell.

A few minutes after two men entered.

Tall, stalwart fellows, without a shadow of pity in their hard features.

"Now," said Radford, "we will commence our task—an ugly one, truly. A hundred and fifty lashes! He'll never stand it."

The wretched man uttered a cry of anguish and terror.

"A hundred and fifty lashes?" he cried. "You must be jesting with me—a horrible jest, indeed! It is murder, sheer murder."

"Those are our orders," said Radford.

"But I am rich; I will pay you all well," exclaimed the earl, frantically. "Set me free, and half my wealth shall be divided amongst you."

Radford shuddered.

"No," he said; "you may keep it. It is the price of blood!"

So saying, he advanced, and tried to tie around the prisoner's mouth a thick handkerchief.

But in vain.

The wretched man, rendered desperate by his position, moved his head and bit at him with his teeth so rapidly, that it was impossible.

"Come," cried Radford, addressing his companions, "this will never do. You must hold him."

Assisted by them, Radford soon succeeded in fastening the gag round the mouth of the doomed man.

Then one of them produced from his pocket a large whip, with several thongs.

"Now," said Radford, "commence."

A shudder ran through the frame of the victim.

Then the whip was raised, and with a whizz, it descended on his bare flesh.

Steadily, slowly, as he had been directed, the merciless agent of a just retribution plied his fearful weapon till the flesh grew blue and the blood trickled down his back.

And all this time, while he writhed and moaned with pain, the countess knelt upstairs before the portrait of her murdered son, and prayed that she might be deemed to be doing right.

At the fiftieth stroke the wretched man fainted.

"Desist," cried Radford. "I must speak to the countess. Give him some spirits while I hurry up to her."

She sprang to her feet as he knocked and entered.

"Well," she cried, "well! Is the punishment over?"

"No, madam."

"Then why are you here?"

"He has fainted."

"How many strokes has he received?"

"Fifty."

"And what did I order?"

"A hundred more."

"Then, when he has received them, come to me again; not before."

Radford gazed in surprise at the implacable woman.

He had known her before as all love and tenderness.

"But, madam, he will die," he ventured.

"If he dies, a just doom will be his," replied the countess. "Complete your work, or, if you are too faint-hearted, let your men do it for you."

Radford bowed, and slowly quitted the room.

"She is like a tigress whose cubs have been killed by a hunter," he murmured, as he descended once more to the prisoner's cell; "yet, after all perhaps, she is acting rightly."

When he was once more in the presence of Lord Milroy, he found him recovered from his faintness.

"Surely," said the victim, in a low voice, "my punishment is over."

"It is not," replied Radford. "My orders are peremptory—there are a hundred lashes yet to come."

"A hundred!" almost shouted the prisoner, "then my fate is sealed. Give me some more brandy."

They placed the bottle to his lips and he swallowed quite half a pint of the burning liquid.

Then he was again gagged, and the punishment commenced once more.

For a long time the brandy enabled him to bear up against the fearful pain.

Presently, however, his strength failed him entirely.

He hung helplessly from his manacled wrists, and the last few blows fell upon a helpless body.

Then they unbound him from the wall and tried to revive him.

But it was all in vain.

"He is dead," said Radford, in a solemn voice.

After placing the lifeless body upon the straw at the bottom of the vault and covering it over with some clothes, Radford proceeded to the room where he had left the countess.

"Well," she said, "how is it now?"

"The young earl is avenged," replied her domestic, solemnly, "Lord Milroy is dead!"

The countess, who had but schooled herself for this great trial, started at these words.

Her bosom heaved violently, and her features assumed a deadly pallor.

"Is it really so?" she murmured.

"Yes, indeed," replied the man, "he is dead; he died, I think, ere the last few strokes were given."

"Well, well, it is best so," she said, "my boy now is avenged and I shall be happy. Bring me some wine, Radford, and send Letitia to me."

Within a few minutes the young girl was by her side.

"You look pale and ill, dear lady," said the betrothed of the murdered youth, as she sat down near the one who would have been to her a mother. "What is the matter?"

"My boy—dear Francis is avenged," said Lady Milroy. "I have undergone a trial which you could not have borne. This night Lord Milroy has died!"

"How died he?" cried Letitia; "not by assassination?"

"No, no; he has died beneath the lash."

Briefly she recounted the manner and the result of his punishment.

The young girl shuddered at the recital.

To her younger and more tender mind the mode of execution seemed too terrible, even though the one for whose death he had suffered was her own lover.

"Oh, it is horrible!—most horrible!" she said.

"What!" cried the countess, indignantly; "what!—where has gone your love for my son? Did he not suffer, too? Did he not come, full of hope and joy, to England—trusting to meet me—trusting to enter upon a gay and happy existence—and did not this coward compass his death? Did he not, because he was too wretched a villain to do the deed himself, place into the hands of a vile poisoner the task of destroying my son? Oh! Letitia, was any punishment too great for him? Is any punishment too great for the other wretch whom he employed?"

Appealed to like this, Letitia soon found her scruples vanishing away.

"You are right, dear lady," she said; "and now, having found and punished one of the assassins, we must find and punish the other."

Lady Milroy pressed her to her heart.

"You are my daughter always," she said. "Had he lived it would have been so, and his wish shall be obeyed."

CHAPTER XXXI.

JEALOUSY OF ROSALIE ST. AUBYN—THE PLAN OF REVENGE—THE RUINED HOUSE—THE ENTRANCE BY THE ROOF—THE VISIT TO OSCAR PENRAVEN.

As I said in a former number, Rosalie St. Aubyn had conceived for Rupert Dreadnought an all-absorbing passion, to gratify which she would have sacrificed anything, and willingly committed murder.

When she saw Helen taking leave of her lover, and receiving from him those loving kisses she would fain have had imprinted on her own lips, she quitted the room noiselessly and quickly, her bosom swelling with ungovernable fury.

The man to whom she had almost confessed her passion, had evidently forgotten her existence.

All her charms, all her fascinations had been in vain.

He had forgotten her!

Such were her thoughts.

She forgot that he must know her as the poisoner—the associate of demons in human form—the head of the female section of the society which had for its object the decimation of the rich!

She was proceeding noiselessly along the corridor when she met with another surprise.

RUPERT DREADNOUGHT; OR, THE SECRETS OF THE IRON CHEST

"IN AN INSTANT THE SHARP POINT WAS BURIED IN HIS CHEST!"

Ere telling what this was, however, we must explain how it was that she obtained entrance into the house of Rupert Dreadnought.

I scarcely remember whether I have already told my readers that closely joined to the residence of the young Earl was a ruined building which had been the abode of a wealthy family, and was of the same height as that of the Dreadnoughts.

To any one, therefore, who was venturesome enough to scale the ruinous staircase, it was easy to pass from the roof of the one place on to the roof of the other.

Once there all difficulty was over.

A series of skylights served to light the upper rooms, and any of these could be easily lifted from without.

Rosalie knew no fear.

She had in her lifetime gone through many and varied adventures, and committed crimes which would have made many a man's hair stand on end.

She had no terror of the darkness, however, and where the men sent by Oscar Penraven to force an entrance into Rupert's house had failed even to think of trying, she at once began.

Under cover of night, she entered the black darkness of the old ruins, and groping about for the staircase began at once to ascend.

It was but a trial truly.

At any point they might stop, and her attempt would stop abruptly too.

But she had not reckoned without some reason.

She had twice or thrice observed from without, through the paneless casements, that a staircase did ascend to the summit of the roofless building.

The only chance of failure, therefore, lay in the doubt whether or not it was broken down in the middle.

However she found no such hindrance.

Protected as they were from the fierce onslaughts of the weather, they had remained solid throughout the whole ascent, and the daring woman who had resolved to penetrate the secrets of the one she loved with such passionate infatuation, soon found herself at the top.

Then she carefully passed to the roof of Rupert Dreadnought's house.

Here she had to act with caution, and without precipitation.

To open any window at random, would be to arouse the inmates and devote herself to certain destruction, for destruction it would certainly be to her to be discovered in such a situation.

She went from one skylight to the other, therefore, till she came to one which, so far as she could see by the moonlight which streamed in, belonged to an untenanted room.

This she gently raised and peered in.

No one was stirring.

A cold air seemed to fill the place.

Evidently it had not recently been used.

So far she had succeeded.

A feeling of triumph pervaded her breast.

"I shall succeed," she murmured. "Caution is all that is now necessary."

The door of the room was unopen.

In a moment, therefore, she was in the corridor.

Here she paused again to listen.

All was very still.

Rupert and Helen were even then preparing to take leave of each other.

So she passed down quickly.

What she saw in Rupert's room we have already seen.

We must now follow her to what I have named her second surprise.

Stepping lightly along the corridor, with the object of retracing her steps to the unoccupied room and there remaining until night and slumber had overtaken all, she came upon a half open door.

With a curiosity natural under the circumstances she glanced in.

Sitting before the mirror was a young girl engaged in her toilet.

Her bright hair hung in curls over her warm, white shoulders, rounded and lovely as those of a statue by a master of the art.

In the glass the face—a sweet face truly—was reflected.

Rosalie St. Aubyn knew at once those exquisite features.

They were those of Lesbia Howard.

Up to this moment Rosalie had been perfectly unconscious of the fact that Lesbia had sought refuge with Rupert Dreadnought.

She started now in wonder.

Her breast heaved with hate and fierce-consuming jealousy.

Rupert would protect and favour any one but her.

Oh, how her heart throbbed!

Oh, how she longed to be able to enter that room and stab her enemy to the heart!

But no, the time had not yet come for vengeance.

Pressing her hand over her trembling bosom, she hurried on once more, and gained the unused chamber.

Here, in the darkness and the cold, this woman, wretched through her own sin, sat on the bare floor and thought of the means of revenge.

Her heart was bursting now with intense fury.

She loving Rupert with a passion unequalled in its strength, was compelled to sit up in a cold room —hiding away in the darkness—while the man she could have sold her soul for was embracing tenderly another woman!

The thought was maddening to her ill-regulated mind.

She forgot that she had no right to be even where she was.

Traitress that she was, she soon conceived a plan by which to further her plans.

She had heard from Rupert's own mouth that he was about to leave England.

Now, therefore, was the opportunity to gratify her desires.

While Rupert was absent she would seek the advice and aid of Oscar Penraven.

He was now the chief—the deputed chief—of the Society.

He had the power, therefore, as well as the will, to aid her in her schemes of diabolical revenge.

Her plans were soon formed.

She would inform Oscar Penraven of the method by which he could enter unperceived the residence of his greatest enemy.

But this would be only on one condition.

He must not delay, in his first visit, to seek for the IRON CHEST, or any treasures of that kind; HE must carry off Helen Penraven, who, by a forced marriage, was his wife.

This marriage once consummated, she imagined —poor, infatuated fool—that she herself would have a better chance of obtaining the one she wanted.

This plan having been decided on, she quitted the

disused chamber, and, descending as she had ascended, made the best of her way towards the retreat where the Poisoners had located themselves.

It was night when she arrived there ; but, having given the password to the man at the gate, she had no difficulty in obtaining the address of Oscar Penraven.

Thither, in spite of the late hour, she at once repaired, and, having sent up her name, and a private password, she was at once admitted to his presence, though he had to rise and dress himself to receive her.

He advanced gallantly towards her, and drawing her to a seat, sat down beside her, and would have kissed her.

"It is long since we met, my beauty," he said ; "why are you here ?"

She drew herself gently from his embrace.

"Enough, Oscar," she said ; "the time of such follies is over between us ; I know whom you love, and come hither to speak of her to you."

"Helen Penraven ?"

"Yes ; see how glibly the name flashes to your lips," said Rosalie, laughing, "but fear not, I am by no means jealous. You will so acknowledge when you know that I am about to place in your power the woman you are seeking."

Oscar Penraven's eyes brightened.

"You are ?" he cried.

"I am," said Rosalie St. Aubyn, "but I make my conditions."

"And those are—"

"Very simple ; but they must be adhered to."

"Name them then," cried Oscar Penraven, impatiently.

"I can, to-morrow night, show you the way by which you can enter the house of Rupert Dreadnought," replied Rosalie. "This, I know, to be your dearest wish."

"It is. Is he there ?"

"No ; but it matters not, his secrets are there. Helen Penraven is there ; and one whom you desire to punish, Lesbia Howard. Now the terms I exact are very easy. I wish you first of all to carry off Helen Penraven, and then return to make any discoveries which you may desire."

This was a matter of wonder to Oscar Penraven.

Not knowing the state of Rosalie's feelings towards Rupert, it was, of course, difficult to understand her anxiety that he should carry off Helen.

But it mattered not to him.

He cared not to pause and enquire motives.

All he saw was the possibility of achieving at once what he had so long desired, and he at once leaped to a determination.

"To-morrow night," he said. "I will be there."

"And you will act as I wish ?" asked Rosalie, again.

"I will."

"In every way ?"

"In every way. Now tell me, how am I to enter ?"

"Next door to the house of Rupert is a ruined tenement. Within this you will find a staircase, leading to the summit of the house. From this summit you can reach the roof of Rupert Dreadnought's mansion."

"And when there ?"

"You and your men must crawl carefully to the third skylight."

Oscar Penraven laughed.

"Which, if it be shut stops at once our whole enterprise."

A cloud passed over Rosalie St. Aubyn's face at these words.

"You interrupt me," she said, "before you understand me. I shall be there to admit you, but you must not then halt to do anything save secure Helen Penraven. You must seize her at once and fly. Be there at eleven o'clock, and she will be fast asleep in bed. Were I near her, I would see she slept more soundly. At any rate, when you have secured her, I will let you in again, and you can then seize all in the house, especially Lesbia Howard, to whom we both owe a grudge ; and we can open, and destroy, too, the Iron Chest."

"Good," said Oscar Penraven ; "we are agreed, then ?"

"To-morrow night at eleven."

"Yes ; we will be there to the minute. And now, since our business is over, can I offer you refreshment and rest for the night ?"

"No," said Rosalie ; "I shall hasten home. My breast is full of strange and conflicting emotions, and I would be alone."

She rose as she spoke, and avoiding the embrace which the young reprobate seemed to offer her as a matter of course, opened the door for herself, saying, as she stood in the entry,

"Remember the time and my terms."

Then she glided away.

"A most lovely and most extraordinary woman," muttered Oscar Penraven, as she disappeared. "Were not my heart so full of Helen, I think that Rosalie St. Aubyn could queen over me entirely."

"A silly fool, in spite of all his roguery," thought Rosalie, as she quitted his house. "I will let him have the girl he so much prizes, and then—well, we shall see how he will appreciate my plan."

CHAPTER XXXII.

A TEMPESTUOUS NIGHT—THE RUINED BUILDING—THE OPEN SKYLIGHTS—THE DELUSION OF PASSION—THE SLEEPING BEAUTIES—THE DRUG—THE ABDUCTION—THE ARRIVAL OF OSCAR AND THE POISONERS—HELEN IS CARRIED OFF—ROSALIE PREPARES TO ACT A NEW CHARACTER.

THE next evening set in very dark and very tempestuous.

It was just the kind of night which favoured a design such as that contemplated by Rosalie and Oscar Penraven.

The darkness would cover their movements completely.

The noise of the gale would drown the sounds of their actions.

About ten o'clock, Rosalie St. Aubyn glided up the unfrequented street, and made her way into the building, which was now enveloped in almost total darkness.

It was, indeed, so dark, that no one unaccustomed to the place could have succeeded in making way at all.

Having once ascended the staircase, however, she knew well its bearings, and experienced no difficulty in making her way up it, and proceeding to the empty room which she had found before so invitingly open.

She found it just as easy of access on the present occasion.

Lifting up the skylight cautiously, she fixed it so that no one could enter without her aid.

Being herself a traitor, she suspected all others to be so.

She had no wish that Oscar Penraven should enter without her aid.

He might take it into his head to make her also a prisoner, and act as he pleased in the house.

Having fastened the casement, therefore, she cautiously opened the door, as she had done on the preceding night, and listened.

Everything in the mansion was more still than it had been before.

Rupert and Allan of the Glen had now departed, and the women had evidently retired to bed.

"Good," thought Rosalie St. Aubyn, while her bosom heaved with intense emotion; "in a few moments Oscar Penraven will be in possession of the one he loves; she will be beyond the power of Rupert Dreadnought, and then, when he has no one whose affections are fixed upon him, *I* may be able to soften his heart."

Deluded girl!

Loving passionately as she did, she ought to have known by her own feelings how difficult it is to shake off the memory of one who has so filled the soul.

Slipping down, she gently opened the door of the room in which she had seen Lesbia Howard on the preceding night.

Glancing in, she saw by the light of the lamp which burned on the table that the two girls were sleeping in one bed, their gleaming arms wound round each other's necks, their soft breasts throbbing one against the other.

"This is awkward," murmured Rosalie; "but I will see that my plan is not marred. Ah! Helen sleeps on this side of the bed; she can be removed without waking her companion."

Gently approaching the bed, she knelt down, and softly, carefully unwound the arms of the sleeping girls, who, buried in the deep slumber of innocence, were not easily disturbed.

Rosalie did not unnecessarily hurry herself.

She had nearly an hour before her, and she recognised the danger of undue haste.

So, having taken Helen's hands from around Lesbia's neck, she drew from her bosom a handkerchief, and pressed it for an instant to the face of the sleeping girl.

Then she turned down the lamp till the room was nearly dark.

Thus she could handle Helen as she liked, without fear of wakening her, for the handkerchief contained a subtle essence, which had rendered her for the time unconscious.

She then cautiously began to draw her from the bed.

Lesbia Howard once or twice moved uneasily.

But each time Rosalie St. Aubyn stopped, and threw her own arm round her, and the sleeping girl was quieted again.

At length she had drawn the insensible girl entirely from the couch, and covered Lesbia warmly up.

Then she took the body of her enemy in her arms, and turning the lamp up, saw where her clothes were placed.

These she seized with a kind of triumphant leer, and hurried up the stairs to the disused chamber.

Arrived here, she locked herself in, and drawing a lantern from her pocket, she proceeded to dress the unconscious girl.

The robing was just completed, when a slight noise heard above the raging of the wind warned her of the approach of Oscar Penraven and his men.

She sat Helen up in a corner and at once opened the window or skylight.

The next moment Oscar Penraven's face appeared.

"Are you there, Rosalie?" he said.

"I am, and some one is with me," she answered.

"Some one with you! Whom do you mean?" he cried.

"Helen Penraven."

"You are jesting."

"I am not. I have occupied my last hour in bringing her from her chamber here, and yonder she sits ready for you to take away."

"She is then, I presume, unconscious," said Oscar.

"She is, but will not continue so much longer," said Rosalie, "and I would advise you, therefore, to hasten her departure."

Oscar Penraven dropped into the room, but remained for some little time silent.

The truth was that he had expected to be able to act far differently.

Rosalie was right.

He had intended treachery.

But he was here utterly defeated.

"Well, well," thought he, "I must make the best of it."

Then he advanced to the skylight and said in a low voice—

"Here, Henry and Roger."

In a moment two faces appeared at the window.

"Be ready," he said, "and I will hand you up a lady. She is quite insensible, and must be taken great care of."

Then approaching Helen, he stooped down, raised her up, imprinted a kiss upon her lips, and then, returning to the opening, held her up for the men to receive in their arms.

"Now," he said, turning to Rosalie St. Aubyn, "it will take me quite two hours to bear her away to a place of safety. Will you remain here, and await my return?"

"Most assuredly I will," she said. "Be quite easy on that score."

It was nearly dark, and he could not, therefore, see her face.

Had he been able to do so, he would have never left her side.

It was pale—deadly—ghastly pale, and over it flitted an expression of demoniacal triumph.

It was difficult to say truly why she should have been so triumphant, but that she was there could be no doubt—triumphant about something or another.

"Very well," said Oscar Penraven. "I will go at once. Be on the alert, and I shall return the same way I came."

Then he swung himself up through the sky-light.

As he did so, Rosalie closed it, and bolted it firmly.

"If you do return the same way that you came," she murmured, as she prepared once more to descend the stairs, "Rosalie St. Aubyn must have less wit in her than of old."

What she meant by these words we have yet to see.

At present we must follow the footsteps of Oscar Penraven and his crew, and see how Helen Penraven fared in their hands.

THE DEATH MILL.

CHAPTER XXXIII.

THE OLD SERVANT ON THE WATCH—THE UNEXPECTED PURSUIT—THE OLD MILL—THE SOLITARY CUSTODIAN — THE LONELY CHAMBER — THE KNOCKING AT THE DOOR—THE THREAT OF DEATH—A NEW WEAPON OF DEFENCE—THE ATTACK — A FRIEND TO THE RESCUE — THE ESCAPE FROM A GREAT PERIL.

In safety Oscar Penraven and his followers conveyed Helen down the dark and rickety staircase, and reached the street, at the corner of which a carriage was in waiting.

Apparently unobserved they made their way out of the ruined building into the quiet thoroughfare.

Apparently only.

Just as the first of the party emerged from the long-disused doorway a man, who had been walking slowly along in the shadow opposite, glided into a doorway and watched.

This was none other than old Robert, one of the most trusted retainers of the Dreadnoughts, the only one who, by his absence, had escaped the massacre of the servants.

It seemed strange to him to see persons issuing forth from a place which he knew had been long disused, and when he saw two of them come out bearing the inanimate form of a lady, he at once saw that something wrong was on foot.

Full of the courage which had been his peculiar characteristic as a youth, he resolved at once on the course to adopt.

He would follow in their track.

He waited accordingly till all had gone forth, and then made his way along the wall until the group of men halted at the corner where the coach was stopping.

Here Oscar Penraven took Helen in his arms and carried her in.

"See yonder tavern?" he said. "You can wait till I return. Where *I* am going there is no danger to *me*."

Having given them money, therefore, he made the necessary arrangements with the driver, and the coach drove off.

The old domestic glided quietly along by the side of the wall, and as soon as the men had departed he ran lightly after the coach, and swung himself on behind.

There was a large back-board to it, and he was enabled, therefore, comfortably to seat himself.

In a few minutes he was rolling away from London; for the coach, upon leaving the corner, was at once driven towards Essex.

Knowing the antipathy which existed between Rupert Dreadnought and Oscar Penraven, it at once occurred to the old man that this abduction of a lady was in some way connected with the Poisoners' Society.

If, therefore, the lady was being hurried away to their retreat, it was in vain to dream of saving her.

In their hands she would be far beyond the reach of the help of one man—and that a man enfeebled with age as he was.

However, he had a hope still that such would not prove to be the case, and resolved not to abandon the victim (for so he considered her to be) until the last, he clung on as the coach rattled along the dark roads.

At length it came to a dead stop in a dark, gloomy spot.

A murderous cut-throat spot it truly was.

A ruined mill threw its distorted shadow across the road.

This mill, like the Bridge of Fate where the count had fought his last duel, had an evil memory.

It had been first the property of a man who had married a young and lovely wife, and appeared to worship her.

Miller as he was, and with a large connection, he had money truly, but he had not the gentle blood which flowed in the veins of his wife, and he often insulted and jeered at her for her "aristocratic breeding."

People heard not these jeers, and imagined that he was a perfect slave to her in every way.

They were mistaken, for he was a perfect brute.

Suddenly, without any warning or expectation of it, a rich relation of the wife's died, and left her a large fortune.

From this moment his manner towards her changed.

He was the most devoted of husbands, and when, after two years, she died, he was the most pale and tearful of mourners.

But suspicions arose.

Her relations would not allow them to rest, and an examination after death disclosed the dreadful fact that the poor creature had been poisoned.

The wretched murderer fled the country, and was never found again.

The wealth passed back to the family of the wife, and the mill was sold.

Again and again it was sold and resold.

Each time to a master of evil disposition.

Murder had again been done, and when the last owner destroyed one of his children by throwing it in drunken fury into the mill-stream, the country people would suffer it no longer.

Assembling in large crowds, they went in a body to the mill, and, without warning, tore the place to pieces.

The wretch escaped, but the mill was never rebuilt.

And now when the time arrived of which I am speaking, the great wheel lay on almost dry land—the blackened walls stood tottering against the sky, and the weeds and the undergrowth choked up what once had been sleeping apartments, and the chambers where lovers had sat and whispered, and children had played and prattled.

One part, however, of the old tenement was habitable—the left wing of the building where one bedroom and one sitting-room had, by means of patching up, been made sufficiently tenable to be lived in by a grim old fellow who paid no rent, but had slunk in no one knew how, and kept it no one knew why.

It was to this man's charge that Oscar Penraven intended to entrust the one to whom he had been united in a forced marriage.

Arriving here, then, as I have said, he knocked at the door, and a roughly-bearded, bronzed complexioned man answered the summons.

"Ah!" he said, when his eyes fell upon Oscar Penraven, "you have then arrived!"

"Yes; and I have the lady with me," said Oscar, "have you the room ready for her?"

"Yes."

"And you are here alone?"

"I am."

"Good; well, I must leave her in your charge entirely till the morning; I have more work to do. Open wide the door, I will bring her in."

Taking the form of the insensible girl tenderly in his arms, Oscar Penraven then passed through the door.

As he did so the light of the lamp fell upon Helen's face.

The old domestic, as he watched, could scarcely repress a cry.

He recognised the face at once as that of his master's betrothed.

"Thank Heaven, I watched them," thought he; "and this man is alone. In such a cause as this, I feel the strength of youth returning to me. I will save her or die."

Then, as he spoke, he crept away under the hedge and waited.

In a very few moments Oscar Penraven again emerged.

"Back whence you came," he said, to the driver, and in a few moments the coach was being driven at a rapid pace towards London once more.

The old domestic waited for more than a quarter of an hour before he commenced operations.

By this time everything was very still in and around the mill.

Rising from his concealment, he commenced a tour of the building.

The first blush of the dawn was now just appearing in the east, as he began his proceedings, and he was enabled, therefore, to see all the details of the place.

He soon found the most vulnerable point.

Of course Oscar Penraven had not chosen the spot because of its strength.

He had only taken it as a place of concealment because he expected no one to follow him, and because, moreover, no one would be likely to suspect her being there.

He reasoned rightly.

If the old domestic had not chanced to see them, her place of confinement would never have been dreamed of.

The vulnerable point of which I speak was at the rear of the building.

There was here an old iron-bound door, half off its hinges, but secured by planks and bolts.

Above it was a small casement large enough to admit the entrance of a man's body.

It was here that old Robert halted at once.

He saw in it a good chance of making good an entrance.

He rapped loudly and imperatively at the door.

For some time the summons was entirely disregarded.

But, as he kept knocking louder and louder, the keeper of the ruins put his head out of window.

"Who is there?" he cried, angrily.

"A friend of the lady whom you have within there," replied old Robert.

The rough-bearded custodian was somewhat taken aback.

But, growling something, he moved away.

The retainer guessed in an instant his intention.

"He has retired to find some weapon," thought he, "and I am defenceless."

As he spoke, his eyes fell upon a long, strong-handled pitchfork, with large, sharp-pointed ends.

"Good," thought he, "that will do."

He had scarcely seized it when the man reappeared.

This time he held a large pistol in his hand.

"Now," cried he, "quit this place or die."

The murderous look in his eyes was sufficient to show old Robert that from him neither he nor Helen could expect mercy.

The man left him no time to think.

In an instant the pistol was levelled at his head.

But old Robert was as quick as he.

In a moment the sharply-pronged fork was raised, and just as the fierce custodian of the mill fired, the iron points were plunged into his chest.

The astonished and terribly-wounded man uttered a cry of horror and pain, and fell back.

"Now is my time," thought the retainer.

But how to enter ?

That was the question.

One easily decided, however, as it seemed.

Driving the wooden end of the pitchfork into the ground, he leaned the pronged part against the wall.

Into this he fixed his feet, and by raising himself upon it, he was enabled to reach with his hands the sill of the window.

Then by a strong effort, he drew himself up, and in a few moments he had entered the room.

A lamp was burning here on a table, and by its light he saw that the man who had so rashly attempted his life, had paid the penalty.

He was dying fast.

Blood was flowing rapidly from a double and deep wound in his chest, and the breath was coming thickly and in gasps.

He opened his fast glazing eyes as old Robert leaned over him.

Then a scowl of hate overspread his features.

"You've done for me," he said. "Oscar Penraven will avenge me."

"You have brought it upon yourself," returned old Robert, "you would have taken *my* life in a bad cause—I have taken yours in a good. I come to save the honour of a lady ; where is she ?"

What the wretched man would have said I cannot say.

He rolled his eyes wildly.

A gurgling sound escaped his quivering lips.

Then his limbs moved convulsively, and all was over.

The last occupant of the Death Mill had gone to his account.

"Well, well," said the old servant, as he took up the lamp, "these are terrible times, very terrible times. It is the first man's death that lies at my door ; but Heaven will forgive me for this, for it was in a good cause."

Passing from the room, he felt his way very carefully.

He had seen enough of the old mill to know it to be unsafe.

He had not very far to go, however.

What was still habitable of the old place was very small, indeed, and in a very few moments he reached the door of a chamber, and glanced in.

Lying in there on a bed was Helen Penraven, and, what brought joy to his heart, she was beginning to awaken.

He rushed in just as the poor girl glanced round her, as one mad, pressed her hand to her brow.

Her last waking memory was the kiss she had imprinted on Lesbia's lips, and the pressure of her arms round her soft form, ere lapsing into peaceful slumber.

And now !

She woke to find herself in a dingy room, in a strange place—alone.

"Oh, just Heaven, where am I ?" she murmured, faintly.

Then her glance fell upon the well-known face of old Robert.

"Oh, Robert," she cried, "where am I ? To what part of this old place have I wandered ?"

Briefly, as far as he knew, the old domestic told the story of her abduction.

Helen Penraven listened in utter bewilderment.

It seemed almost beyond the range of possibility that such a deed could have been done so utterly without her knowledge.

The old servant, too, could not tell her all.

He could only date his story from the moment when he saw the men issuing forth from the ruined house which adjoined that of Rupert Dreadnought.

All that happened within the house of the latter was a mystery.

"Well, this is, indeed strange," murmured the young girl, when old Robert had completed his story. "How did they bring me from the house ? I retired to rest with Lesbia Howard ; I fell asleep, locked in her arms. How could I have been taken from my bed and dressed, unless—unless, indeed—but no ; Lesbia would never betray me !"

"I am sure she would not," replied the old man ; "but come, let us leave this place. Who knows how soon Oscar Penraven may return !"

"You are sure it was he who brought me hither ?" asked Helen.

"Certain ; he was pointed out to me once, and his is a face I should never forget."

"And whither shall I go ?" asked Helen Penraven.

"Well," mused old Robert, "it will not do to return at present to the house of Rupert Dreadnought, for we know not what has been going on there. You can remain one night at the house of my daughter, whither I will take you, and you can then return as soon as the place is once more secure. Come now, let us hasten."

In a few minutes they were out on the high road, making their way, with all possible speed, towards the nearest inn, where they hoped to obtain a conveyance.

Ill and weary as she was, Helen Penraven felt a lightness of heart as she once more stepped along the road when she thought of the danger she had run—alone in the power of a man who claimed to be her husband.

CHAPTER XXXIV.

OSCAR PENRAVEN RECEIVES AN UNEXPECTED CHECK—ROSALIE IN A NEW CHARACTER—THE MASKED LADY WARNS THE HOUSEHOLD—THE ATTACK AND FLIGHT OF THE POISONERS—RETURN OF HELEN—DESPAIR OF ROSALIE.

OSCAR PENRAVEN secure now of his prize, hurried back eagerly towards the house of his enemy.

His heart was full of malicious joy.

His enemy was away from London.

Helen Penraven was in his power.

What more could he desire?

He could enter Rupert's house, secure the Iron Chest, or, at least, all it contained, and then return to Helen and joy!

Such were the thoughts that animated him as he hastened back towards London.

Every moment seemed an age, and when he reached the corner of the street, he leaped out of the coach with an eagerness which nearly upset him.

Paying the man an exorbitant fare, he dismissed him, and then hastening to the inn where he had told his men to await him, he roused them from their carousing and bade them follow him.

This time no one was observing them.

The street was quite deserted.

All was as still as death.

Hastening into the ruined house, he eagerly ascended the stairs, and made his way over the roof towards the skylight.

This reached, his trembling hands attempted to raise it.

But in vain.

It was closely fastened within.

His heart failed him.

What could it mean?

"Give me a lantern, Forrest," he said to one of his men.

The man obeyed, and Oscar cast the light into the room.

Within there he could see several forms—the forms of armed men.

"What can this be?" he said. "Stand to your arms, my men: we are betrayed."

To explain properly how it was that Oscar Penraven received so unexpected a check, we must follow the movements of Rosalie St. Aubyn.

As soon as she had, as I have before described, closed the skylight firmly, she took from her pocket a mask, and placing it over her face, descended the stairs.

Then she made her way into the bed-chamber of Lesbia Howard.

Approaching the bed, she placed her hand upon the shoulder of the young girl, and gently shook her.

After a few moments, the young girl slowly opened her eyes.

On seeing the masked woman, however, she at once sprang up.

"Who are you?" she cried, "and what are you doing here?"

"I am come to save you. Quick; rise and dress yourself," replied Rosalie.

Then it was that Lesbia missed Helen.

"Where is Helen—where is my friend?" she cried; "tell me—tell me where is she."

"I know nothing of any friend," said Rosalie; "perhaps your enemies have been here before me. At any rate, take my warning ere it be too late. Dress yourself, rouse the house, and let the domestics be ready to defend it, or Oscar Penraven and his crew will be its masters ere two hours are over your head."

Lesbia at once sprang from the bed and commenced dressing.

To do as she was desired might do good, and certainly could do no harm.

"Tell me," she cried, as she proceeded with her toilet, "tell me, who are you?"

Rosalie St. Aubyn shook her head.

"No," she said, "I cannot disclose *that*. I am here to save you. If you will not accept my assistance without knowing my motives I will retire; but, for the sake of Rupert Dreadnought, I will save his house from thieves."

Lesbia stayed her as she was about to quit the room.

"No, no," she said. "You perhaps misunderstand me. I am weary and alarmed too, and I know scarcely what I am saying. I am thinking of my friend."

"Who is she?"

"Helen Penraven, the betrothed wife of Rupert Dreadnought, the master of this house."

"Indeed. Why should you think she is gone? She may for some reason have risen. It will be best to search the house before you give up all hope. And now that you are dressed, shall I rouse the house?"

"Yes—ring yonder bell."

Rosalie at once did as she was desired, and a loud clangour rang through the old house.

Within five minutes the servants hurried down, dressed and armed.

Rupert had so ordered it.

The slightest alarm was to be a signal for a general preparation for defence.

A few words from Lesbia explained all.

Then, led by Rosalie, who carefully prevented not only her face, but the details of her form to be seen, they ascended to the upper rooms.

Here they carefully locked and secured the skylights, and, in the disused chamber, they awaited the arrival of Oscar Penraven and his band.

It may seem strange to my readers that Rosalie St. Aubyn should have assumed such a position as this.

It is easily explained.

She had disposed of her rival.

So far she would injure Rupert—no farther.

She would now assume the position of his friend and protector, and thus, as she imagined, win her way to his heart.

In this sweet delusion the treacherous woman waited eagerly for the arrival of Oscar Penraven.

Presently they heard the stealthy approach of men.

"They come," she said, pressing her hand over her bosom; "now, then, disperse. Some of you remain here, and others enter the next room, and if it comes to a conflict fire from the other skylight at them. Quick!"

Obeying the orders of the masked woman who had thus suddenly taken possession, as it were, of the place, the retainers divided into two bodies, and had opened the second skylight, and were ready for action, when Oscar Penraven and the men arrived.

Finding the place closed, Oscar, as I have said, cried loudly—

"Stand to your arms! We are betrayed!"

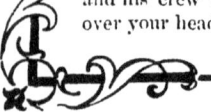

RUPERT DREADNOUGHT
OR THE SECRETS OF THE IRON CHEST

"WHAT MEANS THIS!" CRIED THE HOST. "MURDER IN MY HOUSE!"

Oscar then leaned down, with his face close to the glass, crying—

"Rosalie, what means this? Where are you?"

"I am here," said she, hurrying through the wondering servants. "What would you with me?"

"An entrance, as you promised," returned Oscar Penraven.

A scornful laugh was the only answer.

"I shall force an entrance, then," said Oscar, savagely.

"Do so," said Rosalie, "and you will find all here

well prepared for attack. You have the bride you so much coveted. What more do you want? Go to her, but here you shall not enter. I will defend the home of Rupert Dreadnought even at the peril of my own life."

These words, while they astounded, served also to exasperate Oscar.

"By heavens!" he cried, "you shall rue this hour!"

Then, turning to his men—

"Now," he said "let us enter. There are but a few menials to bar our passage, and within there is wealth and treasure."

The men, who were flushed with the drink they had imbibed at the inn, at once prepared to do his bidding.

But hardly had the first blow broken the glass of the skylight, than a shot laid the bold intruder low, while from behind several bullets rattled forth from the casement of the other room.

Oscar Penraven saw at once that, for the time, all further attacks upon the place were useless.

"We must retire, my men," he said, "we are in a nest of traitors here. Beware, Rosalie St. Aubyn!" in a loud voice. "You will rue this hour. By my voice you shall be denounced to the Society."

But his words gave no terror to her breast.

She had conquered.

She had saved for Rupert his secrets, and she fondly, delusively imagined that she had thereby secured a passage to his heart.

Making their way painfully and slowly over the housetops, Oscar Penraven and his men retired.

They were unmolested.

No more shots were fired, and leaving two men in each room to guard the entrance, Lesbia and the others retired to rest.

When I say the "others" I do not include Rosalie St. Aubyn.

She kept vigilant watch.

Having effected so much as she imagined for Rupert Dreadnought, she cared not to allow the golden opportunity to glide away of proving to him that she was not only his friend, but had risked her very life for him.

She, therefore, could not rest.

Her bosom was full of an eager hope; and all through the watches of that eventful night she sat in her chamber writing a long, long letter, detailing to Rupert the events of the evening, and appealing to his gratitude, if not his love.

The overwhelming, blinding passion that consumed her, however, was evident throughout.

This letter, as soon as the household was awake, she gave to Lesbia Howard.

"Take this," she said, giving her also a sealed packet; "the letter I desire placed in the hands of Rupert Dreadnought; the other I desire you to keep, in order that, in the future, should any doubt arise in your mind, you may know who it was who saved you this night."

Then, masked and mysterious as she was, she was preparing to depart, when a loud ring announced the arrival of some one.

A faint glow of hope invaded her bosom.

It might be Rupert!

Rupert, who would scorn her if they met face to face, when she fondly—foolishly imagined she could win him over.

In any case she was now disappointed.

Rupert, as my readers are aware, was many, many miles away, and when the door opened it admitted old Robert.

He looked fatigued sorely, but, nevertheless, there was a glow of pleasure upon his features.

"Mistress Penraven is saved," he cried.

Rosalie started, and pressed her hand over her breast with an evident feeling of pain.

Lesbia, on the other hand, uttered an exclamation of joy.

"Saved!" she cried, "so soon! and out of whose hands?"

"From the hands of Oscar Penraven," said the old domestic.

"And is she with you?"

"No; she is in a place of safety," replied old Robert, who suspected the appearance of Rosalie, masked and mysterious as she was. "But at present I will keep that place a secret."

"You are among friends," said Rosalie, as calmly as she could.

"Certainly; I believe you," replied the domestic, respectfully, "but until Master Rupert returns, I fancy it will be better to hold my tongue, and hold my tongue I will, no matter what may betide."

Rosalie bit her lip.

But there was no help for it now.

So, with an aching heart, she took her leave, and, full of dread—a dread of some unknown evil, she made her way towards her own home.

CHAPTER XXXV.

RUPERT DREADNOUGHT RECEIVES A SECOND LETTER—HE IS ABSOLVED FROM HIS OATH—HIS PREPARATIONS TO ESCAPE—THE ALARM—THE FLIGHT ACROSS THE LAKE—THE OLD INN—THE SOUNDS OF STRIFE.

RUPERT DREADNOUGHT, of course, was not aware of the death of Count Hendringing.

He knew there was an unusual commotion in the castle.

He saw torches gleaming on the lake, and hushed voices on the stairs, and the carrying of a heavy burden.

But that was all.

He dared not venture to ask what had occurred.

But this he *did* remark.

The count did not make his appearance in the laboratory or in the vast underground work rooms.

On the third night, however, he received a second letter.

A letter sent to him as mysteriously as the first.

It was from Gascoigne, and ran thus:—

"I have met and killed Count Hendringing. Whatever oath, therefore, you may have taken, you are absolved from. Begin your escape at once, and when you are ready, place a light in your window. We are always on the watch.

"GASCOIGNE."

This was brief but to the purpose.

The count being dead, Rupert was certainly absolved from his oath.

He had already commenced his escape.

Beneath his bedstead there was now a large hole in the wall which he had made by repeated workings with a small piece of iron picked up in the workshops.

He contrived so to arrange matters that the bricks as they were moved did not fall into the lake.

Directly he had sufficiently loosened them he drew them inwards, and when he had completed his night's work he piled them up one on the other so as to prevent the ingress of the fresh cold air of morning when the attendant brought his breakfast.

Gascoigne, in his former letter, had spoken of the hole thus made being large enough, not only for Rupert's escape, but also for the admission of men to seize upon the castle.

Without some donouement as this, indeed, Dreadnought's entrance into the Castle of Hendringing would seem useless.

But in his second letter no mention was made of this.

Escape, therefore, seemed the only thing to be looked for.

He knew enough to lay an information before the authorities.

That, perhaps, would be enough.

Enough certainly as regarded his own feelings, for of the sword and of blood he had had sufficient.

Not that he shrank from the fulfilment of his vow.

Far from it.

But the alternative was given him of delivering the villain Henzollern up to the authorities to punishment; and of this alternative he gladly availed himself.

So on he worked steadily.

But all his labour was in vain.

When he returned to his cell on the second night, he found his work undone.

The aperture was bricked up again and everything was more solid than before.

He had been discovered certainly by some one.

By whom he could not guess.

It was not by the attendant.

If it had been he would have spoken to him of it when he re-admitted him for the night.

Whoever it was, however, that had found out his secret, it was quite evident that a desperate effort must now be made.

With eager hands he turned up his lamp to its fullest extent, and placed it so in his window that his friends could not fail to distinguish it on the other side of the lake.

Scarcely five minutes had elapsed before the waving of a flaming torch among the trees of the wood proclaimed that his signal had been recognised.

His heart beat high with hope.

He knew now the secret of the old Castle of Hendringing.

He had the Poisoners of London, as it were, in his power.

And freedom must be his at all hazards.

Standing on his stool he seized the bars of his window and wrenched at them vigorously.

He knew that this mode of escape was perilous because it could not to be effected without noise.

But the risk implied in the attempt was not so great as that implied in remaining.

He guessed rightly, that now that the Count Hendringing was dead, the Chief of the Poisoners would assume command of the old castle.

When, therefore, he was informed of the attempted escape, Rupert's instant death would follow.

Eagerly, therefore, he wrenched at the strong bars.

Wrenched till the skin was worn from off his palms, and the blood started from his nails.

At length one bar yielded, and, in yielding, brought with it a shower of bricks and mortar.

This rendered the rest of his task more easy, and with redoubled energy he worked away at the others.

It was, of course, a work of some little time.

But somehow or another, though everything was so still in the old castle, no one heard the sounds of the falling brickwork.

At length all the bars were out, and he rested for a moment.

Only a moment, however, was it before he renewed his task vigorously.

Dragging away the bricks he thrust his body through the aperture, and sat with his legs dangling over the edge.

From this point he had a view of the country round.

He could see the waving trees of the forest; the light in the inn beyond; and the little black boat which had brought him and his silent guide to the castle.

Presently the edge of the lake was alive with figures.

Then the boat was seized and entered by two figures, Gascoigne and Kamril, and rowed across.

In the dim light it was quite impossible for Rupert Dreadnought to recognise faces.

But he knew at once the voice which addressed him.

It was that of Gascoigne.

"Rupert, are you there?"

In the darkness the cautious detective feared to be careless.

"Yes I am here and eager to depart, I can assure you," said Rupert.

The window where our hero sat was a considerable distance from the surface of the lake.

If he had dropped into the light skiff, therefore, he would have run the risk of upsetting it.

If he had dropped into the water he would have hazarded an alarm.

Gascoigne had provided against this.

He had brought with him a stout rope which he had procured from the inn.

"Catch this," he said; "fasten it securely round the bedstead and then let yourself down to us."

Rupert Dreadnought lost no time in doing as he was desired.

But quick as they had been in their movements they had been seen.

Just as Gascoigne had his oar raised to push off from the side of the castle a second boat shot round from the shadow of the gate.

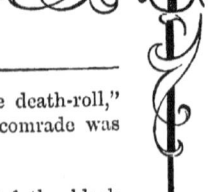

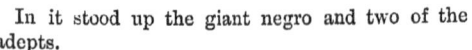

In it stood up the giant negro and two of the adepts.

"What do you here?" cried the black overseer in a voice of thunder.

"We are releasing a friend from a den of assassins," cried Gascoigne; "let us pass or you will rue the hour you assailed us."

The negro uttered a low, guttural laugh.

"If he disliked his work he should have told the count so and *he* would soon have ended it."

"Truly," replied Rupert, who still wore his mask, "he would have ended it by my death."

At a sign from the negro, those who were with him in the boat made one vigorous pull which brought them alongside the others.

Then they all sprang up.

"Have a care," cried Gascoigne, fiercely, "you have to deal with desperate men."

The negro again indulged in his guttural laugh.

"We are desperate, too," he said; "we knew you to be spies and informers, and we do not wish our living taken from us. Deliver your prisoner then, and we will say nothing to the count of this matter."

It was now Gascoigne's turn to smile.

He saw through the ruse plainly.

The negro had been present at the death of Count Hendringing, but he desired not the men to know it, and did not, in the darkness, recognise Gascoigne as the count's opponent.

"My men," said Gascoigne, in the German language, and in a loud, clear voice, "believe him not. Were you to remain in the servitude of the villains who have inveigled you into this castle, you would, at the completion of the term, be destroyed by some hideous agency—no doubt by the very drugs which you are called upon to make. Your servitude is at an end—the count is *dead*—he died by my hand, and you are absolved, therefore, from your vows."

As he spoke these last words, the negro uttered a cry of rage and darted so violently forward as nearly to upset the boat.

"Villain!" he cried "murderer of my master, die!"

And as he said this, he made a violent blow at Gascoigne with a short hatchet he wore in his belt.

But the blow fell short.

One of the men behind him struck his arm, and losing his balance, the black ruffian fell headlong across the gunwales of both boats.

It was evident that Gascoigne's words had taken effect.

Both the men dashed upon him who had so lately been their master, and seizing him, held him in a grip of iron.

But the negro was not only a giant, but one possessed apparently of superhuman strength.

Though thrown thus on his face, he struggled up and seized Gascoigne.

But there were too many against him.

In an instant the two men, Gascoigne and Rupert, were upon him, and as he made a last effort to stagger back and draw his knife from his girdle, he fell over the side of the frail bark, and plunged with a loud plash into the waters of the lake.

"He has gone to join the last on the death-roll," said Rupert; "for undoubtedly your comrade was murdered."

And so it seemed.

They scanned eagerly the surface of the black water.

But he re-appeared not.

The waters of the mysterious pool had claimed him for their own.

"Now, then," said Gascoigne, "let us row ashore. As for you, my men, you are at liberty either to return to the castle, or escape. Choose as you please."

"We shall escape," said the men. "The Count Hendringing being dead, we are absolved of all oaths, and our lives themselves would not be safe in the keeping of the other."

By the "other" they signified the Chief of the Poisoners.

They rowed, therefore, across the gloomy lake with Gascoigne and Rupert.

On the shore they parted company, and were seen no more.

Gascoigne detained his friends by the side of the lake till the strangers were gone.

"We have now two boats," he said; "let us conceal them among the brushwood, so that no one can approach the building until we return, or, at least, so that we shall have ample accommodation for the transit of our men."

Having acted upon the wise advice of Gascoigne, they then hurried on towards the inn, which nestled among the thick woodland.

The night was, as I have before said, very still.

But, as they advanced, its aspect entirely changed.

Loud voices, raised in anger, echoed among the dense trees; and as they approached nearer, the sounds of strife were plainly discernible.

"There is something wrong here," cried Rupert. "We must hurry forward."

So saying, he set the example, and the three advanced at a run towards the entrance of the "Three Shepherds."

CHAPTER XXXVI.

THE "THREE SHEPHERDS"—THE SUSPICIOUS GUESTS—THE ASSASSIN—THE MURDER OF HANS HORSTACKER—THE MASKED LEADER—ALLAN OF THE GLEN IS SURROUNDED BY MURDERERS—THE FIGHT IN THE DARK—JUST IN TIME!—THE ARRIVAL OF RUPERT—THE CONFLICT—ESCAPE OF THE MASKED ASSASSIN AND SURRENDER OF THE OTHERS—THE COMPACT—THE DEPARTURE OF THE EXPEDITION.

In order to explain the commotion which was going on at the inn as Rupert and his companions neared it, we must go back to the time when Gascoigne and his friend set out on their expedition to aid Rupert in his escape from the Castle of Hendringing.

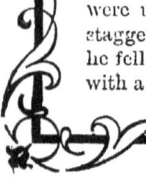

Allan of the Glen and Horstacker the gipsy, remained behind for the purpose of watching the proceedings of certain suspicious characters who had that evening entered the public room of the inn.

Engaged as he was upon a strange and secret errand, Allan was, of course, more open to suspicion than others.

But the men whom we allude to would have excited doubts anywhere.

They were tall, burly fellows, apparently well-fed, but dirty, ragged, and drunken.

They entered the place with an insolent swagger, and though their appearance was certainly not such as to warrant the idea of their being possessed of money, they flourished well-filled purses, and paid their reckoning in advance.

They evidently, in fact, recognised the doubtfulness of their disguise.

Though, as I have said, they were evidently under the influence of strong liquor, they had only taken sufficient to stimulate them in their work, not to affect the clearness of their brain; and as they drank the fine old German ale which the landlord placed before them, they cautiously took stock of all present.

Allan of the Glen and his friends were clearly the objects of their scrutiny.

When, however, Gascoigne and Kamril quitted the inn, the men remained where they were and continued drinking.

This aroused more than ever the curiosity of Allan of the Glen.

"They are certainly watching some of us," said he to himself, "and as they have not followed Gascoigne, they must be after *me*."

Here again, however, he seemed to be at fault.

The men, at length, rose, paid their reckoning, and departed.

The inn once more resumed its quietude; and after a while Allan and Horstacker retired to an upper room to wile away the time in a friendly game of cards.

The time passed swiftly by.

Engaged in their amusement, the two players did not observe the door noiselessly opened.

"AT LENGTH ONE BAR YIELDED!"

But open so it did to admit the two suspicious men and another covered with a cloak and masked.

Stealthily in the dim light they stole in.

Then one glided behind the chair of Hans Horstacker—a bright light gleamed in the air, and a knife was buried between the shoulders of the unconscious victim.

With a yell of agony he sprang up, overturning the table as he did so, and falling prone upon the floor.

This saved Allan from sharing the terrible fate of his companion.

He started back just as the knife of the other assassin was striking, and the man sprang aside to avoid what he deemed an attack.

But they were in utter darkness now.

When the table was overturned, the lamp also was extinguished.

"What is to be done?" asked one of the murderers, addressing the mask.

"One is dead, there is but one now left to destroy," replied a hollow voice, which Allan failed to recognise: "we can easily complete the work. Cut off his approach to the door, and it is as good as done."

Dragging the table before him as well as he could, Allan prepared for a desperate struggle.

But it was not so easy to dispose of him as the man in the mask had said.

The loud yell of agony which had escaped the

lips of Hans Horstacker had reached the ears of the landlord; and as the assassin, whose steel had drank the blood of one victim, was creeping with hideous stealth towards a second, the door was flung open, and the landlord entered, bearing lights.

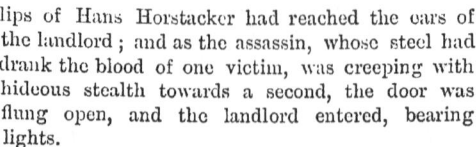

"What means this! Murder in my house!" cried he. "Gentlemen, I must insist——"

"Have a care," cried the masked man, in a stern voice, "have a care that you do not share the fate of the man you see dead yonder. Leave those lights, and quit the room."

"You are mad," returned the landlord, who, though recognising his peril, had no wish to leave honest men to be butchered—and, in fact, to aid in their butchery. "Can you suppose that I will assist in such a thing? Hark! What is that?" he added, a gleam of pleasure overspreading his features.

A loud and peremptory knocking was heard below, accompanied by cries of—

"Host—here—host!"

"In Heaven's name, desist, gentlemen," he cried. "Would you ruin my house by open murder?"

Then, ere the assassins could answer him, he rushed away, carrying with him the lights.

Below he found Gascoigne, Rupert, and Kamril.

"Quick!" he cried. "Follow me. Your English friend is in danger. Hans Horstacker is already dead!"

They had already heard, as I have said, the cries and clashing of weapons.

Without waiting, therefore, for any explanations, they drew their swords and rushed up into the room, where they found Allan behind the fallen table defending himself blindly against the three villains.

In an instant the scene changed.

The two assassins drew back towards their masked leader.

The landlord timidly dragged the table up, set it in a corner, and put the lights upon it; after which he drew aside the body of the murdered man.

There were four against three now, and the villains saw at once their disadvantage.

No time was given them, however, for parley.

The indignant friends rushed at them with drawn swords, and the ragged ruffians had to parry fierce thrusts with the blades of their long knives.

The smallness of the room aided them in this, for there was no room for the display of any swordsmanship, and the longer weapons had to be used almost like daggers.

The masked leader soon saw, however, that a continuous struggle would end in their inevitable destruction.

He kept his eyes, therefore, upon a window which stood partially open.

Here was his only chance of escape; his men must look to themselves.

As he fought, therefore, he yielded towards this point.

Allan, who saw his object, attempted to stay him.

But in vain.

The mask was the only one of the assassins who had a sword.

He knew how to use it, moreover, and as he neared the casement he suddenly made a rush forward, threw up the point of the Scotch youth's sword, and then, leaping back, plunged out into the darkness before any one could prevent him.

A ringing, mocking laugh announced to the combatants that he had reached the ground in safety.

Allan was not slow in following him, but though he fell softly on the turf, and dashed away instantly in pursuit, he was unable to see any trace of his enemy.

The stranger, whoever he might be, had disappeared.

The two minor villains saw the manner in which their leader had abandoned them, and wisely resolved to give up a contest in which, wounded badly as they already were, they had every chance of losing life.

"We surrender!" they cried, with one accord, and flung their weapons upon the floor.

This was scarcely what Rupert or the others desired.

They had the chance now of destroying the murderers of Hans Horstacker without encumbering themselves with legal proceedings; and it was with regret that they felt themselves compelled to give life to two such wretches.

"We accept your surrender only conditionally," said Gascoigne.

"What are the conditions, then?" said one of them.

"That you tell us the name of your employer, that you lead us to his dwelling, and accompany us whithersoever we choose, unarmed. With assassins treachery is always to be feared."

What could the men do?

There was nothing for them to do but consent; and they did so.

"In the first place, then, who was the masked man who fled from the window?"

"His name," said one of the murderers, "is Dr. Henzollern. He sent us hither to avenge the death of the Count Hendringing."

"Who died by my hand in a fair duel," said Gascoigne. "And whither has he fled?"

"To the castle."

"Good," said Gascoigne. "This night the place will be ours."

Rupert at this moment called Gascoigne aside, and held with him a hurried and secret conference.

This over, he turned to the prisoners.

"As we are all going to leave the inn for awhile," he said, "you must consent to be bound. There is no one here in whose custody we should care to leave you."

"Well," returned one of the men, boldly, "if you are going to the castle, you will be making a grevious error if you leave us here. We could be of service."

"How so?"

"We know every turn in the castle, and could lead you by secret ways to the doctor's own chamber. But be warned by me; unless you go in force, it is useless. You will only fall into a trap. The castle is full of workers, who, at a sign from their leader, would rise and destroy you."

"Does he then keep the keys of the rooms in which the labourers are confined?"

"No; the giant negro overseer has possession of them always."

"He can use them no longer, then," said Rupert, "for he is dead."

"Dead!" echoed the men in astonishment.

"Yes; in attempting to kill *me*, he fell into the lake," answered Gascoigne, "and was drowned. However, if you are willing to aid us, we will accept your services in part. One of you must remain here as a hostage for the other. We have no need of numbers now. The keys of the cells being at the bottom of the lake we have no fear of the workers; and we are in numbers sufficient to take the place."

The men could not help acquiescing with amazement.

Being utterly helpless, all they could do was to submit.

After a brief consultation, therefore, among themselves, they settled which was to remain, and the landlord, who had descended, was at once summoned to the room.

"Which one is to accompany us?" asked Rupert.

"Hinrich Alse," returned one of the men, pointing to the taller ruffian.

"Good," said Rupert.

Then he turned to the landlord.

"You have ropes here, doubtless, mine host?" he asked.

"Enough to bind, neck and crop, the whole company here present."

"That is well. Then bring enough cord to bind firmly one of these fellows. The other accompanies us as guide. If aught evil happens to us in consequence of his treachery, pitch his friend, bound as he is, into the lake."

"It shall be done," said Boniface, as coolly as if he were speaking of the proper arrangement of a supper. "You may depend upon my best attention."

Within a quarter of an hour the assassin of Hans Horstacker was lying bound.

Then the others, having partaken of some refreshment, started on their expedition.

CHAPTER XXXVII.

THE STILL CASTLE—THE BANQUETING ROOM—THE BEAUTIFUL SIRENS—THE UNWELCOME INTERRUPTION—THE FLIGHT—THE INTERCEPTED ESCAPE—THE DARK LAKE—THE DEAD PURSUER—THE BATTLE IN THE WATERS—THE HORRORS OF DARKNESS—THE OLD INN—THE PHANTOMS OF THE NIGHT—THE SLEEP AND THE AWAKENING.

EVIDENTLY no one in the old castle suspected what had occurred.

Everything was still gloomy and silent as before.

Dr. Henzollern had seen who it was who attacked him at the old inn, but that any of the number had been within the walls of Hendringing he never dreamt.

He contrived easily to re-enter the castle in spite of the concealment of the boats, for he always had a skiff reserved for his private use—placed away in a manner similar to that adopted by Rupert and Gascoigne.

On entering the castle he asked for the negro.

He was not to be found, but no one had seen the conflict on the lake, and no one consequently suspected his death.

With a heart weary with disappointment, then, he made his way to the large banqueting-hall, where a splendid supper awaited him.

As he tinkled a bell, the door opened and admitted the two sirens whom Rupert had seen on his first visit, dressed in the same daring undress in which they had before appeared.

Neither Dr. Henzollern nor these young ladies seemed in any way affected by the death of the Count Hendringing.

He having quitted this sublunary sphere, the command of the place had devolved apparently upon the Chief of the Poisoners, and the sirens, therefore, both transferred their attentions and blandishments to him.

They were soon engaged in disposing of the luxurious repast.

The scene we will not dwell upon.

Suffice it to say that much of the good wine had disappeared, and the eyes of the demoiselles were beginning to flash fire, when the door was suddenly thrown open, and the attendant who had guided Rupert to his chamber on his first entrance into the castle, appeared in the room.

He looked pale, and his manner altogether was indicative of great agitation.

"What ails you?" asked Dr. Henzollern, in some surprise.

"There is something most strange going on in the castle," replied he.

"Something! what mean you? Do not talk in riddles, but explain yourself."

"Well, then, as I came by the room in which the new workman was placed, I heard the sound of many voices."

"Pshaw! the man is talking to himself to save himself from becoming dumb," cried the doctor, jeeringly.

The man shook his head.

"No, no," he said, "it is not the voice of one man I hear, it is the voice of many—at least, six. If you do not believe me, come and listen for yourself."

For a moment the doctor hesitated.

"It is impossible," he said; "how could they have entered?"

"That is a question I cannot answer," replied the man.

"Well," said the doctor, "I will come with you. Don't be afraid," he added, patting one of the girls on her white shoulder, "I shall not be long, and you will see that it is all a false alarm."

He soon found that he was in error.

No sooner had he approached the door, which he did stealthily, than he heard the steady working of some instrument in the lock.

The murmur of several voices, too, was distinctly audible.

"You are right," said the doctor, turning somewhat pale, "follow me."

He led the way back into the banqueting room where the girls were still drinking wine.

"My dear ladies," he said, "I fear I shall have to dismiss you. There is more truth in what this man told me than I cared to believe. Escape at once. My private boat is at the water-gate; fly."

The ladies waited to hear no more.

Their love for the person of Dr. Henzollern was limited to their admiration of his money, and the good things with which he invariably provided them.

The room was quickly, therefore, cleared of them, and Dr. Henzollern and his attendant were left alone.

"Where is Asnail the Nubian?" asked Dr. Henzollern.

"I know not," returned the man, "he has been for some time absent."

"And has he the keys of the rooms where the workmen sleep?"

"Yes."

A flush of disappointment overspread the features of the Chief.

"Most unfortunate—most cruelly unfortunate," muttered Dr. Henzollern. "What is to be done? We are alone—you and I—with the exception of the old fellow who keeps the lower gate. We shall most certainly be overpowered. Hark! they come! Where can Asnail be? Curse him for a negligent fellow. What means he by thus absenting himself and taking with him the keys?"

"They have broken open the door," said the man. "What shall we do?"

"Extinguish the lights in this room and follow me," cried Dr. Henzollern. "We must fly from the castle. To remain here is to court death. I know well that these men seek my life."

It did not take many minutes to carry out the doctor's instructions, and the banqueting-hall was soon involved in total darkness.

"Follow me," said the Chief, in a low voice.

This injunction there was some little difficulty in carrying out.

In the first place it was utterly impossible to see anything.

In the second place the steps of the doctor were utterly noiseless.

"I cannot unless I know which way to go, or I hear your voice at least."

"Take my hand," said the doctor.

As he spoke, there was a terrific crash, which told that the attacking party had rushed into the large room and come in contact with the table, covered as it was with glass ware and crockery of all kinds.

The fugitives turned aside, after proceeding a short distance along the passage, and, passing down the steps, made their way to the water gate.

But no skiff was there!

The two fair ones who had for so long a time enjoyed the hospitality of the castle and expressed their devotion to its master, had not waited to see if the doctor was obliged to follow them.

Fear not only gave them wings, but made them regardless of the cold wind.

Without hesitation, therefore, they entered the boat, their shoulders bare to the blast, and rowed themselves across the gloomy water, which at any other time they would have feared to pass.

When, therefore, Dr. Henzollern reached the bottom of the staircase, and went out through the water-gate upon the stone steps, he found no boat there.

"Our means of escape seem cut off," cried he, turning in dismay to his companion.

The man laughed.

"Fear has made you forgetful," he said. "It is but a short distance from this to yonder shore. We can swim."

The Chief shuddered.

Knowing, as he did, the terrible secrets which those dark waters hid; knowing how many dead bodies lay beneath that silent lake—dead bodies of men sacrificed to the hideous cause, no wonder was it that he felt a thrill of horror at the idea of plunging in.

"But needs must," &c.—the proverb is well known.

"You are right," he said; "it is our only chance of safety. Let us try it at once. Do not plunge in, for the noise would attract their attention."

Throwing off their heavy coats, the two men then slid down into the water, whose cold waves sent a chill almost of terror to the heart of Dr. Henzollern as he began his noiseless journey.

It was no great distance, as the man had said, from the castle to the opposite shore, and they had, moreover, no current to oppose them.

Everything was very still.

Still as accorded with the name given it by the peasantry.

The Lake of Death.

But there were impediments in the way which Dr. Henzollern had never dreamed of.

Oppressed as he was by superstitious terror, his dread and agony may be imagined when he found himself clutched from below.

A yell of fear escaped from his lips, almost choked by the water.

He tried to swim on.

But in vain.

Something below the surface of the water held him in its clutches, and down he sank.

Sank to find himself in the arms of what was evidently a corpse.

The desire of life was strong within the breast of the wretched man, or he would never have been able to endure the horror of that moment.

The cause was simple enough.

The effect stupendously terrific.

The negro when, in attempting to destroy Gascoigne, he fell over the edge of the boat into the dark lake, had caught himself in a tangled wisp of ropes, which had been allowed to remain fastened from one side of the lake to the other, when it was used by the peasantry round as a place for fishing.

It was for this reason that he had never risen, and had been suffocated at once.

Dr. Henzollern, when his face touched the clammy features of the corpse, felt inclined to yell forth a demand for aid.

Fortunately for himself, however, he restrained himself and tried to extricate his limbs from the perilous clutch of the dead man.

"THE DOOR WAS FLUNG OPEN, AND A MASKED MAN ENTERED."

But a few moments were thus engaged truly.

But in those few moments an age seemed to pass away.

The accumulated agony of years was concentrated in them.

The grasp of the dead man's fingers being at length loosened, the wretched doctor floated to the surface, and gazed about him in bewilderment.

For a time his senses seemed to fail him.

All the evil deeds he had ever done in his life had been acted over again during those few minutes in the water.

The forms of his murdered victims had appeared to float around him in an atmosphere of poison!

Now when he breathed again the free air, and saw the clear vault of Heaven studded with its myriad stars, he, for an instant, forgot that he was a fugitive.

Then the thought occurred to him—

"I am flying for my life from my own stronghold. What if that hideous corpse below there be the corpse of him who holds the keys which keep captive a hundred helpers. What if I dive again and discover this, I can return in triumph."

Courage seemed to return with the thought.

After floating a few moments, to recover breath, he dived.

But he failed in his object.

His struggle with the dead negro had extricated the body from its entanglement, and he had sunk to the bottom.

With rage at his heart, Dr. Henzollern returned to the surface and made his way to the shore just in time to see the windows of the old castle lit up as by a hundred fires.

A demoniacal smile lit up his face as he gazed.

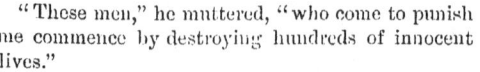

"These men," he muttered, "who come to punish me commence by destroying hundreds of innocent lives."

"Well," said the man, who had reached shore long before him, "you have arrived, then, at length. I thought you were lost."

"No," said the doctor, shudderingly, "no, I have escaped, though, truth to tell, I was nearly lost; but see how the fire has the old castle. They have done a clever deed, these friends of the innocent; two hundred men will perish by their hands this night. But it matters not to me—let them burn, our secret will be all the safer. Meanwhile we must fly. You had better go one way and I another."

"And when and where shall we meet again?" asked the man.

"This is no time or place to make rendezvous," returned Dr. Henzollern, hastily. "I know where you live; when I require your services I will make it my duty to come to you. For the time, good-night."

And, leaving the man to digest these words as best he might, he fled away towards the wood.

As soon as he reached the shade of the trees, he proceeded to make a wonderful change in his appearance.

First of all, he took from his head his heavily-curled wig, and appeared in short, straight hair.

Then he took off his coat, and turned it, so that the gaily-dressed courtier had the semblance of a humble citizen in a snuff-coloured suit.

Then he took off his heavy boots, and took from his pocket a pair of low shoes.

After this he wiped away some of the bronze off his face, drew his hat over his brow, and boldly advanced towards the inn, where, but a few hours before, he had been engaged in a murder.

He knew well that the landlord would not recognise him, and that the others were not there to render his entrance perilous.

His mind was made up.

His horse was in the castle, and he would have to walk to Hamburgh to proceed to England.

The next inn was quite ten miles on, and he was in sore need of refreshment.

Knocking boldly at the door therefore, he demanded entrance.

The landlord, who had had lately to deal with so many rough customers, was at first loth to open, but having glanced out of window, and seen that the doctor was by himself, he came down at length, and admitted him.

Suspicious of every one since the "Three Shepherds" had been made the rendezvous of assassins, he cast one inquiring glance at the features of the stranger.

But the disguise was perfect.

He recognised him not, and, in fact, had only once before beheld him.

"Enter," he said; "though this is somewhat a late hour to crave hospitality."

Dr. Henzollern laughed.

"It would be better were you to throw open your door," he said. "You will have all the people on the country side flocking here presently, for the castle yonder is on fire."

As if to corroborate his words, there was at this moment a rush of crimson light, that lit up the porch of the old inn as with a lightning flash.

"You say truly; there is a conflagration somewhere of no little magnitude," began the landlord.

Dr. Henzollern interrupted him.

"Well, great or small, I am not going to remain to see it. I have travelled long, and desire to get home now. Let me have some Schiedam, and quickly, for the night is far spent, and dawn cannot be far distant."

The host, thus admonished, at once produced a large glass of the strong spirit, which the doctor swallowed eagerly.

Then he paid his reckoning, and bade the host good-night, and plunged into the forest.

He had no sooner done so than his brain began to whirl strangely.

Whether from the effect of the spirit or not we cannot say.

Be this, however, as it may, certain it is that he reeled and staggered as he went, the trees took phantom shapes, the wind seemed to shriek menacingly at him, the earth seemed to swell and burst, and yield up hideous forms.

At length, maddened, he could go no further, but sinking down upon the dewy ground, and covering his face with his hands, he placed his head upon a mound of earth, and lapsed into a deep slumber.

When he awoke the bright sun was high in the heavens, and men's forms were bending over him.

Forms which caused him to shrink, as it were, into himself, and shudderingly crouch from their gaze.

CHAPTER XXXVIII.

THE BURNING OF THE CASTLE—THE FATE OF THE TWO HUNDRED—THE DESTRUCTION OF THE SECRET POISONS—THE CRIMSON LAKE—THE SCENE IN THE FOREST—THE DISCOVERY OF THE DOCTOR—THE DUEL—THE DEATH-POOL—THE DOOM OF THE POISONER.

THE castle truly was on fire.

In this the doctor had not lied.

But he had spoken falsely in one way.

The two hundred prisoners had not been sacrificed to a blind revenge.

Rupert and his men knew well how many beings were there imprisoned.

The first thing, therefore, was to release them.

They had searched everywhere for the doctor.

But neither he nor any of his men were to be seen.

Evidently he had escaped.

So in the great banqueting-hall they went to consult.

"We have lost our prey," said Rupert, as they sat down at the banquet table, which they had restored to its former position. "The Chief of the Poisoners has escaped."

"Yes, but he will easily be recaptured or hunted to his lair," said Gascoigne; "in the meantime let us destroy the place which has harboured these villains, and root out as it were the very foundation."

"But the workmen. What are we to do with them?" said Rupert.

"They, of course, must be saved."

"But how? The negro who had the custody of the keys is dead."

"We must force open the doors."

"That will occupy us all night."

"Nevertheless, we cannot wilfully destroy two hundred lives. Let us break open the door of one of the men, and see what a little questioning will do."

So it was done.

Proceeding to the corridor which, according to the directions given by Rupert, contained the first set of workers, they forced open one of the doors.

A tall, masked man came forth, and gazed at them in surprise.

"What want you with me?" he asked.

"That is the deputy-overseer," whispered the man who had come with them from the inn.

"Ah!"

"Yes; if anyone possesses duplicate keys he does."

"His name?"

"Conrad Hardaber."

Rupert approached him.

"Your name is Conrad Hardaber," he said.

"It is; though how you know it is a mystery," returned the man.

"You are deputy-overseer here."

"I am."

"Where are the keys of the rooms?"

"They are in the hands of Asnail, the negro, the head overseer."

"He is dead," replied Rupert. "But you have duplicates. Produce them."

The man hesitated.

"I know you not," he said.

"There you say truly," answered our hero; "we are come to destroy this place, to burn it to the ground. But we must first of all release the innocent from their danger. Produce the duplicate keys at once."

The man drew back.

"I have them not," he said.

Rupert turned to his followers sternly.

"Let this fellow," he said, "be taken into yonder room and shot at once. We can then proceed to the next."

The words had an immediate effect upon the deputy-overseer.

"Since you have me in your power," he said, "I must obey."

Then he turned back into his room, and after a moment brought out the keys.

"Here," he said, "they are. Now what use are you going to put them to?"

"To save the lives of all in Hendringing."

"But where is the count?"

"He is dead."

"And Dr. Henzollern?"

"He has fled."

"And you?"

"We are the enemies of both, the avengers of murdered friends, the sworn foes of the Poisoners, and, ere we leave this place, we shall level it with the ground. The poisonous drugs it contains will then be destroyed, the secrets which surround the production of the hideous poison will be lost for ever; and England—and, indeed, all Europe, will be freed from a scourge which for too long a time has decimated the people."

"Amen!" said the deputy-overseer. "Since the count is dead, and Dr. Henzollern has deemed it wise to fly, I am no longer subject to them. My oath is nil; and I will gladly aid you. This way; follow me."

One by one the doors were opened, and the masked workers came forth.

It would have taken too long to have explained to each one the cause of their release.

Rupert waited, therefore, until all were summoned into the great vaults beneath the castle.

Then they were told to remove their masks, and pickaxes having been placed in their hands, they were ordered to break through the wall at a point where there was now no outlet from the castle, on the side, in fact, where there were no windows or doors.

In a very short space of time the work was completed.

Then the loud voice of the deputy-overseer addressed them.

He told them all.

They listened in silence.

Then, when they were told that they were at liberty to go, came the trial.

One by one they filed out of the door into the free air of night.

Not a single one hesitated.

The deputy-overseer went last.

"Now," said Rupert, when he was once more alone with his friends, "we will commence the destruction of this den of iniquity. We will begin at the top of the building, and end with the bottom."

So it was done.

Ascending to the summit of the castle, they set fire to the rooms as they descended.

When they reached the basement story, they lit the strong liquids, which blazed up like spirit.

Then they passed out into the wood at the rear, and watched with pleasure the result of their work.

The combustible materials, which filled every department of the castle, soon caused the flames to spread bravely; and it was not long before, amid the smoke and the fire, there was scarcely a possibility of distinguishing any one portion of the building.

When they had seen that the work of destruction was fairly advanced, Rupert and his friends made their way along the margin of the now crimson lake towards the old inn.

Here they found the peasantry gradually collecting.

Here they also learned of the sudden arrival and departure of a stranger, and it at once occurred to them that it must be the fugitive of whom they were in search.

They remained a short time to partake of refreshment.

Then, just as dawn was peeping over the forest, they started in pursuit of Dr. Henzollern.

It was near the verge of the great wood that they came across him.

He was lying with his sword drawn—he had drawn it in his sleep—and with his other hand grasping the grass, as he would have grasped the hair of a foe.

His face was distorted strangely, as with anger and fear mingled, while a ghastly hue as of death overspread it.

They awoke him after repeated shakings, and then, as I have said, he closed his eyes again, and averted his head as if they had been so many demons.

In their presence he read his fate.

He knew now that the Shadowy King was near him.

While they stood there, he could hear the flapping of his wings and the sound of a trumpet voice.

But he was not long suffered to remain at peace on the ground.

They forcibly raised him, and compelled him to stand upon his feet.

"What are you going to do with me?" he asked, with a vague, wild expression of countenance, which almost led to the conclusion that he was mad.

"Your hour of reckoning has come, base assassin," cried Rupert, in a voice of stern anger; "but since I will not constitute myself your judge so far as to hang you up to yonder tree, as you deserve, I will even measure swords with you; though Heaven knows my good weapon will be degraded by being crossed with yours."

Those who were with Rupert Dreadnought now drew back.

They awaited eagerly the result of the conflict which was about to commence.

None the less eagerly, because it signified to them return to England.

They not for one moment doubted the issue of the contest.

The firm wrist, the bright dauntless eye of Rupert was a singular contrast to the trembling hand and the wavering glances of his opponent.

The duel, however, had quite a different termination to what was expected.

The doctor evidently was either out of his mind, or he was so overcome by the bearing of his antagonist, and the position in which he found himself altogether, that he could not bring himself, as it were, to face the danger.

Suddenly, when no one dreamed of such an action, he cast his sword full in the face of his enemy, and, with a wild yell, dashed away.

Excitement had, at length, proved too much for him, and his senses had fled!

For an instant Rupert and his friends were so astounded that they attempted no pursuit.

Then, as if by common assent, they sprang after him, and the extraordinary chase began in real earnest.

The doctor had one advantage over those who followed him.

He knew well the locality and the ins and outs of the forest.

For some time, therefore, he had the best of it, and headed them considerably.

But he had forgotten one thing.

A fatal piece of forgetfulness as it proved.

In a secluded part of the forest, towards which he naturally made to elude his pursuers, there was a deep pool.

It was called by the villagers the Death Pool.

Round it were jagged rocks, overgrown so thickly with trees and underwood that it was impossible to see anything of the water or the grotto-like stones until you were close upon it.

In those superstitious days it was believed to be haunted.

In Germany, especially, such spots are soon peopled with strange hobgoblins; and the *ignis fatuus* which danced above its waters at night, assisted in the formation of stories of a demon spirit that haunted the Pool, and led men on to destruction.

It was said to be bottomless.

How far this was true we cannot say.

At any rate it was stated confidently by the peasantry that any one who had the misfortune to fall in sank to rise no more.

Towards this spot of ill-omen, then, the Chief of the Poisoners rushed at headlong speed.

He was pursued rapidly.

Those who followed were younger and more active men than he.

Though, therefore, he gained, as I have said, at first, the tremendous pace soon began to tell upon him, and with a heart that beat with a terrible fear, he realized—mad as he was—that his deadly enemies were gaining on him.

It was as he glanced back he met his fate.

Seeing only before him a clump of brushwood, which it was easy to leap, he dashed on, and with a wild bound plunged into the Death Pool.

The wild cry that ascended to the heavens told his pursuers that something had happened.

They hurried forward, therefore, with greater speed than ever, and it was not long before they reached the edge of the water.

The eddies caused by the fall of the doctor's body were still visible.

But that was all.

Like Asnail, the negro, he never rose again, and the secret of his end, and the crimes of his hateful life, were alike buried in the mysterious depths of the Death Pool.

END OF BOOK IV.

BOOK V.

THE FOURTH SECRET OF THE IRON CHEST.

CHAPTER I.

HOME ONCE MORE—THE MEETING OF THE LOVERS—THE LETTER OF ROSALIE ST. AUBYN—THE OPENING OF THE IRON CHEST ONCE MORE—THE LAST ACT OF VENGEANCE—RUPERT AND THE POISONERS.

ENGLAND once more!

Glad, indeed, was Rupert to return to it again, and leave behind him that land of mystery where he had experienced such strange adventures.

Hurrying on the wings of love, he made his way towards home, where he expected to find Helen waiting for him with open arms.

She was not there, however.

She had thought it better to remain with the people with whom old Robert had placed her.

Suspicious characters had been seen lurking about the old house, and, not doubting that Oscar Penraven had people constantly in his employ for the purpose of doing injury to Rupert and his friends, neither Lesbia nor Robert cared to run the risk of keeping with them the one upon whom all our hero's hopes were set.

When the beloved form of his master appeared, however, old Robert was not long in starting off to fetch his future mistress.

Rupert had, in fact, scarcely heard from Lesbia's lips the whole of the strange story of Oscar's attack upon the house when Helen entered the room.

"Helen!"

"Rupert!"

That was all, and the throbbing form of the lovely girl was pressed to the breast of her delighted lover.

In a few words he told her of the success of his mission, and how the madness of the Chief of the Poisoners had saved his sword from the necessity of being stained again with blood.

"My missions are fulfilled much more rapidly than my father deemed it probable, my dearest," he said; "and I hope, should my next task be accomplished as quickly as the last, to be able to claim you soon for my own."

Then he kissed the lips of the blushing girl, and turned to Lesbia.

"Give me," he said, "the letter which this strange woman left for me."

Lesbia at once produced it, and Rupert opened it with eagerness.

THE DEATH POOL.

As his eyes fell upon the signature he started in wonder and alarm.

"How little do you know the terrible danger you have been in," he said. "The woman who was here pretending friendship was Rosalie St. Aubyn."

"Rosalie St. Aubyn!" repeated both Helen and Lesbia, in amazement.

"Yes, indeed! See, here is her signature," he cried. "How comes it, Lesbia, that *you* did not recognise her?"

"She was closely masked."

"And you did not even suspect her?"

"I did not, indeed, or I should have feared to touch food while she was here."

Rupert thought a moment.

"Yes, indeed," he said; "I can see now the whole plan. It was she who aided Oscar Penraven in taking Helen from you."

She it was who prevented his entrance.

Rupert smiled.

"Yes, yes," he said; "that is her cleverness. But come, I will finish reading this strange epistle."

He did so, and did so in bewilderment.

As a man who had passed through some of the strangest adventures that ever fell to the lot of a human being, he saw plainly what it meant.

Rosalie was in love with him.

Mad love was evident in every line of the letter.

He closed it with a sigh.

"This means fresh trouble in the future," he said; "but for the next few days I will cast all thoughts of this kind from my mind. We will devote this week to pleasure, and then I must open the next compartment of that Chest which has contained so many strange injunctions for me."

The week passed rapidly by.

Joyous days are always the fleetest.

At length the seventh day arrived.

Then, with a heavy heart, he went once more towards the room where the Iron Chest was kept.

With a sigh almost of regret, he turned the key, and removing the covering of the fourth compartment, saw a parchment merely.

On this was written—

"MY DEAR SON,—After the adventures you have gone through, I need scarcely tell you who is your next foe. Oscar Penraven, the son of my direst enemy, has by this time sufficiently proved to you his character. When *he* is destroyed, the list of enemies to be swept from the face of the earth will be complete."

A flush of pleasure overspread the features of Rupert Dreadnought.

The last task of revenge which his father imposed upon him was not, then, of the same nature as before.

He would not have to search for a victim to destroy.

The one whose life was to be cut short by his sword was already a hated foe.

He knew him to be a villain of the deepest dye.

He knew that his destruction would be but the saving of trouble to the hangman; and he accepted this task, therefore, not only without compunction but with satisfaction.

The question was how to set about it.

Alone it would be unsafe now to attempt such an enterprise.

Oscar Penraven was now Chief of the Society of Poisoners.

He had a large and deadly machinery at work.

Although the immense establishment over which Dr. Henzollern had presided was now no more, the power of the hideous community was not destroyed.

It might be weakened.

But its awful strength might at any time be revivified.

It behoved him, then, to act with due caution.

Either he must work by stealth, or, combining the whole strength of his friends, attack openly the stronghold of his enemies, and destroy the whole crew together.

In this matter there was one whose counsel he liked best of all.

Allan of the Glen, Tom the waterman, Stanley Sherrington, and Richard Penraven might be good friends in open warfare.

But for wily counsel none was the equal of Gascoigne.

To him, therefore, he applied in the emergency.

He laid before him the entire of his thoughts, the task he had to perform, and the manner in which he proposed to perform it, and Gascoigne was just about to give his opinion, when the door was flung wide open, and a masked man appeared, sword in hand.

Gascoigne leaped from the table where he had been sitting, and sprang into the centre of the room.

But the new-comer waved him back with something of dignity.

"I wear my sword naked for my own protection," he said; "put yours up, and I will put up mine. I come as a friend, and to give you good counsel. And——at any rate you are two to one!"

CHAPTER II.

THE MYSTERIOUS STRANGER—HIS STORY—HIS STRANGE ADVENTURES—HE RESOLVES TO QUIT THE POISONERS—HE IS DISCOVERED—HE ESCAPES—HIS DISCLOSURES AND AWFUL DOOM.

THE man who thus strangely thrust himself, as it were, into the presence of Rupert and Gascoigne, was, as I have before said, masked; but, from his general appearance, you would have guessed him to be between thirty and thirty four years of age.

Although there was a certain air of weary melancholy about him, he yet seemed full of vigour and energy, and, indeed, seemed braced up for the commission of some deed of daring.

"Your mode of entering our presence is somewhat extraordinary," cried Rupert; "masked and with a drawn sword. You will excuse us if we feel a doubt as to the propriety of trusting you."

The man bowed.

"Your words carry no offence to my ears," he said, as he sheathed his weapon. "I wore a sword to guard against unjustifiable attacks; I wore a mask that those in the street should not know me."

So saying he withdrew the covering from his features.

But even then they knew him not.

It was the face of a stranger.

The face of a young, handsome man, with a bold, fearless expression, but yet a sad one.

Beneath the eyes was a heavy, dark rim, which told of illness or some strange mental excitement, while the lips had a peculiar tinge of purple upon them.

"Well, since you have unmasked your face," said Gascoigne, "perhaps it will not be too much to ask you to unmask your thoughts. Tell us whence came you and why are you here?"

"I am one of the Society which has proved such a scourge to London," replied the unknown; "I am one of the Poisoners; but to you, Lord Rupert Dreadnought, I have come to unfold what I would not unfold to any but the man whom I know to be their worst enemy. If you will grant me leave I will, as briefly as I can, tell you my story, and you will then no longer be in surprise in regard to my appearance here now."

The permission was, of course, at once accorded and the man began, after first begging leave to drink a glass of wine which stood on the table.

The liquid seemed to revive and stimulate him, yet, at the same time, to put him in pain, for he pressed his hand over his chest as if in sudden agony.

Then he began—

"I am not going to enter into a long account of my life.

"It would, on the one hand, be tiresome, and, on the other hand, I have not the time left me to do it had I the desire.

"I need only say that in my youth, that is to say,

some six years ago, I met and loved a girl whose face and form were something beyond the loveliness I had ever dreamed of.

"I was poor; my father had been rich, and was of good family, but, through misfortune and recklessness he had spent all his estates, and I was left in the world with only enough to keep me from starving.

"The one I loved, on the other hand, was rich, not only in her splendid beauty, but in her worldly wealth.

"There was no hope in my love affair.

"Despair met me on all hands.

"I was nerveless.

"What little chance I had of earning money, I cast aside.

"Of what use was all I could scrape together, either by the sweat of my brow or the workings of my brain?

"To soar to a position equal to hers it would have required to have coined thousands per day.

"So I wandered about in a state of mad idleness.

"Then occurred something to render me more frantic than ever.

"I have said before that I was well connected.

"Chance then cast me into society where I met the one I loved.

"Infatuated, impelled by an insane passion, which, for the time, cast aside all impossibilities, I allowed her to see how wildly I adored her.

"Again and again we met.

"I could see by her eyes—by her manner towards me—by her soft, tender words, that I was not indifferent to her; and, at length, hopeless as was my case, I told her all—the poverty of my position, the wealth of my love.

"She did not rebuke me.

"Far from it.

"With a kiss—whose delicious pressure I fancy I can feel upon my lips as I speak—she sealed a compact with me to be faithful, to love me, and wait for me four years.

"I scarcely liked to accept what she proffered of her own free will so tenderly, but what could I do?

"With her lovely form lying in my arms; her lips trembling against mine; her bosom throbbing with joy at having found a mate; what could I do but press her to my breast, and tell her of my unbounded devotion, and how I would strive to win a fortune that I might claim her?

"Yet in the midst of this what sorrow there was in my heart!

"I could not feel joyful.

"I knew that except by a miracle I could not attain the height to which it would be necessary to attain ere I could dream of her as a wife.

"I left her with vows of mutual constancy, and at parting, she gave me the ring I still wear for her sake."

The man's voice trembled as he spoke.

But he quickly recovered himself, and proceeded—

"Well, I was commencing my career, working hard and mingling in all kinds of strange society, when chance threw me into the society of a man who, though he appeared to do nothing, seemed always in possession of abundant means.

"Some little service I rendered him made him a very close friend, and one evening he disclosed to me in private that there was a mystery of no small magnitude connected with his life.

"'If I could trust you,' he said, 'I could put you in possession of a secret by which you could obtain thousands of pounds.'

"You may imagine how my heart leaped.

"Here was my golden chance—my miracle.

"I swore secresy, and I was admitted by him a Member of the Society of Poisoners.

"I had rich relatives—far distantly removed; but by the aid of the subtle essence they could be quickly removed.

"One by one my scruples were removed.

"I became one of them, and a rich man.

"But where was my reward?

"Where is now the one for whom I perilled my soul?

"The wife of another man.

"The sudden death of my relations, one after another, and the reversion of immense wealth so quickly to me, caused suspicion, and legal inquiries were issued.

"But, as may be imagined, these were perfectly without issue.

"The poison used by the devilish crew was far too subtle for discovery, and though people shook their heads and avoided my society, they could find nothing against me to warrant punishment.

"Wealthy now, in spite of the portion I was compelled to give to the League, I went to seek my beloved.

"The horrible gnawings of conscience were still almost for the time by the delicious anticipation of clasping her to my bosom, and hearing from her her joy at my good fortune.

"When I reached her home I was at once admitted to her presence, not before the servant had informed me, however, that the father was dead.

"'There is now no obstacle whatever,' thought I, as richly clothed I stepped into the drawing-room.

"There I found her awaiting me; her face pale, her eyes ablaze, her bosom heaving with an unaccountable excitement.

"I will not torture myself by referring further to this interview.

"Suffice it to say that I was driven from her presence with scorn and ignominy.

"She not only suspected, but by some mysterious means *knew* my guilt; and, though loth to be the agent of my destruction, she refused to listen to a word I said.

"A month afterwards I had the torture of knowing that she had yielded to another, and had married him.

"Again and again have I sought to quit the League.

"But in vain.

"The only thing which severs your connection with that terrible Society is death.

"I *have* quitted them now, and Death has already claimed me for his own.

"I feel the working of the poison within me. There is no antidote to it. I must die, but I can yet have revenge."

As he said this, his form was convulsed with a

strange spasm, and he was compelled to drink another glass of wine.

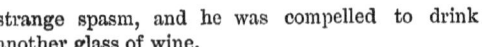

This wine was from a fresh bottle, which Gascoigne had brought from the cupboard.

"Well," he continued, "I can give you the means of always entering the retreat of the Poisoners without fear of discovery.

"Here is a key by which you can enter the retreat at any hour of the day or night, and the general password is ever the same, *Mors Semper* (Always Death). Should there be a special password for a special night, you can plead absence from home.

"I have told you now enough to enable you to understand my wretched life, and to destroy, moreover, the hideous League of Death.

"For my own part, I acknowledge that I have been rightly punished.

"Had I waited, no doubt the love of the one I so worshipped would have been mine, and I should have been a happy husband.

"As it is, the mad greed for gold seized upon me, and I have paid the full penalty of my crimes."

A spasm, stronger than before, now seized the unhappy man, and a greenish pallor overspread his features.

"Yours is a strange history," said Rupert.

"It is, indeed," said Gascoigne. "And are you ready to swear that every word you have said istrue?"

"I swear it, as a dying man should swear, by my hopes of mercy!" returned the man, solemnly.

Gascoigne rose, and drawing the wine to him, took from his pocket a small phial, poured half its contents into a glass, and then, filling it with wine, handed it to their strange guest.

"Drink!" he said.

The man took it without hesitation.

He knew death to be imminent.

If, therefore, the drink were poison it mattered not, whereas there might just be a chance that it would be beneficial.

No sooner had he swallowed the liquid than a glow pervaded his whole form—a kind of stifling feeling invaded his chest—then all the pain fled.

His eyes grew brighter, a heavy weight seemed lifted from his brain, and he said, in a clearer and stronger voice,

"How is this, gentlemen? Have I come into the house of a magician?"

Gascoigne smiled.

"You have come into the house of the enemies of the League," he said, "who have potions strong enough to defy the poisonous compounds they use. You are saved."

The man stood up, walked a few paces, and then sitting down again, said, in a voice full of emotion,

"My fear of the League seems now as a dream. Oh, that all my past life were but a dream also! Oh, that I could live that life over again!"

"It is of no use wishing," said Rupert; "you must spend the remainder of your life in atoning for the past."

"That I will," returned the man, earnestly; "but tell me, how can I ever hope to show my gratitude to you for what you have done for me—a miracle, indeed, to whose fulfilment I have been led as if by the hand of Heaven?"

"Be one of us: aid us to destroy these monsters, and if you do so you will have gone some way towards atonement."

"There will be no fear of my refusing all aid against them," returned the man, whose face was now all aglow with excitement; "meanwhile, if you can afford shelter to such an abandoned creature as myself, I would crave shelter for the night."

"Certainly," said Rupert.

And he was about to ring the bell.

Gascoigne stayed his hand.

"Do not trouble yourself," he said, "I will see to this."

He then beckoned the stranger to follow him, and leading the way to a chamber, said,

"Remain here and rest. If you are in need of anything, yonder bell will summon the servants, whom I will apprise of your presence here."

"I cannot thank you," said the man, with much emotion, "for your kindness to a sin-laden being like myself; but I will prove my gratitude, as I have said, by my actions."

When Gascoigne returned to the room in which he had left Rupert, the latter said—

"Are you sure you have done right in placing sufficient confidence in that man too, to leave him by himself in a room in my house? May not his story as to the poison have been a ruse to deceive us?"

Gascoigne smiled—his peculiar smile.

"No," he said; "*I* can answer for that. If he had *not* taken poison, the antidote I gave him would have caused his instantaneous death."

CHAPTER III.

THE RESULT OF THE COUNSEL—A JOURNEY ON A DARK NIGHT—PERILOUS WORK—IN THE LAIR OF THE POISONERS—THE ANNOUNCEMENT OF THE DESTRUCTION OF THE POISONERS' CASTLE—THE DISCOVERY OF RUPERT AND HIS COMPANION—THE PURSUIT.

It was a dark and somewhat tempestuous night when Rupert and Gascoigne, disguised in masks and heavy cloaks, made their way towards the Retreat of the Poisoners.

They had learned from the man whom they had so strangely saved that this night was appointed for a special meeting.

At this meeting a list of the denounced was to be read, and a number of the League commissioned for their destruction.

Though he would gladly have gone straight to the work of destruction, Rupert's sense of prudence had dictated to him the wisdom of caution.

He had, therefore, resolved to act at first in secret, and again penetrate into the very lair of the enemy.

Both he and Gascoigne were aware of the fearful risk implied in such a visit; but they had nerved themselves for the risk, and well armed, both materially and mentally, they advanced towards the Den of Assassins.

The clock dismally tolled the hour of ten as they saw the dark building looming up before them on the side of the fast-flowing river.

Lights were in the window, and the business of the evening had evidently commenced. Boldly they advanced to the gate and rang the bell.

A tall, masked man answered the summons.

RUPERT; OR, THE DREADNOUGHT: SECRETS OF THE IRON CHEST.

"OSCAR PENRAVEN SPRANG UP, AND DREW A DAGGER FROM HIS GIRDLE."

Furnished as they were with the password, they experienced no difficulty in making their way into the room where the crew of assassins were collected, and in a few moments, therefore, they were standing in the brilliantly-lighted apartment where Rupert had stood on a former occasion.

No notice was taken of them beyond a recognition of the bow they made on entering.

The business of the evening had, as I have already said, commenced; and as they took their seats, Oscar Penraven, who was the only unmasked member, rose to his feet.

"Friends," he said, "there is one amongst us who has brought us strange and woeful tidings. Dr. Henzollern, our respected Chief, is no more."

An exclamation of horror burst from the lips of all present at these words.

"Speak not," cried Oscar; "let me tell you more."

A hush at once fell over all.

Then he continued in a solemn voice, which to Rupert's ears certainly seemed assumed—

"Yes, the Chief for whom we all had so great an affection, who by his able counsels enabled us to reach our present strength, has been basely murdered, the castle where our powerful drugs were manufactured by our army of adepts is destroyed, Count Hendringing also is dead, and we are without a leader."

He paused here to give greater effect to his words.

But there was no response.

He had enjoined silence, and they observed it strictly.

Then briefly he narrated the attack upon and the destruction of the Castle of Hendringing, the duel at the Bridge of Fate, the death of the count, and the subsequent disappearance of Dr. Henzollern.

Oscar Penraven knew well that if there were any doubt as to the death of the Chief of the Dreadful League, his own chance of being at once promoted to the position of leader would be greatly prejudiced.

At this point, therefore, he deviated from the truth, and proceeded to describe not only the death but the subsequent discovery of the body of the Chief, whose corpse had in reality never again risen to the surface of the Death Pool.

"He was pursued into the woods," he said, "by a band of enemies, and was at last compelled to stand at bay against a dozen murderers.

"Bravely he defended himself against overwhelming odds.

"But it was all in vain.

"Wearied by their incessant assaults, he at last turned his sword against his own breast, and deprived his foes of the exquisite pleasure of killing him by plunging it through his heart!

"Satisfied, the assassins then quitted the wood, leaving his body to be devoured by the wild beasts.

"But such was not to be.

"A youth—the son of one of the workmen in the castle, too young to prevent the terrible catastrophe, or, indeed, to render any assistance whatever to his unfortunate master, had watched all the proceedings, and as soon as the enemies of Doctor Henzollern had fled away, he rushed to the spot where the body lay.

"But life was extinct.

"Our Chief lay still and murdered, but he was at least secured a decent burial which the vindictiveness of his enemies would have denied him."

"Liar," thought both Rupert and Gascoigne.

But they kept quite still except when joining in the murmurs of indignation which every now and then broke from the lips of the Poisoners.

"It now becomes our duty to elect a new Chief, and, having done that, to set at once to work to effect the destruction of those who have murdered our leader.

"Need I say that the chief of the band of assassins who went to Germany was Rupert Dreadnought, my hereditary foe, and that he was aided by that mad Scotch youth, Allan of the Glen, and the traitor, Gascoigne?"

A universal groan greeted the latter name.

It was evident that he was regarded as the author of all the misfortunes which had happened to the Society since his leaving its ranks.

While this groaning was going on, Oscar Penraven quitted his chair of office.

Then among the Poisoners there was a hurried whispering, during which both Rupert and Gascoigne were more than once appealed to.

It was evident from the tenor of this which way the feeling of the meeting went.

Oscar Penraven was the one whom they desired to see elevated to the post of Chief.

After a few moments, therefore, one of their number said, in a loud voice—

"I propose that Sir Oscar Penraven shall be made Chief of our Society in the place of Doctor Henzollern, now dead. If there is any other name which any member desires to propose, let him state it at once."

"Penraven! Penraven!" shouted the members, as with one voice.

Among that nestfull of villains at least Oscar was popular, though it might well have made the bodies of some of his noble ancestors shudder in their graves to hear the grand old name shouted out as the proposed leader of a band of such horrid villains.

There was not a dissentient voice.

"Sir Oscar Penraven is elected," said the member who had before spoken. "Sir Oscar, in the name of myself and my comrades, I invite you to again take the chair, this time as the Chief of our Society, which I hope to see regenerated and strengthened in your hands."

Oscar Penraven bowed, and accepted the compliment with as bland and gratified a smile as if he had been offered the leadership of some society confederated for a charitable object.

"I will gladly take the honour which you place so unanimously within my reach," he said, "and will do everything in my power to infuse fresh blood into our great confederation, whose operations will in two years be able to be suspended.

"I will commence my task by giving you a list of all those who are proscribed—who have been denounced, and whom it is your duty to destroy.

"Rupert Dreadnought, Gascoigne the traitor, Allan of the Glen, Tom Braxley the Thames waterman, Stanley Sherrington, Alford, otherwise Richard Penraven, Lesbia Howard, and Rosalie St. Aubyn.

"Such are the names of those who must fall at once beneath your dagger.

"We use poison to clear away from our path those who are possessed of property that we claim.

"But poison is not necessarily the means by which you must destroy enemies whose destruction alone you seek.

"You may use it if possible, but if it is not within your power to do so, use the sword, the knife, the dagger, anything which is at your command.

"Enter their houses as friends or as servants, and destroy them on their own hearths. Use all your energies for one month to annihilate them.

"Let all other business be suspended.

"We shall lose nothing by this.

"Once free from these persons, our Society can work on rapidly to the end.

"Work bravely, and you will receive brave rewards for your success.

"Remember your motto, *Mors Semper!* (death always). Kill, destroy, annihilate!"

A thrill of horror ran through the frames of Rupert Dreadnought and Gascoigne, as Oscar thundered forth these words, accompanying them with a dash of his clenched fist upon the table, which made it tremble.

He seemed transfigured.

His face was crimsoned, and his eyes shot fire like those of a demon.

His whole figure seemed to dilate and glow with excitement; life impregnated with the very spirit of Hate, as he bellowed forth his Proscription, and thundered forth the terms of their terrible mission.

Those whom he addressed seemed influenced by a similar feeling.

He, in fact, inspired them, and, as he concluded, a roar of applause broke out.

"Truly," thought Rupert, "I am in a den of as vile a mass of human corruption as it can be possible to bring together into one spot."

To Gascoigne the scene was not exactly a new one.

Introduced to the diabolical confederation, as will be remembered, by Oscar Penraven himself, he had seen many terrible meetings.

But even *he* was somewhat surprised at Oscar Penraven's manner.

Dr. Henzollern had always acted calmly.

He had gone slowly, calmly, methodically to work at his hideous game.

Oscar Penraven, on the contrary, was animated by a frantic spirit of vengeance, which sent a shuddering horror through the heart of our hero, the more so when a loud and enthusiastic burst of applause followed the words of the speaker.

Truly his father had spoken.

The mission which he now had—that of destroying Oscar Penraven—was one of justice and mercy.

The applause had scarcely ceased, when a low voice sounded in Rupert's ear—

"I know you. You are Earl Dreadnought."

It required iron nerves to prevent a wild start at such an observation in such a place, but Rupert did *not* start.

A cold tremor invaded his limbs.

But that was all.

He had a concentrated feeling within him that banished all alarm.

He would brave all.

Turning slowly round, he sought among the masked men near him the one who had whispered the words.

But his search was in vain.

All had the same facial concealment.

All were stolid, quiet as the rest.

Leaning over to Gascoigne, however, he whispered in his ear.

"Keep close," said Gascoigne. "If it were a great enemy he would discover the fact at once to the assembly. He must be a friend."

"*We* find no such things as friends here," returned Rupert. "We must expect the worst."

As they spoke, there was a rush along the corridor without.

Then the door was flung violently open.

"There are suspicious characters lurking about the house," said the man who entered. "The business of the meeting is well nigh over, and we had better disperse."

"How many are there? Are they in great numbers?" asked Oscar Penraven, impatiently, who cared not, indeed, on the first night of his supremacy, to lead a flight.

"They seem in large numbers," returned the man, "and by their manner are evidently meditating an assault upon the place. We may have nothing to fear, but it is best to act with prudence. Why should any here lose their lives when it is in their power to escape without a struggle?"

"True, true," said Oscar Penraven. "Open the door of the secret corridor, and let the lights be extinguished. This day month we will meet again, friends, and let us hope that before that time we shall be able to exterminate those enemies who are now preventing the due service of the confederation."

He stepped down from his raised seat as he spoke, and the lights were then at once extinguished.

As this occurred Rupert felt a hand slide into his.

Then a voice said—

"Let your companion keep close. I know you well. But I will save you as you are Allan's friend."

Rupert at once guessed who his strange friend was.

It was the old man they had met on London Bridge.

The father of Allan of the Glen.

A word to Gascoigne was enough; and they were soon being led by their unexpected guide into the subterranean passage.

At the extreme end they anticipated that their conductor would leave them.

Even when they went out into the leafy woodlands he kept with them, until at length all members of the Society had dispersed and they were alone with him.

"Now," he said, as he halted in a deeply wooded part, "I will leave you. I have saved you from destruction at a great risk to myself. When I rushed into the room with the announcement that enemies were without, I lied—for not a soul was there. I cannot act thus again—you have had your head in the lion's mouth once and have escaped destruction; in future keep out of it."

He moved to go.

Rupert detained him.

"Stay," he said, "one word with you. We have met before."

"We have."

"On that occasion, though in a strange and unnatural way, you suggested to me the means of saving myself from all peril."

"Well?"

"I take this," pursued Rupert, "as a sign of some goodness left in your heart. You have a feeling of gratitude to me because I have been enabled to do good to your son. Can I not persuade you to leave this terrible Society? can I not induce you to quit them, without betraying them, if you will; but at least let your son know that you are no longer with such a gang of villains and desperadoes?"

The old man shook his head.

"Alas!" he said, "what you ask me to do is impossible."

"How impossible?"

"The oath I have taken precludes all idea of it. But time presses, I must go. Tell my son nothing of what you have heard or seen in regard to me. In a very short time he will hear from me, and when he does so, he will know that I am dead."

Then he quickly turned away, and passed hurriedly into the dark shadows of the trees.

"A strange man, truly," murmured Rupert, as he moved away with Gascoigne, "there is good—great good in the composition of that man. What fearful oath can he have taken that he is so resolute?"

"It matters not," returned Gascoigne, "he has evidently made up his mind to live and die a member of the horrid League. We know enough now to put us on our guard; and we must be ever on the alert. After such a speech as that of Oscar Penraven, we and our friends are safe nowhere."

CHAPTER IV.

OSCAR PENRAVEN'S TREACHERY—THE TRAITOR'S LETTER—THE PRIVATE MEETING—THE LOVE-SCENE—THE INTERRUPTION—THE ENTRANCE OF THE MASKED STRANGER—THE DENUNCIATION—THE ARREST OF THE FAIR DEMON—THE PROMISED DOOM.

It was some two weeks after the return of Rupert Dreadnought from Germany that Rosalie St. Aubyn was sitting in her little boudoir.

She had just emerged from the bath, and had now attired herself in her richest robes.

Not that she expected guests.

Not at all.

She reckoned on being entirely alone.

But so it is with some women.

They revel in their own beauty.

She had dismissed her maid with an injunction to procure as soon as possible some refreshment, when a knock was heard at the front door.

Rosalie started.

A visitor was now unusual.

Now that she was denounced by the Society, and was no longer one of its members, she saw scarcely anyone.

Her victims, too, had ceased.

No longer did lover after lover thrill to the beauty of her deceitful form.

No longer did they tremble as her musical voice spoke of love.

No longer were they carried one after one down into the dreary vaults of death.

Apart from the world she sat brooding over her revenge.

And now——

Wicked as she was, brave in evil doing as she had proved herself to be, she trembled as she heard the loud summons at the door.

Who could it be?

She had no friends. Could it——

Her reflections were cut short by the entrance of a servant.

He had in his hand a letter.

"A gentleman awaits an answer at the door," he said.

Rosalie trembled.

She thought at once of the denunciation.

What might this be?

It might be a summons to a meetiug of the assembly.

However, she opened it quickly, and started in surprise as she saw the signature.

It was that of Oscar Penraven.

"Oscar!" she murmured; "what can he want from me?"

Then she read hastily—

"Dearest Rosalie,—To you in my trouble I fly. Though named Chief of the League, as doubtless you have heard, in place of Dr. Henzollern, now dead, I am not I find above suspicion.

"A number of the members, jealous no doubt of my advancement, have combined against me.

"I am accused of treason to the Society, and am at present hiding from them.

"No doubt I shall in a few days be able to collect round me those true men who know well that all my efforts have been directed to the good of the Society; but, until then, I have need of a refuge.

"Will you give me one?

"If it is only for this night do not deny me; for, though you foiled me in my attempt to carry out my vengeance on Rupert Dreadnought, I bear no malice against you.

"Oscar Penraven."

A strange stifling feeling invaded the breast of Rosalie St. Aubyn as she read, and she sat down, pressing her hand over her agitated bosom, and looking vacantly into the fire.

Vacant, indeed, her eyes might be.

But otherwise she was awake enough.

Her eyes gleamed, her cheeks were aglow with a strange fire, her whole person seemed full of intense excitement.

At length, after a few moments' consultation with herself, she turned to the servant.

"Admit him," she said.

The man bowed and retired.

In another minute Oscar Penraven entered.

He was attired in the height of fashion.

Rosalie noticed this at once.

There was that in his dress and in his manner as he came in which bespoke the man bent upon a love adventure rather than one flying from his inveterate enemies.

"I thought you would relent, Rosalie," he said.

"I have never been so deadly an enemy to you that I need fear your uncompromising hatred."

"He has been upon some love errand and been disappointed," thought she.

But she gave no vent to her thoughts.

"You have not been a friend of mine," she said; "you have deceived me again and again. At first you pretended a love for me you did not feel; that I forgave you, for my heart was never yours. I have aided you again and again. I even enabled you to carry off the one on whom your mind was set, and yet there is reason to believe that you have been since plotting against me."

Oscar smiled.

"Would that be wonderful," he said, "if it were the truth, when you remember how you foiled me in my attempt to destroy Rupert Dreadnought?"

"I love him!"

Oscar Penraven had suspected this.

Nevertheless he started as she spoke.

Her voice was full of such intense feeling.

As I have said, her passion for Rupert was almost a madness, and every fibre of her form seemed to thrill to the words—

"I love him!"

"You love, then, the greatest enemy I have," said Oscar Penraven.

"Truly—but what matters that?" she added with a laugh; "*you* love another; we are simply friends; you come here for safety—I will give it you, as far as is in my power. As for love, that is not for you and me. By the way, I am about to have supper," she added, gaily, "will you join me?"

In a short time they entered the supper room, and sat down to a sumptuous repast.

Alone in the world as she might be, she yet lived like a princess.

The supper it is unnecessary to describe.

It would be but wasting necessary space.

"AN OLD WOMAN, BENDING OVER A STICK, WAS LISTENING AT THE DOOR WITHOUT."

We only mention it as forming a prelude to deadly treachery.

Suffice it to say that the bright wine flowed, and that the eyes of both the banquettors flashed with a more fiery light, and Oscar's arm slid round the round waist of his voluptuous companion, and their lips met again and again.

"What can this mean?" thought the fair demon, as she responded freely to his ardent caresses; "he must require my services to carry out some diabolical scheme."

In the midst of this scene, when matters had so far progressed that both, apparently, were under the influence of the wine, and had forgotten all but the enjoyment of the moment, a loud step was heard ascending the stairs.

There was no attempt at announcement.

The door was opened, and a man attired in a long, black cloak, and wearing a mask, halted in the entry.

Oscar Penraven sprang up, and drew a dagger from his girdle.

"What means this intrusion?" he cried.

Rosalie feared the worst from this vehemence.

"Be patient," she whispered; "you do not yet know that this man is an enemy."

"Does he come as a friend?" cried Oscar.

"I come from the League of which you have been appointed Chief," returned the man.

"Well, am I summoned?" said Oscar, with a sneer.

"No; you are denounced."

"Your Chief denounced!"

"Yes; you are now with a traitress, who has been denounced long since. Our men surround the house on all sides. You cannot escape."

Oscar advanced to the casement, and looked out.

What the man had said was true.

Everywhere out in the grounds were armed men.

"We are trapped, Rosalie," he said, as he returned to the table, with a stern look upon his features, which was but the result of acting; "but I have still power with the League, and will protect you."

Then he turned to the man.

"Whither are we to proceed?"

"To the Retreat."

"Where is your order?"

"I have none," replied the other. "I am acting under the command of the Council; and that is enough. If it were not, the number of our men would be sufficient to do away with all necessity for it."

"Is our trial to take place to-night?"

"No; the special Council does not sit to-night. You will be tried to-morrow. Come, we must hasten."

During all this time Rosalie St. Aubyn had stood by the table with one hand leaning on it, eyeing Oscar with a strange look.

It was a look of deep, intense scrutiny.

Evidently to her mind the idea suggested itself that treachery was at work somewhere.

The question was how and where?

Was Oscar Penraven acting a part?

When the man spoke of the haste he was in she rang a bell.

A servant girl, pale and trembling, appeared.

"Oh! my mistress," she exclaimed, clasping her hands, "what is the matter?"

"Nothing," replied Rosalie, "nothing. It means that I am going on a journey, perhaps a long one. But fear not; *however long it may be, this gentleman will accompany me,* and I shall not be in want of one to aid me."

She gazed full in Oscar's eyes as she spoke, and in the light that blazed full upon him from those brilliant orbs he plainly read her meaning.

Death was the destination she spoke, and, if she were to reach that, she was resolved that *he* should accompany her.

"Bring me my hat and cloak," added Rosalie, quickly, "and put in the pocket what you will find on my toilet-table."

The young girl, who was not one of the initiated, and knew nothing of the misdoings of her mistress, saw, in spite of the latter's words, that something was wrong, and when, on reaching Rosalie St. Aubyn's room, she saw lying on the table a small delicate dagger and a tiny pistol, she guessed at once that she required these for her protection.

Hastily, therefore, she placed them in the pocket, and carried them to the room where the messenger of the League waited in silence.

In a few minutes more Rosalie St. Aubyn and Oscar Penraven had been led out into the open air, and placed in a carriage.

The man who had been the messenger of the Council did not enter the carriage, but mounted on the box, while the men who had surrounded the house walked quietly along by the side of the coach.

"Oscar," said Rosalie St. Aubyn, in a strange, low whisper, "I have an extraordinary idea in regard to this night's work."

"What is it?"

"That *you* have betrayed me."

The voice in which she spoke was so terrible that Oscar fairly trembled.

The traitor saw that he must temporize.

Gliding his arm round the waist of the woman he had betrayed, he pressed her form to him.

"Why should you think so?" he said, in a gentle whisper. "I am denounced as well as yourself."

"That may be a ruse."

"But it is not, I say. You will see when the Council sits that I will endeavour to do all I can——"

"To destroy me," replied Rosalie. "I can see through it all—you who once professed to love me."

She adopted a new plan now.

She saw she was surrounded by enemies—she saw herself fairly entrapped, and she spoke, therefore, in a tender voice, and suffered her lithe and exquisite form to glide into his arms, while her breath fanned his cheek.

Oscar felt the influence of this lovely creature, but he was not thus to be deterred from his purpose.

The chance of greater deception, however, was thus given him.

He kissed her lips and pressed her to him, so that her bosom throbbed against his.

"Fear not; I will save you," he said.

And she, affecting to believe him, kissed him in return, and said—

"And *I* will aid you in punishing your foes."

So the two traitors tried mutually to deceive each other.

Yet in the hearts of both were deadly hate and suspicion.

At length the carriage stopped.

It was in a thickly wooded part of the high road; and Rosalie St. Aubyn at once guessed that they were close to the Poisoners' Retreat.

"Now then comes the proof of your words," said Rosalie; "I shall see whether or not you are deceiving me."

In another moment the armed men drew up closer; the carriage door was opened, and they were invited to alight.

Obeying the order at once, they were conducted together to the door.

Here they separated, Oscar Penraven being led

up a staircase, and Rosalie being led downwards into a cold and dank passage.

At the end of this she was thrust into a cell, in which was nothing but utter darkness.

And here the fair demon was left for the time.

CHAPTER V.

THE OLD HOUSE NEAR THE POISONERS' RETREAT—THE LISTENER—THE CAPTURE—THE CONFESSION AND THE PLAN.

It will be remembered that about the time when Helen Penraven's adventure at Brentwood took place Rupert Dreadnought became purchaser of an old house in the wood, close by the Poisoners' Retreat.

It was here that they hastened after their escape.

So arranged, they found everything in readiness for their reception, as they had only been absent a few days.

The old housekeeper who had charge of the place was always on the watch; and though alone in the place, and so near the home of the terrible Leaguers, she never was once under suspicion.

Neither Oscar Penraven or any of his men, in fact, had any idea that those of whom they were in search had a place of observation so near to them.

On the evening after their arrival, just as the twilight had fallen, Rupert and Gascoigne were seated in their front room talking over what had occurred the night before, and the plan it would be best to employ in the future.

"Now we have seen what unreasoning villany heads them," said Rupert, "and what a savage resolution they have taken to destroy all of us, no matter by what hideous means, I think there ought to be no compunction in our minds. We ought to root them out, no matter by what means."

"Aye, set fire to the place and burn them in it," returned Gascoigne; "such a fate is by no means too hard for them. Did you see Allan of the Glen and our other friends?"

"Yes," returned Rupert, who had only just returned from a flying visit to his own house. "Allan and Tom the waterman, Alford and Stanley Sherrington, will all be here this night, and we will then consult together as to the best mode of destroying these human vultures."

Just as he spoke, the old housekeeper entered, bearing some refreshment, and with a strange look on her face.

Then, as she laid the wine and so forth on the table, she put her finger to her lips to enjoin silence as to her proceedings, and drew Rupert towards the window, saying, in a low whisper—

"Keep on speaking of your affairs."

"I shall be glad enough when the chance comes," said he, as he neared the window, and, following the direction of the housekeeper's finger, gazed out.

An old woman, bending over a stick, was listening at the door without.

"We have spies here it seems," and rushing swiftly to the door, he flung it open ere the old woman could start up from her position as eavesdropper; he seized her by the arm.

"What do you here?" he cried.

The question and the manner in which it was said was so quick that the woman was unable to speak.

She stood there looking at him, and trembling violently.

Rupert drew her into the room, and locked the door.

"A spy, I suppose," said Gascoigne, who at once comprehended the scene.

"I believe so," said Rupert: "but, since I have no proof of her villany, I will force it from her own lips. Woman, what was your purpose in listening at yonder door?"

"To see if anyone was within."

"And for what purpose?"

"That I might crave a bit of bread and a drink of water for one on the point of starvation," she said, in a tremulous voice.

But, though there was a natural reason why she should be full of fear, there was that in the look of her eye which told that she was lying.

"I believe her not," said Gascoigne.

"Neither do I," returned Rupert; "however, it is very easy to discover whether or not she is an imposter. You," he added, turning again to the old woman, "you are, I believe, in the pay of the Poisoners. You are some emissary from Oscar Penraven. To prove the truth or falseness of this you will be detained here on the bread and water you profess to seek, and placed in an underground cell. There you will remain until you think proper to make a confession."

It may seem, at first sight, that Rupert Dreadnought was running headlong to a conclusion, and that he was permitting himself to be carried away by a spirit of injustice.

It was not so.

There is, strange to say, a way of discovering a traitor which admits of no ready explanation.

There is something in the blanching cheek, the unsteady eye, the trembling manner, which speaks of a consciousness of evil doing.

All these signs were evident in the woman before him.

And yet for some time she endeavoured to put on an air of innocence.

"Of course I'm in your power," she said, in a tone of despair and sorrow. "I'm alone and helpless and you can do as you please with me. I don't know why you behave thus, for I'm sure I've nothing on me you can want to steal."

"Come," said Rupert, "we have no time to waste in idle talk with you. Either you are employed by the Poisoners or you are not. If you are not you can give a good account of yourself; if you are, and will confess all you know, you shall not only be rewarded but you shall be released in a few days after being well paid. I will give you half-an-hour to think over it. Here, Masters," he added to the housekeeper, "take her to a secure room at the top of the house and lock her in."

The old woman turned to go.

Then her courage deserted her.

"Well," she said, facing round, "what is it you desire to know?"

"Who sent you here?"

"Oscar Penraven."

"I thought so. Does he suspect us to be here?"

"He does; in fact, he knows it. You were seen at one of the windows last night."

"And what did he think *you* could learn for him?"

"Your progress and your future intentions. I was told to make my way hither, to listen, and report your intentions and numbers. There is a grand council to-night, to decide upon the fate of one of the denounced whom they have caught, and I was to appear before them, and inform them of all I knew."

"Which one of the denounced is it they have caught?"

"Rosalie St. Aubyn."

"Ah! and what will be her fate?"

The old woman shuddered visibly.

"Oh, ask me not," she said; "it will, no doubt, be something terrible. Doubt not that the first one of the denounced will receive a punishment which shall be an example to the rest."

Gascoigne at this moment approached Rupert and whispered something in his ear.

"True," said Rupert; "I was going to ask that question had you not reminded me."

Then, turning to the woman, he added—

"You are, of course, well acquainted with the Poisoners' Retreat?"

"Yes," she said, hesitatingly.

"Come, no prevarication," he said. "You must lead us to the underground portion of the building this night."

"At what hour?"

"When does the Council meet?"

"At nine."

"Then at half-past nine you must conduct us to the secret entrance, then you will be free to go whither you please. Now, Masters, take your prisoner to her room, give her some refreshment, and see that she is forthcoming when she is required."

"This woman's arrival here seems an act of Providence," said Gascoigne, when they were once more alone; "we shall be able to effect our object this very night. But, by the way, although you are resolved to go, you have not yet told me what is your exact plan of operations."

"Well, this providential aid somewhat changes the programme," said Rupert; "in fact, it strangely simplifies it. We and our friends must proceed to the house, enter by the private way, and then set fire to it. Let them all perish."

"And Rosalie St. Aubyn. Will you save her?"

A grave, stern look overspread Rupert's features.

"Ask me not," he said. "She is as bad as the rest. If she is there among them, let her perish. Though I could not see her struggling amid the flames, it would be but a just doom, for her soul is heavy with guilt."

CHAPTER VI.

THE ARRIVAL OF ALLAN OF THE GLEN AND OTHERS FROM LONDON—ONCE MORE ON THE POISONERS' TRACK—THE SUBTERRANEAN CELLS—A SURPRISE—THE BEAUTIFUL VICTIM—THE POWER OF WOMAN'S CHARMS—THE TORTURERS—THE ATTACK—THE CONFLAGRATION.

WHEN darkness once more set in, the little party of horsemen made their way through the wood, and stopped at the door of Rupert's house.

This party comprised Allan of the Glen, Stanley Sherrington, Alford, and Tom the waterman.

They expected their services to be quickly brought into requisition; but they were agreeably surprised to hear the unexpected turn affairs had taken.

A spasm of pain, however, crossed the face of Alford, or, rather, Richard Penraven, as we should call him, when he heard the fate of Rosalie St. Aubyn.

Bad as she had proved herself to be she had been the partner of his wedded joys, and, though she had deliberately sought his death, he hoped even now that she would escape the fate which the Poisoners would award her—a fate which he doubted not would be a terrible one.

After partaking of a hearty meal, and thoroughly arranged their plans, the friends caused the old spy to be released from her room, and then, in a compact body, they proceeded along the wooded avenues under her guidance.

They were not long in reaching a part of the tangled woodland where the bushes grew in such a dense mass that it was with great difficulty they could make their way.

At this spot, which was some little distance from the door of the Poisoners' Retreat, the old woman halted, and pushing aside a mass of thick undergrowth, disclosed a concealed doorway.

This Rupert at once remembered.

It was that by which the father of Allan of the Glen had led them out into the forest a few nights before.

Pushing against this they found it yield, and as it did so they could hear the faint sounds of distant moaning.

"Some wretched victim is being put to the torture," said Richard Penraven, who suspected it to be Rosalie, whose voice was raised in accents of pain. "'Let us hasten forward and see."

Hurrying on as well as the extreme darkness would permit, they at length came to a sudden stop before a doorway, from which a dim stream of light was thrown across the passage.

It was here that the moaning victim, whoever it might be, was immured, and advancing cautiously, they peered in.

What a sight was there!

In the room were four men in masks, while a fifth, a brutal-looking being, was in his shirt-sleeves, and with uncovered face.

Tied up by her hands to a beam was Rosalie St. Aubyn.

Her feet did not reach the ground, and the whole weight of her body, therefore, was on her wrists.

In this helpless position the exquisite demon was the subject of numberless jeers from those around.

RUPERT DREADNOUGHT OR THE SECRETS OF THE IRON CHEST

"'SAVE ME! SAVE ME!' GURGLED THE OLD MAN."

"Again," said one of the number, "again I ask you the same question. Rupert Dreadnought and the spy, Gascoigne, were, a night or two back, admitted to our Retreat. Was it not by *you?*"

"No, no," shrieked the wretched woman, as her form writhed in agony; "no, no, I will not tell you a lie to give you the chance of making my punishment worse. I did *not* betray you."

A laugh of scorn was the reply.

"Now," said Rupert, whose pity was aroused as

he gazed at the form of the woman writhing in her exquisite pain, "let us burst into the room and seize on the torturers, then release Rosalie St. Aubyn, and fire the house."

A gentle push against the door proved that it was not fastened.

The demons appointed by the hideous Council to destroy by hideous torture one of their own number had never dreamed of any one save their own crew entering by that secret door, and when Rupert and his men burst into the vault, they fell back in utter astonishment.

They had no time left them to defend themselves.

In an instant the hands of the brave friends were at their throats, and Rosalie St. Aubyn was cut down ere a single word was spoken.

Leaving her, fainting though she was, the band of adventurers proceeded to bind the hands of their prisoners.

Then they gagged them and placed them together in one corner of the vault.

By the time they had done this, Rosalie, by the aid of some brandy which Richard Penraven administered, had been restored to something like life.

She then rose upon her feet, and looked around her in wonder and fear.

What was to be the next movement?

Was she a prisoner, or would the men who had saved her from torture save her also from all fear of again falling into the hands of her enemies?

This question was soon settled.

"Go, Mistress Rosalie St. Aubyn," said Rupert Dreadnought, solemnly, "go, and let me never set my eyes on you again. There is time yet left for you to repent and mend your ways. Quit the country, and let the fearful doom you have just escaped be a warning to you in the future to leave the hideous track of guilt you have so long pursued."

Oh! such a look of pleading as Rosalie St. Aubyn cast upon the face of the man who spoke was never seen by any there before.

Rupert, the man upon whom she doted so passionately, speaking to her in such terms of contemptuous warning, was too much for her feelings, and a flood of passionate tears burst from her.

Then, regardless of all around her, she flung herself upon her knees at his feet.

"Oh, Rupert!" she cried, "do not be so cruel to one whose life is yours by gratitude, by love, by all a woman holds dearest in life! Oh, Rupert, I ask no more than that you will permit me to be near you. Do not, do not demand from me such a sacrifice as to quit England for ever!"

Perhaps none was more astounded by this exhibition of feeling than Rupert Dreadnought himself.

He could scarcely believe his ears; but, then, as he glanced at the bright streaming eyes he remembered the flashing orbs that had taken such a strong hold upon his mind when he rescued her from the hands of the Mohocks.

It seemed again the helpless school-girl that appealed to him for protection.

But he did not suffer his feelings long to overcome his reason.

The creature who knelt to him was certainly a model of beauty.

But she was also a model of iniquity.

"Rise!" he said, "I am not the one to whom you should kneel. We have no time to lose; rise quickly and quit this place ere it is too late for you to do so in safety. Hark! what is that?"

It was a loud voice calling from above.

A voice that echoed in hollow tones along the subterranean corridor.

"Bertrand, are you ready?"

Gascoigne advanced to the door and said in gruff accents—

"Yes; I will be with you in five minutes."

"Hasten, for the Council waits to hear the confession of the prisoner."

"She will not confess."

"Then she will be broken on the wheel."

Rosalie placed her hands over her eyes and uttered a low moan.

"Oh! horrible!" she murmured.

"You see," said Rupert, "to what a doom you are destined by the wretches in whose crimes you have shared. Go, quickly, I say," he added, sternly, "or remain here to be gagged, and to suffer the same fate as they are about to suffer."

The manner in which he spoke was such as to take from the wretched woman's mind all hope.

So, slowly rising, she quitted the vaulted chamber, where her lovely form had so short a time before been submitted to excruciating agony, and took her way along the cold, earthy passage towards the place of egress.

As she passed out of the door into the wood, with her hands pressed over her eyes, and her form bent, she looked the very picture of despair—like a fallen angel driven out of Paradise.

"I will not leave England—sooner would I die," she murmured, as she made her way among the dense trees, and took up a position where she could see the Poisoners' Retreat without any fear of being discovered herself.

Hating Oscar Penraven as she did, and still loving Rupert Dreadnought in spite of his insulting exhibition of contempt for her, she wished to see, if possible, the triumph of the latter over the Chief of the Poisoners.

How the small and unassisted band of friends would be able to succeed in their desperate venture she could not imagine.

And yet she had sufficient faith in Rupert's courage and skill to make her believe that in some way or another she would see the end of the Dread League that night.

Meanwhile, as soon as she had quitted the vault of torture, Rupert and his friends prepared to act.

Gathering together all the wood they could find—and there was no small quantity of it, seeing that the vault was used as a repository for lumber—they quickly dragged it up, and placed it against the door, which alone formed the communication with the subterranean passage.

Then, casting upon the huge heap some spirit they had brought with them, they set a light to it, and the mass blazed up like tinder.

Having seen that except to rush into certain destruction the conspirators could not quit their room by that door, Rupert and his companions quitted the subterranean passage, and made their way into the open air.

Here they drew from their pockets some packets heavily weighted, and containing combustible materials, and cast them with all their strength through the windows.

They heard the bursting, crackling noise, which told that their missiles had taken effect, and then lurid flames began to hiss and roar through the crashing casements, while yells of agony betokened the torture of those within.

This part of their work was done.

They now bethought them of their prisoners.

"Helpless men shall not burn," said Rupert. "We will bring them out here, and hang them each to the branch of a tree. Death is their proper portion."

They had very little time in which to effect their purpose.

When they entered the subterranean passage, they could feel the hot air surging along it, and see the glare of the exultant flames as they lapped the door at the other end.

The vault, however, in which the torturers had began the pnnishment of the fair demon had not yet been reached by the conflagration.

Indeed, in the position in which it was placed, it was doubtful whether, if the whole place had been wrapped in one immense flame, the heat would have reached the spot in sufficient force to have made it dangerous to life.

They found the five men exactly in the same positions in which they had left them.

Hastily, without paying any heed to the desperate and imploring looks cast upon them by the wretched victims, they raised them up and carried them out into the open air.

"Now," said Rupert, as they reached a clearing where three or four trees showed themselves with conveniently placed boughs, "now let us finish this part of our work. We know not how soon we may be required elsewhere."

Tom the waterman at once produced from his pocket a set of ropes enough to have hung double the number of victims.

Then one by one the villains were placed beneath the boughs, the ropes adjusted round their necks, the bodies raised and then let fall again with a heavy crash.

When the five bodies hung in a row, the flare of the conflagration had spread itself over the whole forest, and they could see the distorted features of the executed Poisoners, who, had they been given time to reason, would have thanked Heaven that they had escaped the awful doom of their fellows.

Hour after hour passed, and the fire still raged furiously, lighting up the old woodland, and casting weird shadows on the green sward.

Then the wailing wind blew out the flames, and scattered the burning wood into a myriad sparkles, like red snow, which floated away slowly towards the silent heavens.

Then the fire died out, and nothing remained but the blackened walls and the smoking embers.

"Now," said Rupert, "our work is done; let us quit this place."

Hastening away through the dusky woods, the little band of adventurers soon reached their own retreat, and flung themselves, wearied, upon their couches, full dressed as they were.

When their forms had disappeared from the precincts of the still smoking pile, there was a movement among a mass of materials where the fire seemed first to have extinguished itself.

Then a man's form—only just distinguishable as such among its rags, or, rather, its burnt garments—rose up and staggered forth into the fresh air, uttering a low, wailing cry as of terrible agony and despair.

Gaining a little strength from the inhalation of the cool breeze, he stood for a few moments in one position, with his hand pressed to his brow.

Then, turning suddenly, he glanced at the wreck and ruin of the Poisoners' Retreat, his clenched fist aloft, and appeared to be uttering some wild, incoherent curses.

Then he turned away again, and with heavy steps slowly crawled away from the scene of disaster.

Who and what was this wild, despairing, wretched creature?

CHAPTER VII.

TIME FLIES APACE—RUPERT'S MISGIVINGS—HIS RESOLUTION TO WAIT AND WATCH—STRANGE EFFECTS OF THE DESTRUCTION OF THE POISONERS' RETREAT—LONDON IS SAVED FROM DEATH.

On the morning following the conflagration, Rupert and his friends made their way to the Poisoners' Retreat, or, rather, what had once been their retreat.

The fire had now completely been got under, and scarcely a wreath of smoke arose from the blackened mound of burnt materials.

Rain, in fact, had fallen during the hours of darkness, and had quenched what few faint signs of life there were.

"We must search these ruins," said Rupert Dreadnought, "for until I see the body of Oscar Penraven, how can I be satisfied that he is dead, and that the fourth desire of my father has been fulfilled."

"True," said Gascoigne, "the task must, I suppose, be fulfilled, but it is a dismal one, to say the least of it."

Carefully they searched the ruins, but although numbers of dismal corpses met their view, it was impossible to recognise any.

Naturally enough, a small band of friends as they were, without proper tools of any kind, they were unable to make a thorough search.

But this evil was soon obviated.

The old woman who had guided them to the spot, and who had escaped the terrible fate which had overtaken the rest of the Poisoners, had carried to the nearest town the news of the utter destruction of the house and its inmates; and the morning had not gone far ere a crowd of curiosity-mongers assembled round the house.

By the aid of these (many of them rustics armed with formidable spades and picks) the ruins were soon thoroughly examined.

But all with no effect.

Ninety-five bodies were there discovered, but among that number scarcely one was there that could be recognised as human at all.

Here, then, was a difficulty.

Was Oscar Penraven dead?

Not having personally seen his death, was Rupert Dreadnought at liberty to open the fifth compartment of the Iron Chest?

How could he satisfy his conscience in this respect.

Certainly he knew that the special Council of the Poisoners numbered exactly one hundred, and a hundred dead bodies had been found, counting those hung on the trees.

But he could not, therefore, conclude for a certainty that Oscar Penraven was dead.

There might have been a hundred and one that night, counting the executioner.

It was too much of course to suppose that Oscar Penraven, the vilest of the vile, should be the only one to escape from the terrible fire in which the wailing, agonised wretches had tasted of the pain which they had aided in giving to others.

What then was to be done?

How could he prove the fact?

There was nothing for it but to watch and wait, and this he resolved to do.

Glad indeed was he for a rest from the terrific whirl of adventures into which he had been cast of late; and he retired to his home to spend his time with Helen and his friends to recruit his energies for the final struggle.

The effect of the destruction of the Poisoners' Retreat was soon apparent.

Not only in London, but for miles and miles around, and in all the great towns of England, was the result felt.

The nucleus of the diabolical conspiracy being destroyed, the members who were spread over England had no one to direct their movements, and on hearing of the death by burning of the Dread Council they left their horrid occupation altogether.

But uncles, fathers, mothers, whose hungry relatives were eagerly watching the thinning of the thread of life, and by insidious poisons constantly aiding the efforts of Death, found themselves suddenly rising and expanding into new strength.

Throughout London the effect seemed miraculous.

Hundreds recovered from beds of sickness where they had lain for months.

However, there were yet among the population wretches who wanted only the opportunity to show their talons.

Of these and their doings we shall speak anon.

We must pass over rapidly and without comment the space of two months, and take our readers with us to a spot on the margin of the river Thames, close by the spot which is now called Southend.

In those days that portion of the river's banks was the abode of numberless fishermen, who reckoned, among their other avocations, those of wreckers and smugglers.

The latter pursuit was one which they carried on with the utmost avidity and adroitness, and numberless were the encounters which took place between the authorities and the hardy sons of the sea.

The huge chalk cliffs, which extend from above Southend to Shoeburyness, and frown there over the German Ocean, afforded scarcely any means of landing, except at one place, and there, at the time of our story, was a huge cave, in which the stores of the smugglers were concealed, and where, also, they caroused on those evenings on which they were awaiting the arrival of their vessel and its illicit freight.

It was a wild, weird place.

Being used only at certain periods by human beings, it was still the haunt of wild sea-birds, who made their nests up in dark corners, and shrieked and swooped about dismally when the smugglers lit their torches.

The cave was covered with barrels and pieces of old timber.

Here and there stood the figure-head or the name-board of a vessel that had foundered at sea, and had been lured on to sand-banks and jagged concealed rocks by the false lights of the wreckers.

The goods which were liable to be spoiled by damp, or which would rouse the suspicions of a stranger, were hidden away far in the recesses of an inner cave, which, at first sight, could not be seen, as its entrance was at right angles with the wall of the outer cavern.

Here one night, about two months after the destruction of the Poisoners' Retreat, was gathered a motley crew.

It was a dark, tempestuous night.

The wind howled fearfully over sea and land, and shrieked like the voices of lost spirits, as it swirled in at the entrances of the caverns.

Not a star was visible.

Black clouds effectually obscured the twinkling lamps of the sky.

The moon, too, had not shown herself.

Land and sea were covered with the same black, monotonous pall.

It was just a night for crime.

And crime was, of course, abroad.

Wretches such as those who lured misguided travellers to their destruction have always an instinctive affinity with darkness.

On the topmost pinnacle of the rugged rocks which overhung the cave stood a man.

He was a tall, broadly-built fellow, evidently full of manly energy.

His wide chest, his massive limbs, his well-poised head, told you this.

Yet this model of manly beauty was a smuggler, and a wrecker, too.

By his side was a pile of wood, which was the beacon, ready to be lit as soon as any unfortunate vessel was approaching.

"Curses on the night!" he muttered, as he strode to and fro on the edge of the cliff. "In spite of the darkness, I can see nothing like a vessel approaching. I hope to-night will bring something for us, for our luck has been little of late."

Then he started and listened.

The sound of footsteps was heard approaching.

"Who comes there?" shouted the smuggler.

"It's Red Orley," answered a gruff voice. "I bring you news."

"Let's hope it's better news than the wind and waves promise then," growled the wrecker; "for that isn't much."

"What, grumbling already, captain?" said the new comer, as he climbed the rocks and stood by the side of the wrecker.

The one who now came upon the scene was a man of middle size, with a thin but seemingly strong and wiry frame.

But his face was a strange one.

It seemed as if it had been seared and eaten away by some corrosive substance, or as if it had been submitted to the influence of fierce and terrible flames.

The flesh was all in heavy seams and scars; the nose was distorted, the mouth awry.

But the eyes still burned savagely.

Awful eyes they were.

They glittered like those of some wild anima

There was in them all the reason of a human being mingled with the ferocity and bloodthirstiness of the brute.

"Aye, Red Orley, it's enough to make one grumble I should fancy," replied the one addressed as captain; "here there have been three dark nights running and not a single wreck."

"Well, of course it's provoking," replied the other; "it's as bad for us as for you, captain. However, I *do* bring you better news. The 'Helena,' a merchantman of eight hundred tons burden, should arrive in the estuary this night. She should have arrived by this, and unless she goes to pieces on the Goodwins, which there is, of course, a chance of, she'll be driven in here. The tide's rolling swift enough, and what with our beacon here and the Shark's Head Rock, it will be a curious thing if our boys should have nothing to do to-night."

The captain, as the other was speaking, had walked nearer to the edge of the cliff, and had approached it very closely, when he exclaimed, in a loud voice—

"Ah! see there, what is that? That surely is a light!"

"A light true enough," cried the other.

Then he sprang to his side.

What followed was the work of a moment.

There was a sudden push, a loud cry of surprise and agony, a dark body crashed over the cliffs, and the second comer stood on the cliff alone.

The captain of the wreckers lay meanwhile a mangled heap upon the jagged rocks beneath.

Red Orley then drew from his pocket a horn, and blew a loud blast.

A blast that startled the sea-birds, and went wailing away on the wings of the mighty wind.

It was instantly answered.

A wild blast echoed up from below.

Then a number of men rushed up the rocky path.

"See below the cliffs there," shouted Red Orley, "the captain has fallen over the rocks. He may still be living. Bring him to the cave ere the sea reaches him."

The men, without waiting to question him as to the manner of their leader's death, rushed at once to the spot which Orley intimated.

There they found him truly.

But he was stone dead.

There was no mark of human violence on his body.

He had fallen headlong on the jagged stones, and his brains were crushed out.

But of foul play there was no indication.

Eagerly, when the wreckers carried the body into the cave, did Red Orley scan their features to see if possible what were their thoughts.

But they showed no evidence of suspicion.

"It's all over with him," said one of them, as he examined the fracture of the skull; "he must have been dead in a moment. How did it happen?"

"Why," said Orley, with the coolest effrontery imaginable, "we were standing together upon the summit of the cliff. He was grumbling about the ill-luck which the band had lately met with, when the lights of a ship suddenly appeared—"

"Ha!" cried several voices at once, "is there a ship in the offing?"

"Yes, there is. But let me tell you," continued Red Orley; "he started suddenly forward to catch a glimpse of what so much pleased him, when he missed his footing, and fell over ere I could aid him."

"Well, well," cried one burly fellow, "he's beyond our reach now, that's one thing. We'd better look after the plunder. Is the beacon lit?"

"No. Go some of you and light it," said Red Orley, assuming at once an air of authority. "I will be with you in a few moments, as soon as I have made Mistress Orley acquainted with the meaning of the dead thing that lies here."

So saying, he made his way to the back of the cavern, and, pushing aside a small door, revealed a strange sight.

It was a small inner cave he entered.

Not that in which the goods were stored.

That was on the opposite side.

This one was a cave which a woman's taste had rendered something like a room.

The white chalk of the walls could not, of course, be concealed.

But over the floor was cast a carpet.

In the centre were chairs and a table, and on one side a bedstead.

Opposite this was a fire-place where a woman was kneeling.

She was engaged in cooking something as Red Orley entered.

She sprang up at once to meet him, however, and, pale and wan as she was, by despair and suffering, she was still recognisable as Rosalie St. Aubyn.

"Oh, Oscar," she said, "have you returned so soon?"

Red Orley, then the seamed, disfigured man—the wrecker—the murderer of the captain—was Sir Oscar Penraven, one of the last of a noble race!

How this came about we must describe in our next chapter ere we describe the strange events which followed among the wreckers.

CHAPTER VIII.

TWO BAD HEARTS TOGETHER.

MY readers will remember, no doubt, that after the destruction of the Poisoners' Retreat, one wretched, half-burned being emerged from the blackened ruins, and, after invoking curses on those who had been the ruin of the League, staggered away into the wood.

This was none other than Oscar—Chief but for a few hours.

Hurrying along as fast as his weary legs would carry him, he came to a stile, or rather a wooden gate, against which a figure was leaning.

On nearing it he saw it was a woman.

"What do you here?" he asked, in a gurgling tone.

His mouth was too parched—too dry with the heat and dust to permit much articulation.

The woman turned towards him a face white with terror.

Then, as the light of the moon fell on it, he saw that it was Rosalie St. Aubyn.

"Ah! you, too, have escaped, then," he said. "You do not know me."

The wretched woman glanced at his burned and blistered face.

Then at his tattered clothes.

"Speak again," she said.

"My voice is gone for the time," he answered.

"Truly, if it was a voice, I know it *is* gone," she said, "for I cannot recollect it."

"A good chance of vengeance, then, is still left me," said Oscar. "If even you do not know me, I am safe from detection. Know, then, that I am Oscar Penraven, the one whom you imagined your betrayer, but who, in very truth, has only escaped because he was in a cell below, just about to be placed in the hands of the torturers."

"You a prisoner?" she cried, doubtingly.

In this doubt she was wrong.

For once the traitor had spoken truly.

Although, in his own base heart, he had intended to betray Rosalie St. Aubyn, whom he had hated for the part she had taken in saving Rupert Dreadnought from his designs, he had not had the opportunity given him of doing so.

Suspected by the Council of not adhering strictly to their rules, he was still more suspected when the messenger of the League informed them of the scene he had beheld at Rupert Dreadnought's house.

They could not conceive the necessity for the treachery exhibited by Oscar to a woman.

They rather saw in it an attempt at eluding punishment for her.

In very truth Oscar Penraven had not been prepared for the rapid interruption of his supper.

As we have seen, he and Rosalie had established a very good understanding one with the other, and the entrance of the man had been very inopportune.

But this was not all.

A paper, dropped accidentally by Oscar Penraven, had disclosed to the astounded Council a plan for the wholesale destruction of the Leaguers.

One passage proved this.

It ran thus:—

"*The present constitution of the Council of the League is altogether unwieldy. A hundred members are not required for the administration of the affairs of the Society. Ten would be quite sufficient, and to that number I propose to reduce it. It can easily be done. I know several whom I can employ at such a duty, and when they have succeeded, the property of the other ninety can be divided among the ten remaining. By this means the ten may be so rich, that further attacks upon the general public of London may be unnecessary. Meet me at ten to see to this.*"

This memorandum was addressed to some one, but the initials only were given.

These corresponded with the name of no one belonging to the League.

Oscar Penraven's name, however, was appended boldly to it, and the writing, too, was well known.

When on that terrible and memorable night, therefore, he took his place as Chief, he was at once seized.

He stood up stern and resentful.

"What means this? Are ye mad?" he cried.

"No," replied one of them; "but you must have been mad to venture into this place, knowing as you do the black treachery of your heart."

Oscar Penraven, as we have seen, was not at all wanting in brute courage.

He stood, therefore, stern and immoveable.

"This seems a dream to me," he said. "Of what folly are you speaking?"

"It is no folly," said another of the members, as he produced the paper. "We have here the evidence of your guilt. Listen, while I convict you with your own words."

Then he read aloud the document I have given above.

Then came a slight change in Oscar.

Only slight.

He became intensely pale, but besides that nothing else was observable.

"A forgery—a base forgery!" he said. "It tells simply nothing but that I have some deadly enemy in the Society—some one no doubt who is envious of my position so recently acquired."

"You were seen to drop it," returned the man; "and there is no doubt, moreover, that this is your writing. Sieze him, my friends, and bear him to the torture room."

Oscar made no effort at resistance.

He thought to awe them into belief by his firm resolution.

"Lead on!" he said. "Torture inflicted upon me by madmen will not lead me to tell falsehoods."

They bore him towards a room on the same floor as the council-chamber, and were just descending the steps when the alarm of fire was given.

This they at first paid no heed to.

Proceeding, therefore, to the cell, they manacled one of his hands with a clasp of iron, and had just succeeded in tying up his wrist by a thick rope, in order to torture him in the same way as they had begun to torture Rosalie St. Aubyn, when the deadly missiles came crashing through the casements, and the yells of the burning conspirators rang out horribly through the night.

The men who had tied him up rushed up to see

what was the cause of the unheard-of commotion, and did not return.

With one arm bound behind his back, one bound to the beam above him, Oscar Penraven stood up helpless, awaiting a fearful death.

But the fire which destroyed, so to speak, his features, saved his life.

It burnt the rope which held him; and when the ruins fell in, the burning beams above him formed a hollow where he could crouch.

All this he told to the wretched woman who leaned against the little wooden gate.

"Here," he said, showing her the iron still clasped around his wrist, and the piece of burnt rope still adhering to it, "here is a proof that what I say is true."

Rosalie saw, indeed, that in this one case, at any rate, he was not lying.

"Well," she said, "and what now do you propose to do?"

"I know not," he answered. "I feel consumed by a terrible heat and thirst. Let us hasten to some place where we can obtain refreshment and also a doctor. I have plenty of money, and I will aid you in avenging yourself on your enemies. Will you accompany me?"

She scarcely hesitated a moment.

What could she do were she to refuse?

She had no friends.

She knew not the utter destruction of the gang.

To them—to Gascoigne, to Rupert—her own home and its awful secrets were known.

Not a soul in the wide world offered her a home and a place of rest save this bad man, whom she had once pretended to love.

Rupert had bidden her to quit the country, but this she was unwilling to do.

Here there was a chance of a protector.

"Yes," she said, "I will go with you. But first let me bind up your face. The cold will affect it terribly; and more than that, the people would remark upon your appearance, and ask you awkward questions."

Oscar Penraven raised his hand to his head.

He pressed his brow convulsively, as if his memory were going.

"Yes, yes," he said, "do as you like. My brain is reeling. There is money in my pockets. Be quick, or I shall die."

Then the woman whom he had tried to betray bound up his wounds carefully, and led him towards a place of refreshment.

Long before they arrived there, he had lost all his senses, and speaking of him as her husband, she obtained for him a bed to rest in, and tended him during his illness.

It was not long before Oscar recovered his health.

But he never recovered his looks.

The redness disappeared, and left an unearthly pallor, crossed by seams and streaks.

This—if it had any effect at all on Rosalie—had an effect in his favour.

"He will be faithful to me now," she thought, "and aid me in avenging my wrongs."

With his recovery came an eager haste to quit the scene of the late disaster.

Not that he feared a meeting with his hereditary foe.

By no means.

But he desired that at that meeting they should be on something like an equality—he in the possession of his full vigour, and surrounded also by a new band of friends.

To gather together this necessary adjunct to his plans, he thought it requisite to quit the scene of his last adventures.

And he was right.

Among a new set of men who knew nothing of his antecedents he was far more likely to become popular.

He made his way, therefore, without delay towards the home of those desperate men whose calling and whose appearance I have already described.

He intended deliberately to fall into their hands, and to trust to chance and his own courage for the rest.

He chose a night suited to his purpose.

A night stormy and tempestuous.

Just such a one as that on which I introduced the wreckers to my readers.

Walking rapidly along the dismal road, right into the heart of the enemy's camp, as it were, as if they had lost their way, they soon had their wish.

Four or five rough-looking fellows, leaping out from behind a rocky ledge, confronted them.

Making a show of hopeless resistance they were dragged rudely down into the cave, and there searched.

Oscar laughed loudly when he saw the glee with which they handled the gold.

"I've plenty more in London," he said, "and I tell ye what, lads, if you'll let me join you, you shall share it with me. I've reasons to be on the quiet."

For some time of course he was not believed, and though they suffered him to remain with them, and treated Rosalie, as his wife, with some sort of rude respect, it was not till a certain incident occurred that they trusted him.

Until this happened he was never suffered to remain behind in the cave when they were out on their marauding excursions, lest, after all, he might be an informer in disguise.

One night he and another had been out reconnoitring up the river, when they saw themselves pursued by a boat in which were six men.

They were excisemen.

"They know me well," said Oscar's companion, "we must pull for our lives."

Oscar laughed—a cruel laugh.

"I can hit a farthing at twenty yards," he said, "give me your pistols. *You* row and I'll pick them off one by one."

The man did as he was desired, and the revenue cutter soon gained on them.

Oscar knew well that this was the chance of making his reputation.

He nerved himself for his desperate task accordingly.

One after another the pistols flashed and echoed.

One after another the excise officers fell back dead and desperately wounded.

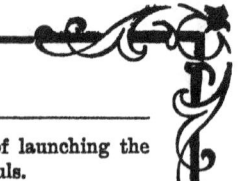

A terrible Providence seemed watching over the man of blood.

Again and again the revenue officers fired at the boat.

But vainly.

Oscar and his companion remained unscathed.

It seemed, truly, as if he were being saved for a more horrible doom.

Then, when only two were left, and ammunition was expended, he stopped his companion's rowing, and let the others float up to him.

"Now, then," he said, "stand up, and at them with your oar."

With an oar each, they made a desperate attack upon the revenue officers, and presently the boat of the latter tipped suddenly over.

Both officers were plunged into the stream.

One, whose skull had been broken, sunk to rise no more.

The other, an old man, the captain of the crew, rose to the surface, his grey hair streaming on the water, his hands outstretched for mercy.

"Save me! save me!" he gurgled; "for life only. I will not inform——"

He had no time to say more.

The oar launched forward by the hand of the merciless Oscar struck him full in the face, and he sunk to rise no more.

This incident, narrated in tones of admiration by Penraven's companion, raised him at once to the pinnacle of fame among the bloodthirsty crew.

He had before been named Orley.

He was now called Red Orley, and by his daring and cruel deeds had made himself far more looked up to among the men than the captain himself.

Having explained so far, I must return to the moment when Oscar entered the cave where Rosalie was kneeling before the fire, and relate the extraordinary results of that night's awful storm.

CHAPTER IX.

THE WRECK OF THE "HELENA"—THE WRECKERS AT WORK—THE YOUNG SAILOR—THE PROMISE OF REWARD—THE UNEXPECTED MEETING.

"ROSALIE," said Oscar Penraven, as he entered the cave, "there is a wreck near at hand. Don't come out, for you may see scenes that will sicken you. I'm captain now."

"Where, then, is the leader?"

"He is dead. He fell off the rocks. See that some hot spirits are ready for all the men when work is done. I must make myself popular here, and then for revenge!"

So saying he quitted her side and rushed out again into the storm.

The night was just suited to the deadly work before him and his horrid crew.

The flaring beacon on the summit of the giant cliff was the only thing visible among the gloom, save the faint light of the labouring vessel as it rose and sank in the far-off darkness.

Presently, above the wailing of the storm, was heard the booming of heavy guns.

It was the signal of distress.

But it had no effect save that of raising joy in the cruel hearts of those who watched there, clinging to every available piece of jutting rock.

No thought was in their minds of launching the life-boat to save poor struggling souls.

All they hoped for was to hear quickly the loud yells of agony as the doomed vessel broke on the rocks and crashed on unseen sands.

Those yells would mean plunder—wealth.

What mattered if they also meant the destruction of a hundred lives?

The lights on the rolling vessel came nearer and still nearer.

With beating hearts the villains watched her.

Then suddenly a last gun was fired.

The lights after this disappeared, and in another moment there rose a loud and prolonged yell, which seemed to hush the storm for a moment with its terrible despair!

"She is gone!" shouted Oscar.

"Aye, right enough," said several of the wreckers, in one breath, "right enough she's gone. We shall soon see something of what it contained. Let's get down on the beach."

They had not very long to wait.

The waves were rolling mountain high, and presently on their foamy crests were seen dark objects, which were hurled in among the surf, where the wreckers rushed in to seize them.

First came the bales of goods, and casks, and kegs, and such like.

But there followed soon more dismal burdens.

Dead bodies of hale, stout men, and women, too, in their night-dresses, with children clinging to their cold breasts with their tiny death grasp.

Some were not dead when they reached shore, but they soon found death there.

Women and men, too, were stabbed unmercifully and cast back into the waves.

The wreckers wanted no living witnesses to their hideous crimes.

All they desired was the jewels and the clothes of the crew, and their appeals, gasped out in their last agony, were unavailing.

Oscar Penraven, standing up to his knees in the surf, was giving directions to his men when he saw coming towards him a dark object.

At first he was unable to distinguish what it was, but presently he saw that it was the body of a human being clinging to a mast.

"Here is a stranger who may give us trouble, if he is not well looked after," said Oscar.

And he drew a glittering long-bladed knife from his pocket as he spoke.

But Providence had not ordained that he should commit this murder.

As he stood there, knife in hand, thirsting for the life of his fellow-being, the wave which bore the stranger on its bosom dashed suddenly over him, and the mast, catching him full on the chest, flung him on his back on the beach.

Before he rose the stranger, who had seen the knife and guessed his intention, had seized him by the wrist.

"You are a wrecker and seek my life; I know it," he said, quickly, "but if you kill me you lose a rich prize. In my belt are gold pieces; they are yours say you by right; but there are those not far from here who would give you a hundred times as much for my safety. Suppose we make a bargain?"

RUPERT OR THE DREADNOUGHT OR THE SECRETS OF THE IRON CHEST

"THE WALL SHOOK AND A DOOR WAS FLUNG SUDDENLY OPEN!"

"It depends upon what the bargain is," said Oscar.

"Well then, I will explain. Do you know Hanley House?"

"Yes," said Oscar, as the other unloosed his hand; "and what then?"

"My friends await me there. Take me there in safety and I will guarantee you a hundred golden guineas."

"And you will inform upon us and bring the officers of justice upon us."

"I will not."

"Will you swear it?"

"I will; by the heaven above us and my hopes of salvation, I will not betray you!"

"Good; then make your way up that rocky pathway and await me. Conceal yourself behind yonder ledge, for if my men see you I can promise they will make short work of you."

The youth, for he was no more, did at once as he was bidden, and Oscar, having seen that he had taken up the position he had assigned him, proceeded with his work.

That youth was the only one saved.

The others, coming in gasping for breath, or already dead, were stripped at once, without distinction of sex or age, and cast into the waters to die.

For hours the ghastly work continued.

Then, drunk with success and blood, the wreckers clambered up the rocks, and entered the cavern.

"Wait," whispered Oscar, as he passed the shivering figure still standing on the rocks. "I will be with you presently."

Then he, too, disappeared in the dark shadows of the cave's mouth.

It was light enough within, and in the course of a very few moments a scene of uproarious jollity commenced.

The drenched smugglers sat round on every available seat.

Spars, barrels, bales, anything was taken into the service, and soon the rocky vault resounded with laughter, singing, oaths, and cheers.

Rosalie was the presiding genius.

Steaming glasses of grog were furnished out to the lawless and bloodstained crew by her fair hands.

Loud and prolonged were the cheers which greeted her every now and then.

But gradually she attracted less notice.

As the drink mounted to their brains, they began to boast of their achievements—to tell of the horrors they had been guilty of—to act over again their murders—and the fair creature who served out to them their refreshment was regarded as no more than an ordinary tavern wench.

Any one less hardened to crime than Rosalie St. Aubyn would have shuddered to hear the terrible crimes of which the men accused themselves.

But, young as she was, she was inured to scenes of blood, and her heart was hardened against pity towards man, woman, or child.

Oscar Penraven, unwilling to call the attention of the band upon himself, left the stranger some time waiting on the rocky ledge before joining him.

Amid loud and clamorous cheering his health was drunk, and he was just appealing to the band to obey him in all things, and promising a rich treasure for them in the future, when a shout from without attracted the attention of all.

The smugglers sprang to their feet, and grasped their weapons.

"It is the voice of Rathsay, our lieutenant," said one.

"There may be danger, then," said Oscar, as glancing round he saw that Rathsay, as the man had named him, was absent. "Let me go and reconnoitre."

Then he quitted them hastily, and rushed up the rocky path in the direction of the spot where he had left the young man.

To explain what he found there, however, we must go back to the time when the young stranger was left standing alone in the cold and the storm.

CHAPTER X.

LIEUTENANT RATHSAY—HIS HATRED OF OSCAR PENRAVEN—HIS MANY EFFORTS TO DESTROY HIM—HE SEES THE YOUNG STRANGER—HIS PLAN OF VENGEANCE—THE STRUGGLE ON THE CLIFF—HANLEY HOUSE—THE UNEXPECTED MEETING—OSCAR SCHEMES A GRAND SCHEME OF VILLANY.

OSCAR PENRAVEN had naturally imagined that amid the noise and bustle of the horrid scene enacted on the beach his proceedings in regard to the lad would pass unobserved.

But it was not so.

There was one in the band who hated him.

This was he who had been spoken of by one of the brigands as Rathsay.

He had long been jealous of Oscar.

He had hoped himself to secure ultimately the command of the band, and he saw with anger and hate the gradual ascendancy which his rival was acquiring not only over the chief but over the men.

He had not seen the murder of the captain.

Yet he suspected it.

Nevertheless, suspect or not, it was of no use to give vent to his thoughts.

Murderer or not, Oscar Penraven had for the time such a position in the band that to accuse him of such a crime would only result in bringing down ridicule on the accuser.

Bloodstained as they were, they would doubtless have regarded the murder of their leader as a bold and daring deed, and have admired him all the more for its commission.

So he resolved to go to work stealthily.

Little did he imagine how soon he would be able to commence his work.

He was in the surf aiding in the hauling ashore of a large bale, when he saw Oscar mounting the rocky path stealthily with another.

As their manner was mysterious, he quitted his work and followed.

He heard Oscar Penraven tell him to wait, and satisfied for the moment with this, he entered the cave with the rest.

As soon as the smugglers were so far engaged that they were not likely to observe his movements, he quickly dropped from his seat, and for a few moments lay on the ground quietly.

Then when one of the noisy ruffians proposed Oscar Penraven's health, and it was drunk with loud and boisterous acclamations, he crawled away among the shadows, and disappeared out over the rocks.

The youth had not moved from the spot where the new chief of the wreckers had bade him remain.

When the lieutenant stole up to him, therefore, he imagined it to be Oscar Penraven, and said—

"I am glad you have come; it is weary work waiting here; and more than that I am wet through and shivering. Besides, I am anxious now to see my friends again."

But he soon saw his mistake as Rathsay neared him.

"I am not he whom you seek," said the latter, gruffly.

"I see my mistake," returned the youth.

"For whom are you waiting?"

The stranger hesitated.

Who and what was this man who was questioning him?

At any rate, he resolved not to trust him.

"I am waiting for some one, truly, but our business is private," he answered, "and I must decline to speak in regard to it."

No sooner had these words left his lips, when the lieutenant seized him by the arm, and uttered that shout, that loud, ringing shout which the men had heard, even above the din of their hideous merriment.

"Help, comrades! help!" he cried. "There is treachery among us."

But the words reached not their ears.

Carried away by the wild wind, they took the form merely of a wild cry.

In a few moments a form issued from the cavern's mouth, and made his way towards them.

It was not help, of course, that Lieutenant Rathsay wanted.

Himself a tall and broad-shouldered muscular man, he could easily have hurled the youth over the cliff side.

What he wanted was to rouse the gang, to give them ocular proof that their chief had a secret from them, and then, while their passions were roused, try and break the rod of his supremacy.

He was surprised, crestfallen, as well as enraged when Oscar Penraven so unexpectedly approached him.

"What want you here, Rathsay?" said the new chief, in a stern and peremptory voice. "Why are you not carousing with the others? Have you some private scheme of treachery on foot that you have thus absented yourself?"

"Nay, that is a question I should rather ask of you," returned Rathsay; "you—who have secrets from your band—who have strangers lurking for you in dark corners for purposes they care not to name. Who is this youth?"

A scowl of hate and rage overspread the brow of Oscar Penraven.

"Who are you, that you dare to question me?" he cried. "I am leader of the band, and their interests are in my hands. Shall I leave it to you to tell me how to serve them best?"

Rathsay laughed jeeringly.

"Oh, I envy you not your captaincy so strangely and so quickly obtained," he said; "but I *am* suspicious as to this meeting, and shall inquire further into it."

Oscar Penraven advanced towards him, threateningly.

"You had best keep your tongue between your teeth," he cried, "or you may find one who will brook no insults."

"Nor stop at private murder."

The words had scarcely left Rathsay's lips when a blow was struck.

A blow, heavy, savage, full in his mouth.

He staggered backward a few paces.

Then his bright, long-bladed knife flashed in the semi-darkness, and he rushed upon his enemy with a growling curse.

Oscar Penraven, however, was quite prepared for the onslaught.

His knife left the scabbard the instant he had struck the blow, and the two ruffians were on equal terms.

The young sailor resolved not to interfere.

So, with his arms folded, and his back against the rock, he watched the struggle.

It was difficult work this hacking and fighting in the dark.

Stab after stab was dealt, but very ineffectually, and at length they sheathed their weapons as if by mutual consent, and rushed at each other with their fists.

One or two blows were smartly administered on both sides.

Then, with one accord, they grappled in a deadly conflict.

Both strong men—both animated by a spirit of resolute hate—it was, as may be imagined, a fearful conflict.

For some time it lasted.

There was no other feeling in their minds now but the desire for immediate supremacy.

Their thirst now was a thirst for blood.

Presently in their struggles they neared the edge of the cliff.

Both saw the danger.

Every nerve was strained.

It was death, perhaps, for both, and each with a kind of supernatural strength prepared to battle against a sudden rush into the great unknown.

Suddenly Oscar Penraven contrived to free his arms, and grasped tightly the throat of his antagonist.

The young sailor heard a gurgling, horrid sound and a curse choked in the utterance.

Then there was a separation of the two combatants, and one stood on the edge of the cliff alone.

This was Oscar Penraven.

He turned round quickly.

"A hardy villain, that," he said, in a voice still panting with strong exertion; "but at any rate he has got his deserts."

"And you, I trust, have liberty now to accompany me," said the sailor.

"Yes: that fellow would have spoiled all; but the other members of my band are by this time well nigh intoxicated and we will therefore to our journey."

He quickly led the way up the rocky path, and they were soon standing on the level above.

Here there stretched away a long, monotonous bank of darkness.

But Oscar Penraven knew well his way.

Telling his companion to keep close by his side, he walked rapidly along the chalky road for a moment, and then, quitting it, struck across a black and desolate moorland.

It was such a lonely and strange place, that the young sailor must be forgiven if doubts arose in his mind as to the propriety of trusting himself to the desperate character by his side.

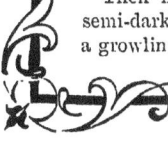

He would have been more than justified if he had slunk away into some dark corner.

Oscar Penraven, indeed, for a moment, when the thorough darkness overwhelmed them, considered whether it would not be better to settle the matter at once—put the young fellow out of the world without any further to do, and take his gold, in preference to running the risk of being deceived at the end of his journey.

He had now, by constant companionship with criminals and constant participation in low crimes, become so thoroughly debased that he could have stooped to the meanest and most grovelling act of robbery or assassination.

But the fancy passed away.

The youth had, perhaps, only some paltry sum about him.

A hundred guineas were promised at the end of his journey, and this he cared not to lose.

True, his property was squandered.

He had lived at a rate that would have swallowed up twenty fortunes.

Now, apart from a few hundreds laid by, he had nothing.

It was gladly, therefore, that he anticipated an addition to his hoard.

If he were deceived?

Why, then, he knew the people at Hanley House to be wealthy, and they would be the sufferers, even against their will.

"Yonder," he said, presently pointing to the lights of a mansion in the far distance, "yonder is Hanley House; you have good friends there, I presume?"

"I have a brother," returned the young sailor, "who believes me lost for ever. He has long given me up as one numbered with the dead, and, unless he be much changed, he will pay even more than I have named to the one who brings me safely to him."

"Very likely," said Oscar Penraven, drily; "but I doubt if he will feel inclined to pay a hundred guineas to one who did not venture his own life to save yours, but simply did not assassinate you."

The sailor was astounded at the straightforward way in which his companion confessed his infamy.

"Well," he said, "perhaps not; but as I, under the circumstances, can better appreciate your peculiar kindness, I will represent to them that you saved me. It is your own fault if you let them know differently."

"Well, that's honest," said Oscar; "so let us trudge on. It's getting towards morning, and I've no wish to be seen in the daylight."

Hastening on still more, they at length reached the heavy iron gates of Hanley House, which they scaled, and made their way to the doorway, where Oscar Penraven loudly pealed the bell.

After some little delay, a head was poked out of a window.

"What want you at this unseasonable hour?" cried a voice.

"To speak with the master of the house," replied Oscar Penraven.

Then, turning to his companion, he added—

"But you have not yet told me whom I am to ask for."

"Ask for Master Chester Rice."

"We wish to see Master Chester Rice," cried Oscar Penraven. "Tell him that I bring to him his long-lost brother."

"That's all very well," said the man; "but seeing as how his brother's been at the bottom of the sea these two years, I can't——"

"Cease your foolish prating," shouted Oscar. "Take your head in, or I will send a bullet through it. Come quickly and open the door."

The voice and the threat had their effect upon the domestic.

The head was quickly withdrawn and the casement closed.

But some time elapsed before the door was opened.

"They surely can't take us for ghosts," said the young sailor.

"No, or he would not have popped his head in so quickly when I threatened to shoot him," said Oscar Penraven. "However, it will be as well to ring loudly again."

A second loud and clanging peal rang out upon the night.

Then a sound of many feet was heard within.

Bolts and bars were withdrawn, the door flung open, and the two beheld a number of gentlemen, half dressed and fully armed.

"What want you at this time of night?" said a tall, fine-looking man, about four and twenty years of age, advancing pistol in hand.

"I've come to see my brother Chester," said the young sailor, "but I did not expect so warlike a reception. Don't you know me, Chester? I am Charles."

The voice checked all further doubts.

The elder brother flung away his weapon, rushed to the side of the new-comer, and drew him into the light.

"Yes, yes, it *is* Charles, my long-lost and beloved brother!" he cried, and in an instant they were clasped in each other's arms.

Oscar Penraven was, of course, drawn into the hall by the young man whom he had rescued, and, for the moment, he was not particularly observed by those around him.

They simply regarded him as one of the young sailor's companions at sea.

But while their attention was taken up elsewhere by Charles's story of the storm, his eyes were busy, and presently they lighted upon a face, the sight of which caused him with difficulty to repress a cry of astonishment.

It was the face of Rupert Dreadnought!

What was he doing there?

What mysterious power had brought about this meeting?

True it was that the disfigured state of his own features would give Oscar some little safety.

But he cared not to trust to this.

Drawing his cap more over his face, and buttoning up his pea-jacket as if ready for the return journey, he said, in a thick, disguised tone,

"Well, Master Rice, I'm off."

This roused the attention of the party, and all looked at him.

But he was unrecognised.

The fire had so utterly destroyed his looks that he would not have been known by his dearest friends.

"This is my preserver," said Charles to his brother. "I promised him when I was struggling among the raging surf, when our devoted vessel was wrecked, that he should have a hundred guineas if he rescued me. Aid me, Chester, in redeeming my word."

His brother smiled.

"AWAY WENT THE LOVERS TOWARDS LONDON."

"If it were ten times as much," said he, "I would gladly do so."

Then turning to Oscar he said,

"My good fellow, my best thanks are yours. Come in the morning, or remain now if you please, and the money is yours."

But Oscar was in no humour to remain.

He felt in the lion's den, where any false move might betray him.

So, assuming the awkwardness of a rough fisherman, he touched his cap, saying—

"I won't disturb yer honour now. I'll come in the morning."

And, opening the door for himself, he hurried out into the darkness.

He cared not for the hundred guineas.

He had a better reward than that in view for himself.

Vengeance!

Rupert Dreadnought was there.

Near at hand were the fierce wreckers.

What now was there to prevent him from slaking his eager thirst for revenge?

CHAPTER XI.

THE YOUNG SAILOR'S STORY—THE CRUEL FATHER—FIRST LOVE—THE QUARREL—FLIGHT, AND CAPTURE OF THE LOVERS—CHARLES RESOLVES TO ESCAPE TO SEA—THE LAST FAREWELL—THE VOYAGE—THE MUTINY—A CRUISE WITH PIRATES—IN A FOREIGN PRISON—THE RETURN TO ENGLAND—THE WRECK—OSCAR PENRAVEN GETS HIS REWARD.

EAGER as every one was to hear the story of the shipwrecked sailor, yet humanity suggested for him a warm glass of grog, a warm bed, and a good rest.

He was in no humour for eating, and, after drinking off the large jorum prepared for him by his brother, he made the best of his way between the sheets, and was soon in the arms of the Sleepy God.

And while he is so, I can explain in a few words how it was that Rupert Dreadnought happened to be so far from London.

It will be remembered that when Henry Clanberris had reached the consummation of his happiness, and become the husband of Margaret Dalrymple, he retired to a house near Brentwood, near which Helen Penraven was carried off when on a visit to them.

Chester Rice was a friend of Clanberris, and it was when Rupert Dreadnought was on a visit at the house of the latter that an invitation was received and accepted to spend a week or two at Hanley House.

By such a simple circumstance as this were the two enemies once more brought face to face.

On the morning after the arrival of the long-lost brother, when they had discussed a hearty breakfast, and retired to the dining-room, it was proposed that Charles's story should be told.

"Well, it is not altogether a very cheerful one, but—"

"I'll tell you how to arrange it," said Chester, "since, in spite of what I whispered last night ere you retired to rest, the first part of your story may be somewhat painful for you to narrate, I will tell all I know up to the time of your disappearance."

This was agreed to.

So, closing round the genial fire, Chester began—

"I and my brother were the only children of our father.

"He was a stern, uncompromising man, and though fond of us, he was a tyrant in his way.

"My mother's death (he had doted upon her) made him harder than ever, and for days and weeks together we never saw him except at meals.

"And yet, recluse as he made of himself, he was hatching the plot which for years has made us wretched.

"There was near this place a family, named Edgetown, with whom, for some reason, unknown to us, our father had a feud.

"It was not certainly the fault of Robert Edgetown that they were bad friends.

"Never was there a kinder or more good-hearted man; and both I and my brother, unknown, of course, to our father, were constant visitors to his house.

"Master Robert Edgetown had an only daughter.

"She was a lovely girl, this Minnie, and my brother at once fell in love with her.

"I need not tell you that the courtship was carried on strictly in private.

"Had one word of its existence been known to our father, he would have stopped its progress in an instant.

"However, stolen meetings were frequent; and at length Charles determined to pluck up courage and ask his father's consent.

"In this proposed interview he was anticipated.

"One evening my father called him into his study.

"'Charles,' he said, 'I have to tell you something which, I have no doubt, will deeply interest you. Chester, your brother, has, as you are aware, chosen for his future partner in life a young lady of beauty and accomplishments' (you see *I* was fortunate enough to secure his approval).

"'I am aware of it,' said Charles, smiling, and with his heart beating wildly; 'and I——'

"'Wish, no doubt, to be as fortunate,' cried his father, interrupting him; 'I have arranged matters so that you shall be as fortunate. You know, of course, that Sir Lionel Radstock, who owns so large a property to the west of us, has an only daughter. She is lovely, accomplished, and young.'

"'I own it, sir,' said my brother, 'but——'

"'You have not seen her, and, perhaps, she may refuse you,' cried my impatient father. 'Don't fear anything of the sort; I will take care that you have an early opportunity of expressing your devotion to her.'

"Charles saw that the crisis had arrived.

"'Sir,' he said, 'I have at present no wish to be married. But, if I had, my affections would not be fixed upon Mistress Radstock.'

"'And pray why, may I ask?'

"'Because they are bestowed elsewhere, sir.'

"'Well, if the young lady is of good family, and of wealth equal to the one *I* have chosen, then I shall have no objection to ratify your choice.'

"'She *is*, sir, quite as lovely, of quite as good a family as Mistress Radstock can be, and has more wealth.'

"'And who, pray, is this paragon?'

"'Minnie Edgetown.'

"I can scarcely describe the rage of my father at these words.

"He raved like a madman, and it was some time before he would permit Charles to explain.

"When he did, the explanation made things worse.

"The very fact of the stolen interviews caused his wrath to rise higher and higher.

"'Mark me,' he cried, 'you have defied me, and what I say to you now is final. If you do not now, in my presence, once and for ever forswear this girl, you are no longer my son. You know how I have divided my property, that you and your brother have equal shares between you. If you do not promise to relinquish this connection, you leave my presence a beggar.'

"Expostulation was useless.

"Charles refused to accede to his father's wish, and without even telling me what he intended doing, he left the house that night.

"He had a few hundred pounds of his own, and with this the lovers resolved to begin life.

"After what had occurred, Robert Edgetown refused to permit the union, and flight was resolved on.

"So meeting one night, my brother lifted his mistress before him on his horse, and away they went towards London.

"But in vain.

"A spy had seen them, and my father was soon in pursuit.

"Fortune was against the lovers, and they were captured.

"Minnie had to return in tears and wretchedness to her father's, and Charles was brought captive here.

"How he escaped I must leave him to tell us; but that he did so is certain, and until this moment, or, rather, till last night, I have never clapped eyes on him since."

"But Minnie, you say, is alive and constant?" said Charles.

"Yes, indeed. That she is alive, I can vouch; in regard to her constancy, I will leave you to ask her."

"Aye, and that I will ere the day is much farther spent," said the young sailor; "but I will tell you briefly before I go how I have fared.

"On finding myself a captive in my room, I thought for a time whether I had better remain quiet, and trust to time to change my father's determination.

"But something told me it was no use.

"He was, as Chester has told you, a stern, obdurate man.

"There was no hope of his relenting.

"So I resolved to run away.

"I made up a bundle of things, threw open my window, clambered down by means of my bed-clothes, and was soon rushing away in the direction of Robert Edgetown's estate.

"I was resolved to see Minnie, to tell her my resolve, and, while taking leave of her, extract from her fair lips a vow of constancy.

"Despair gave me courage.

"I did what I should never have dreamed of doing before.

"Scaling the old black fence, I made my way to that part of the grounds below Minnie's chamber, and with some stones tapped at her window.

"The poor girl guessed who it was, and though in her night-dress, she flung the casement open, and with the chill blast playing on her bare shoulders, leaned out to me.

"'I have come to say good-bye, Minnie,' I said. 'I am going to sea.'

"I need not dwell upon her grief, nor her entreaties to me to try some other calling.

"Suffice it that I contrived to haul myself up to her room, have a last and heartrending embrace, and then, ere I was well quit of the whirl of ideas that thronged upon me, I was away on the dark road again.

"I might have taken Minnie with me that night, no doubt you will say.

"But it was not possible.

"Her clothes had been taken from her to prevent the possibility of escape; and, even if it had not been perilous to take her out into the cold, her appearance in such a guise would certainly have created much astonishment, and have resulted in our being stopped.

"Well, I shipped at the nearest sea-port, and, after a prosperous voyage, reached America.

"There I traded, and made money; and should certainly have returned at once, had not a strange event occurred.

"The captain of the vessel in which I shipped for England was a coarse, brutal ruffian, who could not brook the slightest contradiction.

"It was for this reason that he took a dislike to one poor fellow called Naylor, who was not disposed to let the villain have it all his own way, and one day he struck his brains out with a marling-spike and flung his body overboard.

"This was the cause of a mutiny, which I was utterly unable to quell, and the sailors, having shot the captain, turned the vessel about, hoisted a black flag, and commenced a series of lawless acts, which resulted in our being pursued, taken, and lodged in prison.

"The prisons there, Chester, are but rude places, and I could easily have escaped had I been disposed to club with the others, but I knew that, if recaptured, I should certainly be regarded as guilty.

"So, I remained in my prison until I was brought up for trial, and, through the intervention of the guilty men themselves, I recovered my liberty.

"Then, undismayed by the terrors of the seas, I once more embarked for dear Old England.

"How I was overtaken by a storm and thrown by the angry sea just near your home, I need not tell you.

"I knew not where Hanley House was, though your letter telling me that my father was dead spoke of it and its vicinity.

"And so here I am."

"Yes, and half proprietor of the place," said Chester, warmly.

"Not I, my dear brother," cried Charles, "not I. I will not rob you of what you have justly considered yours so long. I have made money which is now safe in the bank, and I have plenty of wealth and to spare."

I need not dwell further on this day.

I must hurry on to that part of this chain of incidents which refers to Rupert and to Oscar.

The latter, in thorough disguise, came for the promised reward, and obtained it.

He was treated well, loaded with refreshments and thanks, and, having taken good stock of the premises, quitted Hanley House, resolved and prepared to take his revenge.

Even his black heart revolted, however, from the idea of destroying the man whose life he had once saved, and who had kept his word so nobly.

Rupert alone was the object of his search and his hate.

CHAPTER XII.

STRANGE NOISES BY NIGHT—A WATCH AGREED UPON—RUPERT TAKES HIS STATION—THE SECRET DOOR—THE APPARITION—THE SURPRISE—AN UNEXPECTED FRIEND—THE STRANGE NOISES EXPLAINED—THE STRANGER REVEALS TO RUPERT DREADNOUGHT OSCAR PENRAVEN'S PLAN OF REVENGE—PREPARATIONS—THE AVENGER DEPARTS—THE MEETING ON THE ROAD—THE ARRIVAL AT THE CAVERN.

It was somewhat late when Charles Rice—flushed with pleasure—returned from his visit to Minnie Edgetown, from whom, as well as from her father, he received a hearty welcome.

About eleven o'clock all retired to their rooms.

But not to rest.

That was denied them.

Throughout the hours of darkness strange noises were heard in the old house.

They vanished with the dawn.

But, while they lasted, slumber was impossible.

The noise was continuous aud irritating.

A scratching, incessant noise, then sighing and groaning, then the pattering of feet.

In the morning, at breakfast time, a consultation was held.

Chester looked very grave.

"They told me when I took this place," he said, "that it was haunted; but, of course, I never gave credence to such an idea. What all this means I am at a loss to say; but we ought to take immediate measures to discover it."

Rupert, who of all present was the most free from any superstitious feelings, laughed at the serious manner of the speaker.

"If you are at all nervous about this matter," he said, "I will propose a manner of finding out the meaning of it all."

"Well, what is it?"

"That we should each in turn watch in the place where the noises sound the loudest. I will take the first watch."

"Agreed," said Chester, "though I confess myself to be somewhat unpleasantly moved by the odd doings in this place. However, we must not allow ourselves to be alarmed, nor must we allow you to imperil yourself unnecessarily. While one watches, the others must be on the alert to assist him."

It was arranged that on that same night the friends should endeavour to discover the spot where the noises seemed greatest, and then that on the night following the system of watching should commence.

The first night resulted as before in hideous sounds and omens, and towards dawn Rupert had decided that the long, wailing cries which formed the staple of the unpleasant demonstrations proceeded principally from a disused room, or, rather, stone vault, below the building.

Here, then, on the next night, he located himself.

It was a dull place—cold and chill as a sepulchre—but with a good fire, a large tankard, his sword, and a volume, he felt himself to have companions enough.

The hours passed gloomily enough.

The old house was very still.

Chester, Charles, and Henry Clanberris were upstairs, ready to descend on the slightest alarm.

But their conversation could not be heard.

The ghostly visitants, if such there were, made no sound.

"This is very strange," thought Rupert, as among the solemn quietude a distant bell tolled the hour of midnight.

Just as it did so a slight noise was heard.

A slight scratching noise like some animal forcing its way through the woodwork.

Rupert listened eagerly.

"Now," thought he, "now comes the elucidation of the mystery.

The noise seemed to proceed from that part of the wall which was immediately opposite to his chair.

He had not long to wait.

There was a sound as of feet approaching, then the wall shook, and a door was flung suddenly open.

In it appeared a strange being.

It was a man, dressed in an outlandish kind of way, with a long wig, worn seemingly for disguise or to hide some disfigurement.

Rupert's sword was lying on the table next to his glass, and he at once seized it, and sprang up.

"What do you here?" he cried, sternly.

The stranger, who was, to all appearance, unarmed, placed his finger on his lips, and entered boldly.

"Hush!" he said; "I am here on a secret mission."

"It seems so truly," returned Rupert, drily; "and pray will you inform me why you are here?"

"I am here," said the stranger, "to save your life, so put up your sword, and listen."

And with the words, he took a seat, and placed it near the old-fashioned fire-place.

"This is a cool kind of a *ghost* truly," thought Rupert; "not certainly the kind expected by Chester."

Then he added, as he also seated himself near the fire—

"And now, sir, since this intrusion into my friend's house and my room is most unwarrantable, perhaps you will be good enough to explain your meaning."

"I will," said the stranger. "My name is Rathsay. I am, sir, of course a stranger to you. I should be even if you were a resident in these parts, which you are not. I am one who will be regarded as risen from the dead by your enemies."

And then, without further beating about the bush, he narrated to Rupert the story of the attempt upon his life by Oscar Penraven.

"Your friend, Chester Rice, has rewarded him, so I hear, and he has done so wrongly," said Rathsay. "It was not from the wild waves that his brother was rescued, but from the steel of our new captain, who is a murderer and an assassin."

"But these noises we hear at night," said Rupert. "I believe what you have said, but that does not explain the mysterious doings in this house."

"That, too, is easy of explanation," returned the man who had been so miraculously saved after his fall from the high rocks into the sea. "Our new captain has some hatred against a person in this house named Rupert Dreadnought, and he is resolved to avenge himself upon him. Every night they have been working to effect a secret entrance, and it is the wind rushing up unaccustomed passages that has caused the strange sounds which I, too, have heard."

"And when is the attack to take place?" asked Rupert, who now saw that the man was not deceiving him.

"I believe that to-morrow night, as midnight strikes, the assault will be made. You should lie concealed here and you will certainly catch them unawares."

"And you?"

"Oh, *I* will gladly assist you. Meanwhile, having accomplished all I wish—having put you on your guard and saved you from my would-be murderer, I will return again and watch. I have another revenge yet in store for him."

"And what is that?"

"He has a wife."

"Whom he loves."

"He appears to do so, most certainly. I will take her from him, however, even if her death results from it."

"It will be but a poor revenge," replied Rupert; "for to-morrow night, if he makes an attempt at attacking this house, he will lose his life, and it will matter little then to him where his wife is."

RUPERT OR THE DREADNOUGHT SECRETS OF THE IRON CHEST

THE MEETING ON THE SHADOWY STAIRCASE.

"Ah!" replied Rathsay, with a sardonic smile; "but she shall quit him ere he comes here. Farewell."

Rupert stayed him.

"Hold one moment!" he cried. "Can you tell me who this man is who has an enmity against Rupert Dreadnought, for I am he!"

"You Rupert Dreadnought!"

"Yes, indeed; and as a stranger in the place, I wonder to find that I could have made an enemy so soon."

Rathsay shook his head.

"Ah! he is no new enemy," he answered; "who and what he is I know not, for he has been but a short time a member of our band, but his hatred for you is of long standing. He hates you with the deadly enmity of years."

"Who *can* it be?" murmured Rupert. "Can it be that some of that vile brood escaped? No, no; but time will show. I will keep you no longer. When shall I see you again?"

"To-morrow night, at ten o'clock, I shall be with you again," said Rathsay; "and then I shall come by the front door."

And, with these words, he walked hastily across the vaulted chamber, and disappeared through the secret door.

Rupert then hastened upstairs, when he narrated to his astonished friends the adventure that had befallen him.

With very little discussion Rathsay's plan was adopted, and after seeing to the safety of the upper part of the house they retired to rest.

Meanwhile, the vengeful lieutenant of the wreckers pressed on hastily towards the cliff-side.

His escape had been miraculous.

Cast from the summit of a rock quite as high as that from which the captain had been flung by Oscar, he was caught on the crest of a huge wave, and borne out to sea.

Here, as he fought and struggled for dear life, he clutched at a dark object.

He found it to be a spar.

He was saved.

For full an hour he had to cling to this frail support.

But he clung on manfully.

Drifted hither and thither at the mercy of the waves, he was at length flung up upon the beach some little distance from the wreckers' cave; and as soon as he had somewhat recovered his breath and strength, he walked to the village, procured some drink, and then went a few miles off, where he slept, away from all chance of molestation, in an old barn.

Then, on the night following, he made his way to the old cave, where he heard Oscar Penraven's entire plan for attacking and sacking Hanley House.

It will be remembered that the instant Oscar Penraven saw and recognised Rupert Dreadnought, he resolved upon a scheme of vengeance.

He had, as I have before mentioned, intended, all along, to employ the band of wreckers to foward his ideas of revenge.

But he had never dreamed that such a chance as this would be thrown in his way.

Here was his enemy brought to him.

A terrible Providence seemed to hound him on to the commission of new crimes, and his black heart accepted the situation willingly.

So, on the night following the wreck of the "Helena," he collected all his men into the large cavern, and, having served out to them a good quantity of grog, laid before them his plans.

It was something out of the usual routine of their lives.

They had wrecked many vessels and taken many lives.

But an assault upon a house—a burglary and a murder, were things quite novel to them.

However, drink and excitement will work wonders.

By the time they had completed their grog, and Oscar Penraven had done explaining to them, they had all acceded.

Then came another glass of strong drink, and they were told to be ready on the third night, while four of them were chosen for the making of the secret entrance to the old mansion.

Matters then were all arranged, and as Rathsay made his way towards the cave, he knew that the last labour, the subterranean way, would be done that night ere dawn.

For an hour, or perhaps two, therefore, Rosalie St. Aubyn would be alone.

He would now have his revenge.

So eagerly he pressed forward.

Presently he heard voices.

The night was very dark, and it was unlikely that any passers-by would see him.

Yet he would not risk discovery.

Making his way up to a clump of trees, therefore, he concealed himself.

In a few moments the speakers went by.

They were Oscar and his men.

The black heart of the wrecker leaped with joy.

"Now," he chuckled, "not a soul will be near her. I shall be avenged."

And, so saying, he pressed forward once more.

To one accustomed as he was to climb among the jagged rocks, it was a matter of no difficulty, even in the intense darkness, to find the mouth of the cavern.

He entered it eagerly.

A light shone beneath the door of Rosalie St. Aubyn's chamber, who was now half undressed and preparing to retire for the night in her strange home.

He knocked loudly.

"Who is there?" asked Rosalie, hastily, and in fear.

Oscar being gone, she knew no one who had a right to be there at such an hour.

"I want to speak with you, Mistress Orley," said Rathsay.

It will be remembered that Oscar Penraven was known as Red Orley.

"Well, speak. I am going to bed, and can admit no one," she cried, firmly.

Yet she suspected that she would be unable to prevent his entrance, and, accordingly, she quickly slipped on her clothes.

She was right.

In an instant the door was burst open, and Rathsay stalked into the room!

CHAPTER XIII.

ROSALIE'S TERROR—RATHSAY REVEALS HIS PURPOSE—THE FORCED LETTER—THE PREPARATIONS FOR FLIGHT—THE DEPARTURE—RETURN—RAGE OF OSCAR PENRAVEN—THE ROADSIDE INN.

To say that Rosalie St. Aubyn was astounded by

the sudden appearance of the lieutenant of the wreckers, would not properly describe the scene.

She seemed petrified.

What could Rathsay want with her?

She had heard from Oscar that the man had perished in the surf on the night of the wreck.

At first sight, therefore, she felt half inclined to shriek at his apparition.

But his voice revived her.

"You seem astounded," he said, as he closed the door behind him.

"I am," she answered. "What can your purpose be here?"

Rathsay laughed as he flung himself into a chair.

"No doubt your delightful husband informed you that I was dead. He had good reason for believing so, since he flung me over the cliff, as he had flung the captain before me; but the sea saved me that I might punish him."

He little knew the nature of the woman to whom he spoke, or he would not have wasted his words in proving to her that Oscar was a murderer.

"Well," said Rosalie, impatiently.

Rathsay looked at her in astonishment.

"Do you know, then, that Red Orley murdered the captain—that he tried to murder me? and is that all you have to say to it?" he cried, in wonder.

"I have but your word for it, and I prefer taking his," returned Rosalie; "what I desire to know is why you are here?"

"I am here for revenge."

The deep tone and desperate vengefulness with which he spoke caused a shudder to pass through the frame of Rosalie St. Aubyn.

She knew how utterly she was in the power of this man.

"But my husband is not here," she said, tremblingly.

"No, no, it is through you I mean to have my revenge," he said; "be quick, and dress yourself, and follow me."

"Whither would you take me?"

"Where *he* will not find you. Come quickly, for resistance is useless, and if you attempt it I shall carry you away by force."

With a feeling of terror, and a sickening dread of something horrible to come, Rosalie, losing all presence of mind, threw herself at the feet of Rathsay.

"Oh, for mercy's sake!" she cried, "if you are going to kill me, do it here. Do not take me out into the dark night that I may endure an agony beforehand worse than death itself."

A strange smile passed over the man's face.

"I shall not kill you," he said, "I shall not touch a hair of your head. All I require is that you shall write to my dictation a note and leave it here; then I shall take horse, place you before me and ride for thirty miles. At a house, at the end of my journey, I shall leave you. You will never see *me* or Red Orley again."

Relieved thus of some of her fears, Rosalie quickly donned her travelling attire.

While she did so Rathsay told her all.

She started at the name of Rupert.

"You know this man?" asked Rathsay.

"I do; I loved him once."

"Not now?"

Her bosom trembled visibly.

"I know not," she said; "he spurned me once, and a woman scorned becomes a demon. Yet, had you not apprised him of his danger, *I* should had I known it."

"Even against your husband?"

"Yes."

"Then the task of writing the letter I speak of will not be so great. Have you pen, ink, and paper?"

"Yes; here they are."

"Now write," said Rathsay.

Rosalie sat down and took the pen.

"I have left you for ever," dictated the man. "I despise and hate you, and you ought to have long since known it. I have fled with the man whom you thought you had murdered, Rathsay, the lieutenant of the band. Your doom is at hand. The proverb goes, 'Rats desert a falling house.' Your hour is coming, and I care not to share your fate with you. In the hour of your peril think how I laugh at your sufferings.

"ROSALIE ST. AUBYN."

So ran the letter.

It was not written without frequent interruptions.

But a look from Rathsay was enough.

What he had resolved to do she saw there was no chance of persuading him to swerve from.

So it was written.

Then they rose to go.

As they opened the door, there was the sound of approaching feet.

Rosalie's heart bounded in her breast.

Had Oscar come to save her?

Not that there was in her heart the slightest love for him.

But safety with him even was better than uncertainty with one of whom she knew nothing.

Eagerly, therefore, she listened.

Rathsay saw her anxiety.

He guessed her feelings at once.

With a grasp of iron he seized her arm.

"Come," he said, in low, determined tones; "one word, one cry, and this shall enter your heart!"

And, as he drew her out, he showed a long, keen knife.

Hastily quitting the room, he drew her into a dark corner where they could not be seen.

There was scarcely room for more than one to stand.

But this was the better for him.

He stood up with one arm round her waist, while with the other, he held the point of the knife to her breast, so closely, that she could feel the sharp steel against her tender flesh.

Her heart beat wildly enough.

But she saw there was no hope.

One cry would bring Oscar Penraven to her assistance, truly.

But ere he came death would be her portion.

So, although she sickened and trembled in the grasp of her sturdy captor, she dared not move.

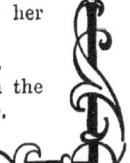

She guessed, of course, that Oscar would be the next object of his vengeance.

But that was nothing.

She had no disinterestedness in her nature.

Had Rupert Dreadnought been in danger, and had Helen Penraven been in the position in which Rosalie found herself, how different would have been the result.

She would have chanced her own death to save him.

Rosalie, however, thought only of her own safety.

Oscar and his men, therefo:e, passed by while she stood trembling in the arms of her relentless captor.

Then came a wild yell of rage.

Oscar had entered the bed-room and discovered her flight.

Not for a moment could it occur to him that she was still within the precincts of the cavern.

He, of course, concluded that she was by this time far on her road.

"Quick, my men," he cried, "my wife has been carried off! We have four horses; let four of us, then, scour the country in pursuit!"

And they rushed forth in a body to carry out this mad scheme.

Rathsay waited till the cavern was once more quiet.

Then he released his prisoner.

"Now," he said, "we must hasten."

Holding her firmly by the wrist, he led her from the cave.

All was dark without.

"They have gone off upon a wild chase, indeed," said Rathsay, chucklingly. "They know rot which way we have gone."

"They have taken the horses, however, and you cannot proceed as you wished?"

This was said inquiringly.

"Look you," he said; "nothing will turn me from *my* purpose. I know well a place where I can obtain horses; so let us hasten."

Rosalie had but thin shoes on her feet, and the stones cut them continually as she walked.

But he cared not.

On, over the sharp shingle, she was dragged.

Complaining was no use.

Knowing, therefore, that she was compelled to advance, she urged on her way as quickly as her captor could have wished.

On reaching a small indentation in the rocks, he turned sharply, and hastened up a natural staircase in the rocks.

At the summit they could see near them the twinkling lights of some inn.

Towards this he hurried.

It was evident in a moment that he was known.

The landlord—who, in fact, owed much of his renown as an excellent spirit retailer to the frequent aid he received from the lieutenant of the smugglers—knew Rathsay at once, and invited him cordially to enter and have refreshment.

"I will right gladly," said Rathsay; "but I have also a favour to ask."

"Name it, then," said Boniface, as he bustled about to prepare a meal.

"I and this lady," returned Rathsay, with a significant look at Rosalie, which warned her of the necessity of keeping quiet, "have pressing need to be at Yarborough by the morning, and we want, therefore, a good horse."

"*One* horse?"

"Yes, one will be sufficient; it is not the first time we have ridden together. You will oblige me, I am sure."

"With pleasure," replied Boniface, "meanwhile, eat and drink. It will soon be dawn, and Yarborough is a long ride. I will see that my own brown mare is saddled for you if you will promise to bring her back in safety."

"Be not afraid of that," cried Rathsay, "I will bring her back myself ere midnight."

The hasty meal over, the unwilling fugitive and her resolute captor proceeded to the courtyard, mounted the glossy steed, which the landlord eyed with a look of deep affection, and were soon hurrying along the chalky high road in the dull twilight of approaching dawn.

CHAPTER XIV.

ROSALIE COMES SUDDENLY TO THE END OF HER JOURNEY — THE UNCONSCIOUS BEAUTY — THE COMPACT—THE AWAKENING—THE GHOST OF THE OLD MANOR—THE MEETING ON THE STAIRCASE —THE STRANGE DISCLOSURE.

THE journey which Rosalie was thus compelled to take at the bidding of her captor need not be described.

It occupied but a short time, during which she clung to him tremulously as they careered wildly—madly over the hushed country.

At length, just as all nature was wavering under the influence of the glorious sun, they came in sight of a large house standing some distance back from the high road, amid clustering trees.

"That is your destination," said Rathsay.

Rosalie looked round eagerly.

This man evidently meant her no harm.

The home to which he was taking her, was manifestly by no means a bad one.

What could it mean?

Was he in love with her?

Was his revenge against Oscar Penraven to include also an attempt to conciliate her affections?

She did not pause long to reflect.

Nor, indeed, had she much time to do so.

Just as they rode up to the great gate, a handkerchief was suddenly pressed on her face.

A delicious aroma surrounded her.

Then earth, air, trees, were mingled in one confused mass.

A strange drowsiness—a pleasant faintness, overcame her.

Then she lapsed into insensibility.

Rathsay smiled.

"Now, my pretty one," he said, as he stooped, and kissed her unconscious lips; "now for revenge upon your husband, and then I will see if I cannot take his place and make you Queen of as brave a band as ever wrecked a ship or run a cargo."

A few minutes after they had passed round to the postern-gate of the mansion.

Rathsay leaped down, aided his senseless burden to alight, and then rang a bell.

An old woman answered the summons.

She recognised Rathsay at once.

But at sight of the lady she started.

"Who is this?" she asked.

"A friend of mine," said Rathsay, "whom I wish you to take care of for me for a time."

The old woman raised her hands in amazement.

"Me take care of her!" she cried; "why, this is not my house."

"I know it," replied Rathsay; "but it is large enough to enable you to conceal anyone in it without fear of discovery."

"But she is ill?"

"No; she is not ill. She is simply unconscious. All you need do is to carry her—or let *me* carry her in—place her in bed, and let her remain quietly for three hours. She will then be restored to her senses."

"And she will ask me where she is."

"Tell her she is in my house, and that you have my orders on no account to permit her to depart. Speak somewhat severely and she will be afraid to anger you."

"And if they find that I have some one concealed in the empty wing?"

"Say it is a poor deranged relation—anything you like—throw yourself a bit on their compassion, and, above all things, see what they do with her. She is my affianced bride," he added, as a sudden thought occurred to him; "but I have offended her, and it will be some time ere she forgives me."

The old woman hesitated no longer, more especially as Rathsay placed in her hand a shining piece of gold.

She held open the door and Rathsay at once entered.

With his lovely burden in his arms, he ascended the stairs as one accustomed to the place, and soon reached a part of the building, the very air of which spoke of its being uninhabited.

Here the old woman opened the door of a bedroom.

"This will do," she said.

Rathsay brought Rosalie in, and laid her on the bed as gently as he would have done a child.

Strange emotions filled him.

Since he had brought her from the cave, a new feeling had sprung up in his breast.

He loved her!

Rough man of crime as he was, he loved her!

Little did he know of her.

Little did he dream of what terrible crimes she had been guilty of.

He only thought that in securing her for himself from the wild wrecker and smuggler he would secure a gentle, pure-hearted being as his future companion.

Vain thought!

Why, rough fellow that he was, guilty of the death of drowning wretches as he was, his soul had not upon *his* conscience the weight of sin that lay at the door of that fair demon—that beautiful murderess of hundreds!

He bent over her and kissed her fondly as he left her.

Then he buttoned his cloak round him, and was soon once more on the road back towards the wreckers' haunt—towards the consummation, too, of his revenge.

CHAPTER XV.

THE AWAKENING — THE CONFERENCE — THE PRISONER AND THE KEEPER CHANGE PLACES— THE CHILL CORRIDOR—THE MEETING ON THE SHADOWY STAIRCASE — THE SURPRISE — THE EXPLANATION — THE FAIR DEMON ENTRAPS ANOTHER HEART—THE DEPARTURE OF THE RESCUERS—THE POISON-PHIAL.

Before following Rathsay, however, we must remain awhile with Rosalie, and see how she fared, and how strangely again the fates of Rupert and his friends were being mixed up with those of Oscar and his hideous crew.

When Rosalie awoke, the shades of evening had fallen.

In the room all was dark.

"Where am I?" she said, aloud, as she raised herself up.

Then she found that she was undressed and in bed.

A chill of horror overcame her.

Whither had Rathsay brought her? and what loathsome fate was it that was intended for her?

She cried aloud.

No answer came.

Then she rose from the bed, and felt round her for a light.

A cry of joy escaped from her as she felt that a lamp was standing on a table near, with a tinder-box by the side of it.

In an instant she had lit it, and was looking eagerly round her.

It was a strange room and a strange bed.

But it did not seem as if she was with enemies.

Her clothes were lying on a chair close by, neatly folded, as if by a woman's hand.

When recollection came freely to her, her alarm in a great measure subsided.

Rathsay had said—

"I shall take you thirty miles, and then leave you until my vengeance upon Oscar is accomplished."

It was only thirty miles, then, from the spot where she now was and the place where Rupert was in danger.

What if she were to send more men to his assistance!

What if she herself were to hie hither and tell him how she had again aided him!

Would he *then* spurn her as heretofore?

The mad passion was not yet extinguished in her breast.

Dressing herself hastily, she went to the door and tried it.

It was doubly locked.

She knocked and called loudly.

But no answer came.

Again and again she repeated her summons.

Still in vain.

At length she desisted from mere weariness, and, after opening the window and seeing that escape by that way was impossible, she sat down dejectedly.

"They will surely send me provisions," thought she; "then I will, if the messenger be a woman, seize and bind her, and make my way into the house."

After about half-an-hour spent in patient watching, a step was heard approaching.

Then some one came to the door and listened.

After this, the key was turned in the lock, and the old woman entered.

A thrill of joy invaded Rosalie's breast.

Here, then, was the chance she had so eagerly sought.

"Where am I?" she asked, quietly, without rising from her seat.

"In the house of Rathsay."

"And am I a prisoner?"

"Nay," said the old woman, "you are not a prisoner, but I am responsible to him for your safe keeping, and I must deliver you up to him when he comes."

You are deceiving me," said Rosalie.

No, indeed," stammered the old dame; "I——"

Nay, deny it not. I have this moment glanced from the window, and I see that this house is a very large one. You and your master cannot use it all. This must be the home of some stranger. Tell me, whose place is it?"

"I have already told you," answered the old woman; "if you do not believe me——"

"I do not," said Rosalie, as she approached the table and seized one of the sharp-bladed knives. "This Rathsay is no friend of mine—he has put me here from purposes of revenge. However, against his own will, I would aid him in his designs against one person, and I shall see for myself what kind of prison I am in, and who are my gaolers."

So saying, she made a movement towards the door.

This was only a feint on her part.

She wished to see if her custodian would follow her.

"Stay!" cried the old woman, frantically, "if you pass that door I shall alarm the house."

This was exactly what Rosalie wanted.

She closed the door, and retraced her steps at once.

"Look you," she cried. "I would have dealt kindly with you, had I thought that you had a woman's feeling for a woman. But, as it is, I must take a man's part. I shall bind you, leave you in this room, and if you make any resistance to my will, I will bury this knife in your heart!"

The old woman was amazed.

The lovely being before her, with her soft features, seemed so utterly incapable of revenge or desperate doings.

"I will not resist," she said; "you need not bind me."

Rosalie smiled.

"No, no!" she said. "I will not trust you."

And so saying, she approached her, and with the bed-clothes firmly bound and gagged her.

"No harm shall befall you," she said, as she took the lamp, and prepared to leave. "I myself will return and unbind you."

The old woman at this made frantic efforts to speak.

But Rosalie understood her not, and simply went on her way.

She knew not how necessary it was to the old woman that no one in the house should know of the part she had taken in her abduction.

So on she went, through the door, and down the wide staircase.

Of course, having first entered the house in a state of complete unconsciousness, she knew nothing of the place.

So every now and then she stopped to listen.

For some time not a sound disturbed the gloomy solitude of the old house.

All seemed like the tomb.

At the bottom of the staircase she came upon a long corridor, wrapped in utter darkness, and filled with a chill and humid atmosphere.

This she traversed at full speed, not without many boundings of the heart as she felt herself thus utterly alone.

When, however, she reached the end, and pushed open the door, a rush of warmer air told her that she had reached the inhabited portion of the building, and with a pleasurable feeling she hurried through it, and found herself on the summit of a broad and massive staircase.

As she began its descent she heard voices.

The voices of a man and a woman.

She hurried on then more quickly, and, as she came to a turn in the staircase, she saw below her in the shadow the two speakers.

The former she did not at first recognise.

The latter she knew well.

It was Helen Penraven!

Neither of them could repress a cry as they saw her descending.

Left here by Rupert Dreadnought, under the care of Stanley Sherrington and Mistress Clanberris, Helen had expressed a wish to explore the old house, and, having heard strange rumours in regard to ghostly visitants to the uninhabited part of it, she, for the moment, imagined the apparition now before her as one of the weird tenants of the old mansion.

Her companion, however, though startled himself at first, quickly recovered his presence of mind.

Dropping the arm of his companion, he advanced towards Rosalie.

"Madam," he said, with a polite bow, "may I ask you how you came here?"

"Strange," thought Rosalie; "he evidently knows nothing as yet of my presence here."

"Sir," she replied, as she stepped down further and joined him, "I came here utterly against my will, and shall be glad when I depart. If you will allow me, I will explain to you my meaning."

She paused a moment.

The sight of Helen Penraven produced an entire revulsion of feeling in her breast.

Here was her rival.

She seemed to have been thrown into her hands by a genius of evil.

What now prevented her from destroying her, and thus leaving the road completely open to herself?

Bloodthirsty demon that she was, she shrank not

from the contemplation of another desperate crime even though the prospect it held out to her in the future was so shadowy.

"Do not be alarmed," she said, as she descended the stairs, and met Helen and Stanley Sherrington.

"But who are you, and how came you here?" asked Stanley Sherrington.

"I will explain, but it must be quickly, for your friend Rupert is in danger," she said, in a voice of great agitation.

Quickly, omitting, of course, all reference to her own connection with Oscar, she told her story.

"This man, who, in his mad love for me, brought me hither," she cried, "may deem himself able to defend Hanley House against the wreckers, but he is wrong, absurdly wrong. They are men who stick at nothing, who fear neither God nor devil. You, sir, whom I know to be a friend of Rupert Dreadnought, *you* will save him, will you not?"

The energy with which she spoke, astounded Helen.

Who was this woman?

And, whoever she was, did she love Rupert?

Rosalie had represented herself as the affianced wife of the man who had brought her.

This her artful nature had suggested, for she guessed what a strange emotion her eagerness to save Rnpert would raise in the bosom of her fair hearer.

"Do you love this Rupert Dreadnought?" asked Helen Penraven, with as much calmness as she could muster.

But the lips were pale that spoke the words.

"Love him!" exclaimed Rosalie, raising her pretty eyebrows in well simulated disguise, "I have never seen him. No, I love another in that house, the handsome young sailor who was saved from the wreck, and it is for *his* sake that I hope you will aid in saving Hanley House from pillage."

Helen was at once satisfied.

Not so Stanley Sherrington.

He fancied he had seen the face of the speaker before.

Where he knew not.

But that he had seen her he felt certain, the more he gazed at her features, and her form.

"We have met before, have we not, madam?" he said, as he led the way to a room.

"Met before!" echoed Rosalie.

Then with a pretty archness, she laid her little hand upon his arm and drew him to the light.

"That face!" she said, knowing well the advantage of a bold stroke; "why, yes, I have seen you before. But where was it?"

She thought a moment.

"Yes, yes, I remember now," she cried; "I remember well. It was when I was rescued with several others from the hands of the Mohocks. You were one of the brave gentlemen who rescued me. But I thought not that you would remember my face among so many."

"I should remember so lovely a face anywhere," said Stanley, whose frame thrilled as he gazed on the exquisite being before him.

Rosalie saw her power.

She saw she had ensnared another.

"This will be my safeguard," she thought.

And so she heaved a sigh, and pressed her hand over her swelling bosom, as if she, too, had caught the amorous infection.

Then she said suddenly,

"But we are losing time. Hanley House is thirty miles hence, and at midnight the assault will begin. It must now be nearly eight."

Helen started.

"Thirty miles!" she cried. "Oh! Master Sherrington, you will never reach it."

"Yes, yes," he said; "I will hasten and collect what men we have. There are six brave fellows, I know; and with good steeds and willing hearts we will reach Hanley House in time to take our station within."

So saying he hurried away, while Helen also hastened to Mistress Clanberris to ask her to give instructions to her followers to obey Sherrington in everything.

In a few minutes he returned, booted, spurred and armed.

Rosalie was alone.

He approached her gallantly.

"Sweet lady," he said, "you have well requited me for any little service I ever rendered you by thus placing it in my power to assist my dear friend Dreadnought."

As he spoke he took her hand and pressed it to his lips.

He was seized with a strange and sudden infatuation.

Glancing up rapidly he caught the eyes of Rosalie fixed upon him.

In them there was a strange and peculiar flush, and, as if attracted by a magnet, he sprang forward, closed his arms round her in a strong and fervent embrace, and pressed his lips to hers.

Then, as he released her, he cried—

"Pardon me, sweet one, if I have transgressed; but the impulse I obeyed was irresistible. With that delicious kiss still upon my lips, I shall the more readily and manfully fight the battle, hoping for another on my return victorious. Say you forgive me."

The entrance of Helen prevented further speech.

But the laughing gleam in the fair demon's eyes told him he was more than pardoned.

"All is ready," said Helen, who was followed quickly by Mistress Clanberris. "Hasten, I pray you, and Heaven grant you strength to aid Rupert, and preserve your own safety."

Another tender glance was exchanged between Stanley Sherrington and Rosalie St. Aubyn.

Then he hurried from the room, saying—

"Be assured Rupert shall be saved, or I shall die in his defence."

His heart, as he vaulted on his horse, was warm with a new life.

Poor, infatuated wretch!

He was in the power—under the spell of the fair sorceress.

As soon as he was gone, the three repaired to the room where the old woman was still bound.

They found her nearly dead with terror.

When she was released, she fell at the feet of Mistress Clanberris.

She knew well that her conduct deserved punishment.

"Oh, forgive me, forgive me, mistress!" she said, grovellingly.

"I do not, and will not," replied Mistress Clanberris; "you might have introduced thieves or murderers into our house. You must quit this place at once and for ever."

Had Rosalie St. Aubyn been of softer mould, these words might have caused her a peculiar sensation of the heart.

As it was she pleaded for the old woman.

"Be not too harsh upon her," she said; "remember her age."

"Which should have taught her better," said Mistress Clanberris. "No, I will not forgive her. I will permit so much grace as this, that she may remain here to-night, but in the morning she must go. And now we had better take some refreshment and retire. Sleep will visit the eyes of neither of us I imagine, but rest by itself is something."

"Sleep!" thought Rosalie, as she entered her chamber and was left alone; "aye, one of us will sleep to-night the long, deep sleep of Eternity!"

And, as she spoke, she drew from its warm concealment in her bosom the phial which, always, and in every situation, she carried with her.

A phial containing the colourless, never-failing *poison* of the Dread League.

She had resolved that that very night should behold the perpetration of her hideous crime.

My readers may imagine that I am painting a monster of iniquity too horrid for reality.

It is not so.

The annals of Paris and of Rome furnish specimens of even worse enormity.

Enormity rendered worse by the loveliness of the demons who perpetrated it.

She locked her door, but did not undress herself.

Throwing herself down on the bed to obtain a little rest, she listened intently to every sound.

In about an hour all was still.

Then she rose and unlocked her door.

Again she listened.

Not a mouse stirred.

She had marked well the position of Helen Penraven's room, and now, lamp in hand, she stealthily approached it.

It was slightly ajar.

Eagerly the murderess approached and pushed it open.

She started as she gazed in.

Helen Penraven was on her knees by the side of her bed.

In this position she had fallen asleep.

Kneeling there, thinking of Rupert, and praying for his safety, slumber had overcome her.

A smile of diabolical triumph overspread the features of the poisoner.

On the table she had caught sight of a decanter of wine, light wine, placed there for the refreshment of the sleeper.

Stealthily approaching, she poured into this some of the colourless fluid.

The drinking water in the room also received a portion, and then, noiselessly, the assassin withdrew, leaving the door ajar, as she had found it, and then crawling away, like the venomous snake she was, to her own chamber.

"She cannot escape me now," she murmured, as she proceeded to array herself for a journey.

It was not safe for her to remain longer.

If Rupert Dreadnought succeeded in escaping from the manifold dangers surrounding him he would hasten with all possible speed to his mistress's house, and her guilt would at once be apparent.

She would, therefore, take a horse from the stable and gallop away to Hanley House to see him ere he could know of the disaster.

Before she went, however, she was guilty of another sin.

She left on her table these words—

"KIND HOSTESS,—I could not rest here in peace while my lover was in danger. I have fled to him. We shall meet again soon.

"MINNIE EDGETOWN."

Thus the guilt of the murder of Helen Penraven would be attached to the innocent mistress of the young sailor.

Having accomplished this last infamy, she had nothing more to delay her.

Taking her lamp, lest a false step might betray her, she advanced leisurely, noiselessly down the staircase, crept out into the darkness, and made her way to what seemed a stable, and tried the door.

Admission was soon gained, a horse soon saddled, and a short time saw the murderess galloping at full speed from the scene of her crime.

Meanwhile we must leave her to the dangers that there awaited her, and return to Rupert Dreadnought, whom we left in such a position of peril and difficulty.

CHAPTER XVI.

HANLEY HOUSE ONCE MORE—PREPARATIONS FOR THE DEFENCE OF THE PLACE—THE WATCHERS IN THE STILL NIGHT—ARRIVAL OF AID FROM CLANBERRIS—THE NOISES IN THE GROUNDS—THE ATTACK.

As may well be imagined, every one at Hanley House was in a state of intense excitement.

They knew, from Rupert's interview with Rathsay, the villanous character of those with whom they had to deal, and felt that a tough battle would ensue.

But no one dreamed that the man called Red Orley was indeed Oscar Penraven.

Had they done so, they would have looked forward to the attack with feelings akin to pleasure.

As it was, the house was placed in a state of good defence.

Every door was so bolted and barred as to effectually prevent any ingress.

Every window had its special guard.

The plan of the besiegers, however, as they knew, would be to enter by the secret way and enter the vault where Rupert had encountered Rathsay; and it was resolved as midnight approached to surround this place as well as they could, and so catch the villains in their own trap.

ON THE WATCH FOR TRAITORS.

The wife of Chester, and all females, had been sent away in the morning to a neighbour's house, as in a beleaguered town, and when night set in, the defenders gathered round the bright fire in the old dining-hall.

Presently they were startled by the loud clattering of many horses' feet, and ere they could think what it meant, a prolonged peal at the outer bell awoke the silence of the night.

"Let me go," cried Chester.

And springing from his seat, he rushed to the front door, and opened it ere one of the domestics were prepared.

Six armed men stood on horseback without.

"What want you?" cried Chester, to whom all were strangers.

"My name is Stanley Sherrington, and I seek Rupert Dreadnought," was the reply.

Had Rupert himself not heard the words, it is more than probable that Stanley Sherrington and his men would have found the door closed in their faces.

As it was, however, Dreadnought and those with him had hastened after Chester, not unreasonably imagining that this open knock at the door might be part of some scheme of the enemy.

He at once, therefore, recognised Stanley's voice, and hastened forward to meet him.

"Admit him, Chester," he cried; "it is an old friend."

Stanley Sherrington and his followers were soon, therefore, standing within the hall, and the door was once more closed and barred securely.

"By what wonderful means have you come hither?" asked Rupert, as Stanley entered the room.

Stanley briefly told his strange story, to which all listened in wonder.

"So, then, it is Oscar Penraven after all to whom I am indebted for this intended assault," cried Rupert, when Stanley had completed his story; "that villain seems to have a hundred lives. But unless, indeed, it be a disguise which he has assumed, his face is so disfigured that he is scarcely recognisable. But who can this be who so opportunely informed you of our peril?"

Stanley's eyes brightened as Rupert spoke of her.

"I know not who she is," he cried, "but at all events she is an angel of beauty; such a face—such a form—such eyes! I have never met with before."

"What!" laughed Rupert, "has the arrow of love entered your heart in the midst of all this turmoil? Well, well, it is a change truly. First a Mohock, then a convert to quiet, then a thorough-paced old bachelor, and then a love-sick swain. I wish you well of your bargain. But you say she is in love?"

"It is so, indeed," returned Stanley, sadly; "she says she loves a sailor—a young sailor who was rescued from the wreck."

It was now the turn of Charles Rice to be amazed.

"It cannot surely be Minnie," said he; "I have seen her this day. *She* knows nothing of the wreckers or their purposes; she was at her father's house not many hours ago, and has not had time to be carried so far by Rathsay. There is some strange mystery here."

"Not so much a mystery as there seems to be, perhaps," said Rupert, smiling. "How know you how many fair damsels have lost their hearts to the sole survivor of the wreck?"

In conversation like this, which did not in any way tend, be it said, to elucidate the mystery in which Rosalie St. Aubyn was the chief actor, the time was spent, until at length the hour approached.

"Now, gentlemen," said Chester, "we must to our posts. Fortify yourselves with another glass of wine, and let us prepare for the assault."

The assembled friends accordingly at once rose, drank off a last glass of wine, and put themselves under the guidance of Chester as being master of the house.

Before, however, they started to their posts, Rupert said—

"My friends, since I have heard Stanley Sherrington's story, a change has come over my mind. I do not see why *you* should all be involved in this peril. Now that I know it is Oscar Penraven who leads the enemy, I know also that it is I alone against whom the attack is meant. Let *me*, therefore, face him when he appears, and fight to the death with him. I have faith in my sword, and in the righteousness of my cause."

"But very little in your friends," said Chester, "if you imagine that they would let you fight this battle alone. No, no; let us to our posts without further delay!"

It was not long, therefore, before they had descended to the vault, where it will be remembered that Rupert Dreadnought had first met Rathsay, and taken positions round it, so that at the first opening of the door not one of them would be perceived.

Then all the lights in the house were extinguished one by one.

It had been arranged that it was to be so; and each party in each room had at hand the instant means of procuring a light if required.

I have omitted to mention that Rathsay had arrived at ten o'clock, as he had promised to Rupert, and was among those who were preparing for the defence of the house.

He was posted among those in the upper story of the house at a window which commanded the view of the road towards the shore.

From this point he hoped to be able to distinguish the forms of the approaching marauders and give notice to those in the house of their coming.

It may be wondered why Chester and his men did not surround the place, so as to render all entrance impossible.

This would have been easy enough.

But they had other plans.

What they desired was to seize upon the ringleaders and deliver them over to justice.

It is a trite saying that time passes slowly to those who wait.

It passed slowly, indeed, to those who waited at Hanley House, with hearts glowing and swelling with intense excitement.

As the time approached, Chester Rice, who was in a room by himself, that in which his men were posted, could hardly contain himself.

Presently he heard a noise.

He started from his chair, and, half kneeling on it, watched the place whence it had proceeded.

Again all was quiet for a time.

But at length there came again a tap at the door of the vault.

Then Chester sprang up, and called to his friends.

All were instantly on the alert.

Then a voice said from without—

"Be ready; they are coming over the heath."

It was true.

Over the dark country Rathsay had seen them coming, for the moon had not favoured the wreckers, but lay in broad, bright patches over the land.

Another half-hour passed.

Then a rustling, as of men's feet, was heard; the wall was felt to shake, and it was evident that the villains had made their way into the secret passage.

Every one of the watchers was on the tiptoe of expectation.

Another quarter-of-an-hour passed.

Yet no show of the enemy.

All eagerly strained their eyes through the darkness at the secret door, expecting to see it open and the rough figures of the wreckers appear.

But no one came.

"What can this mean?" whispered Rupert to Stanley Sherrington. "Surely the villains have changed their plans."

"Yes, it must be so, or Rathsay has deceived us."

This had never occurred to Rupert.

It was a chilling thought in very truth to entertain at first.

But he at once rejected it.

He knew not, of course, that it was Rathsay who had carried off the lady and left her so mysteriously at the house of Henry Clanberris.

Why should Rathsay deceive him?

If he had desired to share in the plunder of Hanley, he could have done so by joining the band of secretly-working villains who had planned the murderous expedition.

Besides, if it had not been for him, no preparations would have been made.

"No, no," said Rupert, "he is not deceiving us; there is no reason for his doing so."

As he spoke, they heard indistinctly, as if at the summit of the house, a loud sound of clashing of weapons, and the shouts of apparently contending parties.

"What can this mean?" cried Rupert. "They must have changed their plans, and begun the attack at the top of the house. Let us at once rush to the rescue."

"And leave this place unguarded," said Sherrington. "That would certainly be unwise. How know we that this is not a ruse?"

"True," replied Rupert; "it would be unwise. I will go myself and see what is the matter."

And so saying, he threw open the door, and rushed, sword in hand, out into the dark passage.

Here the sounds of strife could be heard plainly enough, and directed by these, Rupert hurried as quickly as he could towards the point whence the sounds proceeded.

CHAPTER XVII.

THE SCENE IN THE UPPER ROOMS—THE FIERCE BATTLE—THE MEETING OF THE DEADLY FOES—THE SINGLE COMBAT—OSCAR PENRAVEN FINDS HIS MATCH—HE RESOLVES UPON ESCAPE—DEATH OF RATHSAY AND FLIGHT OF OSCAR—THE PURSUIT ACROSS THE DUSKY HEATH—THE ESCAPE—SURRENDER OF THE SMUGGLERS.

On reaching the second floor, Rupert found a scene of hideous confusion.

Men were mingled in one confused crowd in such a struggling mass that it was at first sight impossible to tell friends from foes.

"What means this?" shouted Rupert.

His voice acted like an electric shock.

The men divided into two factions at once, and glanced in surprise at the new-comer.

But only for a moment was the desperate fight stayed.

One word, one shout from the leaders, and they dashed at one another again.

The combat being renewed now with greater fury than ever, the noise, as may be imagined, was terrible.

But, nevertheless, this did not prevent a loud uproar being suddenly heard from below.

It was evident, then, that a diversion was being made in the vaults, where they had expected to receive the first onslaught of the enemy.

During all this time Rupert Dreadnought had been endeavouring to find Oscar Penraven, who in his turn sought to make his way towards Rupert.

In this Oscar Penraven had, of course, an advantage.

He could tell Rupert Dreadnought's tall figure and recognise his noble features.

But in the case of Rupert it was different.

The disfigured man could not easily be distinguished from the others.

At length in the centre of the room they met.

The light was feeble enough.

But still the enemies knew one another.

It was as if by instinct.

With a muttered exclamation of hate, they at once raised their weapons, and plunged through the thick of the battle.

"At length!" cried Rupert.

"Yes, at length," shouted Oscar Penraven, "we meet, I trust, for the last time."

"Your wish is mine," returned Rupert, "this night you die!"

And then their voices ceased and their weapons met.

No one observed them.

The men, of course, knew that their leaders had joined issue.

But that was all.

It incited them to fresh exertions.

But they had no time to take note of their proceedings.

To describe the various phases of the fight would be useless and tedious.

It was but a series of single combats, then rushes into dark corners whenever one of the men fell.

Then suddenly there came a dash up the stairs, and a shouting throng dashed into the room.

Among these there were no enemies.

They were the victors, headed by Stanley Sherrington, who, as my readers will remember, had headed the band below.

"They have fled, Rupert," he shouted, in a loud voice. "Now let us drive hence these rascals, or take them prisoners, and hand them over to justice."

This was exactly consonant with Rupert's feelings.

To seize Oscar, keep him a prisoner, and see the consummation of his last revenge, was all he desired.

Then came the great hope of his life—the marriage with Helen Penraven, and the termination of a life of adventure which had in it no elements of pleasure.

But to Oscar Penraven the unexpected failure of his expedition signified the immediate necessity for flight.

When he heard, therefore, the shouts of the victors, and knew that some of his desperate crew had fled, he determined, even in spite of his desire to kill Rupert, to make good his escape.

This could only be done by a ruse.

"Fear not, my men," he shouted. "Let us regain the day ourselves; our brave companions will soon return to the rescue. On, therefore, and turn the fortune of the day."

He knew it was impossible.

He saw around him men slipping and stumbling in the blood of their slain friends, disheartened by the coming of the band of victors.

His plan was to incite them to a rush, then to mingle with the crowd, and plunge suddenly down the dark secret staircase by which they had ascended.

This he found was more difficult than he had imagined.

His men, though greatly disheartened, did make a rush.

Then stumbling, or rather pretending to stumble, he succeeded in falling into the rear of the struggling party.

Just as he did so, however, Rathsay, the smuggler lieutenant, made a dash at him, sword in hand.

This was a fatal attempt.

With a savage plunge, made more desperate by his fear of capture, Oscar Penraven drove forward his sword, which was buried up to the hilt in the chest of Rosalie's would-be lover.

Oscar did not wait to withdraw the weapon; but leaving it in the chest of the dead man, rushed away.

One of the men who saw his scheme made an effort to stay his progress.

But the effort was fatal.

A shot from one of the pistols which Oscar drew from his belt sent him staggering back among his companions; and in another instant the private door was closed, and Oscar was hurrying down the dark staircase towards the open air.

"Pursue him! pursue him!" shouted Rupert, and with half-a-dozen men, Rupert and Stanley Sherrington ran hastily down the open staircase towards the basement.

The private way, however, was by far the shortest, and when they reached the postern gate, they beheld Oscar Penraven galloping away towards the dusky heath.

Pursuit seemed useless.

Before they could have reached the stables to bring out the horses he would be far out of sight.

An idea, however, flashed through the mind of Rupert Dreadnought.

If Oscar had a horse, so, also, would the others.

"Follow me," he shouted, without explaining his meaning, and rushing away, he led the way towards a dense clump of trees.

Here he found it exactly what he had expected.

There were six horses ready saddled.

"Come, Stanley Sherrington."

And Rupert mounting, was off ere the others were ready.

The night was fearfully dark.

The moon had completely veiled her face.

The mass of black clouds which had been driving across the sky had now united in one dark mass, and hidden the blue ether, the moon, and the stars.

The heath itself was black beneath, and full of ruts and pieces of stiff undergrowth, which made the horses stumble.

But on pressed the pursuers and pursued.

Oscar Penraven had the lead, and kept it, too, for a long time.

His was the energy of despair.

He cared not if he did stumble.

It was better to risk that than to permit them to gain even a head.

At length they saw the horse disappear an instant.

Then it rose, shook itself, and plunged away over the dusky heath.

It was now riderless.

"On my men," cried Rupert, who felt almost certain now of capturing the fugitive.

But he was destined to disappointment.

When they reached the spot where the rider had disappeared from the horse's back, they found no one, although they spread themselves about in every direction.

It was dark, as I have said.

Yet anybody moving on the ground at their feet could easily have been seen.

Everywhere they sought.

But in vain.

Somehow or another Oscar Penraven had slipped away, and they were forced to abandon the search, and return empty handed to Hanley House.

Meanwhile, the smugglers, cooped up in the room, and seeing the flight of their leader, saw the uselessness of resistance, and yielded.

They were at once disarmed and placed under guard in a room below, there to await the event of the morning.

Then, when Rupert and Stanley Sherrington returned, the house again resumed somewhat of its accustomed quiet.

CHAPTER XVIII.

HOW OSCAR PENRAVEN ESCAPED—ROSALIE'S RETURN TO THE SMUGGLERS' CAVE—HER PLAN OF ESCAPE—THE DISGUISE—THE TRAITOR IN THE CAMP—A SWIFT TRIAL AND A SWIFT PUNISHMENT—THE FATAL BEAM—OSCAR'S PLAN FOR HIS MEN'S SAFETY—THE ROCKY LEDGES—THE ENEMY ONCE MORE IN SIGHT—OSCAR'S EAGERNESS TO DESTROY RUPERT—ROSALIE SAVES HIM.

THE ruse which Oscar Penraven had adopted for making his escape from those who were so hotly pursuing him was one which was more suited to an American Indian than an Englishman.

When the horse had stumbled and risen again to its feet it certainly had no rider visibly upon its back.

But, nevertheless, it *had* a rider.

Clinging along the side of the horse, so as, in the darkness, to be quite undistinguishable from it, was Oscar Penraven.

With a feeling of intense triumph, he saw that his enemies had been taken by the ruse, and, finding that they paid all their attention to the spot where they had fancied they had seen him fall to the ground, he soon was able once more to resume his seat in the saddle and dash away to the cave of the smugglers.

On arriving there he found, of course, that everything was in darkness.

Wounded and fatigued as he was, he uttered a curse as he entered the gloomy precincts.

For the first time he missed Rosalie.

He had asked her to accompany him simply because he desired female society—because she was beautiful, and, being in fear of her own life, would be likely to remain faithful to him for the sake of a protector.

But now he experienced a different sensation entirely.

She was a demon to others.

She had not proved so to him.

While they had been together in the smuggler's cave, she had endeavoured to behave to him with the kindness and tenderness of a wife.

"I wish she was here," he muttered, as he groped his way into the large cave, and sought for a light. "They won't come here after me until morning, and the place will seem lonely without anyone. I never believe she left me of her own accord. Ha! here is a light; some of the men are here."

He was right.

Those who had made their escape from Hanley House when Stanley Sherrington and his men had vanquished them, had made their way as quickly as possible to the cave, and were now indulging in a last glass of grog.

The grog it was that accounted for the extreme silence.

The noisy portion of the drinking bout was over.

They were now relapsing by slow and sure degrees into utter unconsciousness.

They did not even see him enter.

They were soon, however, aroused to a partial knowledge that he was there.

"Ha, cowardly villains!" he shouted, in a voice of thunder. "You are here, are you, carousing, while, for aught you knew, your chief might have been sleeping the long sleep of death! Would that I had been there when you fled; some of you would certainly have seen whether in the hour of danger my hand trembles as it pulls the trigger."

The length of this speech gave time to one or two of the men to rub their eyes, and rouse themselves somewhat from their lethargy.

"Well," said one of them, as steadily as his severe potations would permit, "there weren't a chance, you see, captain. We were overmatched, and the enemy came upon us unawares, too. We were huddled up together in a small space, and thought the best thing we could do was to fly."

"But since *you* are here, captain," said another, "where are our comrades?"

"Prisoners," returned Oscar Penraven.

"Then we're not any of us safe here," said the man. "We'd better take what we can, and be off quickly."

"Cowards still," cried Oscar.

"But what *can* be done," answered the man, "in this place? Cooped up like prisoners in a cell, we should never be able to bear a siege. How could we obtain provisions were they to fail? How could we escape if we came to the last extremity?"

"True; but I mean nothing of the kind," said Oscar Penraven. "I propose that we do not abandon the place entirely, although we may pretend to do so. We can watch from the rocks around, and see the movements of our enemies. Then, as there are very little things they will care to take, except the spirits, which we can remove, we can take possession again when they are fairly gone. Meanwhile, we are, no doubt, safe till morning, so rest awhile, and I will awake you with the early dawn."

So saying, and without even waiting to see whether they agreed or not, he took a lantern and proceeded to his own chamber.

To his astonishment he found the door locked.

"Who can be here?" he muttered, savagely "some traitor, no doubt, who has taken advantage of my absence."

He knocked loudly.

"Who is there?" he cried.

A gentle voice answered—

"Who calls?"

Oscar staggered back in amazement.

Was it possible that voice was Rosalie's?

"Is that you, Rosalie?" he said; "if it be, open quickly; it is Oscar who speaks."

In a moment the door was opened.

It was, indeed, Rosalie who stood there.

On her way a method of disguise had occurred to her.

She would proceed to the cave while Oscar Penraven was absent, and putting on one of his dresses, make her escape once more ere he returned from his expedition.

Arriving there, she had found a suit belonging to a youth among the band, which she at once appropriated to herself.

It was in this attire that she now appeared before Oscar Penraven, an attire which set off to advantage the fine proportions of her bust and shoulders, and the soft undulations of her lower limbs.

Oscar Penraven gazed at her in wonder and doubt.

"How came you hither?" he said, in a voice in which were some traces of sternness. "I thought, from the letter which you sent me, that you had voluntarily left me for ever."

Rosalie saw this was no time for permitting him to think that, although the letter *was* forced from her, she had really thought of making it an opportunity of real escape.

She knew not, moreover, whether he had succeeded or failed in his enterprise.

If he had succeeded, then Rupert Dreadnought, the one she so madly loved, was no more, and all struggles to see him were useless.

If he had failed, his temper would not certainly be such as could well be meddled with.

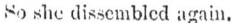

So she dissembled again.

Rushing forward after one look of glad surprise and bewilderment, she threw her arms around his neck.

"Why, Oscar, you must have known that that letter was forced from me," she cried. "You see that I have returned the instant I could."

"And who persuaded you; or, rather, compelled you thus to fly from me?" asked Oscar, returning with pleasure the caress offered him.

"Rathsay, your lieutenant."

"Rathsay!"

"Aye; *he* was the man. He carried me to the house of Lady Clanberris, when he had put me into a state of utter insensibility. Then he left me in the care of an old woman, from whom I escaped, and here I am."

She said nothing of the manner in which she had sent aid to Rupert.

"Well, well, he has paid for his treachery with his life," said Oscar, savagely. "How much more gladly should I have run the villain through the heart had I known how meanly and despicably he had betrayed me."

For an instant it occurred to Oscar Penraven that now he had recovered Rosalie, it would be better to leave the smugglers to do as best they could, pocket what wealth he had, and fly to some place of temporary refuge.

But no.

It would be a matter of difficulty and of time also to collect again a band so strong, so devoted to his interests, and so reckless.

Without them he could not hope to do anything against Rupert.

Mad revenge!

That of Rupert Dreadnought against him was far different.

It was the result of a vow taken at the death-bed of a beloved father—the well-deserved hunting of a villain.

Oscar Penraven's vengeful spirit against him was the result simply of an evil mind.

If he had resolved to abandon all idea of revenge, and to leave the country, he could certainly have escaped.

But this idea never once occurred to him.

He had so resolutely settled to destroy his enemy in punishment for the absolute ruin of his hideous plans, that not even the strong hope of safety made him swerve for a moment from his determination.

"What are your plans now, Oscar?" asked Rosalie, seeing that he had leaned several moments near the fire-place wrapped in deep thought, "did your expedition this night succeed?"

There was the slightest perceptible tremor in her voice as she spoke.

But Oscar did not observe it.

"No, curse it!" he said, fiercely. "By some means or another, we were defeated. That accursed villain, Rathsay, betrayed us, and so they were prepared for us. Otherwise, every one in that house, Rupert Dreadnought and every friend he had there with him, would have slept the sleep of death this night."

As he spoke, he was suddenly startled by a loud and hideous outcry.

He rushed to the door, and, flinging it open, listened eagerly.

The uproar proceeded from the large cave.

"Something is wrong, Rosalie," he said. "Perhaps the enemy are upon us already."

He hurried out as he spoke, accompanied by Rosalie St. Aubyn, who, indeed, was the first to enter the cavern.

There a curious scene presented itself.

In the centre of the cavern were two smugglers, who were with difficulty kept back by two other stalwart men.

"What means this?" shouted Oscar. "Would you murder one another when we have so few of our band left for our defence? What is this mad disturbance for?"

One of the men, who was struggling to free himself, pointed at his adversary.

"I'm a smuggler and a wrecker," he said, "and I've done a rare bit of mischief in my time, I don't doubt, but I ain't a traitor. *He* is."

"What, then, is your complaint against him?" cried Rosalie.

"He has been proposing that we should save ourselves by giving up the captain to the authorities, yield up all we have here, and putting the revenue officers on the scent of the 'Ocean Fairy' that is coming in three night's hence."

"And so you attacked him?"

"I did; and if these lubbers hadn't interfered, I'd have soon settled his business in this world."

"Well, I'm glad you did not succeed, Elston," said Oscar Penraven, with a bitter smile; "it will enable me to punish him in a way he better deserves."

"How so, captain?"

"Why, by hanging him on yonder beam as a traitor. What say you, Compton?" he added, turning to the accused; "you have heard what Elston has stated against you; is it true?"

The man did not answer.

The only gesture he made was a shrug of the shoulders.

"Speak—I shall listen," said Oscar.

"Of what use is it to speak?" returned the man, with a sneer; "these fellows have all heard what I said, and, as they've turned against me, why, of what use would it be to deny it? As they've chosen to sell an old friend for a new one, why, the sooner I part company with them the better, and it don't much matter to me how I do it."

Then, as the men who held him released him, he coolly replaced his knife in his belt, took out his pipe, lit it, and took a strong pull.

"He has confessed, and he shall die," said Oscar Penraven. "My men, throw a rope over yonder beam, and secure it firmly."

The order was soon obeyed.

"Now place a barrel beneath it."

This was done.

The prisoner meanwhile sat on a piece of wreck, and smoked composedly.

What was at work within his dark mind was never known.

But outwardly he was all composure.

"Now," said Oscar, while this had been done, "secure him firmly."

The man stood up, pipe in mouth, placing his arms in position, and never moving while his comrades closely pinioned him, and, at a sign from Oscar, bore him to the tub on which they stood him.

"Now," cried Oscar, as he faced the man upon whom he had resolved to take such terrible retribution, "now, Compton, if, in the midst of your hideous life, you have preserved any notion of prayer and you desire to say anything, say it quickly, for in five minutes you will be launched into eternity."

The man scowled darkly at the speaker.

"If I want to pray I can! You are kind," he said; "but ere I do so I'll tell you one thing. Nothing good will come to you through this exhibition of tyranny and cruelty. Do you think my comrades will admire you any more, or be ready to fight for you any the more readily, because you have strung me up for this thing, which you don't know my reason for. I was only trying their fidelity when I said it."

Oscar Penraven shook his head doubtfully.

"The latter part of your speech I do not believe," replied he; "but I will tell you one thing. If I let you go after this, I know well that our only course would be to fly at once, for as certain as that daylight approaches, we should be delivered over to the enemy. Nevertheless, if your comrades think proper, you shall be released. Say, my men, shall he be saved?"

"No, no," cried they, in one voice, and with a savage ferocity which would have alarmed any other woman but one formed like Rosalie, of steel.

She stirred not.

Not a tremor ran through her muscles, nor did she for a moment take her eyes off the man who was soon to be launched into eternity.

"You see," said Oscar, turning to Compton, upon whose features now there was the slightest shade of greenish pallor, "you are condemned by all. Now, Elston, and you, Bob Ackton, do your duty. Draw the rope a little tighter, and kick the barrel away."

The men at once approached, and, having settled the rope, glanced at Oscar, who stood near Rosalie at the door.

"Would you like to retire, Rosalie?" he whispered.

"No; he is a traitor," replied she, "and would have taken your liberty and life. I will see him die."

It was the savageness of her mind that bade her desire this.

She had seen many deaths, but not a death by hanging.

A morbid wish was in her heart to behold it.

"Brave girl," whispered Oscar, clutching her arm. "Men, finish your duty."

In an instant the barrel was kicked away, and, with a groan, the wretched man fell, and hung dangling in the air.

It was a hideous sight.

No cap or handkerchief had been placed over his head, and his blackening face and protruding eyes could be seen by all.

Even Rosalie shuddered.

"It is a hideous death," she said, turning away her head, "but he deserved it."

"Truly," said Oscar; then to his men he added—"Leave the body till our enemies come; they will see how we punish those who endeavour to act the parts of traitors. It is time we departed. Let us go and take up our positions."

"There is no place near," said one of the men, "where we can avoid being seen."

"You are mistaken there," said Oscar Penraven, "*I* have discovered the spot—one which, although not a cave, is yet a place where abundant shelter can be had even from the storm. Come."

Leaving the man hanging as he was from the beam the men followed Oscar.

They had not far to go.

The spot he had named was scarcely a stone's throw from the cave.

They found he had spoken truly.

The place seemed as if made for the purpose.

It was a rugged set of pathways, among jagged rocks, affording at the same time shelter and abundant points of observation.

There was no possibility of being attacked by an enemy at a distance.

Whoever attempted an assault would certainly have to come to close quarters.

Better could not be desired.

"Well done, captain," said Elston; "this *is* a discovery. We can see over the heath from yonder rocky point."

He pointed, as he spoke, to a rocky point.

Oscar immediately mounted it.

The man was right.

Thence he could see the broad expanse of the dusky heath.

"I will remain here," said he, "and when I behold the enemy coming, I will inform you."

The dawn was now breaking.

Over the sea and land it fell, at first like a grey twilight.

Then indistinctly afar Oscar Penraven could see forms approaching.

"They are coming," he said; "let us each take a post of observation."

Then he descended to the side of Rosalie, crouched down behind a huge boulder, and watched.

From the place he had selected he could see those who approached, and count their numbers.

First came Rupert Dreadnought and Stanley Sherrington, with a man bound walking between them.

This was one of the smugglers.

"See," cried Oscar, to Rosalie, "there come our enemies. See who approaches. The man of all others whom I hate."

"And whom I love," thought Rosalie.

"Oh!" pursued Oscar, "how my hands itch to raise my gun and rid myself once and all of the hateful villain!"

Rosalie placed her trembling hand on his arm.

"Forbear!" she cried.

He turned to her fiercely.

"Why would you save him?" he cried.

She trembled beneath his gaze.

But her quick mind suggested an excuse readily.

"If you fired it would result in the destruction of all of us," she said. "They would be upon us in a moment. See in what numbers they gather."

Oscar glanced again towards the edge of the cliff.

Rosalie spoke in a trembling voice, but he attributed it to her fears, as her words, indeed, were correct.

The numbers which Rupert had brought with him were enough to annihilate any band of the size of Oscar's, and to have fired at Rupert would certainly have brought destruction upon them.

Oscar had only calculated upon their entering the cave, examining its contents, finding it deserted, and departing.

Here he had erred.

Truly enough, revenue officers accompanied the party, who were glad of the chance of seizing so large a quantity of spirits.

But the others were seeking men, not articles of consumption.

Having entered and explored the cave, therefore, and cut down the hanging man, whose life, however, was extinct, they emerged once more into the light of day, and commenced an exploration of the rocks around.

Oscar saw this with a feeling akin to fear.

It seemed truly now as if he were about to be caught in his own trap.

CHAPTER XIX.

ROSALIE'S FEARS—OSCAR PENRAVEN REVIVES HER—THE ATTACK—RUPERT DEMANDS THE SURRENDER OF THE SMUGGLERS—THE BATTLE COMMENCES—UNEXPECTED AID—STANLEY SHERRINGTON AND ROSALIE ST. AUBYN MEET—THEIR DUEL—ITS FATAL ENDING—HORROR AND REMORSE—THE FIGHT ENDS—THE FLIGHT AND ESCAPE OF OSCAR PENRAVEN—THE DEFEAT OF THE SMUGGLERS—RUPERT AND STANLEY BESIDE THE BODY OF THE STRANGE LEADER—RUPERT'S STORY—THE TRIAL AND CONDEMNATION OF THE WRECKERS—THE RETURN OF THE FRIENDS TO LONDON—A HAPPY MARRIAGE AND A VAIN WISH.

Rosalie gave herself up for lost.

Indeed, there was a growing feeling of dread within her heart.

She felt as if some great event was about to happen.

"Oscar," she said, "I feel as if my end was drawing near at last."

Oscar Penraven smiled.

It was the resolute smile of a wild beast, who looks forward with savage delight to the chance of a coming struggle for life.

"Fear nothing," he said, "they will scarcely war against women."

"I am dressed as a man," she answered, "and among those men I have no friends, even if they knew who I was. *You* know that well. Oh, Oscar, I feel now that if I could escape this present danger I would fly from England and never run the risk of another.

And the woman thoroughly unstrung, cowered down, and hid her face in her hands.

"This will never do," said Oscar, with a laugh, "you have a sword by your side, and when the struggle comes, will be expected to fight with the rest."

So saying, he drew a flask from his pocket, and offered it to her.

She seized it eagerly, and raising it to her lips, took a goodly draught, enough at other times to have made her inebriate.

Now it had no such effect.

Her person glowed—a heavy sigh escaped her bosom—her eyes sparkled, and the sense of fear entirely left her.

"This has changed me, indeed," she said: "I feel now that I can fight for my liberty and life."

So saying, she grasped her sword, and drawing it, added—

"The opportunity will not long be wanting; see, they are advancing."

She spoke truly.

Rupert never for one moment imagined that the smugglers had so entirely abandoned their home as they appeared to have done.

It was resolved, therefore, to search the rocks everywhere around.

They had now sought everywhere except the clumps of jagged rockwork pathway the wreckers had, in vain, sought to conceal.

Stanley Sherrington was the first to discover it.

"Here, friends," he shouted, "follow me."

In an instant Rupert and the others had obeyed the call.

"Now, my men," said Oscar Penraven, in a stern, determined voice, "our enemies are upon us. Surely, few in number though we be, we can defend the narrow pass."

Obeying his orders, the wreckers at once crowded down to that part, and when Rupert and his friends reached it, they found a formidable array of desperate men ready to sell their lives dearly.

"What want you with us?" cried Oscar, in a loud voice.

"Your surrender," returned Rupert.

"And who constituted you into a military force to demand surrender from any one?" returned Penraven. "By what authority do you follow us, and ask us to yield our liberty to you?"

"We have officers of the law who have asked our assistance," said Rupert; "but this is not time for parley. Yield at once, or my men must commence the attack."

"We never yield," cried Oscar. "Fire, my men, and aim at the leaders."

Thus exhorted, the men fired in a volley, and aimed by common consent at the leaders.

Either their hands were unsteady or they were bad shots, for not one was hit except Chester Rice, who—wounded in the shoulder—had at once to fall to the rear.

"Advance, my men," shouted Rupert; "now to drive the villains from their stronghold."

The attackers answered with a will.

A loud shout rang through the night air.

THE MOHOCKS SAVE AN OLD FRIEND.—(*See Next Number.*)

Then, with a vengeance, they commenced the assault.

The wreckers had the best of it for some time.

Guarded by the huge boulders, they could fire upon their enemies while they shielded their own bodies from harm.

The attacking party soon saw this.

They saw that their tactics must be changed.

One by one the revenue officers or the retainers were picked off.

"This will never do!" cried Rupert. "There will not be a man left to us by noon."

"What can we do, then?" asked Charles Rice.

"We must stop firing, and take to our swords," said Rupert. "*I* myself will lead the attack."

So saying, he placed his pistol in his belt, drew his sword, and advanced eagerly to the attack.

Now came the tug of war.

The desperate men on the rocks, who had hitherto escaped unhurt, knew that their liberties and lives depended now upon their courage, and with one accord resolved to fight to the last gasp.

Swords were now the weapons.

Hand to hand they fought like demons.

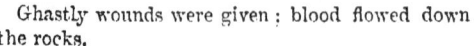

Ghastly wounds were given: blood flowed down the rocks.

Cries of wounded men mingled with the curses of those who fought.

But soon the wreckers found that victory was not with them.

Country people had assembled to see what was going on, and siding naturally with the cause of order and justice, they began to assail the wreckers from above, by casting from the high cliffs huge stones.

Huddled up presently on a small plateau, only partially protected, the wreckers fought hand to hand with their enemies.

Rupert Dreadnought and Stanley Sherrington were in the vanguard of the attack.

It happened thus that the latter became opposed to Rosalie St. Aubyn, who was fighting side by side with Oscar Penraven.

In the heat of battle he observed not her sex.

Neither, indeed, would it have been easy for him to have distinguished it.

Dressed as she was in the garb of the other sex, she had been so constantly in the heat of the battle, that her face was begrimed with dirt and powder.

So Stanley Sherrington fought on.

Little did he dream who she was.

Little did he imagine that that face was the one that had so won his regard; that those lips, compressed now with resolve, were those he had passionately pressed; that that form was the one whose glowing contours had so entranced his soul.

She knew and recognised him.

But she dared not show it.

She was now in her own trap.

If she declared herself, she would run the risk of exposing her treachery to Oscar, and declaring her trickery and deceit to Stanley Sherrington and Rupert.

Not that it truly seemed to matter to her now what became of her.

She seemed full of despair.

The blood shed around her everywhere spoke to her of death.

The clash of weapons told her the same dismal tale.

So did the hushing sea—so did the desperate curses of the men—so did the manifest impossibility of escape, except by surrender.

The latter she dared not risk.

Oscar was by her side, fighting like a demon, fighting with a courage worthy of a far better cause.

If she had surrendered then, he would have cut her down unmercifully.

So she fought on.

Several times during the conflict she had contrived to whisper to Oscar Penraven—

"How long will this last?"

"Not long," was the answer; "we shall soon be victorious."

But this to her was sorry relief.

She saw no prospect of success.

Yet, now, with the shadow of a fearful doom hovering over her, she still fought like an inspired demon.

At length, however, her arms began to tire.

Stanley Sherrington pressed her hard.

Then, at length, as she staggered back, his bright sword was plunged forward, and its point went rushing between her soft breasts.

As she fell, and he drew forth the steel from the flesh, quivering with pain, her jacket was torn open, disclosing her delicate bosom.

"A woman!" cried Stanley Sherrington, in astonishment, as he sprang forward and raised her in his arms.

Her cap, as he did so, fell off, and her long bright locks flowed over his arm.

Then he knew the face.

"Good Heavens!" he cried, "I know you now—it was you who gave us the tidings that saved Rupert Dreadnought. You must be preserved from such a fate as this."

And he raised her from the ground.

"Traitress!" muttered Oscar Penraven, as they passed; "your doom is more than you deserve. The fate of the traitor in the cave should have been yours."

He had heard all.

And his heart had sunk within him.

Truly all deserted him now!

Stanley Sherrington bore the insensible woman away from the thick of the fight.

When he reached a quiet spot, he halted.

Then laying her gently on the ground, he opened her jacket a little more, and examined her wound.

The cut was a wide one, and the blood was welling freely out over the white and tender flesh.

He tried to staunch it.

But in vain.

He placed his hand over her bosom to feel the pulsations of her heart.

It was cold and clammy, that snowy place of beauty.

The beatings of the pulse of life were still.

"Oh, she is dead—dead!" he murmured.

Then, as a slight quiver of the limbs took place, he poured some spirits between her lips.

All in vain.

Her eyes never opened again, and the spirits bubbled back from her mouth.

She was dead!

The fair demon, the poisoner, the member of the hideous League, had gone at length to join the others of that awful crew.

With a sigh Stanley Sherrington, who, of course, even now did not recognise her, drew her out of the way of the combatants, and rushing up the mountain path, joined once more in the fray.

He fought, however, now as one who had no interest in the battle.

He had loved Rosalie.

It was a case of love at first sight truly.

But, nevertheless, in the few minutes in which he had been in her company at the house of Henry Clanberris—ever since, indeed, he had pressed her to his bosom in that warm and passionate embrace he had felt himself bound up as it were in her being.

He had hoped to win her, and his eagerness to see the finish of this combat had in it much of eagerness to be once more in her society.

He paused not now to consider how incomprehensible was her presence among the wreckers, nor to ask why she should be fighting so desperately against him whom it was positive that she must recognise.

He felt only a desolation of the heart, a sinking of the whole system, a disappointment, and a weak feeling of despair pervading his being.

He fought now because Rupert Dreadnought was his friend, and he desired to aid in saving him.

As for himself he cared not whether he died or lived.

So he fought the more eagerly and furiously.

All was nearly over now.

The smugglers had lost several men.

The others were wounded, tired, dispirited.

And Oscar—what of him?

Whither had he disappeared?

That no one seemed able to tell.

Suddenly, just when Rupert Dreadnought was pressing him hard, and was hoping to secure him, there had been a sudden rush, a struggling among attackers and attacked, and a heavy body came tumbling over the cliff.

One of the villagers, eager to see what was occurring, had leaned over too far, and had fallen over among the combatants.

Rupert, struck in the face by the heel of the falling man, had been blinded and staggered for a moment.

This moment was enough for Oscar.

He had no longer anything to detain him.

Rosalie St. Aubyn was dead.

The band was irretrievably broken up and destroyed.

"Fly who can!" he shouted, at the topmost pitch of his voice.

Then he leaped over the jagged wall of rocks, and stumbling, tumbling anyhow he best could, fled away along the beach.

The confusion was so great that no one saw which way he went.

And *he* never looked behind.

Speeding along till he was tired, he at length reached a lonely and precipitous path leading to the cliffs.

Up this he clambered, and seeing before him a quiet old inn, he hurried towards it, and ordering some refreshment, entered the public room.

Here he rested awhile, and, having once more drank heartily, started westward.

His destination was once more London.

Meanwhile, the smugglers, finding that their leader had fled, saw that all chance of success was over.

With one accord, therefore, they shouted—

"We surrender!"

Then, as their foes halted, they flung down their arms, and, in a few moments, as it were, the place had resumed its quiet.

While the men were marched off by the coastguard and the revenue officers, and the dead and wounded were carried away by the others, Rupert accompanied Stanley Sherrington to where the body of the fair demon lay.

"What!" cried Rupert, as he leaned down by the wretched woman, who was beautiful even in death, "can it be possible? Rosalie St. Aubyn!"

"Rosalie St. Aubyn!" repeated Stanley mechanically. "The poisoner! the murderess!"

"Even so," exclaimed Rupert Dreadnought; "the last but one of the horrid brood that is known to us is now dead. One by one they have fallen into our hands."

A deadly pallor overspread Stanley's face.

"Murderess or not, it was she who was at Clanberris House that night—it was she who told me of the peril that threatened you. And to her we owe, therefore, much of our success. I would scarcely have believed that so much wickedness could lurk beneath so fair a skin. When I first saw her, I loved her—my whole heart seemed as it were to go out to her at once; and is she not, as she lies there, beautiful to gaze upon?"

"Truly one of the loveliest and one of the most debased of human kind," said Rupert, "a wonder of Nature in two ways. My men, bear her away with the others."

And so Rosalie St. Aubyn was carried off to be buried obscurely in a grave among smugglers and wreckers.

"There," said Rupert, pointing to the body which the men in wonder were carrying off, "there goes Alford's release. We shall have a wedding in a few days."

"How so?" asked Stanley Sherrington.

"Rosalie St. Aubyn's real name was Rosalie Penraven. She was the wife of Alford, who is no other than Richard Penraven. He is in love with Lesbia Howard, who can now legally become his wife."

And it turned out exactly as Rupert had prophesied.

After the smugglers and wreckers had been bestowed of by the authorities, and a long and fruitless search had been made for Oscar Penraven, Charles Rice and Minnie Edgetown were married amid much rejoicing, and Dreadnought, hurrying to London, lost no time in informing Alford of his freedom.

As may be imagined *he* lost no time in taking advantage of the chance thus offered him.

Hurrying to Rupert's house, he at once put the question to the blushing Lesbia, whose answer we need not record.

"Would that my father's wishes permitted me to follow their example, Helen," whispered Rupert to his betrothed, as the happy pair passed from the church; "but we must live and hope."

CHAPTER XX.

STEPHEN LUCKWORTH—THE STRANGE DOMESTIC—THE OLD HAWKER—A GOLDEN TEMPTATION—THE QUARREL—THE APPOINTMENT AT THE INN—THE MEETING—THE PROPOSAL AND THE ACCEPTANCE—THE GOLDEN REWARD.

THERE were, it will be remembered, a number of new domestics engaged by Rupert Dreadnought for his London establishment after the hideous murder which had swept away all the old and faithful servants who had so long been in the household of the old earl.

Among these was a young man of the name of Luckworth.

Stephen Luckworth was a tall, raw-boned fellow, with red hair, and somewhat of a cast in his eye.

He had an unpleasant way of looking at people altogether, apart from his irregularity of vision, and it seemed strange that Rupert Dreadnought should have engaged one who always looked as if conscious of having committed a crime.

It was easily explained, however.

He had been recommended by Tom the waterman.

And, truth to tell, he had never been known to be guilty of a dishonest action.

He only looked as if it lurked in him.

One evening, some weeks, in fact, two months after the return of Rupert and his friends to London, Stephen was standing in the doorway of his master's house.

Nearly every one was out.

Helen Penraven, Rupert, and Stanley Sherrington had gone to visit Alford and Lesbia, or, rather, Master Richard and Mistress Richard Penraven.

Allan of the Glen and Tom had gone upon courting expeditions also.

Some of the domestics were at the nearest tavern, while others were preparing the glorious supper such as servants, as a rule, think it proper to have in the absence of their masters.

Stephen was glancing up the street, when he saw a man apparently bent with age slowly approaching him.

He had on his back a pack such as pedlars wear, and, in fact, his whole appearance was that of a hawker.

He stopped as he neared Stephen.

"Well, young man," he said, "will ye buy a few things of a poor man? some gloves, some handkerchiefs, some ribbons for your sweatheart, eh?"

"No, no," cried Stephen, waving his hand majestically, "I want nothing of you. I have no money to waste. Such scum as you should be scourged from the earth."

Stephen's father had been a hawker or street-seller of some kind himself.

But this he chose to forget.

The old man, however, was not thus to be put off.

"Scoff not, young fellow," he said; "age should always be respected. I could——but nay, since you mock and insult me, it were idle to talk to you of secrets; but, did you wish to rise in the world, I know how gold is to be got."

He was preparing to move off, but Stephen stopped him with a half laugh.

"Stay," he said; "how sell you your secrets?"

"Sell my secrets, eh?" chuckled the old man. "No—no—no; you mocked at me, and laughed at me, so I'd best go to those who don't jeer!"

And he was moving off, when Stephen caught him by the shoulder.

"Stay!" he said, in an eager whisper. "I did but jest. Stay, and I will get you a tankard of ale that will help you on your journey."

The old hawker laughed.

"Well, well," he said, "a drop of good ale will not hurt me, for I am cold and weary. Go, fetch it, lad."

Stephen at once did as he was bidden, and the stranger peered into the passage of the house.

He seemed highly satisfied both with his inspection and his success, too, with the young man.

He rubbed his hands gleefully.

"Ah!" he muttered, "this is a good beginning—it promises well."

At this moment the serving-man reappeared.

"Here is the ale," he said. "Drink well, and you will find it grease your tongue for the secret you have to tell."

The hawker drank deeply.

"My son," he said, as he returned the tankard nearly empty, "my son, you mistake me. Such secrets as I have to tell cannot be told to every open-mouthed varlet in the streets."

"Then you have deceived me," cried Stephen, seizing him rudely by the shoulder, and speaking in a loud voice.

"Unhand me, young man!" said the pedlar, sternly, "or, mayhap, you may find that you have made an error. I say again that such golden secrets as mine are not to be told to babblers in the street. What is there to assure me that while I talk to you some prating, open-mouthed ass may not be listening at your keyhole, or at some darkened window, or crouching somewhere within hearing? No, no, I tell no secrets in the streets. If you are brave, and are willing to do as I wish you, I can give you instructions that will enable you to win wealth; but not otherwise."

"What would you have me do?" asked Stephen, impatiently.

The old hawker looked round him cautiously.

"Is any one in sight?" he asked.

"No one."

"Then listen. To-morrow night—you know the 'King's Arms' in the Lamb Yard, behind the Eastchepe?"

"I do."

"Then, at nine o'clock I will be there in the public room. I may be changed a little in my dress, but I shall know you. Am I to expect you?"

Stephen hesitated.

As I have said, he was rather acute.

"Why are you so anxious for me to come?" he inquired.

The old man uttered something very like a curse.

"You are playing with me again," he said. "I don't want you—I never wanted you. I can as easily find others. I am selling golden secrets—for I sell, remember, I don't give anything. You detained me rudely just now because I wished to leave you—wished as I do now; but now that I offered to forgive you and meet you again, you say that *I* am anxious. No—no; I am by no means anxious, and am sorry chance brought me this way. Good-night."

Stephen was now fairly perplexed.

He had no desire to let the old fellow escape so easily.

"No," he said, "I did but jest."

"Your jests are sorry ones," returned the old man, "you jest with misery."

"I will jest no more," replied Stephen; "I will

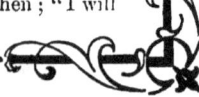

meet you, and, what is more, I will pay you well. You will come, will you not?"

"You will pay me, you say," cried the old man. "Yes, I will see that you do that. I do not work for nothing, *that* I can promise you. I will be there to my time, but if *you* do not keep your promise to the moment you will find that I shall not keep mine. Your jeering has not been lost on me."

And then, without even saying "good night," the old hawker hobbled off.

Hobbled only to the corner.

Then his manner changed.

He stood erect, cast a rapid glance round him to see if he was observed, and then hurried away with rapid paces.

Had Stephen Luckworth seen this, his eagerness for the appointed interview would have been greatly modified.

As it was, he was all eagerness.

He was willing in his heart to perform any mean and paltry action for gold.

Here there seemed a fair chance of his being able to exercise his peculiar talents of roguery and deception.

The whole of that evening and the following day he was strangely pre-occupied.

Every one noticed it.

But they noticed another fact, also.

He took all their jests in good part; and even indulged in an occasional repartee in place of the angry frown and meaningless oaths which he generally gave them in answer.

At length the following evening came, and Stephen, with a beating heart, asked and obtained from Rupert Dreadnought permission to be absent, and set out on his journey.

It must be remembered that in those days, superstition still reigned, broadcast, through the land.

Mingled, therefore, with his anxiety and eagerness was some fear.

Who *was* this old man who so suddenly had appeared before him?

What was his object in mumbling forth his promises—his dark hints about golden secrets?

Might he not have dealings with the Evil One?

However, these considerations did not delay Stephen in his progress.

He went boldly on.

He was naturally possessed of considerable courage, and gold, or rather the anticipation of its possession, will nerve men to almost anything.

At length he reached the tavern.

It was an ill-looking place.

Dark, gloomy, built in the oldest of London's old-fashioned style, its exterior was most forbidding.

Its interior was scarcely so bad.

It was dark, truly, but there were plenty of lights in it, and the old timbers were burnished up with careful hands.

On entering, Stephen found he was before his time.

So, ordering some refreshment, he passed into the public room.

It was empty.

A pang of disappointment passed through his breast.

What if the old man had but jested with him?

He felt half inclined to return.

But then he *was* too soon, and the hawker might have been detained.

So he sat down by the fire.

The hands of the clock had pointed to a quarter to nine when he entered.

The hour of meeting was nine.

Exactly as the clock struck the door opened, and the old man peered in.

A smile broke over his features as he entered and approached the serving-man.

"Ah!" he said, "I am glad to see you so punctual. I am always so. Punctuality is necessary for the obtaining of money. What are you drinking?"

"I have some hot spirit here."

"Good; we will have some more. The night is damp and chilly."

And so saying, the old fellow rang the bell, and ordered of the man who brought it in two strong glasses more.

Matters being thus comfortably settled, the stranger drew his chair up closer to the fire, and began speaking—

"Now, you must understand, young man, that, no matter how you attempt to obtain it, gold is not to be got without trouble and work, and sometimes even danger has to be encountered. You are prepared for all this, I suppose?"

"Yes," said Stephen, being primed somewhat with drink and pleasure at finding that the old man had kept his appoinment, "I am not afraid of peril. Go on quickly and let me know what I have to do."

"That I can do easily," replied the other; "but you must listen attentively and make no remarks, except when I ask you a question."

"Speak on."

"Some years ago your master did a great injury to a gentleman with whom he had always been on terms of intimacy and friendship.

"Well, up to this time, the young Earl Dreadnought has refused to give him an interview.

"It is most important he should have an interview with him, and *you* can contrive it for me."

"*I!*" exclaimed Stephen.

"Yes, you; and I will tell how. On a certain night you must admit this gentleman, who will present himself at once to Rupert and state his case. If you do this you will receive, as your reward, twenty pounds—half now."

And, so saying, the old man took a bag from his pocket, and emptied some of the glistening coins on to the table.

Stephen's eyes gleamed with pleasure as he gazed upon them, and an itching sensation took possession of his fingers.

"Well," he said, "I agree; of course there being no harm intended for my master."

"None, none whatever," returned the old hawker, "I can assure you. But you can earn a hundred, and receive forty of them to-night, if you will do still more."

Stephen flushed, and then turned pale.

"There must be harm in this, or you would never offer so well," he said.

The old man laughed.

"It is for *you* to choose," he said. "I shall tell you all you have to do, and you will not then be working in the dark.

"The object of the interview which the person I allude to so much desires, is to obtain from Rupert Dreadnought a certain paper which he has retained against all justice and propriety.

"He knows well where to lay his hand upon the document.

"All you have to do, therefore, is to admit him, and he will secrete himself near the door of Rupert Dreadnought's room.

"You will enter the room, whether called or not, and proceed to trim the candles.

"In doing this you will clumsily put them out, and leave the room in total darkness.

"He will then rush in, seize the papers, and make off with them."

The old man paused.

"And that is all you require of me?" said Stephen, gazing with eager eyes at the pile of guineas lying temptingly upon the table.

"That is all."

"And who is he who requires of me this service?"

"You know him not," replied the old hawker, "but, nevertheless, I will tell you his name. It is Everard Dalby."

My readers will, doubtless, remember that in the first number of this work the man who was prevented by Rupert from disturbing the last moments of the old earl, stated that he came from Everard Dalby.

Who he was we shall presently see.

We shall see, too, the meaning of the strange amalgamation of interests between him and Oscar Penraven.

To the mind of Stephen Luckworth, the serving-man, however, the name brought no recollections.

He had never heard it before.

"The title is a strange one to me," he said, "and I am as wise, therefore, as before. However, were I able to assure myself that you meant no personal harm to my master, I would close at once with your proposal."

This was said with another longing look at the gold.

The old man could easily interpret it.

He knew that he had in very truth accepted it, and only wanted a few words to settle it.

"Well," he said, "you need not be afraid. I can vouch for this, that *no* harm is intended to your master. Everard Dalby simply wants his rights, and that is all. You will be doing a good action. Dalby has dear ones depending on him, who will be gainers by this, and your master will lose nothing. Shall I count out the gold?"

Stephen took one more glance at the money.

His eyes glared.

The itching sensation once more came into his fingers, and he said,

"Yes; I will do it."

The old hawker at once counted out the promised number of coins.

"These," he said, as he placed them in Stephen's trembling fingers, "these are but a portion of the reward which you will obtain. Golden harvests are yet to come for you in the future, if you are discreet and silent."

Stephen pocketed the coin eagerly.

"Be assured," he said, "that I shall be as silent as the grave. And now, what night is the appointed one?"

"To-morrow night."

"At what hour?"

"At ten."

"And how shall I know who is the proper person to enter?"

"He will give the name 'Everard Dalby,' and now," added the old man, rising, "we will part. To-morrow night at ten he will be with you, and will give you the other sixty guineas. Till then, adieu."

And with these words, he quitted the room, leaving Stephen Luckworth half-stupefied with amazement at his own good fortune and the means that had led to it.

He followed the old man after a minute, but he had disappeared.

Taking another strong glass at the bar, therefore, Stephen hurried away.

"Now," said he, "I've got another full hour to myself, and I'll go and see Lucy!"

Poor, simple Lucy Fotherington, his betrothed!

Little did she imagine how he had obtained that bright, gold chain that he hung around her neck that night, or she would have flung it from her like a poisonous snake.

CHAPTER XXI.

EVERARD DALBY—A POOR HOME AND A DESPERATE SPIRIT—THE TEMPTING DEMON—THE ARRANGEMENTS—THE MEETING AT RUPERT DREADNOUGHT'S HOUSE—THE FAITHLESS SERVANT—THE ENTRANCE OF THE ENEMY—THE LIGHTS ARE EXTINGUISHED!—THE RUSH OF ARMED MEN—THE BATTLE IN THE DARK—THE ARRIVAL OF SUCCOUR—THE FALL FROM THE WINDOW—THE STRANGE DISCOVERY—REPENTANCE ALMOST COMES TOO LATE!

On quitting the inn where he had met Stephen Luckworth, the old hawker hobbled out into the street, and when fairly out of sight resumed his upright walk, and hastened rapidly away.

He bent his steps towards a part of the town where the houses were low and dingy-looking, and the streets generally indicative of poverty and wretchedness.

He stopped at a house which was only distinguished from the rest by its greater squallor and misery, and, without any knocking, pushed open the door, and entered—

On reaching the third floor, he knocked at the door of a room, and a voice said—

"Enter!"

Obeying at once the summons, he passed into a small, ill-furnished room, where sat a man and a woman by a meagre fire.

On a mat before it was a boy of some twelve years,

of age, while two others lay in bed at one side of the chamber.

The man looked emaciated with want and anxiety, more so even than the woman, who seemed as if she had been forced by her husband to have the better share of the poor provision they had.

They both started as he entered.

The wife looked at her husband appealingly, while he seemed to avoid her gaze.

"Ah! you have come then," he said, in a tremulous voice.

"Yes, here I am! punctual, too," said the hawker, who had now resumed his tottering gait, and his semblance of age.

"Yes, very. Well, have you seen the person whom you desired to meet?"

The old man hesitated.

"Yes," he said; "but tell me, can you see me in private? There are various little matters which ladies do not understand. Perhaps Mistress Dalby——"

She at once took the hint.

Rising to go, she approached her husband, and, gently leaning on his shoulder, said in a loving whisper—

"For my sake, Everard, be careful what you do."

The haggard man turned from her slowly.

"Yes, Aveline," he said, "I *will* be careful. Fear not for me. But even peril must be endured when the happiness of our dear children is concerned."

Then the wife slowly left the room, and Everard Dalby and the tempter were alone.

"Well," said the hawker, taking the seat which Mistress Dalby had vacated by the meagre fire, "you are not very comfortable here. A few gold coins would set you up."

A bitter smile crossed Everard's features.

"Gold!" he cried. "It is a dream of the past."

"Well," returned the hawker, chinking some in his pocket, "if what you tell me is true, I have no objection to let you have ten guineas this night."

Everard Dalby trembled.

"Oh! speak not of it," he cried. "It is too great too joyful, to be true."

"Nothing of the kind," said the hawker.

And he drew from his pocket the bag once more, and took from it ten guineas.

"Here," he added, "are the coins. Now tell me, you are persuaded that these papers *are* in the possession of Rupert Dreadnought?"

"Yes."

"And you know where they are kept?"

"Yes."

"You would find it even in the dark?"

"I could, were I once in the room."

"And you have the courage to go thither if the opportunity be given you?"

"The courage," cried Everard Dalby; "and to fight for the possession also."

The hawker leaned over and placed the money in the hands of the trembling man.

"Enough," he said, "the money is yours, and the opportunity will not be wanting. Eat and drink well, and get up your strength. To-morrow night you shall be with me in Rupert Dreadnought's room—at a given signal, the lights will be extinguished by an accomplice of mine. Then we must rush in and secure the papers; *or*, if necessary, fight for them!"

"Have you already arranged it then?" asked Dalby, in surprise.

"I have. I knew well that in such a matter you would not hesitate."

"But we two will be useless against Rupert and his friends in their own stronghold."

The old man smiled.

"Oh!" he said, "I do nothing by halves. I have made all arrangements necessary to securing ourselves in case of an attack."

He rose as he spoke.

"Good night," he said, "at nine to-morrow night I shall be here."

Then, without another word, he quitted the room.

He had scarcely done so when Mistress Dalby rushed in.

"I have heard all, Dalby," she cried, throwing her arms round his neck.

"You have been listening?" he said, sternly.

"I have; it was my right to do," she answered. "But oh, Dalby, I fear this man. I feel that he is tempting you for no good purpose."

"You misunderstand him altogether," returned her husband. "It is quite true that this Rupert Dreadnought has my'papers in a box in his private room; that I have applied again and again to him in vain, and I am only going to obtain my legal right. But come, wife, see here I have ten guineas in gold. I will go out and obtain for you food and drink. See that the little ones are all up when I return, that they may enjoy the best supper they have had for many a day."

And so saying, he rushed away, leaving his wife in a state between pleasure and fear.

On the next night Rupert Dreadnought and Stanley Sherrington were sitting in the room in which was the bureau where were deposited the papers so eagerly sought after by Everard Dalby.

Over the table was a candelabra holding three wax candles.

Both Rupert and Stanley were engaged deeply in business.

"This is a strange communication, Stanley," he said, taking up a letter from among a heap of others. "I will read it to you:—

"'HONOURED SIR,—

"'If you will take the trouble to come down to Exham, in Norfolk, and see me, I fancy I can put you in the way of discovering a secret. It is a most important one, and will lead to the discovery of wealth. I have not written to your father the Earl, as he is ill, and I don't want to worry him; but if you like to ask him, he will tell you he knows nothing wrong of

"'JEREMIAH OLDSTONE,
"'Sexton,
"'Of Exham, Norfolk.'"

"You see," said Rupert, "he knows nothing of my father's death. I cannot understand the matter at all. My father would certainly have told me something of this man, had he been in any way connected with the affairs of the family."

And so saying, he flung the blotched and ill-spelled letter again on the table.

Stanley Sherrington took it up and read it again.

"And what do you propose doing?"

"I propose going."

"When?"

"At once."

"But surely not without some precaution?" said Stanley, anxiously.

Rupert laughed.

"Why, cried he, "you would have me take as much care of myself as if I were some imperial despot ever in fear of an assassination from my incensed subjects."

"Well, it is quite certain that you are almost in as great danger as such a man would be," replied Stanley Sherrington. "I will propose something. Will you be guided by me?"

"That depends upon what your advice is," replied Rupert, smiling.

"Well, said Stanley, "*I* will go down to this place first."

"Alone?"

"Yes, I will go alone, and in disguise; they will know nothing of me; they will simply regard me as they would any ordinary stranger. I should be in no danger where *you* would be in hourly peril."

"No, Stanley, I shall go," said Rupert. "We will both go together. We can be master and servant."

"I will be the master then," returned Sherrington, laughing: "as the master will be the one suspected, not his valet."

"Agreed," said Rupert.

As he spoke, Stephen Luckworth entered; and approaching the fire, laid on some logs.

Then he, with a somewhat unsteady gait, neared the table, and took the snuffers.

Only one moment he hesitated.

One glance at his master, who was busily engaged, and then the recollection of the golden reward overcame all feelings of fidelity and compunction.

He snuffed one of the candles out; then he stumbled, and pretended to fall, knocking out the two other candles.

In an instant the room was in total darkness.

Then came a rush of feet and the traitors were in the room.

"There is treason here!" shouted Rupert, springing up, and in an instant the two friends had drawn their swords and were ready to defend themselves.

Before we describe this scene, however, we must explain how it was that so many persons were present instead of only Everard Dalby, as the old hawker had said.

When the agreed-upon signal was given, Stephen, who was on the alert, and, as may be imagined, was trembling with anxiety, at once opened the door.

The old hawker was there.

"How is this?" said Stephen; "where is the gentleman you spoke to me of?"

"I have come in his stead," replied the hawker; "but quick, let me in. It is dangerous for me to remain here."

So the door was closed, and Stephen was about to lead the old man up to his post of observation, when he said—

"Go quietly down into the kitchen, I know my way. In half-an-hour you can enter the room and snuff out the candles."

So Stephen descended, afraid to lose his reward by disobedience; and the old hawker made a feint of ascending the stairs.

But, as my readers no doubt expect, he did *not* ascend.

He waited until Stephen was fairly gone.

Then he crept noiselessly towards the street door.

Opening it, he peered out and whistled.

In an instant about eight forms appeared, one of them being Everard Dalby.

They entered quietly, the door was closed on them, and they began the ascent.

As they did so, Everard took the hawker by the arm.

"Remember your promise," he said.

"What promise?"

"No bloodshed."

The old man chuckled.

"No, no," he said, "no unnecessary bloodshed. But mark me, if a man is attacked, he must defend himself."

Everard's heart sank at these words.

He heard, too, a chuckle that told him how eagerly the old man desired an encounter.

They posted themselves in the dark shadows outside the door, and listened.

They heard all the conversation between Rupert and Stanley Sherrington.

Then, as we know, came Stephen's treachery, and the rush into the room.

In the dark it was very difficult to distinguish friend from foe.

But Rupert and Stanley retreated, and placed their backs against the wall.

According to Dalby's programme, there should now have been no attempt made at attack.

He simply desired the papers.

When he entered with the rest, therefore, he made a rush towards the bureau where he imagined them to be contained.

With the old hawker, however, it was different.

He whispered to his men, and, leaving Everard Dalby to do as he pleased, they rushed in a body upon Rupert Dreadnought and Stanley Sherrington.

Rupert saw at once that he was surrounded by foes, and that it was a critical moment.

A fight now for dear life in very truth.

They were entirely overmatched, and there seemed no chance of any help, unless, indeed, the servants should hear the noise and rush to the rescue.

Eagerly, with the malignity of an old rankling hate, the old hawker dashed at Rupert.

All his age and infirmity seemed to have left him.

He fought like a lion.

Who was this mysterious man?

Rupert had no time even to think within himself of the meaning of this desperate attack.

He recognised it, of course, as another furious attempt on the part of his defeated enemies.

Given away with No. 20 of "Rupert Dreadnought." "Boys of England" Edition.

LOVE AND HATE.

See an early number.

RUPERT OR THE DREADNOUGHT; OR THE SECRETS OF THE IRON CHEST

"AT LENGTH THE LADDER WAS REACHED."

But that was all.

Whether they were incited by Oscar Penraven he was unable to imagine.

All his thoughts were concentrated upon the one idea that he must conquer, and then in the moment of victory discover his new foe.

Suddenly there was a diversion from an unexpected quarter.

Both Everard Dalby and Stephen Luckworth had bargained that only the papers should be purloined, and that no harm should befall Rupert.

They saw they had been deceived.

While Everard Dalby, therefore, rushed into the midst of the fray to assist Rupert, Stephen ran hurriedly down the stairs to rouse the servants to help their master.

He had no desire to aid in a murder.

His greed for gain did not make him insensible to the sin of shedding innocent blood.

While the hawker and his companions, therefore, were still madly striving to destroy the two brave friends, there was a rush of feet, and the room was in a moment full of armed retainers.

The fortunes of the fight were changed, indeed, now.

Stephen, while the crowd was still in confusion, rushed to the one remaing candle and lit it.

In an instant all was altered.

Now that the light was once more diffused over the apartment, it was possible to distinguish friends from foes, and Rupert's retainers soon ranged themselves on the side of their master.

Very different now was the scene.

The followers of the "hawker," deserted by Everard Dalby and Stephen, were rapidly driven to the wall.

Arrived here, the hawker himself edged his way in among the struggling crew, and, reaching the window, threw it up.

"Everard Dalby," he cried, "I will be revenged for this."

Then, before any one could prevent him, he had plunged through and disappeared.

The men now saw no use in fighting longer, and, with one accord, cried—

"We surrender!"

The fray was at once stopped.

The men were disarmed and led below, while Rupert Dreadnought and Stanley Sherrington stood facing Everard Dalby in wonder and surprise.

"And pray, sir, since you were one of those who surreptitiously entered my house, and afterwards, in the most unaccountable manner, sided with me, pray tell me who you are?" asked Rupert, who had not heard, amid the din, the parting words of the "hawker."

"My name is Everard Dalby."

"Everard Dalby!" exclaimed Rupert, in amazement. "Surely that name is familiar to me. Yes; it brings back to me the saddest event in all my life—the death of my dear father. When he was on his death-bed, a man entered the house by stealth under most suspicious circumstances, and said he came from Everard Dalby. Are you he?"

"I am," said Dalby, in a sneering voice, "I am, and, considering the number of letters which I have written to you since—letters which you have never condescended to answer, though they concerned my rights—I should fancy my name was tolerably familiar."

Rupert glanced at him in surprise.

There was no doubting it.

The surprise was genuine.

"You are talking riddles," he said. "I have received no letters from you."

"None?"

"Not one. Come, sit down here at the table, and let me hear your story."

Everard complied.

Evidently there was some mystery.

One thing, however, was certain.

The "hawker" had deceived him.

Why, he could not conceive.

But that he was either the victim of a present delusion, or a past scheme of villany, there remained no doubt.

So he sat down at the table, which Stephen Luckworth had tremblingly re-arranged.

"Now," said Rupert, "take a glass of wine, and tell me your story."

CHAPTER XXII.

EVERARD DALBY'S STORY—THE DOCUMENTS—THE MORTGAGE—THE OLD CHEST—THE INTERCEPTED LETTERS—THE SEARCH AND THE DISCOVERY.

Having drank the wine offered to him, Everard Dalby said—

"This is a most mysterious matter, and though I fully believe your sincerity, and your ignorance of my claims, it was with difficulty I could bring myself to do so.

"Some years before your father's death, my father, whose name was also Everard Dalby, gave into your father's possession some papers which were requisite to prove his title to certain estates.

"He borrowed a large sum of money from the Earl Dreadnought, which I know he punctually paid, but he did not withdraw the papers because, for political reasons, he had to fly the country, and was afraid that if captured the property would be confiscated, and his family for ever beggared.

"Your father died before mine returned from abroad, and, hearing of his dangerous illness, my father, who was himself confined by a mortal malady, sent me to his house.

"I was refused admittance."

"And you therefore permitted a hired assassin to attempt my life," said Rupert Dreadnought, sternly.

"Indeed, no, upon my soul," replied Everard Dalby, solemnly. "I had nothing to do with that dastardly attempt. I heard the shot, and pursued the villain, but he fled into a dark lane, and escaped me.

"I confess I rushed hastily to conclusions.

"I set down your refusal to admit me to a desire to keep to yourself the property which my father had left yours in trust only.

"I concluded that, in his dying moments, the earl had told you all, and that you, less scrupulous than he, had resolved to enrich yourself.

"Pardon me my freedom, but I have said that I desire to tell the truth."

"Speak on," observed Rupert, "and fear not my displeasure."

"The idea I had formed of you was strengthened by my father, who died very shortly after yours had passed away.

"I came to England resolved to demand my rights, but when I presented myself here I was denied."

"I have been away most of my time," said Rupert, "engaged in carrying out my father's orders."

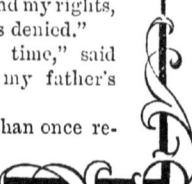

"Truly; but finding myself more than once refused admission to your house, I wrote again and again, but could never obtain a reply."

"For the good reason," said Rupert, "that I never received one. Strange as it may seem, every one of these epistles must have been intercepted."

"I believe it now," said Dalby; "but the most curious part of all is yet to come. The ban of the Government I found still spread over me—as, in fact, it does now, and over me and mine perhaps for ever.

"I feared, therefore, to openly seek redress, and I addressed the most pitiable letter to you, detailing the distress into which my family—my wife and poor little ones—were rapidly being plunged.

"Still no answer.

"This man is a cruel worshipper of Mammon," I said to myself; "he is a very demon of avarice. I will try to pay him in his own coin.

"So I formed a desperate plan.

"Disguising myself as well as I could, to prevent, at first, any resemblance being detected to my dead father, I took my way down to Redburne, where the property is situated.

"I found that the farms were in active working—that everything was going on just as if my father had been there, with the exception that the dwelling-house, which would have been ours, was occupied by a kind of steward and his family.

"Resolved to risk all, I threw off my disguise, presented myself, and was received with delight.

"I thought it surprising at first that they should be so pleased at my appearance among them.

"This, however, was soon explained.

"They had been subject to a tyrannical man, whose name, they stated, was Forsdyke, who had come there as the agent of my father, with papers duly signed; and they were glad enough to escape from his domination.

"One man only was there who seemed in no way pleased by the change.

"This was one of the servants—a common domestic—a rough, uncouth, ill-looking fellow.

"Even in my presence he did not repress his sneering looks, and on the day following my arrival he was missing.

"I had observed this man carefully; and having so long been the child of misfortune, cast hither and thither on the drifting waves of adversity, I felt at once overcome with nervousness.

"I instituted inquiries at once.

"The man, I found, was no favourite.

"He was regarded, in fact, as a spy.

"A spy in the pay of the tyrannical agent.

"A search was willingly instituted by the others when I informed them that I suspected his absence to bode no good either to them or to me.

"But it was in vain.

"He had disappeared as completely as if he had vanished into the earth.

"I guessed some evil was coming, and thinking of those well-nigh starving in London, I resolved to collect some money at any rate, even if I was driven from my stronghold at last.

"I gathered in, therefore, as much money as I could, alleging as my reason for so doing that my journey to England, and the expenses consequent upon my father's death, had drained my purse.

"For one week matters went well enough.

"At the end of this time, however, all was changed.

"I was seated in the library of Dalby Hall, thinking whether I should soon be able to send for my wife and little ones, congratulating myself, in fact, upon the success of my scheme, when a sudden noise in the hall roused me.

"I heard loud voices and the trampling of many feet, and ere I could quit the chamber, the door was flung violently open, and two rough-looking men entered.

"'Pray, master, who are you?' asked one of them.

"I felt bold enough, or, rather, rash enough, for anything then.

"'I am Everard Dalby, master of this house,' I replied, haughtily; 'and who, pray, are you who thus thrust yourself into my presence unannounced?'

"'I am Forsdyke, agent of Earl Dreadnought,' replied the man. 'This property, as you must know, was mortgaged to the earl in consideration of large sums of money lent long since, and——'

"'Repaid,' I put in.

"'Excuse me, *not* repaid,' replied he, 'however I must do my duty, though it is an unpleasant one. You must quit this place at once. The money which you have collected I shall say nothing of, but I beg you to go at once.'

"I resolved not to give up the place without, at any rate, a struggle.

"'You are misinformed,' returned I, 'this money has long since been paid back to the earl. Bring me face to face with the new earl, and I will guarantee to prove it to him. I shall refuse to quit the place until I see him."

"'Very well,' said the man, 'since such is your humour, you must take the consequences. Edgar, he added, turning to the man at his side, 'there is a regiment stationed at the town barracks. Run quickly and tell the colonel to send to the Hall at once, and he will there find the proscribed rebel, Everard Dalby. Quick! Take horse at once.'

"The man at once quitted the room, and in a minute after, I heard the galloping of his horse over the hard road.

"'Coward!' I cried, 'I defy your malice. I am no rebel, and shall abide the result of this attempt to force me from my home. The truth may then be made apparent, and *you* will be driven ignominiously from the property on which you and your master have fattened so long unrighteously.'

"So saying I turned and left the room.

"He made no attempt to stay me.

"I noticed this at the time, and I noticed, too, the peculiar expression of his face.

"I did not understand this then.

"I do now.

"He was alarmed, of course, lest I *should* stop and expose the whole of what I can recognise now as a fraud.

"However, there was no necessity for his alarm.

"I leaned out of my bed-room window, and saw presently, in the distance, the forms of approaching soldiery.

"My courage left me.

"Or, rather, shall I say I thought of my wife and little ones in London, waiting and longing for my return.

"I had now in my pocket over two hundred pounds in gold and notes.

"These would be taken from me, I should be cast into prison, and there I should languish while my dear ones were perishing with hunger, and wrung with sorrow at my unaccountable absence.

"My choice was made at once.

"I hurried on my travelling clothes, saw to my pistols, and succeeded in stealing out of the back gate just as the red-coats galloped up to the front entrance.

"How the fellow managed I know not.

"At any rate there was no pursuit.

"I hastened to the inn, obtained a horse, and never rested night and day till I reached London.

"I will pass over the rest—the joy that greeted me, and the rapidity with which my small store of wealth disappeared.

"Suffice it that in time it all went, and I am now destitute as before.

"In this desperate extremity I was tempted to obtain my rights again by force, though in a different way."

Everard Dalby then briefly narrated the circumstances connected with the hawker, omitting the portion which involved Stephen Luckworth.

"Strange indeed," said Rupert, "but we can easily see whether you have been told correctly. I knew not even of the existence of the box."

"We are doomed to have surprises to-night," said Stanley Sherrington. "First, the singular letter of Oldstone, the sexton of Exham, and secondly the battle and the strange story which has followed."

Rupert at once proceeded across the room, and, opening the bureau, saw before him a small casket.

It was a small, dark, wooden one, clasped with steel clasps.

"I have never before seen it," said Everard Dalby; "but I am certain that is the one."

"Let us open it at once then," said Rupert, who was now deeply interested. "I have, like you, never seen it before."

"You have not the key," said Everard Dalby, smiling; "here it is."

So saying, he handed to our hero a small, finely-wrought key, which he eagerly inserted in the lock.

The lid of the casket then flew open, disclosing a roll of parchment and some small documents.

The former proved to be the title deeds of Dalby Hall.

The latter proved the receipt of the money owed by Everard Dalby to the earl.

"Now," said Dalby, with much emotion, "you will forgive me the manner in which I entered your house."

"Forgive you, yes," cried Rupert, taking his hand. "But who is the villain who has all this time been taking the rents of Dalby estate?"

"That I know not," said Dalby, "nor, indeed, can I guess."

"I fancy I can," said Stanley Sherrington; "it is no doubt another scheme of the Poisoners—another of the fell designs of Oscar Penraven."

"Perhaps it *is* so," returned Rupert; "at any rate we can soon discover whether the rents are still being received by going down there together. We will start to-morrow. You say the Hall is at Redburne?"

"Yes."

"Then it is on our way to Exham," said Stanley Sherrington. "We can form our two expeditions into one."

"Yes, but there is *one* question which occurs to me," said Rupert. "In order to have enabled you to enter this house I must have some traitor among my retainers."

Everard Dalby did not answer for a moment.

Then he said—

"Well, if I were not to tell you I should not certainly be doing my duty to you. You have a traitor, but only to a certain extent. When he saw that personal harm was meant to you, he at once sided with you."

"And his name?"

"Stephen Luckworth."

"Ah!" sighed Rupert Dreadnought, "I wish I had but my father's old retainers—those who were murdered by my villanous rival and enemy, Oscar Penraven. Then, indeed, would my interests be in safety. But now, with new faces round me, who can tell what may happen? I shall take no proceedings against the fellow. I shall dismiss him, and it may be punishment enough to him to know that by one act of dishonesty he has lost a lenient master and a good place."

As he spoke, Stephen rushed in and threw himself at his feet.

He had heard all.

"Oh! my lord, my lord! forgive me!" he said, "and you shall never again have cause to complain.

"Rise," said Rupert, sternly, "and tell me, how came you to be tempted?"

Quickly the fellow recapitulated the story of the hawker.

But even now no further light was thrown on the matter.

He could say nothing in regard to his identity.

"I suspect, in spite of everything, that this was Oscar Penraven in disguise," said Rupert. "Inveterate foe! when shall I meet you face to face, when neither can escape the other?"

CHAPTER XXIII.

THE FRIENDS START FOR DALBY HALL—THE DISCOVERY—THE JOURNEY TO EXHAM—THE HIGHWAYMEN—OLD FRIENDS TO THE RESCUE—STANLEY SHERRINGTON IS WOUNDED AND CARRIED TO THE INN, WHERE HE IS WOUNDED IN A FAR DIFFERENT PART.

ON the morning following the attack on Rupert's house, the trio started.

Furnished with funds by Rupert, Everard left his wife with abundance of money, and removed her and her children to a fresh lodging, more suited to their station.

On arriving at the Dalby estate, they found everything in working order as before.

The old steward still occupied the house, and greeted Everard Dalby with surprise.

"I am glad to see you again, Master Dalby," he said; "you left us suddenly indeed, last time."

"I was compelled to do so," replied Dalby, "or I should not have done so. They induced me by cowardly threats to quit the place; but now I have come to remain. Tell me, where are the fellows who so coolly took possession of my property?"

"Only once since that time have we seen them," returned the steward. "Something very strange must have happened, for we have not even seen Earl Rupert Dreadnought for more than six months."

Rupert smiled.

"No, indeed; and I fancy until now you have never seen him, for *I* am Rupert Dreadnought."

"You!" exclaimed the steward, in amazement.

"Indeed, yes. But tell me, what kind of man was this who assumed my name?"

The steward gave an elaborate description.

Both Rupert and Stanley Sherrington at once recognised it.

"It is as I suspected," said Stanley, "this is the work still of Oscar Penraven and the vile wretches who have decimated London by their poisons, and have been fattening on this property for years. Now, Everard Dalby, you can take possession of your own without fear, for their society is dispersed —nay, not only dispersed, but I believe every soul, save one, and that one its infamous chief, has perished."

"There is yet to be feared the malignant hatred of the Government against our family," said Everard.

"That is less to be dreaded than the undying malignity of such villains as Oscar Penraven, who, after robbing you of your property, endeavoured to lead you into a trap by a promise of securing it to you. Fear not, my interest is good, and I will see you are relieved from this ban."

"That is almost too good to be true," cried Everard Dalby, with a smile, "nevertheless, I will join you in the hope; meanwhile, you will, I hope, accept of the hospitality of my humble place until we start again?"

"Willingly," said Rupert; "and I hope you will find that during the time that no revenues have been paid away to the society of assassins a goodly account of money has accumulated for you."

On the following morning they started for Exham.

They had said truly in declaring that Dalby Hall was on the road.

But it was little more than half way.

The day passed without adventures.

At length night set in.

They had resolved to travel until midnight, and then put up at an inn near the town of Roderham.

The night was very dark and very still.

They could see nothing, but they could hear distinctly every sound.

For a long time they rode on in silence.

But presently an indistinct sound, as of the galloping of horse's feet, was heard.

It seemed neither before nor behind, but all round them.

"What can this mean?" said Rupert, "are we going to have an adventure at last?"

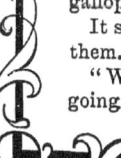

"Perhaps; though I doubt if we are likely to meet many persons on such a road as this."

"Except highwaymen," suggested Everard Dalby.

"Truly," returned Stanley Sherrington; "but though it is not likely, it behoves us to be careful. Ha! what is that?"

As he spoke, four horsemen, two in front of them and two behind, leaped from the skirts of the highway into the road.

"Halt! there, gentlemen," shouted a loud voice, "we should be glad of a word with you."

"A word with us!" cried Rupert; "aye, a dozen if you please."

"We are poor gentlemen," began one of the strangers, as they all approached nearer.

"Doubtless," interrupted Stanley Sherrington; "but, nevertheless, as it is dark, and there is danger of collision, keep to your present stations. There is no need of your being closer."

"Well," continued the other, halting, "we are, as I have said, poor gentlemen. We have reason to believe that poverty is not to be reckoned among your failings. In charity, therefore, give us your purses."

"In other words, you are thieves and highwaymen," returned Rupert. "If poverty, mark you, is not to be reckoned among our failings, neither is cowardice. We fight, but never yield."

"We are four to one, and more of our friends are near," said the highwayman who had first spoken; "therefore, if you have any regard for yourselves, deliver at once all you have with you. Otherwise, you will be left for dead on the road."

"Not so, my boastful friend," shouted Rupert. "Now, then, altogether."

At this signal they drew their swords, and rushed forward.

But to them, ignorant as they were of the road, escape in this manner was far from easy.

The highwaymen in front were stationed in a narrow part of the road, while those behind, seeing their comrades suddenly attacked, at once rushed forward to the rescue.

The mêlée became general.

Rupert and his companions fought, of course, at a disadvantage.

They were three to one, and they knew nothing, as I have said, of the locality.

However, they fought gallantly, and though slightly wounded, maintained their own in spite of odds.

Seeing this, the chief highwayman, who was not used to such tough customers, and who had, moreover, no desire to remain in such a critical position, where the patrol might at any moment come up, drew from his belt a whistle, and gave a long and shrill call.

In a very few moments there was again a rush of horses' feet, and two more highwaymen came on the scene.

It was now becoming serious.

Stanley Sherrington, wounded by a treacherous sword thrust from behind, was becoming so faint that he could scarcely parry the blows of his numerous enemies; indeed, could scarcely sit upon his saddle.

Rupert was in himself a host.

But his arm was also getting tired with constantly whirling his flashing blade, and he was becoming doubtful as to the issue of the combat, when a loud clattering was heard in the distance.

"Help is coming!" shouted Rupert. "We shall be rescued yet."

Already two of the highwaymen lay stretched upon the ground, dead, and the others were now in the centre of the combat.

Otherwise it is likely they would have been inclined to have cut and run.

They had not the chance, however.

Before they could extricate themselves the newcomers were upon the scene.

Like the highwaymen, they were masked, but they were evidently not belonging to the same class or gang.

"How now! what is this?" shouted one of them. "Robbery and murder on the king's highway! To the rescue! to the rescue!"

And with these words they dashed in among the combatants.

They easily recognised friends and foes from the fact that the highwaymen wore crape over their faces, and the gentlemen of the road soon found that their game for that evening, at any rate, was over.

A rapid interchange of words passed between them, and then suddenly they fell back in a line.

Rupert and his new friends then drew their pistols, fired in the midst of them, and, as one of the number reeled in his saddle and fell, the others, seeing the madness of further resistance, wheeled round and fled, followed by derisive shouts.

The victory, however, had not been without bloodshed.

On turning to speak to his friends, Rupert found Stanley Sherrington fainting, and supported in the arms of one of the strangers who had come so opportunely to their assistance.

"I know not who you are, gentlemen," said Rupert, "but I cannot too highly praise and thank you for your noble conduct. My friend, I see, is badly wounded, can you tell me where is the nearest hostelry? We had thought of going on to Roderham."

"He would die ere you reached it," said one of the masked men; "yonder light that twinkles by the roadside is the first inn. But since your friend is so ill, and those villains might return, we will show you the way."

Stanley Sherrington was placed on a horse before one of them, and in a few moments they were making their way rapidly along the high-road towards the inn.

"And so you do not recognise us, Earl Dreadnought," said one of the men, suddenly.

Rupert started.

"You know me?" he cried.

"Aye, and your friend Stanley Sherrington too. He was once one of our society, but he left us suddenly. Well, I suppose *he* had his reasons."

"Then you belong to the Mohocks?"

"We do. The Mohocks may do strange things, but they nevertheless do not forget a friend or leave him to die, if their swords have a chance of rescuing him."

On reaching the inn, Stanley Sherrington, who was still insensible, was lifted gently down and borne by Rupert and two of the masked men into the inn, where, on hearing what had occurred, the landlord quickly prepared a room for his reception.

In the warm bed the wounded man soon recovered consciousness, when stimulants had been administered to him, and, on the arrival of the doctor, they learned that, though he might be compelled to remain in bed more than a week, perhaps, indeed, two weeks, there was no reason to apprehend serious consequences.

The next morning Rupert and Everard Dalby quitted him, therefore, and made their way towards Exham.

For the time, however, we will remain by the bedside of the sufferer, and relate how, in addition to the severe wounds in his arm and shoulder, he received a wound in a still more susceptible part.

On the morning of the departure of his friends, he was lying in bed in no very enviable state of mind.

He was angry with fortune, in fact, because he, of all others—a soldier of fortune—was left there to wile away his time in inactivity while Rupert and a stranger were working out the mystery he had so longed to solve.

It was while in this frame of mind that the door was slowly opened and a vision of beauty appeared.

It was a young girl of about seventeen, bringing him some refreshment.

She was as fresh as a rose.

Her cheeks were beautifully pink and white, her hair auburn, falling in ringlets over her shoulders, whose contours could easily be seen through her gauzy chemisette, which, open in front, permitted just one tempting glance to be taken at a bosom white as snow.

Her pretty form was draped in a tight-fitting boddice, and a skirt just short enough to show a delicately turned calf and ankle tapering down into a sweet little foot.

Stanley Sherrington was, as we have seen, of a highly susceptible nature; yet, excepting Rosalie St. Aubyn, whom death had snatched from him, he had never seen a face which had made any impression on his heart.

Rosalie had attracted him by her bold beauty.

This girl was her opposite.

She attracted him instantly by her intense modesty — the delicate refinement of maidenhood.

As she approached the bedside and placed the refreshments on the table, she gazed pityingly on his pale face, and said, with a pretty blush,

"I have brought you something which will do you good, I hope."

"It cannot help doing so when brought to me by such lovely hands," said Stanley Sherrington. "Are you the landlord's daughter?"

"I am, master; and I'm very busy helping him too," she said, and so tripped away.

"By Heaven! a lovely girl," cried Stanley Sherrington, as his eyes eagerly followed her as she tripped from the room. "With such an innocent little beauty as that one might be happy for many a long year. But, ah! it is of no use thinking of her. She would never believe I meant marriage."

And so thinking, he set himself to work as well as he was able to demolish the comestibles before him.

His thoughts, however, would recur constantly to the fair vision.

He longed for her return so greatly that the time passed heavily on his hands until she came.

After one or two visits, he contrived to draw her into conversation, and ere he had been at the inn a week, he was so head-over-ears in love that the young girl could not but perceive it.

A glow of sweet pleasure entered her mind at first.

But this soon passed away, and was succeeded by a silent sorrow.

The first thrill of love had penetrated sweetly into her bosom.

But reason followed it.

Who was she?

A simple country maid.

And he?

A gentleman who could not think of marrying one so far beneath him.

So she became pale and ill, and Stanley Sherrington, never guessing what was the matter, imagined that his attentions annoyed her.

This idea made him all the more kind and gentle towards her, and thus naturally increased her love for him, while it made her heart more faint and weary still.

And so things went on for a fortnight, during which he had once heard from Rupert.

At the end of this time an accident occurred which settled for ever the love-makings of this strangely-assorted couple.

CHAPTER XXIV.

HOW STANLEY SHERRINGTON WON A WIFE.

At the end of the time mentioned, Stanley Sherrington was, of course, out of bed.

The doctor had promised him a speedy recovery if he had quiet.

The prophecy proved correct.

He was strong enough to walk about for a short time each day, and during these walks in the pretty garden of the inn he was accompanied generally by sweet Dorothea Alson.

These walks made the matter worse than ever.

Each felt that the other was consumed with love.

And yet for some time—some few days, at least—the secret remained undisclosed.

At length, on the third day, as they sat down in a little arbour which was somewhat secluded from the rest of the establishment, Sherrington stole his arm round her waist, stole a kiss from her cherry lips before she could say "Nay," and told his story.

She listened with flushed cheek and heaving bosom to his rapturous words.

Then, as he finished, she turned deadly pale.

"I wish you had never come," she said. "I know all this is folly—I know you cannot mean to marry such a one as I am. It is wicked to tempt a poor girl, and I won't listen any more."

She would have fled from him, but he held her fast by two hands.

"No, no," he cried, "I swear I mean what I say; "I am not tempting you: far be it from me to do so. I will marry you——"

His words were broken short by the approach of the landlord.

All that day Dorothea was absent from his room.

Next day, too.

He inquired for her—boldly asked to see her.

In vain.

"She was too ill to come," they told him.

That night sleep would not come to him.

He thought of nothing but Dorothea.

A deadly presentiment, too, oppressed him.

He tossed and turned in his bed, and, at length, wearied out by endeavouring to court the drowsy god, he got up and dressed himself.

He had just completed this operation when his feet were assailed by a sudden heat, and a cloud of smoke rolled into the room.

"By Heavens! the place is on fire!" he cried.

Rushing to the door, he opened it, in the hope that he could escape.

But, no!

A barrier of fire stopped him.

"Where is Dorothea?" was his first thought.

He ran to the window and threw it up.

The depth was great, but, by the aid of the bed-clothes, he could easily get to the ground.

"I will save myself to save her," thought he, and in a few minutes he had hastily tied the clothes together.

When he reached the ground he hurried to the front.

Here he found all in confusion.

The innkeeper was there, and his wife.

But, where was the daughter?

"Where is Dorothea?" he cried, in frantic accents.

The men in the crowd which had gathered pointed to a window, and shook their heads.

"She is lost," said one; "see: she cannot be saved!"

"How know you," cried Stanley Sherrington, "if ye have not tried. Give me a ladder. Ah! there is one."

Seizing it with a strength which, after his illness, seemed supernatural, he bore it to the window, from which flames were vomiting, and round which those from the old wooden rafters were circling and lapping as if in glee.

But he cared not for these.

All he thought of was that Dorothea, the sweet-faced, gentle, innocent Dorothea, was lying there in the midst of the devouring element.

While a cheer greeted him from those below who had not dared make an endeavour to reach the window, he leaped in at the casement.

There, close to the window, was the bed.

This fact had saved her.

Though she had fainted and lay senseless on the couch, the wind had fanned the flame from her, and,

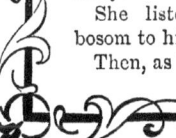

with a cry of joy, he tore the burning bed-clothes off, and seized her in his arms.

Blinding smoke, and red, fierce flames were round him.

Yet he cared not.

The window is gained.

Once more the crowd shouts and yells in wonder and joy.

Then with his lovely burden he steps out upon the topmost spoke of the ladder, and, amid the whirling smoke, descends to the ground.

* * * * *

"And so it was you that saved me," said the blushing girl, when recovering consciousness she found herself lying on a couch in a neighbour's house with Stanley Sherrington bending over her.

"Yes, I did, Dorothea. Does it prove that I love you?" he answered, earnestly.

"It does. I never doubted it," she said; "but it is a love that will bring no happiness."

He bent over, and kissed her.

"You shall be my wife, Dorothea," he said. "Nay, deny me not. I swear that you shall be my own honoured wife. I have already asked your father."

"And he?"

"Consents. It is you now who are the last to yield. Say that you will be mine."

He could have told by the manner in which she permitted his arm to glide around her waist, and his lips to press hers, what the answer was.

Yet the word "yes" sounded no less sweet as it thrilled from her trembling lips, and then, besides, it formed a good excuse for a long and ardent embrace, the first that the lovers had mutually given.

So, leaving Stanley Sherrington and Dorothea to their happiness, we must follow Rupert and Everard Dalby on their way to Exham.

CHAPTER XXV.

OLDSTONE THE SEXTON RELATES TO RUPERT A STRANGE STORY IN REGARD TO THE OLD EARL'S EARLY LIFE.

THE two friends passed on their way without hindrance, and, arriving at the inn where they had originally intended to remain on the past night, they obtained refreshment and the address also of Oldstone, the sexton.

So constantly had attempts been made upon their lives, so unvaryingly had their adventures been crowned by some disaster or some attempted assassination, that they resolved on this occasion to set about their work in the daytime.

Then, at least, they could scrutinise the countenances of those around them.

And, what is more, they could tell their numbers.

The old sexton lived on the margin of the churchyard.

It was a tumble-down, ricketty, gloomy-looking place, and just fitted for such an inhabitant as it possessed.

The gravestones came up close to it, one of them even leaning against the wall in grim friendship, while round the walls of the interior hung religious pieces, interspersed with copies of monumental brasses and tombstones, as if religion and death were naturally mingled, as some preachers make it seem!

On the morning of Rupert's visit to the place, Oldstone was standing at his door brightening and sharpening his spade.

He looked up inquiringly as the two strangers entered the churchyard.

"What may you want, gentlemen?" he said.

"Is your name Oldstone?"

"Yes."

"Sexton of Exham?"

"Aye, every one knows me. I've buried their sons and daughters, fathers and mothers for these forty years," said the old man, grinning.

"Well, my name is Rupert Dreadnought," said our hero. "I have received a letter from you."

The old man's grin lapsed into a smile of pleasure at these words.

"Ah!" he said, "I am glad to see you, Master Dreadnought. Enter, enter, and make yourself as comfortable as my poor place can make you."

Rupert and his new friend at once entered the little hut, for really it was no more, and the old sexton, following them, closed the door.

Then, going to a cupboard, he drew out a bottle containing spirit.

"I am old, you see," he said, "and am obliged to take care of myself. It is cold work, too, down among the graves when the water gets into them."

The old fellow had become so used to his deathly work and deathly talk that he thought nothing of it.

But the way in which he spoke inspired his hearers with something like dread.

He looked so dry and withered, and so thin and gaunt, that he appeared more like a denizen of the other world than anything else.

However, there was not much time to waste thinking of him.

So they drank the spirit he offered, and then began at once.

"Well, Master Oldstone," said Rupert, "I have received a letter from you."

"Yes."

"Well, to begin with, my father is dead."

The old sexton raised his hands in genuine amazement.

"Dead!" he repeated.

"Aye; more than two years since."

"Ah! well," murmured Oldstone, "we must all die; but I never thought he'd go before me. Well, if he's dead, *you* are, I suppose, Earl Dreadnought?"

"I am."

"And his representative?"

"Yes."

"Then my work is made the easier," said the sexton, as he drew himself up by the fire.

"In the first place," he began, after helping himself to another glass of spirit, "I suppose you know nothing of this neighbourhood?"

"Nothing."

"Nor of Luton Hall?"

"Nothing."

RUPERT; OR THE DREADNOUGHT SECRETS OF THE IRON CHEST

"THE OLD GRAVE-DIGGER LEANED OVER THE BODY WITH OPEN MOUTH."

"Nor of the lady that for years wandered listlessly about the place—the lady who loved your father?"

"Nothing whatever!" said Rupert, in astonishment. "You raise my curiosity greatly, I can tell you. Pray go on."

"I will," said the sexton.

Then he leaned forward and placed his skinny hand on our hero's arm.

"I can trust you?" he added.

The old eyes were turned up doubtingly towards Rupert as the words were spoken.

"You can," returned our hero, who could not take offence at what was said by the poor old man.

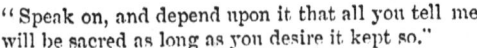

"Speak on, and depend upon it that all you tell me will be sacred as long as you desire it kept so."

"You are the counterpart of your father," returned the old man, "and I *will* trust you.

"I must tell the whole story, or you won't believe it, or rather you won't understand it.

"You know nothing about Exham or its neighbourhood, or you would know Luton Hall.

"It's a celebrated place.

"Celebrated both for its grandeur and its story.

"It has not a good reputation.

"Even now it is said to be haunted.

"Once people saw phantoms there.

"But they were well and terribly accounted for afterwards.

"All I need say of it is that it stands on the summit of the hill yonder, where you can see it now from the churchyard.

"Many years ago your father was down here, staying at the house of a friend, Sir Charles Edridge.

"Sir Charles was a fine old fellow, a jolly, good-hearted man as you could find anywhere, and you may imagine, therefore, that he gave your father leave to go anywhere and do anything in reason while he was here.

"Except one thing.

"Even Sir Charles had one hard point in his heart.

"This was in regard to the people at Luton Hall.

"He had great doubts as to their means of living.

"'Never go near them, never speak to them,' said Sir Charles.

"The earl was, of course, astonished.

"'Are they your enemies?'

"'No; people I never spoke to cannot be enemies,' returned Sir Charles; 'but they are suspicious persons.'

"'People who live in such a place must surely be respectably connected,' urged Earl Dreadnought.

"'They came from abroad, and purchased the place,' replied Sir Charles. 'No one knows whence they came or who they are; but strange sights and sounds have been seen and heard there since their coming, and it is even said that persons who have visited them have never been seen again. However this may, even if it be only a whim of mine, I am sure you will do as I ask you.'

"The earl, though at his early age he was naturally full of curiosity, promised to do as he was asked, and so for a time the matter ended.

"But fate had willed it differently.

"It so happened that Sir Charles's estate and that of Luton joined.

"The best fishing in the famous trout stream was to be got near a spot where only a broken hedge divided the properties.

"At least so thought Earl Dreadnought: or did his curiosity lead him to suppose it?

"At any rate he was often there.

"One evening as he was preparing to go, he turned round attracted by a slight noise, and found that he was not alone.

"Nor had he for some time been so.

"Reclining with her back against a tree was a young girl.

"She was very beautiful, so he saw at once.

"But her eyes were closed in sleep.

"The greatest charm of all therefore was hidden. The earl was even then lamenting the perfidy of one he had loved.

"But such beauty could not fail to move him.

"He purposely made a noise so as to disturb her, and she sprang to her feet, gave him a little frightened look, and fled.

"But that one glance at her eyes was enough to reveal their glory.

"Again and again that spot saw the earl returning to the spot.

"But though he lingered longer and longer, he saw her not again.

"One evening a sudden darkness had overcome the earth; and in spite of the fact that the trout were nibbling grandly, the earl was thinking it best for him to make his retreat, when he was seized from behind: a gag was placed over his mouth and a bandage over his eyes, and before he could make any resistance he was a blind and helpless prisoner.

"They remained near the stream some time.

"Evidently they were waiting until the darkness had become more intense.

"Then they raised him up roughly, and bore him away as swiftly as the unevenness of the ground would permit.

"He could not tell how long he travelled.

"It seemed an age.

"At length he felt himself being carried up some steps.

"Then, from the warmth, he knew he was in a room.

"Here he was laid upon a soft couch, and he was left to himself.

"A dreaminess then assailed him.

"He struggled vainly against it, and presently, despite his knowledge of the danger he was in, he fell into a deep sleep.

"When he awoke, his hands, his eyes, his mouth, his legs were free.

"He was in a large and well-furnished room, comfortable and luxurious in all but one thing.

"It had no window or door.

"He saw he was still a prisoner.

"As he rose to stretch his stiffened limbs, he heard voices in the adjoining soom.

"'And what are you going to do with him?' asked a silvery voice.

"'Wait, and you will see,' answered a man, gruffly. 'Go into his room, and do as I have bidden you.'

"The coarse and brutal manner in which this was said proved to the earl that the owner of the silvery voice acted under compulsion, and he awaited in eager wonder her entry into his room.

"There was no door visible, as I have said, so, seating himself once more on the couch, he waited with his eyes fixed upon the fire.

"Suddenly a voice, the voice of one who had entered noiselessly, and who—for all the door he could see—had sprung from the earth, said—

"'Earl Dreadnought, I desire a word with you.'

"He sprang up at once, and as he did so, he uttered a cry of astonishment.

"The young girl was no less surprised, and stood looking at him with her bright eyes opened wide in astonishment, her hand pressed over her bosom, her cheeks ashen pale.

"It was the beautiful vision he had beheld in the grounds of Luton Park.

"'What means this strange, this incomprehensible mystery?' cried he. 'Who and what are you?'

"She placed her finger on her lips, to impose silence.

"'Here,' she said, 'are pen, ink, and paper; now I will tell you what you have to write.'

"She placed the materials on the table, and in doing so, leaned down, whispering—

"'Do as I tell you, and be silent. *I* will save you. If you address me aloud, we are *both* lost.'

"'I will do all you tell me,' whispered the earl.

"'Now,' she said aloud, 'write to Sir Charles Edridge, and tell him to send by the bearer a thousand pounds in notes or gold, without attempting to follow or discover where he goes, or that within twenty-four hours you will be a dead man.'

"'Am I to say anything of my whereabouts?'

"'Nothing.'

"Earl Dreadnought wrote quickly.

"While he did so, the young girl leaned over him, so that her warm breath fanned his cheek, and her soft lips touched him.

"'I will save you,' she whispered, 'but you must act as I tell you. I shall presently enter with wine and refreshment. They suppose them to be drugged. They will not be, but you must assume drowsiness, and pretend to fall into a deep sleep. You will then hear and see much, but you must take no notice, no matter what happens.'

"A nod from the earl was enough.

"'There,' he said, aloud, 'is the paper you have so infamously extorted from me. But mark me, when I am once more free, I shall take measures to punish you for this.'

"'Provided always,' replied the fair one, in the same voice, 'that you can discover where you are.'

"She then turned and quitted the room.

"This time he saw how she went.

"It was through a panel in the wall, so exquisitely made, that when it closed there was not the slightest trace of any aperture—not even the smallest crack or crevice.

"'Well,' thought the earl, 'this is a strange adventure. 'I wonder how it will turn out?'

"Well might he wonder.

"In the hands of the enemy thus, how could he even guess at the result?

"He resolved to be patient, however, and wait, trusting to his fair companion of a moment ago.

"Well he might.

"Such sweet eyes, such a gentle expression, such a silvery voice he had never before seen and heard.

"He had plenty of food for meditation and reflection thinking of her.

"Who was she?

"How came she there?

"Was she one of such a band of desperadoes as those by whom he had been seized?

"Could she be acting a part?

"Was she deceiving him?

"No, no; she was too beautiful, too full of gentle grace and tenderness to warrant such an idea."

("He had not seen Rosalie St. Albyn or he would have thought differently," was the inward reflection of Rupert Dreadnought, as he listened.)

"Well, after a short time, the secret panel once more opened and the strange beauty appeared.

"She bore a small tray, upon which were wine and some delicate food.

"'Here is some wine and something to eat,' she said aloud, 'we don't starve our prisoners here.'

"Then she made some significant gestures: pointing to the wine, shaking her head, and throwing a small drop into the fire.

"She pointed to the food and nodded.

"He understood her at once.

"In fact the pantomime was very simple.

"He was to eat the food fearlessly.

"The wine he was to pretend to consume and to throw away.

"One thing she was compelled to risk.

"'Pretend to drink up quickly,' she said, in a hurried whisper, "'for one of the men will be here presently, perhaps the chief himself.'

Then she hastened away.

"'Chief!' he thought, "'am I among Rhine robbers or Italian brigands?'

"But he had no time for mental discussion.

"He had as good proof as he could expect in such a situation that she intended all she had said and done for his good.

"So, pouring out a large glassful of wine, he smelt it.

"It had a strong aromatic smell, far from disagreeable.

"Tempting, in fact, when he was so devoured with thirst.

"But he resisted the temptation, and cast it, as he had been directed, into the flames.

"Three more were quickly sent in the same direction, and then he attacked the viands.

"He had scarcely begun, when again the door was opened.

"This time a man entered.

"A tall, burly, swarthy fellow, with a huge beard, and dressed in an uncouth garb.

"A kind of leering grin overspread his face, as he gazed at his forced guest, and saw how quickly he had disposed of the wine.

"He could not for a moment suspect that he had been warned.

"'Well, my friend, what cheer?' he said, as he sat down, with the back of the chair in front of him.

"The earl looked at him fiercely for a moment.

"Then he remembered he had to act a part.

"'Little cheer,' he said, yawning. 'I am not used to being kept in such a place as this against my will. But you treat me well, and as I suppose my friend Sir Charles will not long delay, I shall soon be out of your clutches.'

"'You don't do justice to our wine,' said the ruffian; 'that is the best in the cellar.'

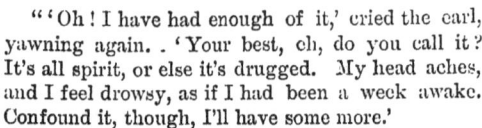

"'Oh! I have had enough of it,' cried the earl, yawning again. . 'Your best, eh, do you call it? It's all spirit, or else it's drugged. My head aches, and I feel drowsy, as if I had been a week awake. Confound it, though, I'll have some more.'

"So saying, he poured out another glass with a trembling hand, raised it to his lips, and then, as if seized with an uncontrollable feeling, he dropped it from his hand, and fell back on his couch as if in a dead sleep.

"The ruffian chuckled.

"'Confound the fellow,' he said; 'he's drank enough to keep a house full asleep for a week. Well, no matter, perhaps it's all the better, and will make the matter easier. Here, Renard.'

"In answer to this call the secret panel was again opened, and a man entered.

"The earl could not see him.

"He had fallen back purposely, so that his face was partially hidden, and those near him would thus have but little opportunity to watch the play of his features.

"'He's asleep already, Renard,' said the man who had entered first. 'See, he has drank enough to send the whole gang of us to sleep.'

"'Well, what do you propose to do, Robert,' said the other. 'Keep him till the messenger returns?'

"'Of course.'

"'But Sir Charles will be sure to send the money.'

"'That may be, but we should be in rather a strange predicament if we killed him before we were certain of the money,' replied Robert. 'No, no, you are impatient for blood to-night, Renard.'

"'*It is murder then they mean, the treacherous knaves,*' thought the earl; 'yet, as they have doubtless murdered so many, why does that mysterious beauty protect me?'

"There was but one interpretation of it.

"One he scarcely liked to think of.

"She must love him!

"'No,' replied the man addressed as Renard, "'no, I am not impatient for blood, as you call it, but I want to be off. I have to meet my betrothed to-night.'

"Horrid villain!

"He was eager to complete the murder that he might visit his betrothed!

"The other ruffian laughed.

"'You can go,' he said, 'and I and Hacker can complete the work ourselves. He is dead asleep, and if the answer is all right, why, two of us can easily settle the matter.'

"'And if Sir Charles Edridge refuses to send the money?'

"'Then we must send another letter.'

"'Good: well, I will take you at your word; but as I am somewhat hungry, I think I will join you at supper in your room ere I start. We can leave him in safety now.'

"'Aye,' laughed the other, 'he'd sleep for a year if we were to leave him.'

"So saying they passed out of the room, and the earl was once more alone.

"'Wretches!' he murmured, 'so it depends upon the kindness of Sir Charles whether I am murdered or not. If he sends the money—which, most undoubtedly, he will—I am to be destroyed by these villains. Ah! they have left me a long-bladed knife on the table yonder; they shall find, if they *do* return before my fair deliverer can come to me, that I shall die hard.'

"So saying, he took the knife from the table, and, secreting it in the breast of his doublet, leant himself in his former position and waited.

"Presently he heard a voice say—

"'Awake.'

"He knew the silver tones at once.

"It was his strange and beautiful friend.

"He sprang up at once.

"'Is all ready?' he asked.

"'Yes; come.'

"The secret door was now open.

"Beyond it there seemed to be a black gulf.

"He hesitated.

"Was she one of the gang?

"A look of pain crossed her face.

"'If you mistrust me,' she said, in a whisper, 'I cannot save you.'

"'No, no,' said the earl, 'lead on; I will follow you anywhere.'

"He could not mistake the mournful pleading of those lovely eyes.

"She led him to the secret door.

"Then she took his hand.

"'Step carefully,' she said, 'there is a descent here. Three steps. Now follow without fear, but noiselessly and slowly.

"They advanced some distance in utter darkness.

"The earl, as they went on, could hear distinctly the voices of the men at their supper.

"But they were evidently convinced that their prisoner was safe.

"In the young girl they appeared to have the most perfect confidence.

"On the fugitives went, therefore, without hindrance in the darkness, until at length a small speck of light was seen in the distance.

"Towards this they made, descending gradually, and presently, as the earl could tell from the smell and the softness of the earth, into some subterranean passage.

"Now the young girl no longer deemed it necessary to preserve silence.

"'We are safe now,' she said; 'at the further extremity of this subterranean way is a horse, and we can make our escape readily.'

"She said 'we.'

"*She* was then to accompany him.

"He felt embarrassed at this.

"But how could he refuse?

"Had she not risked life to save him?

"And could he, then, in the face of this, cast her back into such a den of thieves and assassins?

"They reached at length the end.

"Here they found themselves among a dense clump of trees.

"To one of these a horse was fastened, and in an instant the earl had mounted, and his lovely companion was before him on the horse.

"One thing now was certain.

"He could not return straight to the house of Sir Charles with such a companion, even though she *had* saved his life.

"It would be an unpardonable liberty he fancied, and he galloped, therefore, away into the highroad and took the way towards the nearest inn.

"The girl clung to him with all the confidence of youth, and, as his arm encircled her lovely form, it was not without some emotion being stirred within his breast.

"'Why have you risked all this for me?' he said. 'Would it not have been better to have made it seem that I had myself effected this escape?'

"The girl's form trembled as he spoke.

"'They would have guessed it,' she said. 'Besides I am tired, wearied of being among such an awful crew. I want to be away, free, with some one who loves me; not with demons.'

"There was an intonation in her voice as she said 'some one who loves me,' that told its own tale, and her arms involuntarily clung more tenderly round his neck.

"'And where shall you go now? Have you no friends?' he asked.

"He hardly knew what words to use.

"The girl evidently loved him.

"He, with the wreck of one love still before his eyes, how could *he* love her?

"To simulate it would have been a shame.

"A flood of tears was the answer.

"Then she said—

"'Friends! No, none in the world! *You* have friends. Often—often I have watched you by the fish stream, and envied you. I have nowhere to go. But,' she added, with a sudden vehemence, 'fear not for me. I have hands and a brain. I will work to live.'

"She had hoped too much, and was evidently full of regret at his coldness.

"But he resolutely, as an honourable man, kept from exhibiting any emotion.

"He never then dreamed that he could love again.

"Well, they arrived at length at the inn, where they secured two beds, and having sent a man with a message to Sir Charles that he had escaped, and would be with him in the morning, Earl Dreadnought retired.

"In spite of the wondrous adventures of the night, he could not keep awake.

"But he was not destined to sleep long.

"Awakened suddenly by some one shaking him violently, he found his fair preserver, half undressed, leaning over him.

"In her hand was a lamp, which shone upon her pale and haggard features, showing that she had hurriedly slipped on such clothes as she came to apprise him of some fresh peril.

"'Danger again?' he said.

"'Aye, danger enough,' she said. 'Lose not an instant, but fly. Do not delay to ask me any questions. Suffice it that they have tracked you; that they have received the money, and are even now beneath this window planning your death. Never mind how I know it. But believe me and fly.'

"'And you?' said the earl.

"'Never mind me. You shall hear from me tomorrow. I am in no danger.'

"Then she stooped down suddenly, pressed a kiss of love upon his brow, and fled from the room.

"The earl followed her advice, and had soon passed noiselessly down the stairs.

"Making his way out, he walked through the dark night towards Sir Charles's house, where he was received with eager welcome.

"On the next morning the authorities were communicated with, and a descent was made upon the old Hall, where the earl felt certain he had been taken.

"But the result was nothing.

"The subterranean passage could not be found. Neither could the room where he had been confined. Neither was there any one in the place—man or woman—in any way resembling those whom he had seen there.

"So the visit ended in nothing; and while Sir Charles lost his thousand pounds, the earl never had the chance of revenge."

"But the young lady—my father's preserver," said Rupert, deeply interested, but not being able in the least to comprehend what all this long story had to do with the object of their mission.

"He never saw her again."

"She was murdered, doubtless, poor creature," suggested Everard Dalby.

"No, no," said the old sexton, grinning, "now I come to the most special part of my story.

"Your father never heard of her again, and she evidently did not know where to find him.

"She died but a month ago; but how she lived or what was her ultimate fate no one ever knew.

"Suffice it, that she died rich in some way.

"Having often seen me in my younger days, she wrote to me, and asked me to see the earl, and deliver with my own hands a letter to him.

"I heard from some one I applied to that the earl was ill, but they evidently knew nothing of his death.

"As he is dead, however, you are his proper and legal representative, and to you, therefore, I shall give the the letter."

So saying the old man drew from his pocket a letter, and handed it to Rupert.

The letter was addressed to his father, and read as follows:—

"Loved One—

"I may call you so now, since when you read this I shall be no more. How I have lived since we parted I shall never tell; suffice it that I have never married, and never loved but *you*. I need say no more. The villain who entrapped and would have murdered you died but a week ago. His wealth, *as his daughter*, I give to you. Aye, it was the daughter of an assassin who loved and saved you. The way by which you must win this wealth is strange, yet, nevertheless, I ask you for the sake of my love to accept it. My father died a week since. He is buried in Exham churchyard. Oldstone, the sexton, will show you the grave of the Marquis de St. Lefray. I leave to you the mode of exhuming the body. But you must do it quickly, or my brother, far worse even than my father, will receive all. He is now abroad, but is expected shortly to return. On his return *he* will exhume the body to search for a tablet on the chest of the dead man, which will explain where the treasure lies. On this tablet are letters which will tell you how to act. I

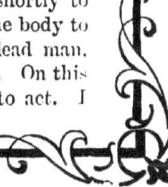

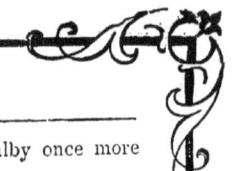

cannot explain further, as one of his associates fastened on the tablet, but, I know the treasure lies somewhere in Luton Hall. The directions are in French. And now, loved one, farewell. A long and mournful captivity alone has prevented me from communicating sooner with you; but, even now that I could ask you to attend me in my last moments, I would not have you here to see the face wrinkled and the locks grey that once were my pride and glory in youth. We shall meet again.

"JULIE ST. LEFRAY."

There was something inexpressibly mournful in all this.

Both Rupert and Everard Dalby were much moved.

For some moments neither spoke.

At length Rupert said,

"I see but one way out of this."

"And that is——"

"To give out that we have reason to suppose that this villanous old marquis came to his death by foul play. Then we can have him exhumed in open daylight."

"Why not by night?" said Oldstone.

"I have no desire to be taken for a resurrectionist," said Rupert. "We shall have some secret work to do at night when we go in search of the treasure. No, no; we will apply to the magistrates. I doubt if any of them will understand French. At any rate, since I am far from being madly eager after an increase of riches, I will take the chance."

"If that is your wish, the day is early yet," said Dalby. "Had we not better see the magistrates at once?"

"Very well," said Oldstone; "I can take you to them."

And then he took another little sip at the spirits, and putting on his old hat was ready for a start.

A sudden idea struck Rupert.

He caught the sexton by the arm.

"There is one thing," he said, "I should like to know. How came you to know this story?"

The old man chuckled.

"Ah!" he said, that is a secret not my own. I cannot reveal it."

"But this lady, this Julie St. Lefray; is she really dead?"

"Alas! yes, poor thing; I can show you her tomb."

"Good; another time I will see it," said Rupert. "In the meantime, let us elucidate this mystery. Lead us at once to the county magistrates."

These worthies, as my readers are doubtless convinced thoroughly, are not very sapient.

They listened in amazement to Rupert's story.

It savoured of the romantic.

Anything that promised excitement was to them a pleasing novelty.

So they at once agreed to give the necessary authority.

Nay, they even went so far in their enthusiasm as to say they would come themselves and superintend the work.

This was not exactly what Rupert desired, but nevertheless it was not possible to avoid it.

Accompanied by the two worthies, therefore, dressed in heavy boots and magisterial robes, and with an immense profusion of hair falling down their ample backs. Rupert and Dalby once more took their way to the churchyard.

As may be imagined, the little band of gentlemen roaming among the tombs, accompanied by the old grave-digger, did not fail to excite curiosity among the country people, who, not having yet been blessed with the advantages of steam, had very few opportunities of seeing anyone beyond their own circle, except, indeed, on those rare occasions when the "gentlemen of the road" took it into their heads to pay them a visit.

When Rupert and the others entered the churchyard, therefore, as I have said, several of the wayfarers quitted the road, and strolled in among the tombs.

The grave was soon reached, and Oldstone, with the assistance of two or three volunteers, began to work eagerly turning up the mould.

All was anxiety.

At length the coffin was reached.

"Now," said one of the magistrates, authoritatively, "break open the lid."

His command was at once obeyed.

There, in a few moments, lay the body of the French marquis cold and still before them.

Upon his breast was a brass plate.

On it were several characters, scratched, with some sharp instrument.

The old grave-digger leaned over the body with open mouth.

He was about to make some observation, but he stopped.

Looking round he beckoned to Rupert.

"See here," he said, "there are strange writings on his breast."

Rupert and Dalby at once approached.

There truly was the writing, and in French as Julie had said.

The explanation was very simple.

"You will find it in the third tomb on the left-hand side of the inner door of the church. The lid is easily removed."

"What does it say?" inquired the magistrate.

"It is French," replied Rupert, turning away, as if not understanding it.

"Ah! well," said the magistrate, confusedly, not liking, in fact, to confess his ignorance before the labourers around; "we can translate it by-and-bye. Let the body be carried to the inn where the doctor can examine it."

So the lid was once more placed on the coffin, the labourers raised it on their shoulders, and away they went towards the inn.

The day passed by.

The body was examined in the evening by the doctor, who pronounced that it had been the victim of natural causes only, and ordered it to be re-buried.

The magistrate, however, desired it to be kept above ground until morning, in order that the French inscription might be deciphered.

"This very evening," said Everard Dalby, "you must seize upon this wealth which has been so strangely bequeathed you. Otherwise, the son of this robber and murderer will return and possess it."

"I scarcely like the matter," said Rupert, "it savours of robbery."

Dalby laughed.

"You are over nice, I fancy," he said, "you should remember that this one whose return I fear, from that lady's letter, is a villain as evil-minded as his father. It would be a sin to permit him to lay his hands upon it. Even if you do not preserve it for yourself, you can use it in bettering the fortunes of those who have proved themselves faithful servants."

"True, true," returned Rupert, "I know where it can be well bestowed. We will go this very evening."

CHAPTER XXVI.

THE OLD CHURCH — THE THIRD TOMB ON THE LEFT—THE TREASURE—THE PAPER—THE SUDDEN APPARITION—THE FOILED VILLAIN—THE RETURN TO THE INN.

THE darkness had fallen thickly when Rupert Dreadnought and Everard Dalby, with the old sexton, made their way towards the church.

Oldstone quickly admitted them into the sacred edifice, where they closed the door, and took out a dark lantern.

Then, from the left of the door of the still building they counted the tombs.

One—two—three.

This third was a square stone tomb, on the top of which reposed the effigy of a knight in full armour.

The sculptured letters were almost effaced by time.

"This is a very old tomb," said Rupert; "it has, no doubt, been chosen because it is hollow. Give me your crowbar, old man."

The sexton handed him a short crowbar.

This Rupert inserted below the lid of the tomb, and raised it slightly.

"It is easily removed," said he. "Now, Dalby, aid me."

It was a matter requiring strength and time; but after some efforts and much difficulty the effigy of the knight was removed and placed upon the floor.

Within the tombstone was a piece of cloth, and, on this being removed, a glittering sight met their eyes.

Gold and jewels were lying there in a confused heap.

"We shall have some trouble to carry all this away," said Rupert.

"There are three of us," returned Everard Dalby, "and surely we can manage it."

"We must cram it into our pockets then," said Rupert. "Let us be quick, or we may be interrupted. Not that I care for the treasure itself, but I would not for worlds be found in such a position."

In a few minutes the treasure was transferred to their pockets, except about five hundred sovereigns.

"Stay," said Rupert; "let these remain."

"Why?"

"Because I will give a chance to this ruffian to reform his life. I have brought with me something which will perhaps explain to him a mystery."

So saying, he drew from his pocket a paper, and laid it on the top of the treasure.

"Now," he said, "let us raise this lid, and replace it."

His companions at once, without even glancing at the paper, complied with his request.

Scarcely had they done so, when a noise attracted their attention.

They started and listened.

The sound was as of some one hurrying along the gravel walk of the churchyard.

"Quick!" said Rupert; "put out the light and let us conceal ourselves."

In another moment all was again dark and still.

Then the door of the church was violently shaken and opened, and a tall man, wrapped in an ample cloak, entered the sacred edifice.

He looked around him triumphantly.

"All quiet!" he said, "all to myself. Truly my father was a wise man.

"A treasure is far safer here than in the maws of some unprincipled lawyer.

"Now, then, for the third tomb."

With these words he drew a dark lantern from his pocket and commenced his search.

"This is the son," whispered Rupert.

He was right.

It was the young Marquis de St. Lefray.

Heir to a title, heir to wealth won by his father's murders.

He had no difficulty in finding the right place.

Drawing from his pocket a crowbar similar to that used by Rupert, he commenced prizing the lid, and in a few moments succeeded in dislodging it so far that he could insert his hand into the aperture.

He started on finding it so empty.

Then his hand touched the paper, and he drew it forth eagerly.

"Marquis de St. Lefray," he read aloud, "I who intend to distribute this wealth among the poor have deprived you of it that you may not have the chance or temptation of following in the footsteps of your father. I leave you five hundred pounds that you may not be subject to want while you are seeking for an honest calling. In the future you will thank me for that which you now curse me."

"No signature—no clue!" shouted the young reprobate, stamping on the marble floor. "Curse him! aye, I *do* curse him! Whoever this may be—man or woman—who has robbed me of my just inheritance, I will follow him to the uttermost parts of the earth until I have my revenge!"

He then seized eagerly yet half contemptuously the five hundred pounds which were left him, and without even troubling himself to replace the stone quitted the church.

After waiting sufficient time to enable him to get clear off, Rupert and his companions followed, and made their way to the cottage of the sexton.

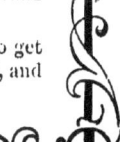

The old man was liberally rewarded, the treasure packed safely, and then proceeding to the inn, the two adventurers procured their horses, and mounting them, proceeded at full speed towards the roadside tavern where they had left Stanley Sherrington.

They had no reason to suppose that they had been seen by anyone during their proceedings at the old church.

And yet they had not gone far before they experienced an uncomfortable feeling that they were followed.

By whom they knew not.

They could see no one.

The disappointed and exasperated son of the dead villain was the only one likely to dog their footsteps.

But they could positively distinguish nothing.

At length, however, when they were not more than a mile and half from their destination, a horseman dashed out of the hedge at the side of the highroad, and confronted them.

"Stand, gentlemen," he said.

A loud laugh burst from the two friends.

"Are you mad, that you thus assail two well-armed men?" asked Rupert.

"No, I am not mad," returned the other, in a voice of suppressed passion, "I know that I am talking to men who take their station in society as gentlemen of honour, or I could not venture to be here. I wish one of you, I care not which, to fight with me for the treasure of which I have been robbed."

They knew now who he was.

He was the son of the dead marquis.

The Heir of the Assassin!

"Who are you who thus oppose our passage?" said Rupert.

"I am the Marquis de St. Lefray," returned the young man.

"The Marquis de St. Lefray—the son of the murderer who once owned Luton Hall," cried our hero. "What want you with us?"

"I have told you," replied the young man, restraining his anger as well as he could, "I have told you what I want. Let one of you—I care not which—descend from his horse and fight me to the death. Then, if *I* am victorious, I will fight the other."

For an instant Rupert hesitated.

Then he remembered that this man was the brother of Julie.

The brother of the woman who had loved his father!

"Marquis," he said, "you—who must be the last born of your mother—I respect because you are the brother of one who saved my father's life, and——"

The young marquis interrupted him.

"Curses on her! curses on her! It was she, then, who betrayed my father when I was but a babe," he cried. "I laugh at your respect. I spit upon you! You have robbed me of my inheritance, and, if you are not a coward, as well as a mean-spirited thief, you will fight me."

Rupert's blood boiled at this.

He could not brook such words.

"Madman! you seek your own death!" he cried: "but I will humour you."

Then he turned to Everard Dalby.

"Remember," he said, "I fight this duel unaided. Whatever happens, let there be no interference."

Then he leaped from his horse.

The road was very dark.

Moon and stars were hidden.

"We cannot see to fight here," said Rupert, as he drew his sword.

The young marquis laughed.

A strange, mocking, unearthly laugh it was.

The laugh of one who had made his mind up for the worst.

"Even that excuse will not avail you," he cried. "See!"

As he spoke he drew from his pocket an unlit flambeau.

In a few moments he had lit it, and a bright light was diffused around.

He handed it to Everard Dalby.

"Now," he said, taking his position opposite Rupert Dreadnought, "now we are ready."

Swords were crossed at once.

Rupert had a strange feeling about his antagonist.

Villain as he might be, he was a brave man.

However, there was no time for compunctious thought.

There was no doubt he meant either death to our hero or to himself.

So the fight began.

It would be useless to describe the fight.

Cut and thrust—clash, clash, clash!—a moment's pause—an oath—another thrust.

Such it was repeated again and again.

But the stranger soon found he had his master.

Yet he would not yield.

He was desperate.

Without his treasure he cared not to live.

In the hopes of being thus one day suddenly enriched, he had lived and waited.

Suddenly despoiled just as he had expected to find himself on the threshold of a career of wild profligacy he cared not to live.

So he fought like a madman.

Wounded severely in the shoulder, he still made violent efforts to retrieve the fortune of the day.

More than once Rupert gave him the chance of yielding.

"Stop," he cried, "while life is left you!"

But no!

The flowing of his own blood seemed only to madden him the more.

He rushed at Rupert savagely; turned to the right, and left; strove, in fact, to harass his enemy by unforseen strokes.

But all in vain!

Rupert watched his opportunity and dashed in.

His sword described a circle in the air, and the next moment his adversary fell staggered back.

The weapon had plunged through his lungs.

He made one effort to draw a pistol from his belt.

But his fingers failed, he gave one gasping cry, and then, spinning round, fell upon his face—dead!

"THE CAPTAIN'S SWORD RUSHED THROUGH HIS HEART."—(*See page 316.*)

"We must hurry on now," said Rupert, as he returned his sword to its scabbard; "we may be assailed again by those knights of the road, who, doubtless, are his friends."

"True!" returned Everard Dalby; "and I for one am anxious to see Stanley Sherrington again, and see how it has fared with him."

CHAPTER XXVII.

THE MYSTERIOUS WATCHER OF THE DARK WOODS—THE THIEVES' DETECTIVE—THE WARNING—THE SUBTERRANEAN CAVE—THE ARMING OF THE BAND — THE ATTACK ON THE HIGHWAY — THE DESPERATE BATTLE—THE ARRIVAL OF AID—THE FLIGHT OF THE HIGHWAYMEN—THE SECRET—A MARRIAGE—THE RETURN TO LONDON.

OUR hero and his friend, however, were not destined to reach the inn where lay their wounded friend without a further adventure.

While they are jogging along, looking to the left and to the right of them to observe whether they were followed again, we will introduce our readers to a strange dwelling, occupied by strange people.

The grand old woods, which made England so picturesque years and years ago, had not at the time of my story disappeared.

On the margin of the road, therefore, could still be seen the majestic oak, the stately poplar, and the thickly-growing evergreens, making it appear like some of the tangled fastnesses of the far west.

For some time before the arrival of Rupert Dreadnought and Everard Dalby in the vicinity, a man had been keeping watch near the only opening that there seemed to exist in the wood.

This was such an opening that a stranger would scarcely have seen it.

It was a round hole, as it were, between the dense verdure, looking more like the hole made by a wild animal than one made by a human being.

The man himself was an oddity.

He was tall and spare, with a long, hooked nose, and a set of blear eyes, and a wide, brutal mouth, overshadowed by fierce moustaches.

His long, lanky hair fell in a wild profusion over his shoulders, and his great, ghastly eyes rolled uneasily in his head.

His clothes were, perhaps, more peculiar even than his personal appearance.

His coat was a half military one, very ragged; his tight breeches a dirty white; his high jack-boots were out of shape and down at heel.

His face, red with frequent potations, was now of a pinkish blue, produced by cold and the absence of the usual amount of fluid.

But, in spite of his peculiar and forlorn appearance, this fellow was a good swordsman and a brave man.

His trade was a peculiar one.

He was what I may call a thieves' detective.

It was he who gave notice to the band of the approach of danger.

It was he who, with a black patch over his eye, wandered through the villages near in the guise of a discarded soldier, and discovered the whereabouts and the means of casual travellers.

It was he who now had watched the proceedings of Rupert and Everard Dalby; had guessed that they had been on a lucrative expedition, and had so informed the band.

He was now watching for their approach.

To his quick ear the sound of their horses' feet came long before they were near.

"Ah! here comes some one. I am mistaken if they are not my game."

Then he stooped down, crept through the hole, and was soon walking rapidly on through the forest.

When he had proceeded some two or three hundred yards he stopped, gave a peculiar whistle, and then passed on again.

The whistle was answered as it were from the bowels of the earth.

Then a kind of gateway of foliage opened, and a man stepped forth.

"What cheer?" he cried.

"They are coming," replied the knight of the ragged coat.

"Good. I will arouse our comrades."

So saying, the last speaker, who was not much better attired than the first, ran quickly down a series of steps into a kind of subterranean cave.

Here a number of ragged ruffians were assembled.

In tales purporting to give the true careers of highwaymen, it has been the plan to describe these villains as handsome, dare-devil fellows — well-dressed, well-fed, polite to ladies, good to the poor, robbing only the rich.

These men are entirely fictitious personages.

They were nearly all like these now before us—squalid, half-fed, brutal, ragged.

The scum, in fact, of society.

"The game is close at hand, my boys," cried the man who had met the first comer at the door: "let us be quick and take our stations."

The men at once drank off what was left of the ale before them, and buckling on their sword-belts, prepared to follow their leader.

Their "detective" led the way, dark as it was, and ere Rupert and Everard Dalby had reached the bend of the road, six villains were ready to receive them.

They belonged to the same band which had attacked Rupert, Everard Dalby, and Stanley Sherrington before, only that now they were less two of their number, who had died on the road that night.

"Are these the same fellows who fought so devilishly before?" asked one of the highwaymen of the "watcher," as they called him.

"The very same."

"Then they shall neither of them reach home to tell the tale," said the leader; "but hush! here they are. Fire altogether, and then rush forward. Curse it! I wish there was more light."

As the villain spoke Rupert and his friend galloped round the bend of the road, and approached the ambush.

In an instant a volley of pistol shots rang forth upon the night air, and the horses leaped back in terror.

Nor was it to be wondered at.

Everything before this had been so hushed and still.

Scarcely a breeze had rustled the branches, and the reports of the six pistols rolled forth on the still air like thunder.

But, above the alarm, no mischief was done.

The two friends rode on as before; but in an instant the road was full of dark figures, and they were unable to force the horses along.

In an instant, without a word being spoken, their pistols had left their holsters, and one of the villains bit the dust, while another staggered back wounded.

But the others seized the horses by the bridles, and commenced cutting the leather, so as to prevent their being managed.

There was no time to load pistols, and a hand-to-hand encounter, therefore, began with swords.

It was an uneven fight indeed.

Even the wounded man could use his right hand.

There were still, therefore, five to two.

But firm in their dauntless bravery, and almost believing now in a sheltering fate, Rupert and Dalby fought on, dealing deadly blows, and keeping their adversaries at bay as with a supernatural strength, until at length the sound of a horse's feet was heard in the distance.

This redoubled their exertions.

"Assistance is coming," cried Dalby; "these villains shall not escape us this time."

This daring speech, in the face of such odds, made the highwaymen doubt after all whether they were not attacking men whose lives were charmed.

But still, knowing what a tremendous booty would be theirs in the event of success, they fought on, and two of them, as if by tacit consent, thrust their swords into the chests of the noble horses.

They reared on their hind legs for a moment, and then rolled over.

But in that minute Rupert and Everard Dalby had succeeded in disengaging their feet from the stirrups; and just at the very moment when the robbers imagined the prize to be theirs, they had sprung from the ground, and were ready to receive the attack.

By this time the horseman, whose approach they had heard from afar, had reached the spot, and, without tethering his horse, he leaped from its back and rushed to the rescue, crying—

"Villains! is it thus ye attack peaceful travellers? Five to one! Cowards! Back, I say!"

The voice told them at once who it was.

It was Stanley Sherrington.

There was no time, however, to think of greetings.

Even now the odds were in favour of the highwaymen.

But the sudden accession of a brave and determined foe lessened their chances.

They began to give way.

This was a ruse.

Stanley Sherrington at once saw it.

They wished to reload their pistols.

"On, my friends," he shouted; "the cowards are loading their fire-arms. Give them no time. Quick!"

Rupert and Everard Dalby quickly acted at his bidding.

The knights of the road had no chance of loading.

Swords were still their only weapon.

With these the fight was continued for some little time.

But soon the tables were turned.

With the coming of Stanley Sherrington all seemed changed.

First one, then another, received severe wounds, while the friends appeared to escape scatheless.

Then one of the villains fell.

This was the "detective," the "knight of the ragged coat."

Upon seeing this, the spirits of the others appeared to receive a damper.

They fought wildly for a few moments.

Then, seized with an incomprehensible panic, they turned suddenly, dived through the green bushes, and disappeared before the victors could oppose their flight.

The friends made no attempt at pursuit.

There was no fear of their being molested again.

"Well," said Rupert, as he grasped Stanley Sherrington's hand, "I congratulate you on two things."

Stanley started.

He imagined that by some magic Rupert Dreadnought had heard at Exham of his proposal and acceptance by Dorothea.

"Upon what?" he asked.

"Upon your successful arrival here, and upon recovering your health," said Rupert. "But you seemed surprised. What secret have you from me?"

Stanley laughed.

"I thought you had discovered it for yourself," he answered; "that was the cause of my surprise. But come, let us mount and away. There is no safety here."

Rupert pointed to two dark masses lying on the road.

"It would be difficult to do so, as you see," he said; "both our horses are killed. All that remains for us to do is to take off our saddles and saddle-bags, and make sure of what they contain, and walk till we reach the inn. We are ready."

Leading his own horse by the bridle, Stanley Sherrington proceeded onward, after Rupert and Everard Dalby had secured their saddle-bags, and on the way told them of his adventure.

A sigh escaped Rupert's breast, as the enthusiastic young lover added,

"I shall not wait long. Dorothea has given her consent to an immediate marriage, after which we return to London."

"We will remain and see the ceremony, of course," said Rupert. "I only wish that I and my dear Helen could be united on the same day."

"Do not be desponding," said Stanley. "Your time will come sooner, perhaps, than you expect."

Rupert shook his head.

"No, no," he said; "there is no hope for me for many a long year. That villain, Oscar Penraven, has disappeared Heaven knows whither. Until I find him, of course there is no peace for me; no hope, until he is dead, of marrying Helen. I envy you, therefore, my friend, but I wish you every joy, and only hope that you will find your bride everything you hope."

We will not give much details in regard to the marriage of Stanley Sherrington and Dorothea.

We have to push on to those stirring adventures which lead to the conclusion of our strange history.

Suffice it, that three mornings after the return of Rupert to the inn, the blushing Dorothea became the bride of Stanley Sherrington.

On the third day after, supplied with fresh horses, Rupert and Everard Dalby started for London,

Stanley Sherrington and his wife proceeding in a post chaise.

Though there was this difference in the style of conveyance, however, the friends kept all together.

The roads were none of the safest, and single travellers were liable to be molested, as Rupert and Dalby had been before.

They met, however, with no adventure on the road, and, in due course, arrived safely in London.

CHAPTER XXVIII.

NEWS FROM AN OLD FRIEND—ANOTHER MARRIAGE—ON THE SCENT AGAIN—A STRANGE PROPOSAL—GASCOIGNE TELLS RUPERT THE POSITION OF OSCAR PENRAVEN—THE COINERS—GASCOIGNE'S PLEASURE IN DANGER—THE COMPACT—RUPERT DREADNOUGHT GIVES GASCOIGNE A GREAT SURPRISE—THE LEGACY BEGINS TO BE DISPOSED OF—THE VISIT TO TOM BRAXLEY—THE LOVERS—HAPPY HEARTS.

On the first evening after Rupert reaching his own house, he received a visit from an old friend.

This was Gascoigne.

The police-spy seemed in better health now than ever.

"Well, my lord," he said, after the usual greetings were over, "two things have occurred since you have been away which will interest you."

"Indeed! What are they?"

"In the first place, Alford, or, rather, Richard Penraven, and Lesbia Howard, are married."

"Another happy couple," thought Rupert.

"Well," he said, "I am glad to hear it. Stanley Sherrington also has found a wife on his travels, and has married her right off. But what is your second piece of news? Have *you* also been to the altar with some fair dame?"

Gascoigne laughed.

"No, no," he said; "while I am free I will remain so. The second piece of news concerns you."

"Concerns me?"

"Yes," replied Gascoigne; "I have found, I fancy, a clue to the whereabouts of Oscar Penraven."

The blood rushed more rapidly through our hero's veins at these words.

Now, indeed, he might have a chance of ending his adventurous life.

"Well," he said, "this is, indeed, good news, the more so because I am sure that your eyes are seldom deceived."

"Very seldom," returned Gascoigne. "when my hate is so concerned. Oscar Penraven, the man who sought my life—sought it as a cowardly assassin, and tried to take it about the command of his horrid Society, will never be free from my search—never escape me when I find him, no matter what disguise he may assume. No, no, I am certain I am on the right scent."

"I am glad, indeed, to hear it," cried Rupert. "I have been never heartily concerned in any of the adventures in which I have been engaged as I have in this one. This assassin—this thorough villain, however, is hardly worthy to meet his death by the sword of an honest man."

"He may meet it now by the hands of the hangman," returned Gascoigne. "The deeds of which he and his companions have been guilty, are such as to leave beyond a doubt their conviction, and the sentence would be the death of a felon. But before I explain to you precisely what I mean, I must tell you what my late researches have told me."

"Sit down, then," said Rupert; "drink a glass of wine, and speak on."

Gascoigne did as requested.

Then he said—

"Oscar Penraven, you must understand, is a thoroughly ruined man.

"This his strange life among the wreckers must have told you.

"A man with any prospect of money would never in his senses have joined so desperate a band of ruffians.

"The Society of Poisoners was secret, silent, treacherous in its action.

"There was every prospect of *not* being discovered.

"The other speculation was a far different one.

"It was a bold, reckless game, fit only for men driven to the last extremity.

"Coming to London, he made acquaintance, as you know, with Everard Dalby.

"Through him he hoped to have his revenge, aye, and secure also a large sum of money.

"He failed in this, and became desperate.

"Desperate men fall into strange company.

"When he leaped from your window, and stood in the street below, he stood there free truly, but without a friend in the world.

"When I say friend, I mean some one who would assist him.

"A 'friend' such a man as Oscar Penraven never could have possessed.

"He went hence furious at defeat and——"

Rupert interrupted him.

"You say he went 'hence?'" he cried. "You mean, then, that *he* was the pretended hawker?"

"Yes."

"I thought as much. Well, proceed; I begin to be interested."

"Well," continued Gascoigne, "he rushed away and made his way towards that desperate locality where Allan of the Glen met you, and you so generously fought to save his life.

"There he entered a low tavern, where upon former occasions he had met some villanous characters, engaged by the Poisoners' League to do the dirtiest of their dirty work, and threw himself recklessly into a scene of hideous debauchery.

"Mad with wine, he let loose his tongue, and said and did many things which, perhaps, in his soberer senses he would never have been guilty of.

"At any rate he must have told them that he was badly off, or they would have never known that he was in a position when so desperate a proposition would find favour in his eyes.

"The men who spoke to him were coiners, and their place of work is well known to me."

"How did you discover them?"

Gascoigne smiled.

"In my usual way," he answered.

"Your usual way?"

"Yes; I am one of them."

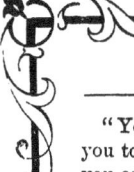

"You brave dangers as if it were a pleasure to you to do so," said Rupert: "and are you certain you are not suspected?"

"I am not only *not* suspected, but I am one of the most trusted in all the band."

"And you are, of course, certain then that Oscar Penraven is one of the number?" said Rupert.

Gascoigne shook his head.

"My eyes rarely deceive me, as I have before told you, and my sense of hearing makes up for any deficiencies they may possess. The man I believe to be Oscar Penraven is seared and seamed about the face as if he had passed through some terrible fire. But his voice is the voice of Oscar, his form is the form of Oscar."

"And what is your proposition? Do you mean to deliver them over to the authorities?" asked Rupert Dreadnought.

"Not at present," answered the police spy. "I care little for delivering up a few wretched, half-fed, miserable beings to the police that they may be hanged. Only if Oscar be there would there be any satisfaction in my mind. Besides, you seem to forget *one* thing."

"What is that?"

"That though my feeling of hatred and revenge against Oscar Penraven is very great, yet *you* are more concerned in his destruction even than I. Unless *you* have a hand in it you do not fulfil the terms of your vow to your father!"

Rupert heaved a sigh.

"You speak truly," he said; "but in what way can I assist you, seeing that it is you that have discovered his whereabouts and his mode of life?"

"I have a proposition to make," returned Gascoigne. "I need scarcely say that it involves danger."

"From which," said Rupert, "I never shrink."

"I know that of old," said Gascoigne. "Well, listen to me and I will tell you what I propose. It is no child's play, I can assure you; yet if you are guided by me you will incur no danger.

"On the second night from this, you and I, disguised as street ruffians, must take our way to the tavern of which I have spoken.

"We must mix unreservedly with the company, and I will introduce you to them as a friend of mine whom I advise them to secure as one of their members.

"You will then be enrolled a member, and we shall have to enter their workshops.

"There you must preserve the strictest silence, and not even if Oscar Penraven comes before you face to face must you express surprise or pleasure."

Rupert smiled.

"You are schooling me," he said, "as if I had never before gone through such scenes. Fear not, I shall not betray anything."

"All I wish to know is that Oscar Penraven is really a member," answered Gascoigne. "We can hardly fail—both of us—in tracing him."

"True; but there is one point in the programme to which I object."

"Name it, then."

"It is this," said Rupert; "through life I think I have endeavoured to act honourably."

"You have."

"You must not ask me to act dishonourably."

Gascoigne flushed.

"Why do you suspect me? Have *I* ever acted towards *you* dishonourably?"

"Not so; but it seems to *me* that this plan involves dishonour."

"Explain it, then, for I would be the last one to wish you to act in any way contrary to your ideas of what is fair and right."

"I am convinced of it," said Rupert. "What I mean, however, is this: in order to enter the workshops of these coiners it will be necessary to take some oath."

"Undoubtedly."

"An oath not to betray them?"

"Yes."

"Then, miserable cheats as they are, I could not take an oath to them, and then perjure myself by betraying them to justice."

"I admire you for it," said Gascoigne, "although it strikes me that among such villains you are over nice. But I do not ask you to act in any way the part of a traitor. I do not wish, as I told you before, to deliver such a wretched set of half-starved fellows to the tender mercies of the law. I simply wish to ascertain whether Oscar Penraven is really among their number."

"And then?"

"We will seize him."

"Good; I am perfectly willing to do that. When is the night?"

"The second night from this."

"I will be ready. You will call for me, and bring the disguise?"

"I will."

He held out his hand and grasped Rupert's, when the latter said, suddenly—

"By the way, Gascoigne, how do you stand for money?"

"I am not overburdened," said the police spy. "I am not now in the pay of the government, and earn very little."

"In that case," said Rupert, "you will not be insulted if I offer you some. I have had a strange legacy, the particulars of which I shall keep to myself; but, at any rate, it will enable me to make handsome presents to my friends. Here, in this purse, are bank-notes for one thousand pounds."

Gascoigne started back.

"A thousand pounds!" he cried; "surely you are jesting?"

"Indeed, no," said Rupert: "take them, and be assured you are welcome. You have more than once aided me in desperate plans, and, more than that, have saved my life. What I give now is but a poor return for all I owe you."

Gascoigne smiled as he took the purse.

"Well," he said, "I shall now retract what I implied in my words just now."

"What was that?"

"You said that I should get married."

"Yes."

"And I said that I was free, and would remain so."

"True."

"I said that because I was poor, and saw no way to get rich. Now, through your munificent gift, all

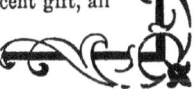

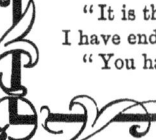

is changed. Once my vengeance is satisfied, I shall marry the one I love, and leave for ever the shores which have been productive to me of nothing but misery. Farewell, generous friend. At eight o'clock on the second evening from this, expect me."

That evening Rupert, having enclosed to Stanley Sherrington a splendid wedding present, took his way towards the house of Tom Braxley's mother.

He knew well that here he should find Tom and Allan.

Nor was he wrong.

As he approached the house and peeped through the curtain, he saw that not only were those there whom he sought, but Mary Macpherson and Agnes too.

The pair of lovers were sitting by the fire without lights, and indulging in those soft nothings and caresses that lovers do indulge in, innocent of all idea that any one was observing them.

Circumstances seemed combining against Rupert Dreadnought.

Everything he saw and heard appeared, as it were, specially designed to remind him of his own loneliness, and the manner in which he was fettered.

"Well, well," he said to himself, ere he knocked, "I suppose that all those around me are to be made happy first, and *my* turn is to come second."

A knock startled the lovers, and, quickly lighting a lamp, they opened the door.

An exclamation of surprise and pleasure burst from each lip at seeing him.

Rupert Dreadnought was always a welcome friend.

"I hope I am not intruding," he said, as he entered.

"How can you think so, my lord?" said Allan of the Glen, while the others eyed him deprecatingly.

"Well, I bring you good news," he added, as he took a seat with them by the fire. "Master Stanley Sherrington is married; so are Mistress Howard and Master Richard Penraven, and I propose now that you, also, should follow their example."

There was a good deal of blushing on the part of the two girls while their lovers said—

"Well, *we* have no objection."

"I, for one," added Tom Braxley, "am quite ready. I don't suppose I shall ever be any better off, and, therefore, if Agnes is willing to take me as I am, for richer, for poorer, I'll marry her to-morrow."

The only reply from Agnes was a sweet smile.

Allan, on *his* part, looked dejected.

"You see, my lord," he said, "I am at present but a soldier of fortune. I have nothing but my sword to depend on. I have as yet not earned enough to carry me through the world if I have a wife depending on me."

"Well, well," said Rupert, "I will remedy all this for you. I have had a most singular legacy left me, and I intend to devote it to the good of those who have served me well. Here, my friends, are two purses; they each contain bank-notes to the extent of two thousand pounds. Go, and be married at once; for, until you set me the example, I believe I shall never get the chance myself."

So saying, he placed the purses on the table.

Then, ere his half-stupefied hearers could understand what he meant, he had quitted the room.

"Now," he murmured, "as I have made them all happy, I might as well be happy myself; so I will go and see Helen."

CHAPTER XXIX.

A SHORT PERIOD OF HAPPINESS—THE PARTING—EN ROUTE FOR THE COINERS' HOME—THE TAVERN—THE JOVIAL THIEVES—THE CAPTAIN OF THE GANG—THE SECRET DOOR—THE SUBTERRANEAN CORRIDOR—THE WORKSHOPS OF THE COINERS—THE ALARM—RUPERT IS SUSPECTED TO BE A TRAITOR AND A SPY—OSCAR IS MISSING—THE DESPERATE CONFLICT.

THE time passed quickly enough.

Although Rupert was eager for the arrival of the moment when he should start on his mission against Oscar, yet the time rushed by as it rarely does with those who wait and watch.

The puzzle is easily solved.

All his time was spent with Helen.

"I begin to think your father's will somewhat cruel," said Helen. "You have no one by your side to comfort you in distress—no one to share with you your joy and woe. How much better would it have been had I been your wife!"

"True, dearest Helen," said Rupert; "and yet, even I, in spite of myself, see a good element in it. I have had to endure unexampled hardships, and incur unexampled dangers. Why, then, should I have selfishly married you, and run the risk of leaving you a widow? Why destroy your young life when another might——"

A soft hand, pressed over his mouth, stopped him.

"Speak not like that, dear Rupert," said Helen; "my love for you, as you ought to know, admits of no thought for another. Had I been your wife but for a day, I would never have married again."

Then, with a loving embrace, the lovers parted, and Rupert arrived at his house just in time to receive Gascoigne.

The latter was in high spirits.

The money which Rupert had so unexpectedly presented to him, had enabled him to do what he had long since given up as hopeless.

Strange-looking, and advancing in years as he was, he had taken a fancy to a little widow more gifted, perhaps, with fascinations than good looks, and he had proposed and been accepted.

He was, as may be imagined, therefore, in the seventh heaven of delight, and was in high spirits apparently, even at the prospect of the dangerous task before him.

The disguises were certainly wonderful.

Rupert was completely transformed.

He wore a stubbly wig, a patch over one eye, a wide-tailed ragged coat, a loose pair of slovenly breeches, and high jack-boots, while his long, unwieldy sword and begrimed face, made him seem like an Alsatian bully.

Gascoigne was equally transformed.

He looked stouter and fatter than was his wont; and thus disguised they started.

The tavern towards which they bent their steps had been designated by Gascoigne as low.

It was far worse.

It was a horrid den of iniquity.

The landlord and the landlady both were specimens of hideous depravity.

They looked what they were.

Batteners upon crime.

The company at the bar was like them.

Ragged, grimy, sallow, drunken.

Men and women stood there to fight, to quarrel, to blaspheme.

And within, the same style of people sat—the same kind of language was indulged in.

But they were more quiet.

They swore none the less, but they did it in an undertone.

When Rupert and Gascoigne entered, there was a slight hush.

But, in a language which was utterly unintelligible to Rupert, Gascoigne spoke, and the men greeted our hero vociferously, and the conversation and drink was resumed freely.

It seemed that one of their number had died off suddenly, and there was need of another.

This was the reason that Gascoigne anticipated no trouble in securing a place for Rupert as one of them.

"Well," said one of the men, turning to our hero, "so you've come to join us, eh?"

"That I have," returned Rupert, in a voice as gruff as he could assume, "and, as I am a new one, why, I may as well pay for some drink. I am not joining because I'm in such terrific want of money, but because I don't want to run short when I've got through all I've got."

With these words, he was about to ring the bell, when the man started up.

"I'll go and fetch it," he said.

Rupert placed a gold piece in his hand, and the fellow at once quitted the room, returning, after a moment, with an immense can of ale.

"Here's the change," he said.

He handed Rupert some silver, suspiciously bright and clean, and our hero placed it in his pocket with the certainty that he had his first share of bad money.

Under the influence of the replenished beer, the men gradually began to become very jovial.

But suddenly all merriment ceased.

The door had opened to admit a young man of handsome countenance, dressed, too, in fashionably-made clothes in excellent condition.

He was greeted with acclamation.

"This, then," thought Rupert, "is the leader."

He was not wrong.

This man, well-dressed, and belonging, as he did, to a class superior to those around him, was the head of the coiners.

He was bold, quick-sighted, always ready at an emergency, and was admired, almost loved by his followers, whom he had raised, by his criminal aptitude, to a position superior to what they had ever held before.

"Here you are then, captain," said one. "We've a new hand here."

"Ah!" cried he, glancing round rapidly, and at once picking Rupert out. "Let us hope he's a good man and true."

"I'll answer for him," cried Gascoigne. "Besides, he will have to take the oath."

"True," laughed the leader, "the oath is enough to keep any man to his work. Well, are we all here?"

"No," returned the man who had first spoken. "Two have gone in already to get the fires ready."

"That is right," said the captain, "that is right. Ah! I see you have some beer there; let me have some."

"My friend paid for it," said Gascoigne, "so you'd best drink his health, captain. He's a good one at spending his money while he's got it."

"He's like all of us for that, then," said the jovial leader of the coiners. "Well, here's your health, my man, and may we find you no traitor."

And so saying, he drank off an immense tankard of ale.

"If I came here to betray any one," thought Rupert, "*you* would be the one, *you* only who lead men less educated than yourself into evil ways."

But little time was given for the indulgence of reflection.

The men, having finished their beer, rose up.

Then the leader went to the door which led into the public bar, closed it, and held it fast, while one of the men touched a spring in the wall.

In an instant a dark aperture was observed, for a panel had sprung back instantaneously.

"You must lead the way, friend," said Rupert, in his disguised voice; "it's as dark as pitch, and I know nothing of the place.

"You'll soon get used to it," returned Gascoigne. "There are six steps and then a long uninterrupted passage. Follow me; it's quite safe."

So saying, he unhesitatingly entered the dark opening.

The captain was the last to follow.

When he came, he closed the door behind him, and until they had reached the bottom of the steps they were in complete darkness.

Then, however, they felt a hot air, and they could discern a small fiery spot in the distance.

"These are the workshops," said Gascoigne, "we shall soon be there."

In a very few minutes they had reached the spot of light, which grew larger and larger as they approached it.

Then a curious scene presented itself.

It was a subterraneous place, evidently the disused cellars of some house, and in the glow of great fires two men were working.

We need not describe the details of the place.

There were the usual appliances for coining—the moulds and dies, and so on, and in a few moments the ragged crew had settled to their work.

Then the captain took Rupert and Gascoigne aside and dictated the words of an oath.

A terrible oath it was.

An oath that Rupert almost shrank from.

But he could not.

He was in the clutches of his enemies as it were.

He must act his part to the letter.

So he repeated the words after the chief, who was about to give him his work, when a sudden outcry was heard without.

"Hush!" cried the captain, in a voice of authority, "stop all work; something is wrong. I trust we are not betrayed!"

And so saying he looked steadfastly at Rupert Dreadnought.

Rupert spoke at once.

"Do not suspect me," said he, "if I had betrayed you I should not have thus thrust myself into the lion's den. Besides, such a thing is impossible. I knew nothing, before this night, of your place of work or your doings except the few hints given me by my friend here when he enrolled me."

"It was but a passing thought," returned the captain, "I do *not* suspect you. But let me count. Are we all here?"

He counted.

"No," he cried, "one is missing. If this noise bodes evil to us we have been sold by him to the enemy. Who is the absentee?"

"The one who calls himself Oscar," replied one of the men.

"Ah!" said Gascoigne, "I knew by that man's face he was a traitor. I know him well, and so does my friend here; if he is absent, and the officers are upon us, I will swear that he is the traitor."

"Why did you not apprise us of it before, then?" said the captain, who was, evidently, in a state of intense excitement, though no fear was visible in his face. "You hear the noises increase, though what they result from, or what they forebode for us, I cannot say."

"I was not sure of his identity," said Gascoigne. "I thought I knew his voice, but his face was so disfigured since I saw him last, that I could not have sworn to him. Now, however, if his name is Oscar, and he has betrayed you, I will swear to him. But, hark!—there is no time for talk—the noise is louder and louder. I cannot understand it—what can it be?"

They all listened.

For some time nothing was heard.

The noise seemed to stop with Gascoigne's words.

Then it commenced again.

All work was stopped.

"We had better return to the inn, and escape," said the captain.

No sooner said than done.

All hurried towards the entrance of the subterranean passage.

Rupert was not the last to fly.

He saw his difficulty.

If discovered in the company of such a set of villains in disguise, too, what would be said?

That he, in spite of his rank and wealth, had consented to place himself in such a position would never be believed; and, being, therefore, one of these wretched crew, for the time, he resolved to act as one.

On reaching the secret door which led into the back room of the "Bull's Head" all seemed quiet within.

They opened the door, therefore, and passed in.

All was still until every one of them had entered.

Then everything was changed.

In an instant a rush was made from the door which opened in the bar, and a number of armed officers rushed into the room.

The captain of the coiners burst into a loud laugh, as, coolly, and with one stern glance at his followers, he sat down in a seat by the fire.

"Ha, ha!" he cried. "Ha, ha! I had thought we Alsatians, as they call us, were the ones to go mad, not the officers of justice. Have you lost a man who has stole a penny, or has some hungry woman taken a loaf? or has some poor bastard, left by its parents, presumed to beg a penny? So ho ruffian, take your hand off me, or it may chance you will have supper with your ancestors."

The latter words were uttered fiercely, as the head of the invading party seized his arm, and in return for the compliment, was hurled full ten feet away.

Then the captain sprang to the floor.

"What means all this?" he shouted. "Friends, draw your swords. Are peaceful men to be disturbed when they are having their glass?"

"Come; no folly," said the chief of the officers. "We arrest you and your gang as coiners. Resist, and it will be the worse for you."

"You are drunk or mad," said the captain, drawing his sword. "As a man who fears not the law, I defend myself. Friends, do likewise."

With these words he placed himself into position, and the others followed his example.

It can scarcely be said that Rupert Dreadnought did so reluctantly.

He had everything to lose by an exposure in such a position.

So he drew his sword like the rest.

Some of the men had no weapons.

But they readily provided themselves with them.

Bottles were seized by the neck, and dashed in the officers' faces.

The captain of the coiners was an accomplished fencer.

This could be seen by the way he handled his weapon.

The chief of the Bow Street Runners instantly singled him out as one he had better secure himself.

He, too, was a good swordsman.

The duel was a good one.

Little difference, indeed, was there between them.

They stood for a moment eyeing each other.

Then a fierce combat commenced.

There was no doubting that upon the issue of this combat depended the fate of the attack.

But still there was just room for a question to be asked as to the meaning of the assault.

"I do not know what is meant by all this," cried the captain, as he skilfully parried the strokes. "I suppose you are some disappointed officer of the law who attack peaceable people in order to secure somebody."

The Bow Street Runner was not in the least degree taken aback by this insolent speech.

He knew his antagonist.

"Feign no ignorance," he said, "you are Desmond Carderer, the chief of a band of desperate coiners. You are well known to the authorities, and this time you will pay the penalty of your crimes on the scaffold."

RUPERT OR THE DREADNOUGHT SECRETS OF THE IRON CHEST

OSCAR MEETS A MYSTERIOUS FOE.

A loud laugh escaped the lips of the captain of the coiners.

The words, too, seemed not only to rouse his merriment, but to make him fight more desperately.

He was cool as one engaged in an honourable duel.

His eye truly shot fire.

But it was the fire of courage.

He was in no way dismayed.

He knew his danger and fronted it.

And so they fought on.

Presently a laugh—a loud, chuckling laugh—announced that the captain had wounded his adversary.

"First blood to me; we win, my boys, we win," he cried. "Now, then, at them; let none escape but ourselves. Those who are buried can scarcely rise up to accuse us. At them!"

And then, as if rendered more desperate by his own words, he made a more fierce lunge at his adversary.

The Bow Street Runner, who was a tall, fine, handsome young fellow, parried the stroke.

But in vain.

His sword seemed to slide up the blade of his adversary.

Then he uttered a yell of pain, and the captain's sword rushed through his heart.

The tables were turned now.

All was confusion.

Those who had bottles and no other weapons fought as if they had swords and pistols.

Loud cheers rang through the room.

In spite of himself, Rupert had to join in the fierce melee.

He had, as I have said, no desire to be taken.

Especially in such company.

There was little fear of it, however.

The Bow Street Runners reckoned upon an easy success.

They were deceived.

Ragged, hungry men, who think they have wealth before them, do not pause to think *how* to fight.

They fight any way.

And the way these fought was like demons.

The Bow Street Runners then found themselves nowhere.

And finding this, they at last thought of retreating.

But it was now useless.

They were in a net.

To get out of it they understood no way except surrender.

This was against the grain.

But what could they do?

"We surrender!" they cried.

No answer.

No answer, I mean, but sword-thrusts and fiercer blows.

They knew what this meant.

Death and no quarter!

This roused them to a still fiercer resistance.

"On, my men!" cried one, more daring than the rest. "We have offered to surrender; they have refused to accept it. Let them have cause to regret it. Let them see that we can beat a set of thieves and assassins. On, friends, on!"

They answered as well as they were able to their comrade's call.

But in vain.

The day was not with them now.

And, more than this, they saw that, fight as they might, they would receive no mercy.

This made an uncomfortable feeling arise in their breasts.

It was bad enough at first.

It became worse when they saw that the outer door was closed, and that no exit was left them.

The certainty was a dread one.

Again, from more than one mouth rang out the word—

"Surrender!"

Still no answer.

Rupert saw now what it would be.

A fearful massacre!

Fighting himself against odds, he managed at last to get near the side of the chief.

"This is unnecessary bloodshed, is it not?" he asked.

The captain's eyes were ablaze with rage and excitement.

"Unnecessary! no," he said. "If we leave one to tell the tale, our lives are not worth a straw. No, no, we must fight on and kill."

This was too much for Rupert.

"Then I for one will fight no more," he cried, resolutely.

"Nor I," said Gascoigne.

"This is rank treachery!" exclaimed the captain, furiously.

"It is not," said Rupert; "it is best for you. If all these men are killed, where will you be able to show your face? You may achieve a trifling triumph now, but you must know that the law is the strongest in the end."

"Well, there is another gone to his account," cried the captain, fiercely, as his bright blade leaped through a fellow's heart. "Give in, my men—they have had enough, and surrender."

The fight at once ceased.

No sooner had the sounds of strife ceased, than there came a furious knocking at the door.

"This comes of taking other's advice," said the captain, sullenly. "Who's there?"

The question was answered by the landlord's pushing his way in.

He pretended to have only just heard the noise.

Poor, innocent soul!

He had heard nothing of the reason why the officers came.

Of course not!

He knew nothing of the coining or anything of the kind.

"If gentlemen," as he told the head of the Bow Street Runners, "if gentlemen rent a private room and pay for it, I've no right to ask what they require it for. Certainly not. Secret doors and passages in *my* house! Absurd, sir—preposterous! Go yourself and find them!"

But, as we have seen, he found his death instead.

"Dear me!" cried Boniface, "what is this all about?"

"These persons interfered with us while we were drinking," said the captain, "and it came to blows. The result is evident to you. Three of them are dead. The others have surrendered, and desire to speak with us in private. To this, doubtless, you have no objection."

A nod, they say, is as good as a wink to a blind horse.

The landlord required no more.

He knew his game at once.

He went out and closed the door.

"Now," said the captain, leaning on his sword, "now, my men, listen to me."

He was addressing not his own men but the Bow Street Runners.

"You have fought well," he said, "but you know that you have had the worst of the contest, and, had we not accepted your surrender, you would now be numbered with the dead. Well, now you are still in our power to kill or save, swear not to betray us—swear that you will go hence knowing nothing of us, our faces or our haunts, or you will die now."

There was no choice left them.

What could they do?

A moment's consultation, and then one of them said—

"We swear."

"Good," said the captain, "then you are free to go."

As he spoke the door opened from without, and they saw their way clear before them.

"Take your dead with you," cried the coiner; "we want none of your carrion here. Quick!—remove them—I like not the sight of dead men!"

"That is true," he said, turning to Rupert, when the officers had departed with their ghastly burdens. "I like not to see dead men. While I am fighting—while they are opposing me with fire in their eyes and fierce words upon their lips, then I can fight and kill; but they are ghastly things to gaze on when the spirit is fled!"

Then he leaned over, and said, in a low whisper,

"You see I took your advice."

"Yes."

"I trusted you."

"Yes."

"And why?"

"That is more than I can tell," said Rupert Dreadnought.

"I will tell you, then," said the captain. "You are not what you seem. You are not here to betray us; but you come for some purpose besides coining. But now there is no time to talk. We will get ourselves in safety, and then you and I will talk, that is, if it be agreeable to you."

"Yes," said Rupert, who, in spite of the criminality of his strange companion, felt a kind of interest in him, "yes, I will see you after all is over."

A smile of satisfaction crossed the face of the coiner.

"Good," he said, in a whisper.

"And now, my men," he added, in a loud voice, "you have fought well and bravely; you shall have your reward. Not one of our number, I think, is dead?"

"Not one."

"Are any seriously wounded?"

"Yes; Alexander."

"Very well. To every man shall be given this night a hundred pieces of our gold coinage, and five real coins, for his courage and trustworthiness; to Alexander a hundred and fifty and ten real coins. Now follow me. Ask no questions, however strange my actions may appear. We will beat the authorities, we will keep still our workshops, and yet they will find no clue. But all our doings must be secret, even from the landlord of this house. We know not what he might do were his neck in the noose."

A buzz of assent was the answer, and the captain at once approached the secret door.

"Follow me," he said, as he dived once more into the darkness, "and close the door behind you."

The men willingly did as they were bid.

They seemed to have perfect confidence in their leader, and Rupert Dreadnought, for his own safety's sake, was compelled to act in unison with them.

When all were on the steps, and the door was once more closed, the captain said—

"Three of you stop here and guard the door; the rest follow me."

Then he hurried away.

On arriving at the workshops, he commenced operations himself, giving his instructions rapidly all the time.

"See these piles of bricks," he said, "this mortar and tools? Carry them to the secret door. We will brick it up so that none can pass through. It is but a small aperture, and we will build against it so solid a wall that they shall not find any hollow sound on trying it. You know now what I mean, so work with a will."

"We shall be burying ourselves alive," murmured one of the men.

The captain paused a moment in his work, and eyed him sternly.

"What! grumbling in the hour of danger!" he cried. "Have I ever deceived you? Have I ever betrayed you, that now, when delay is dangerous, you would refuse to do as I bid you?"

"No, no," said the man, "no, no, I'll leave it all to you, though I must say it's a rum start."

And, having delivered himself of this peculiar expression of opinion, set to work willingly.

By dint of immense exertions, the work was completed in two hours.

Up to this time no effort had been made to attack them again.

"I had thought that, in spite of their oaths, those fellows would betray us," said the captain, wiping the big drops from his forehead, as they returned to the workshop; "but we've fogged them, at any rate, for a time."

Then he went to a cupboard, opened it, and drew out an immense stone bottle and a glass.

"In case of emergencies," he said, tapping it playfully.

Then he handed glasses round of some strong spirit, which had most likely never paid duty.

Having thus revived the energies of his men, he said—

"And now you will see how secretly I have thought of the safety of all of us."

With these words he crossed the workshop, and stooped down in a corner.

Then, as he rose up, a part of the wall seemed to rise in the air.

It was another secret panel working a different way.

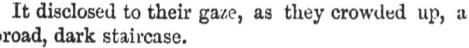

It disclosed to their gaze, as they crowded up, a broad, dark staircase.

"Now," he said, "follow me. There is no fear of discovery here."

The men, with Rupert and Gascoigne, at once followed in surprise.

Then the chief closed the door, and running up in advance, led the way to a second door, admitting to a broad corridor, well lighted by frequent candelabras.

At the door of a room he halted, and ere he could open it, a lovely girl, of some eighteen summers, flew out to meet him.

She started back on seeing the crowd of rough-looking men.

"Be not alarmed, Ada," he said, "these are only some workmen who have been repairing the cellar. Run in; I will be with you in a moment."

He gently pushed her through the open door, and closed it.

Then he said—

"Now, my men, listen. I will be with you to-morrow evening at the 'Rising Sun' in Eastchepe, when we can make arrangements for the future. In the meantime, here are bags containing the gold I promised. Be careful how you use it."

"Then, turning to Gascoigne and Rupert, he added—

"With you I would have a word in private, if you will not object."

"Certainly not," said Rupert, who began to feel a kind of interest in the strange man.

"And," said the captain, "as I am going to take you into the room where that lady is whom you saw just now, I will take you to my bed-chamber, where you can rearrange your costume a little, and wash off the false wrinkles which now deform your face."

For an instant Rupert thought—

"Am I discovered and betrayed?"

But in an instant the suspicion vanished.

He had liberty to go if he chose, and besides, the way in which the words were said was only a bantering one.

"Well, I will confess I am not what I have professed to be, but, nevertheless, I am no traitor. I came not here to betray you."

"I never suspected it," said the coiner; "but, come, follow me."

And with these words he led the way to the door of a sumptuously furnished bed-chamber.

Agreeably to the instructions of this strange man, Rupert removed his disguise, which was only placed over his ordinary costume, and removed the artificial colour and wrinkles that disfigured his face.

The captain laughed heartily at the transformation.

"You will give me credit," he said, "for being a tolerably good judge of character."

"Yes," said Rupert, "better than myself."

The meaning glance with which he uttered these words, did not escape the captain.

"What mean you?" he asked.

"That meeting you under other circumstances I should have been deceived in you."

"Ah, I see!" said the captain, "we must have mutual explanations. Come. You are both ready now. Let us enter the room where I am so anxiously awaited. Whom shall I introduce?"

He turned to Gascoigne as he spoke.

"Richard Gascoigne, Bow Street Runner," replied that worthy, with a smile.

The captain's hand flew to his sword.

"I am betrayed then?"

"Not so. When we have told you all, you will understand it. I am here in my private character."

"And you," said he, to Rupert.

"Lord Rupert Dreadnought!"

"Well," said the coiner, "I am bound to hear of wonders this night. But come, gentlemen, as you have introduced yourselves to me, I will introduce you to my wife."

CHAPTER XXX.

CARDERER'S STORY.

"Lord Rupert Dreadnought and Master Richard Gascoigne Mistress Carderer."

So went the introduction.

Ada Carderer was a lovely creature.

Evidently she knew it.

Evidently, too, she did what all women should do; that is to say, she dressed to look her best to her husband.

She was attired in a tight-fitting, blue dress, low in the neck, and displaying a tempting picture—a soft, white bosom, over which the bright locks wandered caressingly.

Her features were perfect, her figure everything that could be desired, and the glance she cast upon her husband as he entered, plainly told that if strangers had not been present, she would have cast her arms around his neck, and nestled up to his breast.

Another thing, too, was evident.

She knew nothing of his vocation.

To her, at least, he was pure.

On the table were preparations for a sumptuous repast.

"Now, my friends," cried Carderer, as he took his place at the head of the table, "now, my friends, eat, drink, and be merry, and, after our supper, my wife will leave us alone, and we can compare notes."

A jolly supper it was.

Somehow or another, in spite of the fact that their host was nothing less than a coiner, neither Gascoigne nor Rupert could entertain anything but a friendly feeling towards him.

There seemed good points about him which told of the possibility of reformation.

The meal at length was over.

Then Carderer leaned over, and whispered to his wife.

She at once rose with a smile.

Among other things, she had evidently learned to obey.

"Good-night, gentlemen," she said, sweetly.

And then, with a pretty curtsey, she quitted the room.

"Your wife is a most lovely lady," said Rupert.

"Lovely indeed!" echoed Gascoigne.

Carderer laughed.

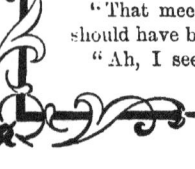

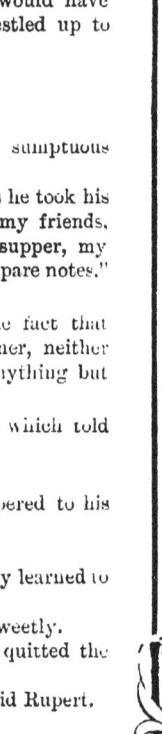

For the first time they had heard him laugh an unnatural laugh.

Evidently hard and forced it was.

"Aye; she *is* lovely," he said, "there are few who do not acknowledge that. She is far too lovely and good for me. But come, friends, now we are alone let us hear your story. Fill up your glasses and proceed. I must consider myself highly honoured. It is not often I entertain a lord and a Bow Street Runner."

Briefly, and without reservation, Rupert told the story of his life, and explained to the coiner the reason why he had sought to join the band.

"Well," said Carderer, "I congratulate myself on my discernment."

"How so?"

"I knew you were not informers, and yet I knew, in spite of your excellent disguises, that you were not what you seemed to be, or rather what you desired to appear. Well, you were right; the villain who is your deadliest foe is the traitor who betrayed us to the authorities. But," he added, while a cold glitter came into his eyes, and a cruel smile played over his mouth, "we shall take a deadly revenge upon him."

"But how will you secure him?"

Carderer laughed.

"It is a certainty," he said.

"But how?"

"Ah! that is *my* secret," replied the coiner; "but depend upon it that we have a machinery at work which makes it a deadly and a dangerous thing to play tricks with us."

"Well," said Rupert, "now that I have made a kind of confession, you will now oblige us with *your* story. I long to know why a person like yourself should, as it seems, willingly accept such a position as you now hold—a criminal, and a dangerous one."

Carderer laughed.

More genially this time.

"Well," he said, "you are not complimentary. Why should you be?"

"No, indeed," returned Rupert. "Why should I in any way act so as to induce you to continue in such a life?"

"True, true, my friend, I am not offended, and in telling you my story, I will endeavour as far as possible to avoid details which would annoy you.

"I shall, in fact, cut it as short as I possibly can.

"I was born in Cornwall.

"I am a second son.

"That is enough to show that I am a child of misfortune.

"In some cases, of course, it is not so.

"But when there is property it always is.

"Well, I was no favourite at home.

"My mother died early.

"My father was a brute.

"My eldest brother was all he cared for.

"I openly told my father so once, and he struck me.

"Then my blood rose.

"All my worst passions were roused within my breast.

"I spat upon the floor, and quitted the house, vowing never to return.

"He died soon after, and I, poor and forlorn, read his will.

"Not one penny was left to me.

"My brother enjoyed the whole.

"I saw him, and being wellnigh destitute, I asked him for assistance.

"He laughed at me.

"I left the house cursing him.

"But retribution was at hand.

"My brother was, and had always been, a great gambler.

"Loss after loss fell upon him.

"His young wife died, his child died, and he became a worse gambler and a worse drunkard than ever.

"At length he has come to that strait that he must sell his estate.

"*I*, aye, *I*, have arranged to buy it, and I shall pay him all in false coin.

"*That* is what my workshops are open for.

"Not to cheat the public.

"It is to punish him."

"But you will be discovered and hanged!" cried Rupert Dreadnought.

"Not so," returned the desperate man, "not so.

"My brother is even now hiding from justice, and wishes to fly the country.

"When he receives—all in gold, as he desires it—the amount of the sale money of the estate, he will leave England, and dare not return to it.

"It is abroad where he will be seized—abroad where he will receive the reward—the just reward of his iniquity."

Carderer's eyes glistened as he spoke.

An evil glitter it was.

"You know what his fate will be," said Gascoigne.

"Yes—death!"

"You are deliberately murdering him."

"Murdering him!" exclaimed Carderer, loudly; "no. He robbed *me*, and *I* am robbing *him*."

As he spoke there was a loud knock at the door.

Carderer started.

"Hark!" he said. "What was that?"

The knock was repeated more loudly.

"It is evidently some one in haste," said Rupert, who began instinctively to be possessed with a loathing of his companion, but who, nevertheless, had no wish for his own sake, and that of Gascoigne, to see the entrance of officers of the law.

Gascoigne, meanwhile, approached the window, and, throwing it open, looked out upon the silent street.

There was only one person at the door.

"What want you?" cried Gascoigne.

"Master Carderer."

"He is in bed."

"But I *must* see him."

"Is your business so important?"

"It is a matter of life or death."

"You hear," said Gascoigne, in a whisper to Carderer. "What am I to say?"

"Ask whence he comes."

"From whence come you?"

"From his brother, who is dying."

"Dying! Great Heaven!" exclaimed the wonder-stricken man. "I will admit him at once."

And he rushed frantically from the room.

"Well," said Rupert, as he passed out, "we have either to do with a great villain or a madman."

"Maybe both," said Gascoigne; "but I fancy that his troubles have turned his brain."

As he spoke, Carderer returned.

"Here's a letter," he said.

And, tearing it open, he read it eagerly, and aloud.

We need give but its substance.

His brother, in a drunken row, had been mortally wounded, and, sending for a priest and a lawyer, made his will, leaving all the ancestral property, which he declared to be wholly unencumbered, to his younger brother.

He was not yet dead, and he wished to see him before he died.

The effect on Carderer was immense.

He seemed crushed by good fortune.

"It is the finger of Heaven," he kept murmuring. "Providence has stepped in to save me."

He was roused by the man who brought the message.

"If you want to see him, you must be quick, sir," he said.

"Is he then so bad?"

"He is near death."

"He cannot well be worse, then," said Rupert. "You will go, of course, to see him?"

"Yes," said Carderer, who was as white as a sheet and seemed quite dazed; "I must go, though this sudden change of fortune comes upon me so suddenly, when I was in the midst of such sinful schemes, that I scarcely know what to say or do. I will trust in you. Will you accompany me?"

He looked both at Gascoigne and Rupert as he said this.

"Well," returned Rupert, "I have had misgivings in my heart of late whether I ought to have remained here so long after what I have heard from your own lips. But now, if this strange, and, indeed, almost miraculous event is really to have any effect upon you, if it will really make you see the error of your ways and endeavour to begin a new life, I have no objection to aid you."

"And, by heavens! I *will* try, I *will* do my best," said Carderer.

"And yet just now you were planning to bring about your brother's death," suggested Rupert.

Carderer made a gesture, as if putting away the thought from his mind.

"Don't speak of it, don't mention it," he cried, "it doesn't bear thinking of. But we must not remain here. He is dying, and I must be near him."

The next few moments were spent in rapid preparations.

Not a word was said to Ada.

What part she had played in the fraternal tragedy Rupert knew not.

At any rate it was Carderer's wish that she should know nothing, and so presently, without a word, they emerged from the house as secretly as possible, and followed the direction taken by their strange guide.

I shall not follow them now.

Before doing so I must pursue the fortunes of Oscar Penraven, and explain how that worthy was making his way in the world at this time.

CHAPTER XXXI.

THE MASKED INTRUDER—THE STRANGE DUEL—A WRETCHED BARGAIN—THE SCHEME FAILS—A A NEW COMPACT.

On quitting Rupert that night, baffled and beaten, he made the best of his way to his own lodging.

Gascoigne had given Rupert Dreadnought a pretty reasonable account of his doings.

But he did not know all.

He remained alone closeted in his room, drinking hard for three days.

At the end of this time he was about to go out, when the door opened, and a masked man entered.

The intruder strode so boldly in, that Oscar Penraven did not utter a word for a moment.

Then he said—

"Pray, sir, who are you? Do you know that this is my bed-room?"

The stranger uttered a dry laugh as he turned and closed the door.

"Yes," he said, "I know it is your room, and that is the reason I am here, as I wish to speak with you."

"And pray who are you?" cried Oscar Penraven, laying his hand on his sword.

"An officer of the watch."

"An officer of the watch!" returned Oscar, sneeringly. "I have no acquaintance among such worthies. Oblige me, therefore, by quitting the place, or I shall fling your dead carcase presently through yonder window."

The masked man laughed.

This exasperated Oscar.

He was inflamed with drink, and, after his ill success, he was in no humour to brook resistance in any way.

He drew his sword.

"I stand no insult from any man," he said. "Draw, for your life."

Again the irritating laugh.

"I will accommodate you willingly," said the masked intruder, "since you wish it."

And they crossed swords.

Both were skilful masters of the art of fence.

There was no apparent advantage.

A full quarter of an hour passed in a constant interchange of passes, without scarcely more than a scratch.

Then the officer drew back.

"This is great folly," he said.

"Why so?"

"This is not what I came for."

"Perhaps you came to arrest me," said Oscar Penraven, with a sneer.

"Not so."

"Then for what, in Heaven's name?"

"To put money in your pocket."

"For what?"

"For doing government a service."

"In what way?"

"I will explain. In the first place I may suggest that you are poor."

"I am. But how did you know it?"

The officer laughed.

"That is my secret," he said. "Well, in the second place your name is Oscar Penraven, and you have been brought up in the lap of luxury. Poverty is detestable to you as it is to all, but most so to men of your stamp."

"Well?"

"I can place in your hands the means of earning easily a large sum."

"Name them."

"I will. But you will incur danger."

"I like it."

"Then listen.

"There is in this metropolis at the present moment a gang of desperate coiners, whom we are at a difficulty to catch.

"They have up to this time defied all our efforts.

"We know their haunts, we know where they meet every night, but we cannot discover any clue to their workshops.

"Until we do this, of course all our efforts are useless.

"We cannot arrest men on suspicion simply, because if we were to do so, nothing could be made out against them, and they would inevitably be let off."

"True. Then what am *I* to do? Act the spy?"

"Something like it," said the masked officer. "I wish you to go to the head-quarters of the gang, which I will point out to you, and there, in the disguise of a poor man, make friends with them and join the band."

"And then betray them?"

"Precisely; though *I* do not use that word: I call it delivering them over to justice."

"And what is the reward?"

"On the day of capture five hundred pounds."

Oscar Penraven smiled.

"The government are good bargainers," he said, sneeringly.

"Why so?"

"They speak of reward when the capture is made. That does not lie in my hands at all. So that if you bungle over the matter, and fail in taking them, I get nothing. No, no, it is not good enough for me to risk my life for."

The masked man laughed.

"It is you who are the good bargainer," he said. "You wish to be *sure* of your reward. Very well. It shall be so. If you consent at once to undertake the affair, I will place in your hands fifty pounds."

The miserable bargain was accordingly struck, the rendezvous of the coiners pointed out to Oscar Penraven, and—we have seen the result.

The very man who had made the compact with the son of the old earl's deadliest foe was the first one who received his death wound at the hands of the captain of the gang.

The expedition having thus miserably failed, Oscar Penraven, of course, could claim no further reward, and for several days he heard nothing more either of spies or coiners.

On the fifth day he was walking along a narrow street, when he fell against one of the latter.

"Ah, Brotherton," he exclaimed.

The man started at the voice, and drew him beneath a lamp.

"Oscar the traitor!" he exclaimed, in a gasp of surprise, and holding him in a tight grasp.

"Traitor!" cried Oscar Penraven, in well-feigned astonishment. "What mean you?"

"Do not pretend to misunderstand me," said the man, savagely; "it is all known. It was you who sold us to the Bow Street Runners—it was you through whom the band was broken up."

Oscar Penraven shook him off.

"You're mad," he said; "I don't know what you are talking about. All *I* know is that I was ill the other night, and I could not come. The next night, when I went, I found that the Runners had been there, and that nothing had been seen of any of you. There's the extent of *my* information."

These words were spoken with such a show of earnestness, that the man was thoroughly deceived.

"Well, it's strange," he said, with a kind of growl, "very strange; we all set it down to *you*; at any rate, the band's broken up."

"How so?—where's the captain?"

"He saw us three nights ago at the 'Rising Sun' in Eastchepe, gave us some money, and said he was going to leave off the game altogether, and quit the country."

"Ah," said Oscar, "I see it all now. It is *he* who is the traitor."

"Impossible!"

"Not so; finding that the game had turned out a losing one, he has sold us all to the police for a large sum. Are you in want of money?"

"Yes, I have spent nearly all *my* share of the division."

"Well, we will break into the captain's house, and help ourselves to whatever he has obtained by his treachery."

"It's rather a dangerous game," said the other, doubtingly.

"Never mind," said Oscar; "nothing is done without danger. Say, will you join?"

"Yes," said the man, "I am not particular. In fact, I'd like anything that would enable me to leave the country. It's too hot to hold any of us, that's my opinion, for the Runners are on the watch for us everywhere."

"Well, to-morrow night I'll meet you anywhere you please; at this 'Rising Sun' you speak of will do. In the meantime, I will take notes, and make preparations for our scheme. And now, as it's very cold out here, I propose we go in somewhere and have something to drink."

They turned into the nearest tavern, drank some spirits, and, having once more made the appointment, separated for the night.

"I'll be deuced careful with that fellow," said the man called Brotherton; "I don't like him at all, and I shouldn't wonder if, even now, he's a spy of the Runners. Never mind, I'll be ready for him, and if he tries any treachery with me, why I'll send a bullet through his head in an instant. *He* shan't reap any benefit from spying, at any rate, if he comes it over *me*."

CHAPTER XXXII.

HOPES FOR THE FUTURE—THE WATCHER AT THE DOOR—A NEW SCHEME OF MURDER.

On the following night Carderer and his wife Ada were seated in their drawing-room.

His features were very stern and serious.

But yet there was no look of unhappiness upon them, rather a look of relief.

He had visited his brother on that night when his mind had been so full of bitter thoughts against him, and when so wonderful a change of fortune had fallen upon him.

He had found him hiding away in a wretched hovel.

It was termed an inn.

It was a wooden shed only just big enough and strong enough to contain the liquor and the wretched creature who drank it.

Here in an upper room they found him lying on a squalid bed, evidently near death.

He had received a sword thrust through his lungs, and the doctor gave no hope.

What was said between the brothers we need not detail here.

They are only passing characters in our story, with whom our hero came extraordinarily into contact.

Suffice it that as Carderer sat thus by the bedside holding his brother's cold hand, he prayed Heaven's forgiveness for his past evil and his evil thoughts, of which that Heaven had so strangely anticipated the result.

On this evening, then, he was sitting with his wife.

They had just finished supper, and had drawn up to the fire.

"Well, Ada," he said, "all my wonderful schemes are knocked on the head now. I shall no longer waste my time in the vain search after what is hidden in the deep recesses of nature. We shall go down to our country seat, and you will be what I always promised you—a lady."

Ada, then, knew nothing of her husband's guilty schemes!

She smiled sweetly.

"I am glad," she said, "for two reasons. I shall have more of your company, now that you have given up your mad plans; and then I love the country."

"Well, I shall be glad enough to escape from London myself," said Carderer: "and now that I have a large fortune at command, I shall not need to visit it often."

"And when do we start?"

"To-morrow."

"And is Carderer House a nice place?"

"If it is the same as it was in olden times," returned her husband, "it is a perfect gem of a place, full of rare paintings, and exquisite articles of *vertu*. However, we shall soon be there; I must go in the morning to the bank and get some money, for I have cleared myself out."

Little did he know what the effect of these last words were.

He never knew it.

But they saved his life!

During the whole of the conversation, a man, whose features were hidden beneath a crape mask, had been standing behind a curtain.

This was Oscar Penraven.

He had listened eagerly to the conversation, expecting to glean some information.

And he had done so.

Carderer had no money in the house.

To kill him, therefore, would be committing a useless murder.

So he motioned his companion, who stood without, to keep silence, and listened still more eagerly.

"I expect you will find the place in a sad state," said Ada.

"Why do you think so?"

"Because your brother, if he is so desperate a character as you have made him out to be, will, in all probability, have torn the place to pieces. Scenes of riot and debauchery cannot take place without destroying a house. But however, *I* will soon set the place in order again for you, dear Desmond."

And, with these words, she threw her arms round his neck, and kissed him fondly.

"Well, I trust in you in everything," said Carderer. "Whom, indeed, could I better trust? We will retire to rest now. It grows late, and I must be up early in the morning."

Hearing this, and seeing them rise, Oscar Penraven slunk away.

His companion was surprised.

"What means this?" he said. "Are you going away without doing anything?"

"Yes; let's get away quickly."

The man grumbled.

But it was of no use.

Oscar Penraven was bent on going.

They passed out of a back window, and into a back street.

Then Oscar's companion stopped doggedly.

"Now," he said, "what does this mean?"

Oscar explained hurriedly, and the man laughed chucklingly.

"You are a clever chap after all," he said. "Well, where have we got to go to when we *do* start?"

"Down in the country somewhere."

"Somewhere! that's not very clear."

"No; but to-morrow we will be on the watch. I've got plenty of money, and when we see them start, we'll follow in a post-chaise. But I tell you what, it will never do to go down in this guise. Here's five pounds. Get yourself dressed out like a gentleman, and meet me at the corner of this street at nine in the morning."

"Right," said the other, gleefully, "I'll be here to the moment."

And so he was.

At ten they saw Carderer go to the bank—at twelve he and Ada left in a private carriage.

Then entering the post-chaise which they had waiting at the corner, they followed on their errand of murder!

RUPERT OR THE DREADNOUGHT; OR THE SECRETS OF THE IRON CHEST

"CAUTIOUSLY HE ENTERED THE CHAMBER OF THE JEWELLER."

Oscar Penraven was at first overwhelmed with eagerness to rush after his prey.

But reflection showed him his error.

Precipitation might ruin all.

So he altered his plans.

Instead of proposing to himself the following up

of the carriage, he saw that the very fact of his doing so would excite, or at any rate run the risk of exciting, suspicion.

So he altered his tactics.

Putting his head out of window, he ordered the coachman to turn his horse's head and drive to the bank.

Banks were different things in those days.

Not great buildings, built up at the expense of credulous shareholders.

They were humble, modest edifices.

At the English bank the coach stopped, and Oscar Penraven leaped out.

He made his way unhesitatingly into the office.

Here he asked to see the chief clerk.

The old man came out, bowing and scraping.

"What is your pleasure?" he said.

"My friend, Desmond Carderer, banks here?" he said, inquiringly.

"He does."

Oscar Penraven smiled at the other's surprise.

"I do not ask from any idle curiosity," said he. "I merely desire to know his residence. I received a letter this day requesting me to come down and see him at his country house—Carderer House—and I have not the slightest conception where that is."

"Oh! if that is all, I can easily tell you," said the old clerk, bowing, and he at once wrote on a slip of paper the exact address:—

"Mr. Desmond Carderer,
"Carderer House,
"Near Ullarton,
"Bucks."

"You will know your road now," said he, as he handed the slip of paper to Oscar Penraven.

"Oh! perfectly."

"It is to be hoped that you will go by day, then," remarked the clerk, "for it is a shocking road at night. So bad is it, that I have heard the joke made, that *none but thieves and rogues go that way at all.*"

And the old man laughed at his own witticism.

Oscar Penraven laughed, too, though scarcely with so much zest.

"We mustn't say that, however," he exclaimed, with an appearance of mirth, "or we shall be including our friend, Carderer. Good morning."

"Curse the old fellow!" he muttered, as he re-entered the coach, "he was quizzing me I am certain."

"Well," said the man, called Brotherton, "have you obtained the information you required?"

"Yes; I know my way now, and you will see that we shall be able to make a good success if we are only brave and determined."

Brave and determined!

What expressions to use in an expedition for robbery and plunder!

"Well, it's a good haul in prospect," said Brotherton, "and you won't find *me* backward in anything."

CHAPTER XXIII.

CARDERER HOUSE—THE OLD MISER—HATRED FOR HIS SON—THE BLUE-EYED WITCH—THE MYSTERIOUS DEATH—OLD CARDERER AND THE BOY GO A LONG JOURNEY—A STRANGE APPRENTICESHIP—THE MAD MISER—THE MURDERS IN THE WOOD—DEATH OF THE OLD MAN—THE HIDDEN TREASURE—A STRANGE DISCOVERY.

Carderer House was a strange old place.

It had been much neglected.

Built full a hundred years before the time of our story, it had an antique appearance, not only in consequence of its shape, but its weather-beaten aspect.

It had a bad reputation.

The former owner had been a man of whom all kinds of evil had been spoken.

This had been Carderer's grandfather.

He was a miser.

Having married early, he had lost his wife when their child—an only one and a boy—was but five years of age.

While his mother lived he had been most tenderly nurtured.

But when she died everything was changed.

His father had other views.

He had watched with great jealousy the manner in which the child had been educated.

The mother desired to educate him as befitted the wealth of the family.

He saw only in his child a kind of vampire, whom he was bringing up to eat up all his wealth!

A true miser, he loved gold for itself.

He had loved his blue-eyed, golden-haired wife at first.

But it took gold to dress her.

It pained him to see her adorned in silks and gold and jewels, whose value ought to have been safe under lock and key.

He used to sit for hours pondering over his money, watching it, handling it, letting it run through his fingers.

And at last—

Well—he said she died of decline.

Others said differently.

They said that there had been foul play at work.

They said that poison and not bad health had carried her off.

But there was no inquiry.

Apparently she had no friends.

He had brought her there from abroad.

So it had been said.

And now she had no one who cared to venture to attack one who would doubtless move heaven and earth, and think nothing of wasting even his dear gold to save his worthless life.

So it was hushed up.

Then came another mystery.

Or rather a second scandal!

The tenderly nurtured boy, who inherited his mother's fair hair, blue eyes, and gentle graces, was no longer to remain at home.

His father, as I have said, regarded him as a vampire.

He must be removed.

So, one day, old Carderer and the boy undertook a long journey.

Whatever his treatment of his poor wife might have been, murder was not *now* his object.

He took him away many miles and placed him in the care of a village pedagogue.

The schoolmaster had definite instructions.

When he had learned enough, he was not to be sent home.

He was to be apprenticed to a trade.

So at fourteen years of age he was apprenticed to a shoemaker.

He the heir of ten thousand a-year!

No wonder is it then that in after years he was stern and severe.

He had served an apprenticeship to misfortune aud sorrow.

Well, the old man was now left alone.

He was alone with his gold.

Was he happy?

No!

Whatever visions they might be that haunted his pillow, he was evidently by degrees losing his senses.

Whatever liking for or affinity with his fellows he *had* possessed, melted now away.

He brooded and brooded until at length he became a perfect recluse, and, it was suspected, a murderer.

He dismissed his servants, and went out only when it was necessary for him to go out for food.

That is to say, he was only then seen out.

They saw, however, that at night he was often abroad in disguise, wandering about the roads in search of some one to attack and despoil.

However this might have been, it is certain that numerous desperate robberies, and several unaccountable murders, were perpetrated, and by no means could the author of them be traced.

So they were ascribed to old Carderer.

The people hated him for his unnatural seclusion, and for the treatment he had bestowed upon his lovely wife and child.

The reports were but natural, therefore.

"Give a dog a bad name and you may as well hang him at once," says the proverb.

And it is a true one.

Very true in this case.

People shrunk from him in horror.

They hardly cared to take his gold.

Yet what could they do?

They had no reasonable excuse; no crime had really been brought home to him.

And so things went on until at length the miser was seized with illness.

The news was received with general interest, and even anxiety.

"Now," thought the neighbours, "*now* the truth will be known."

They were wrong.

That is, if by truth they meant the confession of murder.

No such confession—nothing, in fact, like it, came from the lips of the old miser.

He sent for a doctor—two doctors—the best which the town could produce.

He listened calmly when they told him that his death was near, and said he wished to see his son.

A messenger was dispatched to the old pedagogue, and the son was brought—a sturdy artizan now.

He was told by his father he was rich, that he had concealed the knowledge of his parentage from him that he might grow strong, and not die off young like his mother.

Then tears filled the old fellow's eyes—tears of remorse people said they were—and, taking the young man's hand in his, he pressed it, saying—

"*She* will forgive me now. The house and lands you see around you is not all that is yours. You have more than that—far more than that. There is a treasure——"

And that was all he said.

There was a gasping cry, a gurgle, and all was over.

A blood-vessel had broken, and the old miser—murderer or not—had gone to his account with his secret locked in his bosom.

What the treasure was had never to this day been discovered.

Everything in connection with the estate was in correct order.

But nothing in the shape of an extra treasure could he find anywhere.

People at last said that it was the ravings of a dotard, and the idea passed away.

Desmond Carderer, however, the son of the artizan, had heard the story from his father.

It now recurred acutely to his mind.

No wonder.

He found his fortune sadly unlike what he had expected.

His wife Ada, in fact, had been right.

His brother had recklessly squandered nearly all the money in the bank, and, though naturally the estate was capable of being mortgaged for an immense sum, Carderer had no wish to commence life in such a manner.

He saw, however, no fair prospect of anything else, and it was while brooding over the best arrangements to make to enable him to cut a proper figure in his native place that the thought occurred to him.

"The treasure of which my father spoke. What if I could find that!"

This idea haunted him night and day.

"It must be concealed somewhere in the vicinity of the old house," thought he. "But the clue! how to find that is the mystery."

There appeared little chance of success.

The words that had escaped his grandfather were as vague as any information could possibly be; and there seemed no possibility that one now living could give him any information.

He made a discovery, however, after a short time in a strange and mysterious manner.

CHAPTER XXIV.

OSCAR PENRAVEN'S PLANS—THE LONE COTTAGE—MAGGIE—THE ARRIVAL OF THE JEWELLER—HIS STORY—THE DRUGGED WINE—THE PLAN OF THE ASSASSINS—THE DEATH LOTTERY—THE MURDER.

OSCAR PENRAVEN had, as I have said before, determined not to act hastily.

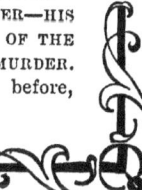

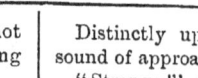

He had saved a few pounds, and he resolved not to lose a chance of obtaining a good haul by being too precipitate.

So, with his new friend Brotherton, he took up his residence at an old cottage not far from the old house.

This cottage was as dreary a place as the home of the Carderers.

It was worse in one way.

It had not for a long time been inhabited, and had a dingy appearance about it, and a dank, murky smell.

Oscar Penraven cared not for this.

He was intent only on the obtaining of his treasure.

So these two men established themselves in their solitary home.

It had two rooms on the ground floor, and two above.

The upper ones were only divided by a partition, and were reached by a narrow ladder-like staircase.

The upper rooms were chosen by them as being the least affected by the damp, for the roof was secure and uninjured by the weather, whereas the front room and the kitchen were oozy with the damp.

For a week they kept up huge fires in the rooms, and at the expiration of that time had made it somewhat habitable.

In the evenings one or the other always sallied forth to Carderer House, and making his way across the grounds approached the rear of the premises.

Whatever kept him here I cannot say; but certain it is, that whichever of them it was that emerged from its dark shadows after remaining two hours or more, returned home under the evident influence of fatigue.

At the end of three weeks, night came on one evening and found Oscar Penraven and Brotherton at home.

Their plans, apparently, were matured: and, sitting now before a blazing fire, they were indulging in some supper and some hot spirits, prepared for them by a young girl of the village, whom they engaged to come in and look after their rooms.

"Well," said Oscar Penraven, with a significant wink over at the girl, as much as to intimate to his comrade that only guarded expressions must be used, "in three evenings I fancy the affair may be expected to come off, and our long expected fortunes may be clutched."

"You are sure everything is right?" asked Brotherton, complacently.

"Yes, it cannot fail to come to us. No matter what happens, you will see that a new tide in our affairs is coming."

He spoke prophetically.

"You may go now, Maggie," said Oscar Penraven, turning to the girl, for he felt desirous of speaking more to the purpose. "You have set the beds to right, I suppose?"

"Yes, sir."

"Very well, Maggie. Run home now, and be sure and be early to-morrow. Ha! what is that?"

They all listened.

Distinctly up the gravel walk was heard the sound of approaching footsteps.

"Strange!" said Oscar Penraven; "travellers at *this* hour! It is not usual."

But, as he spoke a knock was heard at the door.

"Open it, Maggie," said Brotherton.

The girl obeyed, not without some trepidation, and as the door swung open there rushed a gust of strong wind and rain, and in the midst of it a man wrapped in a large cloak.

"Excuse my knocking at your door, gentlemen," he said, "but, being caught in this unexpected storm, I ventured to do so, and take shelter for awhile from its violence."

"Close the door, Maggie," cried Oscar; "and you, sir, sit down by the chimney corner. It shows what good cheer and a good fire will do. We knew not even that there was a storm. But here, Maggie, take the guest's wet cloak, and let us have another glass. Some warm spirit will not do you harm after such a soaking."

The stranger, who seemed unfeignedly pleased by this unexpectedly warm reception, gave the girl his cloak, and sat down by the cheerful blaze.

"Well, gentlemen," he said, "I cannot express my thanks for this unexpected welcome."

Oscar smiled.

"We are used to foreign countries," he said, "where welcome is accorded to every stranger. Drink, therefore, and warm yourself after your journey. Are you travelling far?"

"No," returned the stranger, as he unfastened a large wallet from his side, and placed it beneath his chair. "I am going to Ullarton with some jewellery which I have to take to one of the largest firms in the town, and there receive an equivalent; and, thinking a good walk would not hurt me, I left my horse at the 'King's Head,' on the road yonder, and was caught in the midst of as fierce a storm of rain and wind as I have ever met in England."

"You are a native of these parts?" suggested Oscar.

"No; I come from London. I arrived this evening from that city; but I know this place well. I was agreeably surprised to see a light here, since, when I came before, all was dark; the cottage, in fact, was uninhabited."

"Yes, it must have been a pleasant surprise," said Brotherton. "But I wonder at you, who have the appearance of a master jeweller, if such, indeed, be your trade, travelling these rough roads by yourself."

The stranger laughed.

"I might say the same of you," he said. "How is it that two persons who have the appearance of gentlemen, inhabit this wretched, tumble-down cottage?"

"Ah, that is a secret," said Oscar Penraven. "We are compelled to do so, or we lose a fortune."

"The same, or, rather, similar with me," said the traveller. "I have here in my wallet property that I would not trust to a stranger. Such particular business as this it is always best to transact yourself. But really I must be going. Has the storm abated, my good girl?"

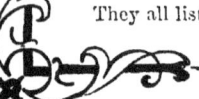

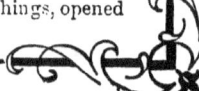

Maggie, who had been busying herself during the conversation in clearing away the things, opened the door once more, and again a roaring wind and a drift of rain rushed into the room.

"Dear me! this is most provoking," said the jeweller. "I had hoped to have been able to have seen my customers in the early morning, and to have slept in the town."

"You will never be able to go on now in this storm," said Oscar Penraven, as he approached the door and looked out. "You had better sleep here. I dare say we can contrive for you to remain; and as for you, Maggie, why, I don't see how *you* are to get home in this storm."

"Oh, I'll run home, I think, sir," she said. "It's only a few yards like to what the gentleman will have to go. I'd better come early in the morning if he wants breakfast before he goes."

"Well, you're exceedingly kind and hospitable," said the stranger. "I think really I'll accept your offer. I fancy I shall keep my appointment better by remaining here than by trudging and stumbling along in the dark and the rain."

So it was settled.

Oscar got up some more spirits.

Maggie ran off home without even a word more of request on the part of Oscar that she should remain.

Then the door was firmly bolted, and the three men gathered round the fire.

They had not remained there chatting long before the traveller complained of being drowsy.

"I feel very sleepy," he said, "and, with your permission, I'll get to bed."

Oscar rose.

"Very well," he said. "I shall follow your example presently. These spirits are strong, and they seem to have got up into my head."

The jeweller laughed.

"So they have in mine," he said; "but, never mind—a good sleep and a walk in the fresh morning air will dissipate all fumes."

Oscar now took a lamp and led the way up the narrow staircase into the bed-room, which was, as I have said, divided into two portions by a partition.

"Here is your bed," said Oscar. "I shall turn in with my friend for the night."

"You are very kind indeed," said the jeweller. "I am afraid I am inconveniencing you very much."

"Not at all," returned Oscar. "Good night. It will not be long before we come up, too."

And so he left him.

When he re-entered the room below, he placed his finger on his lip to enjoin silence upon his companion.

Then he sat down by the fire, took a knife from the table, and drew it with a significant gesture across his throat.

Brotherton nodded.

He knew his meaning at once.

The jeweller was to be robbed and murdered.

Having sufficiently made his companion understand his meaning, Oscar said, again pointing upstairs,

"There is a task to be done, my friend, which we must not forget. We had better draw lots who shall do it."

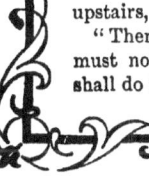

"Willingly," said Brotherton; "and yet since you were the first to propose the affair, suppose you were to undertake it yourself. I should be sorry to take from you the honour of the performance any more than the honour of the invention."

Oscar frowned.

"Remember," he said, severely, "that I am your master in these things."

Brotherton answered him with a laugh.

"Why so?"

"Did I not select you to aid me? Did I not tell you a secret worth thousands of pounds?"

"Truly; yes, you did."

"And you have had no reason to repent it?"

"I *may* have. You said this moment that you gave me a secret that would be worth to me thousands of pounds."

"Well, is it not true?"

"It may be."

"Curse me, you know it."

"Certainly I thought I understood it. But if you give me thousands of pounds, I shall scarcely be in the position of your servant."

Oscar laughed.

"Well, well," he said, "I was somewhat hasty. Let us think no more of it. Let us draw lots now as to the other matter."

So the death lots were drawn.

They took no special care in the matter.

Their minds were now so thoroughly depraved that they thought nothing of the commission of another murder.

The lot fell to Brotherton.

Oscar filled a bumper.

"Here's to your success, my friend," he said; "the old fellow will sleep now like a top. Those last four glasses of drugged wine will make him slumber on till early morning."

"I'll be quick, then, and finish the affair off quickly," said Brotherton, "there's no use in delay."

And so saying, he raised another bumper to his lips and drank it off.

Then he rose, wrapped round him the stranger's cloak, placed his hat on his head and his mask on his face.

After this he took a lamp and a long-bladed knife from the table and began slowly and stealthily ascending the stairs.

Cautiously he entered the chamber of the jeweller.

There was no need of care.

The poor fellow lay in a deep and artificial slumber.

Nearer the murderer crept.

The bed-clothes were partially drawn aside, and a piece of his chest was revealed.

Here was the chance.

The knife was raised, one steady glance was taken, and then it descended full upon the chest of the stranger.

One convulsive movement agitated his frame.

Once his eyes opened.

Then, with a loud groan, he yielded up his life.

Brotherton wiped the blade of his knife upon the

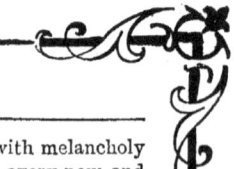

sheet, seized the jeweller's wallet, and then hurriedly descended.

"Well," said Oscar, "is the deed done?"

"Aye, and the gems are here," returned the assassin, with a shudder; "we'll make an even partition of these, although I, as the worker, ought to receive the lion's share."

To this Oscar made no reply.

He saw no use in refusing the division of which the man spoke.

They were man to man; and more than that, they were linked together in another bond of crime which they saw no possibility of breaking, for the simple reason that they could in no way accomplish it singly.

The wallet was emptied on the table.

A cry of surprise as this was done arose from both.

They had no idea that the treasure they had seized would be anything like what was now laid before them.

It was a mass of gems and gold.

Large rings—necklaces—bracelets—brooches.

Ornaments of all kinds.

And all costly.

"Well, this is what I call a good haul," said Oscar Penraven. "This is quite a providential piece of luck," said he.

"Aye, truly," said Brotherton; "if the other affair does not turn out as well as can be expected, why, we should not starve for some time even with this."

No, indeed; but come, now let us divide the spoil, and then dispose of the body."

"And as to Maggie?"

"We can tell her that the traveller went away early," said Oscar. "Leave that to me, and you will see I will arrange all for the best."

The spoil was soon divided.

"Now," said Brotherton, "where are you going to put the body?"

"Dig a hole in the orchard and throw it in; no one will know of his calling here."

"And Maggie—if she suspects or discovers anything?" said the other.

"Why, she must—no; there is no need for unnecessary bloodshed. We shall have seized Carderer's wealth, and be speeding away to London before they hear of anything. She need have no communication with any one, as, while we are away on our expedition, we can drug her."

CHAPTER XXV.

OUT IN THE DARK NIGHT—DIGGING THE GRAVE—THE BURIAL—MAGGIE BEGINS TO SUSPECT—OSCAR'S PLAN FOR DISPOSING OF THE JEWELS—HE IS DEFEATED—HIS RAGE AND DESPERATE RESOLVE.

HAVING partaken of some more spirits to keep up their desperate spirits, they put out the light, so as not to attract any more travellers, and went out into the night.

The wind was still gusty.

But the rain had ceased.

Loud voices seemed in the air.

The trees groaned and creaked with melancholy sounds, and Brotherton and Oscar every now and then glanced round them almost fearfully, as they made their way towards the old tool-house near the dark orchard.

Having found their spades, they soon set to work, and in less than an hour they had dug a wide pit, deep enough to conceal the body.

Then they returned to the house for their ghastly burden.

It was not without some misgivings and tremulousness that they went up into the bedroom and approached the body of the jeweller.

Strange feeling this.

They had not feared to slay him.

And yet now that he was dead, and the ghastly wound in his chest showed *how* he had died, they dreaded to gaze upon him.

However, it was but a momentary feeling.

"Wrap him in his cloak," said Oscar; "it will not do to leave that here, for Maggie would wonder why we had got it."

The body, therefore, was wrapped in a cloak and tied round the neck and heels.

Then it was carried down the stairs and out to its cold bed beneath the fruit trees of the wild, lone orchard.

Here it was placed in its pit, covered over, and the two men hurried back as swiftly as they could to their house.

They bolted and barred themselves in, but they did not dare to sleep in the bed of the murdered man.

Sitting down by the fire, they indulged in more spirits.

Then a drunken drowsiness came over them and they fell asleep.

Morning found them still there.

Maggie, tripping lightly over the fields, tapped loudly at the door.

For some moments neither heard.

Then one of them jumped up with a loud cry.

"It's only Maggie," growled Oscar Penraven.

Then rising he opened the door.

Maggie started at his red, bleary eyes.

"What is the matter, sir?" she cried, "you look ill!"

"Ill, aye, that I am," said Oscar Penraven, "that cursed nuisance of a traveller had us both up here at four o'clock and went away in spite of the darkness."

The girl felt most uncomfortable.

There was something in the appearance and in the atmosphere of the two men she did not like.

However, though she felt intuitively that something was wrong, she knew also that any agitation on her part would be her death-warrant.

So she entered the room and busied herself as usual.

Presently Oscar Penraven whispered to Brotherton, and without waiting for breakfast, they passed out, the former saying,

"We shall be back in an hour; get everything ready for us."

"I'm deuced tired," said Brotherton, as they quitted the cottage, and passed along its wilderness of a garden. "What are you going out for?"

"In the first place," returned Oscar, "because I want to make a call; in the second place, because a little fresh air will do us good, and freshen us for our evening's work."

Brotherton laughed gruffly.

"So you thought that you would kindly include me. I'm obliged to you; but I'd sooner have stopped at home and made love to little Maggie."

"That's just what I imagined likely," returned Oscar Penraven.

"Why?"

"Because you are drunk."

"And why do you object?"

"Because such conduct would assuredly attract the girl's notice to a change in our behaviour. She's a modest girl, and we've always treated her as such, and I've no desire to court too many inquiries."

"Very well, have it your own way," said his companion; "but I shan't be sorry to get back and have a lie-down. Last night's snooze in the chair wasn't enough after such hard work."

And so on they trudged towards Ullaston.

Presently an idea struck Oscar Penraven.

"I have an idea," he said; "one that will put money in our purses."

"Out with it," said Brotherton; "your ideas have generally proved good ones of late."

"Well, it is this simply. The jeweller said he came from London."

"Yes."

"His name was on the wallet—Thomas Hardacre, Lockspur Street, London."

"I saw it."

"Well. *I* will take the jewels to their destination, and receive the money for them. What say you?"

"It is a good plan, for the jewels themselves are dangerous as long as we have them on our persons. But whom will you represent yourself to be?"

"The messenger sent by Hardacre from London, in consequence of his own illness. Give me your portion, and we will replace them in the wallet as we found them."

"And the wallet?"

"Is here."

And Oscar Penraven produced it from beneath his coat.

The jewels were then replaced in the exact manner in which they had been found, and then Oscar Penraven and his companion proceeded towards the town.

The house of the large firm of jewellers at Ullarton was soon found, and leaving Brotherton outside, Oscar Penraven entered boldly.

"From whom come you?" asked the porter.

"From London—from Mr. Thomas Hardacre."

"Good," said the man; "walk this way."

He was ushered, in another moment, into the presence of the head of the firm.

"So you come from Mr. Hardacre?"

"Yes."

"You have some jewels for me?"

"I have, sir."

And he produced the wallet.

The old gentleman took it, opened it, and spreading out the gems, admired them greatly.

"They are beautifully set," he said; "they do Mr. Hardacre much credit."

Then, turning to one of his workmen, he said,

"Gerald."

The young man sprang up.

"Oh, there is no hurry," cried his master, waving him back to his seat; "but I will give you your instructions now in order that you may not forget. These jewels have—as you have heard me say, no doubt—been all ordered by the Countess of Desborough."

"I remember it, sir."

"She *must* have them to-night before eleven o'clock, and you must, therefore, start by the evening coach. Let me see, when does that start?"

"At eight, sir."

"Good; then you will arrive at Desborough House by half-past nine; that will do."

Then he turned to Oscar.

"I must give you a receipt for these things," he said, "so that Mr. Hardacre will know that you have delivered them correctly."

Oscar smiled.

"Your payment to me of the money for them will be sufficient receipt, sir."

"Payment, sir!" exclaimed the head of the firm, in a voice of surprise and indignation. "What do you mean by that?"

"Why," said Oscar, somewhat staggered, but not guessing the extent of his calamity, "Mr. Hardacre told me to ask for the money."

"Mr. Hardacre must be mad, or *you* must be," replied the other. "I will charitably set it down to that instead of an attempt at fraud. *The money was paid a month ago in London!*"

"Paid!" exclaimed Oscar Penraven.

He staggered back white as a ghost.

The jeweller and his clerk stared at him in amazement.

Well they might.

He seemed completely paralysed with astonishment.

He pressed his hand to his brow, gazed wildly round, and then sank into a chair.

"Why, what means this?" said the old man, as he advanced to his side. "This is most mysterious."

The tone in which this was said restored Oscar Penraven to the consciousness that he was acting a strange part, which might end in danger.

"Mysterious!" he said. "No; there is little mystery about it. The words you have addressed to me imply my ruin."

"Your ruin!"

"Yes. It may seem strange, but it is so."

"It does seem strange," said the one he was addressing; "but, nevertheless, it is true."

"Pray explain."

Oscar Penraven thought a moment.

He was really concocting a story.

"Well," he said, after awhile, "as I have been so deceived, I see no harm in doing so. The truth is that, on the faith of the jewels, I advanced to Mr. Thomas Hardacre a large sum, and as security he gave me the task of bringing them to you!"

"This is very bad," said the other, with a shake of the head. "I had always esteemed Mr. Hardacre as a just man of business; this is very like a fraud. But, however, *I* have no hand in it, and all I can advise you is to hasten back to London and do all you can to restore your fortunes."

Oscar started up.

"Thank you," he said. "I will take your advice and hasten back. Of course I acquit you of all blame, and I am much obliged to you for your kind advice."

He then bowed and quitted the office.

"Curse the fellow," muttered he as he went out. "What did he mean by obtaining an equivalent?"

Brotherton seeing Oscar approaching him with such a cast-down look, hurried forward eagerly.

"What is the matter?" he cried.

Briefly, Oscar told him.

The man looked sufficiently downcast at first, and then burst into a loud laugh.

"Well," he said, "we are properly done. We have killed a man for nothing."

"Not so," said Oscar.

"Not so! I think it is pretty clear."

"*I* do not see it," returned Oscar. "I have a plan to save us yet."

"Like this one?"

"No—no; listen, this is no time for jeering jests. To-night the mail leaves the 'Falcon' inn at eight."

"Yes."

"Well, in that coach will be a clerk named Gerald, from the firm of jewellers whom I have just left."

"Well?"

"*He* will have in his possession the jewels of which I have been so cleanly robbed; but now we must attack the coach and secure the jewels once more."

"Good!" said Brotherton, "we must kill a few more people in order to secure what we have already had in our possession. Still, it's a good plan, and I'm with you in it. And now, having so neatly placed our goods in a spot of safety till the night, let us hurry home and get some breakfast, for I am very hungry."

CHAPTER XXVI.

MAGGIE'S SUSPICIONS—THE HORROR IN THE OLD ORCHARD—WAITING FOR HER LOVER—HER RESOLVE TO FLY—THE MURDERERS RETURN TOO SOON—MAGGIE'S BRAVE RESOLVE—THE STRANGER FROM LONDON—A NEW ADVENT OF FORTUNE.

We must now return to the cottage.

Maggie, as we have seen, had been left there alone.

She was far from easy in her mind.

The agitated manner of her two masters made her suspect something.

What, she could not guess.

"Perhaps," thought she, "they have been tempted by the gold, have made the old jeweller drunk, and have robbed him of some of his treasures; and then I shall be blamed too."

She little dreamed how much more terrible had been the scene there enacted!

Having tidied up the front room and made preparations for breakfast, the young girl proceeded upstairs to make the beds.

That of the friends she saw at once had not been slept in.

The other was much disturbed.

"He rose in a hurry, I expect," she said, trying to comfort herself.

But it was small comfort.

She was very much afraid.

Then, as she turned over the sheets, she uttered a loud shriek of affright.

She saw blood.

Evidently not accidentally-placed blood, but big drops that had welled from a wound, and the marks where the weapon of murder had been wiped.

She indulged in no second shriek.

She was far too wise.

Her own life was now in danger.

To show fear was to run the risk of death.

At any moment her ruffianly masters might return, and, if they found her in any unusual state of agitation, they would suspect at once that she had discovered something.

So, only against her inclination, she sang away cheerily, while she made the bed.

Quickly as she could, as may well be imagined.

Then she closed the bed-room door, and hurried as quickly as she could down the stairs.

Her heart almost stood still with horror, and she was glad when she found the room still empty, and was able to run out into the fresh air.

It was a fine morning, and, as she glanced over the grounds, she was struck by a sudden thought.

The colour came once more into her cheeks.

"Ah!" she said! "Peter will be going to his work. I'll go and ask his advice."

Peter was her lover.

Like all girls of her age and appearance, she had her sweetheart.

And he, of course, was the one to consult.

No sooner was the thought matured in her mind, than she proceeded to put it into execution.

Closing the door, she ran across the orchard.

This joined the high-road.

The high-road along which the lover would pass to his labour.

There was an apple-tree here, laden with its rich fruit.

An excuse, therefore, was ready to her hand.

She could accuse herself of having gone there for the purpose of stealing apples.

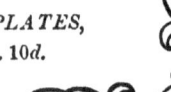

THE ATTACK ON THE MAIL-COACH.

No. 46.—"BOYS OF ENGLAND" EDITION.

So, placing a pair of short steps up against the wall, she peered over.

But no one was in sight.

Peter was either late, or he had gone by already.

She continued to wait.

Yet no one came.

At length a distant clock tolled the hour.

"It is too late," she said, with a sigh.

And she hastened to descend.

As she did so, a shrill cry escaped her.

Then she stood still in horror.

What did she see?

At first she could scarcely credit it.

She imagined herself to have seen some hideous vision.

She rubbed her eyes, and looked again.

There was no mistake this time.

She had seen it, and she knew now that her suspicions in regard to the murder were correct.

There, beneath the apple tree, protruding from the soil, was the right hand of the jeweller.

There was no doubt now.

The question was what to do.

Should she fly and apprise her parents?

That would be best!

But no!

It was not to be.

Just as, with a heart wildly panting in her bosom, she was preparing to fly to the front gate, it was thrown open, and the two murderers entered.

"Now for a trial—now for a day of horror," thought she; "but for my own sake, and for the sake of trapping these villains, I must go through with it."

So she plucked an apple, began munching it, and ran towards the house.

"What were you doing in the orchard, Maggie?" asked Oscar Penraven, sternly.

She cast her eyes down, and stammered forth—

"Please, sir, I went to get an apple. You said the other day I might."

"Well, one or two; I don't allow the place to be stripped," said Oscar; "but, tell me, is the breakfast ready?"

"Yes, sir," she answered, though very much fearing that the fire would be out, and her long absence detected.

But she was in luck.

The kettle was singing merrily on the hob, and the fire blazing brightly.

The murderers, therefore, suspected nothing, but sitting down began at once to talk.

"I say, Maggie," said Oscar, after awhile, just as she was placing before them some broiled ham, with a sincere wish in her heart that it would choke them, "you know that jeweller fellow who came here last night?"

"Yes, sir," said the girl, all in a flutter.

"Well, he left you this piece of silver for your civility."

And he handed her a coin.

She took it as if it were red hot, and dropped it into her pocket.

"Thank you, sir."

"Well, either to-night or to-morrow night—I don't know as yet which—we expect a lady and gentleman to sleep here. We want everything got ready for a nice supper."

"Another murder," thought the girl.

But she only curtsied, saying—

"Very well, sir. I'll see that everything is 'nice.'"

His words had changed her resolution.

She would not fly now.

She would remain to save the lives of the innocent.

"Can you sleep here?"

"Oh, yes, sir."

"If they do not come till to-morrow?"

"Oh, yes, if you will call at my parents' house and tell them."

"I will do so," said Oscar; "they might call to-night while I and my friend here are out. We have to go out on business for awhile, and it would not do for the house to be closed altogether when they came."

"Certainly not, sir," said Maggie, bustling about now more eagerly.

What a blessed chance!

If the unfortunate strangers only could come before their intended murderers arrived, all would be well.

They could be saved, and preparations could be made for the trapping of the villains.

The thought made her quite elate, and her manner of tripping about was such that no suspicion of any alarm on her part could possibly have been excited.

She felt in fact a kind of unexampled gladness at the idea that she would be able to be the prime mover in the affair—in ridding the world of two such reckless and bloodthirsty villains.

CHAPTER XXVII.

THE TWO VILLAINS ONCE MORE AT WORK—THE MAIL COACH ON THE DREARY HEATH—THE ATTACK—THE MURDER OF THE YOUNG JEWELLER—THE ROBBERY.

The evening once more approached.

During dinner the two had slept heavily.

Not at one time, however.

They were too suspicious for that.

They took it turn and turn about.

Darkness fell very quickly when it did once begin, and then, as the clock struck seven, Oscar and Brotherton rose, and proceeding upstairs, procured two crape masks.

Then, with a word of parting injunction to Maggie, they left her.

"We may only be a few minutes," said Oscar; "but keep up a good fire. Lock the door carefully, and don't admit any one of whom you have any suspicion."

"But how shall I know your friends?" said the girl.

"That is easy," said Oscar. "Their name is Carderer."

"The people who have taken the new house?"

"The same."

The girl's face expressed surprise.

But she did not speak.

"You seem astonished," said Brotherton.

"I am, sir."

"Why?"

"If Mr. Carderer wants to see you, why doesn't he invite you to his house?"

"That's *his* business and mine," said Oscar; "Miss Maggie, you're getting quite inquisitive for a little girl. There, good-night! and mind what I'm telling you."

"I'll be sure, sir."

And so she closed the door, and the two precious villains passed out.

They had no need to enjoin upon her the necessity of bolting the door.

She bolted it doubly strong, and, making up a huge fire, took the spirits out of the cupboard and made herself a large glassful.

She had need, indeed, of artificial strength.

Not one girl out of a hundred would have dared to remain in that abode of murder—with the blood of the dead man above, and his body lying without, with his hand pointing to the sky.

Meanwhile Oscar and Brotherton made their way to the "Falcon" Inn.

Here they called the ostler, ordered horses, and, having partaken of refreshment, rode away.

Having ridden away for about a mile, they halted on the skirt of a large common.

Here there was on one side a high embankment, the beginning of a road.

At this spot, therefore, they concealed themselves, after donning their black masks.

"Do you think it safe to leave Maggie in that house alone?" asked Brotherton of Oscar, as they waited for the coach.

"Why not?"

"She might go ferretting about."

"There is nothing to discover."

Brotherton was silent.

He had just remembered that he had forgotten to wipe away the stains of blood!

"What are you brooding over?" asked Oscar Penraven. "Have you remembered something that you have done which may betray us?"

"You remember that I told you how I found the old jeweller, and how I killed him?"

"Yes."

"I stabbed him, and wiped my knife on the sheet."

"And did not remove it?"

"I forgot it."

"Curses on your folly," cried Oscar; "you have betrayed us. The girl will give us up to justice. And yet, had she thought of doing so, she would have acted this morning. She would have discovered the stains then if at all."

"True; there is hope yet," said Brotherton, moodily. "But hark!"

They listened.

Afar in the distance was heard the roll of wheels.

"The coach is coming," said Brotherton.

"I hope so," said Oscar. "You know our plan?"

"Repeat it."

"I know the face of the man who has charge of the jewels."

"Well?"

"*You*, then, can stand at the horses' heads, and *I* will go to the window of the carriage and demand their delivery."

"And in case of resistance?"

"I will shoot the man and you the coachman. We will then despatch the guard, and bundle out the other passengers."

"That is, if we can."

"We *must*. But hush! Here it comes."

Along the road they could see the dark, lumbering coach.

It had two lamps, which swung uneasily to and fro.

It was going at a very jog-trot pace for a mail.

But in those days ten miles an hour was "express."

At length it approached.

The highwaymen's hearts beat high.

"Now," cried Oscar, at length.

And they leaped out.

Their horses were drawn at first right across the road, so that it was quite impossible for the driver of the mail coach to pass without riding over them.

Suspecting their errand, he tried to do this.

But in vain.

The leaders had been startled already by the sudden leap of the highwaymen, and refused to stir, and it was with some difficulty that they could be got to stand at all.

"Stop, on your life," cried Brotherton, as he took up his position, and held a pistol at the head of the trembling coachman.

The guard seemed paralysed with fear, and held his blunderbuss as if afraid to discharge it.

"Fire, and you will be shot at once," said Oscar, to him threateningly.

Then he preseed up to the side of the coach, and leaned in at the window.

There were only four idside.

Gerald, an old woman her daughter, and a farmer.

"Be not afraid," said Oscar. "I come not here to take life, nor do I come as an ordinary footpad to rob you. I seek that young man yonder."

"What want you with me?" cried the other boldly.

"Your name is Gerald?"

"It is."

"You are a jeweller in the service of a firm in Ullarton who employ one Hardacre?"

"You are correct. I know the villain's name well."

"Oh! a villain is he?" said Oscar. "It strikes me that your firm are the villains. Well, your master robbed me this morning of the sum of ten thousand pounds."

"You are mad."

"No, no. He took jewels of me to that amount, and refused to pay me. You know me now, and I know you. You have all those jewels with you in your wallet. Give them to me, or you are a dead man!"

"I will not yield them without a struggle," cried Gerald.

And with the words he drew a pistol from his belt, and presented it at Oscar's head.

"Withdraw," he added, "or I fire."

But, Oscar was too quick.

He had hardly spoken when the murderer fired.

The young man's pistol fell from his hand; his head fell back.

He was dead!

The bullet had crashed through his skull!

The two women instantly fainted.

The farmer alone had to be dealt with.

"Now, sir, are you disposed to trouble me?" said Oscar, presenting another pistol.

The farmer was unarmed.

What could he do?

"I am unarmed and in your power," he answered; "I will not molest you."

"Hand me his wallet, then," said Oscar Penraven, "and quickly."

The farmer doubted a moment.

Certainly it was aiding in a felony.

But how could he refuse?

He had others to think of besides himself.

He was no single man.

He had a wife and children to support.

His danger was, of course, imminent.

If he refused his fate was sealed.

So, "as needs must when the devil drives," he slid the wallet off the side of the dead man, and handed it to the thief.

"Thank you," said Oscar.

And then, without giving the farmer time to change his mind and renew his courage, he drew away from the window, and, going to the side of Brotherton, cried—

"Quick! let us ride away. The jewels are ours.

And, with a rush, they sped across the heath.

The guard recovered himself now that he thought they were safely gone, and discharged his blunderbuss uselessly after them.

And then the coach resumed its journey with its dead passenger, and the two villains returned to their home.

CHAPTER XXVIII.

THE STRANGER FROM LONDON—OSCAR PENRAVEN HEARS OF UNEXPECTED GOOD FORTUNE—HIS CHANGE OF RESOLUTION—MAGGIE'S BRAVERY—HER FLIGHT—DEPARTURE OF THE MURDERERS.

Maggie was nodding over the fire, when a low knock came to the door.

She had been dreaming pleasantly.

Dreaming that she was married.

Dreaming that she was forgetting all about the murder and the murderers in the arms of Peter.

The knock roused her abruptly.

She started up and rubbed her eyes, and wondered how it was she was not in bed, and why Peter was not by her side.

Then the knock came again.

"Oh! here's Mr. Carderer," she said, half aloud; now I'll tell them all."

But she was wrong.

As she opened the door a tall man stood on the threshold.

He was not Desmond Carderer.

Neither was it Oscar Penraven or Brotherton.

"Is this the house of Oscar Penraven?" he said.

"No, sir," said Maggie, in surprise.

"Then I say it is," returned the stranger. "You don't know him so well as I do. Give him that letter, he'll be glad enough to get it. It is as good as three thousand a year to him."

As he spoke, a loud gust of cold wind burst in at the door.

The man looked wistfully at the spirits.

"'Tis very cold," he said.

The girl smiled.

"Would you like a drop of spirits?" she asked.

"Well, now, that's hearty," he said. "I *should* like some if you have any to spare."

"Come in, then," she said.

The man, nothing loth, entered the room.

The girl shut the door, and bolted it behind him.

Then, as she gave him the spirits, an idea occurred to her.

Might not this man aid her?

Might she not tell him all?

Or was he the accomplice of the two murderers?

"Did you say my master's name was Oscar Penraven?" she said.

"I did," said the stranger, stretching his legs before the fire.

"And his friend?"

"I don't know him."

"They have not been here long."

"I know it, and I expect they'll not be here much longer."

"How so?"

"Why, as I have told you, this paper I give you is something worth three thousand pounds a-year to him."

"He has come into some property, then?"

"Yes, from his uncle. He is a baronet this master of yours."

"A baronet! Then that's the reason," she added to herself, "that Mr. Carderer is coming to see him He doesn't know what a villain he is."

She looked round fearfully.

Should she tell the secret?

She almost feared to speak.

The shadows in the corners seemed ready to take shape and speak.

But she roused up courage.

"I will," she thought; "this man will aid me."

But the chance was not given her.

Just as she was about to speak, another knock sounded at the door.

"That's master," she cried, with white lips.

The man looked disconcerted.

"I shall get you into trouble," he said.

"No," she said, and went boldly to the door.

Oscar Penraven and Brotherton hurried in.

"Whom have we here?" cried the former.

"One who brings you good news," said the man, rising from his chair. "Your name is Oscar Penraven?"

The latter frowned.

"What is that to you?" cried he.

"Everything; since to you alone I can bring good news. If you are Oscar Penraven, here is a letter, which tells you of a fortune of three thousand a-year."

Oscar took the letter and opened it.

His face flushed crimson.

"It is true," he said, holding out his hand, "it is true. You have, indeed, brought me great news. We will eat, drink, and be merry. Maggie, bring up more spirits. *You* shall join us, for this man brings us news of great riches."

Maggie saw no use in absolute refusal.

She, therefore, approached the table.

"I will take a glass, gentlemen," she said, "and then, with your permission, I will retire, for I am very weary."

"All right, my girl," said Oscar, slapping her on the shoulder. "Drink away, and do as you like. You're a brave piece of goods."

The girl at once drank the spirits

Then, with a feeling as if the hand of death were on her where Oscar Penraven had placed his, she crept away.

The three men caroused until late.

Then the stranger expressed a wish to go.

"I *must* be in the town before morning," he said.

"Oh, you'd better remain till morning; it is very dark."

"I'm not afraid of the darkness," said the man, rising. "I've travelled too much to indulge in silly fears. Good night, Sir Oscar, and, when you're in possession of your fortune, don't forget the man who brought you the news."

He then shook Oscar and Brotherton by the hand, and went.

Then Oscar closed the door, and returned to his seat by the fire.

"Well," said Brotherton, "you've come into a good stroke of fortune."

"Yes," said Oscar. "I never expected it."

"No, and never revealed your name."

"That's it. I kept my secret well."

"And how comes this money?"

"It is left me by an uncle. You must know that all my fortune has been lost and stolen from me by one method and another, and I have been forced to resort to all kinds of means to restore myself to anything like a position. It is from an uncle, Sir Bertrand Lascelles, that I have received it."

"And now, I suppose, that you will give up all idea of enriching yourself at the expense of Carderer?"

"Why so?"

"You will have sufficient, and will no longer be in need of me."

Oscar laughed.

"You are a most suspicious man. I shall *not* give up my plan. Why should I? No matter how much money I receive thus at the hands of my uncle, I shall still be in want of ready money. So we will carry out the plan proposed, with *one* exception."

"And that is, that you will not share it evenly with me, I suppose?"

"Suspicion again," said Oscar Penraven. "No, no, that is not it. I shall not kill either him or his wife."

"Thank Heaven!" said the voice of her who listened above.

"What then?"

"We will inveigle them here as originally proposed, then we will drug them, enter the house, and fly to London. Who will recognise in the rich and gaily-dressed Sir Oscar Penraven the hero of these midnight adventures?"

Brotherton mused a moment.

"I am of your feeling quite," he said, "and do not like needless murder. But something strikes me."

"And what is that?"

"How will you succeed in establishing your claims, since you told me not long ago that the very semblance of your former self had been obliterated by fire?"

Oscar smiled.

"If a man," said he, "had no other means of identifying himself than that of trusting to the remembrance of other people, he would have a sorry chance of recovering his property, I fancy. No, no; I have other means."

"Well, it's no matter of mine," said Brotherton, "but certainly I am not clever enough to follow your drift."

"I'll explain," said Oscar; "you see, in the first place, my banker knows my signature."

"Yes."

"Secondly, there is a private sign between us."

"Good."

"I have merely to say, 'Between us only, you remember,' with an emphasis, bringing in the words when they are not absolutely required, three times; and no matter what the difference in my appearance might be, old Abraham Moore would recognise my rights in a moment."

"But is your money paid into this bank?"

"I must write and instruct the solicitor of the estate to transfer everything to it; and I must write also to Moore and inform him of my good fortune."

"I should lose no time, then."

"You seem greatly interested," said Oscar, eyeing him sharply.

Brotherton laughed slily.

"Well, now, I am," he said. "I'll not pretend to have the disinterested friendship of an old friend, but you *must* know I have an interest. When you are once more Sir Oscar Penraven, you will not utterly discard me, I hope, or refuse me a handsome present?"

"No, indeed," said Oscar. "At any rate, I'll take your advice, and the first thing in the morning I'll write to the lawyer and the banker; meanwhile, I'll have a doze."

And, with the words, he finished off his glass of spirits and composed himself in his chair.

Brotherton pretended to do the same.

Presently, however, hearing Oscar snore, he opened his eyes.

"Asleep!" he muttered. "I can have a good look at him now."

He leaned over, and eagerly scanned Oscar's features.

"An aquiline nose, like mine. A scar on the forehead; so have I. A wide mouth; so have I. Heavy brows; so have I. The beard is the only thing! Never mind, it will do well, I think. Brotherton, my friend, you have found a gold mine!"

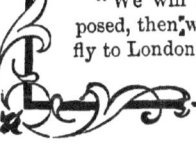

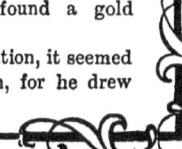

Whatever the truth of this observation, it seemed to have a soothing effect upon him, for he drew a handkerchief over his face, and was soon sound asleep.

"Now is my time," thought Maggie.

Cautiously she opened her door.

Then she leaned forward and glanced down.

She saw all at a glance.

The lamp was still burning, and she recognised at once that the two men were fast asleep.

"Heaven grant me strength," she said, as she crept down.

She knew all now.

She saw the plan they had formed against Carderer.

She would fly, therefore, through the dark night to Carderer House, and inform them at once of the danger.

She reached the floor.

Tremblingly she passed on, for one of the sleepers moved, and threw up his arms wildly.

"He is dreaming of his murders," thought she.

On she crept to the door.

Gently she withdrew the bolts.

Then, seeing a pistol on the table, she seized it, and placed it in her bosom.

"Who knows," thought she, "whom I may meet on my night's journey."

So far all had gone well.

But fate was against her escaping without the knowledge of the two villains.

As she pulled the door it jarred, and one of the rusty bolts, which she had shot back too far, fell to the ground.

In an instant Oscar sprang up.

"Ha!" he cried, "what have we here?"

"Treachery," said Brotherton, springing up also.

"What are you doing there, girl?" shouted Oscar, advancing.

In an instant the gleaming pistol was snatched from its warm hiding-place, and presented at his head.

"Back! murderer!" cried the brave girl. "One step forward, and you die! I know all. I know that you murdered the old jeweller. I know your villanous plots against Carderer and his wife, and I go to warn them. Back! or you die!"

For an instant the two villains were paralyzed by this sudden surprise.

Then Oscar cried—

"At her, Brotherton! We had better risk life at the hands of this mad girl than at the hands of the hangman."

So saying, they sprang forward.

But not in time.

With the energy of despair, Maggie flung open the door, sprang out, and closed it after her.

It was all the work of an instant.

Oscar Penraven and Brotherton once more swung it open, and rushed after her.

But in vain.

Not a sound disturbed the solemn stillness of the night, and search everywhere as they would, they could find no trace of the fugitive.

She had disappeared as completely as if she had vanished into air.

"Ten thousand curses on her!" cried Oscar Penraven. "We are undone."

"Undone!" repeated Brotherton; "not so. We shall have to give up all idea of the attack on Carderer House. But have we not our jewels, and have you not three thousand a-year?"

"True, true," said Oscar; "but to be baffled and beaten by this girl is not only absurd but maddening. We must leave this place at once. The neighbourhood will be perilous now for both."

"Curses on her, she has ruined all my plans," muttered Brotherton.

But, nevertheless, whatever these plans were, he busied himself in getting ready for departure, and in the course of ten minutes the two desperate adventurers started.

They left the light burning on the table, so as to lead those who might approach to suppose that they were still there.

They then started away across country at full speed, and made their way towards the village of Lapston, some twenty miles distant.

CHAPTER XXIX.

A STRANGE MYSTERY.

At the "King's Head," Lapston, they arrived about eight in the morning, footsore and weary.

"We had better rest here awhile," said Brotherton, as they entered the parlour; "there will be no fear of pursuit."

"No; we'll push on another ten miles at right angles," said Oscar Penraven, who seemed under the influence of some great fear, "and then rest until night falls, then we can make all haste to London."

"Very good," said Brotherton, "*you* are the leader, *I* only follow."

"And now that we *are* here, I will send those letters. It will be as well to make sure of a supply of cash, as the jewels may be hard to get rid of."

"True," said Brotherton, with a twinkle of the eyes, which denoted how much he was pleased.

When the waiter entered with refreshment, Oscar Penraven ordered pen, ink, and paper and wrote.

When he had finished he handed them to Brotherton, saying—

"I think they will do. They are short and to the purpose."

Brotherton read as follows:—

"To Alfred Marlin, Esq., Solictor,

"17, Little Harding Street, London,

"Sir,—In reply to your letter of yesterday, I beg to request that you will pay into the bank of Abraham Moore and Co., Lombard Street, the money in your hands, and all deeds, &c., connected with the Wickworth Estate. I will see you on the 15th inst., the third day from this.

"Your obedient servant,

"Oscar Penraven."

The second ran as follows:—

"To Mr. Abraham Moore,

"Lombard Street, London.

"Dear Sir,—Having, by the death of my uncle,

succeeded to the Wickworth property in Hampshire, I have instructed the agent of the Estate to pay into your hands the money in his possession, and also to deposit with you the deeds, &c., of the Estate. I will be with you on the 15th instant. Travel and much trouble have changed me greatly, but we shall know each other by the private pass agreed on.

"Yours sincerely,
"OSCAR PENRAVEN."

"Very short, but very much to the purpose," said Brotherton.

"Yes," replied Oscar, laughing; "and my first request will be very short and to the purpose. It will be a demand for money. I shall deposit the gems as a part of the family property saved from the wreck, and raise money upon them."

"Good," said Brotherton. "And now, since you have written the letters, despatch them, and let's eat and drink. I'm more inclined for something good than for business."

The waiter was at once despatched to the post-office, such as it was in those days, and they felt a certainty that the letter would arrive at least on the second day.

Then they set to work at the drink and the viands, and, these being disposed of, once more started on their journey.

They now, as Oscar Penraven had proposed, made a half detour, so as to throw any pursuers off the scent.

The ten miles were accomplished in three hours, and they found themselves in a comfortable inn about one o'clock in the day.

They had proposed to remain here.

Well would it have been for one of them, perhaps.

But it was not to be.

On entering the bar, they found the mouths of everyone full of the doings of the highwaymen who had robbed the mail and murdered two of the passengers!

There is always something added in these tales.

They say "a rolling stone gathers no moss."

It is different with a rolling story.

So, feeling that the further away they were from such company the better, they drank up their ale, and, weary and footsore, now once more betook themselves to the road.

Not two miles beyond, the friendly shelter of a little inn invited them to stop, and, unable really to proceed further without rest, they entered and sought accommodation.

A hearty meal having been disposed of, they retired to their room, nor woke till black darkness had thoroughly enveloped the whole country.

When they entered the public room, which was now gradually filling, there was a marked difference between them.

Oscar was dejected and moody.

In fact, like a man who had a presentiment of some evil.

Brotherton, on the other hand, was quite the reverse.

He was buoyant and gay, and seemed like one who had just come in for a fortune.

Oscar felt irritated at this.

But he did not speak of it.

He himself had always been used to riches.

It was different with this man.

He had been brought up in the lap of indigence, used to hand work—drudgery, in fact, until he threw it off, and turned thief and coiner.

It was natural, then, that *he* should feel a degree of elation which would have been absurd on the part of Oscar Penraven.

At length the time came once more for departure.

They partook of steaming glasses of hot spirits, and set out.

The road was somewhat dark.

But it became darker presently, when they turned from it, and, for the sake of a short cut, passed through the wood—Edgeley Wood, as it was called in the neighbourhood.

They entered it at ten at night.

At eleven *one man* emerged from it at the furthermost end.

He seemed in a great hurry, or else in great fear, for he ran hard until he got clear of the wood, and his face was ghastly pale.

His companion did not follow, and he took, therefore, his lonely way towards London.

BOOK VI.

THE FIFTH AND LAST SECRET OF THE IRON CHEST.

CHAPTER I.

A NEW SURPRISE.

RUPERT DREADNOUGHT was not surprised at the sudden disappearance of Carderer and his wife.

He had anticipated it, of course, from the fact of his sudden accession of fortune.

Moreover, on the day after his departure, he received a note, stating the situation of his newly-acquired property, and requesting the pleasure of Rupert's company at Carderer's house.

There was a doubt in his mind as to going.

Carderer had lived anything but an honest life.

However the visit, even if made, would be something in the far future.

So he troubled not about it.

His mind, in fact, was far too much perplexed by

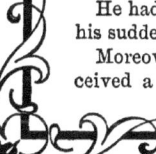

the disappearance of Oscar Penraven to think of other things.

He was, in fact, wearied of his present life.

He saw Helen every day, blooming into fresh graces, and longed to call her his own.

He had seen blood, too, until he was sickened of it.

What wonder, then, that he was weary of his life, and longed to settle down happily in the character of a husband.

He was expressing these very thoughts to Helen herself, when a servant knocked at the door and announced the arrival of Allan of the Glen.

Rupert welcomed the young Scotchman gladly.

Allan was now a tall, handsome man, and had discarded his national costume for the no less graceful garb of an English gentleman.

Both he and Tom the Waterman were married.

They had not hesitated to take the advice proffered by Rupert.

Happy in the love of their beautiful wives, they were not, however, neglectful of their old friend, and frequent were the visits they paid him.

This visit Rupert looked on as merely one of friendship; though somewhat annoyed at an interruption to his tête-à-tête with Helen, he welcomed him gladly.

"I am not disturbing you for nothing this time, my lord," he said. "I bring you news which may be welcome."

Rupert smiled.

"Anything," he said, "would be welcome which would make me able to wed the one I love and release me from my missions, which have, in very truth, been irksome to me."

"Well," said Allan of the Glen, "I bring news of Oscar Penraven."

Rupert started.

"By Heavens! that is what I long to hear. Is he dead?"

"He is not."

"And you know where he is?"

"I do."

"By the saints, then, my mission shall yet be done. Tell me, how did you discover this?"

"In the most singular manner," said Allan. "I will sit down and tell you. You know the 'Fair Maid of London'—the inn near Thames Street?"

"I do well," said Rupert.

"I had been out with Tom for a row on the river, when, feeling tired and thirsty, we entered the 'Fair Maid of London,' and called for some wine.

"While standing there we heard loud voices, and the clashing of swords, and, being ever eager to see a fray, we made towards the room whence came the sounds of strife.

"There we found two men in the livery of servants, engaged in a deadly fray, while the other occupants of the room were looking on in much amusement.

"Both men were somewhat inebriated, and from time to time ejaculated drunken words expressive of disgust at the presumption of the other.

"Tom and I at length succeeded in separating them after very little blood had flown.

"Then we questioned the one who seemed the least intoxicated as to the cause of the fray.

"'That fellow,' he said, pointing to the other, 'is in fault.'

"'How so?'

"'He presumed to put himself on an equality with me—he, the servant of some retired grocer, and I, the servant of Sir Oscar Penraven, a baronet of a fine old English family.'"

"The words must indeed have surprised you," said Rupert.

"They did," said Allan. "But I concealed my emotion, and endeavoured to make peace.

"This was only done, however, by the ejection of the 'low fellow' from the room.

"I then made friends with the other, called him a man of spirit, and called for wine for him.

"I very soon, in this way, opened his heart, and began to ask him questions.

"'I knew once a person of the name of Oscar Penraven,' I said, 'but he has now been absent from London some time.'

"The man clapped me on the back familiarly.

"'That's the very same,' he said, 'he's been away a long time.'

"'And where is he now?'

"'At his own house—his family house in Luxmore Street.'

"'He has changed his secluded habits, then, entirely?'

"He laughed loudly.

"'Secluded habits, eh?' he cried. 'Why, there's not one in London that lives in a more open style, or is more generous to his servants.'

"This was a puzzler to me.

"But he did not notice anything in our manner, and we remained with him until he went home, and then we accompanied him.

"Sure enough the windows were all lit up, and evidently Sir Oscar Penraven keeps open house."

"You could not bring me better news," added our hero; "and yet it excites the utmost astonishment in my mind. How he can dare to show himself openly in London, I cannot conceive."

"It does truly seem extraordinary," said Allan. "But what do you propose to do?"

"We must, by some means or other, enter his house and confront him."

Helen pressed his hand.

"No, Rupert; why should you desire to thrust your head thus in the lion's mouth? No, no; seek some secret meeting with this villain, but do not place yourself in his power."

RUPERT
OR THE
DREADNOUGHT
SECRETS OF THE IRON CHEST

THE CONFLICT IN THE WOOD.

"Fear not," said Rupert. "I have already, I think, proved myself a good general. Leave this to me. I shall not unnecessarily cast myself into danger."

"Well," said Allan. "I have set myself a task which may turn out to your advantage."

"What is that?" asked Rupert.

"Simply this," said Allan: "from what I heard

from the serving man I conclude that a grand ball —a masked ball—is to be given by Sir Oscar Penraven."

"The daring villain!"

"It is nevertheless true, I believe. If it is, nothing is easier than to enter, mingle with the throng, and——"

"Discover, let us hope," interrupted Rupert, "that Oscar is dead, and that some relation has taken his place."

"Let us hope so indeed," said Helen, fervently. "Your mission, Rupert, would then be fulfilled without your being compelled again to draw your sword. But how, Allan, will you obtain your information?"

"From the serving man; and now, as I have said all that I came to say," said the Scotch boy, "I will depart."

"Not so," cried Rupert; "the bringer of such good news must not depart so easily and so unrewarded. You must stop now and sup."

The following evening Allan made his way to the house of Oscar Penraven, where he saw the servant whom he had defended at the inn.

From him he learned that the ball took place in a week, and he obtained also two cards of admission on payment of a bribe.

On the night of the mask, accordingly, Rupert and Allan, well armed and in fancy costumes, were among the guests at Oscar Penraven's house.

CHAPTER II.

THE MASKED BALL AT THE HOUSE OF OSCAR PENRAVEN—THE OLD ROOMS REMODELLED—THE GAY SCENE—THE BRIGHT-EYED WITCH—THE TURK WITH THE SCARLET TURBAN—THE NOTE—ITS DELIVERY AND CONSEQUENCES—SIR OSCAR GREETS OLD FRIENDS—THE PRIVATE AUDIENCE—THE UNMASKING OF THE HOST—A STARTLING DISCOVERY.

MASKED balls have been so often described that I shall not pause to give any lengthened description of that to which Rupert and Allan of the Glen made their way.

The rooms were very full.

Gaily decorated, too.

They had long been unused.

Very soon, in fact, after the death of his father, Oscar Penraven had ceased making use of them.

They had, when after this lapse of time they had been re-opened, an ancient and unpleasant smell.

A smell as of a charnel house.

But this had soon disappeared.

The owner, now he had apparently resolved to dare all, and openly inhabit again the house of his fathers, had spared no expense in the doing up of his house.

Now, therefore, gay festoons hung from the brightly painted pillars, and baskets of flowers depended from the ceiling, and fragrant perfumes floated among the dancers.

These, too, were attired in all the bright and gaudy colours imaginable, and covered with jewels and gold ornaments.

There was every variety of costumes there to be seen.

In strange, incongruous groups, too.

Turks and nuns, monks and soft-bosomed Greek girls, Armenians, Brahmins, cavaliers, Puritans, huntsmen; all mingled in one hurrying, laughing, dancing throng.

Allan and Rupert, both of whom were attired in the garb worn by the gallants of the days of Elizabeth, attracted notice by the brilliant nature of their costumes.

In order, therefore, not to seem conspicuous, they joined in the merry-makings and in the dance, and were soon separated.

They had, however, a sign and a password.

It was not likely, therefore, that they would miss each other for long.

A bright-eyed little witch it was that hung on Rupert's arm after the dance was done.

A little girl she was, of age some seventeen summers, dressed in the delicious Greek dress, which did not impede her graceful movements, nor hide the warm beauties of her budding bust.

"I have not yet seen our host," he said, as he retired with her to a part of the room set apart for refreshment. "I wonder where he is."

The girl laughed a silvery laugh as she raised a glass of sparkling wine to her red lips.

"Ah, you have not yet discovered his secret," she answered. "*I* have. See, he is yonder, with the scarlet turban and the Turkish habit. Shall I lead you to him?"

"No," answered Rupert. "I will introduce myself presently. See, there is another dance; shall we join them again?"

His arm was around her waist in a moment, and they were soon whirling round in the giddy circle.

He had no desire for her introduction.

He knew not how the meeting would end, or, in fact, how it would begin.

It was best, therefore, to be on the safe side.

As soon as this dance was over he made the excuse that he desired to see his friend.

Then slipping away from his companion, whose eyes and manners altogether plainly showed that she by no means approved of his departure, he sought eagerly for Allan.

Allan had also quitted his partner and was seeking Rupert.

They met in a secluded part.

"Well," said Allan, "have you discovered anything, my lord?"

"In the first place your information was correct!"

"In which way?"

"He is acting openly and daringly?"

"Yes; more so than I credited."

"And I have discovered which among these people is the one we seek."

"Which is he?"

"Yonder Turk in the red turban."

Allan was all impatience.

More so than Rupert.

"Let us lose no time," he said.

"We will not," said our hero.

Then he drew from his girdle a little note.

"Take this, Allan," he said, "and give it to him. It demands an interview."

"And where will *you* be?"

Rupert turned and pointed out a kind of alcove behind where he was standing.

"Here," he said, "I will remain here."

Allan took good note of the place and hurried away.

He found the red turbaned Turk talking to some friends.

Very eagerly he was speaking.

But he bowed graciously when Allan handed him the note.

"What!" he cried, as he read it, speaking in a voice of pleasure. "What! my old friend, Rupert. Well I *am* glad. Tell him I will be with him in a moment."

Allan of the Glen bowed and left him.

He was too surprised to speak.

Well he might be.

The note had run as follows:—

"To Sir Oscar Penraven.

"An old friend, Lord Rupert Dreadnought, has taken the liberty of entering your house without permission. He is very anxious to see you, and will await your coming in the alcove near the conservatory. I and the friend with me are in Elizabethan costume."

"Sir Oscar Penraven must be *mad*," muttered Allan, as he moved away.

"Well, what cheer?" asked Rupert, as he joined him.

Allan repeated the words.

Rupert thought a moment.

"There is either some secret in all this which we cannot fathom, or else there is treachery afloat," he said; "however, we will be on our guard, and be prepared for all emergencies."

There was no immediate fear of treachery, however, at any rate.

The red turbaned Turk advanced alone to meet them.

He held out his hand as they met.

"I am glad once more to meet you!" he said.

"This is very strange!" thought Rupert, "but as this can never be Oscar in person, I will take his hand."

He took his hand, therefore, and shook it.

"And this," said the other, genially making a gesture towards Allan, "is this also an old friend of mine?"

Allan removed his mask.

"Ah," said the supposed Oscar, "I see this is not a friend. Will you introduce me?"

"Certainly," said Rupert, beginning now to see through the filmy atmosphere of mystery, "this is Allan of the Glen! He was a foundling and knows no other name, though now he has taken that of Macpherson on his marriage."

"Well," said the supposed Sir Oscar Penraven, "as we are met here let us drink a glass to old acquaintance, and this its pleasant renewal, and as we know one another, we may as well dispense with these tiresome and hot masks."

This was just what Rupert Dreadnought desired.

As soon, therefore, as the servant whom the red-turbaned Turk summoned had brought the wine, the door was closed.

"We'll have a little talk to ourselves," said the supposed Oscar. "My guests will not miss me, and I like to renew old acquaintances."

With these words, which, together with his manner altogether, struck Rupert and Allan of the Glen dumb with surprise, he removed his mask.

As they had expected, it was not Oscar.

The face had resemblances to it.

But it was not the face of their enemy.

"Sir," said Rupert, "who are you? You are not Sir Oscar Penraven!"

CHAPTER III.

EXPLANATIONS—THE MURDER IN THE WOOD—THE INTERVIEW WITH THE BANK MANAGER—THE PASSWORD—MARLIN, THE ATTORNEY—A DIFFERENT KIND OF INTERVIEW—AWKWARD ASSERTIONS—THE COMPACT.

Before proceeding with this interview, however, I must retrace my steps somewhat.

Brotherton—for it was he—was prepared for this reception.

His object for this secret interview had been to try them.

As yet he had experienced very little difficulty in the task he had set himself.

When he had left Oscar Penraven murdered in the wood—for he had murdered him—and left his body to the storms, he had proceeded to London, and, armed with the password, had presented himself at the bank.

Here the bank manager had expressed his inability to recognise him.

But in his letter Oscar had spoken of the change that travel had made in him.

Brotherton smiled at first.

"I thought," he said, "you would scarcely recognise me in this guise."

"I do not," said the bank-manager, stiffly.

Brotherton refused to observe his manner.

"No wonder," continued Brotherton, seating himself comfortably in a chair, "no wonder. The scenes and troubles I have gone through have been enough to change any man. I have been burned in a burning house, been wrecked twice, wounded in a dozen duels, and yet, though my face is scathed, my spirit is the same, though——"

"Your voice is *not* the same," said the other, drily.

"Is it not?" said the supposed Oscar. "No one has remarked it but yourself. My other friends have made a very different remark. However, I will not keep you or waste your time any longer in chattering about myself. Has Mr. Marlin acted on my note?"

"He has, but there is a little difficulty."

"And what is that? Has he failed to do the transfer property?"

"No; but I really—well, I may as well say what I mean at once, eh!"

"Precisely."

"Well, then, the truth is," said Mr. Wickham, the manager of Abraham Moore and Co's bank, "I really am not *quite* satisfied that you are Sir Oscar Penraven."

Brotherton laughed.

"Well, as this interview," he said, "is 'between us only, remember,' I don't mind your joke."

He had acted on Oscar's words.

He had brought in the words when *not* absolutely required, as Oscar had said.

Mr. Wickham at once recognised them.

"That alters the case," he said; "but, indeed, Sir Oscar, you are rarely changed."

"It was for that reason I desired that we should have a password," replied Brotherton; "but now, since you are satisfied, I will draw out a couple of hundred pounds, and proceed to renovate my town house. I shall live there for the future."

"I wonder you have not always done so," said Wickham.

"Ah!" said Brotherton, with a smile, "it would not have been convenient. In fact, I have had scarcely a farthing. I have been swindled out of my property one way or another, and I have gambled away what I have not been robbed of. Now, however, I shall receive my old friends, revive old habits, except the gambling, and enjoy myself quietly."

Enjoy himself quietly!

He—the murderer!

"Well, it's a good thing. You've seen the folly of it, Sir Oscar," said the bank manager; "a very good thing."

And he rang the bell.

"Mr. Wickham," said Brotherton, ere the bell was answered, "all I have said is between us only, remember."

Wickham smiled.

"Yes, yes," he said: "between us only, remember."

Curiously enough, Brotherton had gone to the bank before going to the lawyer's.

He had a motive in this.

If it was not all right at the bank, why should he unnecessarily place himself in a position to be annoyed twice?

Besides, at the bank there was a password.

With the lawyer it was different.

He knew nothing of Marlin.

He had heard nothing of him from Oscar Penraven.

He might be an old friend who would know him well, and be inclined to spoil the game of an impostor at the bank.

So he went to him in the second place.

Mr. Marlin received him at once when he heard the name.

He was a peculiar man, this Marlin.

A tall, thin, colorless man about forty.

A man whose keen grey eyes looked you through.

He glanced, without any surprise, at this visitor, but there was a turning up of the corners of his mouth which told that he suspected something.

"I think you sent up the name of Sir Oscar Penraven?" he said.

"I did. I am Sir Oscar Penraven," replied Brotherton.

Mr. Marlin smiled.

"Indeed," he said, drily.

"Yes. You received my letter, I know, because I have already been to the bank."

"Take a seat," said the lawyer, pointing to a seat near the fire.

Brotherton obeyed.

The lawyer then went to a cupboard, and brought out a bottle and two glasses.

These he placed on a table, and pouring out some fine sparkling wine, passed one to Brotherton; and taking the other himself raised it to his lips, saying—

"Here's your health, sir. I always admire a clever man."

The tone in which this was said was most irritating.

Brotherton could not help taking notice of it.

He drank his wine, and then, setting down the glass, said—

"Now, Mr. Marlin, I must request you to explain yourself. I know from your manner that you are concealing something, and I want to know what it is."

Marlin laughed.

"Guilty consciences, you know, &c.," he said.

"Sir," said Brotherton, "explain yourself, or I shall be compelled to chastise you."

"I will, then," said the lawyer, "since you feel it so forcibly. You are not Oscar Penraven."

"Not Oscar Penraven! This is an insult!" cried Brotherton.

"It may be, or not," returned the lawyer, placidly; "at any rate it is true. You are not Sir Oscar Penraven. I have known him since he was a child, and you have neither his look nor his voice. Tell me," he added, "where and how did we meet first?"

This was a poser.

Brotherton could not answer.

Of Penraven's early life he, of course, knew nothing.

"I refuse to answer your impertinent questions," he said: "I refuse absolutely. All I know is that I have been received properly at the bank, and I mean to stick to what I have obtained. Sir Oscar Penraven or not, you would never recognise me after all these years of toil and trouble. I am going down to the Wickworth estate soon, and if you like to superintend its affairs you can. If not, why do as you please."

The wily lawyer had no need of lengthened thought.

He knew well that Brotherton had by some means or other obtained possession of the fortune, and that if he opposed him, proof would be very difficult.

In a moment, therefore, he decided.

"Very well, Sir Oscar," he said; "I will do all that is necessary, and in the meantime——"

"I am going to rehabilitate the town house, and reside there."

And so, having explained the fate of Oscar Penraven, and how Brotherton came into the property, we must return to the point where we left him with Rupert Dreadnought and Allan of the Glen.

CHAPTER IV.

BROTHERTON IS ASTONISHED—THE RECITAL OF OSCAR PENRAVEN'S DEATH—THE CONFESSION—ANOTHER COMPACT—THE BODY IN THE WOOD—THE WOUND IN THE BACK—THE LAST SECRET OF THE IRON CHEST.

"You do not remember me, then ?" said he, sarcastically, as he saw the amazement expressed on the faces of both his guests.

"No, indeed," said Rupert; "if you are Sir Oscar Penraven, you are not the one of whom I am in search."

"Have you, then, known him long ?"

"Very long."

"He is an old friend of yours then ?"

Rupert smiled.

"A friend," he said, "no, he is a deadly enemy. One of the most deadly enemies I have ever had the misfortune to come across in my life. I came here to see him, because I was astounded to find that after his many atrocities he dared to show himself in public."

Brotherton was somewhat staggered at this.

"Are his misdoings publicly known then ?" he asked.

"They are known by so many that I fear you will have but a short-lived time of pleasure here," replied Rupert Dreadnought. "But tell me, for I long to know it—what has become of Sir Oscar Penraven ?"

"He is dead."

"You can swear it ?"

"I can."

"And how died he ?"

"By my sword," said Brotherton. "We had been engaged together in a little transaction, and on returning through a wood we quarrelled. I drew my sword, and his leaped quickly also to the scabbard. We fought, and he fell; and then reason came to me. I bethought me that we had quitted the inn alone—that we were last seen to enter the wood alone—that I should never be believed if I said that we had fought a fair duel, but I should be accused of murder. Consequently, I left him where he fell, and hurried to London."

"But are you any relation of his that you have assumed the title of Sir Oscar Penraven ?" asked Rupert Dreadnought.

"Yes, I am his cousin," replied Brotherton; "but I have preferred to take upon myself his identity, as it might be awkward to explain in regard to his death."

"But surely," said Rupert, "this imposture—for such of course it is—will be discovered ?"

"Well," said Brotherton, "it looks awkward for me now. But I had no idea that he was so beset by enemies. Was he, then, so great a villain ?"

"A poisoner—an assassin—he could not be much worse," said Rupert. "I was pledged by a solemn vow to kill him, but since he is dead I am exonerated."

Allan at this leaned forward, and said in a whisper to his companion—

"May not this be a ruse ? May not some deeply hidden scheme lie concealed beneath all this ? You have so often been told that Oscar Penraven is dead that it is scarcely right to believe it unless you see the body."

"True," said Rupert.

Then, turning to Brotherton, he added—

"What my friend has just said to me is most correct. I have so often heard that Oscar Penraven is dead that I cannot believe it truly unless I see his body, and satisfy myself in that way. Have you any objection to tell me where I can find it ?"

Brotherton hesitated.

He knew neither of his companions.

He had never before heard their names.

Might they not be officers of justice in disguise ?

"Well," he said, "I know not what to say. I have only your word for it that you *are* the people you represent yourselves to be. You *may* be officers of justice."

Rupert smiled.

"You are very cautious," he said, "and you, no doubt, have good reasons to be so. Nevertheless, your caution is, I assure you, thrown away in this particular instance. I *am* the person whom I represent myself to be, and can prove it."

"Well," said Brotherton, "will you make me one promise ?"

"What is that ?"

"That, no matter what happens, you will not betray me to the authorities."

Rupert Dreadnought had no suspicion of murder.

"It is not my business," he said, "I care not who inherits the villain's property. I shall say nothing."

"Very well," said Brotherton, "I will tell you, then, where to find the body."

Then he accurately described the spot where the dead body of Oscar Penraven lay.

When he had done so he said again—

"You swear not to betray me ?"

"I swear," said Rupert.

"And you ?" turning to Allan.

"And I also."

They little knew to what they were swearing.

After this interview they lost no time in departing, to the chagrin of the pretty little partner whom Rupert had secured in the beginning of the evening.

They, however, had no desire to remain longer under the roof of an impostor.

The next day, early, they started in the direction pointed out to them by Brotherton.

It was no difficult task to discover the wood.

But it was a more difficult task to find the body.

Brotherton had told them to search behind a clump of large evergreens.

But there were so many evergreens, and so many clusters of them, that noon had long past ere they came upon a spot which seemed in any way like that of which they were in search.

Here, however, was the cluster of holly and laurels, and there the stately oak tree.

An awe fell over them.

"I feel," said Rupert, "that we are near the dead."

And so they were.

It was in the very centre of the wood.

A dark and dismal spot, well fitted for such a crime, and its concealment.

Presently they came upon it.

It was lying on its face.

On its face just as it had fell, with the wound gaping—*in its back.*

"See," said Rupert, as he pointed it out to Allan. "See what we have sworn to conceal—it is a murder—the wound was given from behind."

"This accounts for his hesitation," said Allan of the Glen.

"It does most horribly," said Rupert, as he turned over the body and gazed at the face; "but see, he has spoken truly, it is Oscar Penraven, and my vow is fulfilled, or rather I am released from it."

"You will return at once now," said Allan, "and investigate the last secret of the Iron Chest, I presume?"

"I shall," said Rupert, "and I hope I shall find something in it which will release me from my long celibacy. It is cruelty to keep Helen longer pining away the best of her days in uncertainty, after this long engagement. I might at any moment be killed in one of my perilous adventures, and she might be widowed as it were before she was a wife."

"True," said Allan of the Glen; "and as to this body?"

"It may as well remain as it is," said Rupert. "I have not mixed myself up in any way with this ruffian. Let us return to our inn, secure our horses, and away to London."

CHAPTER V.

THE IRON CHEST IS OPENED ONCE MORE—THE FIFTH SECRET—THE WILL AND THE LETTER—ROBERT DANVERS—THE STORY OF THE BOX OF TREASURE—THE MISSION—THE JOURNEY—THE "PETHERINGTON ARMS"—THE INTERVIEW WITH THE OLD LANDLORD—HIS WARNINGS.

It was with greater pleasure than before on any occasion that Rupert Dreadnought looked forward to the re-opening of the Iron Chest.

It had up to the present time been a long list of fierce tasks of vengeance.

But the last visit had proved to him that the next visit would be of a different character.

So that evening he once more passed—alone—into his chamber.

There he locked himself in, and, with a feeling of awe, approached the chest.

He regarded it for a moment with arms folded.

The last secret!

What could it be?

He almost feared, as it were, to turn the key in the lock.

But he took courage, and kneeling down once more opened the repository of so many strange secrets.

There was but one layer of documents now.

The first was a will.

This I shall not give *in extenso.*

It would only be wearisome.

But its sense was as follows:—

"I, Rupert Stackington Ardleigh Dreadnought, being at the time of signing and making this my last will and testament, in possession of my full senses, do hereby give and bequeath the whole of my property, real and personal, wheresoever situate, to my dear son, Rupert Dreadnought, with my best blessing."

The second document ran as follows:—

"My dear Son,—

"You have by this time accomplished all my missions but the last.

"The others have led you through great perils, as I am certain.

"This last one will not be of the same character.

"It is one, in fact, which you will scarcely care to undertake, inasmuch as it is principally to bring to you and your family, when you have any, a still greater degree of wealth.

"However, as it is my wish that you should do so, I am certain that, ere you lead to the altar your beloved Helen, you will carry out my desire.

"And now for the explanation.

"Down in Hampshire, near Petherington Wood, lives a family of the name of Harding.

"There are now, at the time of my writing, a father, a mother, and six sons, all grown up—tall, sturdy men.

"Into the care of Hugh Harding, the father, I gave, seven years ago, a large box.

"This box is full of treasure.

"I gave it to them at the time when foreign commotion was so much threatened; and at the same time I gave into their custody a little boy of ten, the son of a friend of mine—a very dear friend of mine.

"You may wonder why I should not have undertaken his care myself.

"There were reasons (strange reasons which you will *never* know) why it would have been wrong, foolish and imprudent to do so.

"This boy's name is Robert Danvers; and he has not a friend in England.

"I am not wrong, therefore, in supposing that he will find a friend in you.

"I wish you to go down to the house of the Hardings, see the boy, and bring him and the treasure away with you.

"Then give him a choice between the army and navy, and get him a berth either in one or the other.

"Having done so, let him have a thousand pounds and let him go.

"Of course there will be no difficulty about the treasure.

"The box was securely fastened when it was delivered into the hands of the Hardings, and they were told that it contained pictures.

"There *is* a picture in it, at the top, which you will probably find of use to you.

"Having done this I leave you to shape your course of life in your own fashion.

"Marry Helen; be happy.

"Try not to forget your father; act honourably by all men, and receive from me again the blessing which a man owes to a good and dutiful son.

"Rupert S. A. Dreadnought."

Tears stood in the eyes of young Rupert as he read the last words.

"His last recorded sentences," he said, as he kissed the paper, and placed it in his pocket. "Poor old man! he little guessed that this adventure may prove more dangerous still than all. These rough people in whose honesty he so much relies, may be villains of the deepest dye. Gold seems to make all men devils. I have found it so. Well, well, danger or no danger, it is my father's last behest, and I will not shrink from it."

The place named by Earl Dreadnought, namely, Petherington, was some miles distant from London, and in those days communication between him and his friends would have been most difficult.

He resolved, therefore, to take with him those of his staunch friends whom he could persuade to go; so that in case of any resistance on the part of the Hardings he might be in a position to defend himself, and to compel their compliance with his father's wishes.

Upon this point he consulted Allan of the Glen, Stanley Sherrington, and Tom the Waterman.

It is almost needless to say that all agreed to accompany him on his last adventure.

Helen Penraven herself, though sincerely glad that this was, in very truth, the last expedition which her betrothed husband would be compelled to undertake, was yet sorely disappointed at the idea of his being once more led away from London.

She had hoped that whatever other wish of his father he had to fulfil, he would have been enabled to do in the quiet of his own home.

She had even gone so far as to imagine it possible that the last secret of the chest might refer only to their union.

But it was not so.

There was no help for it.

She must submit.

So she took a tender adieu of him and watched him sadly from her window, as, in company with his friends, he rode up the street.

But there was one antidote to her sorrow.

One thing seemed to assure her somewhat of his safety now.

Oscar Penraven was dead.

He would no longer be followed by the malignity of him and his crew of assassins.

Yet her sorrow was well to be excused.

Three years had now passed away since first Rupert passed his arm round her waist, and whispered his declaration of love—three years since their lips had thrilled to the first kiss of mutual passion.

And now, when by reason of the old earl's own words, she had hoped that he would be free from all adventures, he had left her side once more.

However, she kept up a brave heart.

She knew well that he *must* perform his commission, and she did her best to be brave under the trial of his continued absence.

Meanwhile, we must quit her side, and take our way with Rupert and his friends.

They had prepared themselves in every way for a long absence, both in money and in arms, and they quitted London in high spirits.

They started at night time, in order not to attract notice, but they, nevertheless, met with no adventure on the road, and, on the evening of the second day, arrived safely at Petherington.

Here they at once proceeded to put up at an inn—the "Petherington Arms," on the outskirts of the town, both to refresh themselves and horses, and to make inquiries in regard to the Hardings.

When they had partaken of a substantial meal, they sent for the landlord.

He entered with a bland smile.

They were excellent customers.

"Sit down, master," said Rupert, pushing a chair towards him; "you give us such jolly fare, that we have determined you shall do a bottle of your good wine with us."

"Most happy, gentlemen," said he, though with some suspicion that our four well-armed friends were gentlemen highwaymen; "I will go down into the cellar and procure a bottle of my best. I will not keep you long."

Rupert laughed as the old man toddled quickly away.

"I hardly fancy he likes the look of us," he said; "he takes us, I verily believe, for footpads out for a holiday, or 'night adventurers on the watch for prey.'"

However, think as he might, the old man soon returned with the wine, which he carried as if it had been gold, and uncorked it before them.

It was a rich, luscious wine, and the old fellow licked his lips when he had drunk it, both at its exquisite flavour and at the price he intended to make his guests pay for it.

"And now," said Rupert, "now that we are here I should like to ask you a question or two."

"Certainly, sir," said Boniface, deferentially.

"Yes; I wish to speak of the Hardings!"

It was a joke to see the transformation of the landlord's face at this.

He nearly dropped his glass in astonishment.

"The Hardings!" he repeated.

"Yes; don't you know them?"

"Know them!" cried he. "Yes, indeed I *do* know them. They're the biggest vagabonds for many a mile round."

"Indeed!"

"Are they friends of yours?" asked Boniface.

Rupert laughed at this.

It was said so drily.

"No," he answered; "but I desire to see them. They have some property of mine which I desire to take away with me."

The old man grinned.

"Property," he said; "if they have any property ne'er a bit of it will *you* ever see. They know how to stick to it themselves as well as any men on the whole country side."

This was just what Rupert had feared.

But he did not wish to let the landlord see his drift.

"Indeed!" he said; "you surprise me. My father had reasons to trust them."

The old man shook his head.

"They've changed then," he said, "for they live a kind of outlaw life now. Ever since they came into a little bit of property about ten years ago, they've been outrageous. They came into it all of a sudden like, and they spent and squandered it outrageously. Then, when they'd been used to it like, they couldn't do without it, and they were up

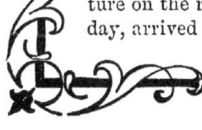

to every kind of trick to keep themselves in the same position."

"About ten years ago did you say?" asked Rupert, carelessly.

"Yes; full ten years."

This was the date when his father placed in their hands the treasure.

But he resolved to say nothing.

"Well, and what do they now for a living?" pursued Rupert, who was anxious to learn more.

"Why, they seem to have started in a kind of Robin Hood fashion," said Boniface. "They live in the woods, and rob every traveller who comes that way."

"But is this allowed? Are there no laws in this part?" asked Stanley Sherrington, who seemed much amused by the old man's style of telling his story.

"Well," said Boniface, "we have our patrols, and our justices of the peace, and our constables, and so on. But they don't seem to be able to do much against Richard Harding."

"That's a son, I suppose?"

"Yes; the eldest."

"And which is the way to their dwelling?"

"Well, you're in the right way here," said Boniface; "you've only got to go straight on when you go outside the door yonder. Keep along by the side of the high hedge and pass into the wood. You'll sure to meet some of the Hardings there; and, if not, another stone's throw will bring you to Hugh Harding's cottage. You'll then see it, for it is the only one near, and stands right in the pathway, with a red-tiled roof, rough log walls, and small, diamond-paned windows."

Rupert rose.

"Well, we'll go and reconnoitre," he said, turning to his friends.

"Surely not at night," said Boniface.

"Yes; why not?" answered our hero. "There are four of us here, all used to perilous adventures, and the use of warlike weapons. I doubt if these wonderful Hardings would have much chance with us were we only to measure swords with them."

"Had we not better wait till morning?" said Allan. "We could see our way better."

"Aye; early morning dawn, let us say," suggested Stanley Sherrington.

"Yes," said Boniface; "I would see that you were called. It would be far better starting then than trusting yourself in such a neighbourhood at night."

So it was arranged.

The four friends, well wearied by their journey, sought repose, and slept on uninterruptedly till daylight streamed in upon them.

Then they rose, and, before the old landlord came, were dressed and ready for their early breakfast.

This being dispatched quickly, they quitted the inn, leaving their horses in the stables, and made their way with all speed towards the wood where they naturally expected to meet with no ordinary adventures.

CHAPTER VI.

THE FRIENDS START—THE SURPRISE—THE SIX DESPERADOES—THE CONFERENCE—THE BATTLE—THE FALL OF YOUNG HARDING—THE SIGNAL—THE INTERRUPTION—OLD HUGH HARDING—THE EXPLANATION—THE WARNING, AND END OF THE BATTLE.

THERE seemed, indeed, in the mission which they had before them, something specially romantic.

The men whom they were about to meet were evidently of a kind of Robin Hood type.

A wild, daring, vagabondish lot, if nothing else.

"I rather anticipate amusement from this enterprise," said Rupert.

"So do I," said Stanley Sherrington; "it is far more pleasant in anticipation than any in which I have been engaged for you yet. And yet I fancy we shall have tough work somehow."

Allan and Tom laughed.

"That is just what we should like," said Allan, "for even now I am married I feel when I am with you all the old spirit of adventure."

Rupert smiled.

"And you, Tom?" he said.

"Allan has answered for me, my lord."

"Well," said Rupert, "I fancy if your fair wives heard you say this, I should be no favourite with them as of old."

"Never fear, my lord," returned Tom the Waterman. "Women like men to show their manliness—I know my Agnes does."

"Aye, and my Mary," said Allan; "she never dreamed of opposing my coming, or of questioning the danger or length of absence, when she knew it was for you, my lord."

So talking, they proceeded onwards until they reached the thick of the wood.

"Now," said Rupert, "we had better cease talking and look about us."

They advanced onwards quickly—as quickly, in fact, as they were able among dense, dark thickets, until presently smoke ascending through the trees told them that a human habitation was not far distant.

"We are approaching the house of the Hardings now," said Rupert. "We had better advance in a body, and make friends with them at once. They may not, after all, be such people as represented by the landlord of the inn; you know how all peculiar people are thought of and reckoned up by——"

RUPERT OR THE DREADNOUGHT SECRETS OF THE IRON CHEST

THE ATTACK ON THE OLD CASTLE.

He was suddenly and fiercely interrupted.

A band of six stalwart fellows burst from among the trees.

"What have we here?" cried one of them, advancing with a drawn sword, and in a bullying manner. "What want you in our domain?"

Rupert smiled as he surveyed the group of desperadoes.

Fine fellows they were—tall, broad-shouldered, with well formed features, and dressed in good clothes of the decided highwaymen "cut."

"Your domain, my good sir," said our hero, "your domain? Are you, then, Robin Hood come to life again, or are you endeavouring to mimic his ways?"

The speaker, who was Richard, the eldest of the six sons, frowned darkly at this.

"Have a care, sir," he said; "we are not used to put up with mockery. We free sons of the forest hold a sway here as absolute as ever your Robin Hood did, and those who make their appearance here with any show of swagger, are apt to remain in our power longer than is good for them."

"We came not to dispute your claim to the sovereignty of these wild acres," returned Rupert, in the same tone of banter, which, in the presence of the insolent brothers, he could not throw off; "we came to see your father, Hugh Harding, who, probably, were he here, would teach you better manners than to insult strangers ere you know their mission."

Richard Harding's eyes shot fire.

"Death, sir!" he cried, "our father teaches us to chastise the insolent; so, be ye friends or foes, ye do not see him save with an apology wrung from you!"

Rupert turned quickly to his companions, who at this speech had drawn their swords.

"You see," he said, "that we shall have to fulfil our mission at the point of the sword. These braggart fellows are either mad or desire to provoke a quarrel."

Then he turned to Richard.

This worthy was engaged in a hurried conference with his brothers.

But he confronted Rupert Dreadnought at once when he addressed him.

"Harkee, sir," said our hero, "I have told you that my business is with your father, and not with *you*, and I intend to see him. I shall make no apology for words called forth by vain boasting. Let us pass, therefore, in peace, or we must pass through your ranks."

The cool, cold, determined manner in which these words were spoken somewhat awed the young desperadoes.

But they were not daunted.

"Well, since you so will it," said Richard Harding, "be it so."

The brothers at once sprang to the attack, and in an instant the unequal contest began.

The wood rang with the clash of arms, the woodland echoes sending forth clearly and distinctly each stroke that the swords gave out.

The brothers, being six to four, of course anticipated an easy conquest.

But it was not so.

They little knew the metal of which their adversaries were made.

They themselves had been used to night attacks and marauding.

But such staunch fellows as these they had now to deal with, were far different persons to conquer.

Presently one of them, the youngest of the brothers, fell.

A groan of rage rose from the others as he rolled over on the green sward and his sword remained in Rupert's hand.

"Death to the villains!" shouted Richard.

And they responded eagerly to the cry.

But it was of no avail.

Rupert and his friends fought like lions.

With their backs to the trees they kept the others at bay, receiving not a wound, while the blood trickling down the white shirt-frills of the others told a far different tale as regarded them.

Presently, in the midst of the conflict, a loud, shrill whistle rang through the forest glade.

The brothers all started.

Richard uttered a loud curse.

"We shall be interrupted," said he, "if we do not hasten. Quick, cut them down."

His brothers responded with right good will.

But in vain.

They might as well have attacked a wall of stone.

Only for a few minutes longer now the fight continued.

The whistle during this time was repeated twice.

It served, from some unaccountable reason, to exasperate them more.

To drive them to renewed exertions.

But, at the end of the few moments, another person appeared upon the scene.

A tall man with grey hair.

An old, bent man now, but one who had evidently, in his youth, been of the same stamina and pluck as his sons.

For this was Hugh Harding.

He rushed in between the combatants.

"Down with your swords, mad boys!" he cried; "do you want all the people in Petherington about us?"

The sons obeyed sulkily.

"It means," said Richard, "that we were insulted, and that we resented it. See, there lies our brother, Morris, dying from the wounds inflicted by these men whom you are protecting."

"A word with you, Hugh Harding," cried Rupert. "What this man asserts is false. I came hither with my friends to see you, and these fellows insolently opposed my passage. Because, forsooth, I refused to apologise to them, when it was they who had given the insult, they drew their swords on *me*. If your son here bleeds from his wound, it is from a wound he sought."

The old man thought a moment.

"This is a serious matter," he said, as he gazed with a look of rough tenderness at the youth who, though not absolutely dying, had received a deep and dangerous wound. "I must be well satisfied that your motive in desiring to see me is a good one before I accuse my sons of acting wrongly."

"Are they always in the right, then?" asked Rupert, "or is it, rather, the case that you have instructed them to waylay, insult, and murder unoffending travellers? When I started on my journey, I had no conception what style of men

I had to encounter; but I shall now begin to believe that the reports I have heard since I came into these parts are true."

Hugh Harding advanced a step, and gazed earnestly into Rupert's face.

"Look you, young sir," he said, "I know you not, but your manner and bearing are such that I am in no way surprised that my sons could not preserve their good humour. What is your name?"

"Lord Rupert Dreadnought."

Hugh started.

So, indeed, did all his sons.

They glanced at their father with a peculiar glance.

But he, disregarding them, put up the sword he had drawn when he had first come upon the scene, and, with a cheery smile, said to Rupert, at the same time advancing nearer—

"Your name alters things greatly. I was a friend and confidant of your father, and I am sure, had you but mentioned your name to my son Richard, there would have been none of this."

"No, indeed," said Richard, gruffly.

But his thoughts were far different.

They said—

"No, indeed; I should have killed him in cold blood."

However, for some reason or another, they all repressed their real feelings.

"Follow me, gentlemen," said Hugh Harding; "I have but a humble home, but, as you come from the earl, why, you are one of the old stock, and will not be ashamed to sit with humble folk in a humble room. Richard," he added, turning to his son, "see that a litter is made for Morris, and that he is borne to his room. *I* will conduct and see to the strangers myself. Now, gentlemen."

"I must correct you in one thing," said Rupert, as they advanced. "I do not come from the old Earl Dreadnought. He is dead."

The old man started.

A gleam, which all recognised as one of satisfaction, illumined his eyes.

"Dead!" he repeated.

"Yes," said Rupert, "he has been dead three years. But *I* am his representative."

He said this with force and evident meaning.

The old man knew at once that the old earl, being dead, had left behind him one of the same grasp of mind and resolution.

"You surprise me!" he said. "I am indeed sorry."

"Rather glad, *I* should imagine," thought Rupert Dreadnought.

But he said aloud—

"Yes; it is three years now since he deputed to me a task which I am here now to fulfil, a task dear to his heart."

"And that is——"

"In the first place, to see Robert Danvers."

"Yes; he is now within. And secondly——"

"Secondly," said Rupert, emphatically, "to take from you and bear to London a box which contains some portraits and other articles of value!"

The old man turned pale, and as he glanced round put his finger to his lip to enjoin silence.

"Hush," he said, "let not my sons hear."

"Why?"

"If they knew I had a box of valuables," he answered, in a whisper, "*you* would never live to tell the tale to others. They are good boys, good boys, but terribly avaricious, terribly avaricious."

"This is an old villain of the deepest dye," thought Rupert Dreadnought.

But he was resolved to dissemble.

"You may depend upon my silence," he said.

Then he turned to Stanley Sherrington and the others who were near him.

"Stanley Sherrington, and you, Allan and Tom," he said, "be careful not to mention to any one the object of our visit. I and Mr. Hugh Harding will manage all."

They heard him, and they understood his words.

But they better understood the looks that accompanied them.

The words spoke fairly to the ears of the old villain of the wood.

The looks said—

"Have a care; we are in a den of thieves and assassins. It behoves us, for our lives' sake, to watch and be careful."

All this, of course, could not be conveyed in silence.

But enough *was* conveyed to assure them that, for some reason or another, Rupert Dreadnought, their leader, considered silence a necessary act of prudence; that danger, in fact, was ahead; and to him, as their leader, therefore, they resolved to look for orders in every respect.

As Rupert spoke, they came in view of the house of the Hardings.

CHAPTER VII.

THE HOUSE OF THE HARDINGS—ITS STRANGE APPEARANCE—THE BREAKFAST—THE PRIVATE CONFERENCE—THE OLD MAN MAKES A CONFIDANT OF RUPERT—THE CASTLE—THE JOURNEY THROUGH THE WOOD.

The home of the Hardings was scarcely the kind of domicile which one would have expected to belong to any one who was possessed of any degree of money.

Outwardly, it was more like the hut of a squatter in the far West than the home of a well-to-do British yeoman.

It was, in fact, a log-hut.

It was built of huge logs cut flat top and bottom, so as to form a thick solid wall, the outer part being left wholly untouched.

Within, there was a tolerable semblance of rough comfort.

The floor was tiled as in France.

The roughness of the walls was in some measure hidden by the mass of utensils and curiosities of all kinds that were hung upon them.

Deers' antlers, boars' heads, old shields, and so on, were mixed with platters, and hams, and so on incongruously; everything, in fact, giving to the observer the notion that Hugh Harding and his sons performed their housekeeping duties themselves, without any aid from the female kind.

Such, indeed, was the fact, in this place.

But, as they discovered afterwards, *this* was only a hunting-box.

These outlaws, as they seemed to delight to consider themselves, had a far better home.

Of this, however, we will speak anon.

Our tale, at present, has to do with the "log-hut" and its inmates.

On entering it, the first thing which Rupert observed was a young fellow sitting by the fire, attending to a huge joint of beef which was there roasting.

He was a tall, handsome youth, of some nineteen years of age, fair, with blue eyes and light brown hair—a pleasant-looking youth, in truth, very different from the rough fellows with whom he was in constant companionship.

"That is Robert Danvers," said Hugh Harding, in a whisper, as they entered; "but tell him nothing as yet, we will have a talk about him presently."

Then he turned to his sons, who were bearing Morris to an inner room.

"Now," he said, "I suppose, lads, you are hungry after your conflict in the wood? So see to your brother, and then we will discuss a good meal."

That meal was a strange one.

It was what they called a breakfast, thought it had all the substantiality of a dinner.

Neither Rupert nor his friends had any fear of joining in the meat or drink, inasmuch as they all partook of it; and so, tired and hungry after their conflict, they all fell to with a will.

After the meal Hugh Harding rose.

"Now, my sons," he said, "if you will retire with our guests into another room, I will speak to Lord Rupert."

He avoided mention of the name of Dreadnought.

Evidently Robert Danvers knew it.

One look passed between Rupert and his friends.

It was a look implying caution.

But it was unobserved by any save those for whom it was intended.

When they had quitted the room, the old man drew two chairs close up to the fire.

In one he seated himself.

To the other he motioned Rupert.

"Now, then," he said, "we've got a little mutual confession to make."

Rupert smiled.

"I don't know exactly about confession," he said; "you may have; but, as regards myself, I must say I have none."

"Very good," said Hugh Harding. "In the first place, you come after Robert Danvers."

"I do."

"What do you want with him?"

"To take him away."

"Good," growled Hugh Harding; "I am glad of it—glad to be rid of him—he doesn't suit me—doesn't suit my sons. It will be a good day for him, and me, too, when he's gone."

"True enough," thought Rupert, "and a better day for him than for *you*, perhaps."

But he remained silent.

The old man continued—

"Well, and when you've got him, what may be your intention?—what are you going to do with him? He's no use."

"No use!—how so?"

"He can't fell a tree; he can't hunt; he can't—"

"Pick a pocket," thought Rupert, as the old man paused.

"There, I've no patience with him!"

"Well, I shall try and make something of him," said Rupert Dreadnought. "I shall make a soldier or a sailor of him; whichever he likes best; but, as Robert Danvers was not the principal object of my visit to you, we will defer speaking of him for a time, and proceed to business."

"Certainly," said Hugh Harding, eyeing him keenly and nervously.

"About ten years ago my father gave into your hands a large chest containing certain valuables."

Hugh Harding nodded.

He had evidently expected this.

"Well, that box I have come to take with me. That is very easily told. And, having told it, I have explained to you my whole mission upon which I am here."

The old man thought a moment.

In his own heart there was going on a strange struggle.

Should he use violence or cunning?

For it was merely a question which to employ.

To keep the box he had resolved, with whatever there was of value or of strange secresy within it.

His mind was quickly made up.

He remembered well the conflict of that morning.

Cunning was the weapon to use with such men as Rupert Dreadnought.

He drew his chair closer to that of our hero.

"I have been thinking what to do," he said, "and I am resolved that if my sons only knew the object of your visit, the result would be extremely dangerous to all of you."

"Are they murderers, then?" asked Rupert, with some sternness.

"No, not murderers," he said, "but they look upon the contents of that box as legitimate property to be divided between them after my death. And even I myself should be afraid to tell them that I had let it go into the hands of a stranger. So we must act upon a far different principle."

"And pray what principle may that be?" asked Rupert, who was somewhat amused, naturally, at being asked to assist this strange old man in hoodwinking his own sons.

"We must use art, not force," said Hugh Harding. "I myself am quite willing that you should have the box; it is your own—your due, and in the obtaining of it, therefore, I will do all I can to assist you."

Then he lapsed again in thought.

After a few moments he said,

"In the first place, you must know that this is not our home."

"Not your home!" repeated Rupert Dreadnought, in some surprise.

"No," said old Harding, "I am not, indeed, telling you wrongly. We sleep here sometimes; but our home is on the other side of the wood. As you are the son of the old earl, I will let you into the truth, but it must be upon a promise of strict secresy."

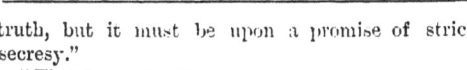

"That I promise."

"Well," continued Hugh Harding, in his confidential tone, "we reside here sometimes for the purposes of hunting and so on——"

"Mail coach robbing," thought Rupert.

"And the rest of our time we spend at our castle, as we call it. It *is* the remains of an old castle, and people imagine to this day that it is uninhabited."

"How do you keep up the illusion?" said Rupert. "Surely sometimes lights must be seen at the windows?"

Old Harding smiled.

"You shall see how we contrive," he said. "I will take you to our castle and introduce you to our wives. My wife still lives, and three of my sons are married, and we all live in the ruins, and have done so for years, without being discovered. Well, my plan is this: I will take you there, then send my sons back to this place on some expedition (one *must* stop here, you see, to see to Morris), and, while they are gone, you must, with the aid of your friends, carry off the box."

This plan seemed pretty feasible.

The man's manner, too, was so plausible that Rupert Dreadnought could not help being deceived in some way by him.

"Very well," he said; "I am agreeable to anything you propose, so that it will not take long to accomplish it."

"Oh, no; we shall not be long over our work," said the old man, with a strange smile. "And now, since we have pretty well settled our matters, we had better call in the boys, and have another flagon of ale, or they'll suspect that we're conspiring."

So saying, the old man rose, and approached the inner door.

The young men entered the room with an amused and a surprised expression upon their faces, and glanced from their father to Rupert, and from Rupert to their father, as if in vain endeavouring to fathom the meaning of the private interview between them.

The old man, however, was as impenetrable as stone.

"Now, then," he cried, "let us mix a good glass of grog. This gentleman has quite satisfied me as to the object of his mission here, and I can only say that I am extremely sorry that such a misadventure should have occurred this morning."

They were soon discussing a good jorum of splendid punch, and an hour or two passed in jovial talk.

Then Hugh Harding proposed a move.

The sons were surprised at this.

"Whither are we going?" asked Richard.

"To our castle," replied his father.

"With the strangers?"

"Yes; I have informed Lord Rupert Dreadnought in regard to our other home. I have done quite right, as you will see in the end. Come, let us bustle about; and you, Henry, can remain here to take care of Morris while we go home."

CHAPTER VIII.

THE MYSTERIOUS DOOR—THE OLD HAG—THE SUBTERRANEAN CORRIDOR—THE CIRCULAR ROOM—THE THREE WIVES—THE NEW MYSTERY—THE UNDERGROUND DUNGEONS—TREACHERY AT WORK AT LAST.

It was not long ere they were *en route*.

About a quarter of an hour's walk through the wood brought them to a dense cluster of trees, a circle of which were planted round a mass of evergreens.

These evergreens Hugh Harding pushed open, and showed a doorway so sunken in the earth that it was completely concealed by the surrounding brushwood.

Here Hugh Harding pulled a bell, and waited.

After the lapse of a few minutes the door was opened by a queer, odd-looking woman.

A woman singularly repulsive in looks, with one of the witch faces we more often see depicted by an artist's imagination than in real life.

Hollow-cheeked, gaunt-eyed, parchment-skinned, prominent-featured, with a wild tragic expression as of a spirit that had given its whole life and thought to one aim and burnt itself feverishly out at that.

She wasd ressed commonly, but the clothing was scrupulously neat and whole.

A few thin locks of silvery white straggled down the swarthy forehead, through which the black eyes, which seemed all pupil, peered eerily with a most unpleasant effect.

She stared at the new comers with a look which was anything but a welcome.

"Whom have we here?" she said, gruffly.

"Friends of mine," said Hugh Harding. "Come, let us enter, my lord."

He led the way, pushing the old woman on one side rudely, as if annoyed by the manner in which she had glanced at his visitors; and they found themselves at once in a gallery fashioned out of the damp earth itself.

"This is the way we reach our castle, my lord," said the old man, with a chuckle; "you see I was right in saying how difficult a matter it would be for any one to find us out."

"Yes, indeed," said Rupert Dreadnought, "this is not a bad method of entrance—though of course it is a mystery to me why you should need all this secresy."

Hugh Harding laughed.

"Ah, ah!" he said, "thereby hangs a tale. But you don't come here to find out my secrets, do you; only to carry away your property? So I won't let you into my little designs."

And, so talking and jesting, they went on, followed closely by Stanley Sherrington, Allan of the Glen, and Tom the Waterman.

These latter were completely at sea.

They had not the slightest conception what was going on.

As yet all had been mystery.

There had been sundry winks, and stern looks, and so on, on Rupert's part.

But beyond this there had been nothing in the way of explanation.

However, they had perfect faith in the wisdom of

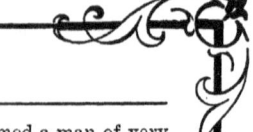

Rupert Dreadnought, and in this faith they went on boldly, keeping their eyes, however, well about them.

The old parchmenty woman, meanwhile, lagged behind to close the door, and then, hurrying after them, plucked one of her sons by the sleeve.

"What is the meaning of all this?" she asked, in a fierce whisper. "Has your father gone mad, or what ails him that he brings strangers?"

Her voice sounded like the growl of some savage beast.

The young fellow addressed shrugged his shoulders.

"Don't ask me," he said; "as far as I am concerned it's all a mystery."

"Ah! I fancy your father is not the man he used to be," she said, still in her horrid undertone "he would never bring a posse of armed strangers into our castle, by our secret way, too, unless—unless—indeed——"

Then she paused and whispered in his ear the remainder.

It was evidently something villanous.

Something that tickled her horrid fancy.

This she did not strive to conceal.

A horrid laugh, like that of some gratified wild beast, or some demon who has destroyed some human soul, went ringing away along the subterranean corridor.

But it did not reach the ears of Rupert Dreadnought and his friends.

If, indeed, it had, they would not have understood it.

At length the extreme end of the earthy gallery was reached.

Here a lofty set of stone steps led up into a large hall.

This was the commencement of what they called "the castle."

"You see," said Hugh Harding, as they halted at the summit of the staircase, "you see, we can have a view here of all that is going on around us."

"And others can see you," said Rupert Dreadnought, with a smile.

"No, no, not as well as we can see them," said Hugh Harding. "Besides, the best proof of it all is that during all these years they haven't seen anything of us, or even suspected a living soul to be here. Now, as we go on, you will see that all our other arrangements are just as perfect."

It might have suggested itself to Rupert Dreadnought as peculiar that the old man should be so anxious to prove to him how utterly unlikely it was that any one from without should ever suspect the existence of human beings within the precincts of the old castle.

But it never once occurred to him as anything extraordinary.

He had been prepared to meet strange people.

He had met them.

And in no respect were they different to what he had expected.

The meeting in the morning had certainly not been a friendly one.

But that was a mistake, and the fault too of the sons.

Old Hugh Harding himself seemed a man of very different stuff.

At any rate, as Rupert Dreadnought advanced he was so interested with the strange people and the strange place, that he thought of no suspicions.

On entering further into the precincts of the house they passed through another doorway into a large circular hall.

Round this were seven doorways.

Above it was lighted by a large skylight, evidently placed in in modern times.

This was the secret.

This skylight enabled them to gather together at meals and of evenings without being in fear of discovery from without.

The seven doors were the doors of the sleeping apartments of the old man and his six sons, with one of whom Robert Danvers slept.

All the food of the family was cooked in this large room by means of charcoal, which emitted no smoke.

The ruins towered so much above this skylight that even when the brightest lights shone below there was no fear of a single ray being seen; while as to sounds, the thickness of the wall, and the fact of the bedrooms being placed in a circular form, prevented the possibility of anything being heard from without.

The old man proudly expatiated upon these matters.

He expatiated upon them with an earnestness which seemed unsuited for the occasion; but his speech was cut short by the opening of three doors and the entry of three women.

They were all young.

Tall, dark, gipsy-eyed, they had fine faces and forms, fashioned in a sinewy yet graceful mould, with long, sweeping limbs, and muscular arms and necks.

Just such wives as one would have expected to find in the homes of such men as Richard Harding and his brothers.

They started on seeing four armed strangers.

But the old man quickly reassured them.

"These are four friends of mine," he said. "They are going to dine with us."

The girls merely nodded acquiescence, while Rupert said, with a smile—

"Well, Master Harding, we had a breakfast that amounted almost to a dinner. It will be late before I have appetite for another meal."

"Oh! no," said Hugh Harding. "When you have explored this place with me, and imbibed a little more of this fresh air, your appetite, you will find, will recover wonderfully. Besides," he added, in a whisper, "I desire an early meal for another reason. I am all nervousness; while knowing myself the object of your visit, I am dreading each moment discovery by my sons."

"Will they go then after dinner?"

"I will see that they *do* go," said the old man. "But come, I will show you a specimen of the cruel refinement of our ancestors. You boys can remain here," he added, turning to the four sons, who had accompanied him; "I will conduct our guests myself."

So saying, he opened a little door, and disclosed a flight of steps.

"I will lead the way," he said. "You know it not, and might fall in the darkness."

There would have been ample room for suspicion had the old man followed them, instead of preceding them; but, as it was, he placed himself in such a position that if any treachery was attempted by the sons, he could be sacrificed at once.

Rupert and his friends, therefore, descended without hesitation.

As the door closed, the old hag, who was the wife of Hugh Harding, scowled darkly.

"What *is* the meaning of this?" she said. "*Who* are these men, and what is he doing with them? To no one in his life before has he thus shown the secrets of the old castle."

Richard Harding smiled.

"Rest assured, mother," he said, "that he is well aware what he is doing. They have proved themselves too strong in open warfare; mark me if he does not lead them headlong into some trap."

We shall see soon whether his prophecy was verified.

As soon as the door of the large room was closed, old Hugh Harding lit a torch.

"We shall now be able to see which way we are going," he said. "Follow me without fear. Where *I* can tread so may you."

"This is, indeed, a dismal place," said Rupert, who was nearest to him.

"Yes. See there through that loophole that dark and dismal den," said Hugh Harding; "not a fit place for a sane being or a mortal soul at all, is it?"

Rupert glanced through.

It was, indeed, a horrid den.

A tiled floor, dank and damp, with only a pile of decaying straw in a corner.

"I am going to show you worse than that," said the old man. "A prisoner there might have the possibility of seeing a human face and of speaking through the loophole, or even peering out into the darkness beyond here. But there—well, you will judge for yourselves."

He led the way on a little further.

Then he stopped opposite a part of the wall where there seemed no door at all.

"Perhaps I am boring you," he said, in his most genial tone of inquiry.

"Not at all," said Rupert.

"Well, truth to tell," continued old Harding, "I would not show these to every one. In fact, you and a friend of mine, whose acquaintance you may make ere long, are the only beings that *I* have ever trusted with my secret."

With this he touched a spring in the wall, and a door swung open.

Nothing but darkness within!

"Well, certainly," said Rupert, "this *is* a frightful den."

The old man laughed.

"Worse than the other I fancy; but I have two more torches. We will light them all, and then you will see what the refinement of cruelty can do to its fellows."

The other torches being now lit, the three were held aloft, and by their red light the black darkness, as it were, was seen.

A square room, without a window or even a loophole—with dank, murky walls, and a dank, murky floor.

Such was what they saw.

"What a place!" said Rupert. "Why, anyone immured in this place would never again be able to hold communion with his fellow man. See here, there is not even a loophole through which he could speak his wants."

"You are wrong," said the old man, stepping suddenly to the door, "you are wrong."

Then he, in an instant,, sprang into the corridor without.

The door closed with a clang, and——

Rupert and his friends were prisoners!

For an instant they did not realise their position.

They imagined naturally that the old man had only gone out for the purpose of showing to them the mode by which they might communicate with a person outside.

But they were soon undeceived as to this.

A loud, jeering, ringing laugh fell upon their ears!

"Ha! ha!" cried the old man, "you are caged then, my fine birds! You thought that after insulting my sons, and nearly slaying one of them, that you would be received as my honoured guests. You are mistaken!—you are mistaken! I said that only one other friend of mine had ever entered the dismal den you now inhabit! I said that you might soon become acquainted with him. You can do so now! See in the corner of your dungeon—his bones whitening—see what will be your own fate! Farewell!"

CHAPTER IX.

THE LANDLORD'S SUSPICION—JOEY, THE OSTLER—THE WATCHER—THE PATIENCE OF AN INDEFATIGABLE GOSSIP—THE MYSTERIOUS DOOR—JOEY HAS HIS SUSPICIONS—AN ACCIDENT AT THE CASTLE—JOEY FANCIES HE HAS DISCOVERED SOMETHING, AND HURRIES OFF WITH THE NEWS.

THE landlord of the "Petherington Arms," who was a jolly fellow in his way, had, as we have seen, no great opinion of the honesty of the Harding family.

He looked upon them as rogues and vagabonds.

And, as we have seen, expressed his opinion to that effect pretty freely.

On the other hand, he had taken a liking to Rupert and his friends, and he saw with great regret their determination to pursue their journey to the Hardings' home without the aid of others.

But there was no help for it.

He watched them as they went for some time.

Then a thought struck him.

He rushed to a window overlooking the yard and threw it up.

"Here, Joey, Joey!" he cried.

A small voice answered quickly,

"Yes, sir—coming."

Then a very small body entered through the front door.

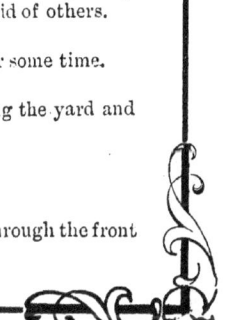

"Here I am, sir. What is it?"

"You know those four gentlemen that have just gone off?"

"Yes, sir."

"Well, they're going to see the Hardings."

"They'll be robbed, then."

"Perhaps worse," said Boniface: "however, I want *you* to save them."

This was just the thing for Joey.

He loved to believe himself of consequence.

"Save 'em?" he cried. "I'll do it; but how?"

"I'll tell you. You must go after the gentlemen."

"Yes, sir."

"And watch what they do."

"Yes, sir."

"And where they go."

"Yes, sir."

"Never mind that eternal 'yes, sir,' of yours, listen to me. You must watch, never mind how long, until you discover something."

"Yes," thought Joey, "and if I can't discover anything, I'll have to stop there for ever without anything to eat and drink."

"Very well, sir," he said, aloud, "I'll go; but as I'm likely to be there a long time, I'd like a drop of ale before I start, and I'll take a bit of bread and meat with me."

The good-natured landlord made no demur at this.

Joey was soon supplied with the requisite comforts, and, in a high state of excitement, he departed on his errand, fully resolved to put a stop, if possible, to the designs of those whom, in his peculiar phraseology, he denominated "those murdering thieves."

Now Joey was a curious being.

But his heart was in the right place.

He had bowlegs, a stumpy body, a round bullet head, red hair, and eyes that squinted terribly.

But he was cunning as a fox.

And, what was more to the purpose, he always used his cunning to some good ends.

Mis-shapen people are generally of the "Wormwood" class.

He was not.

Well determined to follow in the track of those whom he considered about to venture into a den of thieves and murderers, he crept stealthily after them.

Boniface had not told him that he was not to show himself even to those he went to protect.

This he would have done, had time been given him.

But Joey needed no such instruction.

He knew the wise course.

He crept on stealthily, keeping to the grass, which made no noise.

He saw all—the fight, and the interruption by old Hugh Harding.

Then he saw the four friends enter the old log house.

"All right," thought Joey, as he planted himself on the green sward behind a tree; "I'll have my lunch now. I guess they'll be in that place some time. It's a rum thing, after fighting, to make friends like this."

Joey, while the old landlord's back was turned, had purloined a bottle of foaming ale.

So now, with his bread and meat, he made a sumptuous repast, while Rupert and his companions and the Hardings, were breakfasting.

When they issued forth once more, he followed them, and saw them pass in at the mysterious door.

There he lost them.

But Joey was, as I have said, full of cunning.

"Now," he thought to himself, "where can that door lead to?"

As he spoke inwardly thus, his eyes fell on the old ruins.

It seemed like an answer to his mental questioning.

"Good," thought he, "good; I have it now. These villains have somehow lured them into the ruins, for no good purpose, I'll be sworn, so I'll keep a good watch hereabouts."

So he left the mysterious door and wended his way towards the ruins.

The country people were superstitious in regard to them, as I have said.

And Joey had been of the number of the alarmists.

But now he cast all this aside.

He was a great man.

He had a mission to perform.

Besides, his strength was heightened by the strong ale he had imbibed.

So he advanced boldly to a place where he could have a good view of the old ruins.

To his credit, be it said, he went very near, and even peeped in at some of the cavities, but he saw nothing.

The place where he ultimately remained on the watch was a slight eminence crowned by some dense evergreens.

Here he remained some half-an-hour.

Then suddenly, just as his patience was being sorely tried by the continued silence, there was a loud crash, an explosion, and fragments of glass and wood were sent flying up into the air.

"Ah!" thought Joey, "I was right. They're in the ruins, and the Hardings are up to some devilment. I will away at once and give information."

And so off he ran.

He had hardly left his post of observation when a man's head appeared on the ruined battlements.

NOTICE.

"RUPERT DREADNOUGHT"

Will end with No. 52.

Our Readers are requested to observe that A NOTICE *in regard to the* SENDING UP OF THE PRIZE CHEQUES *in connection with this work, to 173, Fleet Street, will be given in our next, and a List of Winners in No. 52.*

HANDSOME COVERS FOR BINDING

Will be issued on the same date as No. 52, Price Ninepence; Post Free, One Shilling.

The work will also be Published in Handsomely Bound Volumes, containing all the

SPLENDID COLOURED PLATES.

Price 4s. 6d.; Post Free, 4s. 10d.

"A VOLLEY OF FIRE-ARMS WAS POURED FROM THE WINDOW."

The head which appeared over the wall was that of Richard Harding.

He glanced eagerly and hurriedly round.

Then he slipped down again into the big room, saying—

"It's all right; no one is near."

This big room was a sad wreck now.

One of the daughters had accidentally thrown a small bag of gunpowder on the fire, and, exploding, it had knocked two of them down, and crashed through the skylight.

Meanwhile, Joey sped away, as fast as his legs would carry him.

He arrived breathless at the inn.

"Well," said Boniface, "have you discovered anything?"

The little ostler was panting for breath.

Yet he managed to cry out—

"Yes, yes! they've got the gentlemen in the old ruins, and are murdering them!"

This rather vague statement, given in a style and with a grimace which was most comical, was all that for a few moments the landlord could extract from Joey.

But after awhile he recovered himself.

Then he gave, in a somewhat disjointed manner, the history of what he had seen—the quarrel—the fight—the reconciliation—the re-appearance of Rupert and his friends—the mysterious door—and the explosion in the old castle.

The landlord fortunately was, as we have seen, a somewhat clever fellow.

He saw how matters stood.

Rupert and his companions had been led nto some ambush.

This was certain.

There was no time to lose.

"Saddle me Molly quickly, Joey," he said.

"Molly was out yesterday, sir," began Joey.

Molly was his favourite mare.

"Don't talk to me, but saddle Molly quickly," said Boniface. "There is no time for babbling when people's lives are in danger; saddle her, and be quick with you."

Joey saw it was no use arguing.

The landlord was roused.

When he *was* roused, no one in Petherington could have altered him.

So, with many a sigh, he hurried to the stable and saddled Molly, the best animal in the inn, which had done good service the day before, but was in reality quite fit for more.

In a few minutes it was brought round to the door.

Not sooner was it there, however, than the old landlord.

He was already waiting, and, losing no time in leaping into the saddle, he was soon speeding away along the road.

He had quickly formed his plans.

In the town, which was not far distant, was stationed a troop of soldiers.

To the colonel of these, therefore, as being far more useful than the constabulary, he resolved to apply for aid to rescue Rupert.

CHAPTER X.

THE COLONEL OF THE GARRISON FORCES—ENSIGN MORNINGTON SMELLS A LITTLE ACTIVE SERVICE—JOEY TO THE RESCUE—THE ENTRANCE INTO THE WOOD—JOEY LEADS THE "ARMY" UP TO THE CASTLE RUINS—HE SHOWS HIMSELF A GENERAL—THE CONFERENCE WITH HUGH HARDING.

NEVER since he had been a young man had he used whip and spur so; and Molly, unused to such harsh treatment, carried him along at a spanking rate.

On reaching the town he lost no time in seeking the colonel.

The latter was a bluff, grey-headed old soldier, and listened with courteous attention to the strange story which Boniface had to tell.

The name of Lord Rupert Dreadnought had an immediate effect upon him.

In those days the army was very loyal.

The name of a member of the aristocracy was quite sufficient to enlist the sympathy of such a man as Colonel Almore.

"Gad! sir, this is a disgrace to the country," cried he. "I'll see to it at once. Sit down, sir."

The old landlord accordingly sat down, and the colonel, making his way out into the barracks, called out one of the young officers, and hurriedly explained to him the circumstances.

Young Ensign Mornington was engaged in a game of cards with a fellow officer, when the presence of Colonel Almore was announced.

"The devil take him!" he muttered, as he flung down his cards. "Some frivolous pretext or other, I suppose."

He never dreamed of active service.

The colonel's information entirely altered his ideas.

He was every inch a soldier, and was delighted at the mere chance of battle, were it ever so small.

To Ensign Mornington, then, the task of relieving Rupert and his friends was given.

In a few minutes, as it were, the men were ready—about a dozen fine well-armed fellows, who, to the surprise and awe of the rustics, marched away at a quick pace, followed by a gaping crowd.

Joey was the one deputed to be the guide of the expedition.

He himself had lost no time in following his master, for Joey, as we have seen, was of an inquisitive turn of mind, and was resolved to see what was coming of it all.

Besides, he didn't at all relish the idea of being suddenly elevated as he had been into the position of a great man, and as suddenly being let down again.

He had a painful notion that now *he* had done all the work his master was going to rob him of the glory and take it all himself.

Resolved not thus to be cheated, therefore, he had closed the stable-yard, given it into the care of his little brother, and started off as fast as his bowlegs would carry him towards Petherington.

Knowing his master to be usually long-winded, he had concluded that, in spite of Molly's speed, he would be able to reach the town long before the worthy Boniface had completed his conference with the colonel.

But for once he was was wrong.

The landlord's wits had been sharpened by circumstances.

When, therefore, the little ostler had proceeded, puffing and blowing, and red with the heat, about two-thirds of the way, he saw the small troop advancing towards him, headed by Ensign Mornington and the landlord, and Molly, while the rear was brought up by a number of wondering and eager peasantry.

The landlord at once saw him.

At any other time he would have been enraged

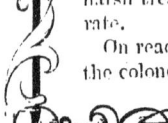

at him for neglecting his duties thus without leave.

Now, it was different.

He was overjoyed to see him.

"There comes Joey!" he cried.

"Who's Joey?" asked the ensign.

"The man who is going to guide you."

The officer laughed as Joe came up, puffing and blowing and admiringly scanning the troops with his squinting eyes.

"He is not a great beauty, nor does he seem particularly acute," said he.

"That may be, to anyone who doesn't know him," said the landlord; "but he's a clever fellow, is Joey; and has got his heart in the right place and——"

Boniface stopped.

Ensign Mornington had left him and was speaking to Joey.

The old fellow, in fact, had gone off into one of his long-winded speeches when he found Joey's sense impugned; and the soldier, who was all impatience for the fight, was in no humour to listen to him.

Joey was in a fluster of delight when he knew what was expected of him.

He was again an important personage!

He was to lead an army!

His own feelings were nothing less.

"Well, captain," he said, addressing the ensign (in *his* idea all officers were captains), "if all you want of me is to lead you through the wood to the place where them poor genelmen has been put by them there murderin' fellers, I'm your man. So foller me, and we'll be there in no time."

"That's just it, my good man," returned the ensign; "lead on, and quickly."

The words "lead on" inspired Joey at once with a desire for martial glory, and feeling like a general he marched forward, and after proceeding a few yards came to a point where the woodland ran close to the high-road.

Here he quitted the road, and dived in among the trees.

The soldiers, being on foot, easily scrambled through after him, as also did the peasantry.

Not so Boniface.

He was on horseback, and there was no inlet for Molly, the mare.

He was thoroughly resolved, however, not to be beaten thus.

He had determined to see the attack on the castle, and so dragging Molly up to the hedge, he tied her to a tree by the bridle, and leaving her there to chance being run away with by a footpad, he dived in among the brushwood, and was soon scrambling through the wood with the others.

Joey knew his way through the forest well.

There were not many along that part of the country-side who did not.

But, as I have before said, the old castle had a suspicious reputation, and few cared to meddle with it, whereas Joey didn't care, and never *had* cared a rap about the superstitious nonsense babbled by others.

If he had been in any way influenced by such feelings, his present exalted position would have certainly caused them to evaporate.

He went on in a direct line, therefore, like a brave little fellow as he was, and before long they came in sight of the castle ruins.

There they were, as quiet and as grey and deserted-looking as ever.

"Everything looks still enough here," said Ensign Mornington, turning to Joey.

"That's their artfulness, captain," returned the ostler; "look here; here's a piece of the glass as was smashed to pieces when the explosion took place."

Sure enough he picked from the ground a piece of glass which had belonged to the skylight of the Hardings' centre room.

"You'd better place a couple of men on watch at the secret door, captain," he added; "and one here and there round the place, as they're mighty artful, I can tell you."

The ensign smiled as he turned to his men.

Joey had forestalled him in his command.

Of course the manœuvre was a self-evident one.

Nevertheless, when Ensign Mornington told off the men for the service, the little ostler was delighted.

"Show these four men the way to the secret door, and leave them there," he said.

Joey obeyed with alacrity.

In a few minutes he had reached and pointed out to the soldiers the mysterious door.

"There," he said, with an air of authority, "there is the point you have to guard. Remain there until further orders."

Without observing how the men were laughing at him, he then ran back to the ensign, just in time to see Richard Harding's head appear on the top of the wall as he had seen it before.

There was a scowling look of defiance on his face as he glanced at the soldiers.

"What do you want here?" he said.

The ensign had knocked loudly at the old door of the ruinous place.

"I might ask you the same question," said Mornington, in reply. "This place is not your property."

Harding laughed coarsely.

"Have you come here to tell me that?" he asked.

"I have not. I come to take with me those whom you have here as prisoners. Be quick about it, for we have no time to lose."

Harding laughed again.

"We've got no prisoners here," he said. "Some one has been making a fool of you. At any rate, we're not going to open the door. You've been set on by Colonel Almore, I suppose, because he thinks we've been poaching; but it's no use. You'd better go away, and not lose your time. This old castle may be in ruins, but it will stand a siege now."

"You refuse to open?"

"We do."

"You refuse to give up the prisoners?"

"We've got none."

And then he disappeared.

CHAPTER XI.

PREPARATIONS FOR ATTACK—THE FIRE—THE MYSTERIOUS DOOR—THE ATTACK AND DEFENCE—THE TRUCE—THE CONFERENCE—THE BATTLE RENEWED—THE DEFEAT OF THE OLD POACHER AND HIS FRIENDS—THE SEARCH FOR THE PRISONERS—THE DISCOVERY OF RUPERT AND HIS COMPANIONS—THE CONTEST AT THE SECRET DOORWAY.

"THERE is nothing for it but to attack the place," said the ensign. "Quick, my men; collect some of yonder dry brushwood and those sticks, and bring them to this doorway, and we will burn them out."

The men at once piled their muskets, and did as they were commanded.

It was not long before a goodly pile was heaped against the old gateway.

It was worm-eaten and dry with age.

It seemed certain that it would soon yield.

In a few moments the pile was fired, and a flame shooting up red and lurid licked the woodwork which crackled beneath them.

Then, with some large pieces of wood, the men battered at the doorway.

As they did so, the report of musketry was heard.

"They're at it now at the secret door," cried Joey, wild with excitement.

"Run there and see," said the ensign.

And Joey ran like the wind.

He was no coward.

In fact the smell of the gunpowder, and the rattle of the guns, and the commencement of hostilities, appeared to act like a spark upon tinder.

When he reached the door by which Rupert and his friends had entered the trap, he saw one of the soldiers lying dead on the green sward.

The door, it seemed, had been opened a few inches, and a face protruded.

Then it had been closed again for a moment, and when opened again, a volley of fire-arms had been poured upon the soldiers, and one had fallen a victim.

The other three, undaunted by the fall of their comrade, stood, pale and determined, watching for the reopening of the door.

"Tell Ensign Mornington what has happened," said one of the men. "We've lost Joe Archer; but never mind, they won't do the trick again. We know too much for them now."

And as he spoke they began hammering with all their might at the secret door.

Meanwhile the ensign and his men had not been idle.

When Joey returned he found the great door half battered in.

The Hardings were, up to this moment, idle at their point.

But when they saw Joey running up again, they began to fear he had come to announce reinforcements.

So from within now there came showers of missiles—bricks, stones, and pistol-shots.

They had no muskets here.

Not for a moment imagining they would ever be wanted at the castle, they had left them at the hunting-lodge.

The female Hardings were busy preparing another means of defence—simple, but horribly effective.

Boiling water!

This was presently poured on the soldiers, just as they were facing the gate, scalding their hands and faces, and disabling them more even than shot wounds.

But they fought on.

Irritated—exasperated,—at the idea of being checked by a parcel of ruffianly fellows like the Hardings, they fought on in spite of their pain.

Presently the great door gave way.

Then the real struggle began.

The Hardings were drawn up here behind an inner wall, the men in front armed with swords and pistols, the women with pistols at the back.

"Hold, one moment!" cried old Hugh Harding, holding up his hand.

The ensign made a gesture to his men to halt.

"What have you to say?" he asked.

"Much," returned the old poacher, with difficulty restraining a desperate oath. "You've come here to attack me for nothing. This ruin mayn't be mine, but I'm doing no harm to it. I know my children live in it and pay no rent, that's right enough. Besides, as there is no owner for it, I don't see as it matters to you or any one else."

The ensign cut this speech short.

He naturally, knowing the state of affairs, considered that the old fellow was trying to gain time for some rascality.

"That's all very well, I dare say," he cried, in a loud voice, "but we've nothing to do with it. I have learned that Lord Rupert Dreadnought and some friends of his are immured in this ruin. Now, I can promise you if any harm happens to them, that every man and woman in this place shall suffer a horrible death. I will set fire to this place, and you shall be driven back into the flames. If, on the other hand, you deliver up your prisoners, you shall not be molested."

Old Hugh Harding laughed loudly.

"Boastful words enough," he cried; "but we are not of the sort that's afraid. We've no prisoners here, and we've got an idea you're up to something that's no good. So keep off, or we'll fire."

"It's no use talking to this old fellow any longer," cried Ensign Mornington, losing his temper. "Charge away, my men, and clear them out."

Leading his men on, he dashed at the old door where the defenders were, and was received of course by a volley of musketry.

But fire-arms were almost at once discarded.

The besieged and besiegers soon came to close quarters, and fought with desperate energy, using their swords and bayonets.

Old Harding's obstinacy was greater than his judgment.

He had imagined that a strong volley would check the ardour of the foe.

He was wrong.

Trained English soldiers are not frightened at the rattle or the effect of musketry.

The fall of comrades, moreover, only renders them more wildly eager for victory.

The sight of blood now acted in the usual way.

It made them desperate.

That blood was the blood of dear friends.

Their own might mingle with it presently.

So, with dilated nostrils, hard breathing, and distended eyes, they fought on.

Soon they struggled over the wreck of the old door, and were just entering the room in a crowd, when a dense smoke arose from the floor, and for a moment blinded them.

The vapour soon cleared away.

But when it did so, the place was empty.

The Hardings and their Amazonian wives had disappeared.

"This is a strange contretemps," said Ensign Mornington, as he wiped the perspiration from his brow (though foremost in the contest, as many a brave British officer before him, he had been unhurt, though his men had fallen); "this *is* a strange contretemps. This place, too, seems full of doors. We must search all."

The soldiers each rushed to a door.

The doors of the bed-rooms were all unlocked.

These chambers were, of course, searched at once.

But no one was found there.

The two rooms which resisted were those which led, the one to the subterranean passage to the wood, the other to the underground cells, in one of which Rupert and his friends were confined.

Fortunately for all, the first door which was attacked was the latter.

A few blows from the butt ends of muskets shivered the panels of the portal, and the dark descent was visible to all.

One of the soldiers eagerly lit a piece of wood, and began descending.

"We had better all go down together," said the ensign; "there is no knowing what devilry these fellows will be up to."

So he hurried down himself.

But he had no cause for alarm.

The place—as far as regarded the Hardings—was deserted.

All was still as death.

But still a search was made.

Ensign Mornington had no idea of doing things by halves.

So into every cell they peered.

They would have utterly failed in their search, however, but for one circumstance.

Rupert and his friends had heard the sounds of battle.

They knew that those who attacked the Hardings *must* be on their side, no matter who they might be.

When, therefore, the soldiers descended to the subterranean passage and began searching, they heard a loud clattering at a door which before had been invisible.

Even now there seemed no way to open it.

"How are we to get in?" cried Mornington.

A muffled voice answered—

"There is a secret spring."

But no spring could be found.

"We must force it open," cried the officer.

In an instant one of the soldiers sprang up the stairs, and in a few minutes returned with a hatchet, which the Hardings had left in the room above.

By means of this the woodwork was—not without great difficulty—demolished, and Rupert and his companions were once more free.

The faces of their rescuers were entirely strange to the rescued.

"Well, gentlemen," said Rupert, as he advanced among them, "I can but offer you my sincere thanks for this speedy liberation, though how you knew of our incarceration here is to me another mystery."

In a few words the ensign explained it.

There was no time for lengthy talk.

What he said, however, was enough.

Boniface and Joey were booked in Rupert's book for a good reward.

"Have you captured the villains?" he asked.

"No; but they cannot be far off," replied Ensign Mornington; "we will start off at once in pursuit."

"And we will aid you," said Rupert; "you see, they did not deprive us of our arms. They were in too great a hurry to secure us."

In a few moments they stood once more in the large room.

Rupert knew at once the door by which they had emerged from the secret passage, and with very little effort it was forced open.

But all in vain.

Not a soul was to be seen.

They traversed the earthy corridor from one end to the other without opposition.

When they reached the door which led out into the forest, they found a second soldier lying dead, while the other two, badly beaten, were lying disabled on the ground.

This was enough to show that the Hardings had passed that way.

"What has happened?" asked Ensign Mornington, kneeling down by one of the soldiers.

"There was a sudden rush from the door there," said the man, "and the whole of the family fired upon us. We attempted resistance in vain; the women fought as well as the men—like devils, too."

"I don't doubt it," said Rupert; "from what *I* saw of the wives, I can fully believe that they would fight like their husbands. But follow me; we will make for the log hut."

CHAPTER XII.

THE ATTACK ON THE HUNTING BOX—THE MYSTERIOUS DISAPPEARANCE OF THE HARDINGS—THE VAIN SEARCH—THE RETURN TO THE INN—THE QUARREL—THE DUEL IN THE WOOD—ITS LUDICROUS ENDING.

By this time some of the peasantry, headed by Boniface and Joey, had reached the place, and leaving the wounded in their care, with directions to make some kind of litter and carry them to the inn, the others set off at once for the log-built hunting-box.

On reaching it, a volley of fire-arms was poured from the windows, and two or three of the soldiers fell wounded.

The troops answered with a rapid discharge, and then dashed up to the door.

One of the Hardings having been severely

wounded in the first encounter in the wood, it was natural to suppose that some human being would, at any rate, be found in the place, and the firing, of course, strengthened the idea.

But it was not so.

When they reached it, they found the door wide open, and everything within indicative of the greatest disorder.

Rupert rushed into the inner room.

It was empty !

There were marks of blood on the door.

Marks of blood were visible, too, all along the floor.

The wounded man had evidently been taken from his bed hurriedly.

But no living being was to be seen.

Not even Robert Danvers.

"This is most mysterious," said Ensign Mornington ; "that they were here a moment ago is certain, and yet now they have disappeared as if by magic !"

"They cannot be far off," said Allan of the Glen, "we had better search."

And search they did.

But in vain.

Mysterious and vexatious it was.

But it was useless to deplore it.

The Hardings had secrets which were not to be fathomed; that was very certain.

The walls were sounded vigorously.

They were solid.

The floor was torn up.

It was nearly level with the ground below.

"Well," said Ensign Mornington, "this is about the most extraordinary affair that has ever occurred to me. If I were superstitious, I might really attribute this disappearance to magic. But at any rate, it is of no use remaining here. We must scour the country with increased force tomorrow."

"Well," said Rupert, in a tone of sincere vexation, "we have failed most signally, and all through my own folly."

"I do not see that," said Stanley Sherrington, "you were misled by the instructions left you by your father. They led you to suppose that this last mission was one in which no peril existed. You had no right to suppose that you would be compelled to use force to obtain possession of the treasure or the boy. But it's of no use remaining here ; we had better make our way back to the inn. After being cooped up in that dark and dismal place, I feel much inclined for refreshment."

"And you will accompany us," said Rupert to Ensign Mornington.

The young officer at once accepted the invitation.

His wounded men had been carried there, and the others, of course, would need rest and refreshment.

On reaching the "Petherington Arms," they found the old landlord bowing on the doorstep.

At the conclusion of the attack on the ruins, he had seen that proper litters were made for the wounded soldiers; and then running off to the spot where his mare Molly was tethered, he had mounted her and ridden off with all speed so as to arrive first at home.

A fine cold collation was soon spread ; and over their wine they discussed the extraordinary events of the day.

"I cannot conceive," said Ensign Mornington, "that such people should have been allowed so long to remain in undisturbed possession of the ruined castle."

"But their occupancy was never suspected," said Rupert. "How should it be ?"

"Their living must have been that of footpads and desperadoes," said Stanley Sherrington, "and in pursuit of it, they must have gone frequently out on the highroad and attacked peaceful travellers. It seems strange, certainly, that with any kind of constabulary they could have been able to carry on such a game."

"So it is, however," said Rupert ; "and the manner in which they disappeared in the wooden house yonder makes it no wonder to me that they have failed to be discovered."

And so the conversation was progressing when a gentle knock came at the door.

"Come in," cried Rupert.

Boniface entered smiling.

"A gentleman to see you, my lord."

"Who is he ?"

"The chief of the constabulary."

Ensign Mornington laughed aloud.

"Now," he said, "you require no further explanation as to the reason why the Hardings have been permitted so long to have their own way. Here, when all this fighting has been done, and when I have had three of the best men in my company killed, the chief of the constabulary comes to know if anything is the matter."

"They have not been asleep, Ensign Mornington," said a voice, and the chief of the constabulary entered the room.

There is always a rivalry between the police and the army.

A savage glance consequently shot from the eyes of Solomon Heavyweight, the constable, who had heard the laugh of the officer as well as his jeers.

"No one accused you of somnolency," replied the ensign ; "but it does seem strange that such vagabonds as those Hardings should have been suffered to exist so long when you and your men have had the patrolling of the highways. I can only account for it by supposing that some of the constables are in league with the desperadoes."

Heavyweight's eyes shot fire.

"Ensign Mornington," he cried, "these remarks are most uncalled for. All my men are quite as respectable as the army, which, as we all know, is filled with the very scum of the earth."

Ensign Mornington sprang to his feet.

His face was crimson with anger.

"Sir," he said, as he laid his hand on his sword, "is that observation meant personally to me ? If so, sir, perhaps you will be good enough to draw your sword, and accompany me into the wood yonder. Lord Dreadnought here will be my second."

Rupert was about to interpose.

But Heavyweight's blood was up.

"I don't care," he said, "whether you take it personally or not. I was an officer in the army myself. You are but an ensign; I am a colonel, sir—a colonel—and I quitted the army in disgust. I will retire with you at once. I am sure one of these gentlemen here will be my second."

The colonel was as fiercely disposed as Ensign Mornington.

Rupert, however, resolved to try and put an end to a quarrel commenced on such absurd grounds.

"Gentlemen," he said, "let me beg of you to reason for a moment."

"I will not," said Ensign Mornington; "he said I was the scum of the earth."

"And *I* will not," said Colonel Heavyweight; "he said I was the leader of a band of thieves."

"Gentlemen," said Rupert, "this is entirely a mistake; it is a quarrel got up in a moment in pure hastiness of temper. Let me entreat you——"

"Lord Rupert," interrupted Ensign Mornington, "will you or will you not act for me in this matter? This is not the first time that I have been insulted by Colonel Heavyweight, and this time, after the manner in which I have fought for you, I really shall claim at your hands this little service."

"Ensign Mornington," said Rupert, "I owe you my liberty: but if it were not so I should none the less act for you in this matter. I had only hoped that this affair might be arranged so that the meeting should not take place at all. However, as you are so thoroughly resolved to fight, I will choose a second for Colonel Heavyweight."

"We are resolved," said the colonel, hot with anger.

Rupert saw that arguing was no good.

He therefore turned to Stanley Sherrington.

"Stanley," he said, "will you be this gentleman's second?"

"With pleasure."

"And you, Allan and Tom, had better come with us to see that we are not disturbed."

The landlord had remained quiet until now.

"For gracious sake, gentlemen," he said, coming up from a window, whence he had been looking out upon the yard, "if you are resolved to fight yourselves, do prevent your men from quarrelling as well. My inn will be ruined."

The ensign went to the casement and looked out.

Sure enough the constables and the soldiers were at loggerheads.

"We will soon settle that," he said. "Now, gentlemen, if *you* are ready, I am."

He hurried down the stairs.

In the yard he passed a word to his men, and they at once left off wrangling with their natural foes, the constables, and passed into the inn.

The two angry disputants then left the yard and crossed the road to the wood.

Here they passed in among the brushwood, and selected a spot where they would be free from all observation, some thirty or forty yards from the high road.

One more ineffectual effort at conciliation was made by the seconds.

Then they measured the ground, and the weapons and the two officers faced each other.

Both were brave men.

Both were good swordsmen.

Both, moreover, looked upon themselves as aggrieved.

So at it they went with a will.

With little effect.

The sword play was brilliant.

But no blood flowed.

This only made them more angry.

They dashed at one another with redoubled fury, and the woods re-echoed with the sound.

Presently they paused a moment to rest.

As they did so there was a rustle in a clump of brushwood near at hand.

All started.

"Something stirred yonder," said Allan.

And he ran towards it.

Tom the Waterman followed his example.

When they reached the place they drew their pistols.

"Now, then," cried Allan, "whoever is in there had better come out. I shall give you one minute, and then I fire."

In an instant there was a violent commotion among the underwood.

Then a man's form rose up.

He was dressed as a constable.

Allan at once led him towards Colonel Heavyweight.

"What are you doing here, sir?" cried the latter, fiercely.

The man was very pale before.

At seeing his officer, his knees shook beneath him, his teeth chattered, and he could hardly splutter forth the words—

"Nothing, sir."

"Oh! nothing," said the colonel, with cold severity; "then you think hiding in bushes is the way to do it. What have you got in your back pockets, sir?"

The back pockets alluded to stuck out immensely.

"Nothing, sir," repeated the man.

"Take it out, then," said the colonel, drily.

Tremblingly the man obeyed.

Out came a large hare.

"Where did you get that from?" shouted the colonel, furiously; "have you been poaching?"

"No, sir—it was given me," said the trembling man.

"By whom?"

"By Dick Harding, colonel."

This was too much.

Colonel Heavyweight heard a smothered sound near him.

Slowly he turned his head.

Ensign Mornington was convulsed with laughter, which, as he met the colonel's serious gaze, burst out into a loud guffaw.

"This is too much, colonel," he cried, while the tears stood in his eyes. "We'd best shake hands and have done with it."

So saying, he held out his hand.

The colonel took it with a rueful smile.

"Well, ensign," he said, "you've won the wager in a way I did not expect."

"At any rate, it is better than bloodshed," said Rupert Dreadnought, who, together with Allan of the Glen and Tom the Waterman, had enjoyed the scene hugely.

"Yes," added Col. Heavyweight, "and it teaches me that I must look more sharply after my men."

Then he turned to the constable, who expected nothing short of a violent death.

"Now, look you, sir," he said, "I will pardon you and say nothing of this on one condition."

"Thank you, sir."

"That you tell me all the truth."

"I will—I will," said the culprit.

"Without any reservation?"

"Yes, colonel."

"I shall know if you are lying," said the colonel. "Now when did Harding give you this?"

"Well, colonel," returned the man, "you see he didn't exactly give it me. We come for it; it's a regular thing."

"Oh, it's a regular thing, is it?" said the colonel, smothering his passion as well as he could; "and pray in what way is it a regular thing?"

The man hesitated.

"Speak out!" cried the colonel. "I told you I would pardon you if you told the truth."

"Well, you see, colonel," said the constable, brightening up again, "you see the Hardings kill a few hares, and leave some here in the bushes for us."

"Oh! then there are more in it than you?"

"All of us."

"And what is this bribe for?"

"To shut our eyes."

"And let them rob and pillage as much as they like?"

The man did not reply.

"Well, well, this is, indeed, a discovery," said the colonel. "I shall make further investigations into the matter. Go about your business now, take your hare with you, and remember, not one word to your comrades in regard to this matter."

The fellow, glad to be let off so easily, acquiesced, as may be supposed, at once, and skulked away gladly.

The two officers, with Rupert and his friends, returned to the inn, and, over a few glasses of wine, swore eternal friendship.

CHAPTER XIII.

RUPERT THINKS OVER HIS FAILURE—THE COLONEL AND THE ENSIGN DEPART—THE BED-CHAMBER AT THE INN—THE DISTURBANCE IN THE NIGHT—THE MYSTERIOUS APPEARANCE OF JOEY THE OSTLER—THE SECRET LETTER—THE OLD COUPLE AT THE COTTAGE—THEIR INFORMATION—THE WATCHERS—VOWS OF REVENGE.

RUPERT DREADNOUGHT had not accomplished his mission.

He had, as he had himself said, failed.

But it was not through his own folly.

Stanley Sherrington had taken the most reasonable view of the matter.

Certainly, the words of the old earl had been enough to banish from his mind all idea of there being any peril to encounter.

He had naturally acted, therefore, in the matter as if it had been only a business transaction.

The question now was—what was to be done next?

He scarcely knew.

He was resolved not to be beaten.

That was a certainty.

Yet now failure was more likely even than before.

The Hardings now knew well that they had to deal with an enemy.

A man full of desire for vengeance.

How, then, was he to circumvent them?

He retired early that night.

The ensign and the colonel departed in the afternoon to concert measures for the scouring of the country side.

But Rupert had little hope in the success of their experiments.

He felt sure that he himself was destined to meet them first.

Stanley Sherrington, Allan of the Glen, and Tom the Waterman, had all joined earnestly in conversation with him on the matter.

But somehow or another he desired to be alone, and he quitted them early, as I have said.

The bed-chamber into which he was placed was a tolerably large one.

It overlooked the yard, and from its windows could be had a view of wood and dale away for miles.

A low outhouse, with a sloping roof, was directly beneath it.

Somehow or another this seemed to Rupert to indicate danger, and he saw well to the fastening of the window.

Then, thoroughly tired out with the adventures of that long day of action, he got into bed and passed off into a quiet sleep.

He had slumbered about three hours when he was awakened by a noise at the window.

He sprang up, and glanced in that direction.

Sure enough he could discern on the outside of the casement a human form, which seemed to be making the most violent gesticulations.

Seizing the pistols which were in readiness on the table, Rupert leaped out of bed and approached the window.

"AT THE GRATING WAS A WHITE, HAGGARD FACE."—(*See No.* 51.)

The night was very dark, but he could see that a man was on the ledge outside.

That was all.

What manner of man he was he could not distinguish.

Presently a voice spoke.

A whispering voice—

"Let me in."

"Who are you ?"

"I'm Joey the ostler."

"Very well; wait a moment," said Rupert.

Then, returning to the table, he lit the lamp, and carried it to the window.

Sure enough it *was* Joey.

In another moment the casement was thrown open, and little Joey rolled in.

He was shivering with cold.

"Oh, it's awful cold out there," he chattered, putting his hands round the lamp to warm them.

"What were you doing there?" asked Rupert, amused; "there is a door to my room. If you wanted to speak to me there was no occasion to come to the window."

"That's where you're wrong, my lord," said Joey. "What I've got to tell's partickler private, and I wasn't even to let the landlord see me a speaking to you."

"Another mystery," thought our hero.

"Well, my man," he said, aloud, "what is it?"

"Well, you see, my lord," said Joey, "I was a closing the yard gates about half-an-hour ago, when I felt some one's hand a gripping hold of my neck, and I was dragged out into the road.

"I hadn't a chance of hollering out, for I felt a cold pistol pressed up ag'in my forehead, and the man says—

"'If yer cry out, I'll blow out yer brains!'

"So I kep' still.

"'What's all this for?' I says, in a low tone.

"'Tell me,' says he, stern-like, 'are those fellows from London gone away yet?'

"I hadn't no idea he meant your lordship.

"'We ain't got no fellers from London here,' says I.

"He swore an awful oath, then, saying—

"'Yes you have; those fellows that were out in the woods with the soldiers.'

"'Oh, if it's them you mean,' I says, 'they're all fast asleep.'

"'And the landlord?'

"'Yes; he's in bed, too.'

"'Very good,' he says. 'I've got some horses up here as wants a feed and a drink, so just bring us some hay and water.'

"It warn't no use saying no.

"He came with me.

"Well, I took the hay and the water out, and, while he was busy putting the feed into the nose-bags, one of the chaps on horseback slips a piece of paper into my hand.

"I guessed it was a secret, so I just slips it into my waistcoat-pocket, and says nothing.

"I was standing near the yard door as the man who had spoken came up to me.

"'You're the chap as set the soldiers on to the castle,' he said, fumbling in his pocket.

"I saw a kind of nasty glitter in his eye, as he was a speaking, and I guessed I was in danger.

"So I flings my empty pail right clean into his face, and slams to the yard door.

"'Now, be off,' I cried, aloud; 'or I'll have the whole inn about yer.'

"And in a few minutes I heard them galloping off.

"Then I comes in and looks at the paper.

"Here it is. It says outside—'To be given to Lord Rupert Dreadnought, without any one's knowing.'

"So, here I am, and here's the paper."

Rupert took it eagerly.

It ran as follows:—

"I am a prisoner in the hands of the Hardings, and cannot say much. When you came to the hut we were among the bushes, but I dared not cry out or they would have murdered me. If you want any information about the Hardings, go to the cottage of Luke Waldron, on the other side of the wood. He will tell you a great deal. I can't write more now.

"ROBERT DANVERS."

"Well, this is most strange," said Rupert.

Then, turning to Joey, he said—

"You have acted very rightly, my man, and you may think yourself lucky you did not fall into the hands of those ruffians. They were the Hardings."

Joey's eyes opened wide with astonishment.

"Well," he said, ingenuously, "well, if I'd a known that, you'd never have had that letter. I'd a run in and took my chance. Why, they'd have murdered me if I hadn't cut away as I did."

"That they would, my friend," said Rupert. "And now here's a guinea for your pains. Say nothing of this to any one. *I* will arrange my plans myself."

Joey accordingly, after sundry expressions of gratitude, passed out of the window again, and descended into the yard.

Then Rupert closed the casement, and once more retired to rest.

In the morning at breakfast he detailed to his friends his discovery.

They were for immediate action.

"Yes," said Rupert Dreadnought; "I shall not let the grass grow under my feet. We will start at once. Perhaps we shall be able to learn from this couple of whom Robert Danvers speaks the exact spot where this family of murderous villains are concealed."

"Or, better still," said Stanley Sherrington, "we may discover such news in regard to the treasure that our further pursuit of these Hardings may be unnecessary. In that case we can give them over to the authorities."

"You forget the boy Danvers."

"Oh, fear not for him," returned Stanley Sherrington. "He is a clever lad, and I'll lay my life he'll find some method of escape."

"No; I must go through with the affair properly now," said Rupert Dreadnought. "But come; if you are ready, we'll go out and see to the saddling of our horses. We'll go mounted this time."

It was not long before, mounted on their fine steeds, which had now had a good rest, the four adventurers set out on an expedition which was by no means without hazard.

From Joey they had learned full particulars as to the best and nearest way to the cottage of old Luke Waldron.

"He's a curious character that old Luke," said Joey; "but I don't fancy he's half a bad sort. He's been mighty thick with old Hugh Harding, but that's only because Hugh's had him in his power. If he only knows that the Hardings are flying from justice, he'll be one to help you, I know."

This information from the acute little ostler was

just the best thing that Rupert could have started with.

It put him on the right scent.

It told him plainly how to deal with the old cottager.

They chose the high road as their route in preference to making their way through the woods.

They knew it to be the nearest way, but they had experience of the danger of penetrating recklessly into the forests.

It was not a long ride.

About half-an-hour's trot brought them in view of the cottage of the Waldrons, standing quiet and alone.

They rode up hastily.

"House!" cried Rupert, not stopping to alight.

He deemed it better for the time to remain mounted while he questioned the old man.

Luke came out grumbling.

It was nearly mid-day, and he was in the middle of his dinner.

"I've got a few questions to ask, my man," said he, as the cottager came out. "I don't come to waste your time for nothing though, so here's a gold piece for you."

Old Luke grinned.

He was a thin, parchmenty, grey-haired old fellow, and his grin expressed about as much merriment as you would expect from a death's head.

"It be something important you want to know, I'm thinking?" he said.

"It is," returned Rupert. "I've come to ask a few questions about the Hardings."

The old fellow's countenance changed in an instant.

"The Hardings, eh?" he answered. "They be dangerous people to meddle with. I'd rather by half have nothing to do with them."

"You need fear nothing from them any more," said Rupert Dreadnought, remembering what Joey the ostler had said, "nothing more. They've got the hue and cry after them, and if they save their own skins it will be as much as they will do, without harming other people."

There was a slight movement in the bushes near as Rupert spoke.

But all were so engaged that it was not noticed.

"They're being pursued, eh?" asked the old man, with a peculiar expression in his face, which seemed to speak of anything but displeasure.

"Aye, right and left," said Rupert; "but it's of no use beating about the bush like this. I want a service from you."

"Well, what is it, sir?"

"Simply this. I want to know where the Hardings are now, or rather where they can be found to-night."

The old man smiled.

"You want me to peach?" he said.

"Well, now, that's not a very unpleasant matter to you," said Rupert. "I know all about you. Old Hugh Harding is no friend of yours; and now you're out of his power, why the best thing for you to do is to tell where we can find them, and earn a good handful of gold."

"How out of his power?" asked the old man.

"Why, he'll never be able to show his face in this neighbourhood again. But, come, we've no time to lose. Is it to be a bargain or not? Here are ten guineas to begin with, and if we find your information correct, you can have twenty more."

"Well, look here," said the old man. "What is it you want?"

"To know where they'll be to-night."

Luke extended his skinny hand to clutch the gold.

He took it with a feverish impatience.

"Well," he said, "do you know Horrock's Mill?"

"I do not."

"Joey at the 'Petherington Arms' knows it well. He'll tell you."

"When will they be there?"

"At ten this night."

"All of them?"

"Yes; and there's more there than *you* know of!"

"How so?"

"Treasure."

The bushes now stirred more eagerly than before.

Still no one observed anything.

"Ah! indeed!" said Rupert, assuming indifference.

"Yes; buried in the ruins. But at any rate they'll be there. Mind now, if you succeed in catching them——"

"I'm to keep silent," said Rupert, "certainly. And so adieu. To-morrow, if we find your information correct, you shall have the other money."

Then turning their horses' heads, he and his companions rode off.

Old Luke hobbled off into his cottage.

As he did so men's forms arose from the undergrowth, and hurried in after him.

These were those who had listened.

CHAPTER XIV.

ROBERT DANVERS A PRISONER—EN ROUTE FROM THE FOREST—AN UNEXPECTED FRIEND—THE ESCAPE—THE SHOT IN THE DARK—THE COTTAGE PORCH—THE HORROR OF SILENCE—WHAT ROBERT DANVERS FOUND IN THE DARKNESS—THE CHALLENGE—THE HARDINGS AT THEIR WORK AGAIN.

WE must return for awhile to Robert Danvers.

When they left together the inn where he had contrived so adroitly to slip the paper into the hands of Joey the ostler, he had been placed for a whole day in charge of three of the Hardings.

The next evening he was strapped on a horse's back behind one of the brothers.

This one, who was the youngest of the family but one—the next to the wounded one—had had always a kind of friendship for Robert Danvers, and he knew well the injustice of his being in his present position.

Hugh Harding had threatened him with death if he attempted escape.

And why?

What was Danvers to him?

The lad himself, as they moved through the wood, felt desperate.

Why should he be forced to join these ruffians?

The horse he was riding lagged somewhat behind the rest.

A thought occurred to him.

What if he were to kill the fellow who rode in front of him, or at least desperately wound him and so effect his escape?

The idea put his blood on fire.

Already his knife was in his hand when——

"Robert," said young Harding, in a low tone.

"Yes. What is it?"

"You don't much like coming with us."

"I hate it."

"I will let you escape!"

Robert's heart bounded joyfully.

"Do you really mean this?" he asked.

"Yes. I have already lagged behind. When I tell you, you must jump down and run. I shall fire a shot after you, and pretend to pursue you. You understand?"

"Yes; and then——"

"You must conceal yourself in the wood for awhile, and then you can go where you please."

They rode on for some time in silence.

At length they approached a dense thicket.

"Now," said young Harding.

In an instant Robert leaped down and was off.

Harding made as if to plunge after him, and then a pistol shot rang out upon the night.

Robert Danvers did not wait to see how matters stood.

He plunged away, not caring whither he went; but after awhile he found that he was approaching the house of Luke Waldron.

Here he stopped.

He heard voices and shuffling feet.

He knew, therefore, that the Hardings were near, and he kept quiet.

The twilight was now thickening.

Birds began to wing for home, and Nature assumed an unwonted quiet.

Still Robert Danvers knew well the danger of being precipitate.

The Hardings were not the men to trust in the slightest degree.

He waited until he could trust to the darkness to screen him from observation.

Then he left the cover of the woods.

He approached the premises in the rear, and reached safely the shelter of a stable.

The house was, perhaps, twenty yards distant.

All was still about it, and there were no lights in the windows.

Neither were there any cattle or any living creature whatever stirring in the yard.

Robert Danvers felt uneasy.

He knew not very well why.

It seemed to him that all was not right here.

He had hoped to meet the old man at the stable or the corn-cribs, and avoid the risk of first entering the house, where there might be visitors he would not like to see.

He coughed.

Then he cried aloud—

"Hullo there!"

In case he had brought out a suspicious-looking character, or any one but the old man or his wife, he was prepared to run for the woods.

The worst of it was he brought no one whatever.

"They have gone to bed," thought he. "I'll just step round where I can see in front of the house."

In front of the house was a porch, and Robert perceived, standing under it before the door, perfectly motionless in the gloom of the early evening, the form of a man.

He waited a moment to see if his presence would be noticed.

No.

The man stood like a statue, his hands behind him, and his head on one side, in an attitude of the most profound and melancholy meditation.

He had on a queer thing in place of a hat.

He seemed very tall.

Or was he standing on something that raised his feet from the ground?

Robert approached, determined to attract attention.

"Good evening, sir," he said.

Still no motion—no response.

The lad's hair began to lift itself with thrilling roots.

A fearful mystery was here.

Still he advanced, resolved to know who the man was, and why he did not speak.

"Good evening," he said again, setting his foot upon the steps, and steadying himself with his hand against one of the posts.

Speechless as a spectre, motionless as the post itself, rigidly erect but for the drooping head, the figure kept its place in the gloom.

But now Robert's attention was directed to another figure.

A woman on the porch-floor—an old woman with a wound in her temples, and her grey hair clotted with blood.

"Who has done this?" he exclaimed, in accents of horror.

He looked up at the man.

His hands behind him were tied.

The queer thing on his head was a handkerchief tied over his eyes.

Instead of standing before the door, as at first appeared, he was hanging by the neck from a rope attached to a rafter of the porch.

That was what made him look so tall!

"Look at 'um! look at 'um!" said a deep voice, hollow with passion and despair; "a pleasant sight, ain't it?"

Where did the voice come from?

Robert did not know at first.

It seemed to be the voice of the present Horror, that was in no particular spot, but surrounding him.

Then he saw a movement in the open door of the house.

A gun-barrel was pushed out menacingly towards him, and behind the weapon he discerned in the darkness of the room beyond, the outlines of a human form.

Robert did not recoil.

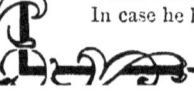

A strange and terrible calmness had come over him.

"It is dreadful, dreadful!" he said. "Who did it?"

Upon this the individual in the house came out.

He stood holding his gun before his breast, while he pointed at the corpses.

He was a young man.

A mere youth, in fact, as Robert could plainly see.

He was in his shirt-sleeves, his throat was open, his head uncovered, his hair tangled wildly over his brow.

His whole aspect was ghastly and savage.

"Look at that old man! Look at that old woman!" he said; "that's my father—that's my mother. I'm their son—the youngest. I was the baby, you know. They set more by me than they did by their own lives. That's the way it happened, ye see."

The young man's chest heaved with a sudden convulsion—a fierce, dry sob—and he gnashed his teeth, leaning upon his gun, and looking down at his mother.

"But how—how did it happen?"

"How! I'll tell ye. Ye ain't one of them I was watching for; lucky for ye," he said, with a hideous laugh. "Ye see I was watching. My gun was loaded ready to kill. I thought they might be coming back."

"They! Who?"

"The Hardings."

"The Hardings," repeated Robert Danvers, in surprise. "Why should they do this hideous deed?"

The boy laughed with a kind of maniacal jeer.

"Why?" he repeated: "truly you may ask why! Wherefore do men do any cruelties? Wherefore does man do evil instead of good, when one is as easy as another? These are difficult questions to answer, I know; so the best thing we can do is not to answer them, or even try to. That man hanging there was my father."

"You told me so."

"And that woman was my mother."

"Yes."

"Well, your friend Rupert Dreadnought and his companions came here to-day."

"I told them to."

The lad drew back.

"Curse you," he cried, "what did you send them here for? You, then, have done all the mischief."

"I!" exclaimed Robert Danvers, in undisguised amazement. "Why, Lord Rupert and his friends never killed your mother and father in cold blood, I'll be sworn."

The lad put his hand to his head, as if its throbbings were more than he could bear.

"No, no," he said, after a moment. "You must forgive me. I did not mean what I said: but this sight is enough to drive any fellow mad. Well, I was telling you how these murders came to be done.

"Your friends came here to see my father.

"Now my father has been friends with the Hardings, because for some reason or another he's been obliged to.

"Well, when he found that the villains had been beaten out of their lair, and had the soldiers after them, he thought he might safely tell where they were, and so he told all he knew."

"And I'll be sworn that Lord Dreadnought did not betray him," cried Robert Danvers.

"I know it. He betrayed himself."

"How so?"

"Why, while he was telling Lord Dreadnought what he could, who should be hiding among the bushes near but Dick Harding.

"As soon as your friends had ridden off, he and two others came in, murdered my mother first, and then hung my father up as you see him in the porch. Oh! if I had been at home, I'd have had one of them, at any rate."

"But why are you stopping here?"

"Because they may return; and then I'll die, but I'll kill them."

"They will not be here again to-night. They're off to Horrock's Mill."

"Not now."

"Why not?"

"Because they know that Lord Dreadnought has been told of their place of concealment."

"That will not deter them," returned Robert Danvers. "I have been with them since they were aware that Rupert Dreadnought had the information, and I know for certain that they *are* on the road, if, in fact, they have not already reached it."

"There'll be another stiff fight then," continued Danvers, "for Lord Dreadnought and *his* party are resolute men. *You* will go too, I suppose, if you are so eager for revenge?"

"Aye, that I shall," replied the lad; "and you—are you armed?"

"I am not; that is, I have only this knife."

"I'll fetch you a musket then."

The lad dived in among the dark shadows of the house, and returned in a few moments bringing a musket and some ammunition.

This Robert took eagerly.

"Now," he said "lead the way. "I've no notion where the mill is. Is it far?"

"About five miles."

Robert's heart sank.

Five miles to walk.

And his enemies had long the start of him, and were mounted on strong, willing horses.

This took much of his pluck out of him.

"It's almost useless our going at all," he said, as the other lad hurried on.

"Why so?"

"All the fighting will be over before we get there. Both Rupert Dreadnought's party and Hardings' party are mounted, and they will have met and decided the affair before we are near them."

"You can do as you please," said young Waldron. "I shall risk it. My mind is made up for vengeance, and I will not be deterred from attempting to obtain it because such and such a thing might be. No, no; I feel that I shall lose my life in this adventure, but I am resolved that Dick Harding shall die with me."

"Why Dick specially?"

"Because I am sure that it was he who murdered my father and mother."

"But if you were absent how came it that you know that it was Dick and his men who committed

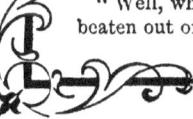

the deed?" asked Robert Danvers, as they plodded quickly along the rough, dark road.

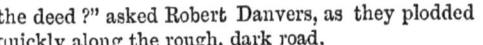

"Why, you see," said young Waldron, "I was on my way home when I met Lucy Alstone. Lucy and I are lovers, you see, and I was going to marry her. I shall never live to be hers now. Well, she met me, pale and scared, and wouldn't stop only just to cry out,

"'The Hardings are in your house. I met them at the door, Dick and two of his brothers, and they're swearing and going on awful. Hurry on.'

"So I did hurry on, and you know what I found. Oh! Heaven's curses on them all. Would they were all one toad so that I could put my heel on them and crush them!"

So talking, they pressed onwards.

But time passed slowly.

Five miles is weary walking to those who have a great object in view, and who have but a short time to walk it in.

They did not lose heart.

There was plenty of excitement in the future if there was none in the present moment.

So on they pressed.

At length, weary and somewhat footsore, they came in sight of Horrock's Mill.

It was a gloomy place.

The Hardings seemed to delight in gloom.

Perched on an eminence, with its rugged arms stretched out across the grey leaden sky, it looked like some huge phantom overlooking the landscape.

"That's Horrock's Mill," said young Waldron.

"It's a ruin, then. I can see the dim light through open windows."

"Yes, it *is* a ruin," said Waldron; "the Hardings choose such places for safety. Let us rest a few moments and listen."

They say sat down accordingly on a stone by the wayside.

All was very still.

The moaning of the light wind through the ruins and the trees that surrounded it was all they could hear.

"It will be best to get in before they come," suggested Robert Danvers.

His companion smiled.

"Yes," said he, "if they are not there already."

"They would not be so quiet."

"Why not? They would wish to lead Rupert into an ambush."

"Well, we can easily ascertain," said Robert Danvers; "we will advance a few steps, and if we are challenged we can make for yonder thicket."

He rose up accordingly.

As he did so a hand was placed heavily on his shoulder.

Turning round he saw a man standing by him, while another had hold of young Waldron.

"What are you doing here?" said a stern voice.

It was rather an awkward question.

The lads had very little account to give of themselves.

"We were resting on our way," said Danvers, looking the man full in the face.

One thing he had at once discovered.

They were not the Hardings.

"And which is your way?"

"To Edenbridge."

This was a town some ten miles distant.

A town perched on the rocky shore.

"Oh, Edenbridge; and what may you be going to do there?"

"Go to sea!"

The men laughed.

"You can tell a good story upon occasion," said the other, who had not yet spoken; "but the worst of the matter for *you* is that we know you both. You are Robert Danvers who was with the Hardings, and your companion here is the son of old Luke Waldron."

"Whom the Hardings——"

Fortunately for the boy's future there was an interruption here which saved him from saying more.

He was about to add the word "murdered."

Had he done so, the fate of both would have been sealed.

As it was, a loud voice from the direction of Horrock's Mill cried out—

"What have you got there?"

"Two lads—Danvers and young Waldron."

"Bring them in, then, quick."

"Come on," cried one of the men, who, though strange to them, evidently know all about their names and characters; "don't try to resist, or you might get a stray shot or a knock on the head."

Danvers assumed a demeanour quite different to that of his companion.

Waldron was savage, stern, full of thirst for vengeance.

He was thinking of nothing but the chance he should soon have of punishing the murderers of his father and mother.

Danvers, on the other hand, pretended not to care either way.

They might take him or leave him.

He had good reason for this.

He knew well his customers.

He was aware that as regarded him personally the Hardings had no enmity.

He was aware, moreover, that they had no desire to keep him with them except to prevent his being with Rupert Dreadnought.

So he advanced boldly.

The two men led them over a kind of bridge—a temporary wooden structure thrown over a broad ditch.

Then they clambered up a dark staircase, and then suddenly emerged into the light.

As they went up the staircase Robert Danvers managed to whisper a word of advice to young Waldron, whom he knew to be fuming with wrath.

"If you desire revenge upon these men, do as I do, and attempt nothing rashly."

This was all he could say.

But Waldron heard it, and knew that it was just.

When they passed into the light so suddenly, they found themselves in a little room, in which were seated the Hardings.

Old Hugh was cowering over a fire, while in a corner lay the wounded son.

"Well, you young devil," said Richard Harding, addressing Robert Danvers, "what have you got to say for yourself?"

Danvers still wore the same jaunty air.

"If I tell you, you won't believe me," he said.

"Yes I will."

"And if I tell the truth I'm not to suffer for it?"

"No."

"Then I'll speak out."

"Yes, mind yer do," growled Hugh Harding, "or it'll chance to go bad with ye."

"Well, I tried to escape because I thought you'd sell me to Lord Dreadnought."

"And why don't yer want to go to him?"

"I wish to go to sea."

"You still wish it?"

"Aye, that I do."

"And you'll go if we give you the chance?"

"That I will."

"And young Waldron here, will he go too?"

Waldron's blood boiled.

He longed to spring upon the speaker.

But a glance from Danvers' eye restrained him.

That glance said plainly—

"Wait."

So he resolved to wait.

"Yes," he said, "I'll go, too, if Robert Danvers goes."

"Very well," replied Dick Harding; "you shall have your wish."

Then he bent over his father, and whispered a few words in his ear.

The old man growled assent.

"Well, youngsters," said Richard, returning, "you can go as soon as you like. We're going to —— to-night, and you can go with us."

As he said this there was heard a loud and prolonged whistle.

"There's the signal," said Harding.

Richard leaped out through the door eagerly.

He was absent only a few moments.

When he entered again he was greatly excited.

"Quick, boys," he said, "we must start at once."

"What," said old Harding, "are they coming, then?"

"Yes, they're on the way," said Richard, "Lord Rupert and his three friends, and a party of twelve soldiers. Their plan was to get us into the mill and surround it. We've got half an hour's start if we go now."

"Leave me at Widow Folston's on the way," said the wounded man. "I shall be in the way."

In a few minutes they were ready.

The country was still wrapped in silence and in darkness as they issued from the old mill.

Nature seemed to favour the escape of the Hardings.

For their own sakes, too, they resolved to act upon the advice of the wounded man.

Very gentle to their own kindred, though so savage to others, they carried him carefully in their midst.

In their midst, too, was carried something else.

A large wooden box.

This was the box of treasure.

There, also in the centre, were Danvers and young Waldron.

There were more than the Hardings guarding them.

Four men, two being those who had seized Danvers and Waldron while they were resting on the stones, accompanied them.

Neither Danvers nor Waldron knew them.

But Colonel Heavyweight and his men would have known them well.

They were four of the most desperate characters on the road.

Cut-purses and villains of the deepest dye.

However, as far as they understood friendship, they and the Hardings were sworn friends.

On they went slowly for a mile.

Not a sign of any pursuit was there.

At the end of this mile they came to a little tavern by the wayside.

Here they halted.

This place was kept by the widow whom the wounded man had mentioned.

One of the Hardings bore him in, and he was soon located in a comfortable bed-room.

Meanwhile, the others had gone into the yard and brought out a number of horses.

Upon these Harding and his sons mounted, and the highwaymen also.

Danvers and Waldron were placed in front of two of the men, to prevent their escape, and once more on they went.

CHAPTER XV.

THE JOURNEY TOWARDS EDENBRIDGE—THE DARK SEA VIEW—THE OLD MANSE—GRANDEUR AND RUIN—ANOTHER HIDING PLACE FOR TREASURE—THE HARDINGS HEAR EVIL NEWS—HOW DANVERS AND WALDRON WERE TRAPPED—ALONE AMONG THE RATS—FRIENDLY VOICES—STARVATION AND DESPAIR!—WHERE CAN IT BE?—HOPE DAWNS AGAIN—THE STRUGGLE FOR LIBERTY.

The journey towards Edenbridge was unmarked by a single incident.

Either Rupert and those who were acting with him had been completely put off the scent, or they had abandoned the pursuit, or—

They were laying a new trap.

Both Danvers and Waldron believed the latter.

But they said nothing.

Waldron now imitated his more cunning young friend.

He simulated gaiety.

Both chatted gaily with the men upon whose horses they were placed.

The men with whom they were riding were, for their part, thoroughly convinced that the boys were both satisfied with their fate.

So it would have seemed to everybody.

The highwaymen were well aware that the Hardings had killed the father and mother of one of the boys.

They had no conception that young Waldron knew it, and was on the look-out for vengeance.

Little did they imagine what a burning fury of hatred was smouldering beneath his outwardly calm demeanour.

A long and tiresome journey was it.

All in utter gloom too.

At length in the distance gleamed a few lights.

"There's Edenbridge," said one of the men.

"Mighty glad of it," said young Waldron.

"Getting tired?"

Waldron suppressed the words which leaped to his lips.

"Yes," he said, "and impatient. I want to go to bed."

The man laughed.

"You won't make much of a sailor," cried he, "if you can't bear a little fatigue. This is nothing to what you'll have to do."

"I know it; but then I shall have my rest as well. Besides, I shall be doing my duty, and earning my living, instead of jogging along uselessly on a horse with a parcel of——"

Ruffians, he was going to say.

But he caught himself up in time.

"Parcel of what?" said the man.

"Men who don't care whether I'm dead or alive," said Waldron. "I know why I'm being taken away."

"Why?"

"So as I can't be a spy."

The man laughed.

"You're about right there," said he; "but here we are."

Here they might be, as regarded the spot they desired to reach.

But it certainly was not Edenbridge town itself.

It was some distance from it.

Edenbridge was built on the sea.

Here they could hear the far-off waves.

And that was all.

Not a single portion of the water was visible.

Near them, moreover, was only one large house, a kind of rustic grange, with a long dead wall overhung by high trees.

"What is this place?" asked Robert Danvers. "This is not the town?"

"No; but it's where you're going," growled old Hugh Harding, as he came up to their side. "Here, get down, youngsters, and be quick."

Robert Danvers and young Waldron at once complied.

Then the men jumped off also and led their horses away into the woods.

The Hardings, meanwhile, made their way up to the rear of the building.

Here there was an old doorway half rotten with age.

"Now, then, Dick," cried old Hugh, "where is the key?"

"They seem to know plenty of secret places," thought Danvers.

But what seemed a mystery was in reality none.

The Hardings, and the footpads who were connected with them, were friends with all the smugglers on the coast, and who, in the days of which I am writing, were not a few.

This old place behind the Grange was a spot which these fellows had used for years to deposit their smuggled goods.

It was, in fact, the base of an old ruin—the ruin of an ancient mansion, whose owners had, instead of rebuilding it, built up a splendid edifice by its side.

As soon as Dick Harding had given his father the key, the old man opened the door, which, swinging open with a creaking sound, disclosed a black and gloomy corridor.

The old fellow then took from his pocket a dark lantern.

"Follow me," he said; "bring the box and your prisoners along. I know my way well."

The men seemed to have perfect confidence in him.

Seizing the box, which seemed very heavy, they pushed Robert and Waldron on before them, and plunged unhesitatingly into the dark passage.

After advancing a few steps, they came to a staircase.

This the old man hurried down with no more care than before.

The place was evidently one that he was accustomed to explore.

He hurried on with all speed, and at length, at the end of a cold, damp, underground passage, he reached the door of a room, or rather cell.

This he opened, and invited all to enter with him.

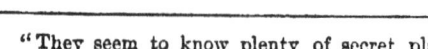

RUPERT OR THE DREADNOUGHT SECRETS OF THE IRON CHEST

"ON THEY PLUNGED THROUGH THE ARCH."

"It's not a very pleasant place," said old Hugh, as they passed into the underground cellar, and closed the door behind them, "but it's, at any rate, safe from our enemies."

"Too safe," thought both Danvers and Waldron.

But they kept silence.

They knew that it would be dangerous to speak.

"Now then," said old Hugh, as soon as the door was closed, "that box must be left here for a time, and these boys must remain to guard it."

This was said with a wink at his sons—a wink, by the way, which was observed both by Robert Danvers and young Waldron.

"Against whom are we to guard them?" asked Robert. "Against the rats? They seem to be the only things which are likely to dispute possession with us."

"You are wrong," said Hugh Harding; "of that you will soon know more. However, you have to remain here; so far is decided, so make your minds easy."

"And when do we go to sea?" asked young Waldron.

"To-morrow night," said Hugh Harding, "we shall return for this box, and we shall all then go on board the cutter that is waiting for us now near Sandy Point."

"And we are to remain here alone till all your arrangements are made?"

"Yes."

"And why?"

"Because, my young sparks, we cannot trust you."

"Have we deceived you so greatly, then?" said Robert Danvers.

"There, don't argue; I won't argue," cried Hugh Harding, savagely. "It's enough that you've got to remain here. Here, Dick, hand us over the food and the spirits, and let us be off."

Richard Harding at once complied with the old man's request.

He took from his pack a large knapsack, and laid it on top of the chest.

"Here, my lads," he said, "you'll find a couple of blankets to keep you warm, and enough food and spirit to satisfy you till to-morrow night; then we'll return for you."

A sickening dread entered the mind of young Waldron.

They had murdered his father and mother!

Why should they not also murder him by leaving him there to starve to death?

"I hope, whatever happens," he said, in a low voice, with a tremor he could not disguise, "I hope you *will* come back. It would be terrible to be buried here, down under the earth, where no one would ever dream of seeking for a human being."

"No, no," cried the old man; "we never took the life of a human being uselessly. We have revenged ourselves (and revenged ourselves terribly) upon those whom we have discovered to be our enemies. But the innocent we leave free."

Then he turned and unlocked the door, saying—

"Now, then, boys, I'm ready."

The Hardings and their rough companions then quitted the cell.

The door was re-fastened directly.

The echoing footsteps died away.

Robert Danvers and Waldron were alone—under the earth!

CHAPTER XVI.

THE "RAVEN'S NEST"—THE SMUGGLERS' MEET—RICHARD ALBORNE AND HIS CUSTOMERS—THE HARDINGS RESOLVE ON EMIGRATING—THEIR ARRIVAL—THE SURPRISE AND THE BARGAIN—THE VAULTS—THE RECEPTACLES OF TREASURE—THE DARK CORRIDORS—THE RECKLESS BANQUETTERS.

THERE was on the rocks at Edenbridge, perched high above the sea, a little inn.

It was a strange structure.

It seemed to have been built up out of numberless stray pieces of wood, any odds and ends which had been picked up by the way.

It was entirely of timber.

Great black beams supported it, shored it up, as it were, and held it firm against the dark rocks on the other side.

A rising land protected it shoreways, while on the other it faced defiantly the broad-rolling sea.

They sold good beer at the "Raven's Nest," as the place was called, and their spirits were something which a prince might have been proud to have on his table.

How they obtained so good a supply of liquor was questionable.

But they did.

And, what was far more to the purpose, they had the good sense not to tell nor to allow any one so to pry into their secrets as to be able to "inform."

Regular customers, who, as a rule, were fishermen, smugglers, and men who picked up on the coast a strange living, knew very well how little profit accrued to the revenue from anything which was sold at the "Raven's Nest."

To these the best of commodities were meted out.

To strangers the most vile concoctions were presented—so vile as to have always the desired tendency of keeping them and their custom at a civil distance in future.

They were not wanted.

Richard Alborne, the landlord, could dispense with chance custom.

All he required was the custom of the fishermen and the smugglers, the aid of the men from whom he got his liquor, and who, at night time, at certain dates, transported large quantities of the brandies to the various places where he had established a "roaring trade."

The Hardings were well known to him.

They had been rare smugglers in their time, and even of late had aided in a "run."

But their business had been principally of a different class altogether—aiding in transporting the goods, and concealing them also when any danger was afloat.

For this purpose the old ruins had always afforded a splendid receptacle.

They had been well paid for this, and, together with the robberies they committed on the road, they made a good living.

It was now all over with them on this part of the coast.

So away they resolved to go to another part of England.

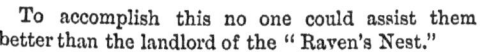

To accomplish this no one could assist them better than the landlord of the "Raven's Nest."

The swift-sailing cutter of which he was owner, and which had made so many daring and successful runs under the very eyes of the revenue officers, was just the craft to carry them swiftly from the dangerous shore, and deposit them safely in some quiet spot where they might once more inaugurate a system of heartless robbery and pillage.

So it was towards the "Raven's Nest" that they made their way.

It was very late when they reached it.

But the "Raven's Nest" was full of people.

At such times, and in such localities, there were no restrictions as to hours.

Loudly over the cliff side rolled the song and merry jest.

A fine run was expected on the following night, and, in anticipation, they were enjoying themselves, and drinking success to their enterprize.

When Hugh Harding and his companions knocked at the door there was a general commotion within.

Every man flew to his sword.

They knew well that though, perhaps, their absolute employment at the moment was innocent enough, they would be recognised by the revenue officers—if these were their visitors—as suspicious characters, and marked for the future.

The old landlord himself was the one to open the door.

He recognised his friends at once, and burst into a loud laugh.

"Why, it's Hugh Harding and his cubs, by all that's holy!" cried he. "Enter and welcome, though you scared us a bit, I can tell you."

The Hardings and their highwaymen friends were received with shouts of welcome.

"You're just in time to help us in a fine run," said one of the guests, a big, burly, black-bearded man, sitting by the fire.

"What, to-night?" asked Harding, dipping heavily into a tankard of ale that was held out to him.

"No! to-morrow night. We expect the 'Jolly Lucy' round the point at eleven precisely," said the landlord, "and we're short of hands. I know you too well to think you could shrink from aiding us."

Old Harding chuckled.

He was not insensible to compliments.

He considered this a great one.

"We'll help you," said he.

And then a bright idea struck him.

He could obtain aid in return.

"Yes," he added, after a moment's thought, "we'll help you, but we want your help also."

"That you shall have," replied the landlord, "and welcome. We're not the fellows to let a friend require help and refuse it. Let us hear what it is you require."

Briefly Hugh Harding told his story.

At the mention of the box of treasure, the smuggler's eyes glistened.

"It will take the 'Jolly Lucy' a long way off her tack," said the landlord, when he had heard all; "but no matter. We won't be backward in aiding a friend out of such a scrape. We'll strike the bargain. *You* aid *me*, I'll aid *you*."

So it was agreed.

The smugglers who, as they said, anticipated the biggest run of the season, were delighted at the prospect of securing to themselves the services of such men as the Hardings and their colleagues, and the bargain being struck, the night was spent in conviviality.

For Danvers and young Waldron they did not fear.

Their object was *not* to destroy them.

No special enmity existing against them in their minds, they had resolved that when they made good their escape they would take the boys with them.

The run was to take place on the following night at eleven.

The lads had abundance of food to last them till the morning following that.

So the villains were satisfied.

They never thought of the wretched misery of their situation; the cold, the loneliness, the terrible proximity of creeping, noisome things, the anxiety lest their deliverers should never come.

Their minds were too brutalised to comprehend such a condition of mind as that which would be suffered by their wretched captives.

So they laughed, and sang, and caroused, and made merry till morning.

Then they retired to rest.

This had to be done surreptitiously.

The constabulary knew well their friendship with the landlord and the frequenters of the "Raven's Nest."

It was here, naturally, therefore, that they would seek for the Hardings, when they found that they had altogether quitted their old haunts.

In an ordinary house, therefore, it would have been a matter of difficulty to find a resting-place.

Not so here.

It had plenty of receptacles for goods of a description which required concealing, and among these, therefore, it was decided to hide away the reinforcement which had so unexpectedly come to the aid of the smugglers.

It was a strange place.

The "Raven's Nest," as I have said, was built upon the summit of high rocks.

These rocks, just below the foundations of the house, had been hollowed out, where a large seam of chalk ran through the cliffs so as to form huge caverns.

An entrance to these had been made in the cellar, and here, after one of the runs, the kegs of smuggled spirits were concealed until the first rush of pursuit and search was over.

Again and again the revenue officers had searched the house from top to bottom.

But in vain.

No one, indeed, uninitiated into the secrets of the "Raven's Nest," would ever have been able to discover it.

You first passed down a ladder leading from the kitchen into the cellar.

Then you passed round some huge casks of beer, and found yourself against an immense disused fire-place.

Here was the secret.

Standing on the iron-work of this, with your head up the chimney, you pressed an iron plate, which at once sprang up, revealing an open space.

Into this you passed, and found yourself on a kind of landing, from which a staircase descended, as it were, into the bowels of the earth.

It was well known to the Hardings, who had often assisted in carrying thither the smuggled goods, and they were soon quietly and comfortably located in the gloomy caves, wrapped in blankets, and hiding away their drink.

It was a strange place.

It was nearly empty of goods now, and the bare chalk cliff was nearly everywhere visible.

It was of great extent.

Great corridors seemed to run away interminably in the darkness.

Weird echoes from afar answered loud voices, while here and there water filtering through the roof fell with a hollow sound upon the rocky floor.

But the smugglers cared not for the dismal aspect of their abode.

They were beyond fear of loneliness.

Pinioned on the scaffold, where mortal help could avail them not, then they might have flinched.

But nothing would have daunted their hardened souls while a weapon of any kind was at hand for use.

CHAPTER XVII.

THE REVENUE OFFICER AT THE "RAVEN'S NEST"—BAD RUM—THE CONFERENCE—RICHARD ALBORNE THINKS IT BEST TO BE COOL—THE WARNING—THE PREPARATIONS FOR THE GRAND RUN—THE DOUBLE ROCK—THE YOUNG HARDINGS AND THEIR SWEETHEARTS—LOVE OR DUTY—WHICH WILL WIN?

DURING the whole of the next day they remained concealed in the caverns.

Well for them they did.

Their visit was not suspected.

But the actions of others had excited in the minds of the revenue officers an idea that "something was in the wind."

What this "something" was they had a very vague idea of.

But there *was* something.

Of that they were certain; and it naturally, in their minds, took the form of a smuggling cruise.

Nothing, however, could have exceeded the quiet reigning at the "Raven's Nest" when old Lieutenant Seaford strolled into the bar and ordered some rum.

"It's very cold," said he, as the landlord placed before him a steaming hot glass of some execrable compound, "and rum is the very thing to warm one."

He had no sooner tasted it, however, than he spat it out again on the floor.

Richard Alborne laughed.

"What ails you, sir?" he asked.

"*You* know very well what ails me," said the officer, with a smile: "but you shouldn't physic me with such a stuff as this, because you fancy I'm here on duty. I *am* here on duty, and am going to ask you a few straightforward questions. But, come, I know you've got better than this, so ——"

"Well, well," said the landlord, with a smile, "I've got a bottle that I use for myself. You shall have some of that. I know it's good, for it was given me by Hugh Harding, one of the veriest smugglers out."

"And one of your special friends," thought Lieutenant Seaford, as Richard Alborne moved away.

But he said nothing.

In a few moments Boniface returned with a bottle out of which he mixed his visitor another stiff glass of spirits.

"You'll find that some of the right sort, I'm sure," said he. "And now, sir, what is it you desire to ask me? Don't stand out there, but step into the parlour."

With his new allies hidden away beneath his house, Richard Alborne felt quite secure.

He knew well that no excise officers could ever penetrate his secret.

Lieutenant Seaford complied.

He was an old hand in the service.

The calmness and politeness of the landlord, therefore, did not in any way put him off his guard or deceive him.

It seemed, in fact, to make him more particular.

"Well," he said, "you have the eyes of the authorities on your house: are you aware of that?"

The landlord smiled.

"Well," he said, "I'd be a great fool if I didn't know that, considering that it's been so for years. But it is no use their trying to bring me into it. I've got nothing to do with the smuggling myself; but. I tell you what, Lieutenant Seaford, I'm not going to ask too many questions. If people come to my house for a glass o' grog, I'm not going to say, 'Are you a fisherman or a smuggler?' before I serve 'em—not I: no, not for the king and all his men. There's no law against serving out my stuff to any one, and I'd like to see the man that'll hinder me."

He waxed excited as he spoke, and brought his clenched fist heavily down upon the table, so as to make the glasses ring.

The lieutenant laughed.

"Why, you're getting quite excited, Alborne," he said; "but you're making one grand mistake in this matter."

"How so?"

"Nobody complains of your serving your customers."

"What then?"

"You pretend not to know?"

"I do *not* know."

"Very well, then, I can soon explain," returned the lieutenant. "Intelligence has reached the authorities that a grand smuggling expedition is on foot."

"Curse them," thought Richard Alborne, "some of them have been babbling."

But he gave no vent to his feelings.

He only smiled.

"And do they give *me* credit for being the leader of the expedition?" said he.

"Not so: but I have been desired to warn you

against any repetition of your conduct in harbouring them," said Lieutenant Seaford, more firmly; "you must *not* allow meetings to take place here."

"Certainly not," said the landlord, "I never do."

"And, furthermore, I may tell you privately that if this run should prove successful, in spite of the vigilance of the coastguard, your house will be placed for a long time under strict watch."

"Ho! ho!" chuckled the landlord, inwardly, "they fancy that the run *may* succeed then in spite of them all."

"Well," he said, aloud, "this of course I can't help, although it is most unfair. However, I've nothing to do with the matter; if the constabulary get it into their heads, I know there is no moving them."

"Then you had not heard of this attempt at a run before?" said Lieutenant Seaford, rising.

"Indeed, no."

"Well, then, if any of the suspected parties come into your house, just warn them that the coastguard will be on the alert, and that an extra body of men will watch them. It will be dangerous for them this time, I'm afraid, if they persist in it."

"Well, you see," said Richard Alborne, drily, "that's just the sort of thing they don't mind. They're used to it; and to some of them it's half the pleasure."

"All right. Good day, Mr. Alborne," said the lieutenant, as he passed out. "I've given you good warning—you must say that. If you don't profit by it, why, it's not my fault."

And so off he went.

Richard Alborne laughed as he saw him disappear along the rocky path.

"Ah! my fine fellow," he cried, "you think yourself a very clever officer, as no doubt you are an honest one, but you've defeated your own purpose. Now we know that you are on the watch we can take our measures accordingly."

Having delivered himself of these words, which augured ill for the success of the revenue cutter and its officer, he whistled, and his wife having responded to the call, he left her in charge of the bar, while he descended to the cellars.

He found the Hardings just finishing their breakfast, which consisted of broiled ham and beer.

Such worthies despised the use of such milk-and-water fluids as tea.

Richard Alborne briefly explained to them what he had heard from the officer of the revenue cutter.

Hugh Harding laughed a chuckling laugh as he listened.

"We'll give them a reception they little expect," he said, "if they try and stop us. We're in more force than ever they will expect. We'll start early; at least, I and my men will, and we'll take possession of the road to Sandy Point; that's where the cutter will come to, isn't it?"

"Yes: up against the double rock."

"Good," said Hugh. "Then we'll give them such a lesson, if they come that way, that they'll be sorry they ever tried to track Hugh Harding and his men, whom they're driving from their old home. Bring us down some more beer, and let us know when it is five o'clock, for my two younger sons here must needs go gallivanting after their sweethearts in the very hour of danger. Never mind; I've not been in the habit of preventing them from having their own way, so I won't begin now."

So the day passed in drinking, and cards, and so on till five o'clock came.

Then the landlord having given notice of the time, the two younger Hardings sallied forth.

Such a proceeding on their part was not safe.

The whole neighbourhood knew that Rupert Dreadnought and the soldiers were after them.

But they cared not.

All they thought of was the girls they loved.

They were going away now for ever from that part of the country, and they resolved to take with them the girls whom they had selected to be their wives.

They set out together.

"You know where I am going, Amos?" said one, after they had proceeded a short way.

"I think so, William," said Amos. "You're going up the creek."

"I am. And you?"

"Never mind," said the other, somewhat moodily. "I'll bet a round dozen guineas I bring back as fair a bride as you."

"That may be, and I hope it, for your sake," said William Harding; "at any rate for me there's only one pretty face on the country side, and that's the face of Lucy Hartwright."

The other made no reply.

He looked dark and sullen, as if the face of Lucy Hartwright was as bright to his mind as to that of his brother, and less hopefully.

But whatever he felt he veiled his feelings.

He had no desire apparently, however, to allow his brother to know the state of his mind.

After a moment, therefore, he resumed the conversation upon another topic, and they passed on rapidly until they reached the bridge which passed over Darman's Creek.

It was a peculiar bridge.

A portion of it—that is to say, the parts which adjoined the land—were of solid stone, while that in the centre was of wood, and could be raised like a drawbridge, to allow of the passage of the ships which were at times compelled to proceed further up the creek.

Here the brothers parted.

"We'll meet again at eight," said William, as he prepared to descend some rough, narrow stairs, which led from the top of the bridge to a landing pier. "Don't be late, Amos, for it seems to me by the look of the sky that we shall have a storm."

And so the brothers parted.

William, without once glancing back, hurried eagerly down the wooden stairs.

Amos, on the other hand, watched him with a scowling face.

Then, as he passed out of his sight, he muttered something very like an oath, and proceeded back on the way they had come.

After he had gone a little way, he entered a little copse on the way side, and concealing himself among the bushes, waited.

He had a deadly purpose in view.

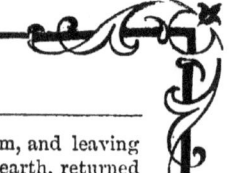

CHAPTER XVIII.

THE DISCOVERY OF ROBERT DANVERS—THE EFFORTS OF THE CAPTIVES TO ESCAPE—ALONE WITH A MADMAN—THE FIRST DAWN OF HOPE—SAVED TOO LATE—THE DISCOVERY OF THE DEAD—FREEDOM AT LAST—THE STRANGE DELIVERER—AN EXTRAORDINARY COINCIDENCE—ON THE WAY TO PETHERINGTON—THE MEETING WITH RUPERT DREADNOUGHT AND HIS FRIENDS—PREPARATIONS FOR AN ATTACK ON THE SMUGGLERS—THE DEPARTURE OF THE EXPEDITION.

A MAN passing by the old Grange at Edenbridge about this time saw a haggard, ghastly face peering up at times from a grating by the roadside beneath the ruins of the former mansion.

He stooped down, and raising his hands in amazement, inquired what ailed the prisoner.

"Release me, for Heaven's sake!" said Robert Danvers, for it was he. "I am here alone with a madman!"

A madman!

It was too true.

For a short time after the departure of old Hugh Harding and his companions all had gone right, except that young Waldron had seemed rather excited.

"We're not going to remain here," he said; "that's very certain. Let's try the wall, and see if we can't make our way through."

On trying the wall, they found it sounded hollow, and they at once began to work at the bricks.

As they had nothing to work with but their knives, it may be imagined that they did not make much progress.

But Waldron worked with violence and desperation, and at last, as night fell, he became thoroughly frantic.

Danvers could see he was exhausted.

But it was of no use attempting to stay his hand, and at length, when a hole had really been made through the wall, he leapt through it with a kind of superhuman energy.

In an instant after his senses gave way.

His brain, wrought up to frenzy by the murder of his father and mother, had now yielded to disappointment when he found that the next room was but a black, gloomy chamber also.

He had not sense enough left him to remember that it was night, and that if he waited till morning he might see some outlet.

To his dazed intellect it seemed that after all his frantic efforts he had failed; and, throwing himself wildly on the floor, he gave himself up to paroxysms of mad grief.

It was hideous to hear him howling and yelling in the dark night.

For pitch dark it was.

Whatever light there might be about to enter in the morning was not now discernible, even in the shape of a faint gleam.

But Robert Danvers did not despair.

Having forced his way through one wall, he concluded, naturally, that he would be able to force his way through another.

So after ineffectual efforts to induce the maddened youth to return into the other cellar, and lie down on his blanket, he threw one over him, and leaving him where he was, grovelling on the earth, returned to his own corner and slept till morning.

When he awoke, all was very still.

For a moment he was so confused that he knew not where he was.

Then a dim notion of the hideous events of the preceding night entered his brain, and, rising, he called aloud for Waldron.

No answer was returned.

But *one* thing excited his curiosity.

Streaming through the aperture they had made in the wall was a faint stream of light.

With an exclamation of pleasure, he sprang towards it, and made his way into the adjoining cellar.

Then his hope was realised.

At the extreme end of the place was a wide grating, through which streamed the bright light of day.

With an exclamation of delight he turned to Waldron.

He was still lying as he had left him.

"Waldron," he cried, kneeling down by him, and shaking him gently, "awake. We are saved."

There was no response.

Again he shook him, and spoke more loudly.

A horrible suspicion then entered his breast, and he turned him over.

The poor maddened youth was dead!

He had grovelled, and grovelled, and bitten the ground in his mad fury until suffocated, and had yielded up his frenzied soul in unconsciousness of all around him.

With a shudder, Robert Danvers drew the blanket over his face, and proceeded to the grating to reconnoitre.

He had, of course, expected to find that in a place which was such an utter ruin the bars could be easily moved.

Not so.

He dragged at them lustily.

But in vain.

They had evidently been renovated by the Hardings to prevent the ingress of any one who was likely to be of a prying disposition, or to be connected with the revenue officers.

One thing, however, gave him hope.

He could see the gates of the grange.

He must, therefore, be on the edge of the high-road, or, at any rate, a footpath.

Some one would, in all human probability, pass that way, and he would call out to him.

So it happened.

He brought his food to the grating, and there ate his meals.

All day passed.

Then when he had shouted again and again at people he heard, but could not see; and when, in fact, he had begun to despair, he saw a man approaching the little gate.

Again he cried out, and, as I have before said, the man, kneeling down, saw his white face at the grating.

When called upon for explanation, Robert Danvers at once saw the necessity for reservation.

With the prospect of safety came the desire to do Rupert Dreadnought a service.

If he were to tell all, to reveal, in fact, the existence of a treasure, he would be defeating the purpose for which Rupert had undertaken the journey which had turned out to be so full of peril.

So, in answer to the question "How came you here," he said—

"Let me out first and I will tell you."

The request was easier to make than to carry out.

But, by their united efforts, they at length succeeded in removing one bar.

The rest was easy enough; and at length Robert Danvers, scrambling through the grating, stood a free man.

"Now," he said, after he had warmly thanked his deliverer, "I wish to replace the bars as well as I can."

"Why so?"

"Because unless I do so I cannot punish my enemies."

"Very well, you know best."

"Yes," said Danvers, "and as soon as I have done this, I will walk with you and explain all."

Having straightened the bars as well as they could, they accordingly replaced them.

Then, fortunately having been observed by no one, they walked away.

"Well," said the man, who was fairly bursting with curiosity, "how did you get into that underground den?"

Robert Danvers laughed.

"I promised to tell you," he said, "but I can't very well. I was taken there in the night by a lot of men, who evidently had a design against my life. They left me there with a blanket and some food, and then went away, saying they would return. This they have not done. I know who they are though, and who are looking for them; so, if they *do* come, why, they'll be taken."

"And who may they be?" asked the other.

"The Hardings."

The man started as if he had been shot.

"The Hardings!" he repeated. "Are you quite sure af what you say?"

"I am quite."

"Well, I always thought they were rogues; now I am sure. You have given me information enough now. Hurry away to any friends you have, and let them secure the villains if they can. I am away to warn others."

And so, shaking Robert Danvers' proffered hand, he darted away.

Strange coincidence this!

Robert's deliverer was the brother of the young girl whom William Harding had that day started to see.

He had always been averse to his sister's consorting with Harding.

Now he resolved to hurry home with the news.

Meanwhile, Robert Danvers having refreshed himself at an ale-house, hastened on towards Petherington.

It was a long and lonely walk, as we have described before.

But he cared not for this.

He was actuated in what he was about to do by a kind of enthusiasm, and the way seemed long simply because he was eager.

In reality, he proceeded at an immense speed, and, at length, with joy in his heart, he beheld the lights of the 'Petherington Arms' shining across the road.

Rupert Dreadnought and his friends were in a private room talking to Ensign Mornington.

News had reached the barracks that the smugglers at Edenbridge were about to attempt a grand run, and that the services of the military would be required, as it was anticipated that a good chance would now present itself for seizing upon the ringleaders of the daring band that had so long held the law at defiance.

The arrival of Robert Danvers and the news he brought, at once offered a clue to the doings of the Hardings.

Rupert and his friends had proceeded to Horrock's Mill after discovering the bodies of old Waldron and his wife; and, as our readers are, of course, aware, they discovered that the birds had flown.

They had then scoured the country round about in vain, and had returned to Petherington to consult with the authorities.

As to the treasure, Rupert cared little, except in so far as his father's wishes were concerned.

But the disappearance of Robert Danvers was a far different matter.

The boy might have been murdered, and they were just discussing as to what plan was the most advisable one to adopt, when Joey the ostler announced that the object of their conversation was there, and desired to speak with them.

Robert's story altered all their ideas.

"We will at once make for the coast line," said Rupert; "for, what I hear from this boy, I have no doubt in my own mind that these Hardings will join the ranks of the smugglers."

"That is my idea," said the ensign; "let us go at once."

In a very short space of time they were ready.

They had some way to go.

But they were all mounted.

Besides, they had time before them.

The "run" was not to take place until eleven, and it was then the attack was to be made.

At that time, of course it was natural to anticipate that the whole gang would be collected together.

So, about eight o'clock, in the dark and now stormy night, they set out with Robert Danvers to guide them.

CHAPTER XIX.

LUCY HARTWRIGHT—THE MEETING OF THE LOVERS—THE PERILOUS JOURNEY—THE GHOSTLY FACE ON THE BRIDGE—A DREAD OF DANGER—THE SHADOWY FOLLOWER—THE THREAT OF VENGEANCE—THE MEETING ON THE CLIFF—THE STRUGGLE—THE LAST CHANCE—THE TERRIBLE END OF ALL.

We must leave Rupert Dreadnought now for a time and return to William Harding.

Villain as he was, he loved the girl whom he was now about to see, and he could not, even in the hour of danger, dream of quitting that part of the country without asking her to accompany him.

Lucy was a splendid girl.

Ripened by the warm suns of southern England, and nerved by the bracing sea breezes, she was a splendid specimen of our English girls—plump, rosy, round-limbed, with sparkling eyes, and lips that seemed to invite kisses; and, as she came out at his summons this night, she looked the very picture of health and beauty.

Her short dress revealed a pair of prettily turned ankles, while her low boddice displayed just a tempting view of a bosom white as snow.

"Why, what brings you here this dark night, Will?" she said, as he caught her in his arms and kissed her.

"Danger brings me," he cried. "I want you to fly with me. I am going to-night from this part for ever."

The girl was all in a tremble now.

He going for ever and she being asked to accompany him!

"Oh, what shall I say? What shall I do?" she cried. "I scarce know what to think. Is it true?"

"Yes, yes; we all leave to-night. The 'Jolly Lucy,' when the run is over, will take us all on board, and away we shall sail for the north. We've money enough in store, and we'll be married the moment we land. Say yes, dearest, as there's not a moment to lose."

"But my father, my mother," cried the girl; "oh! what *can* I do? They would never forgive me."

"Yes, yes," he urged, as he drew her towards the boat; "they are even now beginning to relent; and when we are once married, why, what *can* they do? Come. Nay, we have only a few minutes before us, as it were, for in an hour I must join my father and brothers."

"And I?"

"Oh! you shall be placed in charge of my brothers' wives. You don't suppose, lass, I'd take you down to the beach to join in a smugglers' fight? No, no, we'll get through that, and then—away we are together for happy days in the north!"

He was drawing her into the boat now.

"But to go," she murmured, "without even saying good-bye to my father and mother!"

"Dear girl," he said, as he lifted her in, "were you to wait for that, all would be lost. They would suspect you, and I should have to go alone. Were I to do so, you would never see me again."

They were now fairly out in the stream.

The tide was running out, and the boat, therefore, needed little propulsion.

And so, amid the roaring of the storm which had broken, the flashing of the lightning, and the crashing of the thunder, they dashed onwards towards the bridge.

As they neared this, Lucy uttered a loud cry, and sprang up in the boat.

William Harding had his oars very loosely in his hands, and, what with the sudden rocking, and the effort he made to save her from falling overboard, he lost them.

"Are you mad?" he cried almost fiercely, as he saw his loss, and felt the boat whirling along helplessly towards the bridge, "or are you trying to destroy us?"

"Forgive me, Will," she said, trembling. "It was a sudden impulse of fear I could not restrain myself from obeying. I'll be quiet now."

So they plunged through the arch, the tumultuous water rocking the boat to and fro, so that William Harding had to stand up, and with his hands push the frail barque from the stonework.

This peril was but momentary.

They were soon tossing and whirling along far beyond the bridge.

But still there was danger.

How could he steer without oars?

Suddenly he caught sight of a coil of rope at the bottom of the boat.

He seized this at once; and, breaking a heavy piece of wood off one of the thwarts, fastened it to the end of the coil.

Lucy watched these proceedings with great interest. She could in no way understand them.

However, she very shortly did.

A large ship lay tossing in the creek a little further on.

Towards this they dashed on quickly, and just as they reached it William Harding flung the piece of wood so as to pitch into the rigging, and in another moment the boat was brought up close to the hull of the vessel.

Harding had no desire to speak to those on board.

He left them to wonder, therefore, who had flung the rope on board, and, leaving it there, he gently felt his way along the side of the vessel until he reached shore.

Here they landed, and making their way into the high road, hurried along in the direction of the "Raven's Nest."

William Harding felt comparatively happy.

Not so Lucy.

What she had seen peering over the bridge had fairly disconcerted her.

It was only the face of a man.

But such a face!

The white, ghastly, face of Amos Harding.

NOTICE.

With the next Number, which concludes "RUPERT DREADNOUGHT," will be given the Title Page and List of Winners in the Prize Distribution.

HANDSOME COVERS FOR BINDING

Will be issued on the same date as No. 52, Price Ninepence; Post Free, One Shilling.

The work will also be Published in Handsomely Bound Volumes, containing all the

SPLENDID COLOURED PLATES,

Price 4s. 6d. Post Free, 4s. 10d.

RUPERT; OR THE DREADNOUGHT; OR THE SECRETS OF THE IRON CHEST

"WITH A CRASH THE BOUGH GAVE WAY."

She knew well his feelings.

She understood what was passing in his desperate soul.

He had courted her long and eagerly; and, though William was the one she loved, she had—now she thought blamingly—given him too much encouragement.

The encouragement she had given had been very little.

One smile or a kind word.

But these are a great deal to a man in love.

She knew now that all his evil passions were aroused.

He would risk anything for revenge.

Yet she dared not tell her companion.

She did not care to rouse up his evil nature at such a time of peril.

Besides, she would soon be with the rest of the family, and it was unlikely that Amos would attempt anything against her with them.

And then, after all, his pallid face might only have been expressive of sorrow.

And, with these and similiar thoughts, comforting herself, she kept silence.

But had she seen what was following them, she would have been forced to speak.

A tall, shadowy form, pressing on as they did—keeping in the darkness so as to avoid them. A man evidently bent upon a deadly purpose.

None other than Amos Harding!

On reaching the house where the wives of the Hardings were stopping, William explained hurriedly to them the state of affairs, and begged them to take care of his bride.

She was received with great kindness; and, after embracing her, he hurried away towards the cliff. He had not gone far when a voice cried loudly—

"William Harding—stop!"

Harding stopped at once.

"Who is it?" he said, gruffly.

"I—your brother; Amos."

"And what want you with me?"

"More, perhaps, than you dream of," said Amos. "I saw you just now shoot the bridge with Lucy."

"Well?"

"I've kept my tongue quiet until now," he said, "but I can no longer. I've loved that girl a long time—aye, as long as *you* have—and I'm just hanged if I can bear the idea of her being your wife!"

"Why, you're mad, Amos!"

"No, no, my lad, far from being mad," replied the other. "All I know is, that I love the girl, and to see her your wife would just about drive me mad, though you *are* my brother. So, now, listen to me. I don't wish you any particular harm for it, but I tell you what, as I can't have her, *you* shan't; and so, let's both give her up."

William laughed.

"Well," he said, "that is what I call very good. I've won the girl, she's to be my wife, and now, because you've taken a fancy to her yourself, you ask me to give her up. Why, Amos, there are a hundred as good girls to be found, and so don't let us quarrel over this one."

"We shall if it comes to that," replied the other.

Then he added, raising his voice—

"Will you give her up? Say yes or no, like a man."

The imperative way in which this was said irritated the other.

"Well, then—no!" he answered, fiercely.

"Very good," said Amos. "Then, as we are both armed, we'll just settle the matter now."

The words were said very quietly.

But William knew well their import.

"Stay," he said; "do not be too rash."

He had no desire to kill his brother.

Among these men, hardened as they were to others, there was a feeling of fraternity.

But Amos, although at any other time he could have understood this, and, indeed, would have acted in a similar way himself, chose to regard this as an avowal of cowardice.

He laughed tauntingly, therefore, and spit at his brother.

"You're a coward," he said, "so take that."

In an instant William's sword sprang from its scabbard.

"I won't stand that," he cried, "even from my brother; so draw and defend yourself."

The place where they were speaking was near the edge of the cliff.

A spot of great danger for a duel.

But neither thought of that.

Blood was boiling now on both sides, and all they cared for was the destruction of one or the other.

So the swords were drawn, and to their deadly work they went.

William warmed with the work.

He saw that Amos was resolved, and, in his own increasing fury, he began to view the possibility of his falling, and his brother's gradually working himself into favour with Lucy.

This maddened him.

Before, he had been disposed to laugh.

Not so now.

All was serious with both, and one thirsted for blood as eagerly as the other.

Presently William, in making a blow, slipped and fell on his knee, and, in the clash of weapons, they both broke.

They were on the edge of the cliff now.

The steep, dangerous cliff, with scarcely a tree on its edge, and a sheer fall of five hundred feet on to the rocky boulders and the shingle.

"You shall not escape me," gurgled Amos, savagely, and, springing forward, he seized his brother by the throat.

Thus they struggled on the margin of the perilous gulf, just where a gnarled and aged tree threw some of its branches over.

Again and again they rose and fell—breathing hard, battling violently, forgetting all brotherhood.

At length they were on the brink.

"We shall both perish, madman," cried William, as he strove to force his brother down, and plant his knee on his chest.

Amos laughed.

"Exactly as it should be," he said. "If I cannot have my way by any other means I will try that. *You* shall never possess her, as I cannot."

And, with the words, he made a desperate effort, which put them once more on a level, tottering both on the very verge of the gulf.

One grasp William gave, a grasp which enabled him to reach a thin branch of the half-withered tree.

Then they rolled over.

The bough was far too weak to bear their double weight.

One moment they hovered in mid air.

Then, with a crash, the bough gave way, and, with a yell of agony, they fell in a deadly embrace into the abyss below.

Another moment, and the lovers of Lucy were but a mass of mangled humanity on the rocks beneath.

CHAPTER XX. AND LAST.

IN WHICH THE CHARACTERS AND THE AUTHOR TAKE LEAVE OF THE READER.

Eleven o'clock, the hour for the grand run, was fast approaching.

Towards Sandy Point men had been hurrying for hours along the dark and pebbly beach.

Hugh Harding had waited in vain for his younger sons.

"Curse 'em! they're courting," said old Hugh, with a kind of grim humour, "and I suppose they like that better than fighting. No matter, there are plenty of us without them, and, no doubt, when they are wanted, they will be to the fore."

He little knew that at the very moment his two youngest sons lay a mangled heap below the rocks, while the youngest of all, too, lay pale and still in the cottage of the widow.

So they had departed without them.

The night was just the sort of one to favour such an enterprise as theirs.

The storm of thunder and lightning had passed away.

But it was still heavy and dark.

Not a star could anywhere be seen, and as the crowd of smugglers huddled together beneath the high cliffs, they could nowhere distinguish the line of sea from the line of sky.

"This is a rare night for work," said Richard Alborne to Hugh Harding, who stood with his hands stuck in his belt, smoking his pipe in the very height of enjoyment.

Nothing could please him better, in fact, than such an enterprise as the one on which he was now engaged.

"Aye, if the 'Jolly Lucy' is not behind time," he said.

"She won't be that."

"Well, I hope she won't, or the tide will run down, and we'll have to bring her cargo off in boats. If the revenue officers are on the alert, the only thing to fog them 'll be when she disappears as if she'd sank!"

What Hugh Harding said was just the truth.

The disappearance of the "Jolly Lucy" had been the theme again and again among the coast-guard.

It appeared incomprehensible.

Just as she seemed drifting in, she had again and again given a sudden plunge and disappeared.

The fact was that at a certain place the land arched over so as to form a kind of cave.

Beneath this the water was so deep as to make a still basin wherein the "Jolly Lucy" could ride at safety.

Here all the unlading took place in the stormiest weather, and when the tide ebbed the "Jolly Lucy" was once more far at sea, the smugglers carried the kegs along the broad shingle towards the "Raven's Nest."

Presently the bell of a neighbouring clock boomed out the hour of eleven!

Every man started.

Every heart beat.

Every eye, too, was strained towards Sandy Point.

They were not kept long in suspense.

In a few moments a green light shone out of the darkness, and the black form of a small vessel could faintly be seen.

"She's coming," said Hugh Harding, excitedly.

And so she was.

She loomed nearer and nearer out of the gloom and, after a quarter of an hour of eager suspense she rose with the waves, and glided gracefully and gently into the still basin.

All was now bustle and eagerness.

There was no time for talk or congratulation.

Each man set himself to his work, and in solemn silence the small craft was unloaded.

This occupied about half-an-hour.

Then Hugh Harding became anxious.

There was no sign of his sons' arrival, or his other sons' wives.

"What's to be done?" he said to Richard after the bargain had been struck with the captain.

"Well, we can't wait here to be nabbed, that's certain," said the latter; "but I'll tell you what I'll do."

"What?"

"Why, take a cruise and return to-morrow night for ye."

So it was agreed.

A good stiff glass of raw spirits was drank all round and the "Jolly Lucy" stood out to sea.

In a quarter of an hour the shingle was once more passable, and, each man carrying his load, they began their return journey towards the vaults of the "Raven's Nest."

They went on silently still.

They knew the revenue officers to be on the alert.

They little guessed how much so.

On, on they went until within a quarter of a mile of the "Raven's Nest."

Then suddenly the shadows seemed to take life.

With a rush the coastguard, and the soldiers under Ensign Mornington, with Rupert Dreadnought, Allan of the Glen, Stanley Sherrington, and Tom the Waterman, dashed upon them.

Surrender was called for, and mercy offered to all.

But in vain.

The daring smugglers, who had no belief in the clemency of the law, refused flatly to yield, and a terrible combat ensued.

The Hardings had ever been known throughout the country side for their bravery.

True, indeed, they had fought always on the wrong side.

But that mattered not.

They had been the terror of the country side, and their boast had always been that they had beaten the constabulary in every conflict.

When taken suddenly, therefore, at a disadvantage, it was not likely that they would yield without a good struggle.

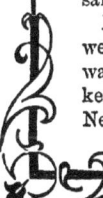

One after another they were beaten down.

But yet they sternly resisted.

Old Hugh Harding himself showed the example.

His stalwart arm cast to the ground one after another of the coastguard.

But at length a bullet through the head sent him spinning back on the body of his eldest son.

It was now nothing but a scene of rout and slaughter.

From that slaughter not one of the Hardings escaped.

It was a general extermination of the family.

The others, seeing all lost, and their companions falling round them, saw the absurdity of further resistance, and reluctantly yielded, and were marched off prisoners to Petherington.

Here Rupert Dreadnought and his friends left them for ever.

Doubtless they paid the penalty due to their crimes.

But he did not remain to witness it.

With the box of treasure which he took from out the vault (together with the body of young Waldron, which he caused to be decently interred), he proceeded to London.

On opening it, he found the greater part of the riches untouched.

But for them he cared not.

On the top of them was the portrait of a lovely woman, whom, by the inscription, he knew to be his mother!

We have little more to tell now.

Rupert Dreadnought, after all he had suffered, was glad, indeed, to give up for ever the roving life to which his father's wishes had condemned him.

There was now another reward, too, awaiting him besides the enjoyment of peace and quietness.

The possession of Helen Penraven.

Who shall describe the rapture felt by those two hearts, when, returning safe from this, his last expedition, Rupert clasped her to his heart, and whispered—

"Now, Helen, at last you can be mine! Now all my troubles are over, and I can claim you my bride!"

No false modesty prevented her from smiling her happiness up into his face.

"Dear Rupert," she said, "I cannot express my joy to you. I had almost feared that from this last expedition you would never return. It has been such a long, dreary time this waiting and waiting, that I began to believe that happiness could never be ours."

"It shall be now, dearest," said Rupert, kissing her again. "To-morrow we will be wed, and over our hearth shall hang in peace the sword which has been wielded in so many a deadly fray."

And so it was.

On the next morning, the lovely Helen Penraven became the bride of her handsome lover, and for many, many years, surrounded by their old friends, did they live in happiness together.

The old sword rusted in its scabbard where it hung, for the necessity for its use seemed to have passed away with the early youth of its master, the gallant RUPERT DREADNOUGHT.

[THE END.]

www.ingramcontent.com/pod-product-compliance
Lightning Source LLC
Chambersburg PA
CBHW080817020726
47501CB00009B/2328
* 9 7 8 1 5 3 5 8 1 0 6 9 2 *